The Price of Ashes

A novel by
Richard Barnard & Sam Hertogs

Louis Hubbard
PUBLISHING

I

The Price of Ashes

Hardcover ISBN: 0-9644751-1-1

Library of Congress Catalog Card Number 95-75128ʹ

Second Printing November 1995

10 9 8 7 6 5 4 3

Cover design by Richard Barnard
Cover artwork by John Keely of Studio West, Minneapolis, MN.

Printed in U.S.A.

Acknowledgments

We gratefully acknowledge the assistance of the following institutions and individuals:

The staff of the archives of the City of Munich, Germany
The staff of the archives of the City of Berlin, Germany
The staff of the National Archives of the United States of America
The staff of the United States National Holocaust Memorial

Mr. and Mrs. Ralph and Ruth Jacobus
Frau Brigitte Schmidt
Mr. and Mrs. Wilhelm Schwartz
Mr. and Mrs. Gottfried Loescher
Mr. Ludwig Hirsekorn
Mrs. Kathy Murphy
Ms. Jean Weissenberger
Ms. Myra Dinnerstein
Mrs. Zemta Fields
Professor Herbert Jonas
Rabbi David Nussbaum of Salzburg, Austria
Mrs. Bobbie Jean Tervo
Ms. Dorothy Fritze
Ms. Jaci McNamara
Ms. Jeri Parkin
Mr. Brett Zabel
Mrs. Tamara Winn
Mr. Noah Anderson
and most especially our families for their sustained support over
the six years in which this novel was researched and created.

We also want to thank William B. Webster III, Randy Eggenberger, Paul Webster and Sara Koller of "Wild Wings"®, whose national headquarters are in Lake City, Minnesota for their help in making "The Price of Ashes" a reality.

It may seem like quite a departure for "Wild Wings"® to offer a book like ours along with their other products, but upon consideration, it is a natural progression. Their's has been a vision of not only the inherent beauty of nature, but also its fragility. They have spent years contributing to the preservation of wildlife as a natural extension of their celebration of wildlife through art.

"The Price of Ashes" looks at the fragile existence of humanity. Its warning is to not lose sight of the interdependence of existence, reminding us that we are all diminished by the absence of justice and that we must keep aware of the world around us and not allow life to just slip away through compromise and rationalization. It talks to those who would stand up and preserve a world and that, after all, has been the guiding principle of "Wild Wings"® for many years now.

Dedication

This book is dedicated to the victims of all historys' holocausts, great and small. Just as there is no reason to the blind hatred, so there seems to be no end. If a prayer might let us learn and in so learning, might reason be our weapon.

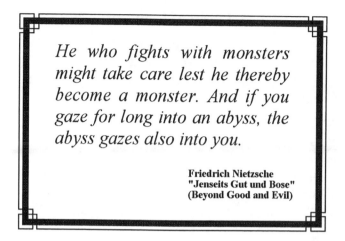

He who fights with monsters might take care lest he thereby become a monster. And if you gaze for long into an abyss, the abyss gazes also into you.

Friedrich Nietzsche
"Jenseits Gut und Bose"
(Beyond Good and Evil)

preface

"The Price of Ashes" is a work of historical fiction. That is to say we have cast a range of real and fictional characters against the backdrop of historical fact. We have made extensive efforts through six years of exhaustive research to produce an accurate historical background, but there are certain historically ambiguous episodes depicted herein with which we have taken a certain amount of license based on popular conjecture of the time.

If there was ever an intent to make a statement through "The Price of Ashes", then that statement would be embodied in the preceding quote by Friedrich Nietzsche. People are all too often eager to find simple answers in their lives and that desire often leads to bigotry, dogma and fanaticism. We believe it's better to live a life ridden with questions than to have an easy answer at hand which promotes misunderstanding, fear and hatred.

Table of Contents

Section I
1918 - 1924

Section II
1928 - 1934

Section III
1938 -1944

appendix

The Price of Ashes

Part I
1918 – 1924

Chapter 1

In a world of such short memory, one might as well be talking about Atlantis or Camelot when considering the world which became engulfed in war in 1914. It may seem we are living in a different place, but of course the moon that shone on blood-soaked battlefields as the Russian people rose against hundreds of years of Czarist tyranny was the same moon touched by man little more than half a century later, the same moon that watched unimpressed as the Russian revolution failed three-quarters of a century after its inception. As for mankind being different, the same petty nationalism and mindless ethnocentric hatreds which focused attention on Sarajevo eighty years ago now thirst for the blood of new generations in these late days of the twentieth century.

It is obviously the same world, a world in the care of beings who are so blinded by the present that they quickly forget the hard-learned lessons of the past.

In terms of the history of man, the First World War is an historical boundary of such magnitude that it seems almost like a physical wall separating the nineteenth and twentieth centuries in the European community, a wall which had been carefully pieced together brick by brick, conflicting treaty laid atop conflicting treaty and all held in place by a mortar of rabid nationalism and oppressive colonialism. There had never been an armed conflict such as the Great War in the history of mankind up to that time, played out with the cooperation of so many human beings from so many different cultures and fought with modern weapons which, compared to weapons of the previous century, leapt beyond all superlatives of horror.

German armies stood within one hundred kilometers of Paris as the Autumn of 1918 came to an end. The Great War had dragged on for four long years and the front lines cut deep into French territory. Erich von Ludendorff, the quartermaster general of the German high command, had gambled on one final offensive to break the stalemate of trench warfare and bring victory to Germany, but when that final offensive failed, it became apparent to Ludendorff that his troops could not hold out much longer. He knew that the German armies simply didn't have the men or materiel to stand against the French, Britons and most of all, the fresh manpower

1

resources and great industrial strength of the Americans. He therefore advised that emissaries be sent to discuss the terms for a peace settlement.

The armistice on November 11, 1918 brought great disorder to the German front lines as many soldiers began to leave their posts. There was a rising revolutionary sentiment sweeping across Germany and once word of the armistice came through, many of the German soldiers at the front line who would have fought to the end felt there was no more reason to stay. German officers began sending reports stating that the troops were disappearing so fast, there might not be an army left to march back to Germany by the time the high command issued such orders. When those orders finally came, senior German military officers had the unpleasant duty of informing the Kaiser that, while the troops would "be honored" to have him return among their ranks, they would no longer obey him.

Hundreds of thousands of families then began their wait for a moment that would become a dramatic part of personal histories; the day when father, son, husband, brother... when "he" came home.

One might also note, as an aside, that at that time of humanity's lost hope and virtue, a prayer so childlike in its innocence and so seemingly hopeless in the face of man's apparent nature began to spread across the world. It was a prayer from the battered victims on all sides asking humanity and God that this war might be the war to end all wars. The war to end all wars...

There are moments of definition in every man's life, a moment against which all other times will be compared, and this was such a moment for Gunther Metzdorf as he waited for the whistle. He looked up at a pale cloud floating by. It reminded him of the head of the Medusa as it drifted lazily over the upturned mounds of black dirt. The cloud, residue of a final exploded artillery shell over the battlefield, added a salty taste to the air.

The haunting silence was prelude to an impending charge across the field by the Austrians... or the Russians... It was easy to lose track as one army would charge and the other retreat and then the reverse as the loser tried to regain and the winner tried to hold.

He had perched on the earthen wall of the trench by digging his feet into the dirt. He looked down into the wash of mud below him. The water looked gray, but he decided that the grayness was just the sky reflected in the water. Its real color was a sickly reddish-black made red from the blood of his comrades. The dirt was black and brown. "It must be good for farming" he thought for an instant, but suddenly it seemed ridiculous to think about life springing from that earth. This was the same earth that had consumed so many of his friends. Pictures replayed in his mind of his friend Luther Scheutzman being blown to pieces with all the bits of arms, legs and the rest raining down into a neat pile as great mounds of dirt fell in after him into one of the man-made craters that became his grave.

It occurred to Gunther as his mind wandered that something wasn't quite right. Why was he, as a Captain, huddled against the dirt wall awaiting a brass whistle's call? He should have been the one calling the men up, sending them over the top of the trenches to rush out with their fixed bayonets hoping to cut deep into the belly of some poorly trained Russian peasant. There wasn't much time to wonder about such things, however, as the eternity which stretched between the silencing of the artillery and the charge was suddenly ended by the shrill whistle. He and his men began scratching and clawing their way to the top of their trenches and out into the cannon plowed fields which were carpeted with the broken bodies of Russians and Austrians alike. They no sooner cleared the trenches when the deep, guttural barking of enemy artillery warned of another volley hurtling towards their lines and they all threw themselves to the ground as though the cannon were some pagan god demanding their devotional submission.

3

Gunther rose up from the mud as the artillery paused for a moment and looked out across the field where his comrades were starting their labored, hunched-over charge towards Russian guns. A strange feeling came over him and he stood tall, almost at attention, as he watched.

A machine gun began to sputter its lead issue in a staccato melody from somewhere across the field and the bass of the cannon sounded a mighty counterpoint. It was a symphony, a ballet. He saw the dancers here and there fly off one foot and land gracefully in the dirt. There was a rifle flying over a man's shoulder as he convulsed in pain and yet further down the line a boy tumbled with the perfect form of a well-trained acrobat.

All at once Gunther wanted a better view, he wanted to understand it all and thought that maybe if he could just see it all at once he might understand. But how? It somehow came to him that if he could fly... And with that he jumped. He jumped up as high as he could, feeling his feet leaving the ground and not allowing himself to consider that he might fall. He just kept rising higher and higher. He saw the whole battlefield, the place that was the whole black world to him, made up of burnt trees and battered little buildings and rotting human flesh. He flew higher and saw that the whole great, black, bloody battlefield was only a spot on the countryside, getting smaller and smaller as he flew.

And he felt so free.

"Time to go" the corporal said as he shook Gunther awake. Gunther desperately grabbed the corporal by the coat, holding on for dear life so he wouldn't fall.

"It's all right Captain. You were just dreaming." The corporal continued without a laugh or a sideways look, for it was so common. They all had nightmares there.

Even months later, far from what had been the Russian front, Gunther sat at a table with a blank expression. He had thought the terrible visions would disappear when the guns fell silent, but he still found himself lost in the memory of it. Why couldn't he get the face of Lorenz Weber out of his mind? There he was again in that wooded hollow, Lorenz looking back at Gunther and waving him ahead and then suddenly there was a bayonet in Lorenz's chest. Gunther didn't know why he was so constantly haunted by that particular incident

4

out of all the others. Maybe it was that look of complete surprise on Lorenz's face. A lone Russian who seemed to come out of nowhere giving all his strength to the thrust of that rifle as though he might lift his impaled victim off the ground. Although it seemed like a long time, it was only an instant before the forest erupted in gunfire. They had stumbled into an ambush.

Some men had made it through without these scars. Gunther had believed in the war. His belief in some holy cause of courage and glory was the drug that had kept him going. He had joined the infantry as a common soldier, but was soon promoted in the face of horrific battles which decimated his brigade. He managed not only to stay alive, but also to rally and lead the others in his squad as the Austrians and Germans drove into eastern Galicia. Through the next years of seemingly endless attacks and counterattacks he received more field promotions, achieving the rank of Captain by the time of the Armistice.

When the time came to go home, he had to travel out of his way because of problems with trains and transportation in general throughout Europe. He had to go to Berlin and then travel south from there and that was how he came to be sitting at a table in a restaurant on the Alexanderplatz*. He had never been to Berlin before and found it vastly different from his home near Salzburg. Even the Munich of his youth couldn't compare. Munich had a personality while Berlin just seemed to happen somehow in its vast, sprawling randomness. Berlin simply was.

Gunther was musing over these differences when he suddenly looked up. It was one of those times when a person senses that there is something he ought to look at without knowing why. There across the dining room of the restaurant stood Klaus Grunewald. It was an incredible chance of fate that Klaus and Gunther should meet again.

At the onset of the war, Germany's Austrian allies agreed to defend Germany's eastern border while German armies marched off to France, but additional troops were soon required to hold off the Russians and so German soldiers were brought from France to fight alongside the Austrians. That was how Gunther and Klaus met, but Klaus had returned to France with the rest of the German troops after the treaty of Brest-Litovsk. The Russians had made a separate peace

---

* "Platz" is the German equivalent of "place", referring to a city square. Alexanderplatz is a famous square in the eastern part of Berlin.

with the Germans when they signed Brest-Litovsk, quitting the war to concentrate on their revolution. The Austrians were then left to Garrison the border for the last few months of the war.

"Klaus!" Gunther shouted, almost knocking over his table as he jumped up and began working his way across the crowded room. He threw an arm around his friend as they came face to face. "You made it home."

"Metzdorf? What are you doing in Berlin?"

"Waiting for a train or horse cart, anything going to Salzburg. I'm trying to get home."

"Home? Are you out?"

"I'm just waiting for paperwork. It should be done tomorrow."

"Why? Do you have something else lined up?"

"I'm going home." Gunther said solemnly, as though it were the answer to a four-year-long prayer.

"No. I mean work" Klaus countered with a lighter attitude, "What are you going to do for work?"

"I don't know. I haven't planned that far ahead yet."

"You should have stayed in. Believe me, with all these others coming home, it's going to be hard to find work."

"I just wanted to get home." Gunther insisted, "I've got a wife and son that I hardly know."

"What good is it if you get to know them while you're all starving?"

"Haven't you had enough?" Gunther asked incredulously as the two of them went back to his table and sat down. "You had it harder than me. I haven't had much of a war since the Russians quit, but I hear it was far worse in the West than it ever was in Galicia."

"Worse?" Klaus asked with a sardonic smile that quickly faded. "I don't know if you can say it like that. It's like the weather. If it's zero degrees out, how cold would it have to be to be twice as cold?"

"...But you're staying in?"

"Yes." Klaus answered adamantly, "I decided before leaving the front. I'm just waiting to see where they send me... That is, if they keep me. The army will be cut down to nothing. And just when they need us more than ever at home. You've heard about the mutiny in Kiel?"

"Yes. They say it's like that all over."

"Damned Communists."

"I thought it was Social Democrats."

"It's all the same" Klaus answered. "Different brands of anarchy."

They faded into silence for a moment, but the silence was soon broken as they abruptly changed to making plans for the evening. They decided to go out drinking, or at least looking for something suitable to drink in a city whose only bounty was its abundance of shortages after years of war.

Within a day Klaus found himself assigned to the Munich Garrison. Gunther conceded that if he insisted on staying in, then Munich was the place to be. Since Munich was so close to Salzburg, Klaus managed to secure passage for Gunther on the same train and they traveled together for the first leg of Gunther's journey home.

It was on the train that Gunther confessed to his friend that he had some misgivings about returning to Salzburg. His father had all but disowned him for marrying a Jewish girl and besides that, Salzburg, while not being a little town, was not large enough to supply returning soldiers with jobs.

Klaus had the good fortune to inherit an apartment from the officer he was replacing in Munich and so he volunteered to let Gunther stay the night before taking the train to Salzburg the next morning. That night Gunther gave Klaus a grand tour of Munich, at least as much as he remembered from his childhood, and then they spent the night talking. It was Klaus who brought up the idea of Gunther and his wife and son staying with him while Gunther looked for work and a place to live in Munich. Klaus even argued for it, fighting to win his friend over so that the four of them might share the one bedroom apartment. The next day Gunther sent word to Amalie that they were going to live in the city where Gunther had lived as a boy and they all waited with excitement, and apprehension, for the day when it would happen.

It was only a couple of weeks later when an Austrian train groaned in tempo with the repeated "clanking" of its steel couplings as the line of cars drew taut and the train began to move into a dark, overcast night.

Amalie was so anxious about the journey that she had remained awake for some time after the kerosene lamps in the battered old coach car were turned down, but eventually she was lulled to sleep by the roll and sway of the train.

She awoke with a start as another train going in the opposite direction passed by, causing a sudden explosion of wind through the narrow slit of a partially opened window. She suddenly realized that she had fallen asleep on the shoulder of the old woman sitting next to her. The woman appeared to be asleep and didn't stir as Amalie pulled away, but Amalie looked at her for a moment just to make sure. The old woman's head was slouched forward and her many chins, which cascaded down to large breasts and a huge stomach, moved in rhythm with a pronounced wheeze of a snore.

The only light in the compartment came from the faint glow of a kerosene lamp in the passageway along with a hint of moonlight occasionally filtering into the windows through the cloudy December sky. Amalie looked around at the other people in the crowded, stuffy compartment. It was cold and smelled of musty clothes and people who hadn't bathed. Many people were on the move since the Armistice. They were soldiers returning home and families, like Amalie and her son Jakob, going to be with their soldier-husbands and soldier-fathers.

Her thoughts began to drift to the things she was leaving behind in the city of Salzburg where she had been born and raised. Her mother, Ruth, had died there in 1908 after a brief battle with influenza, leaving twelve year old Amalie and her ten year old sister, Eleonore, alone with their father, Ethan. Amalie, as the eldest daughter, became the woman of the house and remained in her father's house even after Eleonore married on the eve of her seventeenth birthday and moved with her husband, Louis, to Vienna. Amalie even remained after she herself married a few months later in 1914 and her husband, Gunther, volunteered for duty in the Austrian infantry just as the war began. She attended a university as she waited for the war to end, partly from an interest in getting an education and partly just to pass the time so that she would have somewhere to go rather than sitting about the house all day.

In October of 1916, nine months and ten days after Gunther had managed to get a rare one week pass from the Russian front in Galicia, their son was born. She named him Jakob after her mother's favorite Emily Dickinson poem, just as Amalie herself was named after the American poet.

Amalie's father never acknowledged that his daughter was

turning away from her Jewish heritage and took it for granted that Jakob would have a bris, the Jewish ceremony of ritual circumcision, even though Jakob's father wasn't Jewish. Ethan arranged for it while Amalie was still recovering from a difficult delivery and so she didn't even know about it until it was over. Ethan's presumption put an even greater strain on his relationship with his daughter, but Amalie didn't say anything outright. She decided that she would just bide her time until the war was finally over and Gunther would return for good so that they could start their own life together.

She finally received word from Gunther a week after the Armistice was signed. He wrote her that they were going to live in Munich and that he would meet her there a few days later. Amalie was put off because the instructions sounded more like an order issued to troops rather than a decision made between husband and wife, but she was tired of waiting. She was tired of living in her father's world as though it were her own, and so she accepted Gunther's plan without question, preparing for the day when her journey would begin.

It had been a long day, but she managed to get everything together just in time to board the late train. Jakob, who was usually such a good and quiet little boy, had fussed and cried incessantly. He was upset about leaving his home in Salzburg and his grandfather, as though he knew he wouldn't be seeing either again for a long time.

One of the many thoughts that ran through Amalie's mind as she sat in the shadowy train compartment was a picture of how Gunther might look now. They had been apart for so long. What would it be like living together for the rest of their lives in Munich?

She could only remember him as he looked when he held her face in his hands at the train station when they last said good-bye. The end of a furlough more than a year before. A last kiss. The way she had pressed her face so tightly against his so that he could not forget her, forget her touch, so that she could still feel him when he had gone...

"Mutti*...?" came a little voice from beside her.

"Sleep darling. It's late... Very late" she replied as she gently brushed Jakob's hair from his eyes, placing his head against her side and putting her arm around him. Jakob had his father's light blue eyes. He had only seen his father once, for those few days of his last pass.

---

* "Mutti" is the familiar German of "Mutter" which means mother in english.

Amalie thought how strange it was that Jakob wouldn't know his father and then she realized that she might not recognize Gunther either.

What a frightening thought! Here she was traveling from her home in Austria, leaving all her friends and family, heading to Munich which she had heard was bordering on anarchy since the war ended, to be with her husband whom she hadn't been with for more than four months in the four years that they had been married.

Jakob looked up at Amalie from his nesting place in her dark wool coat and laughed as he pointed at her head. She reached up and found that her hat had been pushed to one side when she had fallen asleep on the old woman next to her. She thought of taking it off and putting it up with her luggage, but then she realized she would probably wake the old woman and possibly everyone else in the compartment, so she just pulled out the hat pin and straightened the hat before settling back into place on the wooden bench.

Jakob looked up at his mother again and, almost as though he had read her thoughts from a moment before, asked "Mutti, vatti*? Vatti?"

Amalie looked down with a tender smile, interpreting and answering the question of her two-year-old son in a quiet voice, almost a whisper, "Yes, we'll see your father soon." Jakob's question was like a reflex at this point. Amalie had tried to explain to Jakob over and over again where they were going and why they were leaving Jakob's grandfather. By the time they left Salzburg, Jakob was filled with excitement that he was going to meet this wonderful new person in his life; someone named "vatti".

"Would you like to hear a story about your father? Did I ever tell you how I met your father?"

"Ja." Jakob quickly replied, eager to hear a comforting bedtime story in this strange place, "Story."

"Let me see if I can remember... It was a long time ago in a much different world." Jakob settled back against his mother's coat as she continued. "My father, your grandfather Ethan, is a publisher. That means he prints and sells books that other people write." Amalie stopped and looked at Jakob to see if he was asleep before she continued. "Well a long time ago, almost ten years, father took me to Paris with him when he had to go to buy a book."

* "Vatti" is the familiar german form of "Vater", which translates to father in english.

"Book." Jakob said sleepily.

"Book?" she asked, surprised that Jakob would repeat that word as though it had great significance, but then she realized he only spoke to show that he was still awake.

"I don't remember what book it was, but the important part is that we were in Paris. It was so wonderful! I was only fourteen and I could do as I pleased while Grandfather Ethan was busy with his book, even though he had told me to stay at the hotel while he was working. One day I went to a great museum in Paris called the Louvre."

"Loove" Jakob repeated without stirring, having found a word he had never heard before.

"No." Amalie chided gently "It is a French word and you say 'La Looo vv rr eh '." Amalie made a funny face as she exaggerated the pronunciation and put her face close to her son's, touching her nose to his as Jakob giggled.

Jakob dutifully tried to repeat the correct pronunciation, making the same funny face as he said "La Looo vvv".

"Very good!" Amalie complimented and then went on with the story as Jakob put his head back against her coat. "I entered one room in particular and saw a painting by a man named Raphael, a great Italian painter who lived long ago, and there was a young man standing in front of it... He was tall and awkward, a couple of years older than I was. I noticed something special about him, but I pretended as though he wasn't there... I guess it's a kind of game that boys and girls play." Amalie paused for a moment as she gathered her thoughts to continue the story, "But it was strange... even though I was pretending not to notice him," as she spoke, it was only then that she realized she was telling this story for herself rather than for her son, "I had a picture in my mind, as though I had taken a photograph of him in the best possible light at the perfect moment of his revealing his true nature. He was such a beautiful boy, like a colt which only recently learned to stand. A mix of boy and man. He was a bit clumsy... And shy. I remember him fumbling with some pamphlet and almost dropping it and then clenching it tightly as we talked. I felt so wicked, a young girl daydreaming of him taking me in his arms. As I recall, I lost the power of speech when he looked at me. And when he tried to be friendly and say hello in that horrible French he spoke, I couldn't respond."

When Amalie finished she looked down at Jakob, wondering

11

what her little boy would make of her ramblings. He was asleep.

The train was now slowing down as they approached a station on the German border. Salzburg had been her home for all of her twenty-three years and, even though she had often gone with her father when he traveled for business, this felt like she was leaving for the first time because she feared she might never return. At the same time, however, leaving Austria behind also filled her with excitement and anticipation. It was going to be a new life! Life in Salzburg had been comfortable before the war, but the war had changed the whole world and now it was time to change along with it.

She had certainly done her share of changing already. She had married a gentile, kept her last name and even ignored Kashrut, the Jewish dietary laws. Amalie Stein-Metzdorf was not going to be a typical Deutscher hausfrau*. And oh, what a scandal for the Stein household! Amalie's mother and father knew she was headstrong as a child and she became even more so after her mother died, but this was too much. To marry out of the faith... Amalie could still hear her uncle reminding her of the words of the rabbi; "The lost tribe of Israel is not lost as one would be lost in the wilderness, they are lost as a drop of wine is lost when spilled into the ocean."

Amalie looked up as the conductor stopped a moment to check on the crowded compartment. "How much longer before we get to Munich?" she asked softly.

"About three hours" the conductor replied.

"Three hours?" Amalie repeated with surprise in her voice. The trip to Munich from Salzburg would only have taken one-and-a-half hours total from station to station before the war, but with fuel scarce and so few trains running, it took three hours just to go from the German border to Munich.

"Thank you" she said quickly so that the conductor wouldn't think she was blaming him for something that was obviously not his fault. She then curled around Jakob on the hard wooden bench to keep him safe and warm.

"Three hours to Munich..." she thought to herself as she drifted off to sleep while the weary old train pushed its way through the darkness towards morning.

---

* "Deutscher Hausfrau" translates as German houswife. In that time a "typical german houswife" would be a reference to the stereotype of a woman who was completely subservient to her husband, always agreeing with everything he says.

12

In Munich, Klaus and Gunther decided to kill time in one ofMunich's famous beer halls until the time came for them to go to the train station.

"I have to thank you again, Klaus. It'll be crowded, but I'm sure we can all get along until I find work."

"I told you not to worry about it." Klaus said sternly, "We old soldiers have to stick together. Besides, after all those years of living in trenches with hundreds of other men, I'm afraid I might get lonely all by myself." Klaus laughed and waved to the barmaid across the crowded room of the Hofbrauhaus and as she came close enough to hear over the dull roar of the crowd, he pointed to Gunther and himself, "Beer! And keep them full! We're celebrating."

Gunther put a hand on his friend's shoulder. "Not too much Klaus or we might not make it to the train station on time."

"That would never do." Klaus retorted in mocking fashion, "Not seeing your wife for almost two years and then missing her train..."

"Miss the train?" Gunther repeated ominously, "God in heaven... The war would seem like a schoolboy row compared to the fight Amalie would put up."

"She's a fighter?"

"No, no... well, not often, but when she does fight, she comes from out of nowhere with everything she has." Gunther paused, "And I, of course, being a gentleman, raise a white flag."

"You? The regal captain Metzdorf, sprung from generations of proud officers, a tiger on the battlefield, surrendering to the wrath of a little woman?"

"She was a little woman when I last saw her," Gunther answered with a smile, "But I haven't seen her for a while. She might have put on weight."

"So you think that by now she may be able to wrestle you to the ground in a fair match?" Klaus asked, baiting his friend

"One never knows..."

Klaus looked down at his beer for a moment as the sounds of the other people in the hall rose and filled the room. "How did you ever meet this terror of a woman?" he finally asked.

Gunther smiled and looked as though he were daydreaming. He began to speak slowly and thoughtfully as he recounted a cherished memory. "It was on holiday. My parents had taken my younger brother and sister and me to Paris to visit my father's uncle."

Gunther snapped out of the daydream and leaned forward to inform Klaus of the details; "My great aunt Greta had sent word that great uncle Berchtwald was on his death bed and that the family should come to pay final respects. By the time we got to Paris, Berchtwald was up and around and as a matter of fact the last I heard he's still a strong old bull ready to take on the world. Aunt Greta, however, died the next year of pneumonia after insisting for weeks that she only had a cold, but anyway there we were in Paris without a funeral, so father proclaimed it our holiday for that year."

"What else could he do?" Klaus interjected facetiously.

"As I was saying" Gunther continued, leaning back in his chair and looking upward with his eyes closed as though he could see everything just as it had happened. "I had just turned 15 that year and to my embarrassment, I found that I was often the unwilling victim of spontaneous sexual arousal."

"Ah! a sexual deviant even at that tender age." Klaus piped in exuberantly.

Gunther opened one eye, looking at Klaus crossly, clearly annoyed at the unsolicited interruption. Klaus reacted like an unruly child being scolded by a disapproving teacher.

"It was extremely unnerving" Gunther continued as he turned back to the ceiling, "especially since I considered myself at the time to be so well endowed that no one in the vicinity could help but notice."

Gunther stopped again and looked at Klaus, almost daring him to comment, but Klaus just sat quietly waiting for Gunther to continue.

"One day Father took us all to the Louvre and, being 15 years old, I certainly didn't want to tag along with my family, so with guide book in hand I pestered my father until he finally agreed that I might go my own way providing I agreed to meet them all later at the place de pyramid by the river. So there I was, standing in front of a fantastic Raphael nude, a buxom pink skinned beauty with dark hair and just the slightest hint of a mustache, sporting the ever-present erection..." This time Gunther interrupted himself as he offered an aside to Klaus, "Mine, not hers."

"Thank God" Klaus whispered.

"...When there appeared beside me, a vision. I would have sworn before God that the girl beside me was the younger sister of

14

the immodest lady rising above me in that incredible portrait. I quickly adjusted the guide program to disguise my interest in this great work of art." Gunther gestured discretely, demonstrating for Klaus' benefit as he covered his groin with his hand. "...And turned ever so slightly towards the girl. I wanted to sound clever, but she saw through me. I was fluent in French and I said something about the unequaled artistry of the renaissance, but she just stared at me as though I had told her that my parents were pigeons and I could spread my arms and fly if I really wanted to."

"Does she still look at you like that?"

"Only sometimes, but, of course, now she knows my parents... As I was saying, There was an awkward pause when I could have just walked away and not risked further embarrassment, but we stared at each other as I noticed her deep brown eyes."

"Ah yes, the eyes. A typical woman's trap." Klaus interjected.

Gunther sat up and turned to Klaus, trying to explain, "I still stare into her eyes. We talked. I told her where I was from and we found to our amazement that we lived within a few kilometers of each other. She was with her father who had come to Paris for business and she was staying at a hotel not far from my family. It seems our lives were almost parallel up to the time of our meeting. We spent that week together as much as we could and talked about school studies and friends and other such nonsense. She returned home the day after my family and we began to see each other as often as we could. Three years later we married."

"How old were you?" Klaus asked.

"The men in my family always married young. I've never been one to break with family tradition. Nineteen. I've always followed in the footsteps of my father and my fathers father. That's why I joined the army so quickly. They certainly would have joined if they could have."

"Yes," Klaus agreed. "My father said the same thing."

"But Klaus, look where it's brought us. What have we become? The world has changed and men like you and me just sit and wonder at it."

"My God you take a quick turn." Klaus said with annoyance "From the sublime to the morbid with hardly a pause."

The conversation soon took a lighter tone as the two old friends began to talk about the early times of the war, when they were the victors and still boys. It seems that youth is not always a matter of age, but of the roads one takes. They were still young, but now they were on a rough, darkened road as they trudged through the defeat which Ludendorff had orchestrated, the defeat of the Kaiser and all that the monarchy had meant to the imperial German Reich which Bismarck himself had fused together through sheer force of will some fifty years before.

The animated discourse was about the antics of two boys. They spoke of romantic adventures, real and imagined, and their experiences before they met. They competed in telling stories of times they had bent the rules, such as when Klaus had "found" a stray goat that became a feast for his squad and the time when Gunther disappeared in the smoke of an artillery burst and Klaus rushed in to save him, only to find that Gunther had fallen into a wine cellar and the blood which covered Gunther turned out to be wine hoarded and hidden by a farsighted merchant. They laughed away the hours until they were due to leave for the station to escort Amalie and Jakob to their new home.

At three o'clock in the morning it had already been snowing for hours as Klaus and Gunther stumbled out of the beer hall on their way to the train station. It was a heavy snow that was quickly filling the dark streets of Munich. A strong wind rose, sending flocks of snowflakes stinging against their faces, blinding them now and again as they worked their way along.

They were weaving from side to side as they walked, each with his arm around the other in a fruitless attempt to steady one another. They both knew, though they never spoke of it, that they only allowed themselves to feel drunk. They wanted to be numb and they allowed it as long as they could. Gunther knew how to drink. He knew how to feel full of laughter in the most damned places that a man could find himself, but he knew also to be ready to fight. He learned young to always be a soldier and it would be with him for the rest of his life. The two young-old comrades leaned against the dirty gray cornerstone of an old bank building, laughing at their apparent inability to negotiate the turn around the corner when they noticed a delivery man getting down from his horse-drawn wagon to push it through a snow drift in the middle of the street.

"Wait!" Klaus yelled exuberantly to the old delivery man, "We'll be right there to help!"

The delivery man was startled because he hadn't noticed the two men in the shadows, and he stared at them to see who they were as they moved into the glow of a guttering street lamp. It became apparent as the two men struggled through the snow in their military great-coats that they were drunken soldiers and the delivery man waved them away. "Gott in Himmel..." he said under his breath, "just what I need."

Gunther shouted even though they were now close enough to be easily heard, "Ja, we are experts at pushing wagons. The army only let us in because of our strong shoulders."

Again the delivery man waved them away. "Go back, you'll only get hurt, you drunks."

"Drunks?" Klaus said indignantly as he looked at Gunther.

"Nonshennsshhh." Gunther replied.

"What?" Klaus asked, laughing at his friend.

"I said 'nahhn... sehhnssse...' " Gunther said slowly and deliberately, so as to be understood this time, which made Klaus laugh even more.

"We've pushed wagons through mud... snow... even fire... Why, we pushed wagons all the way to France." Klaus said through his laughter as he once again addressed the delivery man.

"Ja, ja " said the exasperated old man, "Do what you want, but it's none of my fault if you fall under a wagon wheel." He started to move ahead of the wagon, but then stopped and turned back, shaking a stubby crooked finger at them for emphasis as he spoke, "and if you do fall, don't think I'll stop for you when I get moving!"

Gunther looked at Klaus as they got ready to push and said "I'm beginning to like the old bastard."

The delivery man trudged up to his horse and pulled the reins from the driver's seat and gave the horse a pat on the rump. "Come Gertie, show them how it's done."

The delivery man positioned himself in front of the horse to urge her through the snowdrift.

"When shall we push?" Klaus shouted impatiently.

"Whenever the spirit moves you." came a curt and sarcastic reply from in front.

"I'm not so sure he appreciates us" Gunther said to Klaus as they put their shoulders to the back of the wagon.

"Come Gert! Come on!" urged the driver and Klaus and

Gunther threw their weight against the creaking back gate of the old wagon with little result.

"Verdammt!" muttered the old man. He now realized that he would really need the help of the two soldiers and addressed them seriously for the first time.

"Once again, when I count to three." shouted the delivery man as he patted the horse on the shoulder. He then wrapped the reins around his hands a couple of times and drew them up tight in front of Gert.

"Eins*..." the old man shouted.

Gunther re-positioned himself for a better stance and in so doing turned his back to Klaus.

"Zwei**..." came the call from in front.

Gunther looked up the street as he put his left shoulder to the wagon and suddenly saw a sparking blue light appear around the corner.

"Jump Klaus!" Gunther shouted.

"What?" Klaus asked as he turned towards Gunther in time to see the electric street trolley moving towards them. Klaus and Gunther leapt through the snow away from the wagon and the delivery man's eyes filled with horror as he tried to pull his horse out of the way just as the trolley plowed through the snow drift and rammed into his horse and wagon, driving them into the snow bank and dragging the old man along with his hands tangled in the horse's reins.

The impact of the crash was muted by the snow, creating a strange sound like "whuummppff" that filled the empty street. The old man was cursing at the top of his voice "Damn! Damn! My Gertie! What have you done to my Gertie?"

The trolley operator had been thrown over the horse and wagon into the snow bank while the only two passengers on the early morning trolley had merely been forced against the wall at the end of the bench without being hurt.

The windows of the apartments quickly filled with faces as Gunther and Klaus worked their way over to the wagon. The delivery mans horse had been pinned between the snowdrift and the trolley and the old man, who continued to rant and swear at the trolley and

---

* "Eins" is german for "one"
** "Zwei" is german for "two"

the snow covered trolley driver, had broken his right hand and dislocated the wrist of his other hand.

They were all surprised to see a policeman come around the corner within a few short moments. He checked on the trolley passengers and the old man and then stood looking down at the horse. Gert was struggling and panting heavily as she lay pressed up against the snow bank with her front legs bleeding and twisted under her. Without saying a word, the policeman drew his revolver and pointed it at the horse's head.

The old man's shout of protest was disharmony to the explosion of the bullet as the horse instantly stopped struggling in the snow bank.

The first to come out of the apartment buildings was a short, middle aged woman in a night gown. She slipped and slid in the deep snow as she rushed towards the wagon while the policeman and Klaus and Gunther untangled the delivery man's hands from the reins.

"I'll get help. You just wait here." the policeman told them.

As the policeman made his way through the snow, other people in various states of dress started coming out of the apartments, some in pajamas with overcoats, others with only pants and shoes.

Klaus caught only a glimpse of the knife in the woman's hand as it flashed a reflection of the dim streetlight when she drew it above her head and fell upon the horse, driving the knife into its shoulder.

"No ..." whispered the delivery man in disbelief as tears filled his eyes. Klaus and Gunther held onto the old man as he tried to get up and pulled him back a few yards, away from where Gertie was being set upon .

"There's nothing to be done..." Gunther said in a low voice next to the old man's ear while he held him down.

The people from the apartments, who hadn't seen meat for months, butchered the horse in less than a quarter of an hour. They greedily carried the heart and liver and chunks of meat still dripping with deep-red, warm blood back to their apartments, trying to get in from the cold as quickly as they could while struggling through the deep drifts.

Klaus, Gunther and the old man witnessed it all as they waited with the old man for the policeman to return.

"Just like the war..." Klaus finally said in a low, overly-dramatic tone, "Some would feed upon the still living body of our Germany.

They cut it up and take it for themselves so they can grow fat and strong off our demise." It was a statement that showed Klaus' theatrical nature, but nonetheless, Gunther nodded in agreement without comment as they watched the last man in pajamas and overcoat slip in the snow and fall flat on his back, spattering himself with Gertie's blood all down his front and on his face. He then got up without saying a word, not even a curse at having fallen, and made his way through the snow back to his apartment.

In a few moments, the policeman returned with a wagon to take the old man to a hospital and Klaus and Gunther continued on their way to the train station. When they reached the station they found that Amalie and Jakob's train was behind schedule they would have to wait for more than an hour. They didn't talk.

The snow had delayed the train even more and so it wasn't until four-thirty in the morning when the train finally dragged into the almost deserted Hauptbahnhof*.
Gunther and Klaus got up from the cast iron bench in the open waiting area and walked toward the train as it came to a stop. Gunther waited for a couple of minutes and when no wife or child appeared, he threw an anxious glance at Klaus. Klaus snapped to attention and clicked his heals together "You've waited long enough mein Kapitan, it is time you took the train."

Gunther waved off Klaus' sarcasm and rushed up the steps of the passenger car, working his way down the narrow passageway as he checked the compartments one by one. Everyone had already left the first compartment and the next was crowded with people getting their baggage down off the racks over the seats. Once he could be sure Amalie was not in that compartment, he turned quickly and almost knocked down the large old woman who was trying to pass by him in the narrow aisle at the same time. "Entschuldigung Sie, bitte**" he said, apologizing as he slid past and twisted around to look into the compartment from which the old woman had just come.

He had found her. She was still asleep with Jakob curled up beside her. Gunther couldn't move. She was more beautiful than he remembered, her face more gentle, her son, his son, so handsome and frail and safe beside her. All the war was done in that instant. He knew it was right that they had come here to be together This would

---

* "Hauptbahnhof" is german for "main train station"
** "Entshuldigung Sie, bitte" translates to "Excuse me, please"

now be their home, the home he would build for his own family.

Gunther slowly and quietly knelt down in front of his Amalie. He took her hand gently and kissed it. She still didn't stir. He kissed her again and this time nuzzled her hand with his mustache. She awoke with a start and pulled her hand away. She hadn't seen Gunther with a mustache before and she started to protest "Oh my God! What are you..." and then she realized it was him. "Oh Gunther!" she said, still confused, having been awakened from a sound sleep, "Are we home?"

"Well, we're at the Munich station..."

"Mutti?" Jakob said sleepily as he rubbed his eyes. When he saw the man kneeling in front of his mother, he drew back into the folds of her coat.

"Good morning, my fine little soldier. Do you know who I am?" Jakob slowly shook his head "no" and then a bright expression raced across his face as he was struck with a revelation; "Vatti?"

Gunther smiled a great smile and he could feel a tear sting at his eye, even though he would not show it, but his strained voice betrayed emotion as he replied "Yes, yes. It seems about time that we should meet."

Chapter 2

The role of General Erich von Ludendorff in the events of 1918 far exceeded the authority of his position as quartermaster general of the German high command. Ludendorff's victories at the beginning of the war earned him a reputation that carried him far beyond the time of German victories and likewise earned the confidence of Kaiser Wilhelm to a point that even eclipsed the Kaiser's respect for Paul von Hindenburg, the chief of the German high command.

Ludendorff determined in September of 1918, after a final failed German offensive, that Germany could not continue the war. In that desperate moment he decided he must somehow salvage the honor of the German military by finding a way to end the war without admitting military defeat. The answer was handed to him by Woodrow Wilson, the President of the United States. Wilson, acting as spokesman for the Allies, stated in no uncertain terms that the first condition of any peace talks was that the Kaiser must step down as Emperor. Based on this demand, Ludendorff decided that if the government were turned over to a group which was in opposition to the Kaiser, then they would be the ones to actually sue for peace and bear the onus of surrender.

The Social Democrat party was just such a group. At one time, some fifty years before the Great War, they had been considered a radical revolutionary force in German politics. Over time, however, their leadership had moved towards a more conservative position and so, although they spoke of republicanism and democracy in contrast to Germany's autocratic monarchy, they were no longer considered to be radical revolutionaries. For Ludendorff's purpose they were certainly the lesser of evils in a choice between them and the Communists. The Social Democrats represented the scent of rebellion without the fires of revolution.

It was Ludendorff who told the Kaiser that Germany must surrender before the war was pushed onto German soil and in order to achieve that end the government must be turned over to the Social Democrats with Friedrich Ebert installed as president of a new German republic.

Months later, completing his plan to produce a scapegoat without ever acknowledging his role in the transfer of power,

Ludendorff would say that the Social Democrats had betrayed Germany; that they had stabbed the army in the back by surrendering while the army still held the field. "Dolchstoss", or "the stab in the back", became a catch-phrase among those opposed to the Weimar republic for years to come.

The abdication of Wilhelm Hohenzollern was in itself a strange example of the turmoil of the times. The Hohenzollerns had been Germany's only ruling family from the time of German unification in 1871 until 1918 when Kaiser Wilhelm was informed that he no longer had the support of the military. On November 9 of 1918, Prince Max von Baden, an intermediate Reichs-Chancellor, announced the abdication of the Kaiser and the formation of the new German Republic led by Friedrich Ebert.

The Kaiser, however, had not intended to abdicate! He had been willing to step down as emperor, but he had expected to continue influencing his country by retaining the title of King of Prussia.

Original intentions aside, once the Kaiser heard of the premature and incorrect announcement of his abdication he shouted angrily that he had been betrayed and then fled to Holland, fearing for his life in the face of a revolutionary uprising. That fear was certainly well founded considering the fate of his cousin, Czar Nicholas II of Russia, less than a year before when revolution had swept the Romanoff dynasty out of power. Nicholas and his family disappeared without a trace.

It was not until some three weeks after Prince Baden's announcement that the Kaiser officially abdicated while in exile in Holland.

One of the often-cited examples of the revolution which the Kaiser feared was the mutiny by German sailors in Kiel. The irony, however, is that it wasn't a Communist revolution even though it certainly had all the earmarks of such. The mutiny was not a spontaneous act of revolution, but a response to an attempt by a group of naval officers who sought to defy orders from the new Weimar republic to stand down and wait for developments in the peace talks. The officers decided that they could not allow Germany to go down to defeat while there was still a functioning military. Their reasoning was not unlike the course of action being attempted by Ludendorff, but while Ludendorff sought to set up scapegoats to take the blame for the surrender, the naval officers were determined to renew hostilities.

It was at this point that the sailors mutinied. If you look at the events from this perspective, the truth would seem to be that it was the naval officers who were engaging in mutiny against the government. The sailors were putting down that mutiny and standing up for the new republic by refusing to fight on.

Gunther was wearing civilian clothes for the first time in years and he felt out of place. He was a soldier and now he was pretending not to be. He still wore his military coat and highly polished boots but only because he had no others.

The brilliant sunlight cutting through the frigid blue sky and reflecting off the fresh white snow was enough to blind a man. The snow crunched loudly with each step as he walked down Arcisstrasse*.

He had been looking for work for over two weeks since Amalie and Jakob had joined him in Munich and was once again off to beg for a job. He stopped for a moment and felt through the deep pockets of his greatcoat until he managed to fish out a small red book. "Baedekers München und Südbayern**" was spelled out in gold type against the red cover. He opened the book to one of the delicate fold out maps that he had marked off the night before.

When he had left the army, Gunther thought he would be able to put his leadership experience to good use in civilian life. Unfortunately there were hundreds of thousands of other men across Germany with the same delusions. Amalie, Klaus and he had sat around the small kitchen table in Klaus' apartment the night before, suggesting possible jobs, and had all concluded that Gunther should try at the Hauptbahnhof.

When he returned to Munich he was sure that he still knew the city like the back of his hand, but when he had attempted to give Klaus a tour of the city on that first night, he found that his memory was not as clear as he thought. He then resigned himself to the embarrassing experience of being a native who had to buy a tourist's guidebook. He traced the route with his finger toward the main train station when the street was suddenly filled with the explosive sound of an old truck coming around the corner, its four cylinders banging irregularly, indicating a desperate need for repairs.

Gunther looked up as the Lastkraftwagen came into sight. The lorry was filled with soldiers of the revolution. Almost a dozen men rode on the running boards and front fenders of the beaten and abused old truck, all with rifles slung over their shoulders and one of them holding a crimson flag of the revolution which was unmoved by

---

* "strasse" is german for street. Arcisstrasse is the name of a street in Munich.
** "Baedeckers" is the name of a series of international tourist guides popular for decades. "München und Südbayern" means "Munich and southern Bavaria"

25

the slow pace of the truck.

One of the soldiers waved at Gunther as they passed and Gunther found himself reflexively raising a hand to return the greeting to fellow soldiers before catching himself. "What am I doing?" he thought to himself. "Dolchstoss" he whispered bitterly under his breath.

This was what many Germans said to themselves. These were the back-stabbers who had betrayed Germany in its hour of need. They were part of the revolution begun by the sailors who had mutinied in Kiel. They had forced a disgraceful surrender by their revolution and suddenly Germany was caught up in a political, economic and social nightmare.

Even though the streets of Munich were quiet, there had been great political upheaval across the country. Kaiser Wilhelm had fled to Holland and left the ruins to Friedrich Ebert, head of the Social Democrats, and "his friend", Kurt Eisner in Bavaria.

Kurt Eisner was the head of the Independent Social Democrat party in Bavaria and it certainly didn't help matters that he was Jewish since it added a distinctly anti-semitic quality to the "Dolchstoss" sentiment in Germany. It was Eisner who had marched to the royal residence on November seventh and, with the support of the royal guard, declared the Freistaat Bayern, the Bavarian free state, in place of the Wittelsbach's provincial monarchy which had ruled the regency of Bavaria since 1180.

Members of the Wittelsbach family, including Ludwig III, quickly left the royal residence as Eisner began to set up office. The royals raced out of Munich in their great black automobile, eventually ending up in a ditch outside of town, the result of a minor accident caused by their excessive speed.

The end of over two hundred years of Hohenzollern rule, the defeat of Germany in war, the imposing threat of Communist rule, it was all too much. It was unbelievable. But Gunther had his wife and son to care for and so his was not a political world. He needed to put bread on the table and find a place to live so that he would not have to continue imposing on Klaus' hospitality. They couldn't go on forever with Gunther and Amalie sleeping on the floor in the living room and their son sleeping on a couch.

He returned to the map and once again found the Hauptbahnhof before carefully folding it and continuing his journey.

He soon arrived at the station, stamping his boots and shaking off the cold as he stepped inside, but when he turned to find the station-master's office he almost walked out again. There were more than two dozen men lined up by the office and Gunther could tell by looking at them that they were in the same situation as he, looking for the same job that he had hoped for. Even the rumor of work would bring men from miles around to apply; well-qualified men, young and strong. It was all power to the man with a job to offer and many employers knew it and took advantage. New men would be paid less, expected to work longer and not complain. Gunther became angry at the thought of going from an officer in the army to nothing on the streets of Munich.

He stood for a moment, indecisive, until he remembered Amalie and Jakob and then walked over to the group of men and leaned against the cold whitewashed wall. The young man sitting on the floor beside him looked up, sizing up this new competitor for the job and then turned back towards the opposite wall, picking a blank space to stare at.

Gunther reached into his pocket for a cigarette, a rare commodity at the time, and as he did he heard a crunching sound. He noticed the man sitting on the floor surreptitiously eating an apple. Gunther looked at his last two cigarettes as he pulled them out of his pocket and put one in his mouth, offering the other to the young man on the floor. The man continued to stare at the wall until Gunther tapped him on the shoulder and extended the cigarette to him again. This time the man smiled as he took the cigarette. He then took out a pocketknife and cut the apple in half, offering half to Gunther. Gunther thanked him with a nod and slipped the piece of apple into his pocket. He then ran a wooden match against the wall to light his cigarette.

"Which division?" Gunther asked as he offered a light to the young man.

"Medical corps." The man replied as he took a draw on the cigarette, "I drove ambulance. And you?"

"Austrian infantry. Galicia."

"I was in Rhiems at the beginning," the young man explained, "but then I was transferred to drive at the Russian front. I was far south of Galicia."

"I heard Rhiems was bad."

"It was hell. After I was sent to Russia, my brother ended up at Paschendale. He died there just before the end."

"Those are the hardest" Gunther said, trying to offer sympathy. "When they die just before it's over."

There was an awkward pause as they each thought of what they might say next.

"Now if there was just some way to find work." the young man finally said with a forced smile.

Gunther just shook his head from side to side and took a long drag on his cigarette. "It's the revolution. First they defeat us on the battlefield and now they terrorize the businessmen, trying to get them to either close down their factories or turn them over to the workers."

"When I first heard," the young man explained, "heard about the revolution, I was on the Russian front and I had come to town to get the rations for my squad and the quartermaster laughed at me. He tells me I'm an idiot for not knowing. 'They have quit the war' he says, and now we should just leave and find our way home."

"Chaos." Gunther interjected, "At least when I came home, it was on a troop train..."

"I had to get rides where I could. Horse cart, even a motorcycle once." the young man said, "My suit had been stolen, the one the army gave me, and one day there I was at the door of my family's apartment."

The young man paused for a moment as he thought about it. "My mother..." he began as a flash of emotion suddenly raced across his face, but he quickly composed himself. "My mother cried out 'Friedrich! Friedrich is home at last!' and I stood there in that damned flea ridden uniform. It was so strange because my father died earlier this year of a heart attack and my brother died in the war. We were the only two left. There was no one else to hear her when she called out."

There was another awkward pause until Gunther reached out his hand, introducing himself. "Gunther, Gunther Metzdorf."

"Friedrich Haas." The young man countered as he reached up from his spot on the floor.

"How long have you been waiting here?" Gunther asked.

"Almost two hours."

"What's the job?"

"I don't know. I heard they might be looking for baggage men, but I don't know for sure."

A short, bald man with graying hair and thick round glasses came out of the stationmaster's office and stopped dead in his tracks when he saw the line of men. His face instantly turned red and he began to shout "What is this? What do you want here? I have no work, do you hear? No work! When there is a job, it is posted. When there is no work, nothing is posted. Nothing is posted, so stop blocking the hallways. Get out! Get out all of you, or I'll call the police."

One of the men, a gaunt and drawn young veteran who had been waiting longer than most, was clearly angry and started to walk toward the stationmaster. The stationmaster took a small step backwards, but then, determined not to appear afraid, he stood up to the young man.

"No trouble!" the short man said in a loud, threatening voice as he raised a finger. The other men in the hallway froze as they waited to see what would happen. The angry young man stopped and glared at the stationmaster for a moment without saying a word. He then spat in the little man's face and stormed out the door.

The stationmaster pulled a balled-up handkerchief out of his back pocket as he removed his glasses. "Little bastard" he cursed under his breath as he cleaned the glasses and angrily wiped his face.

The rest of the men started moving toward the door one by one. They moved slowly, not wanting to let the stationmaster to win so easily, but he had won. The little gray-haired man with the thick glasses did have power; he decided who would be able to eat and pay rent and who would not.

Gunther closed his coat as he moved for the door, but stopped when he heard something fall behind him. He turned and saw a wooden cane on the floor.

"That's mine." Friedrich said as he struggled to his feet, reaching for the cane. Gunther quickly scooped up the cane and held it out for Friedrich to take. "Thanks" Friedrich said as he quickly buttoned his coat and buckled the belt around his waist before taking the cane.

Friedrich didn't wait for Gunther to ask about his limp. "This was a last minute bit of bad luck. My squad drove ambulance and about two months before the war ended I took a corner too fast and the damned thing rolled over. I wasn't carrying any wounded, but when I came to, the cab was crushed in around me and I turned my head to see my boot next to my face."

"It came off?" Gunther asked.

"No, no" Friedrich continued, "My foot was still in the boot. My leg had snapped like a twig and twisted back up toward my head."

"Weren't there any doctors?" Gunther asked with a wince of empathy and astonishment in his voice.

"You might better ask if there weren't any good doctors. They set the leg wrong and every time I told them it felt like something was wrong, they told me that I was bound to be uncomfortable and I should just take their word that everything would be all right. Now it's too late. Nothing can be done to correct it."

"That's a horrible shame." Gunther said.

"Well, it should get better to the point where I won't need the cane in a few months, but it'll never be the way it was."

Gunther didn't know what to say and Friedrich sensed the awkwardness. "Well, I guess I'll be off. We'll see if there isn't better luck tomorrow." With that, Friedrich extended his hand to Gunther. "Weidersehen*."

"Where are you going now?" Gunther asked, stepping up beside him.

"I might as well head for home." Friedrich answered. "I'm living with my mother until I can get a job and find a place of my own."

"I was just about to meet a friend of mine at the Sterneckerbräu. Would you care to come?" Friedrich looked at Gunther for a moment, considering the offer. "Ja." he finally said. "I can afford one beer." and with that they left the train station to meet Klaus.

When they arrived at the small beer hall, Klaus was waiting. He had been leaning back in his chair, just watching the world go by the window, and he brought the front legs of the chair down with a bang as Gunther spotted him.

"What a day!" Gunther grumbled.

"I take it you have not yet joined the proletariat?" Klaus asked with a grin.

"To hell with you." Gunther tossed back. "Klaus, this is Friedrich. We've come for beer after a long day of chasing down non-existent work."

---

* "Wiedersehen" is a shortened colloquialism of the phrase "Auf Weidersehen" which means "Until I see you again."

"Yes," Friedrich added, "but maybe that stationmaster will think twice before shouting out a group of soldiers."

"Why?" Klaus asked. "Did they kill him?"

"No, no." Gunther replied. "One of the men spit right in his eye."

"Did he get the job?" Klaus asked with a straight face. Friedrich started to laugh.

"I don't know..." Gunther replied pensively, "I don't think they had a job opening for men to spit on people, I think that's a government job."

Gunther then glanced casually around the room and was surprised to see Amalie working her way across the room with Jakob in tow.

"Amalie." Gunther called while waving to her. She had obviously already seen them as she made a straight line to their table.

"Gunther, at last some good news." Amalie said as Gunther held open his arms for Jakob who gladly jumped up on his father's lap.

"What news?"

"A letter from father" Amalie said excitedly. "He has contacts with a couple of publishers here in Munich and sent a letter of recommendation for you."

"Publishers? What do I know about publishing books?"

"Well, there are many things you might start with..." Amalie began to explain.

"I'm not a writer! I don't really have much interest in books." Gunther interrupted.

Amalie looked hurt. She had come running in so excitedly and Gunther had closed the door on her.

"I'm sorry Liebling," he said after a moment, "I just don't think I would be much good at that sort of thing."

"I just thought..." Amalie interrupted, "Jobs are so scarce. I thought maybe just for a little while you might try."

"This sounds more like something you might like to do." Gunther said, "I was raised with soldiers, architects and builders. I know absolutely nothing about books."

"You're right" Amalie said quietly, looking down at the floor. "I just know how badly you want work."

"Don't worry Liebling" Gunther said as he reached for her hand. "I'll find something soon."

Gunther then realized that Klaus and Friedrich had been paying close attention to their conversation. "We certainly can't continue to stay in the asylum" he continued as he looked at Klaus and Friedrich, acknowledging their presence with a nod and wink.

"An asylum?" Friedrich asked incredulously, "Where do you live?"

"...with me." Klaus said dryly.

"Well," Amalie said as she picked up Jakob off Gunther's lap, making a moaning noise as she strained at the weight of the little boy, "I will take our chubby little boy home and get dinner ready. Will we have another for dinner?"

Gunther was embarrassed as he realized that he hadn't introduced Amalie to Friedrich. "Oh! I'm sorry... Amalie, this is Friedrich Haas. Friedrich, this is my wife Amalie."

Friedrich struggled to get up and extended his hand, "A pleasure to meet you Mrs. Metzdorf."

"Are you able to join us for dinner, Mr. Haas?"

"Oh no. I couldn't impose."

"But you must!" Klaus piped in, "I've just come back from the country with a suitcase full of food."

Friedrich's eyes grew large for a moment at the thought of a decent meal, but then he reconsidered. "No, my mother would be all alone."

"Bring your mother along. For a couple of days we eat well. You shouldn't refuse hospitality in times like these." Klaus continued.

"Yes, you really should come." Gunther added.

"Are you certain?" Friedrich asked, giving them a chance to change their minds.

"Absolutely." Klaus insisted.

"Then I would be honored."

A few hours later in the Schwabbing district of Munich, Gertrude Haas looked up from her book with a start when she heard footsteps stop at the door to her apartment. Her body tensed and she sat very still and quiet, waiting to see what would happen next. Her instincts told her to rush to the bedroom and lock the door and get the long kitchen knife which she kept under her bed for protection.

Ever since her husband had died, and especially now with revolution in the streets, she was constantly afraid. Suddenly it came to her as she sat there holding her breath... "Friedrich!" She had almost forgotten that he had come home from the war. She was sure it was just Friedrich coming home, but she still held her breath as she heard someone try the door.

"Mother" Friedrich called as he came in, "I'm home."

Gertrude didn't even realize she had been holding her breath until she let it out in a loud sigh which startled her son. "Oh, there you are." he said as he turned. "Have you started dinner yet?"

"Started what?" Gertrude asked with a cutting edge to her voice. "All we have is a potato and a molding turnip. Have you found any work?"

"No, but today I found something better."

"Better than a job?"

"Yes. I found a couple of friends who have connections in the farmlands. They've invited us for dinner."

Gertrude looked at her son's smiling face, but didn't share his sense of triumph. Friedrich was confused at her lack of enthusiasm. "What's wrong? We'll have a good meal tonight."

"Tonight." Gertrude repeated as she suddenly started crying. "Tonight we can eat, but what about tomorrow?"

"Mother," Friedrich started, about to explain to her the way that things were now, now that they were the defeated and the world was turned upside down.

"Damn!" Frau Haas shrieked.

"Mother!" Friedrich exclaimed with surprise. He couldn't remember ever hearing his mother swear, not that it was such a horrible thing, but this was his mother, a soft spoken, gentle woman of impeccable manners.

"I hate being poor!" she cried "I hate being alone! I hate being afraid all the time and not knowing whether or not there will be food to eat." Gertrude then began to sob uncontrollably as her son knelt beside her.

Friedrich's father had always been there to take care of his mother and Friedrich had never given it a second thought. He knew his mother and father would always be together to take care of each other.

Friedrich's father had been a great, barrel-chested, bull of a man. Friedrich was sure Manfred Haas would outlive his own children. He was a man who could carry the whole world on his shoulders if need be. Friedrich couldn't believe it when he received a tear stained letter

33

six months before, when he was still on the Russian front.

The letter was unlike the perfect examples of calligraphy which his mother had always sent him before. She had written down the wrong day on the date at the top of the letter and then scratched it out. Scratched it out! His mother would never leave a mistake on a letter. Each letter was a work of art in grammar and style and penmanship and now he had received this smudged note with scratched out mistakes and he knew something was terribly wrong as soon as he saw it.

"Heart." The word was written larger than the other words on the page, perhaps because it spoke of two broken hearts, or perhaps because Frau Haas had to remind herself that it was true. Manfred Haas had gone to work on a Monday morning in March where he operated a metal lathe in a small machine shop which made parts to supplement the enormous industrial war production of the Krupp Works in Essen, far to the North. Manfred picked up a half empty box of parts to be finished and started carrying them to his lathe when he suddenly stopped in the middle of the shop floor. One of the other workers, Karl Werthers, an old friend of Manfred's, noticed him standing there staring straight ahead and asked if something was wrong. Manfred looked at his friend, smiled a half smile as his chin began to quiver uncontrollably, and then staggered a half step before dropping the wooden crate. Manfred's arms fell to his sides and he watched as the shiny metal cylinders bounced out of the fallen crate, seemingly in slow motion, each piece ringing like a bell as it hit the cement floor, and then tinkling softly as they continued to roll in a broadening pattern, like ripples rolling away from a stone dropped in a pond. A couple of the other machinists rushed over to help Manfred and Karl heard him whisper in such a sad, low voice "Oh Gertie..." as his knees buckled and he collapsed on top of the wooden crate, crushing it as he fell. It was a massive coronary just a week short of his fifty-first birthday.

"You're not alone," Friedrich said, "I'm here."

"But not for long." Gertrude said amid her sobs, "I know you'll leave too. You'll find a girl and make your own life and I'll be all alone."

"Mother, don't think of that. I'm here now and I won't be leaving for quite a while. We've got to just get through today. The whole world is changing and you just have to try to be strong."

34

"I can't" she sobbed even more than before. "I can't be strong anymore. I don't want to be strong."

Friedrich stood up beside her and said matter-of-factly, "I'm afraid you have no choice mother. I'm sorry, but the world has not stopped and I'm not going to let you stop. Now get dressed and we're going to have dinner with my new friends and we'll both feel better."

"I'd rather not go out." Gertrude said as she wiped her eyes.

"Of course you'd rather not go out." Friedrich scolded, "You'd rather sit here and feel sorry for yourself."

"Friedrich!" Gertrude shouted indignantly, "How dare you speak to me like that. If your father were here..."

"He would say the same thing." Friedrich said, finishing her sentence smugly.

Gertrude looked at him coldly and continued drying her eyes, getting up without saying a word and going into her bedroom, not slamming the door, but certainly closing it with force.

Friedrich went into the kitchen and put water in the tea pot. He called out to the bedroom, hoping to resume the conversation casually, "Would you like tea?"

Normally, after such a confrontation, his mother would stay in her bedroom for the rest of the night and remain cool to him for days. It had been like this for the past month, ever since he had returned home. It certainly portended a depressing Christmas-time with just the two of them left of the family, no money coming into the house and his mother's meager savings running low.

The bedroom door opened. "What time will we meet your friends?"

Friedrich stopped for an instant, surprised that his mother had changed her mind. "Half past seven" he replied.

"How far away do they live?"

"By the Schwabbing barracks on Turkenstrasse."

"Schwabbing barracks? Are they soldiers?"

"Yes" Friedrich replied.

"Are they part of that revolutionary mob?" Gertrude asked with a note of apprehension.

"I'm sure not" Friedrich said reassuringly "They were infantry officers in the trenches, not sailors."

"Are we to have dinner in the barracks?" Gertrude asked in a disapproving tone.

"No mother." Friedrich said, clearly annoyed at her insinuations, "They're two officers, one married with a little boy. One of the officers just came back from the countryside with food. I met the other man at the train station while looking for work and we got to talking and hit it off and the next thing I know, his wife invited us to dinner."

"Just the same," Gertrude cautioned, "You can't be too careful these days."

"They didn't seem to care much for Ebert or Eisner or the rest of that Social Democrat bunch, much less for Communists."

"Well," Gertrude continued "if the conversation turns to politics, just agree politely with whatever they say. It's worth it for a good meal, even if they are Communists."

The teapot began to whistle and Gertrude walked into the kitchen, brushing past her son and taking over the preparation of the tea. "You should take a bath." she said, "We might at least pretend that we are still civilized."

Friedrich smirked as he headed for the bathroom. "Please Mutti dear, have the maid bring my tea to the drawing room while I draw my bath."

"Friedrich, Friedrich..." Frau Haas lamented, "when did my little boy become so insolent?"

"Mother, dear mother," Friedrich retorted, "the world became insolent... I have only joined in" and with that, he moved towards the bathroom as his mother found herself watching with sudden sadness the measured movement of his cane and the accompanying limp that had been returned to her in place of her little boy.

Frau Haas and her husband had lived in the southern part of Schwabbing district for almost twenty years in an apartment at 23 Franz Joseph Strasse. South of them in the Schwabbing district of Munich there were army barracks still full of soldiers, many of them caught up in the revolutionary fervor of the time, disillusioned by the drawn out war and the abdication of the Kaiser.

These troops had played a significant role in the revolutionary uprising of the past months in the area by their refusal to act against the revolutionaries. While the streets were alive with voices calling for a new government, a leftist government, the soldiers stayed in their barracks playing cards.

It was about eight blocks to Klaus' apartment, but Gertrude and

Friedrich couldn't spare the few pfennigs for the trolley car, so they started their journey across the city at about six o'clock to make sure they would get there in time. Friedrich knew his mother was worried about walking through the area at night, but he had traveled there in his uniform many times at night and never had trouble. There was still a bond between soldiers and when the army had refused to fire on their fellow soldiers who had taken up flags of revolution, that bond seemed even stronger.

Gertrude was only 52 years old, but she made constant noises as she moved over the snow encrusted sidewalks. Friedrich thought she sounded like an old lady. It seemed to him that she had adopted the role as a consequence of his father's death. She was now meant to be the little old widow lady who needed help with everything. He found it pathetic and worse, he found himself growing constantly more annoyed and angry with her. She was giving up. She was joyfully leaping into the role of the downtrodden old grandmother who no one cared about. While she constantly said that she knew Friedrich would be leaving her soon for his own life, her implication was that he must stay. He had to stay because she was old and feeble and could not care for herself and now that Manfred and Kurt had left her, there was no one left but Friedrich to care whether she lived or died. When Friedrich dwelled on it he could feel himself become enraged. How dare she place that on his shoulders! Just because she had given up her hope of living and being happy didn't mean that she could expect him to leap into the grave she was digging for herself.

Friedrich slowed down a bit and let his mother walk ahead of him as she carefully navigated the snow and ice under her feet. She kept looking down, paying no attention to the road ahead of her. She was afraid of falling.

Friedrich had fallen behind so that she would not see his face, so that she would not see the anger there and ask him what was bothering him. He truly was just living for the day as he had told her at the apartment. If he could only get through the day without another argument. If he could just get through until he could get work and move away. A little distance. That was all he wanted. Not that he would never see her again. He would certainly help her as much as he could. He knew that he still loved her and that she loved him, but he was not going to be a replacement for Manfred.

Friedrich regained his composure and caught up with his mother as they came to a street. He took her arm and stopped her as she was about to step off the curb in front of an oncoming truck and she looked up with a start.

"Careful!" he said, "You've got to watch where you're going."

"It's a good thing you're with me." Gertie said as she smiled up at her son, catching the glint of annoyance, but not quite understanding why and not wanting to ask him what was wrong.

"Yes... Well, it's only a couple more blocks" he said while looking ahead at the street signs of the dimly lit streets. They walked in silence until they reached the apartment house.

"Here we are." Friedrich said as he opened the door for his mother and then walked to the mailboxes "Klaus Grunewald" he said while looking through the names "Grunewald, Grunewald here it is. Apartment two-B." With that Friedrich bounded up the stairs, using his cane expertly to vault his bad leg up each step as his mother followed behind at her own measured pace. Friedrich leaned against the door jam, waiting for Gertrude to catch up before he knocked on the door.

The door only opened a crack and Friedrich smiled as a little boy peered out at him, looking him up and down. The little boy then looked at Gertrude as she stood stiffly, looking straight ahead, pretending to be oblivious to the little boy's impolite stare.

"Jakob, you have to move so they can come in" Amalie said as she opened the door wider. "Grüss Gott" she said warmly to her visitors in the traditional Bavarian greeting which translates to "greetings from God" in english.

"Grüss Gott" Friedrich replied. "Mother..." Friedrich said hesitantly as he realized that his mother was still staring straight ahead, not even making eye contact with Amalie, "This is Frau Metzdorf." Gertrude finally looked over once she had been introduced, as though a curtain had been opened and now she could acknowledge the young woman's presence. "...and Amalie," Friedrich continued, "this is my mother, Frau Gertrude Haas." Gertrude extended her hand to Amalie who took it gently.

"Welcome to our home Frau Haas, Won't you please come in?"

Amalie almost knocked Jakob over as she turned into the apartment. "Oh! Frau Haas, you haven't met my little Jakob." Amalie positioned Jakob in front of herself and knelt down, presenting him to Gertrude. Gertrude's manner instantly softened as she looked into the big blue eyes taking her in warily. "Good evening Jakob" Gertrude said. Jakob did not reply. He just continued staring at her. Friedrich was then astonished as his mother took the little boy's hand. "How old are you then, little one?" she asked.

"He just turned two last month." Amalie answered for her son. "Klaus and Gunther should be here any minute now" she continued as she took her visitor's coats. "Dinner will be ready in about half an hour."

"It smells terrific." Friedrich said enthusiastically as he caught the smell of food cooking in the kitchen.

"It's only Kartofflesuppe mit Wollewurst" Amalie said apologetically. Potato soup was standard Munich fare and it was common to slice a couple of sausages into the mix when one had such. There are many different kinds of sausages in Bavaria although the name rarely reflected the ingredients. For example, there isn't any wool at all in the wool sausage.

"It sounds wonderful." Gertrude reassured Amalie, "It is so kind of you to have us, especially with food being so hard to come by these days."

"Yes, well, our friend Klaus travels to the countryside regularly for the army and he has friends..."

"You are very lucky Frau Metzdorf." Gertrude said.

"Yes, I thank God for Klaus. Not so much for Gunther and myself, but for Jakob... Children shouldn't have to pay the price for the war, they shouldn't have to starve when they had nothing to do with it."

Jakob had warmed up to Frau Haas a bit and now stood beside her. It seemed so natural as she reached over and lightly stroked his hair. "I'm afraid we will all have to pay the price" Gertrude said in a soft voice.

"Now mother..." Friedrich reproached against her prophesy of gloom. "These hard times are only temporary. Things will settle down."

"Friedrich, I was only five years old when Bismarck's war with France ended, but I knew even then how much the French hated us. All my life I've known how the French hate us and now we're at their mercy. Our soldiers aren't in France ready to fight. They're in the streets of German cities carrying red flags. Even the Emperor has left. We have no Bismarck now. Nothing will be the same."

"Maybe we could just leave that behind tonight?" Friedrich asked plaintively.

Gertrude looked at her son. Her first reaction was anger, but then, at the same instant, she thought how nice it might be to leave the war behind. "You're right..."

"Shall we sit?" Amalie asked as she motioned her guests to the living room. "I'll be right in. I have to check the soup."

The two old chairs and settee in the living room were close in style, although they didn't quite match. The two chairs were covered in a worn, coarse, dark red fabric which showed that it had seen neglect at one time, but still, the entire apartment and contents were very clean. The settee looked brightest, upholstered in a dark blue. It must have been a more recent acquisition. The furniture was obviously second hand, but it was comfortable. Friedrich sat on the settee where Jakob joined him while Gertrude sat in one of the chairs. Jakob looked down at Friedrich's cane which leaned against the settee between them.

"What's that?" Jakob asked.

"I need it to help me walk" Friedrich replied.

"Why?" Jakob asked.

"Because I hurt my leg in the war."

"Vatti and I saw a man... a man hurt his leg" Jakob said in the measured cadence of a child, "...in the war ....they cut it off." Both Gertrude and Friedrich were surprised by such a comment from a little boy, but it wasn't unusual to see wounded men those days. Lost arms, amputated legs, blind men trying to survive in the streets of Munich. What should a father tell his son of such things? Their surprise showed as they exchanged a quick glance, but Jakob, oblivious to the looks, and certainly oblivious to the macabre nature of what he was saying, continued; "Will they cut your leg?"

"Child!" Frau Haas exclaimed in amazement at the question.

"I don't mind, mother" Friedrich said calmly "He shouldn't be afraid to ask questions." Friedrich then turned back to Jakob. "No, they won't cut my leg off because it wasn't hurt as badly as that other man's leg must have been... I suppose I was lucky..."

There was a crackle from the fireplace as the coals settled and Jakob's attention turned quickly, as always with young boys.

"Mutti... the fire?" Jakob called out to his mother in the kitchen, using the shorthand communication that families use with small children, in this case asking if he could put more coals on the fire.

"No." Amalie said as she entered the living room "You're not old enough to tend the fire yet."

"You can help me do it." Friedrich offered as he moved to the fireplace.

Everyone watched as Friedrich used his hands to bend his leg and knelt in front of the fireplace. Jakob knelt beside him and offered him the small coal shovel. Friedrich scooped up a couple of briquettes and stopped for a moment as he read the words which had been stamped into each piece. "Gott vernichten Engländ."

"I always thought this was ridiculous." Friedrich said to the piece of coal.

"What's that?" Amalie asked, thinking he was talking to her.

"God destroy England" Friedrich replied, "God destroy England stamped into each piece of coal. What possible reason could there be?"

"Perhaps they thought the soot would be carried up to God and he would get the message?" Amalie offered.

Friedrich and his mother started laughing loudly and Jakob smiled, although he didn't understand the joke. Klaus and Gunther arrived amidst the laughter, making a noisy entrance as they put up their coats and hats.

"Vatti!" Jakob shouted as he ran to his father's side. Gunther picked up Jakob and gave him a hug and a peck on the cheek as he spun around in a circle. "Grüss Gott Friedrich." Gunther said as he put Jakob down and entered the living room. Jakob followed closely, clinging to his father's leg. "...and this must be your lovely mother." The two young officers snapped smartly to attention and brought their heels together as though they were meeting a general. "We are glad you could join us this evening Frau Haas." Klaus said as he bowed slightly.

"Thank you so much for inviting us Herr Grunewald. As I was saying to Frau Metzdorf, this is especially kind of you in times like this."

"Please Frau Haas, we are all friends here. Call me Klaus."

"My friends call me Gertie."

"Well, I'll be ready to serve in a moment, so everyone should come to the table" Amalie said as she got up and put her hand on Jakob's shoulder. "Come Jakob, you can help me."

Klaus, Gunther, Friedrich and Gertie began to move towards the small table in the dining area of the apartment as Amalie handed Jakob a plate with slices of heavy, dark "war bread".

"War bread" was made from old potatoes, old bran and, more often than not, sawdust. It had been a staple of the German diet for both civilians and soldiers throughout the war.

The thing which caught Friedrich's eye, though, were the slices of fresh, yellow-orange cheese which accompanied the tired, old black bread.

Jakob walked slowly and steadily towards his father, keeping close watch on the plate as he walked, as though it might unexpectedly fly off into space at any moment. Gunther loved watching his son's face. He loved seeing that intensity and seriousness. He was sure it was a sign of intelligence and character.

"Thank you son." Gunther said as he finally relieved Jakob of his burden and found a place for the plate on the small table.

"He is a charming little boy" Gertrude commented after watching the exchange as Amalie began to serve the soup in mismatched bowls.

"Excellent!" Friedrich proclaimed as he took a drink of water after tasting the soup.

"I'm sorry it could only be soup and cheese." Amalie said.

"One forgets" Gertie responded, "Just how good simple meals can be... until one has to do without."

"Yes," Amalie said, feeling a bit guilty at their good fortune, "We eat well for a couple of days a week thanks to Klaus, but the rest of the time we just barely manage to get by."

"But let's not forget the cook." Klaus interjected good-naturedly, countering Amalie's apologetic tone. After all, there was certainly nothing wrong with their good fortune,

"Yes." Gunther concurred, "One of the best in Munich."

There was an awkward pause as they in silence until Jakob finally popped up his head. "Mutti... marmalade?" he asked with his eyes aglow in anticipation.

"No" Amalie replied.

"Why?" Jakob whined.

"Because I said 'No'" Amalie said authoritatively. She was embarrassed in front of her guests and peeked to see how Frau Haas reacted. Gertie looked down at her soup and continued eating slowly.

Jakob whined again "Why Mutti?"

"He knows what he wants." Gunther said, trying to keep Amalie in good humor, but she was clearly exasperated.

"Dear," Amalie started out, now almost snapping at Gunther, "how will Jakob learn manners if we always give in to him?"

Amalie then addressed Frau Haas. "I'm sorry for Jakob's behavior." She then turned to Jakob. "Jakob, we haven't enough marmalade for everyone and it is very bad manners to have something that you cannot offer to your guests."

Amalie's disapproval affected Jakob deeply. Jakob had never felt a disciplinary swat on his bottom because it had never been needed. Just his mother's or father's disapproval was always enough to get him to change his behavior. Now he felt bad at having been scolded and felt like crying, but he did not. He just looked sad, so sad that It prompted Gertie to speak.

"Actually," she began "we've never cared much for marmalade." Amalie looked up.

"No." Friedrich concurred "We rarely had marmalade in the house... I think Kurt was the only one who cared for it."

Friedrich almost caught himself as he said it. He had invoked the name of his dead brother. He usually tried desperately to avoid it. Not that he didn't think of Kurt, in fact, he thought of him often. He had admired Kurt and loved him deeply. Gertrude, however, wore her grief like a crown and now he had given her license to pull out Kurt's death shroud and wrap it about herself.

But Gertie only made passing mention of it. "Kurt was my other son. He died at Paschendale. Yes, he loved his marmalade." She lost only a moment in wistful memory of her dead son and his love of marmalade and then came back to the matter at hand. "So you needn't deny little Jakob because of us."

Amalie recanted, asking Jakob; "Do you want some marmalade then?"

"No thank you." Jakob said quietly and politely.

"Very well." Amalie replied, not even thinking of trying to make him feel better and reconsider his about face. Friedrich couldn't help but smile at Jakob's contradiction. The dining room was silent again as the dark little cloud floated over Jakob's head.

Finally Gunther addressed Friedrich across the table. "Have you heard any good rumors about jobs?"

Again Friedrich smiled as he kept eating. "It seems, my friend, that the rumors far outnumber the jobs."

Klaus laughed. "It's the damned revolutionaries!"

"Please Klaus..." Amalie said softly under her breath, "Children repeat what they hear."

"But it's true." Klaus insisted "They want everyone to share equally in the poverty."

"Yes, you're right" Frau Haas agreed, "If only the Kaiser were still with us."

Friedrich was surprised that his mother spoke out like this. It was the first time he had ever heard her say anything political. It was certainly not unusual in European households that children were unaware of their parent's financial situation or political beliefs. Parents rarely discussed matters of money or politics with their children in those years, but now apparently that was all different with Frau Haas. With the death of her son and husband and the uncertainty of the future, politics were now a very personal thing to her.

Friedrich found himself responding automatically as he always had to discussions regarding the Kaiser's abdication. "He ran away!"

Everyone looked at Friedrich. Perhaps he had spoken a bit loudly.

Gertrude responded in the tone of a school teacher correcting the error of a below average student. "No Friedrich. He was forced to leave by the revolutionaries."

"Mother," Friedrich started, speaking slowly, as though speaking to an elderly woman who had lost her faculties "The revolutionaries were his people. If the Kaiser had been a good leader, they would not have rebelled against him."

Klaus, Gunther and Amalie had listened quietly to the exchange, realizing it was just family bickering, but Klaus couldn't help expressing his opinions.

"The revolutionaries" Klaus began "want something for nothing."

"So you think we would be better off if the Kaiser were at the head of the government?" Friedrich cautiously asked his host, clearly not wanting to offend him.

"No, certainly not." Klaus replied "Wilhelm was not the man for the job, but we do not live in a country whose people are inclined to be ruled by committees."

"Not by speeches and majority votes are the great questions of the day decided," Gunther said, rattling off a quote, "but by blood and iron."

"Bismarck" Friedrich responded reflexively, accrediting the quotation.

"You're all so young," Frau Haas said, interrupting the exchange "but your politics must acknowledge a frightening reality. We have lost the war..."

"...lost the war from within." Gunther interrupted.

"We lost because of the Jewish revolutionaries" Klaus said almost simultaneously in a knee-jerk response.

Amalie felt a strange twinge at Klaus' statement. Certainly there were Jews among the revolutionaries and some of the leaders were Jewish, but the two were not synonymous. She didn't say anything, though. She didn't consider herself a Jew and she wouldn't defend someone just by virtue of their being Jewish. Her family had lived in Austria for hundreds of years and she considered them Austrians who practiced the Jewish religion, not Jews who lived in Austria. Now she was a German who had left her Jewish past behind her, not in the sense of denouncing her past religion, but in the sense that she no longer practiced any religion. She merely left it behind along with other things that she had decided not to take with her when she left her father's house to be with her husband. She would not stand up and defend the revolutionary radicals, and yet she felt that her husband and Klaus were wrong when they linked the Jews, revolutionaries and Bolsheviks all together with the defeat of Germany. They were only parroting what they had heard from others.

"I was saying" Gertrude continued persistently "that we lost, for whatever reason, to the French."

"An excellent point" Klaus conceded "and all the more reason that we need a single strong leader, someone representing the interest of our nation as though we were his sons and daughters. Someone to keep faith with his people in their most desperate time of need."

"Perhaps you?" Gunther mused with his right eyebrow comically arched.

Klaus looked as though someone had just poured a bucket of water on him... a huge bucket of water... from the top of a building. He glared at his friend.

"Well Klaus, you're constantly telling me that I should let you

45

know when you're getting carried away." Gunther said, defending himself from his friend's venomous stare.

"Yes," Klaus responded "but this is something I know about."

"We would all like to be able to draw simple lines. It would make life so much easier if we could tie all the different parts of our world together into one comprehensible, great truth. But I don't think it's possible" Amalie said, responding to Klaus' great declaration.

"Well this is a fine state of affairs!" Klaus said theatrically, "The whole family turns against me." Klaus then turned to Jakob "How about you Jakob? Do you have any comments?"

Jakob looked up at Klaus innocently. "Dessert?"

Everyone at the table laughed as Klaus commented "Now there's a true proletariat."

"But what about God?" Gertrude asked Amalie, "Don't you think he links everything together into one great truth?"

Friedrich was beginning to get a little nervous as his mother broached the subject of religion. Wasn't she the one who had said less than two hours before that they shouldn't risk offending their hosts by discussing politics or religion? And now she had brought up both topics.

"God certainly was not on the battlefield." Gunther answered for his wife, "How could he then possibly have a hand in politics? No, that has to be the devil's field."

"It's not unusual" Frau Haas countered "for young men to lose faith after seeing the ugliness of war."

Suddenly Klaus was serious, without his usual retreat into sarcasm and facetiousness. "With all due respect Frau Haas, you cannot possibly know what it was like for any of us, even your own son, perhaps especially your own son, and we could never completely explain what it was like."

"I know that." Gertrude said as she looked down at the table in a defensive gesture, as though Klaus had physically attacked her. "I only mean that we cannot know what God knows and so we cannot understand what God does."

"Then how do we even know that there is a God?" Klaus asked.

"You can see it in the good in the world, in the beauty of nature, in the best of men and the greatest things that men have done in the world." Gertrude countered.

"If I was to tell you the truth of life Frau Haas," Klaus began thoughtfully, sadly, "it would be that there is something missing in the reality of life, an absence if you will, an absence of honor, love, justice... an absence of superlatives in our little world. Who is the best, who is the worst, who is right and who is wrong. We are constantly surprised in our lives, such as when a good man commits an evil deed or, even more surprising, when an evil man commits a good deed. Yes, there is a distinct absence of superlatives in our little world."

"My father would say" Amalie offered after a brief pause as she contemplated Klaus' pronouncement on the nature of modern man, "That all men are capable of good, if only they make a personal commitment to honor, justice and love."

"But my point is that you will not find many men willing to make that commitment" Klaus countered.

"I agree with Frau Metzdorf." Gertrude said "It is like a living testament to Christ."

Klaus laughed a little at this. "But Frau Haas, Amalie's father is an old Jew."

"A Jew?" Gertrude exclaimed

Amalie was embarrassed at Gertrude's shock and for an instant was in conflict between a strange feeling of shame, mostly because of the way that Klaus could make the word "Jew" sound like such an insult, and a feeling of anger that Frau Haas would be upset because Amalie's father was Jewish.

"Of course, there's nothing wrong with being Jewish," Gertie bubbled as she tried to cover her *faux pas* "I just didn't know... still, your father's words show a Christian hope, that we must work against evil."

"Well, actually," Amalie ventured in again "to me the point has always been to work for good, not to work against evil."

"Isn't that the same thing?" Frau Haas asked.

"I don't think so." Amalie said "When we concentrate on fighting something we consider evil, we fail to see those things that we consider 'good' as well as we might. And once you center your life around looking for evil, then you come to change your whole perspective of the world from what it might be, to what a terrible place it is."

"You must often be disappointed." Klaus said.

"Well," Gunther said with a heavy breath, "Is there any

dessert?"

Friedrich laughed at Gunther's attempt to lighten up the conversation.

"Yes, as a matter of fact, I made some apfeltaschen for our guests." Amalie said.

"Apple pockets?" Gertrude exclaimed in disbelief. "With flour? I haven't seen real flour for so long."

"We so rarely have guests, I wanted to do something special" Amalie confided.

"Just for the guests?" Gunther asked "What about Klaus and me? ...and little Jakob." Gunther picked up his son and set him on his lap with their faces close together, both expressing sadness at this terrible news.

"Why don't you all go to the living room while I dish up dessert?" Amalie said as she started taking the dirty dishes to the sink.

"This is so kind of you." Gertrude said as she got up and moved with the others to the living room. "It reminds me of times before the war. I had almost forgotten what it was like." She wiped a tear away from her eye. "My God!" she said loudly with a great gesture of the hand she had just used to wipe away the tear, "I really am a foolish old woman! Crying over Apfeltaschen."

"It's all right Frau Haas." Gunther said in a comforting tone, "We take things for granted in easier times and then suddenly we associate these little things with times gone by."

"Ah yes," Friedrich mused, "the things we take for granted. I was only seventeen when the war started. That was such a long time ago."

"Let me see..." Gunther began, "Amalie and I had just gotten married a few months before the war broke out."

"...and I" Klaus interjected, "was a fresh young lieutenant in the greatest army the world had ever known."

"The greatest army the world had ever known..." Friedrich repeated wistfully as he looked over at the modest orange glow of the coal in the cast iron fireplace. "I just heard from a friend of mine about another friend who was a lieutenant in the cavalry. He and another officer had found a bottle of cognac in a bombed out restaurant in a small Belgian town and they were drinking it when they heard about the surrender. They finished off the bottle and then each put his pistol in the other's mouth and on the count of three they fired."

"The thing I miss most are the Christmases." Gertrude said, appearing to ignore her son's story, and Friedrich was content to let it go by.

"A big goose roasting all day." Gunther offered, stuttering a bit, recovering from Friedrich's story.

"As a child, I always loved the candles on the tree" Klaus added.

"When Gunther and I got married," Amalie said tentatively as she entered the room, passing out the apple pastries to her guests and family "I saw my first Christmas celebration, and I shall never forget the great crowd of family on the evening before and the closeness and warmth."

Gunther smiled at his wife at the thought of this shared memory.

"I wonder what we'll do this year, with only a couple of weeks to go." Gertrude said to no one in particular.

"What is it now? Two weeks?" Klaus rejoined.

"Ten days" Amalie answered.

"Well, at least we'll be together" Gunther said, knowing that there would be no Christmas feast this year and no wonderful gifts for his son. He couldn't even find candles for a Christmas tree.

"I do have some 'coffee'." Amalie offered meekly.

"...from roasted corn?" Gertrude asked with a smile.

"Ja." Amalie said, now at ease with her ersatz coffee.

"You have given us such a lovely evening." Gertrude said, "There is no need to be embarrassed."

"No, of course not." Friedrich added emphatically, "You've been so kind."

"We were happy you could come" Klaus said, "In these days, we soldiers who fought at the front must stick together."

"Well, I didn't actually fight at the front" Friedrich said, correcting his host.

Klaus shot a look of surprise to Gunther.

"I didn't say he 'fought' at the front, I said he was 'at' the front" Gunther explained.

"I was in the medical corps" Friedrich added. "I drove ambulances."

"Ah..." Klaus replied "Then you were still in the thick of it."

"Yes" Friedrich said "I often went right to the trenches to take men out."

"Is that how you hurt your leg?" Klaus asked.

"No..." Friedrich said as he now explained his injury to a third member of the household, "My ambulance tipped over on a bad stretch of road by the Russian front. The ironic thing is that it happened after all the fighting was over." Friedrich paused a moment and then added "That's how I earned this lovely cane."

"Well," Klaus explained "When I speak of soldiers at the front, I mean to say those who really knew what the war was like. You would certainly qualify."

"You make it sound like a club, some kind of fraternal organization." Friedrich said in an analytical tone.

"Exactly." Gunther explained as he jumped into the conversation. "A brotherhood of front-line soldiers. We have experienced things first hand which others could not imagine, much less endure."

"I see what you mean." Friedrich said thoughtfully as a thousand images raced through his mind, experiences that he could only tell to other soldiers. Who else could understand? Who else but another soldier could appreciate the things a man feels when he hides from a relentless artillery barrage in a tiny hole in the ground with the entire world threatening to collapse in on him. Who but another soldier could imagine the things that a human body can endure? One moment you and a friend dive into a trench to escape an incoming artillery round and in the next instant a mass of splintered bone, blood, mud and intestine gives up a pitiful whimper and calls for it's mother as your friend falls dead into the water at your feet.

Friedrich quickly looked back at the glowing embers in the fireplace so that he would not have to look into anyones eyes. What if they looked into his eyes and saw within him the terrible things that he had seen? Surely they could never look at him again.

Jakob had just been sitting quietly next to Friedrich through all this, slowly eating his apfeltaschen, knowing, even though he had not been told, that it would be a long time before he ever got such a treat again.

Jakob knew that Friedrich was feeling sad, as did all the others in the room, and he climbed up on Friedrich's leg and rested his head against Friedrich's chest. Friedrich was surprised at first, but then he put his arm around the tired little boy. Everyone else just watched in silence and they all knew that Jakob was the only one who could have gotten close to Friedrich at that moment. This sad young man, only just turned twenty-one years old, marked by this hellish war for the rest of his life.

Gradually the conversation returned and touched on lighter topics than those of war, defeat and religion and the remainder of the evening became a pleasant diversion. Friedrich and his mother got up promptly at ten o'clock and insisted that they must be getting home. They were both keenly aware that they did not want to overstay their welcome. On the cynical side, they hoped to be invited back to share in the good fortune of their hosts, but they really had enjoyed their evening and genuinely liked their new friends. Frau Haas even picked up Jakob and rested him on her hip as she gave him a little peck on the cheek. "You must promise to be a good boy until we meet again..." she said with a smile.

"Christmas?" Jakob asked innocently.

Amalie shot an embarrassed glance at Klaus and then looked down at the floor. None of them had any idea if their fortune, such as it was, would continue, and to plan ahead even two weeks seemed ridiculous.

Klaus looked at Gunther and then at their guests. "Of course," Klaus said "you must come for whatever kind of Christmas dinner we have."

"But we can't promise a goose!" Gunther added.

Frau Haas smiled appreciatively, realizing that they had made such a generous offer based on a child's slip of the tongue.

"Thank you so much, but I think we have plans" she said as she turned to Friedrich for support.

"Yes," he said, "I think we promised to visit family and we would be gone for most of the week."

Amalie stepped over to Frau Haas to relieve her of Jakob. "If..." Amalie started hesitantly, "your plans with your family fall through..." Amalie looked at Klaus and Gunther for a glimmer of acquiescence which she saw in their eyes, "...we would very much enjoy your company."

Frau Haas then knew Amalie was being sincere. "Well, if things don't work out, and if you allow us to bring something with us next time," Gertrude stressed sternly, "then I think we would be happy to come." Friedrich agreed with a nod and offered his hand to his new friends and with that, they left.

51

Klaus returned to the living room while Gunther took Jakob from Amalie who went into the kitchen. A dirty dinner dish never saw daylight in Amalie's kitchen, even if it was really Klaus' kitchen. Klaus went about reading the daily newspaper while Gunther hoisted Jakob up on his shoulders for a piggy-back ride into the living room. "Now young man, It's long past your bedtime."

Klaus went to bed soon after and Amalie and Gunther were left alone to lay their bedding on the floor in the middle of the living room. Once they had settled in, Amalie with her head on Gunther's chest, Gunther spoke quietly, so as not to wake up Jakob.

"I don't know how we're going to get an apartment. I didn't think it would be so hard to find work."

"It's not your fault" Amalie said. "No work, no food. I'm afraid to say anything that might offend Klaus because I don't know what we would do without him."

"You shouldn't worry about Klaus." Gunther reassured her, "He's been a good friend and he knows how hard things are."

"He worries me."

"Worries you? Why?"

"Well..."

"Go ahead and say it."

"He hates Jews."

"So what?"

"How can you say that?" Amalie asked as she sat up.

"What do you mean?"

"How can you say 'so what' when you know I'm Jewish?"

"But you're not that kind of Jew." Gunther said in a comforting tone, trying to placate his overexcited wife, "Klaus doesn't mean you."

"Then who does he mean?" Amalie asked.

"Well, he means the Bolsheviks, of course!"

"But they're not all Jews. If he means Bolsheviks, then why doesn't he say that?" Amalie continued to press..

"You're being too sensitive. He doesn't mean all Jews." Gunther replied as he put his arm around Amalie, returning her head to his chest, "In any group of people you have good and bad. There are good Germans and bad Germans, good Frenchmen and bad Frenchman, and just like that there are good Jews and bad Jews. Klaus hates the bad Jews."

"You make it sound so reasonable, but it frightens me when I see that look in his eyes. There's such a strange edge to his voice sometimes."

"You're just anxious because you feel we're imposing. Just hold on. Things will be better after Christmas."

"Christmas..." Amalie said with a hint of foreboding as the subject changed and she found that she was happy to let it go. She was afraid that if she dwelled too long on Gunther's anti-semitism, well, she just didn't know how they could ever resolve it. It was like a monster hiding in a closet waiting to rush out someday and devour them both.

"Yes." Gunther said as he planted a little kiss on Amalie's forehead. "Christmas... That reminds me, It's been a long time since you've given me a gift..."

"A gift?"

"Like this..." he said as he began to kiss her on the shoulder.

"Gunther! Our son is right there."

Gunther looked over at Jakob curled up against the back of the couch.

"He's fast asleep. We can be quiet. I've heard that if you hold your breath at the last minute, it can make it even better."

He then slid his hand gently under her nightgown and across her stomach, kissing her on the lips and then on her throat, moving his hand slowly up her side.

Chapter 3

Kurt Eisner.
Rosa Luxemburg.
Karl Liebknecht.

These were the names and faces of revolution in Germany in 1919. There were certainly more, tens of thousands more, but these were the names known across the country. Karl Liebknecht had been one of the few voices in 1914 that called for peace instead of war and in that time of war fever he was sent to prison for his beliefs. Rosa Luxemburg had been a Communist for most of her life, fighting for the rights of the poor and disenfranchised and believing that the only way their lot could be improved was through Communist rule. She, too was put in prison for her willingness and commitment to speak out about those beliefs. Both Liebknecht and Luxemburg were released from prison just days before the end of the war. Although their political philosophies were different on many points, together they led a group known as the Spartacists, named after Spartacus, the slave who led a revolt in ancient Rome. The Spartacists were a Communist organization in Berlin and many believed that they were the leaders of the revolution in Germany. The truth, however, was that the actual revolution that spread across Germany was a more popular rising of ordinary citizens. Those citizens just wanted the war to end and they believed that they were merely supporting the new Social Democratic Republic.

It was that idea of a new German Republic putting an end to the Kaiser's war which emboldened Kurt Eisner to stroll into the Bavarian provincial palace and declare the new republic in Munich and Bavaria.

Trouble lay ahead in Munich, however, as it always does when a change of such magnitude is begun. As an anonymous revolutionary once so appropriately put it: "The problem with revolutions is that they always degenerate into governments."

Christmas came and went quickly in 1918. Frau Haas and Amalie had become fast friends. It was to their mutual benefit since Frau Haas enjoyed sitting with Jakob and Amalie was willing to share whatever she could with Frau Haas and Friedrich as repayment for services rendered.

Gunther and Klaus quickly adopted Friedrich. They often went to one beer hall or another whenever they could afford it. Friedrich and Gunther would find odd jobs about the city, filling in the time until they could find steady employment.

They all felt that Christmas was a time for children and so when they met for Christmas Eve, the presents for the adults were modest and utilitarian while Jakob was showered with presents. Jakob's gifts were mostly home-made toys from the men and clothing which Amalie and Frau Haas had made by cutting down adult clothes.

Friedrich was especially proud of himself. While everyone expected that Klaus, with his connections in the countryside, would be the only hope for a Christmas Eve dinner, it was Friedrich who had "gone weaseling", as they called it in Munich, into the countryside by Rosenheim and traded some of his father's old metalworking tools to a farmer in exchange for two large chickens.

Gunther had liberated a small Christmas tree for the apartment. He never told anyone where that tree came from, but his silence caused his wife and friends to speculate that it must have come from somewhere in the English garden by the river, a practice that was all too familiar to the park managers in the time after the war.

Gunther's mother, Marie, had sent a few treasured tree ornaments with Amalie when she left Austria. Marie had been upset all along at the way her husband, Oskar, had treated Amalie and the way that he ignored his own son, but Marie was not strong enough to stand up to him. When she heard through friends that Amalie was leaving for Munich, she packed a small crate with some personal things for Gunther, the son she hadn't seen in four years and didn't know if she would ever see again, and managed to sneak out of the house without her husband's knowledge. The meeting with Amalie was very emotional for her as she tried to excuse her husband's actions and then embraced Amalie with tears in her eyes. "Take care of him" was all she could say as she left Amalie at the train.

There were no candles to be found for the tree that year because of continuing wartime shortages. Klaus, however, managed to improvise "ersatz" candles. He polished empty rifle bullet cartridges so that they shone like little brass mirrors and filled them with carbon sticks such as the miners used in the lamps they wore on their hats. The candles were traditionally lit for only a short while, which was a good thing because the burning carbon gave off a bad smell along with a dirty, sooty flame, but at least they had candles. Everyone commented on how nice they were. They were just tiny smoldering candles on a Christmas tree, but as revolution shook their world and they waited to see what the price of peace would be, those candles were a tiny light against the darkness of tomorrow.

There was a sizable snowfall in Munich a couple of weeks after Christmas which meant a lot of shoveling work for Friedrich and Gunther and so, with a few coins in their pockets, they decided to meet at the Hofbrauhaus. Friedrich was passing through the "altstadt", or "old city district", on his way to meet Klaus and Gunther when he heard someone calling his name from across the open air market.

Friedrich turned to see who it was and immediately recognized a mop of red hair settled atop a young man crossing the Viktualienmarkt. At first he couldn't put a name with the large, oafish looking face coming towards him, but then he remembered. Werthers. That was it. Richard Werthers. He was the son of one of the men who had worked with his father in the machine shop.

"Friedrich!" Richard repeated as he slapped a meaty hand on Friedrich's shoulder, "I haven't seen you for years! How are things?"

Friedrich looked at the young man as though he were a child even though Richard was only barely two years his junior. The difference wasn't so much their ages as the fact that Richard, in his clean new uniform, had never left Munich during the war. Richard had only been conscripted some two months before and had barely finished training when the armistice was announced.

"Fine. Just fine." Friedrich replied reservedly.

Richard's gregarious mood changed immediately as he remembered the death of Friedrich's father. "We were all so sorry about your father" he said earnestly, "You know, my father was with him at the last."

"Yes, we were glad that his friends were with him." Friedrich said, grasping for some sort of acknowledgment.

"So... What are you doing now?" Richard asked.

56

"Anything I can until I find steady work. And you?"

"Me? Well, I've just started as an apprentice machinist with father."

It was strange how those words hit Friedrich. Even though Friedrich had never wanted to follow in his father's footsteps and become a machinist, he was still somehow offended that Richard should not only be spared from the horror of war, but he was even spared the economic hardships visited against veterans.

"You're very lucky" Friedrich commented coolly.

"Yes. I know." Richard agreed in an embarrassed tone. He could tell what Friedrich was thinking. "Where are you off to?" he asked, trying to change the subject.

"Hofbrauhaus. To meet friends" Friedrich said.

"That sounds like a good idea. Would you mind if I tag along?"

Friedrich was not thrilled with the idea, but he had grown a bit cynical. Perhaps his lucky friend would buy.

"Sure, why not?" He laughed to himself. He knew that Klaus and Gunther would have this young upstart for dinner and yet he would lead Richard into the lion's den of his friend's company.

It was just after three o'clock as they walked through the cobblestone streets, passing the Heiliggeistkirche* and the city hall with its gothic spires. The streets were dark and ominous under a shroud of gray winter clouds. People seemed to move slower than they had before the war. The smiles seemed more forced and infrequent, the buildings more faded and inhospitable.

So much of the city seemed homogenous with its gray five story buildings all with the same basic structure, the same windows, the same doorways, interrupted here and there by a gothic church or a square. It was the embodiment of a Germanic sense of order and utilization of space.

The Hofbrauhaus, however, was its usual loud and boisterous self. The patrons always made a good show of being loud and hearty. This had been the tradition of the beer hall for generations as patrons banged their two-liter, earthenware beer steins on the tables and sang along with the carnival-like music. It was a garishly decorated hall with its canary Yellow walls ascending to renderings of bright green vines and red foliage with berries all climbing up to the pinnacles of

---

* The Church of the Holy Spirit.

the cathedral vaults. The ceiling did much to emphasize the noise from the crowd below, amplifying the song and conversation of even a small crowd. It was an embellishment. It made these people much larger than they were, stronger and more alive.

Richard followed Friedrich as he made his way to a table against the far wall where Gunther and Klaus waited. Klaus was smoking a cigarette and he and Gunther sized up the well turned out stranger in his flawless uniform.

"Parade inspection today?" Klaus asked.

Richard was quickly on edge as the officer put him on the spot.

"No," he replied, "I just wanted to look good for the meeting of the soldier's council."

Friedrich almost laughed. Of all the things Richard could have said to antagonize these two men, that was the most damning comment, given with the most innocent delivery. Friedrich expected an explosion.

"The soldier's council?" Gunther repeated, "Are you a member?"

"Oh no!" Richard responded emphatically "I have no qualifications for such work."

"Then why are you going?" Klaus asked.

Friedrich was surprised by the tone of his friend's questions, the lack of condemnation, the seeming acceptance. He didn't say a word though, he just pulled up a chair and offered one to Richard.

"I was curious" Richard offered as he sat down.

Gunther and Klaus had seen a lot of boys like Richard and just as Richard was curious about the soldier's council, they were curious how such young men got swept up in this revolution.

"About what?" Klaus asked.

"Well, I guess I thought there was more to a revolution than this." Richard replied.

"More?" Klaus asked.

"More blood." Gunther said to Klaus, answering the question for Richard.

Richard was a bit embarrassed at Gunther's astute observation and broke eye contact as he meekly replied; "I suppose."

Klaus stared at Richard relentlessly as he ominously prophesied "It may not yet be over... There might be a few cards left to play."

"Cards to play?" Richard asked as he looked up and returned

Klaus' stare.

"Look to Berlin." Klaus said, nodding his head, referring to the formation of counter-revolutionary forces called "Freikorps" or "freebooters" which had been organized under Friedrich Ebert's defense minister, Gustav Noske. Noske sought to abolish the worker's, soldier's and sailor's councils in Berlin and had begun to do so with machine guns and artillery in the heart of Berlin just the day before.

"Well..." Richard offered in defense of the councils, "Almost everyone agrees that they've done some good."

"What good?" Gunther challenged.

"They..." Richard started, trying to gather his thoughts, "raised old age benefits... helped men without jobs..."

"They destroyed jobs, betrayed the nation and dishonored us all." Klaus interjected.

"Gentlemen," Richard said curtly as he stood up, realizing he had been led into a trap, "it was interesting meeting you, but I'm afraid I must be going." Richard stopped an instant and turned to Friedrich who had not said a word through the entire exchange. "My best to your mother." he said, and with that he wound his way through the hall to the door.

"Coward" Gunther said under his breath as he took a drink of beer.

"Why on Earth did you bring him?" Klaus asked Friedrich.

"He has a job." Friedrich said morosely, "I thought he might buy."

Gunther almost spit out his beer as he began to laugh and Klaus gave Friedrich a good-natured slap on the back.

Richard walked briskly as he left the Hofbrauhaus and quickly covered the five blocks to Marienplatz. He should have seen it coming, he thought to himself, that an officer would try to pick a fight when he mentioned the council, but he couldn't understand why Friedrich had let it happen like that without saying a word.

Richard reached the trolley stop just as a trolley pulled up to the siding and people disembarked. "Excuse me!" he said as he almost stepped on a tiny woman who was getting off just as he stepped up on the running board. "No harm done" Rosa said as she stepped off the trolley, making her way through the Marienplatz square and down the street to one of the nameless gray buildings.

Rosa had traveled for six hours to get to Munich from Berlin so she could approve galleys for a book of her speeches. The publisher tended to the left politically, to the far left at that time, and they were far enough away from Berlin that they dared to take the chance of publishing her works.

She had been in prison during the war and was only released within weeks of the armistice, just as many political prisoners were being released by the Social Democrats. It was one of the great paradoxes of the revolution in Germany that she was considered to be a leader of the revolution when, in fact, she had no hand whatsoever in the overthrow of the Kaiser.

Rosa Luxemburg was a Communist and a big name in the cause of revolution in Germany. She had opposed the war from early on and it was this opposition that landed her in prison, but the revolution at the end of the war was a spontaneous movement of the people. This concept of a spontaneous movement of the people is most clearly demonstrated by the revolution's tragic, and eventually self-defeating, lack of leadership and direction. Rosa was associated with the revolution by virtue of her revolutionary career prior to the war, not by her actions during the revolution. It was the speeches she had made before the war which were about to be published.

Amalie sat patiently with her hands folded in her lap, the letter of recommendation that her father had sent for Gunther held tightly in her hand. She had left Jakob with Frau Haas and had been waiting for Mr. Freider for over half an hour, but she wasn't about to raise a fuss because she was so nervous that she considered just walking out. Gunther had made it obvious that he was not interested in using her father's connections to get a job, but Amalie was afraid that Gunther wouldn't be able to find anything else. On the other hand, Amalie was pretty sure that Gunther would not be happy with her getting a job, but they had to find a way to get their own apartment and stop living off Klaus' good nature. Perhaps she wanted to get her husband away from Klaus because of his anti-semitism and right wing politics. Whatever the reasons, here she was, afraid to get a job and just as afraid of not getting a job.

Rosa was tired after rushing up the three floors to Mr. Frieder's offices and she let out a loud sigh as she entered the lobby area. Amalie, who had been caught up in her thoughts, reacted with a startled jump that was so exaggerated that Rosa couldn't help laughing.

"I'm so sorry!" Rosa offered apologetically through her laughter, "I didn't see you. I didn't mean to frighten you."

"No, no. It's not your fault, I didn't realize how nervous I was."

"Oh, are you waiting for a verdict on a book?"

"What?" Amalie asked, not at all understanding the question.

"Are you an author waiting to hear about a book?" Rosa asked, re-stating her question.

"Me? Oh no, I'm just looking for a job, something in administration."

"I see," Rosa said measuredly, not sure what to make of Amalie's reaction, as though Rosa's suggestion that Amalie might be an author was a criminal accusation.

"Well, good luck." Rosa said as she went up to the receptionist's desk and asked for Mr. Frieder.

"Do you have an appointment?" the receptionist asked.

"Yes, I'm a little late though. Luxemburg. Rosa Luxemburg."

"Of course, Miss Luxemburg. He's been expecting you. Go right in."

Amalie was impressed. She may have been kept waiting, but at least it took someone like Rosa Luxemburg to do it. And she had even talked to her! This was certainly not something she would talk to Gunther about, but someday she would tell her father, and she knew he would be impressed.

Amalie waited for another half hour and finally Rosa came out of the office with Mr. Frieder. Once they had finished saying good-bye, Amalie got up and extended her hand.

"I didn't realize who you were, Miss Luxemburg. My name is Amalie Stein. My father... My father and I, have admired your work, your courage."

"Thank you." Rosa replied politely. "Are you a member of the party?"

"No," Amalie said meekly "but I agree with many things you've said and I have a great deal of respect for you, for the way you stand up for what you believe in."

"Well," Rosa said, once again smiling and with a bit of a laugh, "that's a start." She then became serious and looked Amalie in the eye. "But remember," she said "now is the time to stand up for what you believe in." Rosa shook Amalie's hand one last time and left, returning to Berlin that same day.

Mr. Frieder then invited Amalie into his office and they went over her hand-written resume' listing her educational background and experience working with her father, some of it actual and some conjured. She then showed him the letter of reference from her father and eventually, she talked her way into a job.

She had no idea what she was going to tell Gunther. How could she tell her husband that she had gotten a job when he could find nothing? Would he let her keep it?

The impending confrontation with Gunther loomed before Amalie's eyes. It was the only thing she could think about as she walked home, as she made dinner and while they ate.

The dinner was certainly nothing to talk about. They ate boiled turnips and war bread with only water to drink. Klaus and Gunther were content to talk between themselves as Amalie ate in silence. She didn't seem mad. She didn't snap as she sometimes did when she was angry. She merely ate in silence and then cleared the dishes and washed them. She then put Jakob to bed and finally laid out the bedding on the floor for Gunther and herself.

"Could you make us some coffee before you go to bed?" Gunther asked, still not questioning her silence.

Amalie made the coffee as Gunther and Klaus continued talking at the table and then went to change into her nightgown. Klaus looked at Gunther and rolled his eyes as Amalie went into the bathroom. "I don't know what you did," Klaus said sympathetically "but you must have really upset her."

"I can't imagine what." Gunther countered emphatically as he shrugged his shoulders and tossed a glance at the closed door of the bathroom.

"A women's thing?" Klaus offered feebly.

"No, that was just over a week ago..." Gunther said just as Amalie came out of the bathroom.

"...and then they threw them out." Klaus said, completing an imaginary sentence so that Amalie wouldn't know that they were talking about her.

Amalie paid no attention to them as she put a last scoop of coal on the fire and banked the ashes before laying down on the bedding on the floor.

The two men continued talking for another hour and more as

Amalie lay still, eyes open, facing Jakob as he slept on the couch, wondering if she would be able to sleep at all.

When Gunther finally came to bed, he kissed her on the cheek as she lay on her side facing away from him. He noticed she wasn't asleep.

"I'm sorry. did I wake you?" he whispered.

"No" Amalie whispered back.

"Can't you get to sleep?"

"No" she answered again.

Gunther reached his arm around his wife to embrace her and rolled her on her back at the same time. He kissed her on the lips. Amalie didn't respond.

"All right," he said quietly, "what's wrong?"

"It's nothing."

"Nothing? You've been moody all week and you haven't said two words all night. You didn't even read to Jakob tonight."

"I'm just tired." she offered unconvincingly.

Gunther rolled onto his back beside her. "I'm not always sure how to love you." he said as he looked up at the ceiling.

Amalie felt sad when he said it. "I know" she replied. "I know it isn't easy. We were apart for so long... We were so young."

Gunther thought this was such a strange turn for the conversation. He had hoped it would be some sort of little problem and now they were talking about the quality of their love.

He couldn't have known that the past week had been a time of decision for Amalie, the time she first thought of getting a job and then deciding where to get a job and finally, working up the courage to actually do it. Gunther only noticed the sudden change. She had become withdrawn and quiet and he was becoming convinced that it was him, that he was not being a good husband, that she was losing faith in him because he couldn't find work and support his family. He was accepting the charity of his friend and beginning to think his wife was giving up on him because of it.

"Do you love me?" Gunther asked.

Amalie was astounded. This was something he might have said when they were first married, but not since he went to war, not since the war ended. It seemed to be a given. She could imagine herself asking him, but not Gunther asking her. When she asked, she wanted to be reassured, to hear the words and know for certain, but he seemed to ask as though he thought the answer might be "no".

"Of course I do." she whispered as she drew close and put her head on his chest.

"I don't know what I'd do without you and Jakob. You're all I live for." he said quietly.

"Oh no, no, it's nothing like that." Amalie said warmly as she kissed him on the cheek and wrapped her arms around him tightly.

"Then what?" Gunther asked as he took her chin in his hand and raised her face to his, looking into her eyes in the pale moonlight.

"I guess..." Amalie started slowly, averting her eyes as she ran a finger across Gunther's chest, hesitating, "I guess I want us to move to our own apartment."

"We've talked about this before." Gunther said calmly, "We will find a place as soon as I get work."

"I know," Amalie said, "but... Gunther, I have something to tell you and I don't know how to say it."

"Just come out with it." Gunther said firmly.

"Do you remember the letter father sent?"

"Letter? What letter?"

"The letter of introduction. The recommendation to that publisher."

"Yes, yes." Gunther said, "Now Amalie I told you I wasn't..."

"I used it." Amalie interrupted.

"You 'used' it? What do you mean?"

"Gunther, I got a job with a publisher."

"You what?" Gunther exclaimed in a loud whisper that roused Jakob who then began to toss and turn.

"Shhh." Amalie said as she touched a finger to Gunther's lip and turned to watch Jakob as though her watchful eye would keep him from waking, but her real goal was to distract Gunther from his temper. Jakob made a little sighing noise as he turned towards the back of the couch and settled in.

Gunther turned on his side, moving Amalie from on top of him onto her side, so that they faced each other.

"What have you done?" Gunther asked in a tone that was once again calm.

"I told you. I got a job with a small publisher. An assistant editor."

"What about Jakob?"

"Gertrude said she would be glad to watch him. Her apartment is on my way." Amalie said, ready to meet any obstacle that Gunther might bring up.

Gunther sighed. "My wife working while I shovel sidewalks." he said and then sighed again. "I don't know Amalie, I just don't know. It doesn't seem right. What will people say? What will my friends say?"

"What can they say? Most of your friends are out of work too."

"Oh Amalie!" Gunther said, clearly exasperated by his wife's attitude "This is just too much."

"Please, darling." Amalie said as she put a hand on his cheek "Please let me try. Let's just try it and see how it goes."

Gunther sighed again and rolled onto his back. "Don't you know how this makes me feel?"

"I know, dear." Amalie said sympathetically.

"Women only work until they get married." Gunther asserted, "I have never met a man whose wife works, except for farm women. Peasants working in the fields." He put a hard emphasis on the word "peasants" which made it sound as though they were animals of some kind and now his family had sunken to that level.

"Gunther," Amalie started delicately, "these are unusual times. We need to do whatever we can to get by." They laid in silence for a moment until Amalie added; "I'm not doing this to hurt you."

"...as soon as I find work, you must quit." Gunther said with finality, acknowledging that they would try it, but still making the point that he was the master.

"Yes, captain." Amalie said contentedly and she smiled as she kissed him gently on the cheek once more and then turned on her side to go to sleep.

"You're so easy to get along with when you get your own way." Gunther commented acidically as he too turned on his side, turning his back to Amalie.

Amalie turned over onto her other side and moved close to Gunther, putting her arm around his stomach and pulling her body close to his as they drifted off to sleep.

Klaus was the first up the next day, off to his administrative duties at the Schwabbing barracks after a quick breakfast of bread and coffee. Gunther didn't say anything about Amalie's job as she got herself and Jakob ready for the first day of her new routine. It wasn't that he was cold, just apprehensive. For that matter so was Amalie. Gunther picked up Jakob and tossed him into the air and then gave him a kiss on the cheek. Amalie smiled as she watched and then Gunther handed Jakob to her and gave her a quick peck on the cheek too. They all went out the door at the same time with Gunther watching as his wife and son left while he locked the door.

The day went by quickly and before she knew it, Amalie was on her way to pick up Jakob. Neither Gunther nor Amalie told Klaus about her job at dinner that night, but they did the next day and, although Klaus didn't betray the sentiment to his friends, he was glad that Amalie was taking the first step toward their imminent move to their own apartment. It was this sentiment on Klaus' part that saved Gunther from the endless stream of jokes and barbs that Gunther had feared.

Amalie learned her job quickly at Frieder and Son Publishing and was glad that she had chosen that particular company. She read the galleys of the speeches by Rosa Luxemburg at the office, mostly because she had met Rosa rather than for any political reasons, but she wouldn't have dared to take it home for fear that Gunther or Klaus might find it. She finished reading it just before going to pick up Jakob on the tenth of January.

In Berlin on that day, Rosa was staying in a house in Wilmersdorf. She was actually in hiding since the Freikorps, the soldiers of counter revolution, had named her as a leader of the revolution and put a price on her head.

Karl Liebknecht was another revolutionary figurehead who was staying at the same house. He was much like Rosa in that he was associated with the revolution because of his pre-war activities and his open opposition to the war even though he actually had nothing to do with leading the revolution. Liebknecht likewise had the dubious honor of a Freikorp's price on his head.

Someone betrayed them both to the freebooters and this was the night when the Freikorps came to "arrest" the two of them. The troops, lead by a lieutenant Linder, invaded the house and caught both Rosa and Karl at home.

Rosa was writing a letter as three men exploded into her room.

"What is the meaning of this?" She shouted as she stood up, knocking over the chair and surprising the soldiers for an instant.

"Rosa Luxemburg?" one of the soldiers demanded.

"Yes" Rosa asked, not backing down, "What do you want?"

"You're under arrest" the soldier said as he took a step towards her.

"Under arrest for what? By what authority..." she began, but before she could go on, the soldier slapped her with the back of his hand, knocking her to the floor. He saw her coat on a hook on the wall beside him and threw it at her.

"Put it on" he said.

She slowly and deliberately put on the coat as she thought about what she would do next. This was certainly not the first time she had been arrested. In a way, it was a good sign. It meant she was being taken seriously and still had an effect on the politicians, but now she was thinking of who she would call and how she would get some money to bribe her way out.

"Take her." the soldier said to the other two men. It looked comical as the two large soldiers dragged the small woman between them, but the men's faces showed no humor. It was clear that these men hated what she represented and they enjoyed the thought of torturing her. Rosa missed a step as the men pulled her along and when she tripped they let her go, making a joke and laughing as she tumbled down the rest of the stairway. She was pretty banged up, but the soldiers took no notice as they met at the front door of the house with another group of soldiers who had rousted Karl from his room. He had been beaten.

From there the group drove over to the Eden hotel with Rosa and Karl in separate cars. Rosa and Karl managed to exchange glances as they arrived at the hotel where they would soon be questioned by a Captain Pabst. Both of them had been through this type of thing before, but it seemed strange that they were both there together. Their paths had only crossed by coincidence before, but now they were both working on a Communist newspaper called "The Red Flag."

Rosa's politics were farther left than Karl's. If you were to try to define the difference, you would probably come up with Rosa trying to scrap the whole government and start anew, while Karl would try to rebuild the current government, saving what he felt was useful.

In the final analysis, of course, these differences meant nothing because they would both share the same fate, and ironically, they would share that fate because of what they appeared to be rather than what they were, although there was another more immediate reason for people wanting them out of the way.

The newspaper, The Red Flag, was making constant and accurate statements about the connections between the Social Democrats and the Freikorps. The Freikorps were right wing German military units not associated with the regular army. Neither of the Freikorps nor the Social Democrats wanted to be associated with each other and they especially didn't want such associations to be made public. These groups at opposite ends of the political spectrum had only allied out of what they all believed to be the absolute necessity of crushing the revolution. The task at hand demanded that Luxemburg and Liebknecht be stopped not only because they appeared to be leaders of the revolution, but because they were exposing the alliance of the Social Democrats and the Freikorps.

Rosa and Karl were taken in turn to a room on the first floor where Captain Pabst was to question them. Rosa began to get nervous, although she didn't show it, when she found that the questions were only to verify her identity. There were no charges or outrageous accusations as there had been before whenever she had been arrested. Now they only wanted to make sure they had the right person.

After Pabst had finished, Karl and Rosa were taken to a side door of the hotel where cars were waiting in the side street which had been closed off to traffic. Just as they got to the door, a guard who was stationed there suddenly brushed past his fellow storm troopers and brought up his rifle, bringing his whole body into a powerful thrust as he drove the rifle butt up against Karl's cheekbone. There was a distinctive cracking noise as the impact fractured bone and Karl then fell to the floor with blood flowing freely from the wound.

Rosa was knocked aside in the melee' and ended up flying against the wall by the stairway where she fell to the floor. This was where the assailant found her as he thrashed his rifle around and struck her, the blow finding it's mark as his rifle butt fractured her skull, leaving her unconscious. Karl was still conscious, but bleeding badly from the head and speaking incoherently.

The guard had been paid and ordered by an unknown party to kill the two Spartacists, but since he had only wounded them, the officers moved on to the next step of their plan and had the soldiers load their victims into cars. A young Lieutenant named Vogel was in charge of Rosa's fate.

Vogel took out his pistol as soon as he got into the car. Once the car pulled away from the curb he pulled her coat up over her head and doubled the heavy but worn fabric, using it to muffle the sound of the explosion as he shot Rosa in the temple while she lay unconscious on the seat beside him. Vogel then had the driver go to the Liechtenstein bridge and stop in the middle, ordering the other two soldiers to carry Rosa's body to the side of the bridge and throw her into the canal. They watched for a moment as the body was quickly swept away.

In the end, when doctors examined Rosa's body after it had washed up on the banks of the canal months later, they could not determine the cause of death. It seems that they found water in her lungs indicating that even after the vicious bludgeoning and the gunshot, Rosa actually survived all that and may have finally drowned as she was carried away by the frigid water of the canal.

Karl Liebknecht had also been killed that night. The soldiers who drove him away from the Eden hotel drove him out to the lake called Neue See and politely asked him to step out of the car. When he did, they shot him once in the back of the head and threw his body back into the car. They then drove to the local morgue and left the body there, saying that it was the body of an unknown man who had been murdered.

All of this was only overture to the fate of revolution in the South, in Munich.

Less than two weeks after the deaths of Luxemburg and Liebknecht, Kurt Eisner was walking through the "old city" part of Munich on his way to a ten o'clock meeting of the provincial assembly with a letter of resignation in his pocket. His organization, which had come about so unexpectedly, his bloodless revolution, was now falling apart under the weight of petty demands of parliament members, each wanting more than the others. Perhaps the resignation was his final answer to parliament or maybe it was just a threat. No one will ever know exactly what Eisner might have done.

It had been typical weather for Munich at that time of year. They hadn't seen the sun for almost a week as light rains periodically swept through the city, not drenching, but keeping the streets dreary and wet. The dark clouds were mirrored on the wet cobblestones and in the puddles on the sidewalk so that one could almost become confused as to which was earth and which was sky.

A nameless doorway held a young man in it's shadow. He dropped the butt of his last cigarette on the damp threshold, glancing down at the fading orange glow as it hissed and crushing it out with his heel. He knew Eisner would be there. He knew it would be soon. He had something to prove. He knew in his heart that the German people did not want this revolution. They had been seduced. They were tired of the war and thought this was the only way to end it, but he could forgive them for this. It was understandable that they wanted the war to end, but Eisner had taken advantage of their war-weariness.

The young man in the doorway, Count Anton Arco-Valley, knew that he was one of the rightful rulers of Germany, a member of the nobility, and that he had to stop Eisner. Anton was half-Jewish and eager to prove to his friends at a right wing club, "friends" who had rejected him for membership because of his Jewish background, that a half-Jew could do something great. In his mind, Anton felt he was doing something great as he stepped out of the doorway. Kurt Eisner came around a corner on to Promenadestrasse and Anton slipped his hand into the pocket of his black raincoat, drawing out a revolver and firing point blank at Eisner's head.

Richard Werther, the young apprentice machinist whose father had worked with Friedrich Haas' father, was stunned when his two friends told him what had happened.

"Where?" Richard asked as he stared at the table around which the three young men were sitting in Alfred's apartment.

"Promenadestrasse." his friend Alfred reported.

"Do they know why he did it?" the third young man, Otto, asked.

"Right wing." Alfred said, "I don't know... Maybe he wants the Kaiser back."

"I want to see where." Richard said after a short pause.

The other two looked at him and agreed.

"But I'm going to bring my rifle." Otto said.

"What for...?" Alfred started, but then he answered himself. "I suppose they might try something."

"We might as well." Richard said, and with that Alfred went and got his rifle and slid the bayonet in his belt and the three of them left his apartment, stopping at the apartments of the other two as they

70

armed themselves on their way to the sight of Eisner's assassination. When Richard stopped at his apartment for his rifle and bayonet, he stopped and picked up a picture of Eisner that he had on a small table by the door and slipped it into his coat pocket.

It was almost dark by the time they got to Promenadestrasse. The Glockenspiel* in the Neues Rathaus** chimed off four o'clock a block away from the square. A mist spread over the crowd of hundreds who had come to see the blood stained sidewalk.

Once the three young soldiers were sure that there was no battle brewing on the street, they worked their way through the crowd, and after about twenty minutes, they found themselves in front of an elliptical red shadow on the sidewalk that represented the last moments of Kurt Eisner. His blood had pooled about his fallen body and then ran down to the curb.

The three stood there in silence, not moving, their eyes darting up and down, taking in the color and size and shape, contrasting the gray street with the red blood. They didn't know what to do next.

Richard slid his rifle off his shoulder and fixed the bayonet. Otto and Alfred watched intently, wondering what he was up to.

"Fix your bayonets." Richard told his friends. Otto and Alfred exchanged confused glances, but then followed the order. Richard rested his rifle on the sidewalk as he waited for his friends, taking Alfred's rifle and hooking it to his bayonet catch, completing a tripod with Otto's rifle. He then took off his coat and cloaked the tripod, forming a tent and finally he took the picture of Eisner out of his coat pocket and placed it on the ground in the tent to protect it from the rain.

"A shrine." Alfred said.

"What about your coat?" Otto asked pragmatically.

"I've got another." Richard said.

"What if they steal it?" Otto persisted, but just then a young woman walked up to them and knelt in front of the picture. They watched as the young lady produced a red votive candle from her pocket and lit it, placing it beside the picture.

"Never mind." Otto said.

---

* Literally, "Glockenspiel" means bell chimes, but it also refers to the intricate set of clock works in the clock tower of the town hall which chimes and sets a display of metal statues into motion at the striking of the hour.
** the new city hall.

71

The three men stepped back, not knowing that the doorway in which they sought shelter was the very same doorway that had sheltered the noble assassin. They watched for a while as the crowd passed by quietly and reverently as though they were viewing the blood of the revolution itself, and one might say that they were. By shear force of will, Kurt Eisner had focused the desires of the people and formed a government which matched the mood of a bloodless revolution, he had ridden a wave of sentiment that could best be described as populist.

By shear force of will, a single man had seized the spirit of this part of the German nation and molded it into the image of a government. It was not unlike the spirit in which Otto von Bismarck had brought together hundreds of small German kingdoms and principalities in 1871 to form the modern German nation after the Franco-German war.

Who would be the next man to harness the power of this fickle crowd? Eisner tried to focus a democratic will of the people, but the demagogues who would come after Eisner would capitalize on the fears of these same people. Subsequent leaders of Bavaria would seek control and order above all else, certainly above the freedom of the individual and the right of the individual to have a voice in his government. The comment "a republic without republicans" seemed to strike a chord deep within the essence of German existence, as though it were not only their history, but their destiny as well.

Chapter 4

The assassination of Kurt Eisner set a tone of urgency throughout Munich as local politics took a turn even further to the left. The revolutionaries knew they would have to fight to keep control from other factions, and the counter-revolutionaries saw it as a collapse of the government. Another member of Eisner's cabinet was attacked within an hour of Eisner's assassination while still other cabinet members fled, leaving only two of the original eight members of the cabinet to try to keep the provincial government running.

After a few days of confusion, a council was formed to run the government made up of members of the worker's and soldier's councils that had been created when the revolution began.

The next change came a couple of months later. Inspired by the success of a man named Bela Kun who took over the Hungarian government to form a Communist state, a poet named Ernst Toller formed a new government in Munich in yet another bloodless revolution.

It was only a few days after the formation of this new government that a former schoolteacher named Hoffman, a member of a right wing political faction, led an attempted overthrow of Ernst Toller's government. The soldiers of the Munich garrison did not fight for Toller's government, which gave Hoffman an advantage, although it wasn't enough to help him win. The Hoffman Putsch came close enough to succeeding to motivate Eugen Levin, a Russian Bolshevik who had been sent to Munich to lead the faltering revolution, to force Toller out and take over the government of Munich. This move, of course, lent credence to the Freikorp's assertions that the revolution had been a product of Russian Bolsheviks all along.

All the while, the counter-revolutionaries were gaining strength.

The Freikorps were engaged in a dance of propaganda in 1919. On the one hand, they wished to maintain the illusion that the military was no longer a force in Germany in hopes that they might thereby elicit less severe terms of peace from the Allies. On the other hand, they were driven to organize an effective military force that would crush the revolution. A paradox of the times was that the

73

Allies were already inclined to close an eye to the military force of the Freikorps because the Allies wished the defeat of a Communist revolution just as much as the German counter-revolutionaries. Proof of this is found in the fact that it had only been little more than a year since the Allies had each sent military contingents to Russia to try to crush the embryonic Union of Soviet Socialist Republic.

The Freikorps, however, still went to great lengths under the watchful eye of the occupation armies of the Allied governments to appear as civilians protecting their country from Russian Bolsheviks.

In Munich and throughout Bavaria there is something called "gemutelichkeit", which translates in the English language as an easy going attitude towards life and is most often characterized by Bavarian natives in traditional costumes drinking beer. The Freikorps propaganda in the Munich area often dressed its soldiers in Bavarian costume for photographs: lederhosen* and mountain climbers cap with a feather tuft, and this was complimented with a rifle, bayonet and forty rounds of ammunition. It was supposed to represent a "gemutelichkeit counter-revolution." It was an interesting political strategy, but Gunther and Friedrich, along with hundreds of other Freikorps recruits, had no such costumes. They only had their old uniforms which had been changed to try to make them look more like civilian clothes.

Klaus told his friends when they first heard of Eisner's assassination that it was time to offer their services to one of the Freikorps units. Noske's counter-revolutionary forces had been moving south for a couple of months by that time and posters recruiting for Freikorps units had been seen in Munich for quite a while by then. Gunther and Friedrich waited for weeks, through all of the changes of governments and political personalities in Munich, for when the local fighting was about to begin.

Meanwhile, in the midst of this political chaos, Klaus, who was still a member of the small forces left to the regular German army, decided to move into the barracks for a few weeks as he waited to see how events would unfold. For the first time in their family life, Gunther, Amalie and Jakob were alone together as a family.

Then Gunther finally got word that he would be needed in his Freikorps unit the next day. His plan was to put Jakob to bed early and then spend the evening making love. This was Gunther's plan, a night of passion before going off to join up with the Freikorps, but he hadn't considered Amalie's feelings.

Gunther had a hard time explaining the Freikorps to his son. He finally just put Jakob to bed on the couch and told him that his father would be gone for a little while and Jakob would have to be especially good while he was gone.

He had a harder time yet explaining it to his wife.

"But why does it have to be you?" Amalie asked as she closed

---

* "Lederhosen" are short pants with suspenders classically made out of dearskin. They are part of the traditional Bavarian costume.

the bedroom door.

Gunther felt that Amalie was pushing too much. Why didn't she just accept his decision like a wife was supposed to do? His mother never would have questioned his father in a situation like this. They turned away from each other as they began to undress for bed.

"What would you expect me to do?" Gunther asked with an angry edge to his voice as he stopped in the middle of taking off his shirt. "Do you think I could stay here, safe and quiet, hiding with my wife and son while men are fighting in the streets?"

"You wouldn't be hiding" Amalie corrected in a pleading voice, "You've done enough fighting."

"Enough fighting? It is not enough until it is done."

"But the war is over!" Amalie shot back, raising her voice, "It's over!"

"No!" Gunther said adamantly as he spun around to face her, "The war didn't end... It just moved to within Germany itself."

Amalie seemed stunned at this argument. The war was not over, the war would never be over until her husband said it was. She quietly sat down on the bed with her back to Gunther. She didn't want to cry. Gunther had no respect for tears. She was determined not to lose this argument by default, by crying and giving Gunther what he would consider justification to storm out. Her head felt as though it were spinning.

"It seems," Amalie began slowly, trying to maintain her composure, "that you've just come home. We have really only started to get to know each other again and now you want to go back to war."

"It is not what I want." Gunther said firmly, "It is my duty."

"Duty?" Amalie exclaimed as she turned to face him, "What about the duty to your family? What about your son? Don't you think he should know who you are?"

"He will know who I am through the things that I do." Gunther shouted dramatically as he waved his hand through the air as though cutting through words to command action.

Just then they heard Jakob from the other room as he tossed and let out a little cry as though he were having a nightmare.

"I'll take care of him." Amalie said as she rushed out to the living room, closing the bedroom door and not giving Gunther a chance to respond.

By the time she got to the living room, Jakob was fast asleep after rolling over, but Amalie knelt down beside her son for a moment in the dark living room, watching him sleep and thinking about her argument with Gunther. She knew he had made up his mind and there was nothing she could do to change it.

Suddenly Gunther's shadow ran up on the floor beside Amalie as he opened the bedroom door, filling the living room with muted light. Gunther looked at his long shadow pointing to his wife, dressed in her white nightgown as she knelt before their sleeping son, looking up at Gunther with a single tear on her cheek.

She quickly brushed the tear away. No victory through the default of a tear.

"Is he asleep?" Gunther asked.

"Yes."

"Are you coming to bed?"

"In a moment."

There was a pause as Gunther watched while Amalie gently brushed the hair away from her sleeping son's face.

"I have to go." Gunther said matter-of-factly, ending the argument with this declaration.

Amalie stood up and moved to the bedroom. Without looking Gunther in the face, she said coolly "The truth is that you want to go." and with that she passed him in the doorway and got into bed.

Her words were like a slap in the face. He said nothing. He stood in the doorway for a moment, considering his next move, and then followed her into the bedroom and got dressed. When he said he had to go, he had meant that he would be leaving in the morning, but now he couldn't stand it. He packed a small bag and finally stood at the door once again. Amalie had not once turned to look at him all the while that he had been dressing and packing.

"Someday you'll understand." Gunther said, like a father talking to a child. He might have even used those same words earlier when he tried to explain to Jakob. "I'll spend the night with Friedrich and leave in the morning."

"Will you come back?" Amalie asked without emotion, still hugging a pillow and not looking at her husband.

"Of course..." Gunther said with an exasperated sigh. He then turned and made no effort to be quiet as his boots fell against the floor, making his way out of the apartment.

Jakob cried again and Amalie returned once more to the living room, this time to find Jakob awake and crying.

"Oh Jakob, Jakob" she said soothingly, "What is it?"

"I had a dream," Jakob said in a quiet, little boy voice as he rubbed his face with the back of his hands, "I dreamt that daddy went away again."

It was only ten-thirty at night as Gunther reached the Haas apartment, but Frau Haas had a habit of going to bed early, so Friedrich was sitting alone, reading, when Gunther knocked at the door.

"What are you doing here?" Friedrich asked with surprise.

"It seems Amalie doesn't support us."

"Oh." Friedrich said sympathetically "Well, she certainly has spirit."

"Perhaps too much."

Only a few blocks away from the Haas apartment, as Gunther and Friedrich were settling in to sleep, a man sat watching a shadow dance around the base of an old brass candlestick. His mind wandered as he wondered absent-mindedly where the shadow came from and then he realized that of course it was the shadow of the candlestick itself as the flame shifted in some breezy draft of unknown origin. He thought it was symbolic of the recent turn of events. The light of the candle casting a shadow on itself because they went hand in hand. The light and the shadow. One could not exist without the other and now with the revolution, the light of its hope created the shadow of politics.

Now that Eisner's government was collapsing, the Communist party had sent Eugen Levin to Munich to try to save the revolution or rather, to turn it into a Communist revolution.

Suddenly the man looked up as he realized that the other men around the table were looking at him. They must have asked him a question he thought, but he didn't have the slightest idea what that question might have been as he snapped away from his communion with the flickering flame.

"Will you support him, Ernst?" one of the men finally repeated.

Ernst still hesitated. Now that he knew the question, it was no easier to answer. Would Ernst Toller support Eugen Levin as Levin tried to reform the faltering revolution into some organized form of government? Ernst was not a Communist, well, he was certainly not a Russian Bolshevik. These were difficult times for Ernst and his friends. It had been easy in the past to sit and join in the debates and political banter at Alten Simpl, the cafe in Schwabbing district that catered to radicals who did much talking and writing without committing those thoughts to action. He now had to face the realities of this faltering revolution, putting his words and great ideals into action. Would he ally with Levin when his own political beliefs were actually quite distant from the Russians, just because Levin might stand the best chance of organizing the forces of revolution and keeping that revolution from total collapse?

"I don't know." Ernst finally said, giving the answer to himself as much as to his three comrades gathered around the table in the dark apartment.

They all knew this was a critical time. That was why they were so cautious, sitting in the dark apartment, away from the window on the street, with just a single candle to light this dangerous meeting.

"We must decide!" said Hans, a middle aged man with bushy, unkempt sideburns. "In a few days there will be no time for discussion. We have to decide where we stand and who we stand with." he continued, clearly frustrated at the impasse in the discussion.

"I will not oppose nor endorse Levin" Ernst interrupted his friend. "I will stand for the councils, not for politicians."

"That is not a decision Ernst!" said Peter as the reflection of the flickering candle slipped across the round lenses of his wire rimmed glasses. Peter was a young man who was surprisingly controlled for his age, considering his passion for his politics. "Hans is right. This is an important decision if we are to represent a unified force on a field of battle."

"Peter, I think you two are missing a point here. The men we are talking about leading into battle are defending their homes. We are not leading them, we are merely trying to help them do what they would naturally do."

Finally the fourth member of the group spoke. "Ernst, you are naive" said Stefan. Stefan was about the same age as Hans and Ernst, but he was the only one in the group who had seen action in the war. He was very clean cut and quite reserved, but when he eventually joined a conversation, it was usually with a keen grasp of the different positions being offered.

"Any fighting army needs clear leadership and direction" Stefan continued. "Their cause and leaders must be kept constantly in front of their eyes..."

"Their cause above any leaders" Ernst interrupted.

"No!" Peter added.

"Their leaders" Stefan started again, "are the focus of the cause. They are a concrete representation of the cause."

"But Levin does not represent our revolution!" Ernst countered. "He has his own revolution in mind."

"That is not important..." Hans said patronizingly in a measured cadence, as though he might slow down Ernst and make him understand through simple words and careful enunciation.

"Of course it's important." Ernst said, verbally brushing Hans aside.

"I'm sorry to be the one to tell you," Stefan said as he laced his fingers together and put his elbows on the table, moving closer to Ernst and bowing his head for an instant before looking up at Ernst, "but soldiers need simple truths. One leader, one direction, one cause."

"With all my being," Ernst began, "I believe that the men, the soldiers you talk of, have found the greatest truth, the greatest justice they could hope for, held within the spirit of this cause, of their own popular revolution. Not Eugen Levin's vision of revolution, but the revolution that these people brought about on their own, a revolution that deserves to live by its own virtue. I will not sell this revolution for political expediency."

"I hope your idealism will stand up to the point of a Freikorp bayonet." Peter said as he stood up from the table.

"I suppose this means we just go on as we have been." Hans said as he also rose to leave.

Stefan and Ernst remained seated as Stefan took Ernst's hand in a firm grip, a tactic Stefan had developed through a career of presenting arguments that he knew would get his adversary's complete attention. "Think about it Ernst... consider what is the best hope against counter-revolution."

Ernst looked Stefan in the eye and Stefan knew that Ernst would consider it. Ernst then pushed back his chair as Stefan released his hand and the two men walked to the door, bidding each other good night as Stefan was finally left alone in his apartment. Stefan crossed the room to the candle and drew close to the flame, blowing it out in a single short breath.

The next day, Gunther asked Frau Haas if she would be sure to watch Amalie and Jakob while he was gone and he also mentioned that they had managed to stockpile some black market food since there was sure to be trouble in the next couple of weeks. Gunther and Friedrich then shouldered their rifles and their homemade packs and left for the northern outskirts of the city where the Freikorps were waiting for their time.

In the weeks that followed, there were a number of battles for Munich. In the beginning, the revolutionaries, led by Ernst Toller, pushed back the Freikorps soldiers. Toller's great shortcoming in the battle, however, was that he was too fair in his treatment of the enemy. Not only did he see to it that prisoners were not mistreated, he even released the prisoners at the end of the battle, long before the war was done.

Levin, who was now head of the revolutionary government, issued orders for Toller to be arrested for his lenient attitude towards the freebooters, only to later release Toller to once again lead the troops when the Freikorps counter-attacked the next day.

This time the prisoners of the revolution were not as lucky. At some point during the battle when a group of Freikorps officers was to be moved from one building to another building further away from the fighting, a group of overzealous soldiers of the revolution rushed in and shot the officers.

This was all the Freikorp's leaders needed to whip their troops into a murderous frenzy. The freebooters had been known for their cruelty towards the men they took prisoner and they had certainly murdered many revolutionaries who tried to surrender, but somehow the thought of the revolutionaries fighting back in such a way was different. It seemed the life of a Freikorps officer or soldier had meaning while the life of a revolutionary soldier had none, and this triggered the psychotic rage that gave many of the soldiers license to commit any atrocity. The goal of the leaders and many of the soldiers of the Freikorps was not just the defeat of the Communists in battle, they wanted to break and purge the spirit of Germany, carving the German soul to an image of their liking with the blade of a bayonet. This is how the cobblestone streets of Munich, which had carried a thousand years of growth in the heart of Bavaria, came to run red with the blood of its own citizens.

Friedrich had never actually fought in a battle before. As an ambulance driver there had been a few times when he had been in the wrong place at the wrong time when some officer had thrown the rifle of a dead soldier into his hands and ordered him to man the trench, but it had never come to much. He was usually back in the ambulance driving casualties to an army hospital before there was any assault by enemy troops. He had seen a lot of artillery barrages, but he had never faced a charge or been a part of one... until now.

His leg held him back as he limped forward with the other troops into the city once they had finally broken through the revolutionary's defenses. He stopped for a moment at the corner of a small house before entering the street so that he could check before going out into the open.

He cautiously looked around the corner and saw two other Freikorps soldiers who had captured one of the revolutionaries. He decided it was safe to enter the street and started to cross as one of the two freebooters took a rifle from the revolutionary's outstretched hand. Friedrich looked away to see if there was anything going on at the houses in front of him, but as he turned away, the picture of the three men flashed in his mind, telling him there were something significant about the picture that he had overlooked. A tousled heap of red hair.

Werthers. It was Richard Werthers that they had captured. Friedrich turned back and took a step towards them, just about to say something, when the free-booter who had been standing in front of Werthers while the other disarmed him, put the muzzle of his rifle up to Werthers chin and pulled the trigger.

Richard Anton Werther's head exploded and his lifeless, nearly decapitated corpse fell, no, it dropped, to the street. Friedrich stumbled. His legs fell away before him as he watched while the world spun down to slow motion, Werthers falling body, the freebooter who had been standing beside Richard moving out of the way so as not to be splattered by the bits of brain and flesh and pieces of skull. He was laughing. It was a joke!

Friedrich began to throw up. He retched, doubled over in the middle of the street, but he had had so little to eat that there was nothing in his stomach to vomit out. The two soldiers who had murdered Richard saw Friedrich and began to laugh as they went on their way, certainly heading toward more victims.

Now the battle was even worse for Friedrich. Now it was not only killing, now there was a face, a face he knew. Now he was fighting beside men who laughed at the most inhumane carnage. His mind suddenly flashed back to his youth when he would see paintings that were meant to depict Hell, and he pictured the demons who stood at the edge of a fiery pit, flaying and torturing the damned before forcing them into the pit, laughing at the pain and suffering of their charges. But Richard had not been damned, these men were no part of a divine judgment between Heaven and Hell, they were less then men. They found power in killing. They felt more alive when they proved that they had the power to take life.

Just then Gunther came up by Friedrich and almost passed him before realizing that it was him.

"Friedrich?" he called out. "Are you hit ?" When Friedrich didn't answer, Gunther knelt down beside him and put his hand on Friedrich's back and repeated his question.

"No." Friedrich finally gasped out.

"What happened ?" Gunther asked.

"They shot him."

"Who?"

"Two of ours... They shot him" Friedrich said as he swung his arm out away from his stomach and pointed at the mutilated corpse in the middle of the street.

"It was Werthers" Friedrich continued.

"Who ?" Gunther asked again.

"Werthers!" Friedrich gasped before retching again and then he finally straightened up so that he was now kneeling in the street. "Werthers was the man I brought to the Hofbrauhaus to meet you and Klaus a couple of months ago. I knew him since we were kids. Our fathers worked together." Friedrich paused for a moment, fighting back tears. "He had given up his gun and had his hands up and those two bastards shot him."

Gunther looked hard at the corpse and finally realized how badly it had been mutilated.

"Christ!" Gunther said. He then put his arm around Friedrich and helped him to his feet. "There's nothing we can do about it" Gunther said. "Let's get out of here... It's almost over."

Gunther was only partially right. The final battle ended in

victory for the Freikorps units, but there were still weeks of bloody retribution to be visited against the Munich population by their Freikorps conquerors.

After the battle, defense minister Noske ordered the Freikorps to go from door to door in the city of Munich, searching for revolutionaries. The order stated that each house would be searched and if weapons, if a single weapon, were found in a house, then all the inhabitants were to be taken for questioning, harsh questioning which could easily lead to summary execution under the weight of martial law which gave the Freikorps ultimate power in the city.

Amalie thought it strange as she stood in the living room with Jakob wrapped about her skirt watching the two men who were now searching the apartment. She thought it strange how the fate of everyone in the building depended on what was found in this apartment, and that her fate depended on what was found in the apartments of the others in the building, people who she didn't even know.

"Have you any guns ?" one of the soldiers barked at her.

"No." She replied, but then as she thought about it, she modified her answer, and in so doing betrayed her anxiety. "I don't think so... You see, this is the apartment of a friend, an army captain who is letting us stay here."

The interrogator smiled. He assumed that the captain had taken advantage of the housing shortage and the difficult situation in which a war widow might find herself in these times. Perhaps he had taken in this handsome woman and her child in exchange for sexual favors. He looked at the other soldier and winked.

This further unnerved Amalie as she tried to explain. "He took in my husband, son and myself because they were friends from the war."

"Where is your husband now?" the soldier asked, thinking he was now on to something.

"With you!" Amalie answered, "He joined the Freikorps."

The soldier was a little disappointed that he had not stumbled upon the wife of a revolutionary as that might have put him in good standing with his superiors. He didn't altogether believe her since she certainly wouldn't tell him if her husband was a Communist. "...and the captain. Where is he?"

"I don't know. He went to stay in the barracks just before the fighting began."

"In the barracks? You mean he's still on active duty?"

"Yes."

"What does he do?"

"I'm not sure."

"What is his name?"

"Grunewald. Klaus Grunewald."

The other soldier who had been searching the apartment came up to the interrogator during this exchange and stood silently as the other man wrote down Amalie's answers. "Nothing" he finally said when the interrogator looked up from his notes, indicating that he hadn't found any guns or incriminating papers. "Let's go. We have a lot more buildings to search."

"Very well Frau..." the interrogator began as he searched the report he had just written for her name, "Frau Metzdorf. Guten tag." He forced an insincere smile as he nodded at Amalie.

"Good day" Amalie repeated reflexively as the two soldiers finally left, not even realizing she said it as a sudden overwhelming sense of relief swept over her like a rush of cool air.

It wasn't until they had asked her if there were guns in the apartment that she realized she didn't know one way or the other. After all, Klaus was an army officer. It was very possible that he could have had a gun in the apartment.

They were lucky so far. If something turned up in one of the other apartments she and Jakob would soon be ordered down into the streets. She had seen it from the window as one of the other buildings had been evacuated. The people on the street in front of that building looked so lost. They were herded onto a truck and taken away. Who had kept a gun in that building? Was it a revolutionary or just a soldier who had brought his rifle home from the war as a souvenir? Who would pay for that indiscretion? It was a frightening thing to let your mind wander like that, especially when you knew that yours was the next building to be searched. Then you began to sweat as you wondered who your neighbors were.

Amalie soon realized that her fears were unfounded as the soldiers finally left her apartment building and moved on to the next. Just as the last of the soldiers had left, there was the sound of gunfire off in the distance and Amalie rushed to the window to see if anything was happening in the street. The only people on the street were the soldiers who were now moving to the next city block. She wondered how Gunther was doing and where he was. Somewhere in the back of her mind, a thought she could barely acknowledge, she wondered if he was even alive.

She felt torn up and confused. Suddenly she had the idea that she needed to see the whole city, that she needed a view where she could see everything and sort it out. She gathered up Jakob and a couple of the toys.

Jakob sat on the gravel covered roof playing with a little wooden horse and wagon as Amalie walked to the side of the building. It was already the middle of May and the English Garden to the east was filled with flowering trees and a fresh green carpet of grass, but Amalie couldn't see that from the top of the apartment building. She looked out over the sea of buildings covered with dark billowing clouds moved about by a damp spring breeze. It was late afternoon and she could see flashes of lightning in the distance, so far off that she never heard the thunder, so far off that it only lit small domes in the clouds like blossoming flowers of light which faded in the next instant.

She remembered the argument that she and Gunther had had when he walked out of the apartment in the middle of the night. She hadn't said anything about the very nature of the Freikorps that night. The stories of the Freikorps in the North frightened her along with the hysterical tone of their posters with raging anti-semitic slurs lashing out against "the Jewish Bolsheviks." She was horrified at the fate of Rosa Luxemburg, that graphic demonstration of the fierce brutality of which these men were capable, and these were the men that her husband now fought beside. These were the men with whom Gunther had cast his lot.

Amalie thought of Gunther's parting words when he had said that the war had not ended, but that it had merely moved within Germany. He had sounded like a man bent on revenge. Amalie had heard the term "November criminals" at the publishing house and when Mr. Frieder explained it to her it suddenly came together in her mind. That was why Gunther joined the Freikorps. He wanted revenge against those who had betrayed him and his comrades, he wanted to punish those who had lost the war. He could not accept the possibility that it was the army that had lost the war.

Amalie was overwhelmed. Her life wasn't supposed to be this

complicated. This had nothing to do with two people falling in love and getting married and raising a family. She suddenly found herself getting angry. From out of nowhere she suddenly grabbed the wall against which she had been leaning and shouted "Why?" at the top of her voice and then crossed her arms on the ledge and put her head down and began to cry. Jakob was startled when his mother shouted and he looked up suddenly to see what was wrong. She just stood there crying and Jakob dropped his toys, got up and walked over to his mother putting his arms around her legs.

"Mutti." Jakob said, not understanding why his mother didn't answer him, why she didn't even look at him.

"Mutti, mutti" He repeated and finally Amalie looked down. When she saw the bewilderment in his eyes, she smiled.

It's nothing liebling" she said as she wiped away her tears, "Mutti is just sad."

"Why?"

I guess I just miss your father" Amalie said as she tried to find a simple answer that would satisfy Jakob.

"Me too" Jakob said and with that, Amalie picked him up and rested him on her hip just as the rain finally broke. It started as a sprinkle and Amalie walked casually over to pick up Jakob's toys as he still clung to her, but then suddenly the rain turned to a downpour and Amalie let Jakob down as he let out a squeal and raced for the door with his mother close behind. Once they got in, Amalie quickly closed the door and laughed as Jakob shook his head from side to side like a little puppy shaking himself dry. Amalie then did the same, but when she did it, her longer hair wrapped around her face and they both laughed at her veil of wet hair.

Amalie then took Jakob's hand and led him down the stairs to the apartment. Just as Amalie got to the door and unlocked it, she heard someone coming up the stairs in the hallway and turned to see Gunther coming up the stairs.

"Vati!" Jakob called out as he ran to his father who swept him up in his right arm while he re-adjusted his rifle and packs on his left. Gunther gave Jakob a little kiss on the cheek and nuzzled his ear.

"Vati, you smell bad." Jakob exclaimed, causing Gunther to laugh as he let Jakob down and walked over to Amalie who was still motionless in front of the door.

"He's right. I haven't had a chance to bathe in days." He put his arms around his wife. "It's done" Gunther said as he let her go while he slipped off his pack and rifle and let them fall to the floor and then took her again in his arms and actually lifted Amalie off the floor as he held and kissed her.

Chapter 5

When a war ends, people often hope for a return to "normalcy", a period when things calm down, the shooting stops and there is a time to rebuild. The problem in Munich in 1919 was that their "war" was only a sideshow to Germany's other problems. The treaty of Versailles was not officially released until the end of June, 1919, more than six months after the armistice and weeks after the bloody suppression of the revolution in Munich.

There has long been a question when it comes to the fate of a transgressor as to whether that antagonist should be punished or reformed or perhaps a medium somewhere between those two options. The treaty of Versailles was clearly a bitter and vengeful punishment of Germany. The Allies politely denied any complicity in the situation that led to the war and fixed all of the blame on Germany, citing her as the responsible party for all civilian losses. It was to cost the nation dearly. Maps were quickly re-drawn to acknowledge where parts of Germany had been confiscated and given to other countries such as Poland, Belgium and France while other parts of Germany were to be occupied by foreign troops for the next fifteen years. Germany would be made to pay.

"Are you all settled in then?" Klaus asked.

"For the most part." Gunther replied.

"Well, you've got a job, a new apartment and your family with you... you've survived the revolution and become a regular member of the bourgeoisie" Klaus said with a subtle smirk. He considered this a de-evolution of a soldier and that sentiment was in his voice and Gunther heard it.

Gunther had finally found a job in July with an architectural firm as a drawer. His father was an architect and so Gunther had learned through casual observation of his father at work even though Gunther didn't have formal education in architecture. He had made some drawings when he heard there was a job available and, mostly because of his experience in the army, having gone from private to Captain in his four years of service, he got the job.

The work was just enough to get by and, considering the shortage of building supplies and subsequently the shortage of building projects, even that was surprising. There was a drawback for Gunther, however, in that Amalie had to keep working so that they could still meet expenses.

Amalie was afraid that as soon as Gunther got work he would insist that she quit on that day, but he hadn't said a word. The time when he couldn't find work had made him pragmatic. He knew he would have to swallow his pride and that they would both have to work to get caught up with expenses and keep their heads above water.

"You're jealous" Gunther countered.

Klaus laughed. "Maybe a little" he finally conceded.

"You understand Klaus..." Gunther began, "when I first heard the war was over, my first thought was to do just as I have done, to become ordinary. But now it feels so strange."

"There is something about war" Klaus said absent-mindedly as he took a drink of his beer.

"If someone had told me five years ago how I would be feeling at this moment, I would have laughed in their face."

"How do you mean?" Klaus asked.

"It is just so different. I hated the war, the bloody murderous war, but now life is just so..."

"Boring?" Klaus asked, finishing the sentence.

"It's crazy!" Gunther said with a laugh. "I know it's crazy. I love

90

Amalie... and Jakob is a wonderful boy, but..."

"I know what you mean" Klaus commiserated. "It's a common complaint of soldiers in peacetime."

"It seems like heresy!" Gunther replied in a shocked tone, shocked at his own feelings. "To make it through that war alive and then to somehow miss it when it's over."

"Did anyone ever tell you that life was a simple matter?"

"No," Gunther replied, "but I never asked."

"Well, if you had asked, only a fool would have said things would be simple... simple to do or simple to understand."

"Maybe life is simple, if you're a fool." Gunther mused.

It was still hot in Munich as the summer of 1919 drew to a close. Klaus and Gunther were spending the late afternoon of a Thursday in September at the Sterneckerbraü. When Klaus and Gunther would go out for beer, and they still did so two or three times a week even though Gunther and his family had moved out of Klaus' apartment, they often chose Sterneckerbraü because it was quieter than the famous Hofbrauhaus a couple of blocks away.

At the same time that Klaus and Gunther were washing down their conversation with the watered-down beer typical of all the beer halls so soon after the war, Amalie was taking Jakob down to the bank of the Isar river in the English garden. It was unusual for Amalie to go out like this on a Thursday, but she knew Gunther would be out late and she wanted to take advantage of the beautiful weather that would all too soon become a typical cold and windy Bavarian Autumn.

The Isar is an excellent example of a German river. In 1156 Emperor Barbarossa gave the Duchy of Bavaria to duke Heinrich der Löwe. Heinrich promptly destroyed the bridge on the Isar at Oberföhring. The bridge had been owned by the bishop of Freising and had earned the bishop toll money because it was on the salt trade routes. Heinrich then built a new bridge at a small settlement called Ze den Munichen where Heinrich then began to collect the tolls for himself. Over centuries, while the little village of Ze den Munichen was becoming the city of Munich, the river was mastered and controlled, locks installed, more bridges built and the waters diverted through canals for factories and mills. The river was molded and fit into the fabric of Munich's life. It conformed.

The banks by the English garden however, were allowed to run broad where the river ran shallow in a western fork as it split and found its way around the islands in the river. The banks were covered with smooth white stones that swept up to the grass of the English garden and this was where mothers would lay out their towels and watch as their children play in the gently moving water at the river's edge.

"Be careful" Amalie cautioned Jakob one last time as he moved towards the water.

Jakob left his shoes with his mother, but when he tried to walk on the stony ground, he only got a few steps as the rocks began to burn his feet. He quickly danced back to the safety of his mothers towel, wincing and whining all the way.

"Mutti, my feet are burning!"

Amalie laughed and helped him on with his ersatz shoes made with wooden soles and cloth tops. He was growing fast and it was bad enough that decent clothes and shoes weren't available, but how could they afford to keep replacing them every few months on top of that?

"There you go" she said as she gave him a little pat on the bottom, sending him on his way.

Jakob stepped tentatively into the cool water, ready to step back if it was too cold. He watched his submerged foot carefully as he decided on the condition of the water. The water distorted the sunlight as it sparkled and flashed and Jakob was transfixed as the image of his foot moved about as though reflected in a funhouse mirror. He then jumped in with both feet, making a splash and screeching with delight as he twisted around to look back at his mother to see if she had been watching what fun he was having. Amalie smiled and waved. He then walked over, splashing as much as he could as he moved through the water, to a group of children who had already been playing in the water when he first arrived.

"Hello" Jakob said to a little girl and two boys who were sitting in the shallow water splashing each other. The girl was about the same age as Jakob, who was now almost four, and the boys were about a year or so older. The other children greeted him and immediately included him in their play. They played for over half an hour as their mothers lay on their towels and blankets, taking in the Sun. The children eventually grew tired of the water and ran up to the patch of trees bordering the stony beach. They began a game of hide and seek in the lush green undergrowth, running back and forth around the small forest and then diving back in to catch one of the others hiding among the trees. The older boy showed Jakob a fortress of green brush which the two boys and the little girl had found when they had played there before.

When their energy was collectively spent they finally took shelter in their castle of underbrush, hiding from the rest of the world. The oldest boy peeked out to see if they had been missed by any of the mothers on the beach. There were still a number of other children making noise and playing in the water and so the mothers of these missing four hadn't even noticed their children's absence.

Once the older boy was sure of their privacy, he joined the other three who were sitting cross-legged in the center of the small canopy formed by the dense foliage. The roof of their hiding place was speckled with sunlight filtering down through the tall trees. The older boy finally spoke as he tried to suppress a smile while he revealed a secret plan he had been working on ever since he led the others to this hiding place. "Why don't we play like we did yesterday?"

The other boy and the little girl began to giggle, but Jakob had no idea what they were talking about.

"Ja!" the other boy said with excitement and the girl also agreed.

"What?" Jakob asked, wondering what their funny secret was. The little girl looked at Jakob with a big smile through which she could barely talk. "We... pretend like... like we're babies... and we take off all our clothes!" she finally said, punctuating her sentence with more giggling.

The thought seemed strange to Jakob. He had never seen, or at least he couldn't remember seeing, other people without clothes before. He didn't ever remember seeing his parents without clothes... As he thought about it, he began to laugh too. It seemed funny and yet he also felt funny in the pit of his stomach, as though it might be wrong. The fact that they were hiding here seemed to make it clear that it should be a secret thing, but he didn't understand why. The other boys had already started to take off their swimming suits and once they had, they watched as the little girl followed their lead. Jakob stared.

He looked at the other boys as they sat naked, and semi-erect, watching as the little girl stood up and slipped off her suit, letting it fall into the dirt.

She had no penis! Jakob sat there, staring between the little girl's legs as she stood in front of him giggling and watching his face while he discovered the secret that she and the other two little boys had already found out about each other.

"Now you!" one of the other boys said to Jakob, smiling as he insisted that this new boy join in.

Jakob, still hypnotized by what he saw, slowly wiggled out of his swimsuit as he remained sitting in the black dirt that was the floor of their hiding place. The earth felt cool as he sat there and he felt somehow free as he found himself naked with the others, all of them looking at one another. Jakob was surprised as his penis started to grow a bit.

The little girl pointed at Jakob's circumcised penis. The other two boys, not being Jewish, weren't circumcised and Jakob found himself in a terrible position among children. He was now different.

"What's wrong with it?" the little girl asked the other boys.

"I don't know" said the younger of the two boys.

"He's a 'joo'." said the older boy with an air of authority that the others didn't question.

"What's a joo?" asked the younger boy, asking the same question that Jakob was about to ask.

Jakob had been circumcised because Amalie was still living with her father at the time Jakob was born, but he had never been told that he was Jewish, at least not in a way that he could remember. It had never been mentioned and he had never had any reason to ask questions about such things.

"I don't know," the older boy admitted after a thoughtful pause "but my daddy... He said that joos were the ones that made the war."

Something clicked in Jakob's head and he suddenly remembered his father and uncle Klaus talking about Jews, but he had never known before that they were a kind of people, he just knew that they were bad.

"How could I be one of these 'joos'?" Jakob thought to himself in a confused panic, feeling as though he was being accused of something bad.

The older boy continued talking. "My father said you can tell a joo because they cut off the end of his thing..."

"Why?" the younger boy asked.

"I don't know," the older boy said "but look..." and he reached down and held his own penis, sliding back the foreskin to expose the glans and then pointing to Jakob. "They cut off the part on the end." The other children watched as though in the presence of a scholar. Once he had shown the others the difference, the older boy continued his lecture.

"My father says joos are dirty and you can't go swim in the water if there is a joo in the water because he makes the water dirty." The boy said it without emphasis or emotion, as if it was an old poem that some adult had made him memorize by rote, words without any meaning.

Jakob was hurt and confused. The other boy was talking about him, but neither of them really understood what it all meant. The older boy also felt bad because now he had put a face to this terrible thing that his father called "a joo" and it was a little boy who didn't look any different than he did.

Jakob started to cry. The little girl, who had been sitting and listening carefully to the lecture, moved over to Jakob and sat beside him, patting him gently on the back, both of them oblivious to their nakedness. She didn't know what to say either.

"Don't cry," she finally said, trying to find some way to make Jakob feel better, "maybe you don't have to be a joo."

Jakob soon managed to stop crying and, without saying a word, without any of them saying a word, they all put their swimsuits back on and left their sheltered little world which living green nature had built for them.

Jakob walked dejectedly towards his mother who was still laying on her towel, reading a book. Amalie didn't actually see him as he came toward her from behind and off to the side, but somehow she knew he was there, and that he was... that something was wrong.

"What is it?" she asked as she laid the book on the stones beside her.

"Can we go home?" Jakob asked.

"Yes, it's getting late." she said as she looked first at the Sun lowering towards the city's skyline and then into Jakob's face.

"What's wrong?" she asked as she looked into his eyes and saw that they were red, as though he had been crying.

"Nothing" Jakob said meekly, with a note of whininess to his voice as he looked down at the rocky ground and shifted stones around with his feet. "I'm tired... I want to go home."

95

Amalie knew her little boy and she knew she would have to wait until he felt like talking. He was a lot like his father in that respect. When something was wrong, he wanted to work it out alone and would only talk about it after he had spent time trying to fix it himself.

Amalie gathered up their things and they started walking through the English garden to their new apartment, but just as they left the riverbank, Jakob looked up and saw the little girl from earlier. She was a pretty little girl with blond hair that seemed to glow in the sunlight. She was smiling and waving good-bye, but Jakob didn't acknowledge her in any way. He just kept walking hand in hand with his mother. He didn't know the names of the other children, but he would always remember pieces of that afternoon that had stirred up so much confusion within him.

The early evening hours found Klaus and Gunther still at the Sterneckerbraü. By six o'clock Friedrich had also joined them just as the hall began to fill with people. There were about forty people, mostly handarbeiter, laborers who work with their hands, who apparently were gathering for some kind of meeting.

It was hard to get drunk on the terrible beer that they served, but the trio did their best. They laughed loud and long on this particular night as they sat at their table along the wall at the back of the room, but they managed to stay fairly subdued as the meeting began. It turned out to be some kind of worker's party, one of the many political factions that kept appearing in Munich at the time. There was to be a speaker, some man named Eggert or Ekert, some name which the semi-drunken trio could not hear nor recognize, but it seems this man was now sick and so the task of addressing the group fell to a man who talked about getting rid of capitalism. The three comrades paid no attention, but they did make an attempt to keep their conversation quiet because they didn't feel like moving to another beer hall and so they didn't want to get thrown out. This was a little strange because Klaus and Gunther rarely felt compelled to avoid confrontation, especially on their nights out, but maybe this just wasn't a day for fighting.

The group who had come for the meeting sat quietly and attentively, but it turned out to be a boring evening spent listening to an economist. The speaker finally concluded his lecture and some of the group began to leave as a free discussion period began.

One man, a professor, stood up and made a suggestion that

Prussia and Bavaria should be recreated as separate states. He went on to say that these regions were so politically different, with Prussia's specifically militaristic history being a contrast to Bavaria's gemutlichkeit attitudes, that they seemed irreconcilable.

Another man, who already had his coat over his arm as he was preparing to leave, took great exception to such a suggestion, that the German state should once again be separated into unorganized states as it had been before 1871. He stopped and challenged the professor, laying out what many of the others considered to be a clear case for keeping Germany a strongly unified country. The man went on to completely discredit the professor's argument to the point that the professor not only returned to his seat in silence, but soon beat a hasty retreat from the beer hall.

Klaus actually stood up as the challenger finished speaking and applauded him and was joined by a few others. The man flashed a quick glance at Klaus, sizing him up along the other two men at the table where he stood. Klaus was the only army officer in the hall and as such he stood out in the group.

The man was about to leave again when one of the meeting organizers caught up with him and introduced himself as Anton Drexler and gave him one of the group's pamphlets and asked him to come again. The man looked at the door, but then turned and walked over to Klaus' table.

"Thank you" he said, "for your kind applause."

Klaus stood up and offered his hand. "You spoke well. It is good to hear such voices in times like these."

"Yes" Gunther said as he also stood up and extended his hand to the man, introducing himself. "Gunther Metzdorf... formerly captain Metzdorf of the Austrian army."

"Austrian?" the man exclaimed, "I also come from Austria."

"I was born in Munich, but my family moved to Salzburg when I was a boy" Gunther explained.

"I was born in Braunau" the man added.

"You speak more like a German than an Austrian" Klaus interrupted.

"Even when I lived in Austria, I felt I was a German" the man replied with a good-natured laugh.

"I am Klaus Grunewald" Klaus interjected, "and this is Friedrich Haas."

Friedrich stood up with the others and shook hands.

"Adolf Hitler" the man said, introducing himself.

Back at Gunther's apartment, Jakob was finally ready to speak as he and his mother were finishing their dinner of turnip soup.

"Mutti..." Jakob began cautiously, as though he might not really want an answer to the question he was about to ask, "What is... a joo?"

"So that was it!" Amalie thought to herself. This was a big question, one that would not be easy to answer, especially considering Gunther's attitudes.

"A Jew is a person" Amalie offered, wanting to keep it as simple as possible, so that she could offer Jakob answers to his questions as he thought of them rather than overwhelming him with too much information at once.

"What makes a person a joo?" Jakob continued.

"Are you finished with your soup?" Amalie asked.

"Yes." Jakob said, as he was always willing to be finished with turnip soup, but he wondered why his mother didn't answer his question. Jakob watched as she got up and cleared away their bowls and water glasses to the sink and then reached up to the highest cupboard above the sink. She found that she couldn't quite reach and so she walked back to the table and got a chair and dragged it back to the sink, climbing up so she could reach into the back of the high cupboard. She looked at him and smiled as she pulled out a small white box and then climbed down and returned the chair to the table.

"Come in here" she said as she went into the small living room of the apartment and sat down on the couch which Klaus had given them as a gift when they moved out. Jakob followed and hopped up on the couch beside his mother, all the while watching the small white box she held and wondering what was inside. Amalie slowly removed the cover, revealing six dark brown pieces of chocolate each set within a white paper cup with scalloped edges. Jakob's eyes grew big with excitement.

"Chocolate!" he said with a great deal of surprise as it had been a long time since he had had such a wonderful treat. It was so hard to get decent food, but to get something like this was truly rare.

"Please mother, may I have one?"

"No," Amalie said playfully, "they're all mine."

Jakob looked crestfallen, but Amalie quickly took one out and pressed it to his lips and they both laughed as he took it from her and began to eat it in tiny nibbles so that he could make it last as long as possible. Amalie then took one for herself and set the box on the arm of the couch as she sat back and put her arm around Jakob and drew him close.

"What makes a Jew..." Amalie said thoughtfully, surprising Jakob who thought that she had wanted to ignore it because "joos" were such bad things that they shouldn't be talked about.

"In the bible" she began, gazing into the air as she tried to gather her thoughts, "There was a man named Abraham. They say that Abraham was a good man and he knew God, they say he even talked to God and he was the first Jew."

This all sounded like just another story to Jakob as he listened to his mother's gentle voice. They never talked about God. Jakob had seen all the great old churches in Munich, but only from the outside. Amalie and Gunther believed, though they didn't actually discuss it or say it outright, that God had somehow abandoned man. They were non-religious. When Gunther spoke of Jews, he spoke of a race of people, not of a religion, and he didn't pursue the Lutheran religion that his family had practiced. It was because of this that Amalie's words had no ring of truth for Jakob, no passion or deep meaning. This was now Amalie's time to repeat an old poem she had been made to remember by rote by her parents, these were her words without meaning. It was important for Amalie to tell Jakob that being Jewish, contrary to what Gunther said, was a matter of religion and not race, because if she acknowledged a link to a people, the people of Israel, then it would be impossible to leave being a Jew behind as she had so easily done.

After Amalie seemed to conclude her talk of Abraham and Egypt and Moses and so on, Jakob still wanted to understand why the other boy from that afternoon had said that he was bad because of how his penis looked. This seems like such a strange question, like the sort of funny question that only a little boy could ask, but when considered, from such a ridiculous little question looms up all the viscous lies and hatreds of prejudice and bigotry, all of the nameless victims piled on top of each other from century to century.

"Am I a 'joo'?" Jakob finally asked.

Such a simple question, a questioned to be answered "yes" or "no", but Amalie was hesitant.

"Half" she finally answered.

"Half?" Jakob asked, not only not understanding the concept of being partly a "joo" and partly not a "joo", but not even yet understanding the meaning of a fraction.

Amalie offered him another chocolate and took one for herself. This was definitely going to be at least a two chocolate discussion.

She got up and found a piece of paper and a short blunt pencil which, as true thrifty Germans, they kept long beyond the point where it was easy to hold. She then drew seven little circles, four above two above one, with names below each circle and lines to connect them from one generation to the next, grandfather and grandmother to father and then father to son and then she drew the same on the other side of the family.

"Look," she said. "This is our family. these two circles are my mother and father and these two circles are your father's mother and father, and this little circle is you." she said as she drew in two dots for eyes and still another for a nose which she underlined with a little smile.

"My mother and father were Jewish and so I am Jewish. Your father's mother and father were not Jewish, so he is not Jewish. You are part of me and part of your father, so you are part Jewish."

"Which part?" Jakob asked as he looked up from the paper and into his mother's eyes.

"What?" she asked.

"Which part of me is 'joo' and which part is not?" Jakob repeated.

Amalie laughed as she realized that she was facing another of those never-ending series of questions which children always seemed to come up with for their hapless parents and she tried to figure out how to explain it all.

"Is my pisha 'joo'?" Jakob asked innocently, at which point Amalie burst out laughing so hard that tears came to her eyes and she leaned to the side of the couch as though she might fall off.

"Where did you ever come up with that?!" she asked as she continued to laugh.

Jakob was somewhat bewildered at his mother's response, although he seemed not at all shaken in the face of such roaring ridicule. He knew what the question meant and it was a perfectly good question to him, so he pressed on, undaunted.

"A boy told me that they cut off the end of my pisha because I am a 'joo'."

"Oh! my, my... Now I see what you mean." Amalie said, regaining her composure. "Remember what I said about Abraham?"

"Yes" Jakob said, even though he hadn't really been paying much attention to the story.

"Well, first," Amalie began "before I tell you this, you must promise not to keep asking me 'why' because I'll tell you right now that I never knew why this was done."

"What was done?" Jakob asked.

"Well, way back when Abraham was talking with God, Abraham told everyone that God had said he should make a mark on his body that would show he really believed in God. He called it a 'covenant', like a promise between him and God, so that any man with this mark would be known as a Jew and this mark was when they would cut off the piece of skin at the end of the penis."

Amalie hoped that going through it quickly and clinically would finish the conversation as she found the subject embarrassing, even just talking to her own son.

"Why?" Jakob asked.

Amalie just stared at Jakob.

"I told you before that I don't know why" she finally answered. She wasn't really upset, but she did want to stop Jakob from going on.

"Jakob," she started, changing the subject, "Can you do something very important for me?"

"What?"

"Don't talk to your father about this" she said seriously.

Jakob's first reaction was to ask "why", but then he thought a moment and said sadly to his mother "Father doesn't like joos, does he?"

It almost brought tears to Amalie's eyes when her little boy said this. It hurt her that somehow he knew this terrible thing and would have to live with it as a child. Especially since she knew that even she, as a grown-up, was having so much trouble dealing with it.

Meanwhile, back at the Sterneckerbräu, Gunther and his friends were just about ready to call it an evening.

"An architect?" Adolf repeated.

"Well, I do drawings" Gunther admitted with a little

embarrassment, "I just fill in things for the real architects, rough outlines and so on."

"I used to paint," Adolph said with a hint of pride, but without giving details so as to leave the extent of his career to the imagination, "I was very good with buildings. I would have liked to have been an architect."

"What do you do now?" Friedrich asked.

"Now I am still in the army, but I think I shall somehow become a full-time politician" Adolf replied without hesitation.

"Excellent!" Klaus piped in, "It is about time we found some politicians who can do some good and help us put Germany back on the right road."

Chapter 6

The reparation payments levied against Germany as a result of the treaty of Versailles were the coup de grâce *for the German economy after four years of total war. An almost immediate response to the demands on the economy was a steadily increasing inflation which had already been a problem at the end of the war. When the terms of the treaty were announced, however, the inflation began to rise to unprecedented levels. The money that would have been considered a good annual salary one day could hardly pay for a single loaf of bread a few weeks later.*

The economic problems along with military occupation in certain areas of the country made fertile ground for those who wished to reap power from the discontent of the German people. Many small political parties on the extremist fringe were formed during that period. One such group was the Deutsches Arbeiter Partie which, under the new leadership of a former corporal of the Kaiser's Imperial army named Adolf Hitler, soon changed its name to the Nationalsozialistiche Deutsche Arbeiterpartei or "nazis" as it became known.

Time is a funny thing. When we look back on our lives, it is rarely a chronological process. Most often we remember things, perhaps an object or maybe a single event that we consider important and then we try to rebuild the world which existed around our important memories in order to make sense of them.

Amalie's memory of 1922 was a brown briefcase. It was made of the best leather with shiny brass catches and shiny brass buckles on the leather tie-down straps. She had looked it over a couple of times in the store window as she passed by to work one week. She finally decided that she deserved to buy herself a gift, an anniversary gift for the three years that she had been working for Frieder and Son Publishing.

The other reason for such an extravagance was that people were then prone to spending their money as soon as they got it because the longer they held onto it, the less it was worth. The common wisdom was that it was better to buy a luxury item now that you might be able to trade later rather than holding on to the currency.

There were a lot of reasons for what happened to the German economy in the first years of the Weimar Republic. Chiefly of course, as with any inflation, the basic problem was money being printed without anything to back it up. The inflation problem began with the development of the ersatz economy during the last half of the war when Germany directed all of its resources and production to the war effort. Civilian goods were made of substitute materials ranging from shoes made of wood and cloth to bread made with sawdust and coins made of pewter. The next situation to exacerbate the economic problems was the harshly punitive nature of the Versailles treaty. The German economy had no chance to recover from the economic strain of total war before having to pay a huge indemnity to the victors. There were a few people who benefited from the state of the economy. Imagine, for example, having a loan that was scheduled for a twenty year repayment and suddenly being able to pay it all off with a single paycheck, but on the other hand the frugal German middle class found within just a few weeks after reparation payments began that the money they had saved to get them through their old age was now only enough to get through one day.

Amalie had only managed to hang on to her job by default over those years. Gunther had told her that she must quit when he found work, but then when he first got the job drawing in the architectural

104

firm they wanted to get an apartment so badly that Gunther agreed that Amalie should keep working until they "got over the hump" financially. Then the money went crazy.

Amalie walked into the offices of the Freider Publishing company with the coveted briefcase wrapped up in a bag and tucked under her arm while she carried a cold lunch in a small bag in the other hand.

"Good morning Mr. Frieder" Amalie said in a cheerful tone.

She was a "morning person". Mr. Frieder was not. Amalie still called him "Mr. Frieder" even though she had worked with him for years now, but she did it out of respect rather than convention, even though "David" was creeping into her conversations more and more as they became better friends.

Their friendship was strictly platonic. In many ways Amalie felt that her boss was more intelligent than her, but the truth was that while he had a better memory for facts, Amalie made better use of the things she knew. She was a better thinker.

"Something new?" Mr. Frieder asked as he pointed at the bundle under her arm.

"A present." Amalie replied with a smile.

"A present? From who?" David asked.

"From whom..." Amalie corrected.

"...And me a publisher." David said as though apologizing. "From whom have you received this gift?" he asked, rephrasing his question.

"From me." Amalie said with a smile.

David smiled too. "Well, at least that way you know you'll get a present you like."

They laughed as Amalie stopped at her desk and put down her packages. She unwrapped it to look at it again and also to show it off to David.

"Very nice."

"Thank you." Amalie said.

"Expensive?" David asked in a way that a friend would, in a way that wasn't presumptuous.

"Very." Amalie answered.

"I hope you can trade it when you need to."

"Well, actually I bought it as an anniversary present."

"For your husband?"

"No. not a wedding anniversary. I bought it for myself because I've worked here almost three years now"

"Three years!? Already three years?"

"Yes. In four days."

"Amazing... Oh yes, I remember now. You showed up on that day, the last day I saw Rosa Luxemburg. It seems like a lifetime ago."

"Rosa Luxemburg." Amalie said thoughtfully "I haven't thought about her for quite awhile. Come to think of it, I heard there is to be some sort of trial, they are trying some military officers in connection with the killing of her and Karl Liebknecht."

"They won't get too far." David prophesied.

"Weimar and the Freikorps. Back in bed together." Amalie said with a smirk.

David smiled and turned to walk away, but he stopped when Amalie began to ask a question.

"Mr. Frieder," she began, but then she decided to change her approach. "David," she started over, "I've wanted to ask you something for a while now, but I wasn't sure how to start."

"What is it Amalie?"

"It's very strange."

"Oh! It sounds interesting already."

"It's also very serious."

"Is it money? If it is, I'm afraid I can't..."

"No, no. I know how things are and you've already... No, it has nothing to do with money."

"Then what?"

"David, I've never talked with you much about my husband..."

"Is there trouble?"

"In a round about way. Gunther is involved with some men."

"What kind of men? Black market?"

"No. It's a political group."

"Which one?"

"It's a small group called the National Socialists Workers party."

"Oh Amalie!" David said with shock.

"You know of them?"

"Yes. I've heard a lot about them. Far right. Vicious rhetoric. But Amalie, aren't you Jewish? They hate the Jews. How could your husband belong to a group like that?"

"He tells me they just hate Jewish bankers and politicians."

"I've heard that fanatic, Hitler. I went to protest with some friends at one of their meetings last year and he didn't sound like he made any distinctions in which Jews he hated."

"That's why I'm worried. Do you know anything about this Hitler?"

"Not much. Why do you ask?"

"I want to find out where he comes from and how he got to where he is now."

"Do you want to bring him down? Discredit him?"

"To tell you the truth, I'm not sure. I just want to find out who he is. He seems dangerous."

"Well, he's vicious, but there are so many of these little groups around. I think this Hitler is just a sign of the times. He'll disappear as soon as things improve."

"Maybe you're right, but just the same I'd like to find out more about him."

David stopped and thought for a moment, stroking his chin as he looked up at the ceiling. "My father" he finally said, "My father might know at least where to start. Since his retirement, he keeps close tabs on the political scene. It's like a hobby with him."

"All right" Amalie said.

"Sam" David said as he began to write down his fathers address. "Sam Freider over in Furstenreid."

"Thank you David" Amalie said as she took the note and tucked it in her purse. She then set the purse under her desk as she started organizing the days work.

Throughout the day, Amalie began to develop a plan for how she might visit Sam Frieder. She knew that it would all have to be secret. She didn't want Gunther to find out. She seemed to think that she might find a way to save her husband from his extremist friends, as though he had been coopted against his will by these people and she might find some way to bring back her Gunther instead of the Gunther who now sometimes frightened her with his politics.

Just before lunch, Amalie asked if she could take off early for the day.

"Yes, I suppose... Oh," David replied, stopping in mid sentence as he realized why she was asking. "a trip to Furstenreid?"

"David," Amalie said as she looked plaintively into his eyes, "you mustn't tell Gunther."

"Amalie, I've never even met your husband."

"I know, but just the same, promise me you'll never say anything about our conversation today."

"You have my word."

Furstenreid was, and still is, a residential area in the southern part of Munich. It took Amalie over half an hour to get there from her office, but once she got to the Furstenreid station, she easily found the right house since David had even drawn a little map on the note with his father's name and address.

The house was a pretty little red brick country cottage with an orange tile roof around which other newer houses had begun springing up before the war.

"Mr. Frieder?" Amalie asked as a partially bald, white-haired man with thick glasses answered her knock on the door, "Samuel Frieder?"

"Yes?" the man answered in a tone that implicitly asked what she wanted.

"My name is Amalie Stein-Metzdorf"

"That's quite a name." the man replied good-naturedly.

"Yes," Amalie said, trying to be polite while getting to the point of her visit. "But the reason I'm here..." Amalie was having trouble getting her thoughts together. "Mr. Frieder," she started again, "I know your son... I work for your son David."

"Oh yes." Sam said as his face grew more pleasant. "Amalie... That's right. David called me and said you might be coming by."

"He called?" Amalie asked with a note of surprise, but then she realized that of course that was what David would do.

"Please come in" Sam said.

The living room was dark. Dark wallpaper and heavy dark oak trim at every corner of floor to wall and wall to door. The only bit of lightness was the sheer white curtains at the windows which had suffered neglect since Sam's wife died a few years before. In a way it reminded Amalie of her own father, this man who kept things a certain way as a momento of his wife rather than for his own preference or taste. There was a bit of a musty smell to the house, but that was understandable in the winter. It was now just the end of January and the windows had obviously been kept closed for almost four months now. It was nothing that fresh Spring breezes wouldn't cure.

There were books everywhere. Books of all sizes and colors, of all qualities and languages. It was apparent that long ago great care had been taken to fit proper bookshelves and organize the books, but now they were strewn about, stacked on top of the bookshelves and piles sitting beside the couch and chairs. It was clear that these books were not for display, these books were meant to be read. They looked lived in.

Sam quickly and unpretentiously brushed some crumbs off the seat cushion of one of the chairs and directed Amalie to sit down while he moved around a low table in front of the couch and sat facing her. Amalie felt a little uncomfortable as she sat down because she wasn't sure exactly what it was that she wanted to know or how to go about investigating this friend of Gunther's and she knew that would be Sam's first question. "Mr. Freider..."

"Please," Sam interrupted "Such a pretty young lady, it would make me feel much better if you would call me Sam."

"Yes, yes" Amalie said with her nervousness becoming more obvious in her voice, "and you must call me Amalie." They both smiled awkwardly for a moment and then Amalie finally continued. "When David called... to tell you I was coming... Did he also tell you what I was looking for."

"No." Sam said as he settled back into the overstuffed couch.

Amalie realized as Sam made himself comfortable that she had been sitting on the edge of her chair. She was sitting so close to the edge that it was amazing she hadn't fallen right off! She then took a cue from her host and settled into the chair, becoming noticeably relaxed as she did.

"Sam... All my life I've tried... to be..." she paused for a moment as she reached for the right word, "rational."

Sam smiled as he concurred; "Me too!"

Amalie flashed a smile but then became serious again. "My husband has become involved with a political party..."

"What kind of party?" Sam asked.

"One of those extremist groups."

"National Socialists?" Sam asked.

"Yes. How did you know?"

"They've grown quickly over the last few years. Even though they still aren't very big, they make a very loud noise. Was your husband a soldier?"

"Yes." Amalie said again, pleased with the fact that he grasped the situation so quickly.

"I see..." Sam said thoughtfully. "They've made a real effort to recruit soldiers who fought in the front lines. Well this is strange indeed." Sam said, sitting up and folding his hands together while resting his elbows on his knees. "Amalie, I assume by your name that you're Jewish."

"My family was, but no, I'm not Jewish." Amalie responded.

"What do you mean? If your family was Jewish... unless... Was your mother a gentile?" Sam asked, trying to understand Amalie's denial.

"No, she was Jewish. I just mean I don't follow the Jewish religion."

"Have you converted to another religion?"

"No. I don't follow any religion"

"Amalie... We don't know each other, but I've got to tell you at the risk of offending you that that is not a consideration. When the people who hate Jews use the word 'Jew', they mean all people of Jewish ancestry."

"I don't mean to contradict you," Amalie said almost apologetically, "but my husband says they mean bankers and politicians and business men."

Sam paused, not because he was considering the plausibility of what Amalie had said, but because he was trying to think of a response that would open Amalie's eyes to the reality of this anti-semitism.

"Amalie," he began, "sometimes when faced with ugly things, we look away and close our eyes so that we don't have to see, but that doesn't mean those things are not still there, waiting for us as soon as we open our eyes again."

Amalie looked down at the floor. She couldn't look Sam in the face. She knew he was right, but she had tried to make life bearable by hiding behind the same things that allowed her husband to stay with her. Gunther's rationalization had become a thread that she held onto, which allowed them to stay together. Even now she would not say it out loud. She felt she was on a mission to save her husband and so she continued the conversation without acknowledging the truth of Sam's statement.

"Sam, the reason I'm here is because I want to find out about the man who leads the group."

"What do you want to know?" Sam asked.

"I want to know where he comes from and how he got here." Amalie answered directly, showing that she was no longer nervous.

"Why?"

"I think he's dangerous."

"...and you want to stop him?"

"I don't know. I'm not sure what I'll find. I don't even know what I'm looking for."

"Amalie, this could be a dangerous game you're thinking about."

"I know. I don't plan on telling anyone. I'll be careful, but I need to start someplace and I thought I could trust David."

"Yes, my son is a good man..." Sam said, drifting off as he thought about what Amalie was asking. "This man, his name is..."

"Hitler" Amalie interjected.

"Yes... Hitler. I know he comes from Austria... Let me see.." he said as he got up and crossed the room to a desk piled high with notebooks and papers. After a bit of shuffling he pulled out a notebook and returned to the couch. "I make notes on people" he explained to Amalie before burying his head in the pages.

"Your hobby" Amalie said with a smile as she repeated what David had told her.

Sam returned the smile as he looked up again. "Yes, some people collect butterflies, I collect politicians."

He dove back into the notebook and then held up a finger as he came to the matter at hand. "Braunau, about a hundred kilometers east of us." Sam stopped and thought again. "I know he was in the army, I think a corporal or sergeant. No, definitely a corporal... in the trenches. I'm afraid that's about all I know."

"What would you suggest Sam?"

"Well, an investigation is a tricky thing. First of all, you don't want people to know who you are or what you're up to."

"Yes, of course" Amalie agreed.

"You might pretend to be a reporter. Use an assumed name."

"But who do I ask and what do I ask them?"

"Well... first you'll want to find out what his family was like. If I were you I would go to Braunau and see if you can't check the church records. Then you would not only be able to find out who his parents and grandparents were, but you might also find out where the family went from there. They might still be living in Braunau."

"Go to Braunau?" Amalie exclaimed. Even though it was a logical suggestion, it stunned her. How would she find money to travel? How would she find the time and how could she possibly hide the purpose of the trip from Gunther?

"Amalie, this may be presumptuous of me, but maybe you could talk to David" Sam suggested.

"Why, what could he do?"

"David travels a lot,"

"Yes, I know."

"If David thinks what you are considering is important, and I think he might, then he might send you on a business trip to Braunau and you could do research while you're there."

Amalie was lost deep in thought for a moment as silence filled the room. Finally she looked up at Sam and asked "Do you think so? Do you think he would? David, I mean, do you think he would send me to Braunau?"

"Judging from the way he spoke of you on the telephone..."

"What do you mean?" Amalie asked.

"He obviously holds you in high regard Amalie. He says you are an intelligent woman and if my son has a flaw, it's that he doesn't compliment people easily. It's high praise when he compliments someone."

Amalie was embarrassed by this revelation and turned her eyes down. "Thank you Herr Frieder."

"Sam." he corrected, "and thanks for what? It was David who said it."

"Then thank you for repeating it."

"You're welcome." Sam replied "Well, I'm not sure where you can go with this or what you may find, but now it remains to talk to David and see what he has to say." Sam stood up and crossed over to Amalie, extending his hand as Amalie also stood up. "It was nice meeting you and I wish you luck."

"Thank you Herr... Sam" she corrected herself, "you've been very kind."

"If I can help you, let me know. ...and I assure you I will tell no one."

Amalie felt a sense of relief after she left the house. She was no longer alone in this risky venture.

The day after visiting Sam, she brought up the subject of possible business travel with David and he agreed. He was scheduled to go to the city of Reid in Austria in a couple of weeks to go over galley proofs with an author. The author had written a few books already and so the proofs were just a formality which Amalie could certainly handle, and the town of Braunau am Inn was between Munich and Reid. The work would take from ten o'clock in the morning until two o'clock for about four or five days and then Amalie could spend about three hours a day in Braunau for the whole period if necessary.

Gunther was not overly excited when Amalie told him about her "promotion" and how she was being sent to represent the publisher out of town, but then after all, this three year job was only temporary. Gertie Haas agreed to come over and make dinner for the week, so it wouldn't be a terrible inconvenience. Amalie had told everyone that she would leave at eight in the morning and be back by eight at night and they all sympathized with her for the long hours she would have to work.

It was the week after Valentines day when Amalie finally found herself on the train to Reid. After about an hour and a half, the train made it's stop at Braunau station where the border guards went from car to car on the train asking for passports and customs declarations.

The border guards were humorless and curt. There had been so much illegal traffic from Austria to Germany and from Germany to Austria that the guards trusted no one and since it was a Monday when there were relatively few travelers, they had time to make virtually all of them feel uncomfortable and suspect.

Amalie was particularly nervous, but not because she was carrying any contraband. She was nervous because she was in Braunau. She would return in a few hours to begin her clandestine research. Would she find anything? Would she find scandal or disgrace in Hitler's family that she could somehow use to get Gunther away from the party? It all seemed so complicated as she tried to figure out how it might all come together. She finally decided to take it step by step, to just try to find out what she could in Braunau and then see where that might lead her.

When Amalie got to Reid she got lost and ended up being over half an hour late for her meeting with Otto Maus, an author of a series of books on the American west. Stories of the American

113

Western frontier were big sellers with German and Austrian boys. Perhaps the romance of a great frontier being conquered by heroic white men struck a chord in the psyche that revered the legends of Teutonic knights.

David had been right in thinking he could send Amalie in his place to work with Herr Maus. Otto trusted David since this was his sixth book and Otto knew that David was a careful professional, bordering on being a perfectionist. It also didn't hurt that Amalie was pretty. Otto was a rather shy man and he especially enjoyed taking Amalie out to lunch at the restaurant around the corner where he always ate lunch during the week. The two waiters and the bartender were all smiles and made admiring remarks as Otto came in and directed Amalie to his usual table in the corner.

The lunch was surprisingly good for such a small out of the way cafe', but it soon became apparent that this had been a special effort by the waiter and cook for their friend Otto and Otto's "date". The lunch was pleasant and went by quickly as did the next couple of hours checking over the proofs. The only problem was that they didn't get as much accomplished as Amalie had hoped, but that was just as well, since it meant Amalie was virtually guaranteed five days work and therefore she would have more time in Braunau if she needed it.

It was a little after three o'clock when Amalie arrived in the small train station in Braunau again. She had decided to leave the galley proofs with Otto rather than dragging them along with her each day, especially since she would be stopping in Braunau along the way. She did carry her new briefcase though, in hopes of impressing the people she might be "interviewing". She decided on using the name of Liesl Kraus who was a new reporter for the Munich Taggblatt. She hoped no one would question her story, but if they did, she felt that by using the name of a new reporter she might be able to talk her way out of any trouble if someone checked with the newspaper.

She walked out onto the cobblestone street in front of the station and immediately spotted a church steeple and quickly covered the few blocks between the train station and the church. When she got to the church, she stopped for a moment, deciding whether or not to go in and decided instead to first look through the headstones in the small graveyard.

114

The short wall around the graveyard was built of mismatched stones and needed repair in a number of places where stones had come loose. After looking for a while she found a stone which read "Otto Hitler, born 1887, died 1887, beloved infant of Klara and Alois". She wondered if this was the same Hitler family. She went on to find three more headstones, all of them for children with the oldest being six years old, with the name Hitler. There were no adults named Hitler. She would have to go ask the priest.

Amalie had never been inside a Catholic church before and it seemed very foreign to her. The building was old and worn, but also very clean. The candles at the altar flickered as a cold draft swept by. Her eyes were immediately drawn to a garishly painted statue showing the crucifixion of Christ that was hung on the wall behind the altar.

"The Jews killed Christ." The thought raced through her mind, an echo of childhood taunts from when she had gone to school in Salzburg. The little boys had not attacked her, but she had heard them shouting at a little Jewish boy. She was a witness. Now here was the proof. This was what the Jews had done to their sacred Christ. This was what those children saw every week when they went to their churches on Sunday and they blamed a little schoolboy for the bright red blood running from the mouth of Christ, from the nails in his hands and feet.

"May I help you?" came a high pitched voice from behind her.

Amalie turned with a start and let out a little scream since she had been so engrossed by the dramatic presentation in front of her that she hadn't heard the priest when he came over.

"Oh! I'm sorry!" she said as she composed herself. "I thought I was alone!"

"We are never alone in the house of God." The priest said with the confidence of a man who knew God personally.

Amalie nodded and smiled, not being sure how one might respond to such a statement.

"I'm Father Kreuger" the priest continued, "Did you need help?"

"Yes, yes... I was wondering" Amalie began, but she then decided to start over so she could tell the whole fabricated story and try to convince the priest to believe her. "My name is Liesl Kraus" she began.

"Kraus, Kraus..." the priest repeated thoughtfully. "Are you a daughter of Artur Kraus from Simbach?"

"No." Amalie shot back quickly, wanting to get on with her story so she could get it all out and not give the priest a chance to critically analyze each point. "I'm a reporter from Munich. A new reporter with the Taggblatt. I'm doing a story on a man who was born here..."

"A man?" the priest asked.

Amalie was grateful that the priest had asked a question about the story she was writing rather than questioning her credentials and she got a little excited.

"Yes, he's a politician now. In Munich. He's doing rather well and they... My editor thought it might make a good story talking to his family, finding out what he was like as a boy and what might have contributed to his success."

"Very nice" the priest said. "There are so many terrible things in newspapers these days. It's a nice idea to talk about someone's success. Who is the man? I might know his family."

Amalie went into her briefcase, holding it high, almost in the priest's face as she pretended to go through notes looking for the name. "Hitler. Yes, that's it. Adolf Hitler"

"Well of course," the priest said pleasantly. "Alois' son"

"Alois. Does he still live in town?" Amalie asked.

"No, I believe Herr Hitler passed on. I think it was... could it be twenty years now?" the priest asked rhetorically. "Let me check our records".

Amalie's heart leapt. This was what she was hoping for and it had been so easy. It took everything she had to hide her excitement as she followed the priest to his office where he began pointing at the labels of the record books on a shelf as he went from book to book, his lips moving as he silently read the names on the labels to himself. "Here we are!" he said triumphantly. "Hitler, Alois and Klara... nee Pölzl" He began to click his tongue as he read. "I had almost forgotten. How sad. First Otto and then the twins and then Edmund. The poor woman lost four children, four little lambs" he shook his head as he continued reading. "Yes, here we are, Adolf. Born April twentieth, 1889." A piece of paper fell out of the book when the priest turned the page. "Ah!" he said with surprise as he bent over picking up the fallen note. When a family leaves the parish we generally don't keep further records on them, but I like to make notes

116

on where they move to and anything else I might hear..."

"So the family moved?" Amalie asked.

"Oh, yes." the priest replied without looking up from the note as he tried to make out all of his own scribbled writing. "To Leonding. Before the war."

"Leonding?" Amalie said with surprise as Leonding was only a couple of kilometers from her mother's childhood home in Linz, Austria.

"Yes," the priest replied, still lost in the task of translating his writing and taking no notice of the tone of Amalie's voice. "Alois died there in ought-three. Klara died of cancer in December of ought-seven"

"Is there anything about his grandparents?" Amalie asked.

"Oh, no." the priest said, finally looking up from his papers. "I believe they came from Spital. The older records would be there."

"Spital?" Amalie asked. "Spital am Pyhrn or Spital am Semmering?"

"Am Pyhrn" the priest replied.

It seems there are three cities with the name Spital in Austria. One on the river Pyhrn, another on the river Semmering and, just to make things a little more confusing, there is also a city called Spittal on the Drau river.

All of this was good news and bad news. The good part was that Amalie had made a good start and found the family. The bad part was that she now had to travel to Spital am Pyhrn and Leonding. Spital was about one hundred kilometers southeast of Reid. Perhaps her father could help by going to Leonding for her, but how would she get to Spital and how could she involve her father in this? This could easily get out of hand. She would have to impress upon him the importance of the task without getting him concerned about Gunther.

Suddenly she came upon a plan. At the end of the week she would suggest to Gunther that she might visit her father since she was already going as far as Ried and then she could make her side trip to Leonding and Spital over the weekend.

Amalie was worn out by the time she boarded the train for Munich. All of this plotting and planning and the accompanying anxiety had taken everything out of her. She pinned her ticket to her coat lapel and asked the conductor to make sure she didn't sleep through Munich. She couldn't help thinking, as they crossed back over the Austrian border, of the trip she had taken three years before when she first went to Munich and then she drew up into the corner of the compartment and went to sleep holding her bright new briefcase on her lap under her coat.

Amalie made it to the apartment just a few minutes after eight-thirty to find Mrs. Haas asleep in the old, overstuffed chair in the living room as Jakob, dressed in pajamas, played with his wooden toys on the floor at her feet.

"Mutti!" Jakob said exuberantly as he jumped up and ran over to his mother's waiting arms.

Gertie was startled out of her sound sleep and put a hand to her chest, feigning a heart attack. "God help me!" she said with a little laugh and a heavy sigh as she lifted herself out of the chair, "You almost scared me to death Jakob!"

"I trust Jakob has been good" Amalie said as she set down her briefcase after Jakob returned to his play.

"As always!" Gertrude said in a cheerful tone. "He and Gunther have eaten and Gunther, Friedrich and Captain Grunewald have gone out."

"As always..." Amalie said, commenting on the tendency of her husband to continually go out even when there wasn't a pfennig to spare. "Well Gertie," Amalie continued, making a special effort to sound pleasant and friendly as she changed the subject "How are things going with you?"

"Well enough" Gertrude said briskly, brushing the question aside as she began to busy herself with picking up a dish and taking it into the kitchen.

Amalie assumed that Gertrude was feeling put out. She really didn't want to deal with a problem after her long day of work and travel. She then found herself getting annoyed because Gertrude had seemed so willing to help when Amalie first asked her to stay with Jakob, especially when Amalie offered to pay her, but now it seemed that Gertrude was upset. Amalie then thought that maybe taking care of Jakob day and night had been a little more work than Gertrude had expected and Amalie immediately forgave her. After all, taking care of a child is demanding enough when you're a young mother, but when, like Gertrude, your children are grown with lives of their own, you grow accustomed to your time being your own and suddenly taking care of a child again for a long period can be quite a shock.

"He's a wonderful boy," Amalie said softly so that Jakob wouldn't hear as she entered the kitchen behind Gertrude "but it takes a lot of patience.."

"What?" Getrude asked, looking up from the dishes she was rinsing off.

"You seem tired..." Amalie said, "I thought Jakob may have been more of a handful than you expected."

"Oh no, really... Jakob was wonderful. We had fun today" Gertrude replied almost defensively.

There was a pause for a moment as Gertrude continued with the dishes in silence. Amalie leaned against the counter beside her deciding whether or not to ask what was wrong even though she really didn't feel like getting into a long discussion of Gertrude's problems, but Amalie had grown very fond of Gertrude and she really cared when Gertrude was upset.

"What's wrong?" Amalie finally blurted out, looking down at the floor, fairly assured that she would have to drag the information out of Gertrude.

"Nothing."

"Come now... I can tell that something's got you upset. I know you too well."

"It's nothing"

"Is it Jakob? Did he do something wrong?"

"No. I told you he was fine."

"Gunther?" Amalie asked, grasping at straws, looking up and watching Gertrude's face for a reaction as she ran through possibilities "Friedrich? Klaus? Money?"

That last word hit a nerve as Gertrude looked as though she had been stung and stopped washing dishes and leaned against the sink, adjusting her feet, changing her stance slightly as though she needed to get a better footing in order to hold herself up.

"Money?" Amalie repeated, moving a little closer and trying to look into Gertrude's downcast eyes "Is it money?"

Gertrude said nothing and Amalie didn't know what to say. Amalie couldn't possibly offer her more money because they could barely afford to give Gertrude what she was getting now, they barely had enough for food and rent, so there was nothing to say and another silence filled the small kitchen, a silence only interrupted by the sounds of Jakob playing with his toys on the floor in the living

119

room.

Finally Gertrude found her voice and in a low, labored, almost hoarse voice, a hoarseness born of the emotion, the terrible sadness of the words, she finally admitted to Amalie "I will have to leave my apartment."

Again, Amalie had nothing to say.

"Manfred and I," Gertrude continued slowly, keeping her eyes closed as she spoke, trying to fight back the tears, "We lived in that apartment for twenty years. We raised our two sons. We could never afford a house, but we always thought we would be able to get by. We were sure we would manage to get by, but now... now..." Gertrude was overcome. "There is no 'we' anymore..." Finally the tears came. Not sobbing, just the tears running freely from Gertrude's closed eyes, crossing her cheeks, running along the wrinkles in her face and sparkling in the light, accentuating the wrinkles. "It's just 'me'" she concluded as she now began to shake while trying to stop crying, but not being able to hold it back anymore.

Amalie could hardly stand to watch and felt the sting of her own tears as she gently put her arms around Gertrude, speaking softly and trying to comfort her.

"It's all right" she said, gently patting Gertrude's back and holding Gertrude's head against her shoulder as Gertrude continued to cry, "It will work out somehow..." but the truth was that Amalie had no idea what Gertrude might do and she could imagine Gertrude out on the street with nowhere to go, just as so many people now found themselves. First they had survived the war and then the revolution or "the war after the war" as they called it, and now the inflation that ravaged the German economy destroyed their life's savings and robbed them of their homes.

They stood there for awhile until Gertrude stopped crying and eventually moved into the living room. Amalie convinced Jakob that it would be a good idea for him to go to bed a few minutes early. When Amalie rejoined Gertrude, she began to analyze the situation.

"Friedrich hasn't found any work yet?" she asked.

"No..." Gertrude replied "He joined the army when he was only seventeen and so he hasn't even learned a trade yet. He doesn't even seem to know what he wants to do. He talks about leaving Munich, as though it will be better in Berlin or somewhere else, maybe even out of the country. He's getting so desperate that it worries me. I feel like I don't know what he might do next. He says I'd be better off without him, but I can't imagine how he would think..." Gertrudes sentence just trailed off as she felt overwhelmed at the prospect of Friedrich leaving her.

"How long do you have before you have to leave?" Amalie asked

"I think I should leave by next month. By then I should still have enough money to last another year if I just find a single room somewhere." Gertrude said dejectedly.

"Well," Amalie said slowly "let's just think about this for a few days and see if we can't come up with something..."

"Something?" Gertrude asked in a surprised tone, "Something like what?"

"I don't know yet, but there must be something that can be done."

Gertrude took Amalie's hand. "Thank you Amalie."

"For what? I really don't know if there's anything we can do."

"At least" Gertrude said with a half smile "You've made me feel a little less alone."

"Well, that's something..." Amalie agreed.

"I should be going now" Gertrude said as she got up and started gathering her coat and bag. "I will see you and Jakob bright and early tomorrow."

It was only a little after nine o'clock and Amalie knew Gunther wouldn't be home for at least another couple of hours. She hoped it wouldn't be much later than that because she wanted to talk to him about going to visit her father and maybe even about Gertrude. The more she thought about it, the more she thought it might be possible to have Gertrude move in with them. It would be convenient to have a live-in baby sitter, but what if they couldn't get along living in the same apartment day after day? Suddenly the apartment seemed a little smaller than it ever had before.

It would mean Jakob giving up his bedroom, a bedroom of his own that he had done without for so long and now he would have to sleep on the couch again for God only knew how long. She decided to talk to Jakob and see how he felt about it first. That way she might be able to diffuse Gunther if he said that Jakob shouldn't have to give up the room.

Amalie opened the door to Jakob's bedroom a little and watched as the light from the hallway lit his face where he lay, pretending to be asleep, on his stomach. She could tell he was only pretending because she could see his long eyelashes move when he blinked while trying to keep his eyes closed enough so that it would appear they were closed while he could still see what was going on.

"Jakob" she said softly as she went into the bedroom and knelt beside him. She lightly touched his shoulder while placing a gentle kiss on his forehead. "Jakob" she said again and Jakob carried out his charade, as though he was being awakened from a sound sleep.

"Mutti?" he asked as though confused.

"Yes." she said, "Jakob... do you like Mrs. Haas?"

"Mrs...?" he said as he rubbed his eyes, not knowing for an instant who Amalie meant, but then making the connection. "Oh! Grandma Gertie!" he said.

"Grandma Gertie?" Amalie asked with a bit of surprise and amusement as her question was answered in that phrase.

Jakob thought his mothers tone of voice might be a rebuke and replied apologetically "That's what she told me to call her."

"I see..." Amalie said smiling "Then it's certainly acceptable. It's nice that you two are friends."

Amalie paused for a moment, stroking Jakob's hair, thinking that it was time for a haircut as she ran her fingers through the long brown strands that were starting to show a curl at the ends.

"Jakob," she started again, "can you keep a secret?"

"Yes." Jakob said seriously

"You must promise not to tell anyone until I say you can."

"Even Vatti?" Jakob asked.

"Especially your father." Amalie said quickly.

"Why?" Jakob asked.

"Because this is something that I need to talk to him about, but I wanted to talk to you firs⁺ because it also concerns you."

"What?"

"Jakob, Grandma Gertie needs our help."

"Because she has to go away?" he said as he sat up in bed.

Amalie was taken aback. "How did you know?"

Jakob averted his eyes and said nothing.

Amalie suddenly realized how he found out. "You were spying!" she said accusingly, but she couldn't help smiling a little at how well he had done it. She had no idea he had even left his room and she usually heard his every move, or at least she thought she heard his every move.

"I just heard you talking..." Jakob finally said, still not able to look his mother in the eyes.

"My little boy... Jakob the spy!" Amalie said letting out a little laugh and reaching over to tickle him under the arms. Jakob giggled, partly from being tickled and partly out of relief at not being punished for his transgression.

Amalie then tried to get serious, changing her expression and repressing her laugh "Now, you know it's wrong to spy on people."

"Yes mother."

"We'll let it go this time, but don't do it anymore" Amalie said authoritatively. She then sat on the bed beside Jakob.

"Now Jakob, what I have to say is very important. Grandma Gertie needs our help and I thought she might stay here with us. All the time."

"That would be wonderful!" Jakob said excitedly.

"Yes" Amalie replied calmly, trying to quiet Jakob down to make sure that he would consider the situation and not just respond out of excitement, "but there's something else. If Gertie came to stay here, she would stay in your bedroom."

"With me?" Jakob asked.

"No. You would sleep in the living room again."

Jakob was struck by this and became silent. He liked having his own room and it would be hard for him to give it up, just as Amalie knew it would be.

"How long?" Jakob asked pragmatically.

"I don't know... a few months... maybe even a year."

Amalie watched Jakob's face as he knit his brow and pondered the situation, balancing his feelings for Grandma Gertie against how much he wanted a room of his own. Amalie studied his face, the blue eyes, the straight thin nose he had inherited from his father's side of the family and she watched as he sat there thinking hard about this grave problem.

"Ja!" he finally said in an exclamation of righteousness, knowing that it had been the answer that he had intended to give all along. He knew how happy it would make Grandma Gertie.

"Thank you, little love" Amalie said as she gave him a hug and laid him back down in his bed, pulling the sheet and blanket up around his face. "And remember, you mustn't tell anyone we talked about this until I've had a chance to talk with your father and Gertie."

"Yes, Mutti."

"Now go to sleep for real. Gute nacht liebling. Schlaft gut.*"

She went to the front closet and got her briefcase, bringing it into the kitchen as she sat down at kitchen table and began to spread out her papers. She began to map out her plan of attack, the method by which she would track down Hitler's family and his past. She spent the next couple of hours going over a map of Austria and train schedules and finally, writing a letter to her father telling him that she and Jakob would be coming. She had decided that it would be a good time for Jakob to see his grandfather again and it would also give her a good cover so that no one would suspect it was anything other than a social visit.

At eleven o'clock she put all her papers away and sealed the letter. She then sat on the couch in the living room reading the newspaper, waiting for Gunther to come home.

It was just a little after midnight when Gunther came in.

"Amalie! You're still up."

"Yes, I hoped you wouldn't be too late."

"What time is it?" Gunther asked. He seemed just a little drunk.

"Not too late." Amalie said, not wanting to challenge him since she needed to talk to him about the trip to Salzburg and also about Gertrude.

"Well," Gunther began "It was a special night, a farewell party."

"Oh?" Amalie said feigning interest, "Who's leaving?"

"Friedrich." he said.

"What!?" Amalie shot back.

"Friedrich has decided to try his luck in Berlin." Gunther said calmly as he put away his hat and coat and walked into the living room. "He hasn't found a job and he says he can't stand living off his mother. He says she can't support the two of them much longer."

There was a silence as Gunther sat down on the couch next to Amalie and watched her face, waiting for her response.

"Gertie knew this might happen." Amalie said sadly, "We just talked about it tonight."

"Well," Gunther countered, "I told Friedrich that we would watch out for Gertie."

---

* Good night little love, sleep well.

"Good... good." Amalie said thoughtfully, "Gunther... I want to ask you something, but I want you to think about it before answering. Just promise me you'll think about it."

"This sounds ominous."

"Gertie told me that she has to give up her apartment next month and find something cheaper..."

"I didn't know it was that bad."

"Well..." Amalie continued cautiously, "I thought... perhaps..." She then blurted out the rest. "If Gertie moved in with us, she could pay us a little rent and we could have a live-in baby sitter for Jakob and I talked to Jakob and he said he wouldn't mind sleeping in the living room and we could somehow get by together."

Gunther was stunned, not only at the thought of Gertie moving in, but also by Amalie's ability to say all that in one breath. "We could try it."

Amalie was completely taken off guard by his sudden acquiescence. "We could?"

"Yes. I promised Friedrich we would watch out for her."

Amalie reached over and hugged her husband. "Sometimes I forget how wonderful you are."

"...and then I remind you" he said with a smile, returning her hug. "Well, we better get to bed. It's late."

"One more thing..." Amalie said as she held onto Gunther's hand, stopping him from leaving the couch.

"What is it?" he asked cautiously.

"I know we can't afford it, but..."

"Oh no. What can't we live without now?"

"No, really." Amalie said playfully "Since I'm already going to Reid, and since Mr. Frieder is paying for that, I thought maybe I could take Jakob with me on Friday and after I'm done working we could go on to Salzburg to visit father."

"I suppose we could manage that" Gunther again conceded. "Is there anything else?" he asked playfully, "...or can we go to bed now?"

"No, that's everything" Amalie said as she snuggled up close to her husband as they walked to the bedroom.

Chapter 7

1923 was clearly the worst year of the runaway inflation associated with the Weimar Republic. The Germans had been consistently running behind on reparations payments until finally they were asking for a complete moratorium on reparations to give the German economy a chance to revive. The proposed moratorium made for a number of stormy meetings of the reparations committee which resulted in the departure of the British representatives. The French, left without opposition, issued orders for a military occupation of the industrialized Ruhr region of Germany where they would have their own troops run the factories and deliver the finished products directly to French markets. The German government reacted swiftly to the military occupation by devaluing their currency even more so that they would be able to meet the French demands for reparations with virtually worthless currency rather than allowing the French to cripple German industry. This resulted in a Pyrrhic victory for the German government as opposition to the new republic grew even stronger among an embittered German population who was ultimately paying the price for the Weimar economic strategy.

Otto Maus, the author in Reid with whom Amalie was working, was not terribly comfortable with children although he didn't dislike them. When he opened the door that Friday, he found not only Amalie, but her six year old son standing at her side looking up at him.

"Are you my grandfather Ethan?"

"No Jakob!" Amalie said with a bit of embarrassment, "I told you I had to do some work here and then we'll go to Salzburg. That's where your grandfather is."

Amalie smiled at Otto. "I'm sorry Otto, but I had a chance to visit my father in Salzburg after we finish today and I hope it isn't a problem, but I brought my son Jakob...Herr Maus, this is Jakob. Jakob this is Herr Maus."

"Guten tag, Jakob" Otto said as he bent over a little, taking Jakob's hand and shaking it lightly.

"Hallo" Jakob replied shyly.

"I'm sure he will be no problem" Amalie said apologetically "He can be very quiet while we finish up."

With that, Otto ushered them into his home, leading Jakob into the living room which, like most of the other rooms in the house, was filled with bookcases, but this was not like Sam Frieder's book filled home which Amalie had visited the month before. Otto's house was meticulously cared for, which Amalie found surprising since Otto was a bachelor and she assumed that any bachelor's house would be a shambles.

"Do you read well?" Otto asked Jakob as he placed a hand on the little boy's shoulder and directed him to a large, shiny leather chair.

"Yes he does" Amalie answered for Jakob who was now acting very shy as he was overwhelmed by the luxurious surroundings.

There were heavy leather chairs which looked so new that they could have just come from a store that morning and the lamps had shades with green and almond colored tiffany all set on brightly polished brass bases. There was a deep blue carpet thicker than the grass of the English garden which showed no wear at all and went from wall to wall of the room. Even the leather bound books in the book cabinets with their lead crystal windows in the cabinet doors looked as though they had been polished just that morning.

"He was reading when he was four." Amalie continued, "My

father is a publisher and he started me reading young and we did the same with Jakob."

"Excellent!" Otto said, looking at Amalie and acknowledging her pride without question. He turned to one of the bookcases and unlocked the door, pulling out a book and then locking the door after himself. "What kind of man locks up all of his books?" Amalie thought to herself.

Otto knelt in front of Jakob who was in danger of being swallowed up by the huge leather chair surrounding him.

"Here is a book..." Otto began as he opened it and paged through to the title page, "This is the first book I wrote. It did very well. Many boys about your age.... well, maybe a little older... Well, I've gotten a number of letters from boys saying how much they liked it..." Otto closed the book and tapped the cover thoughtfully with his finger as he looked out a window at the snow filled street. "The Tears of the Desert." he said absent-mindedly, repeating the title of the book out loud. "I was just starting then." He suddenly slapped the book against his other hand and turned back to Amalie and Jakob. "...but that was a long time ago. You read it now while your mother and I do our work and then you can tell me if you think it's any good." He handed Jakob the book and gave him a little chuck under the chin and a pat on the head before wandering off to his study where Amalie would soon follow.

Amalie stayed behind for just a moment until Otto was out of earshot and turned to Jakob. "Now liebling, please don't touch anything. We should only be an hour or so, and please, please don't play with anything. We could never afford to replace anything here if you break it!" She then gave him a quick kiss on the cheek and followed after Otto.

Jakob sat in the chair and opened the book, looking at the title page. "The Tears of the Desert" he thought to himself. "What a dumb name!" The book smelled funny. It smelled old and musty as Jakob opened the book and glanced at other pages and when he quickly flipped through the pages, a fine dust blew up from the book and the smell filled his nostrils. He suddenly looked up as the dust from the pages floated into a sunbeam and created a small cloud above him. His eyes drifted as he looked up and he noticed a painting above the fireplace.

It was a picture of American Indians on a buffalo hunt as they rode up beside a buffalo, aiming arrows at its shoulder. Jakob climbed out of the chair and crossed the room to the fireplace. He had never even heard of Indians or buffalo and so he didn't really understand this picture of half naked men with outstretched arms, arms that were holding bows, riding on horses without saddles as they gathered around a big, dark brown beast. He then looked beside the fireplace mantel and saw a table that looked like a box with a glass top. Inside the box were little figures of men, some half naked like the ones in the painting and the rest in blue uniforms. He couldn't have known that this was Otto's careful reproduction of the battle of little Big Horn, but nonetheless he was fascinated by the little toys in the glass covered box. He suddenly remembered his mothers warning about not touching anything and even though he really wanted to open the box, he didn't. He dutifully returned to the big leather chair and opened the book, doing just as he had been told.

The next couple of hours passed quickly as Jakob found himself immersed in Otto's book about cowboys in the old west killing Indians. The Indians had killed poor innocent settlers and little settler children who hadn't done anything to make the Indians hate them. The Indians were mean and murderous, even the Indian woman and the Indian children, and the cowboys were strong and good and determined to bring the Indians to justice.

Otto and Amalie were laughing as they came out of the study. "Jakob," Amalie called out, "we're going to leave now." Jakob continued reading without moving as Amalie and Otto continued talking.

"It's been a pleasure, Otto" Amalie said.

"Yes indeed" Otto concurred "It has been very nice having such company."

"Well, I thank you for putting up with Jakob."

"Oh, not at all! I never heard a sound out of him." Otto then turned to Jakob and smiled as he saw the close attention the little boy was paying to Otto's first published work. "You like it then Jakob?" he asked.

Jakob, with his mouth open as he read, didn't even turn to look as he shook his head "yes" while continuing to read.

"Jakob," Amalie interjected, "It's time to go now. Leave the book and come put on your jacket."

Once again Jakob did exactly as he was told and closed the

book, handing it to Otto as he passed him.

"No Jakob, you take it. It's yours." Otto said.

"That's very kind of you." Amalie said, "Jakob, what do you say?"

"Thank you Herr Maus" Jakob rattled off.

"But there is something you can do for me in return." Otto quickly rejoined.

"Certainly Otto. What is it?" Amalie asked.

"One last lunch together?" he asked in reply.

Amalie smiled. "Otto, you've been so kind. We couldn't possibly impose..."

"Amalie," Otto said as he took her hands in his, "I so rarely have guests and all this week you've been like the first gentle breeze of Spring here. Please do me the honor."

"Thank you Otto" Amalie said graciously and the three of them went around the corner to the small cafe' where Otto always had his lunch.

Through the course of the lunch Otto told Jakob some of his experiences in the American west although all of the information was only second hand and Otto had merely been a tourist tramping around the old battle grounds and the sites where unarmed Indians had been massacred by American troopers.

Otto actually had a fairly good grasp of the situation of the American Indian and the disgraceful treatment the United States government had visited against them, unlike some of his contemporaries. Many other German writers of the same genre had never even been to America when they wrote their dramatic stories, but even though Otto had a good idea of what had really happened to the American Indians, he rarely told the truth in his books because he felt it lacked dramatic impact. Where was the nobility in trained, well armed US Cavalrymen riding down on unarmed innocents and slashing them with sabers and shooting them? Where was the glory in forcing the defeated Indian nations onto reservations where hunting tribes were supposed to suddenly change to farmers, farming land that wasn't even fit to grow rocks? What would his book be like if he told of the great general George Armstrong Custer routinely delivering disease infested blankets to reservation Indians in the hopes of infecting them so that an epidemic would ravage the few remaining tribes? More importantly the question was how many books could he sell if he told of these things? and so he simply ignored the facts and wrote books designed to make money, to excite the young boys who might buy them and create a great heroic myth of the American frontier where great white men were destined to tame and rule a savage land.

The mythology of the American Western frontier wasn't much different from the world view fostered by the rampant nationalism and Pan-Germanism that had permeated German society at the turn of the century and up through the early years of the war. Although that attitude certainly waned during the bad years of the war and through the Weimar years, it would soon become stronger than ever, accompanied by the musical score of a new national anthem: "Deutschland uber Alles*".

Amalie slept for most of the trip on the way to Salzburg while Jakob continued to read his new book. When they finally arrived, Amalie became a bit anxious because this wasn't just a welcome reunion, this was to be a mission to coopt her father and convince him to join her in her strange plan.

Ethan Stein was waiting on the platform, watching each window as it passed, looking for his daughter and grandson. It had been such a long time, and such an important time for Jakob. How much he must have changed in almost four years. Was he already six years old? Or was he still five? Ethan tried to remember the birthday and run the years through his mind when he suddenly found himself face to face with his daughter as she leaned out the window of her compartment and was almost close enough to kiss him as the train kept going slower and slower and she continued past him the last few yards until the train finally gave one last rumbling shake before coming to rest.

"Father! Father!" Amalie called out just before ducking back into the compartment and gathering the two old suitcases, the precious new briefcase and, of course, Jakob, and quickly working her way down the narrow passageway of the coach car. She dropped her bags unceremoniously in front of Ethan and wrapped herself around her speechless father and kissed him several times on the cheek. She then picked up Jakob and fairly threw him into his grandfather's arms.

"Come Jakob." she said excitedly, "It's your grandfather Ethan."

---

* Germany above everything

Ethan was usually a rather reserved and dignified man who wouldn't dream of making a scene in public, but after all these years... He at first seemed stunned at Amalie's aggressiveness, but then he looked at his beautiful grandson and hugged him tightly.

Jakob didn't think he would recognize his grandfather. Back in Munich when his mother told him that they were going for a visit, Jakob tried to picture him, but couldn't really remember him. There was the picture in the living room on the table, but it seemed so stiff and formal. Suddenly it was all right. The old mans touch. The smell of pipe tobacco. The look in grandfather Ethan's eyes. Yes, this was Jakob's grandfather.

They all went to the front of the station and Amalie started to hail a cab.

"Amalie!" Ethan called out "There's no need."

"Oh father," she said, "don't worry! I can afford it, we don't need to take the trolley."

"No Amalie!" her father protested again "I've bought a motorcar. It's over here."

"A motorcar?"

"Second hand" Ethan replied.

"Well! Things must be going nicely."

"Things are... well, they are going well enough now, but who knows about tomorrow?"

"Oh father. Always the pessimist." Amalie said, but as she said it she thought of how things were going in Munich. She suddenly thought of Gertrude and Friedrich.

"It's not that." Ethan said as Amalie caught up to him while he walked to the parking spot where the small touring car waited, "I bought it because a friend begged me to. I feel as though I took advantage of him."

"Did you pay a fair price?" Amalie asked, knowing that her father would never intentionally cheat a man, no matter what the conditions.

"Yes, but still..." Ethan hedged.

"...and if you hadn't bought it," Amalie continued "someone else would have who probably wouldn't have been fair."

"I suppose," Ethan acknowledged "but I still don't feel good about it."

"You did the best you could father." Amalie said, understanding his ambivalence and trying to put his mind at ease as they loaded her luggage in the back.

Ethan turned out to be a good driver which genuinely impressed Amalie since she had never remembered her father as being mechanically inclined. When something broke in their house, even if minor in nature, it was either stored so that is could be repaired "someday" or thrown away and quickly replaced. She remembered as a child thinking that she must never break a bone or she might end up on the curb, waiting to be picked up by the rubbish man.

Amalie talked incessantly throughout the car ride to the house. Unlike many other people, when Amalie slept on a train, she found it to be a restful sleep and so by the time they got home she was wide awake and filled with excitement at returning home. Jakob, on the other hand, was ready for a good nap and Ethan showed him to his bedroom as soon as they arrived.

Father and daughter sat at the table in the dining room and talked for hours, catching up on family and politics and discussing work and the state of the world. Ethan was pleased to find that his daughter had become significantly more mature from the time when she had left home just as the war was ending. He found it easy to talk intelligently with her about a wide range of subjects. She had even seemed to lose some of her childish prejudices against Judaism which had been born of that period of rebellion that all children go through as they try to separate from their parents.

"I heard from Eleonore the other day" Ethan said, continuing the discussion as he moved on to a new subject.

"Eleonore! My God. I can't believe how long it's been since I've seen her" Amalie said.

"Not since you left... Almost four years now."

"How is she and her professor?"

"She's fine. Louis is almost tenured at the university."

"I always thought it was funny that my sister would marry someone who became a botany professor and her with her terrible hay fever."

Ethan laughed as he thought about it. "I remember how she would stay inside for a whole month at a time."

"She lost so many boyfriends because she couldn't stop sneezing and blowing her nose" Amalie said, laughing along.

"I received a very unexpected letter just a few weeks ago"

Ethan said once the laughter subsided.

"From who?" Amalie asked.

"Do you remember the Steins from Breslau?"

"Breslau?"

"Yes... in eastern Germany"

"Of course Breslau is in Germany!" Amalie said as though her father was patronizing her, "I just don't remember hearing about the Stein family in Breslau."

"They're distant relations... Third cousins twice removed or second cousins thrice removed" Ethan said facetiously, "I can never keep those things straight. Anyway, the point is that I received a letter from Edith who said that her mother said she should send greetings and that she was changing from a Jew to a Catholic."

"What do you mean?" Amalie asked, pretending ignorance "Is she changing from one boyfriend to another?"

"No Amalie" her father said as they both laughed. "But I don't understand why someone would change from a Jew to a Catholic. It seems that both have their share of problems. I might understand changing from Jew to Protestant. Who ever heard of a pogrom against the Protestants?"

They both started laughing at the thought of it, but it was graveyard humor. Pogrom was a Russian word meaning devastation and eventually came to refer to attacks on the Jews throughout Europe. The Jews had been persecuted since the time of the Diaspora, the time when the Jews were forced out of their homeland of Israel. Although some Jews remained in what would become Palestine, the majority traveled throughout the continent of Europe looking for new homes and for centuries they were faced with pogroms ranging from the crusades and the inquisition to all the other smaller tortures that were visited against them from Vladivostok to Toledo.

"Where does Edith live now?" Amalie asked.

"Gottingen" Ethan replied.

"The university? "

"Yes."

"Is she a student?"

"She was. She graduated last year."

"What course?"

"Something strange. Some sort of philosophy called

134

'Phenomenology'."

"What on Earth...?" Amalie asked, not having any idea what phenomenology could be.

"Well," Ethan began pensively "...as near as I can make out, some professor named..." he paused, trying to remember. "Husserl!" he said proudly, as though he had pulled the name out of thin air like a magician "Yes. Husserl. He started it and he says that an event that does not leave physical evidence can only be explained in terms of that phenomenon, a description of the event itself."

"It sounds like some sort of theological study." Amalie said

"Strange you should say that. That's exactly the way that Edith put it. She says all her college study ties into the Catholic theology and their faith in miracles and so on."

"Well," Amalie said, "you know I've never been much of one for religion."

"There might be something else behind it though" Ethan said as though he were just now making a connection from the rest of the information in the letter. "She said that she had been denied some sort of chair position at the university and there wasn't much else that she could do with her degree other than teaching."

"You think she's converting because the university turned her down?" Amalie asked incredulously.

"Oh, no." Ethan said, defending Edith's decision, "I wouldn't go that far. I wouldn't say that was the whole reason, but maybe it has something to do with it."

"Maybe..." Amalie allowed.

The conversation stopped for a moment and Amalie thought this might be a good time to bring up her "mission".

"Father... There is something going on that I need to talk with you about. I need your help."

"What is it?" Ethan asked with a concern that matched his daughter's serious tone.

"First of all, I want to tell you that this might be nothing and you can certainly say so if you feel I am just being ridiculous..."

"Yes Amalie, yes. Just tell me what it is."

"There is a political group in Munich that has me worried."

"Only one?" Ethan said, making a statement about the confused state of politics in Munich since the war.

"Yes. One in particular."

135

"Which one?"

"They are called the German National Socialist Workers Party."

"I've heard of them" Ethan said as he tried to remember, "Right wing... antisemitic... they draw strongly from ex-soldiers."

"Yes."

"Why them? Why do they worry you in particular?"

"That's not important..." Amalie said evasively.

"Well there must be a reason. There must be something that... Oh my God." Ethan said with a stunned look on his face as he made the connection between ex-soldiers who fought at the front and his own son-in-law, "It's Gunther, isn't it?"

Amalie said nothing. She kept a poker face, but she then realized how ridiculous she had been to think that her father wouldn't have guessed.

Ethan persisted although now he was calm again. "Gunther has joined these..." Ethan was at a loss for a derogatory epithet and finally rephrased his question in the most direct and accusing manner, "He's joined them hasn't he?"

Amalie couldn't see any way to deny it. "It's not like you think" she offered passively.

"Then why are you worried? If it's not what I think, then why have you come all this way? That's why you came, isn't it? This is the real reason. There is trouble and you need my help." Ethan sounded almost hysterical as he piled question on top of question, trying to get a straight answer without giving his daughter a chance to speak.

"I just want to avoid trouble" she said quietly and calmly. "Gunther only joined because a lot of soldiers who fought in the trenches have joined. He joined because he had friends who joined, because he was a soldier, not because he hates Jews. He's a good man, a good husband and father who just needs to have his eyes opened."

There was silence as the father and daughter faced each other. Ethan felt betrayed. He had just been thinking how mature and intelligent his daughter was and now she sat there insisting that she should stay with a man who would join a political party of avowed anti-semites.

Amalie also felt betrayed. She felt her father was just jumping to conclusions, assuming that this was all that there was to Gunther, assuming that he couldn't be saved, that he wasn't a good man.

"What do you want? What do you want me to do?" Ethan finally asked as he stared down at the table.

"I want to find out about their leader. It seems as though he is the whole party. If he were discredited, the whole group might fall apart." Amalie said, finally revealing her plan and for the first time admitting to herself that her goal was to try to destroy the party.

"Amalie," Ethan said as he raised his head and made deliberate eye contact with his daughter "These are dangerous people! They are extremists. Who knows what they are capable of or what they might do to someone who interferes with them."

"I have to do this father. I don't know if I will find anything, but I have to try and I was hoping you would help. I will do it with or without you, but I really hoped you would help."

Suddenly Ethan was afraid for his daughter as he saw that familiar headstrong attitude which Amalie was so known for in the family and he knew she wouldn't back down, but now he also saw something more, he saw courage in her eyes.

The next day Amalie made the trip by train to Linz while her father took care of Jakob. She had to change to a bus to get to Leonding from the Linz train station and she soon found herself at the foot of a small hill which led up to a Catholic church where she once again decided to start by looking through the graveyard. She quickly came upon the stoic and forbidding picture of Alois Hitler set in a weathered granite stone which seemed to spring from the heavy Austrian snow. The stone was not so much decayed as it was blackened by the constant wash of chimney soot and dirt. "Born 1837, died 1903" Amalie said to herself as she looked the monument over. She then brushed away the snow and found another picture, this one of Klara Hitler, Born 1860, died 1907.

Amalie then went in to the church and succeeded with the same story she had used in Braunau, convincing the priest that she was Liesl Kraus, a reporter looking for information on a local man who had made good in Munich. She found out that Adolf and his mother and sister had lived in the house just past the wall of the cemetery for years after Alois Hitler had died. She also found that after all the confusion over Spital am Pyhrn, Spital am Semmering and Spittal, there was actually another place named Spital, but this was a small village by the town of Weitra, only about 40 kilometers from Leonding and, contrary to what the priest in Braunau had told her, it was this small town where Adolf Hitler's mother, Klara, was born and where Klara eventually met Alois Hitler, Adolf Hitler's father.

The trip to Leonding only took Amalie a total of about three hours before she returned to her father's house and all during the return trip she was planning for the next day. Would she take the train or might she convince her father to drive her in the car?

When she entered the house, she found Jakob sitting on his grandfather's lap, holding a menorah in his hands. Ethan stopped speaking as Amalie entered. He was embarrassed by the fact that he was explaining what a menorah was to Jakob and he wasn't sure how Amalie might react. He remembered how antagonistic his daughter was towards the Jewish religion by the time she had left for Munich and he had no reason to believe she had changed her attitude. Jakob was Jewish by virtue of his mother being Jewish and so when Jakob asked what the funny candle holder was, Ethan felt compelled to explain the meaning of Hanukah.

"So," Amalie said with a playful lilt to her voice as she broke the silence, trying to join in on their lesson "I see Jakob found the menorah."

Ethan was intuitive enough to see that his daughter was giving him permission to continue, and so he cautiously resumed the lesson.

"Well... I was just telling Jakob how we start by lighting one candle and then we light two and then three and so on, so that as Hanukkah continues, each night we are bringing more light into the world."

"...and did you tell him the rest?" Amalie asked as she knelt in front of her father and son, looking into Jakob's eyes "dredles and Hanukkah geld and all the family coming for dinner..."

"I wasn't sure you remembered" Ethan interjected as his daughter attempted to create a fantasy of her childhood memories.

"I remember being a child," Amalie said pointedly to her father, "but I left childish things behind me."

"Now you're quoting the new testament?" Ethan countered.

This remark cut Amalie but she didn't want to get into it.

"What is a 'new testament'?" Jakob interrupted.

"Well..." Ethan started as he turned his attention back to his grandson, "the first five books of the Bible are called the old testament, or the Jews call it 'the Torah' or 'Pentateuch'."

"The Jews?" Jakob said absent-mindedly as he looked down at

the menorah that his grandfather was still holding, saying it just because he remembered that he was a Jew.

"Yes," Ethan continued, "God chose the Jews to receive the Torah."

Jakob looked up at his grandfather. "Father doesn't like the Jews."

Ethan was struck by this much in the same way that his daughter had been struck years before when Jakob and Amalie had first spoken about what a Jew was. The emotion was overwhelming to Ethan. It was bad enough within the Jewish community to fear the outside world, but to have fear like that within ones own family.

Ethan looked up at his daughter who looked upset, as though her son had revealed a terrible secret. She took Jakob's hand and pulled him off his grandfather's lap.

"Come along Jakob," she said, trying to pretend there was nothing wrong, "Let's make lunch together, you and I."

There was no more talk about it. Lunch consisted of sandwiches and small talk and the afternoon drifted aimlessly until Amalie finally found the resolve to ask her father to make the trip with her to Spital the next day. He agreed without question. It was clear that he was with her. He now had some idea of what she faced at home and knew that it must be hard enough on her, so he decided to let the past be and try to help however he could.

It was a Sunday morning in February when Ethan, Amalie and Jakob arrived in Spital. Amalie was lucky that her father offered to drive since Spital was such a small village that there was no train station and bus service was unreliable. Amalie told Jakob that she was going to visit an old friend by herself as her father drove past the small church and dropped her off a couple of blocks away. She wanted to make sure that Jakob didn't see her go into the church and start asking questions later. Ethan was in on the plan and told Amalie not to worry, he and Jakob would just go riding in the motor car and be back in about an hour to pick her up.

It was in Spital that Amalie found the family history of Klara Pölzl, Hitler's mother, and traced her family, Johann Pölzl and Johanna Hiedler, to another small town about forty kilometers to the east called Dollersheim. Amalie had just left the church as Ethan pulled up with Jakob and she said that they had to make one more stop.

139

The Austrian back roads between villages were rough and icy with steep hills that made the travel slow in the cold, open little car. Ethan was afraid that the car might not make it up some of the steep icy hills. It took two hours to travel from Spital to Dollersheim, a trip that under better conditions would have taken less than half that time. It was almost two o'clock in the afternoon, with only a couple of hours of daylight left. They had not yet had lunch and even though they had eaten a large breakfast before taking off that morning, Jakob was beginning to fuss and complain. Once again Ethan dropped Amalie off and Amalie said she would have lunch with her fictitious friend while Jakob and her father would find a restaurant.

Amalie was beginning to wonder if any of this was worth while until she finally saw the records of Alois Hitler. The entry under his birth listed him as Alois Schicklgruber and at some point the name Schicklgruber had been crossed off and the name Hitler had been written in without any further notations. Finally she had found something curious, but what did it mean?

The priest she had been talking to was evasive at first and then suggested that she might talk to the priest who had served the Dollersheim parish before him, father Brumgart, who was now over eighty years old and living in a monastery by Weitra.

"Did you have a good lunch?" Amalie asked as she got into the car.

"Yes, we brought a sandwich in case you were still hungry..." Ethan said, still staying to the story that Amalie was visiting an old friend.

"Thank you" Amalie said appreciatively as she quickly unwrapped the sandwich. "You know," she said thoughtfully between bites, "There is someone else I would like to visit..."

Ethan shot a glance at her and as Amalie looked, he could tell that she was on to something.

"Oh yes... your school friend in... where does she live now?"

"Weitra" Amalie said after swallowing a large bite of her sandwich.

"Yes. Weitra... But it will be getting dark soon. We could only just make it home before it starts getting really cold."

"I know" Amalie said, "I thought I might call Gunther and tell him we're staying one more day. I could go to Weitra by train. Is there any chance that Jakob could stay with you tomorrow?"

"I think so" Ethan replied. "I don't have much planned tomorrow and I have a wonderful woman who comes in to clean every Monday. I think she and Jakob would hit it off for a couple of hours. Yes, I think we could do that."

By the time they got home, it was after dark and the temperature had dropped to well below freezing. They all rushed into the house and Ethan hurriedly began a fire that quickly filled the living room with warmth and the scent of pine as he threw a few pine needles into the blaze. He and Jakob watched the fire as the needles hissed and popped with tiny explosions of yellow flame.

Amalie had gone into the kitchen to check on their dinner, a venison stew which she had started on a low flame in the oven before they had left that morning, and she soon returned to the living room to join her father and her son. She stopped in the doorway, watching as the two knelt before the fireplace where Ethan was allowing Jakob to throw a few of the pine needles on the fire by himself and warning him not to put on too many. It was a pleasant scene as she saw the wonder on Jakob's face with the light of the fire dancing about the room and her father with his hand on Jakob's shoulder.

It took awhile, but Amalie finally managed to get a telephone call through to Munich after dinner. Gunther wasn't home, but Gertrude was there. Gertrude had made dinner for Gunther and was cleaning up, almost ready to leave. She took Amalie's message and left a note for Gunther that Amalie would be staying one more day, coming back early Tuesday, and Gertrude also agreed to call Mr. Frieder and tell him that Amalie would be a day late.

The next day Amalie arrived in Weitra at eight-thirty in the morning and about an hour later she found her way to the austere looking monastery a couple of kilometers west of the city. Once again introducing herself as Liesl Kraus, Father Brumgart agreed to talk with her, but he seemed as cautious as the priest who had directed her to Weitra. Amalie at first thought that he was put off by her saying that she was a reporter and that he wouldn't be of much help, but it soon became apparent to her that father Brumgart's cautious attitude was more a product of a man who rarely had visitors rather than the attitude of a man who had something to hide. He soon warmed up to Amalie and was happy to have a visitor who had come to talk with just him, someone who treated him as though he were important and interesting rather than just another resident of the monastery to be bathed, dressed and fed.

Amalie let the father talk awhile before directing his conversation to Alois Hitler and to her pleasant surprise, father Brumgart remembered the occasion of the notation made in the birth records at Dollersheim.

"I don't tell you this lightly Fraulein Kraus..." the old priest began, pausing and looking Amalie directly in the eye to make the importance of his point clear to her, "I will tell you this because I believe the truth is important. Father Strauchler was a good man, a good priest, and he only did what he thought was best..."

"Who was father Strauchler?" Amalie asked, afraid that the old priest was getting lost in his thoughts and wouldn't be able to give her any useful information.

"Father Strauchler" the old priest began laboriously, as though he was trying to keep the story straight while having to go back and deal with Amalie's interruption, "was the priest at Dollersheim when I arrived. He was the one who actually dealt with... the problem."

Amalie was about to ask what problem Father Brumgart meant, but she thought better of it as the priest was apparently struggling to form the story into its proper chronology.

"They came to say that the boy, Alois, who was born a bastard, was now accepted as the son of...Hiedler, but it was actually Alois' uncle who came to correct the name since Alois' father was dead by then."

"Hiedler?" Amalie asked "Don't you mean Hitler?"

"It's all the same. The same man." Father Brumgart said, brushing aside the question as pointless.

"Father Strauchler spelled it wrong?" Amalie asked

"Spelling wasn't important" the old priest said.

Amalie thought a moment and then checked her notes. Wasn't Hiedler the name of Klara Polzl's mother? This was getting confusing. Adolf Hitler's grandfather on his father's side was named Hiedler and his grandmother on his mother's side was also named Hiedler.

"Was this the same Hiedler family from Spital?" Amalie finally asked.

"Yes, they were from Spital."

"Do you remember a woman named Klara Pölzl?" Amalie pressed on.

"Yes, yes." the old priest said with a hint of a smile. "I see why you look confused. The son... Alois... he married more than once and his last wife was..." Father Brumgart stopped a minute and squinted as he tried to remember the relationship between Alois and his last wife. "Yes, that's it! His third wife was his niece! Klara was Alois wife and also his niece" the old man said with a smile and a little laugh at the scandal of it.

Amalie was careful to not react so that he wouldn't think he had said too much. They went on to discuss the gossip that the priest had heard about the family over the years. He told Amalie that Alois had left home when he was about thirteen, two years after his mother had died at their home in Spital.

"Father Strauchler..." Amalie started her question as she looked over her notes, "It looks as though he wrote in Alois' fathers name after Alois mother and father were both dead."

Father Brumgart hesitated before answering, knowing that it was illegal to enter a change in those records without the proper documents that would have included a statement from the mother. Such a statement would have been impossible in this case, however, since Alois' mother had died years before the Hiedler family had come forward to accept paternity. That was why the change in the church records hadn't been dated.

"Yes" the priest finally admitted after a long pause. "Like I have stated, father Strauchler was a good priest and tried to do what was best. What good would be served by denying the man his father's name?"

They continued talking for awhile, but since father Brumgart had no more information about the Hiedler family, Amalie tried a couple of times to break off the conversation. It wasn't easy though, since it was apparent that father Brumgart was a nice old man who hadn't had any visitors for a long time and wasn't willing to let Amalie go.

When Amalie finally escaped, she determined that she had to go back to Spital again and see if she could find out anything more from other sources.

It was almost ten o'clock at night when she finally returned home to find Ethan sitting in a chair in front of the fireplace, reading a book.

"My, my" Amalie said, obviously in a good mood as she hung

her coat in the hall closet and breezed up to the fireplace to get warm, "I thought I'd never make it home."

"I was beginning to wonder myself. I was getting nervous." Ethan admitted, "I trust it was a successful trip."

"You'll never guess!"

"Skeletons in the closet?"

"His grandfather was Jewish!"

"What?" Ethan asked incredulously.

"Well," Amalie started as she sat down next to Ethan, calming a bit as she spoke, "I don't have any proof yet, but I talked to a few people in Spital after talking to the priest in Weitra and the... Well, they say that Hitlers father, Alois, married his own niece, Klara. Alois was a bastard and the rumor in Spital is that the father was a Jew, but it was covered up by the Hiedler family.

"Hiedler?" Ethan asked, "Where does Hiedler come into it?"

"Hiedler is Hitler" Amalie explained, "It was a misspelling in church records. Hitler's father... well, his grandmother, was named Schicklgruber and for some reason a man named Hiedler said he was the father when this Alois, Hitler's father, was almost forty-years-old."

"Amalie, I don't understand this at all. Hiedler was Jewish?"

"It's all very confusing... I don't think Hiedler was Jewish and the rumor seems to be that Hiedler wasn't Alois' father even though Hiedler said he was the father, but he didn't come forward until Alois was middle-aged."

"But if only the father was Jewish, then the boy isn't Jewish."

"Father, we're not talking about Halakah*. These people consider any Jewish blood a curse."

There was a pause as they both considered the implications of this revelation.

"Proof" Amalie said out of the blue.

"What?" her father asked, having been lost in his own thoughts.

"How do we get proof? What would be good proof and just how important is this?" Amalie said, laying out the problem to her father.

"Well, I don't know how far he carries his anti-semitic

---

* A simple definition of Halakah would be to say that it is the legal code of Judaism, but it's more involved than that, having to do with the oral tradition of the Talmud.

program," Ethan responded, analyzing the possibilities, "but I would say that the key is whether his anti-semitism is just rhetoric or if it the foundation of their party. If this hatred of Jews is a large part of his program, then this information could be his downfall, but only if you have good, solid proof... and if that proof is presented by gentiles, not by Jews."

"I have to leave tomorrow" Amalie said, once again seeming to pull a thought from out of nowhere, but of course this thought was the next logical step because if there was proof to be found, it would most likely be in Spital.

"I know" Ethan replied.

"Is there any chance that you..." Amalie started.

"Of course " he said simply.

"You don't even know what I was going to ask." Amalie said, pretending to be incensed at her father's presumption.

Ethan picked up his pipe from the small table beside his chair. "You want me" he began and then stopped as he lit a match and drew on the pipe to light it, completing his sentence once the pipe began to produce its sweet smelling smoke, "to spend some time in Spital trying to find some foundation for these rumors"

"I think this might be important" Amalie said seriously.

"So do I" her father replied.

"Thank you father" Amalie said as she got up and gave her father a kiss on the forehead. "I'm going to get something to eat and then I had better get to bed so we can catch our train in the morning." The next morning Amalie felt sad at leaving and yet she was happy she had come because she and her father had gotten past a very strained period in their relationship that had culminated in her leaving home in 1918. It seemed to her that he had changed so much, but when she thought about it, it became apparent that she had been the one who had changed, or at least she had changed the most.

Jakob wrapped his arms and legs around his grandfather in an expression of childish abandon and Ethan held his grandson tightly, showing the same love in return.

Ethan realized that he had not been so open and demonstrative, with his daughter when she was a child, "but then", he thought to himself, "perhaps I've changed a lot since then" and he smiled as he let Jakob down.

"Take care of yourself" Ethan said seriously to his daughter as they embraced. "Remember what I said" he cautioned, "be careful. These men could be dangerous."

"Oh father," Amalie said as an afterthought before getting on the train, "when you are looking for information on that matter we spoke of..." At this point Amalie left Jakob standing by the steps of the rail car and walked to her father, glancing around to make sure no one was within earshot. "I was using the name Liesl Kraus. She is a reporter for one of the Munich papers. I wanted to tell you just in case you hear the name, you'll know it was me."

Amalie then walked back to the train and she and Jakob boarded, waving good-bye when they reached their compartment as the train started drifting away from the platform.

About a month later Amalie was re-reading a letter from her father as she ate her Monday morning breakfast. She had received the letter just before the weekend and there was a single sentence that particularly interested her. Ethan wrote that even though he had made further inquiries, he had found out nothing more about "aunt Klara." Amalie knew he was referring to Klara Polzl, but Ethan wanted to make sure that Gunther wouldn't suspect anything just in case he happened to see the letter.

Amalie hadn't found any new information about the Hiedler family either and she was beginning to doubt that she had any chance of finding or proving anything that would compromise Hitler's standing in the party. Small towns and villages were always full of gossip and rumors. The rumors could have come about because someone felt they had been cheated by the Hiedlers at some time or another or perhaps there had been an argument years ago and someone wanted a petty revenge.

Calling someone a Jew in the Waldviertel region in those days was considered an epithet, but to say that they were born a Jew, to make people believe through gossip and lies that the family was Jewish, that was a real revenge.

Amalie was beginning to think that she was on the wrong track as she picked up the newspaper, but then she saw the story at the bottom of the page.

"Newspaper reporter beaten to death" read the headline.

"The battered body of Fraulein Liesl Kraus, a reporter for the Münchner Taggblatt, was found on the bank of the Isar river yesterday afternoon. Detective Dietrich of the Schwabbing precinct, the officer in charge of the investigation, believes that Fraulein Kraus was attacked at some other location and then the body was left at the edge of the English garden where it was discovered early Sunday afternoon by a group of children playing in the park. Detective Dietrich went on to say that motives for the murder are unknown and that the victim had not been robbed or sexually assaulted. Relatives of Fraulein Kraus last saw her on Saturday afternoon and the police request that anyone who may have seen her after that time or anyone having any possible information regarding the murder please contact Detective Dietrich through the Schwabbing police precinct."

Amalie felt a sudden heaviness in her chest as she read the story and suddenly she couldn't seem to catch her breath. She couldn't believe what she read. It couldn't just be coincidence. It couldn't!

Her father had said these extremists were dangerous, but could they be this vicious? Could they have beaten this woman to death just because they had gotten information that a reporter named Liesl Kraus was checking into Herr Hitler's family history? If that were the case, then it meant that Amalie had caused this woman's death. The worst thing that Amalie had thought might happen was that Gunther might find out and divorce her. She never in her wildest dreams could have imagined this!

Amalie had to talk to someone.

No. She had to go to work.

She was shaking. She suddenly thought that she should call her father.

David. She could talk to David at work... or maybe his father Sam? Maybe she should talk to Sam.

Amalie just sat for a moment and tried to calm down, finally deciding that she should go to work. She said a hurried good-bye to Gertrude who had been helping Jakob gather his schoolwork just as Jakob was ready to leave too. Jakob asked if they could walk together and Amalie said yes, but Jakob soon knew as they walked that something was wrong. His mother didn't usually walk so quickly and all the while they were walking, Amalie didn't say a word.

"We're here." Jakob said as they almost passed the school.

"Oh. Yes, yes" Amalie said in a tone which tried to cover up her impatience as she gave Jakob a kiss on the cheek and immediately turned back to the street, rushing off towards the trolley.

Jakob just stood a moment, watching as she rushed away,

wondering what was wrong and then turning dejectedly towards the school as he worked his way slowly up the sidewalk.

When Amalie got to work, David was about to say good morning when he noticed the strange, panicked look on her face.

"Amalie, is something wrong?"

"David. I have to talk to someone. It's..."

"Come into my office" David said as he put his hand on her elbow, guiding her to a chair and closing the door behind them.

They sat in silence as David waited patiently for her to begin, but after a few moments he finally asked "Is it Gunther?"

"No, no. This is something terrible..." Amalie said.

"What is it?"

"First David, you have to promise that you will speak to no one about this."

"Certainly. You have my word."

"In Linz, Leonding... That weekend when I was checking into things... I used the name of a newspaper reporter. I thought people might talk to me if they thought I was a reporter, and they did. But David, this morning... they killed her."

"What? killed who? Who was killed?"

Amalie started to speak slowly after she realized that he couldn't follow what she was saying. "I picked a name from the paper, the name of a reporter, Liesl Kraus. Her body was found yesterday. She was beaten to death."

"...and you know who did it?" David asked incredulously.

"No, not exactly. I'm just afraid."

"Afraid of what?"

"I'm afraid I caused it."

"You think someone from the National Socialists did it?" David asked as he tried to follow Amalie's conversation.

"Yes." she said simply as she suddenly made eye contact with David.

"Why? Because they thought she was asking questions?"

"She wasn't robbed. She wasn't raped." Amalie said, listing off reasons, "It's just like all the other political murders. Maybe a hundred people shot or beaten to death just in this city."

"Maybe she was investigating something else" David offered, "Maybe she found something completely different and she was killed for that."

"Do you have any contacts at the paper?" Amalie asked, trying to form a plan, "Could you try to find out?"

"I'll do my best." David answered.

Silence again filled the office.

"I guess there's nothing else to be done" Amalie said despondently after getting up from the chair, "I better get to work."

David got up and stopped her at the door as she was leaving. "You don't know what happened. Even if it was the National Socialists, you couldn't have known it would turn out this way."

"I keep thinking of Nietsche" Amalie said.

"Nietsche?"

"That old quote: 'He who fights with monsters might take care lest he thereby become a monster'."

By the end of the day David hadn't found out anything about the murder that would ease Amalie's conscience. Amalie was constantly unnerved by the incident as the thought of it kept weaving through everything she did, or more accurately, through everything she tried to do since she didn't accomplish anything at work that day.

She forced herself to be bright and pleasant that night until she was alone when she was finally able to make a telephone call to her father, warning him of the possible danger.

It was a couple of weeks before David finally came up with some information on the Kraus murder. He found out that Liesl had been working on a story about a particularly bloodthirsty Freikorps unit that had killed hundreds of unarmed civilians in Munich at the end of the revolutionary period and even though all the Freikorps units had been ordered to disband after the final assaults on the revolutionaries in 1920, this particular group was still together. Apparently Liesl was going to name the men involved and tell about how they were still operating, even though they insisted they were a just a political party and not a vigilante group intent on ridding Munich of all Communist influences. David even had a few names of likely suspects who may have actually carried out the assassination and none of these men were directly associated with Hitler although they and their party were considered sympathetic to Hitler's cause.

Amalie believed David when he told her there was no connection between her visit to Austria and Liesl's death, but still she had been so shaken by the experience that she stopped. She realized that even though Hitler hadn't had Liesl murdered, he could have.

149

Amalie finally realized the kind of business her own husband was involved in and it had a sobering effect on her.

The summer of 1922 passed quickly for Amalie. She was no longer aware of the days, the sunlight or warmth of the Bavarian summer. It all passed her by in a haze as she gradually became swallowed up by a state of depression. She began to wonder what the whole world was about, what it all meant. She was afraid of Gunther even though he had not changed much in that year. It was Amalie who had changed, her perception of Gunther. She feared the things that he might become, as though he were a monster, a werewolf who might become a killer with the change of the moon. Amalie began to spend more time at work, which she justified by talking about how bad the inflation was and how she had to work longer just to make enough to keep up, but the truth was that she was hiding.

Everything started to get strange around the apartment as Amalie not only stayed away from Gunther, but she also started to isolate herself from Gertrude and Jakob. It was a very dark period for all involved, but strangely enough, no one would come right out and ask what was happening or why. Gertrude began to think that maybe she wasn't welcome, but she was afraid to ask because she had nowhere to go. Jakob couldn't understand why his mother had stopped being his friend. Gunther had a habit which had been getting increasingly worse whereby he avoided Amalie when it looked like they might get into an argument. He didn't want to get involved in a fight because he found more and more that he didn't understand Amalie. He didn't know why she didn't like his friends and he didn't know why she insisted on keeping her job. He didn't know why his marriage was so much different than he had expected it to be.

In the last week of September, David Frieder was sitting at his desk. It had been a particularly long week. He had gone begging and scraping to keep things afloat, negotiating with a printer and a book bindery on his latest project, a college level textbook on geology which could potentially lead to more work with educational materials if he could bring the project in under budget. Under budget! Of course when one talked about budgets these days, everything had to be indexed against the instability of inflation. Where he once talked about Deutchmarks and pfennigs, he could now only refer to percentages.

"The price will go up," he would explain to the buyers from

some university "but the cost will be no more than twenty-three-point-five percent of your selling price."

It was almost eight o'clock in the evening as David lit up a cigarette and exhaled loudly, as though he couldn't decide whether to sigh. He leaned back in his chair, propping his feet on the desk, something that he rarely did.

After a moment, he found himself staring absent-mindedly at the ceiling and suddenly felt that someone was watching him and he self-conscientiously took a quick look out the open door of his office. No one was watching, but as he looked out he could see a reflection in the window of the door. It was a reflection of Amalie still at her desk, her head almost buried in a stack of papers. David was suddenly fascinated as he watched the intensity on Amalie's face and the few strands of hair that fell about her face while she read through the papers in front of her. He realized that he and Amalie were probably the only ones left in the office and so this might finally be a good time to talk with her. He had been meaning to speak with her for some time now as he realized that she was spending more and more time in the office even though there had been no significant increase in her work load.

He slowly, as though he were an old man, slid his feet off the desk and righted his chair, lifting himself out of the chair and carrying the cigarette with him as he casually walked out to Amalie's desk.

"Long day" he said as he stood beside her chair.

Amalie was startled. She smiled and nodded and immediately turned back to her work.

David pursued the conversation. "Which one is that?" he asked, referring to the pages Amalie was reading.

"Proofing the copy for the pamphlet from the department of tourism."

"Tourists..." David said with a smirk "American soldiers taking advantage of the inflation. What is it now?"

"I think about 7,200 marks to the dollar" Amalie answered. David took a puff from his cigarette, perplexed at Amalie's obvious attempt to ignore him which certainly seemed ridiculous considering that they were the only ones left in the office,

"You know everyone else has gone home?" David said in a lilt that made the words half statement and half question.

"I'm almost finished" Amalie said in an appeasing fashion.

"Amalie," David said as he pulled a chair from one of the other desks next to Amalie's and sat down beside her, "I couldn't help noticing..."

At this point Amalie was looking down at her desk, but she was no longer reading. David stopped in mid-sentence and broke off his gaze, but then he suddenly found himself reaching out to Amalie and lightly touching her chin with the tip of his fingers, directing her to look at him. "What is it Amalie? What are you hiding from? Why can't you go home?"

Amalie pulled away, turning away from David as tears misted up in her eyes, "I don't really know" she finally said.

"Amalie, I usually don't get involved in the lives of people who work for me, they have their lives and I have mine, but I consider you a friend and I do get involved in my friend's lives."

Amalie was genuinely touched by this statement and found that she could look at David as she quickly brushed away the unwanted tears.

"I had a dream" she started slowly "it keeps coming back. It started after that terrible murder. The Kraus murder"

"Well it's no wonder" David offered sympathetically. "That must have been a terrible shock... under the circumstances."

"Yes, but the dream wasn't really about her, although she was in it. I dreamed I was running." Amalie began to gesture as she told about the dream as though she were painting it on a canvas in front of David, coloring in all the pieces as she got caught up in the telling, "I was running from something, but I never knew what it was. I ran into a house, or something like a house. It looked so small as I came up to it, almost like a doll's house. I looked behind me as I got to the door and it was all dark and then I ducked into the house and suddenly it was a huge room. It was all dark, too, except for some small windows that I could look out, but the windows were too small for me to get through to escape and I started to panic because I could see a beautiful sunny day outside the windows, but there was no way that I could get out and I suddenly knew I was trapped by whatever had been following me and then I found a door that seemed to come out of nowhere and I went through the door into another room and the doorway disappeared behind me and new doors suddenly appeared around the room. I ran from door to door opening them only to find that there was only a mirror behind each door and once

152

I found that all the doors had mirrors behind them and it looked like a carnival fun house, I kicked one of the mirrors and broke it and I screamed because there behind the mirror was my mother's dead body blocking the door and then I threw something that I had been carrying at another mirror and when the mirror shattered, there was the body of Liesl Kraus in the doorway."

Amalie's eyes filled with fear and she grew anxious as she told about her dream and the tears returned. David was surprised by how emotional she was becoming while telling the story.

"...and then I kicked the next mirror and Gunther appeared from behind that mirror and I thought I was safe and I ran to his arms, but instead of holding me, protecting me, he suddenly grabbed me, stopping me from going through the door and he held me so tight that he was hurting me and he turned me as he held me, making me watch as the wall opened up behind me and the darkness began to swallow us up and I screamed. Whatever it was that was chasing me was there and Gunther wouldn't let me go!"

Once finished, Amalie appeared exhausted. Telling someone about the dream was cathartic for her. David didn't know what to make of it all at first, mostly because he hadn't expected Amalie to be so emotional and the emotional outburst distracted his attention from the things that Amalie was saying.

He felt that he should hold her, comfort her, but it was more of an intellectual directive than an emotional response and that showed in the awkwardness of his move towards her as he cautiously put an arm around her.

"I'm sorry to drop this all on you" Amalie said, "You're the only one I've told about this."

"It sounds frightening" David said softly.

"Yes"

"Do you believe in dreams?"

"How do you mean?" Amalie asked, as though David had asked her if she believed in witches and fairies, "Do I believe that dreams tell the future?"

"No." David said in a clinical tone, rephrasing the question, "Do you believe in some kind of psychological basis for dreams?"

"Well," Amalie began as she turned a little towards David and his arm slipped naturally from her shoulder, "I suppose I believe there is some purpose. I believe there is something to Freud's approach."

"What do you think your dream means? Where did it come from."

"Now that it's out in the open like this" Amalie said thoughtfully, with a little smile that showed the relief she felt at finally having someone she could talk to about it, "It seems pretty clear. I think it's about this whole affair with Gunther and maybe I'm afraid of what Gunther... maybe I'm afraid that Gunther isn't the same man that I married."

"Well Amalie," David began, "I'm not a psychiatrist or anything and I don't even know Gunther except for the couple of times we met here, but it seems your dream might be about something else."

David seemed to brace himself in the chair as he offered his thoughts on her dream. "Amalie, I think you're letting things that you think might happen stop you from living now. I think you built the whole Liesl Kraus thing up in your mind and even though you found out it had nothing to do with you, you never forgot it."

David paused to see what Amalie's reaction would be to his hypothesis. Amalie considered what he was saying, but her expression didn't really give David a clue as to whether she accepted or rejected his explanation. David pressed on anyway.

"Amalie, you can't worry about everything that might happen as though it already has happened. You have to just deal with things as they come."

Amalie thought about what David was saying and finally replied "You're right..."

David was surprised at her sudden agreement. "I am?" he asked.

Amalie laughed a little as she wiped her eyes a final time. "Yes you are" she said, "I was so afraid of what Gunther might do, afraid I guess, that he might have been involved with Liesl Kraus' death, and I never let go of that fear even after I was sure he had nothing to do with it."

"Well that would certainly be a terrible thing to think" David said, "to think that Gunther might have..."

"But David," Amalie said, "I still don't know what to do"

"About what?" David asked.

"I don't know what to do about the party. The National Socialists."

"Amalie, there might not be anything that you can do."

"But Gunther..."

154

"Amalie. You have to be realistic."

"Realistic?!"

"Amalie, admit it. Admit it to yourself. There might not be anything that you can do about Gunther... or the party... or anything else. What is going to happen will happen. You just have to live with it. Look at yourself now. Could it be any worse? You're obviously hiding here. You seem to be at one extreme or the other. You either want to change the world or hide from it."

When David finished talking, an almost overwhelming silence filled the room. David was afraid he might have gone too far. He thought that he might have offended Amalie or hurt her, but he didn't know what else to say. He didn't feel he should take back what he had said.

Amalie decided that David was right. She was tired. For all of her fears, nothing had happened in all that time since her visit to her father. She had been feeling that the world had been closing in all around her and now suddenly with this simple conversation she realized that the world had just gone on as it always had. The world went on without even noticing that Amalie Stein-Metzdorf was insisting to herself that the world was ending.

"I think it's time to go home" Amalie said simply as she looked David square in the eye.

David smiled and, as she gathered her things and stood up to leave, he found himself putting his arm around Amalie again, but this time it wasn't awkward or strained. A gentle squeeze and then they said good night.

The conversation with David broke Amalie's isolation and started her thinking and she felt an almost miraculous change as she rode the trolley. She began to see what she had been doing and how she had been running away, just like in her dream, running from the unknown.

She also felt sad as she realized that it wasn't only Gunther she had drawn away from, but Jakob too and she thought how hard it must have been for her son over the past couple of months.

Gertrude was surprised to see Amalie before nine-o-clock.

"You're home early" she said.

"Actually I'm late" Amalie countered.

"Well," Gertrude backtracked, "It's only after six now and you've been working late for so long..."

"I think that's done now" Amalie said, "Things should be getting back to normal now."

Gertrude wasn't quite sure what to make of that, but she didn't question Amalie. "That's good..." Gertrude said, "You've seemed so tired lately."

"Well," Amalie said as she stepped around Gertrude. "I'm going to put this away" and she went to the closet of the bedroom to put her purse and briefcase up. Then she found Jakob in the living room, laying on the floor with sheets of paper spread around him as he drew with pencils. When Jakob first saw her, he flinched and started to gather the papers together, thinking that his mother was going to be upset that he had made a mess, but instead Amalie knelt down and started to spread the papers out again as her son tried to pick them up and then she laid down on the floor next to him.

"What are you drawing?" she asked and Jakob's face lit up. "I'm drawing houses like father does!" Jakob chirped. He was so happy that Amalie was there beside him like that.

"And so nice..." Amalie said admiringly as she held one of the drawings up in the light.

After looking at the other pictures for a moment, Amalie changed the subject. "Your birthday is coming soon."

"I know" Jakob said with a smile.

"Oh! You know" she said, smiling back at him, "Have you thought about what you might like for a present?"

"A little" Jakob said coyly.

"Well... what did you decide?"

"A dog."

"A dog?" Amalie repeated as she thought of all the difficulties of owning a dog, but apparently Jakob had no such concerns.

"Yes, like Mr. Scheiderman has down the hall."

"Mr. Scheiderman? The man with the big German shepherd?" Amalie asked incredulously.

"Yes" Jakob said with conviction as he nonchalantly went back to his drawing, "That's what I want for my birthday."

"I don't know..." Amalie said as she got up from the floor, "We will have to see what your father says about it."

Gunther was also surprised when he got home and found that Amalie was already there. She made up a story about business slowing down so that she couldn't put in anymore long hours.

156

Gunther was pleased, so pleased that he stayed home all evening, winding up the night by playing cards with Amalie and Gertrude and trying to teach Jakob the card game until it was time for him to go to bed. Amalie made a point of reading a story to Jakob and tucking him in and Gertrude cleaned up the dishes and went to bed. Amalie and Gunther retired soon after.

"Jakob's birthday is coming up" Amalie said as she got ready for bed.

"My God... It's almost October already" Gunther responded.

"Two weeks... Seven years old already on the twelfth of October."

"That little boy is starting to make me feel old" Gunther said with a smile.

"And it's only going to get worse" Amalie countered.

"I thought we might have a party on that Saturday" Amalie continued.

"Saturday? The fourteenth?" Gunther said as he tried to remember something, "I think Klaus said there's something going on that day"

"Something? Like what?" Amalie asked.

"A party function. Some rally out of town."

"A political rally? Must you go?"

"It's important. Especially now with things starting to happen."

"Like what?" Amalie asked.

"People are starting to pay attention. We're getting more and more interest."

"Some say it's only because times are bad. Once things improve, people will stop paying attention." Amalie said, taking a chance on contradicting her husband.

"They don't know. Those people aren't at the rallies. They haven't seen the way Hitler can embrace a crowd and lead them. No, the people who say Hitler is just a passing face aren't paying attention. They aren't listening to the streets."

"Well, as far as Jakob's birthday," Amalie began as she worked out a compromise, "I suppose we could have a little party on Thursday when you're here and then have a childrens party on Saturday while you're at... Where is the rally?"

Gunther stopped as he was hanging his trousers on a hanger and looked up at the ceiling, trying to remember where Klaus had told

157

him the rally would be held "Ah... Oh yes, Coburg."

"Well, that should be an all day trip" Amalie said.

"Yes, we were thinking of going up on Friday night so we'll be fresh in the morning."

"I suppose Jakob will understand."

"Of course he will!" Gunther said, the thought never having entered his mind that Jakob would question his father's decision. Jakob, of course, never would bring up such a thing, but that didn't mean that Jakob wasn't hurt by the many times that his father wasn't there. Jakob just accepted that his father had many more important things to do.

"Oh" Amalie said as she remembered, "I asked Jakob what he wanted for his birthday..."

"And what did he say?"

"He wants a dog. A German shepherd like Scheiderman's down the hall."

"We're already pretty crowded" Gunther said as he considered the possibility.

"That's what I thought" Amalie responded, pleased with the thought that Gunther was also against the idea.

"...but maybe a smaller dog" Gunther continued and Amalie was crestfallen as she suddenly realized that it was as good as done.

If Jakob wanted a dog, that was one thing, but if both Jakob and his father wanted a dog, then it was as good as done.

Jakob's birthday quickly arrived along with a springer spaniel puppy named "Honig" that made Gunther a hero to his son before Gunther went off to Coburg with Klaus on the following night. The following Saturday not only brought another birthday party for Jakob while his father was away, it also began a new phase for the National Socialist's plans for Germany.

Adolf Hitler and other members of his party had been very impressed by the political successes of a socialistic, anti-Communist politician in Italy. A former newspaper editor named Benito Mussolini had created a party based on the concept of ancient Roman rule where one man led the government and directed all its authority. Mussolini derived the name for his party from an ancient Roman symbol of the emperors power and the unity of the state, a bundle of sticks held in an eagles claw. "Di fascisti", which literally meant "bundle", soon became known to the English speaking world as the fascists and eventually the name would come to refer to any similar form of totalitarian, anti-Communistic government.

Mussolini, in his drive against the Bolsheviks, had simply marched into certain cities in Italy, accompanied by his black-shirted troops, and laid claim to the town in the name of the fascists. There had been some resistance by Communist factions, but the fascists received widespread support, including support from the Vatican which opposed the Communists because of their atheistic stand against all religions.

Leaders of the National Socialists in Germany studied Mussolini's success and decided to emulate it on that Saturday in Coburg. It was a grand show of bluff and bluster complete with brass band and eight hundred fully uniformed storm troops, many of whom, just like Klaus and Gunther, paid their own way to Coburg for the "attack". There were jeers from the crowds and street fighting with rocks, fists and sticks as the troops entered the town, but the street was soon cleared by the storm troops and the next day when the National Socialists marched through the streets again, they were cheered by the crowds.

Amalie was shocked as she read in the Sunday newspaper that "Coburg was under the control of Hitler." This was Gunther's "rally", the takeover of a town by brute force. Suddenly, as Amalie read, a spark was rekindled in her. She had agreed with David Frieder's conclusion that she couldn't change the whole world, but at that moment, reading the story of Hitler's takeover of a single city, she determined that she would try to find something that could be used against him before he could take over the entire country. She had to reassess her plan. She had to decide how far she would go and what her ultimate goal was and then commit herself to that goal above all else and, most frightening of all, she had to decide what she would be willing to lose in exchange for that goal. Would she be willing to lose Gunther? For the first time, she began to think that instead of saving Gunther, the loss of her husband would be worth bringing down Hitler.

Amalie felt that her fears were more than justified when, only ten days later, Benito Mussolini rode the train into Rome and took over the Italian government without firing a shot. She knew this was Hitlers plan. He wanted to follow Il Duce's lead except for one important factor: Mussolini wasn't sending troops into the streets with money collection boxes labeled "for the massacre of the Jews".

Christmas in 1922 certainly wasn't as bad as some of the other Christmases the Metzdorf family had experienced in Munich. It was certainly more materially festive than that first Christmas just after the end of the war. Even if the inflation made things difficult, at least this year there were now some goods and food to be bought although still quite limited. This time Amalie, Gunther, Jakob, Gertrude and Klaus used regular candles for the tree and there was even a lot of talk about the new electric tree candles that appeared in a couple of the large department stores in the Karlstor district, but the electric lights were still very expensive. The group repeated their traditional Christmas Eve gathering begun in 1918, but this time Gertrude put a single candle in one of the living room windows as a remembrance of Friedrich, as she put it, "wherever he might be." Gunther and Klaus reassured her that even though she had received no word from him, no letter or message in almost ten months, he was probably doing just fine and was just too busy to write.

There was a new addition to their group this year as Klaus brought a friend with him. Katrina Holzmann was a beautiful young strawberry blond whom Klaus had met through his friends in the party. Katrina was a few years younger than Klaus, she was nineteen and Klaus was now twenty-eight, but they seemed well suited to each other and Amalie even noticed that Katrina seemed to be a calming influence on Klaus. Klaus had been seeing Katrina for a few months and Amalie hoped that Katrina might draw Klaus away from the National Socialists, at least so that Klaus might become a bit less fanatical and possibly loosen his influence on Gunther. Amalie realized this was a lot to hope for, but she hoped nonetheless and welcomed Katrina warmly whenever she came to visit.

It wasn't long after Christmas when there was a new crisis in Germany. Things were not going well on the reparations committee, the committee made up of officials from the French and English government who where deciding on the terms of the punitive payments demanded from the German government, and as a result, the English representatives walked out of the committee hearings in the first part of January in 1923. The French, newly freed from the protests of their English counterparts, determined that they would take action against the Germans because the German government had fallen behind on the reparations payment schedule. On January eleventh of 1923, French and Belgian troops marched into the Ruhr region of Germany and occupied the area.

The rumors drifted in one on top of another. "The French had sent in Black Algerian troops." "German women weren't safe on the streets." "German women found on the streets after dark were raped." "The Algerians raided the zoos in the German cities of the Ruhr region and killed and ate the animals that were native to their lands."

The response of the German government was almost immediate. The inflation of German money went completely out of sight. The Germans devalued their money so that the reparation payments would become a farce. Where the exchange against an American dollar was about seven thousand Deutschmarks before the occupation, within a couple of weeks after the occupation the exchange was fifty thousand Deutschmarks for a single American dollar. This was the final straw for the German middle class. Those who were still above water financially, who had not already been ruined and thought they might sneak by the inflation ebbing against their life savings were now swept away by a new tidal wave of inflation.

Within the next few months, the reality of the German economy became worse than anyone could have ever feared or imagined. One day Gunther was amazed as a fellow worker told him that because he had missed the trolley to the bank, in the time between the first trolley and the next, his paycheck was worth less than half of what it had been when he started out!

Large companies began to issue their own currency, notes for their employees to use in the small towns where the companies sponsored the stores.

The Weimar government, unable to keep up with the incredible pace of the inflation began to authorize the printing of larger denominations over smaller bills. A ten thousand mark note would have "ein millionen mark" printed over it in red ink, thus making it a one million mark note. By the time Amalie was to travel to Ried again in April, when Otto Maus had specifically requested that David Frieder send her as David's representative, her train ticket cost almost half a billion marks.

In those four months between the beginning of the year and Amalie's return trip to Austria, she had finalized her plan. She felt she

161

already had enough information to justify her continuing an investigation into Hitler's background and, beyond that, she decided to coordinate with others, people she trusted like David and Sam Frieder and her father, to gather evidence wherever possible and build a history, a file as it were, that would one day destroy the party.

She made what she considered the most important decision in her plan when she decided that the file must remain a secret until she had enough to bring the party down. She didn't want bits of information coming out that the party could simply downplay or deny completely. Amalie felt that she had to find information that would turn the members of the party against the party leaders and that information had to be irrefutable and furthermore, the file would have to be delivered from impressive sources in the world community. She felt if it came from a Jew like herself, the party would simply say it was an unfounded and libelous attack by its mortal enemies.

The time for striking seemed to be closing in quickly as the inflation catastrophe moved more and more people to extremist views against the democracy of the Weimar government. The Nationalist Socialists German worker's party in particular was growing faster than ever.

When Amalie was in Austria working with Otto, she again tried to find more information in the area around Spital and Weitra and she managed to track a bit more of Hitler's family, but in so doing, she found a mistake in her earlier information. When the old priest told her that Hitler's father had married his own niece, it seemed to conflict with records that showed Hitler's father's third wife to be his cousin, not his niece.

During her time in Austria, Amalie thought about involving Otto Maus in her circle of confidants, but she decided that even though she liked him and he seemed like a good man, she didn't really know him well enough yet to risk it.

She found herself stymied in her investigation by the time she returned home. It seemed there was nothing more she could do without becoming far too obvious and drawing unwanted attention. She had to satisfy herself with just keeping up on newspaper articles and rumors and keeping in touch with Sam Frieder who had the time to pay close attention to the political scene and keep Amalie informed. Amalie decided that the best way to keep the information was to send it to her father. Now and again Gunther would mention that he was surprised by the sudden increase in correspondence between his wife and her father, but he never really thought much of it.

That summer was a good one for the family. Just as Amalie had made it a point to make a special Christmas for Jakob the year before, she wanted to spend more time with him during the summer. She wanted to make sure that Jakob didn't have to get caught up in it when things got strained between her and Gunther. She wanted to protect her son from the things she was seeing and from Gunther's politics.

The National Socialists had held many rallies during the summer and fall and Hitler had been getting a lot of coverage in the newspapers for his aggressive challenges to the authority of the Bavarian government. The challenges had been fairly minor, but it was as though a street tough were trying to start a fight in a bar. He constantly hurled insults, postured and made threats. It got to the point where his influence began to be questioned as more and more people came to believe that he was a man of words, but no real action. Amalie began to think that she might have overestimated Hitlers role in the party.

"They changed the date!" Klaus said as he rushed into the apartment when Gunther opened the door, "It's tonight."

"Thursday?" Gunther asked in surprise.

"Yes. I just heard" Klaus explained, "Get ready. We've got to go. We can't miss this one."

Gunther looked at Amalie. She pretended not to be paying attention as she sat on the couch reading her book. Jakob ran up to greet uncle Klaus and Gertrude came out of the kitchen.

"What's this?" she asked in a good-natured voice "Another for dinner?"

"I'm afraid not" Klaus replied, "We have to leave now."

"Right now? Not even time for a quick sandwich?" Gertrude pressed.

"No, really, we have to run" Klaus insisted.

"I'll get my things" Gunther interjected.

"What are you talking about? You've got to change here. We have to go directly to the Bürgerbräukeller" Klaus insisted.

"Well...it will take a minute" Gunther said reluctantly, and then he turned to Gertrude "You might as wall make a sandwich for me while I'm changing. I am starved."

"It will only take a minute" Gertrude said with a smile as she went back to the kitchen.

Gunther was hesitant to change into his brown shirt and armband because he had never done so at home before. He knew that Amalie was nervous about the Nazis and didn't really understand what they were all about, so he tried to avoid upsetting her by never wearing his uniform at home although it wasn't really a uniform since he wasn't a member of the Sturmabteilung. He was just a volunteer who helped support the S.A. at rallies and sometimes he went along with S.A. troops to disrupt Communist meetings and so on, but he certainly never told Amalie the details of these outings. It wasn't the sort of thing you discussed with your wife when you went out and beat up leftists and Jews. She seemed especially sensitive about the Jews even though he had tried to explain to her so often that these were a specific kind of Jew that had to be controlled. Gunther tried to keep a low profile at home, not out of fear or embarrassment, but more in the way that a parent tries to get a child to take castor oil, telling the child that it's certainly unpleasant, but once done with, everything will be better. Gunther knew that he was fighting for a better world and one day his wife and son would thank him for having the strength to do the unpleasant things that must be done.

Gunther quickly pulled on his overcoat and was struggling to get his arm in the sleeve as he stopped at the kitchen to pick up his sandwich on his way out. Amalie glanced up from her place on the couch just in time to catch a glimpse of the brown shirt and the red, white and black arm band sewn to the sleeve. Gertrude set the sandwich down as she took the sleeve and straightened it, helping Gunther get his coat on. Klaus smiled from the doorway as Gunther surrendered to Gertrude's assistance.

"Thank you mother" Gunther said sarcastically with a big smile, giving Gertrude a little kiss on the forehead. Gertrude laughed and gave Gunther a playful slap on the chest.

"Don't wait up." Gunther said to Amalie almost as an afterthought as he stuck his head into the living room, "This could be a long one." Jakob again ran up to his father and Klaus for good-night hugs and then Klaus and Gunther were suddenly gone.

The glimpse of Gunther's brownshirt and swastika armband made Amalie shrink back into the couch involuntarily. She suddenly remembered an afternoon a few months before when she saw three of the S.A. collecting money for the party. They stood there with that look on their faces, that sneering contempt, the look that dared anyone to challenge them, and one man did. A man told them to leave. A stranger who just happened to be passing by stopped and told them they had no right to do what they were doing and the three suddenly set upon the man, punching him in the face and stomach. Once they had drawn blood from a punch to the face, they seemed to go crazy. They became frenzied as they knocked the man to the ground and kept beating him while he was down and a few people stopped and watched, but one of the three S.A. warned them to keep moving or they would be the next to be beaten.

That was one of the chief weapons of the nazis. They were not afraid to use violence. On the contrary, many of the young nazis enjoyed the power of violence, the power they felt in intimidating others. Gunther was certainly not in that class, whether Amalie really knew it or not. Gunther had the attitude of a soldier. He used the same techniques on occasion, but he used it as a soldier uses a weapon, a means to an end, not because he enjoyed it.

"From what I understand," Klaus began to explain to Gunther on the trolley, "they changed the date because Kahr is holding a meeting at the Bürgerbräukeller tonight."

Gustav von Kahr was the state commissioner of Bavaria under Bavaria's Minister President Eugen von Knilling. Kahr had announced that he would outline his plans for the future of the economy on Thursday, November eighth at the Bürgerbräukeller, the largest beer hall in the city with a main hall that could hold three thousand people.

It was just after six o-clock as the trolley crossed the bridge over the Isar. Gunther and Klaus soon got off and made their way to the beer hall and passed through the huge wrought iron gates set in the arched gateway of the high wall around the beer hall grounds and through the large yard which served as a beer garden in the summer. Perhaps Gunther was just nervous, but the skeletons of the barren trees in the abandoned yard set against the cloudy sky seemed foreboding.

Von Kahr's meeting wasn't scheduled until eight o'clock, but Klaus had been told to get there early so that he and other party members could be sure to get key positions in the hall. Klaus wasn't sure exactly what was going to happen, but he was sure there was going to be some sort of action. They kept their coats on so as not to give themselves away until the right time came.

"Hey friend!" Gunther said jokingly as they sat down, "Can you spare a billion marks for a beer?"

"Only a billion?" Klaus said, playing along, "That's a bargain. I heard it's a billion and a half at the hotels."

Neither of them laughed and Klaus went to the bar for the beer while Gunther looked around the room.

"What do you think?" Gunther asked as Klaus returned to the table, "Maybe we're just supposed to disrupt it?"

"No, I think it's something more" Klaus said non-chalantly, speaking to his beer mug as he took a drink.

"Do you know something you're not telling me?" Gunther asked.

"No. It's just the mood..."

"The mood?" Gunther asked as he tried to pin his friend down.

"I don't know... It just seems that... well, the S.A. leaders that I know have been saying that now is the time to make a move. They seem anxious."

"That could just be talk" Gunther replied.

"Perhaps"

Gunther thought about it and suddenly had an uneasy feeling as though he had just been told that the group at the next table had a loaded gun and he didn't know what they wanted or what they would do. The feeling was exhilarating while at the same time being unnerving. Gunther and Klaus were quiet for the next couple of hours, making small talk and keeping to themselves. They nursed their beers and waited.

The hall began to fill gradually and by eight o'clock the room was packed. Klaus kept an eye on the door, waiting expectantly for whatever might happen next while Gunther settled in as Kahr began his speech which turned into a boring lecture on economics. After about a quarter of an hour Klaus nudged Gunther's arm and motioned to the bar. There was Hitler in a black morning coat.

"Now things will get interesting" Klaus whispered to Gunther and he had no sooner finished the sentence when storm troops pushed their way into the hall shouting "Heil Hitler". Klaus and Gunther threw off their coats and jumped to their feet, joining the chant of the storm troops. Hitler and other nazis, brandishing pistols, pushed their way toward the stage as the storm troops at the door barricaded the exit. The crowd went into a panic and tables were overturned as some in the crowd sought cover while the storm troops began beating people who tried to get out.

Suddenly Hitler climbed up on a chair and shouted for quiet and when the uproar continued, he fired his pistol into the ceiling. Once the crowd had quieted down a bit, he shouted out "The national revolution has broken out! The hall is surrounded."

Gunther could hardly believe it. Klaus was right, things were certainly getting interesting. Klaus smiled at Gunther for an instant, overwhelmed that their time was finally at hand, and then quickly turned back to the crowd with a menacing expression, ready to attack if need be as he and Gunther stood in front of the stage while Hitler made his way through the crowd and onto the speaker's platform.

Kahr was not the only member of the Bavarian government on the stage. Next to Kahr was General Otto von Lossow, the head of the army in Bavaria and Colonel Hans Ritter Von Seisser, the chief of the Bavarian state police. When Hitler crossed the platform to speak with the three officials, Colonel Seisser's aide suddenly put his hand in his pocket and Hitler stopped suddenly and pointed his pistol at the aide, warning the major to take his hand out of his pocket. Hitler then ushered the three men into the side room, leaving the crowd to ferment.

The crowd soon grew restless with many people making light of the affair and jeering the storm troops until Hermann Goering, one of Hitler's compatriots who had come in with the storm troops at the beginning of the event, emulated Hitler and fired another shot into the ceiling. Goering tried to keep the crowd calm until, finally, Hitler returned to the speaker's platform amid a renewed outburst and demanded silence, threatening to set up a machine gun in the hall.

Hitler then began to speak and Gunther, still facing the crowd rather than Hitler, watched the crowd as it became transformed. Hitler told the crowd that the three members of the Bavarian government were going to support him and he then went on to win over the crowd with his standard points of a strong Germany freed from the Weimar government and restored from the disgrace of the November criminals who betrayed Germany in her darkest hour, surrendering Germany to her enemies.

The crowd cheered. The crowd that had laughed at him and insulted and jeered him just moments before, now cheered him. Gunther knew it would happen. He had seen it before. He had even been a part of the crowd once, another crowd from years ago that had been skeptical and then similarly swept up and moved, transformed by the power of... not just the power of his words, but the power of his conviction, the power that he was. That man, swept up within the feeling of the crowd and the power of his rage at the world, became more than he was in the beginning. The demons within him seemed to create a greater him.

When Hitler finished speaking, the crowd roared out the words to "Deutschland uber alles".

That, however, was the high point of the evening. From there things quickly started to degenerate as the Nazis tried to coordinate their efforts with other party members in other parts of the city. They also had trouble trying to convince Bavarian government officials that Kahr, Lossow and Seisser supported the uprising and that the officials should also support the overthrow of the government. The coup began to collapse as Kahr and the others managed to get out word that their compliance had been forced and they did not, in fact, support Hitler's putsch.

Another blow was dealt to the uprising when Hitler decided to leave the Bürgerbräu to personally settle a dispute between his men and some city engineers. General Erich Von Ludendorff, who had been in on the plan to overthrow the government from the beginning, but had not been informed in advance about the change of date, arrived at the beer hall in the meantime and Hitler decided to leave the general in charge when he left.

Soon after Hitler left, General Lossow convinced Ludendorff that he should be allowed to leave so that he could return to his headquarters to issue orders to his troops. Ludendorff, unaware that Hitler had been lying when he said that the three men supported the overthrow, agreed not only to let Lossow leave, but Kahr and Seisser as well.

Hitler was enraged when he returned to find that the three men had been allowed to leave. Ludendorff insisted that there would be no problem as the three men had given him their word that they would not oppose the overthrow.

Gunther and Klaus knew nothing of this intrigue, of course.

They only knew that things were becoming tense and tempers were flaring. They finally left at about two o'clock in the morning when they were told to go home and get some sleep and to return in the morning.

There was still much activity on the streets as they made their way home. S.A. troops headquartered throughout the city roamed the streets looking for "criminals" to bring before hastily assembled tribunals. Socialists... Communists... Jews... anyone they considered an enemy of the party would be brought before the tribunal and those found guilty of crimes against the German people would be sentenced to death.

Gunther decided to stay with Klaus that night rather than going through all the discussion and explanations with Amalie. They got about six hours sleep that night, returning to the Bürgerbräu by ten o'clock Friday morning.

The feeling at the beer hall seemed even more strained than the night before. There was no euphoria of victory to be found there. It was obvious there had been complications during the night and Klaus went about asking questions and returned to Gunther, telling him about the Kahr, Lossow and Seisser fiasco and that Ernst Röhm, the leader of the S.A., was trapped at army headquarters with some of his troops. Gunther took the news stoically although he was shaken. Just like Klaus, he had been waiting for this for a long time and now it appeared to be falling apart. What were they to do now?

After a couple of hours, Hitler and Ludendorff decided to march through the city. Hitler told the men gathered in the hall that they would attract others to join them as they marched and make a popular success of their revolution by shear numbers. When the march began, their direction was unclear, but then Ludendorff decided that they should head to the army headquarters to rescue Röhm and his men. After a few blocks they were met by armed police, but when they found Ludendorff to be a member of the group, the police voluntarily turned over their guns. This success inspired the group as they continued the march, almost reaching the Feldherrnhalle on the Odeonplatz before they were once more met by police, but these police were ready for battle.

One of the Nazis fired first, killing a police officer, and suddenly there was a hail of gunfire from the police force. Gunther and Klaus and the other former soldiers and storm troops instinctively fell to the ground, returning fire. It seemed to go on forever, but then it stopped as suddenly as it had started. Hitler was one of the first men to rise. Gunther could see that he was hurt by the way he held his arm, but he didn't see any blood. The next thing Gunther knew, Hitler rushed past him and the other troops who were still laying on the ground and threw himself into a car that had appeared from nowhere. The car then sped away. Gunther couldn't believe it. Hitler had turned and run. He didn't care about any of his comrades who had followed him into this battle. He ran! When it became clear that the shooting was over and the cause was lost as the police began to round up the nazis, Gunther grabbed Klaus and pulled him away from the crowd. The two of them disappeared down an alley and finally made their way to Klaus' apartment.

Neither of them talked as a cold gray afternoon wrapped itself around the apartment house. They threw their coats on the couch and Klaus started making a pot of coffee while Gunther sat at the kitchen table.

Klaus disappeared into the bedroom while Gunther stared out the window, going over the mornings events in his mind. His trance-like state was broken as something landed on the table at his elbow.

"Here," Klaus said as he motioned to the non-descript white shirt that he had thrown at his friend, "you might as well change out of that smelly thing."

Gunther smirked as he pulled off his home-made swastika arm band and traded his brown shirt for the white one.

"I'm going" he said as he finished buttoning up the shirt.

"Might as well..." Klaus said with a certain paternalistic air, as though Gunther was asking permission to go and Klaus was granting it.

The truth was that Gunther was confused. He wasn't sure what to make of what they had just been through. He picked up his coat and draped it over his arm as he walked to the door and then stopped with his hand on the door knob, looking down at the floor as he addressed Klaus. "It's over, isn't it?"

"I don't know. All the cards haven't been played yet." Klaus responded thoughtfully, as though he knew some deep secret about what might happen next.

"You and your Damn cards" Gunther shot back. He was tired

and beaten and he didn't want any of Klaus' dramatics at that point. "Do you think there's a chance?" he continued, wanting to know if there really was something that Klaus knew that he didn't.

"For today? No."

"Then what are you saying?"

"Maybe this was just another battle. We won't know what is what until the smoke clears."

"Do you think many were killed?"

"Well, Adolf was in front and he survived."

"He ran" Gunther corrected.

"He retreated" Klaus euphemized, "You've been in a retreat before."

"Yes, I've seen a retreat before" Gunther said in a challenging tone, "He ran. He left everyone and ran to save himself."

"So did we..." Klaus rejoined.

"After our leader..."

"The point is that we survived... He survived. That's why I say all the cards haven't been played yet."

"Well, I better go. I'll have to see if I still have a job."

"What?"

"The man I work for doesn't like nazis. If he finds out that I was at the Feldherrnhalle..."

"Well, good luck. I'm going to bed" Klaus said as he turned and walked away.

Gunther didn't even bother to tuck in his borrowed shirt as he put on his coat in the entryway of the apartment house. He turned up his coat collar and stepped out into the cold foggy afternoon, heading for home.

"Oh my God!" Amalie said as her eyes filled with tears, "You're safe. You made it."

"Yes, we got away after the shooting. We went to Klaus' apartment"

"I didn't sleep at all last night."

"I didn't sleep too well either."

"Why didn't you send word? How could you let us go on, not knowing whether you were alive or..."

"Everything was crazy. There wasn't time to get word out."

"Well," Amalie said, beginning to calm down, "What next? Are you home for good? Do you have to go out again?"

"I think" Gunther began, faltering, his voice breaking off as he forced himself to admit his unspoken fear, "it's over."

Amalie's heart leapt. She was at once astonished and overjoyed, but she kept silent for a moment, composing herself, afraid that she would incite Gunther to rage if he could see that she was happy that the nazis had fallen. She wanted to appear sympathetic, but first she wanted to be sure of what her husband meant. Did he mean this was a setback, that the putsch had failed, or had he given up on the nazis altogether?

"What's over?" she asked, as Gunther wearily leaned against the doorjamb.

"Everything."

"What everything? You and me, we're not over." Amalie insisted to her husband.

"No, of course not" Gunther said as he began to take off his coat, "You and Jakob, I feel like you're all I have left." and with that Gunther hugged his wife.

Amalie was a little frightened by this. She began to wonder if this was like a little boy running home to his mother after a bully had beaten him in a fight. Gunther had been so distant when he was immersed in the party and now, with the battle lost, he came back to her. She was confused. Here was Gunther, without the party and holding her in his arms, something she thought she had wanted more than anything else, and now she wasn't so sure. "Damn it!" she thought to herself. She wondered what was wrong with her. She questioned everything. She couldn't seem to ever just let herself be happy with things. "Just for this moment" she thought to herself, "I will be happy" and Amalie and Gunther continued to embrace each other.

After a few moments, Amalie looked up at Gunther. "I called your office this morning when you didn't get home..."

Gunther suddenly tensed up in Amalie's arms as thought he had just been hit with an electric shock. He suddenly thought that Amalie had told his employer where he had gone the night before and now there was certainly no way that Gunther could talk his way out of losing his job. His eyes flashed at Amalie, but before he could say a thing, Amalie put a finger up to his lips.

"I told them you had a bad case of influenza and wouldn't be in Friday and maybe not even on Monday." she said pre-emptorily.

Gunther managed a little smile. "You did that on purpose" he said in a teasing manner.

"Did what?" Amalie asked innocently.

"You know what" he said as he gave her a swat on the butt.

"Gunther!" Amalie said with a little laugh and just then Jakob heard them and then Gertrude realized Gunther had made it home and suddenly the apartment was in an uproar as everyone tried to speak at once.

The next couple of weeks found Adolf Hitler in jail, having been tracked down to the country house of one of his nazi party comrades and arrested. He was soon sent to Moabit prison and, by whatever sense of political hierarchy existed within the prison, he occupied the same cell that had held Anton Graf Arco Valley, the man who had assassinated Kurt Eisner some four years before and Arco Valley was moved to a new cell.

Amalie thought everything would become very quiet after that, but she was mistaken. Klaus proposed to Katrina, the girl he had been seeing for over a year, and Gunther, Amalie and Gertrude got swept up in the planning. Klaus said they were going to get married the week before Christmas because that would be the greatest Christmas gift he could ever wish for. Gunther was to be the best man and Amalie was going to be one of the bridesmaids while Gertrude offered to help Katrina's mother with the reception dinner.

It was a fairly small wedding, about seventy-five people, and Amalie had never seen Klaus smile so much. Jakob sat beside Gertrude in the huge Catholic church that seemed to swallow up the small party of friends and family and he watched the priest in his white robes and listened, not understanding the Latin liturgy of the wedding ceremony. The whole thing was very confusing to him. Jakob had never been to a wedding before and he had never been in a Catholic church before, but this was certainly not like the first time Amalie had been in a Catholic church just a year or so before. Amalie, being raised as a Jew, had endured many childhood taunts and threats that caused her to be uneasy, to almost fear Catholic churches.

Jakob was overcome by the church as any little boy would be sitting within the huge structure towering over him with it's spires and stained glass windows and sad looking statues in every corner. All the saints in heaven looked down on him as he looked up at the ceiling with his mouth wide open, taking in the scope of the church.

That Christmas was the best Gunther, Amalie, and Jakob had ever known as a family. It was as though they were now freed from the weight of the world. Gunther spent a lot of time at home since Klaus was now "occupied" with his new wife. The only thing that could have added to the festivities of that Christmas Eve would have been Friedrich coming home, but there was still no word after all that time. Even though everyone tried to encourage Gertrude that she would hear from her son soon, she didn't talk about it as she once again lit a single candle and placed it on a table in front of a window in the living room.

The greatest gift of that holiday didn't come until the first day of the new year. None of this group of friends had ever heard of Hjalmar Schacht, the new Reich Commissioner for National Currency before that day, but it was on New Years day of 1924 that he established the Golddiskontbank*. It was through a number of loans from banks of other nations that Schacht established a new German economy based on gold and issuing currency in pound sterling. It was a coordination of the British empire currency and German currency that solved the most pressing problem facing the German people. With the signatures of a few German banking officials and some foreign banking representatives, the inflation problem in Germany was ended.

"We've won" Amalie thought to herself. Hitler's putsch had failed and Hitler was in jail. The economy was restored and that had been one of Hitler's greatest focal points in arousing the people who came to his rallies. Her husband had become disillusioned with the leader who abandoned him when the bullets started to fly and this led Gunther to leave the national socialist German worker's party. It seemed certain to Amalie that there was no question that the vicious little man who came from nowhere was destined to return to anonymity.

"We've won!"

---

* Gold discount bank

174

The Price of Ashes

Part II
1928-1934

Chapter 8

The period from 1924 to 1928 in Germany was marked by a major change in the pattern of political unrest when Friedrich Ebert died in 1925. It is no small thing to note among the web of political assassinations in Germany that Ebert, first leader of the Weimar Republic and the man marked by the right wing extremists as the worst of all the November criminals, died of natural causes. The event which actually marked a change in the violent unrest in Germany, though, was the election of General Paul von Hindenburg to the office of President as the successor of Ebert. Here was a man who represented a political compromise between the right and the left. He was elected President, which meant that Weimar would stand, satisfying Germans of the moderate left, and he was a military man with a history reaching far back to the days of Imperial Germany, which satisfied most of the moderate right. The extremists on both the left and right, however, were still constantly agitating. The Communists and the nazis still pursued their now common practice of street fighting, especially in Berlin where Joseph Goebbels was trying to perfect his skills at demagoguery through his new vision of political propaganda fostered by his mentor, Adolf Hitler. When Adolf spewed his rambling and bitter commentary of hate, "Four and a Half Years of Struggle Against Lies, Stupidity and Cowardice", a title that was later shortened to "Mein Kampf" or "My Struggle", he stated outright that the common people would easily be convinced of anything if it was "handled" properly. "The big lie" became a part of the party's propaganda policy from that time on.

Anna giggled as she watched Lissa stick out her tongue. The old priest holding out a wafer paid no attention, but Anna heard Sister Angelina making a clicking noise with her tongue. When Anna turned to look, Sister Angelina pointed a finger and made a cross face which told Anna that her first communion was no place for giggling. Anna quickly turned back toward the alter, looking straight up at the statue of the Virgin Mary

Once Anna had been properly chastised, a little smile crossed Sister Angelina's face as she confided to Edith who was standing close beside her. "Lissa does look silly the way she sticks out her tongue... One might think she was trying to catch a fly!"

"Sister Angelina!" Edith whispered back with mock indignation.

After a moment the two women found themselves transfixed as they took in the warmth and gentleness of the scene. "This is one of my best memories of teaching." Edith said in a hushed and emotional voice, "All the preparation and then... the looks on their faces, the feeling in the chapel. It made the rest of the problems worth the trouble."

"I remember my white dress..." Sister Angelina reminisced, "and all the excitement... even though I didn't really understand how important it was."

"I was much older," Edith explained, "over thirty when I had my first communion. It was a completely new life for me."

Sister Angelina knew that Edith had converted from Judaism, but she had never broached the subject even though it interested her. "Why did you do it?" she asked after a brief pause.

"Convert?"

"Yes, why did you convert? Wasn't it hard to change from being Jewish to being a Catholic?"

Edith didn't hesitate with her answer because she had been asked so many times before and had long ago had to answer that same question for herself.

"No, not at all. It was as if I had been looking for something all my life and then some people, some friends at the University in Gottingen, introduced me to Catholicism and it seemed to be the thing I had been looking for all my life and just didn't know it."

"All your life?"

"It's hard to explain, but when I really started to find an interest in Catholicism and accepted Jesus as the messiah and savior, it all just felt right, as though that was how it should have been for me all along."

"That must have been comforting"

"It felt like a homecoming."

"How did your family accept it?"

"Some well, some not so well" Edith said with a note of sadness, "My mother has come to accept it, but my father still seems to hope that I'll come to my senses and give it up. Some of my relatives haven't spoken to me in... It's almost six years now."

"I'm sorry to hear that."

"That's just the way it is, I guess. Some people only accept you if you are what they want you to be."

"That's the philosopher in you coming out again." Sister Angelina noted with a smile. "I understand you're lecturing tonight" Angelina continued, changing the subject.

"Yes. My first. I've been offered a chance to speak on educational issues. I'm a little nervous, especially since I have a relative coming to hear me speak."

"Your Mother?"

"Oh no! She's in Breslau. It's a cousin that I've only met once when we were little girls. She works as an editor for a Munich book publisher and she sent me a letter saying she would be in Speyer on business."

"A woman editor?" Angelina asked.

"I was surprised, too. I started corresponding with her when I heard that she was in Munich. It's been interesting and friendly, especially since she accepts my new faith."

"Oh, how nice."

"She's a wonderful letter writer. It will be good to meet her face to face after all these years."

Amalie was impressed with the city of Speyer. It was one of the cities on the Rhine which had been occupied by French troops in 1923 and it was this event which had prompted Amalie to begin corresponding with Edith. There had been many rumors of the mistreatment of Germans by the French occupation troops including stories that German women couldn't walk the streets at night because they would be raped by French soldiers. There were also strange rumors that the Black African groups in the French occupation army had taken animals from the zoos which were indigenous to their

177

homelands and killed and eaten them.

Edith had written to Amalie's father that she was moving to Speyer to teach in a Catholic girls school and Ethan passed on the information to Amalie who started writing directly to Edith to find out what was really going on.

Edith didn't have much to say, except that she had never personally seen anything that would substantiate the rumors. The letters were a little awkward at first as the two of them were really strangers to one another, but after a few letters their correspondence became less formal and each began to get a better picture of the other's world.

Amalie was not only interested in Edith's conversion, but also Edith's study of the methods and nature of education. Edith, on the other hand, was impressed that Amalie was an editor with a publishing firm. It was such an unlikely profession for a woman in 1928, especially a married woman with a child.

Amalie had gotten an early start that morning and so she had time to stop occasionally to scrutinize the old churches as she walked through the city on the way to her meeting. The city was older than Munich and the architecture reflected the strong influence of the Holy Roman Empire with the many churches of Romanesque style as opposed to Munich's Gothic cathedrals. The buildings were certainly less ornate, but they were more substantial, almost as though they were part of the earth. They were like mountains which a selective volcano had erupted on chosen sites as earthly reminders of an eternal prescience.

Amalie continued to wander for a while until she was surprised to find herself in front of a tiny synagogue nestled within a row of bleak looking buildings. She stopped. The Hebrew school had just let out and a group of boys rushed by her, laughing and shouting as they made their way down the street. She thought of Jakob. He had just turned thirteen. Thirteen is the traditional age in Judaism when a boy goes through the ceremony to become a "Bar Mitzvah" or "son of the commandments" and accepts the responsibility of learning Torah, but of course this wouldn't happened with Jakob. The topic of raising Jakob in the Jewish faith, to any degree, was a taboo subject with Gunther. Yet Ethan had written a letter so full of anticipation and hope asking that Amalie might consider the possibility that she found herself torn...

"No." Amalie said to herself. She knew it would hurt her father, but she couldn't talk about it with Gunther and worse yet, she couldn't bring it up to Jakob. She had a much greater problem than the question of a Bar Mitzvah, though. Jakob was turning away from her. It was probably just his age and it wouldn't have been such a terrible thing in and of itself since it's normal for a boy as he enters puberty to seek out his father more as he tries to develop into manhood, but Amalie was afraid that he was also being molded. Gunther had once again become sympathetic to the nazis and it was clear that it would not take much to move him back to the party. Amalie was terrified that he would take Jakob with him.

It was a moment of reckoning for Amalie as she saw this terrifying possibility for her son. She desperately wanted to turn him away from it and just then she realized how her father must have felt as he saw her turning away from him so many years before. The irony of generations. All the promises we make to ourselves about not making the mistakes with our children that our parents made with us. That feeling of *Deja Vu* as we watch our children struggling through their lives and we try to shout out that we know the answer to this problem or that problem because we went through it before and survived, and yet so many times our children can no more hear us than we could hear our own parents. We find ourselves only able to look on, as though we are encased in glass, unable to be heard. Everyone feels that their situation is different, the parent who insists that they really do know the answer or that they really can tell what will happen next, but Amalie's complaint was more specific. She had wanted to save her husband and then decided that she might have to let him go in order to meet an even greater crisis, but how could she ever even think of giving up on her own son?

There was nothing unusual, nor interesting for that matter, about Amalie's meeting and she had plenty of time to get back to her hotel, get some rest and wash up before going to Edith Stein's lecture.

The lecture was mercifully short, only about forty-five minutes, and it was well laid out and easy to follow even for lay-people such as Amalie. It was only about nine o'clock when Edith finished and Amalie went up to introduce herself and compliment her cousin, inviting her out for a cup of coffee so that they could have a chance to talk.

179

The conversation was mostly small talk, centered around the Stein family until Edith started talking about when she first came to Gottingen from Breslau.

"Of course everyone looked down on me at first" Edith stated as a matter of fact.

"Because you were Jewish?"

"Worse. I was a Jewess from the East. They all assumed we had come from Poland."

"Oh yes, of course that would be worse" Amalie said with an intonation of disgust at not just the German prejudice against Jews, but even the prejudice of German Jews against Polish Jews. Before the word 'kike' became a common slur against all Jews, it was originally the word German Jews used for the Russian and Polish Jewish rag pickers. "It seems that everyone is always looking for someone to look down on" she said, finishing her thought.

"That was the most difficult part of attending the University," Edith continued, "things would be going along nicely and then someone would make some stupid remark and all the hatred and stupidity would be right there again. Another kike from Galicia..."

"It's all part and parcel of the same thing," Amalie said angrily, "scratch a German and find an anti-semite."

Edith was taken aback by the damning statement. "You don't really think it's that bad, do you?"

"You don't know" Amalie said, staring at Edith defiantly, "Certainly you've heard of Hitler. I thought they were done with, but I was wrong. As soon as Hitler got out of jail, he addressed a crowd at the same beer hall where he had started the putsch in '23 and so many people came that they were turned away at the door. Thousands of them, just waiting for him to return." Amalie stopped for a minute and composed herself as she realized how upset she was getting.

"The nazis are rebuilding. There aren't many of them, but they're spreading out, expanding into other parts of the country. Hitler is just waiting to try again and he hates us more than ever. Have you read his book?"

"His book?" Edith asked.

"Yes, he started it while in prison. He says he will send all the Jews out of Germany and even more, he wants to take the east for Germany and throw all the Jews out of those areas too."

"But he's a madman. No one takes him seriously" Edith countered.

"I don't think so. They can't seem to stop him. There is something about him. Something that he touches in the soldiers who fought at the front that makes them fanatical about him, and worse, people who lost all their money during the inflation are starting to listen."

"But how can all these people believe...?"

"The Jews have always been a target."

"But that comes and goes. It doesn't stay for long."

"No one I've heard of has ever worked so hard at it before. He doesn't just want the land of the Jews or their money, he wants them gone forever. He's started talking about Darwinism in his speeches more and more."

"Darwinism?"

"They call it 'social Darwinism'. The talk has been around for some time. They say survival of the fittest applies to mankind as well as the animal kingdom and that man with his intelligence and reasoning should 'assist evolution' for people. He says man should conscientiously remove inferior people from society so that society can improve faster than if things were left to natural selection."

"Well, it's just talk" Edith said with resignation in her voice, "We just have to trust in God and hope for the best."

Amalie was stunned. "Trust in God? Hope for the best?" she thought to herself. Was this what it meant to be a Catholic? She changed the subject after realizing that she might get carried away if she kept dwelling on the nazis and she and her cousin spent the next hour talking about family before they finally said good-bye and Amalie made her way back to her hotel.

Amalie had been careful over the past years to cultivate her conversation so that she would not casually betray her feelings about the nazis. She was determined not to be outspoken because it would make her conspicuous in Gunther's circle of friends and she decidedly wanted to hear all that she could about the progress and direction of the party. As it was, Gunther's friends in the party, such as Klaus, knew that she had no taste for the particulars of what the nazis did, but Klaus just thought of it as "a woman's distaste" for the necessity of violence rather than opposition to Hitler and his party. After all, this was the same sort of attitude that Katrina, Klaus' wife, expressed,

181

but Klaus had always enjoyed shocking people with his stories of demonstrations and beatings and other such actions in the war for control of the streets.

Klaus had remained a member of the nazi party throughout the time when Gunther had gone through his crisis of faith after the beer hall putsch in '23 and now Klaus was more adamant than ever that Adolf Hitler was destined to lead the German peoples to their own great destiny.

Katrina hadn't calmed Klaus as much as Amalie had hoped she might. Granted that in the four years they had been married, Katrina had managed to improve Klaus' manners a bit, but she would never dream of contradicting him in public and she had no desire to engage in conversation about current events or politics. She was content to have babies and be a good housewife. In the four years of their marriage Katrina had already dutifully presented her husband with three sons. After being childless for the first two years of their marriage and beginning to fear that something might be wrong, it suddenly seemed as if she could hardly make her way out the front doors of the hospital before announcing to all her friends that she was expecting "another little gift from heaven," as she was so fond of saying. Her lack of political awareness was more than made up for by her prolific nature regarding heirs to the throne.

Amalie returned to Munich the day after she met with her cousin Edith. It was June sixth, Amalie's thirty-fourth birthday. She realized that she had lived in Munich for ten years now and thought about how happy she had been in the past few years when she felt she had finally gotten Gunther back from all the distractions of the world. She laughed to herself as the thought crossed her mind that a World War and a Revolution should be considered something more than just "distractions", but she felt as though all those other great dramas had closed in on the world of her family and when the crisis were finally over, she, Gunther and Jakob finally had time to be a normal family.

Thirty-four! Not that thirty-four is old, but she couldn't help but wonder where those years had gone. For the first time in her life she had vivid memories of things that happened twenty years before! That sounded like something her grandfather would say... "Why, I haven't seen old 'so and so' in over twenty years." She now had a teenage son who was taller than she was.

Thirty-four. Thirty-four. Thirty-four. It didn't sound good.

Turning thirty wasn't so bad. Thirty was an accomplishment, but thirty-four was just carrying it too far.

When Amalie arrived home, her lugubrious attitude was obvious to Gertrude. The past five years had been rather good to Amalie and Gunther financially. Gunther's boss had taken a liking to Gunther and even helped him go to school while still working so that he could become a qualified architect. Amalie had been promoted to an editor position with Frieder and Son Publishing and soon Gunther and Amalie were able to buy a small house in the Furstenried district, coincidentally not far from Sam Frieder's house. Gertrude had moved with them as though she were a member of the family. Amalie and Gunther had insisted on taking her with when they went to find a house and had listened to her opinions on each property and they all, including Jakob of course, were in on the final decision as to which home they would buy.

"Don't tell me the birthday girl is feeling sad." Gertrude said as she stood in the kitchen doorway while Amalie dropped her briefcase and overnight bag unceremoniously in the living room.

"Don't remind me" Amalie said as she plopped into a chair in the living room.

"Well you certainly better not expect me to cry for you!" Gertrude said good-humoredly as she headed back into the kitchen, "I turned sixty-two this year, so don't talk to me about thirty-four! You're still a child. You probably only finished packing away your dollies a few months ago."

This made Amalie laugh a bit and she got up and went into the bedroom to change.

"Are you off for the day?" Gertrude asked since it was only a little past noon on Friday.

"Yes, David said I should take the weekend and have a good birthday"

"Will you?"

"What?" Amalie called back as she had been slipping her blouse up over her head and hadn't heard what Gertrude said.

"Are you going to celebrate?"

"Well, right now I'm going to take a long bath..."

"In the middle of the day?" Gertrude asked, wondering how someone could disrupt their schedule by taking a bath in the middle of the day. After all, normal people just wash at the sink before going to bed or in the morning before going to work, but take a bath in the middle of the day? Never.

"You should try it some time" Amalie called back, "A little change in routine... You could shake things up a bit."

"You're crazy" Gertrude said, laughing as she poured her cake batter into a pan for Amalie's birthday cake for after dinner that night.

"Gertie, we've known each other a long time and I thought at least I've taught you that."

"Taught me what?"

"A little craziness, it's good for the soul."

Gertrude laughed louder this time as she started to clean up the kitchen.

Amalie slid slowly into the bathtub, but then realized how stuffy the bathroom seemed and she got up again, opening the window over the tub and then quickly re-submerging in the soapy warm water. She sighed heavily as a fresh spring breeze suddenly floated into the bright white bathroom, bringing with it a scent of the recently opened blossoms from the plum tree outside the house. She closed her eyes just for a moment and smiled and didn't even realize that she was drifting off to sleep.

"Mother, please!" came the voice through the door as Amalie bolted awake, splashing water over the side of the bathtub. "I really need to get in there!"

At first Amalie was confused and couldn't figure out what was going on, but then she realized she had fallen asleep and it was Jakob at the door needing, rather desperately it seemed, to relieve himself.

"Just a moment" she called out as she clambered out of the tub and put on her robe. Her skin was all wrinkled from soaking in the water for so long. She hated the feeling of her robe against her wrinkled fingers, but forced herself to move quickly for Jakob's sake.

Jakob quickly brushed past her as soon as she opened the door and rather pointedly closed the door behind himself, almost hitting Amalie as she stood in the hallway.

"You're welcome" she said curtly.

An image suddenly flashed through Amalie's mind. The river. She hadn't been near the river that day. When was it? Why did she suddenly remember standing by the rivers edge? The thought seemed to panic her as she tried to remember. It must have been a dream. She looked at the clock in her bedroom. It was almost three o'clock. She had been sleeping for over two hours in the bathtub.

"Happy birthday, mother" Jakob said as he stuck his head in the bedroom doorway, startling Amalie.

"Oh! Thank you liebling" Amalie said, and then, calling out to Jakob as he continued down the hall, "Stay close to home. Your father will be home early tonight."

"I will" Jakob replied without breaking stride, "I'll be next door with Karl."

Amalie finished getting dressed and went into the living room, leaving the traces of an incomprehensible dream behind and picking up the morning newspaper from beside the chair where Gunther had left it that morning before he had gone to work.

"Did you enjoy your bath?" Gertrude asked puckishly.

Amalie just looked up from her newspaper with a slow burn. "You let me sleep in there for two hours!"

"...and it wasn't easy" Gertrude laughed, "I didn't think I could hold my water that long!"

"That wasn't very nice."

"I know, I know... but I just couldn't resist."

Just then Gunther came home from work, catching the tail of the conversation as he came into the living room. "...couldn't resist what?" he asked.

"Gertie's being mean to me, and on my birthday too."

"Gertie! How could you? But don't worry dear, your present will make up for anything that might have gone bad today."

"Oh, that sounds promising... What is it?"

"It's a surprise, of course."

"...and a pretty good one. I've been looking around for a week."

"That's what I figured, so I made sure it wasn't in the house. I'm having it delivered tonight at seven."

"During dinner?"

"Just before."

"Not even a clue as to what it might be?"

"I promise you'll love it."

"I'll hold you to that."

The afternoon passed quickly as everyone pitched in to get everything ready for the birthday dinner. Klaus and Katrina would be coming with all three children and, even though Klaus had his sons regimented into a strict obedience, Amalie wanted to make sure there was nothing breakable within three feet above the floor.

Jakob soon came home from his friend's house with Honig, the spaniel which Gunther had gotten him for his eighth birthday, close at heel and Klaus and Katrina arrived soon after that. Jakob and the boys played with Honig while the adults talked and Gertrude put the finishing touches on dinner.

At one point, Gunther caught Amalie glancing anxiously at the clock and laughed, letting Klaus and Katrina in on the joke. Amalie felt like a little girl as she anxiously awaited seven o'clock and then finally, a few minutes before the magic hour, they all heard a car drive up in front of the house and park. Amalie started to get up, but Gunther jumped up and raced her for the door, the two of them laughing as they almost crashed into the front door. Gunther pressed his wife against the door, and put his lips to her ear. She thought he was trying to kiss her and pushed him back playfully, laughing all the while "Not now!" she said, "First the present and then the kisses."

Everyone in the room laughed as Gertrude came into watch the excitement. Gunther put up his hands to quiet Amalie. "No," he said, unable to stop laughing himself, "I'm not trying to kiss you this time! I have to tell you something!" and then Amalie stopped struggling as he drew close. "There's more than one surprise." he said, "Whoever is at the door, don't say anything until he comes in." Amalie looked very confused, but she nodded in agreement. Gunther reached for the door knob and made sure to obstruct the doorway from everyone else in the room as he slowly opened the door.

Amalie was dumbfounded. It was Friedrich. Gertrude's Friedrich. None of them had seen him for almost six years. He had gone to Berlin to make a living and had all but disappeared for a couple of years until finally Gertrude got a letter at Christmas of 1925. It said that he was doing alright and that she shouldn't worry, but the fact that he made no mention of visiting and gave no mailing address made it clear to Gertrude that he was struggling to get by. Gertrude took it in stride and never complained to her friends.

Over the next couple of years the letters became more frequent, a letter every couple of months until finally there was a very special letter. It had a return address. That little note at the end made Gertrude so happy because it meant that Friedrich was doing better. If he couldn't come home, at least he had a place of his own. Then it turned out that he was becoming involved with politics. There was a lot of effort to strengthen cells of the nazi party in the North and Berlin was the territory of Gregor Strasser and his new assistant, a short man with a club foot named Joseph Goebbels. Friedrichs connection with the first days of the party in Munich and his experience with the Freikorps had put him in a position to make good contacts which eventually got him work as a clerk and chauffeur at the small headquarters of the nazi party in Berlin. He also managed to supplement his income with part-time work for businessmen who were sympathetic to the party and therefore willing to allow him to work his schedule around party duties.

Gunther took Amalie's arm and guided her, moving aside so that Gertrude, who had been smiling at their antics and standing behind them, could see her son. The smile drained away from her face as she looked into the smiling eyes of her long lost son and she broke into tears. It was as though her feet couldn't move as she opened her arms to Friedrich who swept into the room and embraced his mother. Gunther and Amalie smiled as they looked on and Amalie slipped her arm around Gunther's waist, pulling him close. Klaus explained to his wife that it was Gertrude's son, returned from Berlin after many years away, and their three little sons looked up at Gertrude as she cried, not understanding what was wrong Jakob quickly moved in and corralled the little boys, spending the next few minutes trying to explain that grandma Gertie was crying because she was happy.

Why didn't you tell me you were coming?" Gertrude finally said through her tears.

"I wanted to surprise you." he said, still embracing her. All of the problems from years ago had been swept away and Friedrich was overcome to see her and his old friends again. The others finally came over and greeted Friedrich too, welcoming him back home.

"This really is the most incredible surprise" Amalie said excitedly as she stepped in to give Friedrich a hug.

"Oh," Friedrich said, "I almost forgot. It's your birthday Amalie. I'm not the present, I'm just the delivery boy." and with that he headed for the door with Amalie in tow. "There" he said, "It's yours."

"What?" Amalie asked as she looked out.

"The car. The car, of course. Gunther's gone and bought a car for you."

Again Amalie was dumbfounded as everyone else poured out of the house in the dwindling light of the early spring evening to look at the used touring car.

"Oh Gunther..." was all that Amalie could manage to say. Jakob immediately jumped behind the steering wheel and pretended to drive as Gunther and Klaus looked the car over, discussing the engine and how far it could go on a tank full of gas and so on. Jakob startled everyone as he honked the horn and it was Gertrude who reprimanded him, telling him he shouldn't do that because he might wear out the car before his mother even gets a ride in it. After a few minutes, Gertrude wiped her eyes, still wet from the emotional reunion, and insisted that everyone come in for dinner and everyone started to file in slowly, Gunther and Klaus, followed by Katrina and then Gertrude and Friedrich until Amalie and Jakob were alone as she looked the car over closely, admiringly.

"Is it really ours mother?" Jakob asked dreamily.

"No. It's mine. Your father gave it to me" Amalie said playfully.

"Won't you even let me ride in it?"

Amalie smiled and gave Jakob a hug, struggling as she managed to pull him out of the drivers seat. "Ja, Elch-kind"* she replied as they walked towards the house, Jakob standing a full two inches taller than his mother. When they joined the others at the dinner table, Gunther told his wife that Friedrich had a wonderful suggestion, that they should all pack a lunch and take a long drive to the mountains for a picnic the next day. Klaus said he would drive and they could take both cars so that everyone could go.

"... and Friedrich can show me how to drive." Amalie added.

Friedrich, Klaus and Gunther exchanged amused glances without saying anything, but Amalie caught on immediately.

"Now you all stop that. I'll be a good driver!"

"Yes, I think she will too." Katrina added supportively, taking Amalie by surprise.

"Thank you, Katrina" Amalie acknowledged with a nod.

The meal was delicious and made even better by the unexpected presence of Friedrich, whose adventures in Berlin fairly dominated the conversation throughout the evening, not by Friedrich's choice, but by virtue of the continuing stream of questions from everyone else.

The time that Friedrich had been in Berlin had been a particularly decadent period in the history of the city. Friedrich was

---

* Yes, moose child.

careful to use euphemisms in his descriptions of the night life in consideration of the attentive presence of the women and children. Katrina felt a little out of place, having not met Friedrich before and not having much interest in the terrible things going on in Berlin, and so she ended up in the living room with her sons, playing with them and keeping them occupied.

Finally the time came, almost midnight, when Klaus got up and declared it was time to leave and went into the living room to gather up his sleeping wife and children.

"We'll be at your door at ten o-clock tomorrow morning, so you should all be ready to go or we'll leave without you" Klaus declared pretentiously.

"But you don't even know where we're going." Friedrich said with a laugh since he was the one who had mysteriously suggested a spectacular picnic location without revealing where it was.

"No matter." Klaus said boisterously, "We'll just drive south until we see a mountain."

"Katrina," Amalie said, "Maybe you should drive home tonight..."

"No, I'm so tired that I don't care where we end up. It's up to Klaus where we go."

Everyone managed to help Klaus and Katrina gather up toys and childrens jackets and blankets and all the rest and get them on their way in under half an hour, which was no small accomplishment. There was a collective sigh of relief once they had gone and only then did Gertrude think to consider where Friedrich would sleep.

"He can sleep in my room." Jakob offered excitedly, happy that he had something to offer the great adventurer. "I can sleep on the floor and you can use my bed" he continued, now addressing Friedrich directly.

"I wouldn't want to put you out of your bed" Friedrich replied with a laugh.

"No, really, I wouldn't mind." Jakob insisted.

"You might as well." Gunther agreed and then Friedrich went out to the car to get his bag.

When Gertrude and her son met in the hallway, she got up the courage to ask him how long he would be visiting.

"I think I might be moving back for good" he said and once again Gertrude couldn't help but embrace him.

Her first thought was that everything could be the way it was, but she quickly dismissed the thought. Nothing could be like it was. None-the-less, it was a wonderful feeling, knowing that he would be living in Munich again.

The house finally quieted down as everyone went to bed. In the eerily brilliant moonlight which drifted in through the window of Jakob's room, Jakob looked over at Friedrich.

"Friedrich?" he whispered, "Are you awake?"

"Yes," Friedrich answered in a mumble as he lay on his stomach with his face in the pillow, "what is it?"

"Tonight..." Jakob started tenuously as he carefully chose his words, "when you were talking... What's a 'lady of the evening'?"

Friedrich lifted his head and looked over at Jakob. "How old are you?"

"Thirteen... and a half."

"Thirteen..." Friedrich repeated as he considered his response.

"...and a half" Jakob repeated, hoping to influence Friedrich to give him a man's answer rather than the answer a man would give to a little boy.

"Well... it's a woman... who offers herself... who agrees... to stay with a man if he pays her"

"A whore?"

Friedrich smirked as the unexpected reply registered. "If you knew what a whore is, then why did you ask?"

"I'd never heard them called 'lady of the evening' before."

"Oh."

"Did you ever?"

"Ever pay for..? No" Friedrich lied.

In truth, when Friedrich first arrived in Berlin and was all alone in the city, he found that he could get a room and a girl for almost nothing. Soon afterwards he was using the proceeds from some black market transactions to avail himself of such accommodations. He certainly didn't think that was the sort of thing he should reveal to Jakob, as a matter of fact, as it turned out, Friedrich would never speak to anyone about such particulars of those days in Berlin.

"How old were you when you first..." Jakob pressed on cautiously.

"You shouldn't think of such things." Friedrich admonished sanctimoniously, "When you get married, you will..."

190

"Are you married?"

"No, not yet."

"Are you going to get married soon?"

"I don't know, but there is this girl..."

"In Berlin?"

"No, she lives down here."

"Munich?"

"No." Friedrich said, and then after a short pause he asked Jakob if he could keep a secret.

"Yes." Jakob replied seriously, "Absolutely."

"Tomorrow's trip... We're going to see her."

"What's her name?"

"Angela... but everyone calls her 'Geli'."

The next day, true to his word, Klaus and his family drove up in front of the Metzdorf home at ten o'clock, honking his horn. It was a perfect Bavarian spring day and everyone was ready to go. At the last moment Jakob insisted on bringing Honig so that she could enjoy a romp in the fresh mountain air too, and even though Gunther protested, Amalie sided with Jakob and Honig's passage was secured. It was a tight fit, but Honig rode on Jakob's lap while he and Gunther sat in the back seat and Amalie and Gertrude sat in front with Friedrich driving. Amalie watched carefully as Friedrich worked the clutch and shifted gears and he tried to give her instruction on the shifting pattern of the stick as they went along.

They soon drove through the small town of Grunewald and laughed as Klaus started honking and waving as they passed through the town that bore his last name.

They had driven for almost an hour when Friedrich suggested they stop and all get out and stretch their legs in the town of Rosenheim. Gunther wanted to visit the house his grandfather had owned, so Friedrich followed his instructions and stopped across the street in front of the simple cottage.

"It seems so much smaller" Gunther said as he got out and looked at the house. Jakob put Honig on a leash as everyone else got out of the car and Honig immediately began to bark at another dog in one of the yards.

Gunther was lost in thought as he crossed the street and walked up to the front yard of the house. It needed painting, but the yard was well kept and planted with flowers.

"Ten years... eleven years..." Gunther said.

"Eleven now." Amalie said as she stood beside him, confirming how many years it had been since his grandfather had died.

"This was one of the places that got me through, during the war." Gunther said thoughtfully, "You and Jakob... my mother... and here. I never said it before, but I loved him more than I loved my father."

"I know" Amalie said as she took his hand and squeezed it gently. He didn't think it had been that obvious and was surprised that she knew. He put his arm around her and they crossed the street back to the car by which time Klaus and Katrina and the boys pulled up and Klaus asked why they had stopped. Gunther had told Klaus about his grandfather during the time that Klaus and Gunther were together at the front during the war. Gunther went on to tell a couple of the funny stories that the old man used to tell over and over, like the first time they saw a train locomotive and the stories about being a stable boy for a baron when he was a boy.

When it was time to get going again, Klaus and Friedrich insisted that Amalie take the wheel and try to get them out of town. Amalie tried to perfect letting out the clutch at the right time while pulling out into the street and then shifting into second and third gears. After a while she managed to get them to the edge of town where she turned things back over to Friedrich.

It turned out to be a rather long trip, eventually stretching out to over two hours and a couple of more rest stops before they reached the small town of Berchtesgaden at the foot of the mountains.

"I want to say hello to someone" Friedrich said unexpectedly as he pulled up to the driveway of one of the mountain villas. Klaus pulled his car up beside them and got out, walking over and once again asking why they had stopped.

"We must be close. We certainly don't want to go up any farther. It's still awfully cold up in the mountains." Klaus said.

Just then Friedrich came down from the house with a pretty young woman with light brown hair, both of them smiling and laughing. Klaus looked at the two of them walking towards the car for a moment and then turned to Gunther with a big smile. "So this is why we drove for two and a half hours. The perfect picnic spot..."

Gertrude shifted in her seat, suddenly feeling uncomfortable as she watched her son and a strange girl walking towards them.

"I had to stop since we were so close." Friedrich said when they got to the car, "I thought maybe Geli would like to come on the picnic with us if it's alright with everyone."

"Geli?" Klaus said in a tone meant to needle Friedrich as it became apparent that this had been Friedrich's plan all along.

"Oh... yes. This is Geli. Geli, these are my friends. Klaus, Gunther, Gunther's wife Amalie, their son Jakob and this is my mother, Gertrude." It was apparent that Friedrich was uncomfortable as his transparent plan was exposed and he wasn't very good at covering his embarrassment.

Amalie seemed to be the only one willing to let him off the hook as she held out her hand to Geli. "Hello, it's nice to meet you. You're certainly welcome to come along. We have plenty, don't we?" she said as she turned to Gertrude.

"Yes," Gertrude said curtly, "we have plenty..."

Geli agreed, saying she just needed a moment to tell her mother she was going. Friedrich explained to everyone that there was a terrific picnic area on the Konigssee, just a few kilometers to the west.

Geli was very talkative and pleasant as they drove, explaining how she and her mother had just moved to the villa from Austria to take care of the villa for her Uncle Alfie.

"Uncle Alfie?" Gunther asked from behind her.

"Yes," she said as she tried to turn enough to make eye contact. "He's some sort of politician in Munich."

"Adolf Hitler?" Gunther asked in a funny way that made the question a statement.

"Yes! Do you know him?"

"We're from Munich. Everyone in Munich has heard of him."

"I knew he was popular, but I didn't realize he was that important." Geli said.

They soon pulled into the picnic area by the Konigssee where everyone's first instinct was to get out and stretch. Amalie and Gertrude started to unpack the food while Jakob unleashed Honig and ran to the lake. Katrina started getting the boys out of the other car and the men gravitated together.

"Hitler's niece?" Gunther asked with a smile.

"What!" Klaus shot back as Friedrich just smiled. "You're trying to seduce the Fuhrer's* niece?"

"I wouldn't say that." Friedrich said impishly, "I met her a week ago and she said I should stop by sometime."

"Do you think she really meant it?" Gunther asked.

"If she didn't, she certainly covered well when I showed up at the door." Friedrich replied, "She seemed really happy to see me."

"Come over here!" Gertrude suddenly called out to the three men, "It's time to eat. Everything is ready."

Gunther then called out to Jakob who had taken off his shoes and rolled his pant legs up and was running along the shore, splashing in the cold water of the Konigssee as Honig chased happily beside him. Both of them turned and ran towards the picnic sight when they heard Gunther calling.

Just before they reached the blankets which Amalie and Gertrude had carefully laid out for everyone to sit on, Jakob called Honig back and leashed her to a tree about twenty meters from the cars so that she wouldn't bother everyone while they were eating.

The weather had held up nicely all morning. It was fairly warm for early June in the mountains, warm with just a light breeze. The conversation was pleasant and Klaus resisted the urge to embarrass Friedrich in front of Geli and Geli managed to hold her own whichever way the conversation turned. She talked very casually about how her father had died and her mother had welcomed "Uncle Alf's" offer to come and keep house for him at the villa he rented in Berchtesgaden. She had met Friedrich just a week before in Munich when she had been visiting with her mother. Friedrich explained that he had actually been in Munich for over a week, but he had had a bit of trouble tracking down Gertrude until he caught up with Klaus through some of the nazi party members and Klaus had then gotten in touch with Gunther.

It was just after they had finished eating and everyone was either laying back and relaxing or cleaning up when Amalie noticed the dog out of the corner of her eye. It moved slowly and tiredly, straying from place to place in the sparse pine trees near the picnic ground. It didn't seem out of place, in fact Amalie's first thought was that it must belong to one of the other families who were out enjoying a picnic along the lakefront.

---

* While the word "Fuhrer" means leader in german, "Der Fuhrer" or "the leader" was a form of address reserved solely for Adolf Hitler.

When the dog got closer, Amalie could tell it was a Doberman and it suddenly occurred to her that Honig was tied out between the Doberman and the picnic area and she told Jakob to go get Honig so that the two dogs wouldn't start fighting, after all she thought to herself, the strange dog wouldn't come near the family.

Amalie looked back to what she was doing as she packed dishes in a basket and then looked up just in time to see the strange dog as it caught sight of Jakob running over to Honig. The strange dog's head jerked up as though it had just noticed the people even though the whole group of them were less than twenty meters away. Honig suddenly started barking at the Doberman and the Doberman charged. Amalie was frozen. It was as though she was watching in slow motion as the dog charged toward Jakob and Honig. She finally managed to break from her trance and reach out to Gunther.

"My God! Look!" she stuttered as she shook Gunther, "It's going to attack." Gunther immediately jumped up, but by that time the Doberman had already pounced on Honig, immediately clamping down on her throat and lifting her off the ground, flailing her body as it tried to break her neck. Jakob was only a few steps away and he jumped on the Doberman, knocking it down sideways and reaching his left arm around the dog's torso while clutching at the Doberman's throat, trying to force it to release his beloved Honig. The dog let go of the mortally wounded Honig and turned on Jakob, slashing his forearm with a twist of its head and then biting down on the fleshy part of Jakob's hand between the thumb and index finger. Just then Gunther's foot came up and kicked the Doberman in the back just below the neck. The dog suddenly turned on its new attacker and Jakob fell off, writhing in pain and holding his right hand and forearm against his chest. The Doberman was now back on all fours and just about to lunge at Gunther as their eyes locked. The dog hesitated for an instant for some unknown reason as his muscles tensed and then he sprang. The Doberman didn't even see the tree limb as it struck him down to the ground short of his prey. Klaus had run over to the trees and found a fallen limb and used it as a weapon, continuing to beat the Doberman after it had fallen. It was as though Klaus went crazy, hitting the bloody corpse again and again.

Amalie hadn't even heard herself shrieking and screaming as the attack occurred. It wasn't until the others had run over that she realized she was hoarse. Once Klaus and Gunther were sure the dog was dead, Gunther walked over to his son. Jakob was crying uncontrollably. He was petting Honig's bloody fur and just repeating over and over "Oh Honig, Honig. My beautiful little Honig."

Gunther picked up his son and held him tightly against his chest as Amalie rushed up with Geli and Gertrude close behind. "I know the way to the doctors house in town." Geli offered and she helped as Gunther got into the back seat of the car, still holding Jakob across his lap. Friedrich got in front to drive while Geli got in on the front passenger side to navigate and they sped off down the road.

Those remaining just stood by in disbelief as they watched the dust rise up from behind the car. "I'll have to take the dog in." Klaus said quickly as he walked over to the dead Doberman and wrapped it in one of the blankets and threw it into the trunk of his car. He hoped he could catch up with the others because he didn't know where they were going.

"I'm going with." Amalie said. It seemed natural that she would want to be with Jakob, but the others had left so quickly that she didn't even have a chance to get in the car.

Katrina came up to the door just as Klaus was going to take off. "What about us?"

"You and Gertrude and the boys wait here. Once I find out where they are, I'll come back and get you." He then stepped on the gas, throwing up dirt and rocks behind the car as he began the race to catch up with Friedrich.

Gertrude stepped back and finished gathering everything up and then she turned and caught sight of Katrina's sons standing in a row, staring at Honig, bloody and still, and she started crying. Katrina called the boys away and then walked over to Gertrude and embraced her.

"Why did you bring the dog?" Amalie asked quietly as she and Klaus raced down the road after the others. Klaus didn't answer and Amalie repeated the question even though she knew the answer. She didn't want to know it, but she did and for some strange reason she had to have Klaus confirm it.

"Rabies..." he said without looking at her. Nothing more was said as they drove into town.

Amalie was numb by the time they caught up with Jakob and Gunther at the doctor's office. The doctor did what he could to clean up the wounds, but told them they should take Jakob to the hospital in Salzburg for the best care. Klaus pulled the doctor aside to explain that he had the body of the dog in his trunk and the doctor said it should go to the same hospital so that they could run tests and get results as soon as possible.

Klaus took Geli home on his way to get Gertrude and his family, telling Katrina and Gertie what had happened and suggesting they might as well go home to Munich.

Anger flared in Gertrude's eyes. "If you think I'm going back to Munich while little Jakob..." she started "Klaus Grunewald, I've loved that boy as if he were one of my own for as long as I've known you and I will walk to Salzburg before I leave him lying hurt in a Salzburg hospital. He needs his Grandma Gertie as much as he needs his mother and father!"

Klaus looked at the expression on Katrina's face as she held his own youngest son in her arms and he knew they had to go to Salzburg with the others.

It turned out that the Doberman was not rabid. He was just an old dog that had apparently wandered away and gotten lost in the woods. The doctor said the dog was so old that he could probably hardly see and from what Gunther explained about the incident, the doctor said it was probably the movement of Jakob's running and the other dog's barking which prompted the attack. In short, it seems that Honig and Jakob just got in the way of the lost and confused old dog as it lashed out in its last fit of energy and rage at a foreign and frightening world.

Even though the dog was not rabid and the doctor in Berchtesgaden had done a good job of cleaning Jakob's wounds, there was still a great danger of infection as with any animal attack and the doctor insisted on keeping Jakob there until the following Wednesday. Since they were in Salzburg, Amalie called her father and told him what was going on and he immediately came to the hospital.

Klaus and Katrina decided to leave after a couple of hours when they felt they had done all they could.

"I think I'm going to leave with Klaus" Gunther said to Amalie as they stood by Jakob's bed.

"Leave? Please don't go" Jakob interrupted.

Gunther turned to his son, taking his hand, "You'll be fine now. I've got to get home to work. Your mother and I can't both take off work. She'll stay."

"But I want you to stay, too. I..."

"No, I'm sorry son, but it's best I go. You just have to understand."

Jakob did understand. Other things always came first for his father. This was just one more time when Jakob was an inconvenience to him.

Amalie called David Frieder at home to tell him that she would be staying. Gertrude and Friedrich both decided to stay too, Gertrude because she wanted to be with Jakob and Friedrich because he knew Amalie wasn't able to drive the car by herself yet, and Ethan offered to put them all up in his home.

The days passed quickly as Jakob returned to good spirits and the feared infection never materialized. He knew his bandages and the scars they covered would impress everyone at school and he wore them proudly as proof of how he had fended off a wild beast in the woods with his bare hands. He became very quiet as they passed through Berchtesgaden on the way home as he thought of Honig and wondered if she was still laying out in the forest somewhere by the Konigssee, but he couldn't bring himself to ask if it was true.

Gunther was already home from work by the time the group arrived. They were all glad to be home again to familiar beds and back to normalcy. No one spoke of Honig or the attack. Gertrude went about making dinner after changing into clean clothes and Amalie walked over to the apothecary to get the bandages and ointments necessary for changing the dressings on Jakob's wounds. Friedrich immediately monopolized the telephone as he began to call his party contacts so that he could find work and move back to Munich for good.

Jakob disappeared into his room, laying on his bed and reading the latest book by Otto Maus. Otto hadn't forgotten Jakob and whenever Otto finished a book, he made sure to send an autographed copy to his young fan. Jakob found the books to be light reading, but he respected that Otto considered him a friend and dutifully read each book as though it were an obligation.

Gunther looked in as he walked by his son's bedroom. "Jakob, if you have a moment..." he said in a way that caught Jakob off guard. It sounded like a request, a marked contrast to Gunther's usual draconian tendencies. "I'd like you to come outside with me."

Jakob immediately sat up on the bed, quickly marking his place in the book before following his father out to the back yard.

It was a very small yard, just enough to hold the little vegetable garden that Gertrude tended and a garage.

"I guess we'll have to clean up the garage now that we have a car" he said off-handedly as they walked. Gunther stopped short of the outbuilding and turned towards the garden where there now stood a little rhunic marker, a stake with a gabled roof on it and the inscription "Honig, treu kleine freundin".*

Jakob was speechless as he stopped and looked. His father had taken the time to bring Honig home and bury her there. It was something he never would have expected. He didn't think his father cared about the dog and suddenly Jakob realized that he hadn't even known how much his father cared about him until they took that panicked ride to the doctor's office. His father had held him so tightly, so close, as though he would never let go and never let anything hurt him.

What a confusing time it is to be thirteen. A boy thinks that he has begun to know certain things, He identifies and passes judgment on people in his life, thinks he is well on his way to being a man, singular and independent. Then things happen that make him feel like such a child again, so frightened and helpless. People constantly surprise you, for better and for worse.

"You brought her home" Jakob half-whispered.

"She was a good dog," Gunther pronounced as he put his arm on Jakob's shoulder, "We couldn't just leave her there."

Jakob turned under his father's arm and hugged him, surprising Gunther. Gunther then turned back to the garage as though that had been their true destination all along, as though he had wanted to discuss cleaning out the garage so that the car could be stored there and they had only happened upon the little grave next to the garden by accident.

---

* Honey, true little friend.

Chapter 9

It wasn't long after Adolf Hitler's release from prison that the nazi party began to grow again, soon becoming even larger than it had been before the failed putsch in Munich. The trial had generated enormous publicity for Adolf Hitler throughout the world, transforming the nazi party to a growing national movement.

As with any political group, the leaders in the nazi party tended to socialize within their own ranks and a result of this was the formation of a youth association for their children based on national socialist political views. The nazi youth organization called the "Hitler Jungend", or "HJ" for short, was developed along the lines of other groups such as the Catholic youth organizations and the Communist youth organizations which had been around for quite some time by then.

Eventually, when the nazi party and Adolf Hitler came to power, membership in the Hitler youth would become obligatory for both boys and girls from the ages of ten to eighteen. Over time the HJ would split into different age group and gender subdivisions while other youth groups would be outlawed in Germany. The evolution of the Hitler Youth programs paralleled the development of the nazi party within Germany. The HJ would become a forum for the political indoctrination of those who were being forced to join. Ultimately, as Germany moved past the re-armament period and towards seemingly inevitable military confrontations, the Hitler youth programs became para-military training grounds for the young people of Germany. The HJ and its related programs would virtually deify Adolf Hitler in the minds of these impressionable children.

"You know she was born close to there, don't you?"

"Who?"

"Geli, of course!"

"Friedrich, why is it that whenever I talk to you these days, you always manage to turn the conversation around to that girl?"

"Well, I guess I just think about her a lot."

"That's pretty obvious..."

"But don't you like her, Amalie?"

"Of course I like her, but I like a lot of people."

"But don't you think she's something special?"

"Special?"

"Yes... almost like you would think she was a princess or something... if you didn't know better."

"Oh Friedrich! You really do have it bad!"

"Please don't joke with me Amalie. She's making me crazy! She seems to like me well enough, but nothing ever happens. Even when we've gone out alone once or twice, it's as though I'm just an escort that "Uncle Alf" has arranged because he's too busy to go himself."

"I hate to be the one to say it, but hasn't it occurred to you that she might just be flirting with you? Have you ever just come out and said how much you like her?"

"...No, not really."

"Well then, what's this all about? Why would you expect her to pay any real attention to you if you never even declare yourself?"

"I'm afraid she doesn't feel the same about me and I'll just embarrass myself."

"Can that be any worse torturing yourself like this?"

"Yes!"

"How? How could it be worse?"

"Amalie, if I tell her how I feel and she rejects me, she could tell Uncle Alf that I'm annoying her. That would be terrible. Who knows what he might do? He's very protective of her."

"Friedrich, I don't want to be the one to hurt you..." Amalie fumbled with the words as she tried to find a delicate way to explain the situation, " but there are certain things... Friedrich, there are a lot of people who say that Geli and her uncle are... 'involved'."

"Oh Amalie, you can't believe all that talk. Geli has even told me she's heard the talk and it's just not so."

"Well... I guess people will always talk. Especially when it involves someone so well known."

"Yes, that's it. It's just talk... I need someone to help me."

"Help you? How?"

"I thought maybe someone might ask her if she cares about me. Someone who could save me from making a fool of myself. I couldn't stand it if she laughed at me. I need someone to find out if there's even a chance..."

Amalie couldn't hold back a smile as she asked the question for which she already knew the answer. "Who?"

"Well, I thought maybe you might... You seem to like her..."

"I hardly know her. We've only met a couple of times."

"That's the beauty of it. You're going to Vienna on business and she told me that she wanted to go back there for a day or two to pick up a few things from her mother's house. You could go together."

"Well, I guess I could... If she wanted to..." Amalie said hesitantly.

"Excellent! When are you going?"

Amalie told him about her plans to visit Vienna where David Freider had entrusted her to negotiate a financial agreement with a retired archeologist who had written a book in connection with several excavations in Egypt, including his very limited contact with the men who eventually uncovered the tomb of King Tut Ankahmen. The book was only significant in that the author had a number of contacts in the teaching community who had committed themselves to using the book as required reading for beginning archeology courses in universities across the country.

The commitment by the author's friends was just a ploy to give the old man a little something extra for his retirement income, but David only cared that he had a product with a guaranteed market and so it was a chance to continue Amalie's education in the publishing business with the rare opportunity of a learning experience with limited variables. In other words, there was no chance of Amalie making any big mistakes that could ruin the company while she still had the latitude to make a good deal for the publisher if she worked at it.

After Friedrich left, Amalie began thinking about the implications of Geli accompanying her to Vienna. She wondered to herself how it might help the cause she had abandoned almost five years before when she had been investigating Hitler's background and couldn't find any leads for evidence of anything that might hurt the party.

She decided to take a quick trip to Sam Frieder's house. Maybe she would start looking around again, but this time with the assistance, albeit unwitting, of a member of the Hiedler family.

Sam was now sixty-seven years old, but there was no sign of him slowing down in his hobbies and clubs.

"Amalie," he said warmly as he opened the door, "how are you?"

"Very well, Sam, and you?"

He thought about it for a moment and then smiled. "Pretty good. Yes, I'm doing alright. So," he continued as he motioned for Amalie to sit, "what brings you out so late to see David's crazy old father?"

"Oh, it's not so far now. Didn't David tell you that my family has moved out here? We're practically neighbors now. I only live a few blocks away."

"Well, that's nice news."

"Yes, it's a very nice neighborhood."

"That's good... very nice... so, how are things at the office?"

"Business is good... Hasn't David talked to you? He says he calls every week."

Sam smiled at this and cupped his hand to his mouth, delivering a stage whisper "I'm checking up on him."

Amalie laughed and reassured Sam that things were going very well for the company and then her expression changed as she brought up her reason for visiting. "Sam, do you remember when we first met and we talked about... an investigation."

"A what... Oh, yes. You were checking up on Hitler. Well things certainly have changed since then. Most say he'll just fade away pretty soon."

"I've heard that too, but I don't believe it."

"Why?"

"I know it might sound foolish, but it's my husband. He supported Hitler in the beginning, until the putsch..."

"That's what got you started in all this." Sam interjected.

"Yes. Well, Gunther let it all drop after Hitler was arrested, but lately he's started listening again. It seems that Hitler has changed his approach. He's not as..."

"Reactionary?"

"Yes. I think he's just changed tactics to appeal to more people. I'm not really sure, but that's the feeling I get when I listen to Gunther's friends."

"So what is your question Amalie?"

"Sam, I can't tell you everything, because I just think that the fewer people who know what I'm doing, the better. Not that I don't trust you..."

"I take it you're going to start looking into things again."

"Yes, but this time there is a difference. I think I may have a connection in Hitler's family. He's always gone to great lengths to keep his past under wraps... Have you read his book?"

"I tried, but it was such meandering drivel..."

"Absolutely," Amalie concurred, "but I forced myself to read it all and he never talks about his family except for brief mentions of his mother and father..."

"So you think he has something to hide?"

"I'm hoping."

"What do you want from me?"

"I need some advice. When I went out before, all I had to go by was gravestones and church records."

"Did you find anything?"

"There was one discrepancy in particular..." Amalie stopped, realizing how easy it would be to tell everything to Sam, but he noticed the look on her face as she stopped.

"Never mind." he said, "It's not important that I know the details. What advice do you want?"

"Sam, what would be considered proof? Do you have any ideas what I might be looking for?"

Sam laughed at this. "You can't tell me what you're looking for and now you want me to tell you what you're looking for."

Amalie smiled weakly at the paradox, but didn't comment.

"All right then," Sam said thoughtfully as he stroked his chin and looked up at the ceiling, "As near as I can figure, you must be talking about some scandal in his family... perhaps heredity... Well, if you're looking for his family, I can only think of a couple of sources that would go back more than two generations. You mentioned headstones and church records. Beyond that, the only sorts of records for that time would probably be a family Bible, or if their was any land ownership, a will. If the family was important, there could be city records, but if they lived in a village or small town, chances are that there would be no reliable town records. There might be tax records... other than that I wouldn't know."

Geli Raubal did accompany Amalie on the trip to Vienna on a Friday morning some two weeks later. Geli went directly to her mother's house while Amalie met with the retired archeologist.

Everything in the Raubal house was covered for storage, so Geli took a room at a small hotel nearby for her and Amalie to share that night. Amalie arrived at the house some four hours later and when she knocked on the door, it swung open and she just walked in, looking around as she slowly followed Geli's singing upstairs to one of the two small bedrooms. Geli was startled when she looked up at the doorway to see Amalie standing there.

"That didn't take very long" Geli said pleasantly.

"No..." Amalie said with a hint of defeat in her voice.

"Didn't things go well?"

"They went well enough..." Amalie admitted, "I just took a look at this old man who had never written a book before and probably never will again..."

"You think you gave in too easily?"

"Maybe a bit."

"So," Geli began facetiously, "You probably should have pushed his face into the ground and forced him to take half of what he wanted."

"You're absolutely right!" Amalie said with a laugh as she pointed a finger at Geli to punctuate the point.

Amalie sat beside Geli who was going through her things. They discussed Geli's treasures, Amalie asking about different things as Geli set them aside and explained the history behind her prizes. This came from the fair in Linz, that was a gift from the first boy who ever kissed her, and so on. It was clear that Geli planned on staying with Uncle Alf for quite awhile and she wanted to bring prized childhood momentos back to Germany to make it more like home.

"Are we going to try to take everything with us?" Amalie asked.

"of course" Geli rejoined.

"I mean why don't you get some boxes and pack it up to ship as freight to Berchtesgaden."

"That sounds like a good idea" Geli agreed, "Let's get some

crates now so I can pack things as I go through them."

"If you don't mind, I'd really like to just take off my shoes and sit for awhile ." Amalie said as she dropped a shoe and started to rub her foot.

"You wait here then. I'll be back in a few minutes."

When Amalie had visited Spital years before and asked about Alois Hitler, Adolf Hitler's father, the local people pointed out a house there and mentioned Alois' daughter and son-in-law. Angela Raubal, Geli's mother, was that daughter. She was Alois' daughter by his first wife and she had married Leo Raubal. They had moved to Vienna some time after that.

Amalie hadn't had a chance to get into that house in Spital, but now she felt that if such a record as a family Bible existed for the Hitler family, she might be able to it in this apartment in Vienna. That was why she had contrived to have Geli leave the house so that she might look the apartment over.

Amalie started methodically going from room to room, checking for any books at all. Geli had to go to a couple of places looking for boxes and ended up walking to the train station where they had crates for sale at the freight window. It was a little awkward carrying the boxes back to the house and all told, Amalie had about an hour to go through the house uninterrupted, but even so she couldn't find what she was looking for.

Geli didn't suspect anything as she cheerfully pushed her way into the house with the boxes falling about her. She started recounting her adventure of finding the crates as she went into the kitchen and started digging under the sink for a hammer to open the empty boxes. She then opened the door off the kitchen, complaining how stuffy the house was after being closed up for the past couple of months. When Geli started walking back to the living room, a breeze caught the door and slammed it shut so she went back to open the door again, this time reaching up on a shelf in the closet by the door and pulling down an old box which she used to prop the door open.

Amalie helped Geli pack up her things in the boxes and then nailed the lids on as Geli finished labeling the boxes for delivery.

"There! that's all done" Geli said as she fumbled through her pockets for keys "I suppose we better lock up."

"Don't forget the kitchen" Amalie said, reminding Geli of the other door.

"Wouldn't that be a joke! Take the time to lock the front door and leave the back door wide open." Geli said as she breezed into the kitchen.

"Mother would kill me if she saw that!" she called out to Amalie in the other room.

"Saw what?" Amalie asked, humoring Geli as she rattled on.

"Using that old Bible to prop open the door."

Amalie just smiled, but her heart leapt as she took a couple of quick steps toward the kitchen just in time to see Geli pick up the old, hand-made wooden box and put it back on the shelf in the closet.

"Well, I have some friends I promised to meet..." Geli said as they both headed for the front door, "Would you like to come along?"

"No. I promised my sister I would stop by."

"Oh, you have relatives here."

"My sister and brother-in-law and their daughters."

"Do you come often then?"

"No, not at all. As a matter of fact I haven't seen my sister in ten years."

"Ten years?"

Amalie was a little embarrassed. It had really been more like twelve years, but she thought just saying ten sounded better. "I know... It sounds terrible, but when our mother died when we were young, we grew apart. Eleonore left home when she was seventeen to marry and... well, months become years and then you find it's been five and then ten."

"I always wished I had had a sister."

"There are no guarantees Geli."

"What?"

"I wish my sister and I could have been more... I wish we could have gotten along, but it just didn't work out that way. Just because we were sisters wasn't enough to make us best friends."

"Don't you like her at all?"

"Certainly I... I mean, she is my sister. I love her like a sister, but she just isn't the sort of person I'd choose as a friend if we weren't related."

"Ten years?" Geli repeated with a note of astonishment, "Well, I hope you have a good reunion. I'll see you later at the hotel."

This was the first time Amalie had been to Vienna since the war.

She had visited Eleonore and Louis soon after they had married and moved into a dingy little apartment there. It was an awkward visit. Amalie had thought she would stay with them for the two days, but Eleonore insisted there wasn't enough room and told Amalie very pointedly that she must find a hotel room. The visit ended on an even more unpleasant note as they got into an argument which culminated in Eleonore shouting at Amalie that Amalie was her sister, not her mother. Even though apologies had been exchanged and the two corresponded regularly, there were still buried resentments between them. After all It wasn't just Amalie who hadn't visited Eleonore in ten years, Eleonore hadn't made the trip to Munich either.

Amalie mentioned in a letter that she would be in Vienna on business and Eleonore said it would be the perfect chance for her to stop by. Amalie had never even seen Eleonore's daughters, three-year-old Rachel and five-year-old Sophie.

"Amalie!" Louis said as he embraced his sister-in-law in a great bear hug. Amalie couldn't help staring. He had lost a great deal of hair and put on considerable weight since she had last seen him, but even so he looked better than when he was younger. He had looked so strict and humorless back then with his large black-rimmed eyeglasses at the top of a triangular face with long wiry black hair growing out of control. Now the features had softened as they expanded and the brass of his wire-rimmed glasses complemented his slightly tanned pinkish complexion.

Louis and Eleonore's apartment was much nicer than the one Amalie had visited ten years before.

"Louis... how are you?"

"Wonderful. Things are wonderful. Come, you've got to meet the girls."

"Where's Eleonore?

"You just missed her. I'm surprised you two didn't run into each other on the stairs. She went out for coffee. We don't drink much and she forgot to check and then when she went to make some, we were out. She'll only be a minute. It's funny, she said you'd come while she was gone."

"It's always like that. A watched pot..." Amalie interjected, trying to slow down Louis' rapid-fire ramblings.

"Yes, that's right" he continued as he ushered Amalie into the living room, "Never boils... never boils."

He stopped in the doorway and drew in a loud breath. "Well," he said as he smiled proudly, "here are the girls."

It was obvious that the pretty little girls had been told to sit and wait quietly until their Aunt Amalie came, as though they were prized possessions on display.

Seeing the two girls fidgeting as they waited for inspection reminded Amalie of herself and Eleonore when they were young girls.

"This is Rachel" Louis bubbled as his daughters stood up, "and the oldest there is Sophie. Come girls. Give your Aunt Amalie a kiss."

Eleonore came in just as Amalie knelt down and took the two girls in her arms, in more of a gathering gesture than an embrace, and Rachel and Sophie offered up their obligatory kisses.

"So, you've met my little darlings."

"Eleonore..." Amalie said as she abruptly stood up, leaving Rachel and Sophie in mid-kiss. She was stunned. Eleonore had put on weight too, but that wasn't what shocked Amalie. Eleonore looked just like Ruth, just like their mother had looked in those happier days so long before.

Back in Munich, Friedrich, Klaus and Gunther were having a reunion at the Sterneckerbräu on Herrnstrasse.

"Here's to your return!" Klaus said as he raised his beer stein to toast Friedrich.

"It's been a long time" Gunther mused, "Remember that night we first met the Fuhrer?"

"Of course. How could anyone forget?" Friedrich replied, "Just about ten years ago now... You were with him in '23, weren't you?"

"Yes," Klaus said. "That was when this one left!" he continued, referring to Gunther's departure from the party.

"I thought it was over." Gunther said defensively, "The police and army against us, Hitler in jail, the Deutschmark stabilized... It just didn't seem to make a difference anymore."

"Just wait," Klaus replied, "the time will come again when it will make a difference."

"Are you thinking of rejoining?" Friedrich asked Gunther, ready to sell him on the party and its war against Bolshevism.

"I'm older now. I choose my battles more carefully. It's not enough to fight just for the sake of fighting."

"It sounds like you've grown fond of the republic" Klaus said with an air of contempt.

"Oh come now Klaus! Having von Hindenburg as president is not like having Ebert or Eisner running the country."

"But it's still a republic. A confused, pathetic, rambling collection of committees" Klaus declared with a finality that just left Gunther exasperated at his friends' intransigence.

"Can't we talk about something else?" Gunther asked.

The next morning, a bright and sunny Saturday morning, Amalie and Geli got up at about nine o'clock and had a leisurely breakfast at the hotel before getting ready for the train home.

"So... How was your sister?"

"Good. Very good. It was probably the nicest visit we've ever had. She has two darling little girls and her husband has become..." Amalie paused as she looked for an explanation.

What?" Geli asked impatiently.

"I don't know. He just seemed so happy to see me and they were all so nice. Now I wish I had gone sooner."

"You see! People can change." Geli said triumphantly.

"I'll tell you what." Amalie began, changing the subject, "Let's split up the work... You go to the station and send the freight man out and I'll go to the house and wait for him and then ride back to the station with him."

"That sounds fair enough." Geli replied, "Here's the house key. And for God's sake, don't forget to lock up like I almost did."

Amalie hurried off down the street to Geli's house. Once she got there, she found she was much more nervous than she thought she would be. She went through the house directly to the back closet in the kitchen where she took out the box and opened it. There was the old Bible just like Geli said. It was stuffed with papers and there was something that looked like a family tree in the front pages, but she didn't have time to go over it. She had thought about it the night before and decided that the best thing to do was to send it off to her father in Salzburg where she could go over it in her own time when she managed to get away for a weekend to visit him. That way it would be safe and hopefully, with the Raubal home unoccupied, it would be some time before it was even discovered that the book was missing.

Things went well when the freight man came. He had a number of packages on the wagon already, so even if Geli somehow saw the wagon come into the station, the extra package wouldn't be noticed and he also asked for payment when he picked up the packages which allowed Amalie to pay for the extra package out of sight of Geli.

"Did everything go all right?" Geli asked when she met Amalie walking into the train station.

"Yes. I made sure everything was locked up. Here's the key."

Back in Munich on that Saturday morning, the house was quiet. Gertrude had made breakfast, done her marketing and then gone off to visit friends for the day. Gunther sat reading his newspaper while Jakob lay on the floor with the parts of the newspaper which his father had discarded. When Gunther finished, he put the paper down and watched his son. Jakob was intent on an article about a soccer game as he chased the story from one page to the next and Gunther watched his every move.

The incident in Berchtesgaden had surprised Gunther. It had awakened in him something intangible about the passage of time and how he had taken things for granted. These were the good times and he just assumed they would always go on like this, but with the attack on Jakob, with the frightening thought of losing his son, he began to think about a lot of things. Who was his son?

Wasn't that funny? It had all seemed so clear to him before. You grow up, get married, have children and then they grow up and get married and so on. A neat, clear cut line of succession of the human race, but now he suddenly began to wonder who his son was and who he might become. It was almost like an identity crisis, except that the crisis was Gunther's and the identity was Jakob's! Gunther was just beginning to realize his changing role in his son's life and his son's changing role in his life. Jakob was becoming a different and distinct person who would become more and more separate from his father and Gunther was just awakening to that inevitable truth.

None of this is any great revelation to those who have thought about it, but at that moment it was stunning to Gunther. Gunther's father had been cool and distant and Gunther grew up thinking that that was just how father's were supposed to be.

Another thought hit Gunther as he sat there watching his son. It had been eleven years since Gunther had left his father's home and he had never heard from his mother or father since and he couldn't remember ever bringing up the subject of his parents in conversation in his home. It was as though they were dead and Gunther realized that he wanted something different than that for himself and his son.

Many of Gunther's childhood memories were unpleasant. His father was strict and unyielding towards him and his brother and sister. They lived in fear. Any transgression brought swift and cruel retribution. Gunther swore as a child that he would not be like that and he had done well to keep his promise. He had rarely raised a hand to Jakob and on those occasions when he felt he had to hit his son, it never amounted to more than a couple of swats on the backside with his hand.

"So... what do you have planned for today?" Gunther asked.

"Nothing special" Jakob said as he looked up.

"We could do something together..."

"Like what?"

"Let's go out to the park and just see how it goes..." Gunther answered.

Jakob smiled and popped up from the floor, picking up the newspaper. This was a bit unusual, but he liked the idea of spending the day with his father, just the two of them. He started for the front door, thinking they would walk the couple of blocks to the park by their house, but Gunther called him back.

"Let's go out this way" Gunther directed as he headed for the back door.

"Are we taking the car just to go to the park?"

"I thought we'd go to the English garden and then pick up your mother. Her train will be arriving at about two o'clock."

They talked of superfluous things as they drove; the weather, sports and things they saw on the road as they drove. Before they knew it, they were pulling up next to the park. They walked for a while until they unexpectedly came upon Klaus Grunewald.

"Klaus!" Gunther called out, "What brings you out? Where are Katrina and the boys?"

"They're at home" Klaus said as he gave Gunther a good-natured slap on the back, "I'm here with that group" he continued, pointing to a group of boys about the same age as Jakob. "It's my turn to watch over them."

"Who?" Gunther asked.

"The youth group... Hitlerjungend."

This didn't mean much to Jakob as he looked on, watching the other boys as they were moving bales of hay and unrolling some kind of small banners. "What are they doing, Uncle Klaus?"

"Well, this week we're going to set up an archery range."

"Archery?"

"Yes. You know," Klaus insisted, "bow and arrows. They shoot at targets on the hay bales."

"Bow and arrows! Like the Indians in America?"

"Now you have his interest" Gunther said with a smile as he put his arm around his sons shoulder, "he's been reading those books about cowboys and Indians for years."

"Of course the Indians weren't the only ones to use bow and arrows..." Klaus said professorially "the bow and arrow have been in use in Germany for well over a thousand years."

Jakob took Klaus' declaration as gospel and was eager to try shooting a bow and arrow. "Can I try it Uncle Klaus?"

"I don't know Jakob... I mean, since you aren't a member of the group."

Gunther knew what Klaus was pushing for. He wanted Gunther to rejoin the party and then Jakob could enroll in the Hitlerjungend.

"I suppose we could let you try... At least today..." Klaus continued teasingly, and with that, Jakob ran over to the group of boys and immediately blended in with the cacophony and motion.

"Should we help?" Gunther asked as he watched one of the bales of hay fall over for the third time as some of the boys tried again to make it stand up so that they could tie the target onto it.

"No... no. That's the point" Klaus said passively as he watched, "They're supposed to do it themselves. Youth leading youth. I'm just here to make sure nothing goes wrong."

When the targets were finally set up, the boys separated into six squads of three. The other boys told Jakob that they had done this before and that they gave each ring of the bull's-eye a different point value, just like on a dart board, with each boy getting three tries and then the scores of each squad would be compared. Jakob was teamed with two boys named Johann and Thomas.

Thomas was the first to go on their squad and Jakob watched closely as he slid the arrow down the grip until it came to the bowstring and he fit the fork at the end of the arrow on the string. Even then, the first time Jakob had ever been this close to a bow and arrow, Jakob noticed how awkward Thomas was with the bow as he held the bow across his chest, completely unaware that the arrow was dangerously aimed down the line of other boys while he tried to line up the arrow, taking a long time as he got ready to shoot. When Thomas was finally ready to shoot, he drew back the arrow quickly and the string seemed to slip out of his fingers as the arrow arched up and over the target, not only missing the target, but completely missing the bale of hay and stabbing into the hill beyond.

Thomas was not the only one to suffer this embarrassing fate as one of the other boys down the line also overshot his target, but Thomas grimaced and stomped his foot, swearing under his breath. He then followed the same ritual of slowly setting the arrow and quickly sending it off, this time catching the outermost ring of the target and raising his arms in a silent victory cheer. Inspired, Thomas then quickly dispatched his third arrow, hitting the bail of hay just below the target.

Once Thomas was done, everyone waited until a couple of the other boys finished with their arrows so that the first set of archers could all go out and retrieve the arrows for the second set of boys.

Johann was a bit shy and was more than willing to let Jakob go next. Jakob had learned from Thomas' failings and decided that Thomas' downfall had been his impatience. Jakob thought of his Indians on horseback as he made sure to aim the arrow at the ground when he slid it across the bow's grip and then pulled it up, lining the shaft of the arrow up with an imaginary line that he drew in his minds eye linking himself to the bull's-eye. Before he let go, he thought of how the arrow had arched down when Thomas had shot and decided to raise his aim slightly. The bow was hard to pull, forty pounds of draw, but he forced himself to pinch the fork of the arrow and hold the string as long as he could until he was sure that he was lined up and then he quickly released the arrow, as quickly as one might snap one's fingers. The arrow suddenly took flight, but not like Thomas' arrow. This arrow didn't arc high up into the air and then slip lazily into the bale of hay. It drove straight and hard, straight and hard into the very center of the bright red bull's-eye!

Jakob was surprised, and yet he wasn't. He somehow knew instinctively that his was the right way to do it, but having never shot an arrow before, he hadn't really expected to succeed at the first try.

Gunther, who was talking with Klaus and only watching Jakob out of the corner of his eye, suddenly tapped Klaus on the shoulder and Klaus, who had his back to the boys, turned to see what Gunther was pointing at just in time to see Jakob release another arrow with a deadly accuracy that put the second arrow slightly below the first, but still securely within the red bull's-eye. Before the two men could walk over to Jakob, he had mechanically repeated his performance with his final arrow, setting it above the other two, almost in the bull's-eye in the next ring.

Johann and Thomas, especially Thomas, were stunned at the display and finally Thomas managed to comment. "You must have been shooting for a long time!"

"No," Jakob said coolly, "this was my first time."

"The mighty Orion!" Gunther said as he tousled his son's hair.

"Excellent Jakob! Excellent!" Klaus said.

"I didn't get the last one all the way in the bull's-eye" Jakob said apologetically at which point Klaus and Gunther laughed.

"Jakob!" Gunther said, "Don't be so hard on yourself! This is incredible for your first time."

Jakob looked up and smiled meekly and Gunther couldn't help but wrap his arm around his son, pulling Jakob close. By that time everyone else was done shooting and a number of the other boys had gathered around Jakob's target as Jakob went out to retrieve the arrows for Johann.

Gunther was proud of his son in a way that he had never been before. Both Gunther and Jakob realized that this was something different between them. An acknowledgment by Gunther that his son was not just a child, but there was a person there, a person Gunther could like, could actually love. And Jakob craved this love and acceptance from his father, and would do anything to achieve it.

"You should really join us" Klaus said to Jakob, "Hitlerjungend could help you develop your talents and make you even better and stronger."

Jakob looked up at Gunther. Gunther knew that his son didn't understand everything that this suggestion entailed. He wondered if Jakob had even made the connection between 'Hitlerjungend' and the nazi party. Gunther knew Amalie could never accept it and he knew that the Hitlerjungend would not accept Jakob if they knew his mother was Jewish.

"Do you think he could get in?" Gunther asked Klaus.

"It could be arranged." Klaus said thoughtfully, for he was certainly aware of the difficulties involving Amalie, "but you would have to become a member of the party again."

215

Jakob wasn't really sure why he wasn't supposed to tell his mother about Hitlerjungend, but it seemed like a grown-up thing between his father, Klaus and himself. The kind of a confidence that men would keep among themselves, for whatever reason.

"I can tell mother about the bull's-eyes, right Vati?" Jakob asked later as they sat in the Hauptbahnhof waiting for Amalie's train to come in.

"Yes" Gunther said as he watched the crowd milling about them in the station, "just don't mention the club... just say we came upon a couple of boys and they let you try your hand."

Amalie was traveling alone after Geli changed trains to go to Berchtesgaden. She hadn't expected to be met at the station and so was about to shout when she felt someone tugging at her overnight bag until she realized it was Jakob. He had seen her getting off the train and ran to help her with her things.

"How was everything?" Gunther asked

"It went well."

"...and Geli?"

"Fine. It was nice having someone to talk with on the train. And what did you two do last night?"

"This morning I got to shoot a bow and arrow!" Jakob interrupted.

"You did?" Amalie said, matching her son's excitement the way a mother does when she sees that spark in her child's eyes.

"Yes." Jakob continued, "Some boys in the park let me shoot."

"He made a bull's-eye." Gunther added.

"Two!" Jakob corrected, "Almost three!"

"Just like Orion." Gunther rejoined.

"Who is Orion?" Jakob asked his father as they all began to walk out of the station.

"Orion was a great hunter in Greek mythology. When he died, he became a constellation of stars."

"How did he do that?"

"I don't know. That's just the way the myth goes." Gunther said, hoping to avoid a long line of questions.

"Let me see..." Amalie began as they walked, taking over from Gunther as she tried to recall the legend, "Orion was blinded by... Oenopion, I think it was... And then he had a child lead him back to the light of the rising Sun and there he regained his sight."

"Why did he blind him?" Jakob asked.

"Who?" Amalie asked as Jakob had broken her train of thought.

"Why was Orion blinded?"

"Oh. Orion had attacked Oenopion's daughter."

Jakob let the subject drop as they got into the car. Amalie was surprised when Jakob jumped into the front seat with his father instead of getting in the back with her, but she didn't say anything about it.

"The trip reminded me how long it's been since I visited father" Amalie said as they turned onto Goethestrasse, "Jakob, maybe we should take the train to Salzburg next weekend."

Jakob just looked at Gunther without answering, as though he wanted his father to rescue him.

"Well," Gunther started hesitantly, "I think Jakob has an appointment at the park next Saturday."

"Oh, I see" Amalie said with a hint of disappointment, "maybe the week after."

When the week had almost passed, it became obvious to Amalie that Jakob didn't want to go with her to visit his grandfather although he never came right out and said it. He just kept avoiding the subject and coming up with excuses until Amalie finally decided to go alone to Salzburg two weeks later.

"Did you get the package?" were the first words Amalie spoke to her father when she got off the train. She had written a note and put it in the box on top of the Bible in which she asked Ethan not to go through the book because she wanted to be the first to go through it. She also explained that they couldn't discuss it in any way through letters or telephone conversations.

"It arrived almost two weeks ago."

"Good" Amalie said breathlessly as she rushed Ethan through the train station, suddenly stopping when they got outside as she realized that she didn't know where the car was.

"This way." Ethan said dryly after waiting to see how long it would take his daughter to see that she would have to follow him instead of leading him, "The car is over here."

"What is this all about? Where did you get this Bible and why is it such a secret?"

"I stole it" Amalie answered, letting her words land heavily and plainly on the muffled roar of the cars engine.

Ethan didn't take this admission easily. It seemed so foreign coming from Amalie and yet she said it a defiance that said it was necessary.

"You stole it? From who? Why would you steal a Bible?"

"I'm not sure, but I think it's what I've been looking for in this Hitler affair. I didn't get a chance to go over it. I sent it off as quickly as I could. Right under her nose."

"Whose nose?"

"Geli. Hitler's niece. I found it at her house while she was packing and I don't think they'll notice it missing for quite some time."

"Well, I'd say you're taking quite a chance, but then again, it is just a family Bible. Even if they did trace it to you, what would they do?"

"That depends on what I find. It may mean everything."

There was little conversation after that. Even when they got to her father's house, Amalie, after putting her bag in her room, immediately, silently, cleared the table in the dining room. She then got the box from Ethan along with a stack of writing paper for notes as she prepared to go through the book. Ethan stopped as he was walking through the dining room when he saw Amalie just sitting and staring at the box. She hadn't even lifted the cover yet. She just sat there with her note paper and pencils with the box in front of her.

"Is something wrong?" Ethan asked.

Amalie looked up at him and tried to smile. "I don't know why I'm so nervous." She then looked back at the box. "Yes I do." she rejoined, "This might be what I've been looking for all these years. Success or failure. And I'm not sure I'll know one from the other."

She then let out a deep sigh and took the lid off the box, carefully lifting out the book and all the papers that had been pressed into the pages from one generation to the next.

The cover was a bright red which had aged to a dull reddish brown. It had aged as it's owners had, but instead of wrinkles, there were cracks in the cover and binding and the edges of the pages were withered, brown and brittle.

The first pages showed the names of family members starting with Annaliese and Edmund Hiedler who were married in 1818 and their children including Johann Georg Hiedler and Johann Nepomuk Hiedler. The next generations showed Johann Nepomuk's daughter

Johanna, who married Johann Pölzl and had a daughter named Klara Pölzl, but that page ended with that generation and seemed to show only one side of the family. Amalie tried to figure out why Geli's parents would have had this Bible and then she turned the page and that next page started with Johann Georg Hiedler and Maria Schicklgruber married on May tenth of 1842 and below them was Alois Hiedler without a birth-date. It showed Alois' marriage to Franziska Matzelsberger in 1883 and their children, Alois junior and Angela. Angela married Leo Raubal and had two children; Angela's daughter who was also named Angela and nicknamed Geli, and Leo Raubal junior.

This was the sort of thing that one could look at over and over again, trying to draw lines between the two parts of the family on those two separate pages. The name Klara suddenly hit her. "Of course." she thought to herself, "Klara! Adolf Hitler's mother."

How strange that Alois and Franziska were on one page and Klara, without mention of Alois as her husband, was on the other. The family must not have wanted to acknowledge Alois' multiple marriages. Amalie suddenly realized, after studying the entries, that the first page clearly had different people making entries from one generation to the next as there were obvious differences in the writing styles, but the second page, although different inks were used from generation to generation, was all written by the same person.

"Why?" she silently asked herself.

Since she had stolen the Bible she couldn't ask anyone in the family about the discrepancies.

She called out to her father.

"What is it?" Ethan asked nervously as he quickly came into the room, "What's wrong?"

Amalie realized that she wasn't the only one on edge. "Nothing serious. I just had to ask you a question." She then went over the pages and the different generations and explained how she thought one person had made all the entries on the second page.

"My guess would be" Ethan said thoughtfully, "someone omitted some skeletons in the family closet and then someone else tried to put together the missing pieces..." He then arched his left eyebrow as he looked up from the Bible. "It sounds just like what you're trying to do."

"Oh father! Don't do that!"

Ethan was caught off guard. "Do what?" he asked.

"That thing you do with your eyebrows... It looks like two unfriendly caterpillars wrestling on your forehead."

This was a fairly recent development in Ethan's physiognomy as he was now fifty-six years old and his eyebrows had seemed to suddenly start growing out of control and becoming excessively bushy.

"I don't think that's relevant to the subject at hand." he said.

"I know" Amalie countered with a smirk, "but I think you're right. That must be it. If I were to guess, I would say it was Geli's mother, Angela, who filled in that second page. After all, the Bible was in her house and that page shows her side of the family."

"That makes sense" Ethan said as he turned back to the Bible. "What are these other papers?" he asked as he started to page through the book.

"I don't know, I haven't gotten that far yet."

"Would you mind if I helped?"

"No. That would be fine... but let's go slowly. I want to check each piece of paper."

They then started going over every page of the Bible and each piece of paper. Amalie wanted to make sure there was no writing in the Bible, no clues written on the pages of text or in the margins, and they looked over each piece of paper as they came to it. There were tax receipts and letters, letters from sons to mothers and mothers to their mothers, letters about the weather or about births and deaths, but there didn't seem to be anything monumental. They were halfway through when they came to the thickest letter, still in it's original envelope, in the same place within the book where it had been for many years where it caused the most severe crack in the binding of the book of any of the breaks. It was addressed in a beautiful, elaborate German script; "To be delivered to Alois Hiedler solely upon the death of Johann Nepomuk Hiedler"

Amalie looked up at her father with a look in her eyes that was a combination of excitement and trepidation. Could this be it?

"A will?" Ethan offered.

Amalie gently opened the envelope, handling the pages as if they were the petals of a fragile flower. The text of the pages was written by the same careful hand that had addressed the envelope.

"The following document represents the deathbed confession of

Johann Nepomuk Hiedler as told to brother Marcus of the monastery of Weitra in November of 1881" Amalie read aloud to her father.

"He had his confession written down and addressed it to his son?" Ethan asked in confusion.

"Alois wasn't his son." Amalie corrected "He was his nephew."

"Perhaps not" Ethan said slowly, "maybe that's the confession."

Amalie was clearly surprised by this suggestion and quickly immersed herself in the papers, handing each page to her father so that he could read them as soon as she finished.

The document started by relating a rambling litany of Johann Nepomuk Hiedler's recent sins in business dealings and other small affairs and then as he apparently became lucid for a period of time he began to talk about his mother and father. His father was from the Waldviertel, but his mother came from Graz. He made it clear that he was only doing this so that Alois would know and then Alois could do whatever he wanted with the papers. Johann just wanted to get it off his chest, to tell the truth before he died. His mother Annaliese, was a Jewess. Her maiden name was Frankenburger and she came to Spital from Graz when she ran away from home when she was seventeen.

Annaliese was unhappy with her home and had thought about running away many times, but it wasn't until the maid, Maria Schicklgruber, was leaving that she got up the courage. Annaliese and Maria had become friends and when fifteen-year-old Maria decided to return home to the Waldviertel district, Annaliese went with her. Eight years later, Annaliese married Edmund, Johann's father.

Amalie read all this with interest, but there was nothing shocking until she got to the fourth page. It was there that Johann Nepomuk Hiedler said that when he was seventeen years old, he and the woman who was once his mothers maid, Maria Schicklgruber, who was twice Johann's age, "knew each other" as the monk who was taking the notes so delicately put it. It was during this single episode that Alois Schicklgruber was conceived. Maria agreed to raise the child alone with the assurance of her friend Annaliese, Johann's mother, that Annaliese would give her money on a regular basis to help her raise the boy. Annaliese had been an only child and had inherited a substantial amount of money upon her father's death in Graz even though she had run away from that home so many years before and it was this money that she shared with Maria.

Later, when Johann Nepomuk Hiedler got married, he convinced his brother Johann Georg Hiedler to marry Maria so that she wouldn't be alone and Alois wouldn't be without a father. In consideration, Johann Nepomuk agreed to forego his share of the remaining inheritance from his mother when the time came. Maria died five years after she and the brother married and Johann Georg wandered off a short time after that, leaving Alois to live with the family of his real father, Johann Nepomuk, even though Alois didn't know the truth. Alois ran away from home when he was thirteen, leaving house number thirty-six in Spital never to return, never to retrieve the confession after Johann Nepomuk Hiedler's death.

It had been Johann Nepomuk Hiedler who, as an old man, pressured church authorities to legitimize Alois Schicklgruber as Alois Hitler in the name of Johann Georg Hiedler when Alois was in his late thirties. Alois apparently never knew the real motive for Johann Nepomuk's actions, Alois thinking that since he had become somewhat successful as a customs official that the old man wanted to claim him as a member of the family for the aggrandizement of the family name.

Amalie came up for air. She had gotten so immersed in each turn of this document that her head was swimming by the time she was done reading. This was the key! This was the explanation that tied the two parts of the family together. Hitler's father, Alois, had in fact married his own niece as one of the rumors had suggested when Amalie first went to Spital so many years before. It was the confusion of Alois' paternity that gave rise to the contradicting rumor that his third wife had been a cousin, not his niece, but here was proof and now the other rumors, the rumors of Jewish blood were clear. They had said that Maria, Alois' mother, Adolf Hitler's grandmother, had worked for Jews in Graz and that the son of her employers had gotten her pregnant, but it was Annaliese who had come with Maria to Spital and then had a son, Johann Nepomuk, who got Maria pregnant. So the rumor was true! Johann Nepomuk was, on his mother's side of the family, the son of the Frankenburger Jews from Graz who had gotten Maria Schicklgruber pregnant!

And this confession was the only proof of all this. A single piece of paper, a deathbed confession unregistered with any legal authority, written by a monk almost fifty years before. Below the well crafted

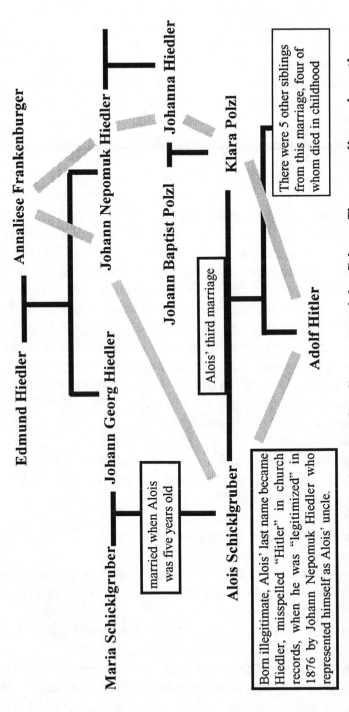

Edmund Hiedler

Annaliese Frankenburger

Johann Nepomuk Hiedler

Johanna Hiedler

Johann Georg Hiedler

Johann Baptist Polzl

Klara Polzl

Maria Schicklgruber

married when Alois was five years old

Alois' third marriage

There were 5 other siblings from this marriage, four of whom died in childhood

Adolf Hitler

Alois Schicklgruber

Born illegitimate, Alois' last name became Hiedler, misspelled "Hitler" in church records, when he was "legitimized" in 1876 by Johann Nepomuk Hiedler who represented himself as Alois' uncle.

Part of Adolf's family tree that Amalie diagrammed for Ethan. The gray lines show the connections that Amalie made from the Johann Nepomuk Hiedler deathbed confession.

223

script of the monk from Weitra, it was signed by the shaky hand of the dying man. "May god forgive me my sins and have mercy on my soul. Johann Nepomuk Hiedler. September 14, 1881."

"I don't know what all this means" Ethan said to Amalie when he finished the final page and she sat considering her next step.

"By itself, not much" Amalie started to explain, "because it speaks only in terms of Alois and his place in the Hiedler family. This becomes important when you go to the next generation, to Adolf Hitler. Hitler and Hiedler are the same family"

"Yes, you told me that before" Ethan interrupted.

"The importance," Amalie continued, "depends on how important anti-semitism is to the nazis. They seem to have eased up. This document, with the other things I've found, says that not only did Adolf Hitler's father have a Jewish father, his mother also had a Jewish grandfather and they were both the same man." Ethan still looked confused, so Amalie tried rephrasing the declaration, "Johann Nepomuk Hiedler, the son of Annaliese Frankenburger of Graz who was Jewish, was both Hitler's maternal great-grandfather and his paternal grandfather and this confession is proof of it." Suddenly Ethan's eyebrows started challenging each other again as he began to understand the significance of Amalie's discovery.

They sat in silence, going over the pages once more until Ethan finally broke the silence. "What are you going to do with it?"

"I'm not sure... What do you think?"

"The newspapers?"

"No," Amalie said quickly, as she had considered it before and dismissed the thought, "That would just be a splash on the front page that Hitler could brush away."

"Then what?"

"It might be worth more as a weapon."

"You mean blackmail?"

"His fear of what this might do to his career might be greater than any actual damage if it were made public, after all, he's the one who's the fanatic."

"That sounds like quite a gamble..." Ethan said with obvious concern in his voice, " How would you approach him?"

"That's the catch. The timing. And the messenger. I don't think it's necessary now. It may never be necessary" Amalie mused, "He's lost a lot of popularity. Some say he's already finished in politics."

"That's what I've heard" Ethan said, finally speaking his mind, "I know this meant a lot to you before, but I keep hearing that since the putsch he's just faded farther and farther into the background. He's just a... a caricature. A joke. A novelty whose time has past."

Amalie felt that her father's outburst was belittling.

Ethan saw the look in her eyes as he continued. "Amalie, I love you and I care deeply about you... maybe now more than ever, and I just feel I have to tell you that you might be obsessed with this beyond reason. Maybe it was your trouble with Gunther in the past that kept you searching, but even that's over, isn't it?"

Ethan waited for his daughter to answer.

"Isn't it? You told me he walked away from them years ago."

"Yes" she said quietly.

"Then what is it? Why would you go on about this?"

Amalie said nothing. She did something she had never done before when she and her father had a disagreement. She just got up and walked away, without a word, going up to her bed and lying down to rest.

Ethan didn't know what to make of it. When he used the word "obsessed", he meant it in a casual way like someone who plays cards too often or gets too engrossed in a hobby, but this behavior seemed even more serious. It seemed like an obsession that no one could challenge and that frightened him.

Ethan watched his daughter go up the stairs and, not knowing what else to do, went in and made dinner for the two of them.

Over dinner they talked about publishing and Jakob and any other subject they could think of that would keep them clear of talk about the papers still spread out on the table in the other room.

The next day, Saturday, Amalie got up early and packed up the papers and the Bible in the box, keeping out the confession. She had coffee with her father and then went into town, hoping to find a photography shop that might be open. She was lucky. She stopped at the window of a shop that was closed, but saw somebody inside brush past the window and so she knocked at the door. A bespectacled eye peeked out from behind the drawn shade on the door which had the word "geschlossen"* painted in green, descending from the upper left corner of the door's window to the lower right corner. The man's finger then appeared, pointing

* Closed.

225

emphatically at the sign on the shade.

"Please!" Amalie said to the eye in the door, "It's very important."

The eye and finger disappeared and Amalie knocked again, this time knocking loudly as she called out again, "Please!" She stopped knocking as she heard the lock being turned on the door. This time a face appeared as the door opened slightly. The bespectacled eye sat with its partner below a very large, bald forehead and above a full beard and mustache with a small mouth lost somewhere in the whiskers. "Es tut mir leid, meine gnadiges Frau,"* came a strained, high voice, "but we are closed today. I am only finishing up some work on my own today."

"But please," Amalie said, using her eyes to show desperation, "I just need this document photographed."

"Yes, well, we will be open on Monday..."

"...but I have to leave tomorrow!" Amalie interrupted.

The man sighed and looked down at the thick envelope and suddenly Amalie knew that he would agree.

"It's only ten pages... Just a document... Black ink on paper." she said as she tried to convince him that it would be an easy job.

"When do you need it?"

"I need the papers today."

"No, I mean when do you need the prints?" the man said with a note of exasperation.

"Oh yes, of course...I don't know... If you can mail them..."

"Yes. How about two weeks?"

"That would be fine" Amalie said as the man opened the door and let her enter, "I'd need the negatives too."

"Of course" the man said, "we always send the negatives."

"Yes, well I just wanted to make sure in case I needed more prints later" Amalie added as she tried to cover her anxiety.

It took about thirty minutes to set up and photograph Johann's confession and Amalie had the photographs sent to Frieder and Sons in her name. She thanked the photographer profusely for accommodating her and even gave him an extra fifty schillings, causing him to smile for the first time during her visit.

"Thank you." he said as she walked towards the door, "the fact

---

* I'm sorry (literally: it does me pain), my dear woman

226

of the matter is," he added with a smile, showing gratitude for the extra consideration as she stopped while he unlocked the door for her, "I think maybe I can send these to you in one week instead of two."

"I appreciate that" Amalie said as she offered her hand and then left for her father's home. When she got there, she put the original of the confession in the box with the other papers and asked Ethan if there wasn't some place to hide it. He assured her that he had a safe place and then disappeared into the cellar.

That night and the next morning passed without incident and Amalie was soon packing for the trip home when Ethan came in.

"I have something for Jakob" he said cautiously, not sure how Amalie would feel about the gift. "It's a watch" he continued as he took it out of its box.

It was a gold pocket watch with the inscription "To Jakob on his 13th birthday from grandfather Ethan" and below that was the Hebrew spelling of the word "schema", the first word in one of the oldest and most important prayers in Judaism. Amalie said she was sure Jakob would love it. She knew that it had been meant for the bar mitzvah that never took place. Ethan had sent Jakob money on his birthday instead. Amalie guessed her father hadn't sent the watch because he thought it might be inappropriate and now he was having second thoughts.

The ride to the train station was quiet and tense. Amalie didn't say a word until Ethan parked the car and they both sat there as Ethan obviously struggled to say something.

"Thank you for your help father" Amalie said before Ethan could speak, "I hope you're not too angry with me."

Ethan smiled. "Amalie, I'm not angry. I love you. I still care about you as if you were still my little girl. I'm just worried."

"I know" Amalie said as she turned down her eyes, pretending to inspect her handbag which she held in her lap.

"Please promise me" Ethan continued, "that you won't do anything drastic without talking to me first."

Amalie looked up, into her father's eyes. "Yes, I will, but you must promise me that you will tell absolutely no one about the Bible."

"Of course not!" Ethan said defensively, "I know what this means to you." They didn't talk much once they were at the platform, but as Amalie was about to get on the train for Munich, she turned back and hugged her father before boarding.

Gertrude was the only one there when Amalie got home. She told Amalie that Gunther and Jakob had been gone all morning with Klaus and she didn't know where they were or when they would be home.

What a difference from the last time she came home. It was a long ride on the trolley from the Hauptbahnhof and it was hours before Gunther and Jakob came home. They rushed in full of laughter and good spirits.

"You two must have had a good time." Amalie said, trying to match their enthusiasm.

"We played soccer!" Jakob said excitedly.

"We?" Amalie asked, at which point Gunther smiled sheepishly. "They didn't have enough boys, so Klaus and I were the goal tenders"

"Father blocked them all." Jakob said with pride.

"Really Gunther, you should have let them win at least a few" Amalie admonished.

"I know. I got carried away. It wasn't like I was playing against the boys, it was more like playing against Klaus."

"Well, at least you had fun together."

"Absolutely." Gunther affirmed.

"Yes, let's do it again next weekend" Jakob piped in.

"We'll see." Gunther said. "but tonight, let's go out to eat."

By that time Gertrude had come into the room.

"What do you say Gertie?" Gunther continued, "A night out of the kitchen? We could try one of those Chinese restaurants by the Hauptbahnhof."

"Chinese?" Gertrude asked incredulously, "I've never eaten Chinese food. I've heard it isn't good for you."

"Isn't good for you?" Amalie exclaimed, "Why Gertie, it's just vegetables and meat cooked a little differently."

"Yes Gertie," Gunther agreed, "you should try it at least once. Let's go early and avoid the crowds."

It took longer than expected for everyone to get ready since both Gunther and Amalie felt they needed a bath, Gunther after his soccer game and Amalie after her train trip from Austria, and so the streets were crowded by the time they drove up Goethestrasse while the sun drifted down to the Munich skyline. It had been an extremely hot July day in the city and the early evening didn't bring much relief

228

from the heat. The gentle breeze streaming in through the car windows was a welcome benefit as Gunther spent almost twenty minutes looking for a place to park near a restaurant. His tenacity was finally rewarded as he came upon a car pulling away from the curb right in front of a dimly lit sign advertising "Yen Chi Loo restaurant" and Gunther quickly and expertly maneuvered the car into the parking space.

"What is 'Yen Chi Loo'?" Jakob asked once he had gotten out of the car and stood under the sign waiting for everyone else to catch up with him.

"I'm sure it's some strange Chinese concoction." Gertrude said once she had struggled out of the car and stood looking apprehensively at the sign above her, "Probably made with opium."

"That's the name of the owner." Amalie said with a smile as she took Gertrude's arm and led her down the stairs from the sidewalk to the restaurant entrance down below street level. "I can't believe you've never eaten at a Chinese restaurant." Amalie continued as they entered the restaurant which was as dimly lit as the sign on the street had been.

A waiter called to them in a strange accent, asking how many there would be and then sat them at a table crowned with a large hanging lamp. The lamp, with its large paper shade and tassels made of bright red string, hung down almost at eye level, obscuring everyone's view. Jakob reached up and brushed his hand against one of the tassels as Gunther sat down beside him.

Gunther watched with amusement as Jakob carefully studied the drawing on the lampshade. It was a stylized oriental rendering in red and black ink of oriental men and women with only a single line slashed up at an angle on either side of the nose to depict eyes and all the human figures dressed in kimonos with their black hair drawn up into a ball on top of their heads.

"How come we've never come here before?" Jakob asked of no one in particular as he again stroked one of the tassels from the lamp while still staring at the shade.

"We did." Amalie said as she unfolded her napkin and put it on her lap, "A few years ago, but you put up such a fuss that we haven't been back since."

Jakob looked at once disbelieving and ashamed of the forgotten incident, as though he had denied his mother entrance to such an exotic place by his bad manners. "I'm sorry." he said.

"I didn't mean it like that." Amalie answered, "It's just that sometimes young children are so sure that they won't like something different even before they try it... We shouldn't have brought you then. Now you're so much more mature. I'm sure you'll find something now that you like."

Jakob smiled at the compliment even though it came in such a round about way and then looked up as the waiter came to the table.

"You ready order now?" the young man asked in broken German. Gunther looked at the others and then said that they needed a few more minutes and asked the waiter to bring tea for now.

"Tea?" Jakob asked, "but father, you always drink coffee."

"It's customary," Gunther replied, "we always drink tea in a Chinese restaurant."

Jakob seemed satisfied with that answer, but all the while the question had been asked and answered Jakob had kept his eyes on the waiter as he walked away. "Did you see his eyes?" he asked quietly of his father in the tone that a young boy would use when telling a dirty joke for the first time.

"Come now." Amalie said, not so much as a scolding, but more in disbelief, "You've seen a China man before."

"No I haven't" Jakob contradicted as he shot straight up in his chair, turning towards his mother, as though his sudden improvement in posture would put his statement beyond reproach.

Amalie just looked at her son and the look was enough to cause Jakob to qualify his remark. "Well, not in real life." he said thoughtfully as though making an effort to search his memory for the truth, "I've seen them in movies and pictures, but not a real person like this."

"Well," Amalie chastised in a whisper, "You certainly know it's not polite to stare."

"Yes, of course." Gertrude piped in supportively of good manners, even though she had done her own fair share of staring, making a close inspection of the waiter's face when she thought he wasn't looking.

"But father, why do they look so strange?"

Gunther felt that Jakob was putting him in the middle and cast a quick glance at Amalie to see if she was going to correct Jakob again, but when Amalie didn't say anything, he thought he might educate the boy.

"Well," he started slowly, "first you have to understand that man is a kind of animal..." Gunther knew that in a discussion like this with Jakob, he would have to give plenty of time for questions, as Jakob had always been full of questions ever since he first learned to speak, so Gunther paused and waited, but Jakob also waited in silence.

"...and there was a man named Darwin who studied animals for a long time and learned that through the course of time, animals change. He called it evolution." Gunther paused again, but this time only for an instant, as though lending weight to his declaration rather than waiting for possible questions. "...and man, like animals, has gone through evolution, and some of the former stages of man still exist today along with modern man."

Amalie's stomach turned as she listened to Gunther's lesson in the development of man.

"Some people," Amalie interrupted, surprising Gunther who had expected that Jakob would be the only one to interrupt him, "say that the differences in man relates to the place he lives."

"Only to a point." Gunther countered, "Different lands do not account for the difference in intelligence and industry."

Amalie suddenly imagined a loud argument developing as Gunther argued nazi party line about social Darwinism. This was the moment she knew for sure that he was back in their pockets. They had him. Worst of all was that now, even right in front of her, he was teaching it to her son.

"Like the Jews?" Jakob asked innocently.

The effect that simple question from Jakob had on Amalie can hardly be described in words. It took the breath out of her. It made her head swim. She had been betrayed. Jakob had been stolen from her. She couldn't believe it and she tried to remain outwardly calm as she found herself forced, almost against her will, to ask her son: "What do you mean?"

"The way the Jews have to live off other people." Jakob said without any idea of how the statement affected his mother.

Everyone was silent at the table. Gertrude was embarrassed and Jakob didn't know what he had said wrong. Gunther just didn't want to talk about it, not because he thought his son was wrong, but only because he knew how unreasonable Amalie could be in these matters.

Amalie couldn't speak.

Just then the waiter returned to the table and Gunther ordered a lot of different things and pretended to be jovial to distract everyone from their uneasiness and insisted that they would all just take a little bit of everything. "It will be an adventure." he said with a smile as he winked at Gertrude who also wanted to gloss over the awkwardness of the moment.

The silence overtook the table again once the waiter left until Amalie finally spoke. She had suddenly made the connection between Klaus and Gunther and soccer and realized what was going on. "Jakob, who are the boys you played soccer with today?"

Jakob looked at Gunther, uneasy because of the accusing tone of his mother's question and not knowing what to say since his father had told him that his mother shouldn't be told about the youth group.

"It's just a group of boys who meet in the park on the weekends" Gunther said, answering for Jakob and trying to casually brush the question aside.

"A group? A youth group?" Amalie asked.

"Well... yes." Gunther said, still trying to avoid a messy argument. Gertrude watched nervously as they talked and Jakob, who was sitting between them, sat silently and uncomfortably looking down at the table.

"Is it that the youth group that Klaus had talked about? The one for the children of party members?" Amalie asked in a final accusation that caught Gunther in his lie of omission.

Gunther knew there was no way out and found himself getting angry at being trapped. "Yes" he said defiantly after a brief hesitation.

"But darling," Amalie said sarcastically, trying to keep her voice from shaking, "I thought you weren't a member of the party anymore."

"I only did it for Jakob" Gunther countered with a resolve that came across as little more than pathetic as he blamed the lie on his son. "He wanted to play with these boys and I had to be a member before he could join."

"But," Amalie said again, this time holding up her index finger as she made her point, "how can he join when his mother is a Jewess?"

This time Jakob looked up and, hoping to comfort his mother and show her that he and his father had thought of that and taken care of everything, said: "It's all right mother, we didn't tell them."

Amalie just looked at Jakob. She knew he didn't understand, but that couldn't stop the tears. It occurred to her that this was just what she had done so long ago. Just as she had cast off being Jewish when she came to Munich, so Jakob now denied his mother so that he could belong to the Hitler youth. She could almost hear her father's sad laughter in her ears, laughing at the irony of it. Amalie couldn't bring herself to continue talking about it and mercifully, the food arrived. She quickly dried her eyes with her napkin and busied herself with dishing up for Jakob and Gertrude, explaining what was what as she put things on their plates.

Their dinner conversation was sparse after that and Jakob contented himself with studying the restaurant and taking in its exotic smells and trying the different foods while the three adults tried to avoid a scene in public.

Amalie was especially quiet on the ride home while Gertrude tried to make conversation about how nice the restaurant was even though it was so strange. Amalie was thinking, not so much about how hurt she was, but what she might say to Jakob later, or if she could even bring herself to talk to him at all about it. She played the hypothetical conversation through in her head, trying different approaches and phrases, but she realized that she didn't know at all what he might say. What did he understand about all this? What did he think was going on? She had thought that her father had won him over in the course of their visits to Salzburg in the past few years. Jakob seemed to be interested when Ethan would tell his stories and teach him about the Jews, but it must not have been enough. Maybe it was just because that's the way children are at this age, as though they are re-inventing themselves, trying to create a person in themselves who replaces the child that they were such a short time before.

"Well? What do you think?"

Amalie was caught off guard as she snapped out of her trance, and suddenly realized that Gunther was talking to her.

"What?" she asked.

"You haven't heard a word I've said, have you?" Gunther said with a smile as he tried to make up with her.

"No." Amalie said quietly, "I was just thinking. What did you say?"

"I said we should do something together tomorrow. It's been a few weeks, and the summer goes so fast."

"Yes, fine. Whatever you think..." Amalie said passively.

"An outing on the Isar. You haven't been to the English garden in quite awhile, have you?" Gunther asked as he tried to keep the conversation going.

"No, not at all this summer" Amalie said, still maintaining a quiet monotone, forcing Gunther to work at the conversation.

"Good! I'll call Friedrich and we'll all meet there."

The next day, Gunther called Friedrich and invited him to the park. He also called Klaus to tell him about the confrontation with Amalie.

"Don't worry about it..." Klaus said, lacking any real sympathy for his friend, "Maybe I'll see you tomorrow at your picnic. We'll be down at the park again with some of the older boys from the HJ."

It was a hot day in the English garden without a cloud in the sky. Amalie hadn't had a chance to talk with Jakob about the incident in the restaurant and so she resigned herself to waiting for a better time and decided to try to make the best of their outing. She couldn't help thinking of the last picnic as she and Jakob got out of the car and she found herself subconsciously scanning the park, looking for possible danger.

"You made it!" Gunther exclaimed as Friedrich walked up to the car, "...But you're alone! I thought you were going to ask Geli to come."

"I did" Friedrich responded with a note of despair in his voice as he pointed to a car pulling up to the curb about a half a block away, "She insisted that Uncle Alf should come..."

Gunther watched as Geli playfully floated out of the car. She reached into the car and pulled at someone's hand and suddenly there he was; Adolf Hitler walking towards Gunther and his family picnic.

"He's going to join us?" Gunther asked incredulously.

"Yes" Friedrich said, "a chaperone. I'll never be alone with her."

"He's going to eat with us?" Gunther asked, ignoring Friedrich's lamentation.

Gertrude and Amalie paid no attention to the event unfolding by the car as they laid out the blankets and food.

"Hello" Klaus called out as he walked up to Amalie and Gertrude.

"Klaus!" Gertrude replied with surprise, "What brings you to the garden?"

"I was here with the boys and I saw you. So... where is your husband?" Klaus asked with a smile as he addressed Amalie.

Amalie nodded casually towards the car since her hands were full and looked over just in time to see Adolf shaking hands with her husband as they were being introduced by Geli.

"Well this is certainly unusual" Klaus said, transfixed by the scene while trying to be nonchalant, but not doing very well at it, "He rarely comes down here... It's so... public."

"Who?" Gertrude asked as she turned to see what Klaus was talking about.. "My God!" she said, "It's him... with Friedrich and Gunther. They're coming over here!"

It was Geli who made the introductions, doing very well to remember everyone's name and identifying Amalie as the one who had been so kind as to go with her to Austria when Adolf had been so busy, and Adolf made a point of addressing Amalie and Gertrude with a gracious acknowledgment and a genteel kiss on the hand which completely won over Gertrude in that instant.

Adolf had asked his chauffeur to bring along some folding deck chairs and they were quickly set up around the blanket as Adolf proceeded to hold court under the shade of an elm tree. One of the boys from the youth group had gone looking for Klaus and once he found that he was in the company of the Fuhrer, all of the boys soon got the news and quickly joined the congregation. Klaus, acting as though the leader of a platoon, immediately took control of the situation and organized the boys so that they could meet Adolf one by one.

Adolf soon loosened up in the company of these people who revered him and he was clearly impressed when Klaus dispatched the group of boys to serve as a sort of body guard unit to keep people away from the little gathering as they sat and talked.

Jakob, Gertrude and Amalie sat quietly and listened as the others talked, Jakob because he was too young to join in, Gertrude because it was the thing to do and Amalie because she felt like a spy who had managed to get into a secret meeting. The men talked politics as they ate sandwiches and drank beer from dark brown bottles.

"Jakob," Klaus called out as the conversation lulled for a moment, "bring us another beer, would you?" and Jakob dutifully got four bottles and began handing them out until he came to Adolf, who politely refused.

"I don't drink much" he said by way of explanation as he glanced at the bottle and he noticed the scar on Jakob's arm. "What's this?" he asked, pointing at the four inch scar on Jakob's forearm, "An old battle wound?"

"That's from a dog attack" Gunther explained as Jakob stood silently while Adolf held Jakob's wrist and examined the scar. Jakob was uncomfortable at being the center of attention and didn't know what to do.

"It looks recent" Adolf said with the authority of one who had seen many scars and wounds.

"Only... what is it? Two months now?" Gunther asked as he consulted Klaus.

"Yes, about that." Klaus confirmed "but our Jakob, he took it like a man."

"Our Jakob?" Amalie thought to herself. Maybe Klaus felt that Jakob should have two fathers... and no mother.

Adolf soon turned the conversation to the early days of the party and Friedrich piped in with his story of how they had met Adolf so long ago at the Sterneckerbräu and Adolf smiled.

"Are you a party member?" Adolf asked of Friedrich.

"Absolutely!" Friedrich said proudly, "That was how I came to meet Geli," he stopped and cast a smile at her before continuing, "through party members."

"Good, good" Adolf said as though anyone who joined the nazi party was to be considered of the highest character. "I'm happy that Geli has the right kind of friends here in Munich. So what work do you do?"

"I'm an inventory foreman at a factory here. The owner is a party member."

"The party is growing steadily" Adolf said in a way that defied contradiction as though the party were inevitable, and so, its victory.

"Yes, even in the factory, some of the men are joining."

"But only the best of them, right?" Adolf said, like a lawyer asking a question for which he already knew the answer.

"For the most part..." Friedrich said evasively.

Adolf was surprised at this equivocation when he had been so sure that the young man would say exactly what his Fuhrer wanted to hear. "The most part?" he asked, prompting Friedrich to explain.

"Yes, well... There is one other party member in my department at the factory, I mean a man who is ready for anything, but he does have one shortcoming..."

"What's that?" Klaus interrupted as his curiosity got the better of him,

"Well, I'll give you a hint," Friedrich said with a smile, "his nickname at the factory is 'Zeigel'.*"

"I see..." Klaus said with a growing smile and even Adolf couldn't hold back a laugh.

As Uncle Alf laughed, he suddenly broke wind in a most convincing manner, bringing the conversation to a sudden halt as everyone found themselves at a loss. What does one say when the Fuhrer passes gas?

"I know what you mean," Adolf said, forcing a smile and getting the conversation going again while completely ignoring the embarrassing situation, "but it's important to remember that strong backs are just as important to the party as strong minds. Maybe even more so!"

The rest of the men agreed whole-heartedly as once again there was a pause and Klaus and Gunther exchanged glances as each took a drink of his beer. Gunther had been amazed that Jakob, or any of the other boys for that matter, hadn't said anything or laughed when Uncle Alf had...

"Those first days in the Sterneckerbräu We went through a lot." Adolf finally said to his bottle of mineral water in the way that any soldier would reminisce about a hard battle from his past.

"Well, to be honest," Gunther said quietly, somewhat ashamed as he dared admit his terrible failing to Hitler himself, "After the..." he faltered for an instant as he tried to find a suitable euphemism, "'trouble' in '23, I left the party."

Adolf didn't comment, and there was an awkward pause until Gunther perked up a bit as he continued, "but I'm back in now. I've just rejoined."

This resolution brought a smile back to Adolf's face. "To tell you the truth," Adolf said as though confiding to a close friend, "I felt like leaving the party, too after that fiasco at the Feldherrnhalle." and

---

* Brick

237

with that, he started to laugh and everyone else joined in, relieving the tension and showing Gunther that he was forgiven, forgiven by the Fuhrer himself.

"But I learned from that mistake and now we have rebuilt the party and will continue to make it stronger, for we cannot afford to abandon the cause of Germany's resurrection. I've said before that the will of the German people was as strong as steel, but I was wrong... The spirit of the German people is stronger than steel. But like steel, this spirit must be tempered, it must feel the heat of that passion which would rebuild Germany to be great again, in fact to be greater than it has ever been before."

By the time Adolf had finished, even though he had spoken calmly and quietly, using the old orator's trick whereby the listener must listen closely to hear what is being said, it felt to Klaus and Gunther and Friedrich as though their leader had been shouting from some gilded podium at the head of a great crowd. Amalie had listened too, but her perception was of how easily Adolf's invectives fell upon the ear, how he swept them up without his message of hatred. She suddenly realized what they meant when some of his followers called him a genius, coarse and vulgar, but still a genius in his way. This captured Amalie's imagination. She stared at him as one might watch a primate in a cage at the zoo, amazed at how much it was like a human, but fully aware that it was certainly not. Amalie caught Klaus' eye as she stared at Adolf and he smiled to himself thinking how incredible a personality Adolf Hitler was that he could even captivate a Jewess like Amalie.

The conversation soon turned to more mundane topics as thoughts floated about, caught in mid air, light and elusive, caustic and amusing, not one tied to another, but chasing and rolling like dogs at play on a warm summers day. After a half hour or so it became apparent that Adolf was restless. Throughout the time the group was eating and talking, a few people had recognized Adolf as they strolled through the park or sought to lay out their own picnics near by, and they had come over to meet him, but the sixteen and seventeen year old boys from the youth group followed their orders and stood their ground, refusing to let anyone approach the Fuhrer. After a while though, Adolf began to feel exposed in the public park.

"It has been a pleasure meeting you all," he said abruptly, interrupting Klaus in mid sentence as Klaus went on about something his three boys had gotten into, "but I'm afraid we must be going now."

Having said that he stood up from his chair and his chauffeur immediately snapped the chair closed and waited behind Adolf. Adolf then offered his hand to Geli, who was still sitting on the ground, talking with Amalie and Gertrude in a conversation separate from the men. "Come Geli" he said as he waited for her to take his hand, but Geli wasn't ready to leave and there was just the hint of a flash of something in her eye. Perhaps it was anger at being summoned to his side and expected to immediately come to heel, but whatever it was, it passed just as quickly.

"Can't we stay just a bit longer?" she asked, "It's so nice out today."

"No, It's almost three" he said as he looked impatiently at his watch to confirm his statement, "We have an engagement tonight and we'll need the time to get ready."

"Well, why don't you go and send the car back?" Geli suggested. It was clear, especially to Amalie who was sitting behind Geli in a place where she could see Adolf's expression, that Geli was testing his patience and, worse yet, she was embarrassing him in public by not doing as she was told.

He apparently decided on a tactical retreat as he quickly agreed and he and his chauffeur started for the car. Klaus and Gunther followed behind with the other two folding chairs, using them as an excuse to have a final word or two with Adolf along the way.

Geli went on talking with Gertrude as though what had just happened was just a pleasant exchange between her and Uncle Alf and not a test of wills. Amalie thought to herself how interesting it all was. The rumors of something between Geli and her uncle must have been true, although she wondered just how far their "something" went. After all, she had found out that Hitler's mother was his fathers niece... Maybe it was a tradition in their family. The thought struck Amalie as funny.

"Your uncle is so charming." Gertrude said in a way that schoolgirls might talk about a new boy in their school, "and those eyes... they look right through you"

"Yes," Amalie agreed, rejoining the conversation, "They are piercing."

If Gertrude had known Amalie better, that is, if Amalie had let

239

Gertrude know her better, Gertrude might have wondered how, or why, Amalie sat through the whole afternoon in such company without raising a word of objection. Especially in light of the trouble in the restaurant the night before. But Gertrude didn't think in those terms. She thought the issue at the restaurant was about Gunther keeping a secret, not about the content of the secret, and so it never occurred to Gertrude that Amalie hated Uncle Alf.

Amalie felt even more like a spy as she tried to find out even more about Adolf through his niece.

"Wasn't that horrible?" Geli asked rhetorically a few moments after Adolf had left.

"What?" Gertrude asked.

"The way he... the way Uncle Alfie makes such a noise and a smell and everyone has to pretend that nothing happened."

"Oh, don't be silly" Gertrude answered unconvincingly, "It's natural... he must just be having stomach trouble. It's not like he did it on purpose."

"But he does it all the time. All the time! We've even been to formal dinners where he has..."

Amalie couldn't help but laugh out loud as Geli went on.

"Amalie!" Gertrude scolded, "The poor man can't help it."

"I know, I know, but I just had a picture of him in evening dress bowing to some bejeweled dignitary's wife when..." she was unable to complete the sentence as she laughed even louder. Geli joined in laughing right along and even Gertrude couldn't hold back a little laugh.

Geli said that she was very fond of her uncle, but he only thought of her as an escort, someone he could call on at a moments notice to accompany him to social functions. When she said this, Amalie wondered if Geli didn't feel something more for her uncle than fondness, since she was beginning to sound like a wife who felt she was being taken for granted.

Gunther, Klaus, Friedrich and Jakob soon returned to the blanket under the elm tree and Friedrich strategically placed himself between Geli and Amalie.

"So," he said as he made himself comfortable, "what have you girls been talking about?"

He was so obvious about insinuating himself between Amalie and Geli that neither could resist laughing. Gertrude glared disapprovingly at her son as he sat helplessly disarmed by the other women's laughter.

Chapter 10

If Germany listened closely, it might have heard a bell tolling in the distance on that crisp afternoon of October 24, 1929. It was a historical day on the American stock market when the prices of stocks began to fall faster and farther than they ever had before. The plunge culminated in a week long stock panic that sent the stock market crashing to undreamed of lows, destroying family fortunes in a matter of minutes and driving many stock speculators to suicide. The 1920's had been an unprecedented period of growth in America, as always seemed to happen in that country after a war, but there was always a leveling. 1929 signaled more than just an economic leveling, however, as Black Thursday became the final call for not just the American economy, but the global economy as well. The economic depression would soon reach out to touch virtually every industrialized nation on Earth.

The rumbling ground of a faltering Weimar economy was an incredibly fertile land for the seed of a new revolution, a national socialist revolution, but this time it would not be Adolf Hitler in the midst of a street fight in Munich. Though there would certainly be countless bloody street confrontations between the nazi Sturmabteilung and Communists, this time Adolf Hitler and his followers were biding their time. They sat comfortably in the belly of their Trojan horse known as the Berlin Reichstag, waiting as the German mittlestanders* began one by one to take the horse's reins and pull it into the courtyard where Germany would finally be taken from within.

---

* Mittlestander is a term referring to a business middle class, those
businesses between small family owned businesses and large
international concerns.

Joseph Hubert was just a passing acquaintance of Amalie's. He was a boyhood friend of David Frieder's who often dropped by the publishers office, waiting for David when they were going out for lunch. They had invited Amalie along a few times and she had come to look forward to Joseph's visits.

When he entered the office, the receptionist would smile and deliver the reflexive "Grüss Gott" while Joseph would only smile and give a slight nod, heading straight for Amalie's desk and launching into the set-up for a joke which, no matter how well executed, would never make up for the content. But Amalie was always polite enough to muster a good laugh.

"Are you coming with us today?" Joseph asked with a smile.

"Am I invited?" Amalie countered with a flirtatious smirk.

"Let's ask the boss." Joseph said as David walked up, "Is Amalie coming with us today?"

"Well, that's up to her, but I certainly don't think I better leave the two of you alone together."

"No. Much too dangerous!" Joseph concurred.

"Yes, like storing the matches with the gunpowder..." Amalie played along.

"Ratskeller?" Joseph asked in the shorthand one uses among friends, asking if Amalie and David wanted to go to the Ratskeller restaurant in the basement of the neue Rathaus for lunch.

They nodded in agreement and gathered up their coats as Joseph started in on another joke that had been around for years: "Did you hear about the Nazi rally the other day?" he asked as they worked their way down the stairs from the office, "Hitler went into one of his rages and shouted 'and who is to blame for the troubles of Germany?' and a little voice from the back of the crowd called out 'the bicycle riders'." Joseph continued even though Amalie and David appeared inattentive. "So Hitler gets a confused look on his face and finally calls back 'the bicycle riders? Why the bicycle riders?' and the voice from the back of the audience calls back 'Why the Jews?'." Joseph laughed at the joke while Amalie and David only smiled politely. "I guess you heard it..." he finally said with defeat in his voice.

"Everyone's heard it." David said as he opened the door onto the street.

It was a cloudy day and a cool, late September wind filled the hallway as the trio started towards the new city hall just as the glockenspiel in the city hall tower began dutifully chiming off the arrival of midday with its brightly painted statues dancing out their farewell to the morning. Marienplatz was filled with people milling about from store to store, many of them people from the country who had come to Munich for Octoberfest who were now window shopping and passing time as their vacation time drew to a close. It seemed as though everyone stopped to watch the clockwork action as the glockenspiel chimes sounded.

Amalie couldn't help but smile to herself as they entered the square to see all of these people stopped in their tracks, staring up at the spectacle in the tower. She wondered if everyone in Munich was a tourist that day as she, David and Joseph made their way to the Ratskeller restaurant, which was as crowded as the square had been.

"Order what you like," Joseph said once they sat down at a table and began looking over the menu, "I'm buying lunch today."

"Oh my God," David said, "is it the end of the world already?"

"No," Joseph replied as he picked up his napkin and unfolded it, drawing out the word as though there was more than one syllable, "It is a celebration... or perhaps more accurately, a party. A farewell party."

"Farewell party?" David asked, "What are you up to now?"

"Yes," Amalie interjected, "What sort of crazy scheme is it this time?"

The question went unanswered until they had all placed their orders with the impatient waiter and then Joseph continued as the waiter slipped away through the crowded room. "It's not a scheme, just the decision of a lifetime. I have decided to seek my fortunes elsewhere."

"Oh God," David said as he rolled his eyes, "not that nonsense about Berlin again! You have the same chances of making a living here as you would in Berlin."

"Not Berlin" Joseph said as the waiter came to the table with their beers.

"Then where?" David pursued.

"America."

"Oh Joseph!" Amalie exclaimed before David could respond.

"America? Why America?" David asked with a certain abrasivness, "Do you even know anyone in America?"

"I have..." Joseph began defensively, faltering as he tried to find a proper description, " 'distant' relatives."

"What does that mean?" Amalie asked, turning to David for a translation.

"That means" David said as he stared at Joseph, defying his friend to contradict him, "that they might let him stay with them for two days, but they won't lend him any money."

Amalie laughed, but neither David nor Joseph laughed with her.

"Do you even know what you'll do there?" David asked, "You've tried everything here from publishing to radio to salesman..."

"You were in radio?" Amalie asked.

"A little while." Joseph offered weakly.

"Two weeks." David corrected.

"Two and a half weeks." Joseph corrected defensively.

"I just don't understand..." David said with frustration in his voice, "If you have all these problems finding work now, here where you have family and friends to support you..."

"I just think that a new start, a new country..." Joseph tried to explain, and then suddenly his eyes lit up as he remembered the old cliché, "A land of opportunity!"

"Where the streets are paved with gold." Amalie said with a laugh that was meant to point out what a ridiculous proposition it was, but Joseph took it as a sign of support.

"Yes." he said, "streets of gold."

"Amalie," David said as he furrowed his brow, "don't lead him on with this idiocy."

Amalie nodded. "Joseph, he's right" she said, "It's not easy to get into America and if you do, you need money to get by and it is best to have family or friends who can sponsor you and help you get started."

"I have some money" Joseph said, still on the defensive.

"But passports, immigration, visas... all of this takes time, and you have to show..."

"That's all done" Joseph said defiantly.

"Done?" David shot back with surprise, "When are you going?"

"The week after next."

"Two weeks? It's all done and settled?"

"Yes."

David looked at Amalie, who didn't know what to say.

"Why didn't you tell me earlier?" David finally asked after a long pause.

"I didn't want you to try to talk me out of it."

"Oh Joseph..." David said sadly and then there was another long pause as the waiter brought them their food. "You know I just worry about you as a friend."

"I know."

"Is there anything I can do?"

Suddenly Amalie popped up from her lunch. "Otto!" she said, trying to address both David and Joseph as her head shot back and forth between them, "Otto Maus... He has a brother in New York. Brooklyn, New York."

"Yes," David agreed, "The writer from Ried. He once told me that if I ever got to New York, his brother would put me up for a week... He's a... Damn. I can't remember what he does. He runs some kind of factory."

"He owns it." Amalie corrected, "Otto told me his brother owns a factory which makes..." at this point Amalie realized she couldn't remember either what it was that Otto's brother made and she stopped in mid sentence. "Ice boxes!" she finally proclaimed as the answer popped into her head. "That's it, he makes ice boxes for homes."

"Yes," David agreed, "At least let me call Otto and see if he won't send a letter of introduction for you."

Joseph agreed and they finished their lunch with David eventually wrestling the check away from Joseph, saying that Joseph would need every pfennig he had for the journey.

The Ratskeller was still filled as they left the restaurant, perhaps even more so as the afternoon wore on. David's good-bye to Joseph at the door leading up to the office had an added meaning as prelude to the farewell that would see Joseph off to America a few short days later.

It was the tenth of October in 1929 when Joseph Hubert boarded the train for the north of Germany where he would then board a ship for America. He didn't really understand the significance of the stories he heard a couple of weeks after he arrived in New York, the stories about stock brokers jumping out of the windows of their tall office buildings, but he was not alone. He was about to be enrolled in the same school of economics as the rest of America as

246

they all learned the lessons of Black Thursday.

Black Thursday in America fell about a year and-a-half after Friedrich had introduced Geli Rabaul to his friends. It is hard to say whether Friedrich was an eternal optimist or just blinded by infatuation, but he held out hope that he and Geli Rabaul might get together long after it was obvious to everyone else that Geli's attention was somehow reserved for her Uncle Alfie. The exact nature of her involvement with her uncle was the topic of conversations all over Munich.

Adolf and his party had made gradual but significant advances across the country in the five years since his release from jail and he was once again considered to be an important man in Germany, especially in Bavaria. Geli was living in Uncle Alfie's nine room apartment on Prinzregentenplatz, with her bedroom right next to his, while Adolf had sent his half sister, Geli's mother, to keep house at his mountain retreat in Berchtesgaden.

Amalie, in seeing the advantages of being Geli's friend in order to get any possible information on Hitler, had made a point of appearing to be the loyal wife of a devoted party member whenever she was around Friedrich and especially Geli. This pleased Gunther because he felt he had finally won his wife over and she had gotten rid of her unreasonable criticisms of the party. It was becoming obvious to Amalie that Uncle Adolf was closing Geli off from the outside world. Apparently Geli was to escort Uncle Alf to parties and other events, but she wasn't allowed to go out with other men. Amalie was sure, however, that in shutting Geli off from the world, she might confide more in the few people who were sanctioned by Adolf as suitable friends and so Amalie went out of her way to appear to be one of those suitable friends, to be on the perimeter of Adolf Hitler's inner circle.

It is an interesting aside that Klaus Grunewald never once referred to Amalie as a Jew to anyone close to Hitler. It is an insight into Klaus' character that it never even occurred to him that Amalie, as a woman, as the wife of a Nazi party member, could ever in any way pose a threat to the party or Hitler. Perhaps even more significant to Klaus, with his cynically political nature, was the importance of having Amalie as an ally since she was a friend of, and apparently quickly becoming a confidante of, Hitler's beloved niece. It made sense therefore, that since Klaus wanted to become part of

Hitler's inner circle, that he would not compromise Amalie's position as his possible link to that inner circle.

In spite of all of these intrigues, life went along smoothly for the next few months, in fact things around the Metzdorf house were the picture of bliss since Amalie had managed to, seemingly overnight, change her opinions of the party.

Jakob, who turned fifteen in November of 1929, had matriculated from the JV, the Jungvolk division of the Hitler youth which accepted boys from age ten to fourteen, into the actual Hitler Jungend program which accepted boys from age fourteen to eighteen. The youth group had been growing steadily along with the membership in the Nazi party and by 1929 the Hitler Jungend had more than ten thousand boys across the country and with this growth, the group was also becoming more organized and restrictive. It was developing a much more militaristic nature as Hitler, in particular, began to see the value of indoctrinating children into the ways of national socialism long before they were actually of age to join the party.

Jakob was still known by the nickname "Orion" among his friends in the HJ, the name his father had given him when Jakob showed his natural talent for archery on that day when he had first met the group in the English garden. Jakob was prized by his friends as a natural marksman and as the group progressed to small caliber rifle competitions, Jakob adapted to the new medium easily. Some of the older boys even suggested that Jakob might be good enough for the Olympic team from Germany in a couple of years at the 1932 Olympics in the city of Los Angeles in America.

It was proposed in the spirit of the Olympics that some of the different chapters of the Hitler youth should get together for an intramural competition in the summer of 1930. By the time summer came, it was all too obvious that the economic problems of America were sweeping across Europe and the unemployment rate in Germany in particular was rising dramatically. Many of the parents saw the games as a pleasant escape and so the attendance was expected to be high. The interest level got so high that some of the other boys groups, like the Catholic youth league, asked if they might also participate. Suddenly the competition was becoming an event, an event that even warranted an appearance by Hitler himself.

Adolf was not worried about the economic crisis which

248

Germany was facing as 1930 wore on. He saw it as an opportunity to discredit the German Republic and win even greater support for the nazi party as he worked to get ready for the Reichstag elections to be held that autumn.

When the day of the competition finally came, the event was held in a recently harvested farmers field outside of Munich which volunteers had spent weeks preparing. Hitler made his speech, a "volkish" speech in which he admonished his listeners to look at how the Italians, under their fascist government, had managed to withstand the depression and how Germany too could survive and even prosper under the auspices of German national socialism. The nazis in the crowd went wild as the speech concluded, but the others merely offered up polite applause. Polite applause, however was quite a change from the bloody confrontations Adolf and his followers had gotten in years past when he would speak. Polite applause meant that he had been accepted as a candidate entering the political mainstream, it meant victory was not so terribly far away.

Once the competition was under way, Jakob won the archery competition with little serious challenge from any of the other groups. Hitler stayed to observe the excellence of his Hitler Jungend. Geli was, of course, by his side when he arrived, but when Adolf had to leave unexpectedly as he always did, Geli remained with Amalie and Gunther to watch the rest of the games. When everything was over, Gunther and Jakob went off to talk with the other fathers and sons about the races and contests while Geli and Amalie stayed in their seats in the small bleacher section.

"It looks like it might rain" Geli said as she looked up at the growing cloud cover, trying to make conversation.

"...and it was so nice this morning" Amalie said, keeping up her end of the chatter, "That's always the way in Munich at this time of year. The weather can change so quickly."

"It's so nice to have an afternoon away." Geli sighed.

"A break from your busy schedule?"

"No... it's not that... I just can't... Adolf doesn't like me to be away from him. We're always together. Always."

"Is that so bad? I mean, having someone who cares about you that much."

"Yes, in a way."

"But?" Amalie asked.

"What?" Geli asked in response

"It seemed as though you were going to say something else."

Geli looked down at her feet and then looked back up at Amalie, making eye contact and then quickly looking away as though she were ashamed and couldn't look Amalie in the face.

"Can I trust you? I mean, could you promise not to tell anyone if I told you something?"

"Yes."

"I mean really not tell anyone. Your husband or family or anyone. It might even be dangerous for you if you did. Do you even want to hear it if that's what it means?"

"Geli, I've known you for quite a while now and I consider you a friend... and love you as a friend... and I've noticed how you've changed since we first met. If you need someone to talk to, a friend to confide in, I can be that friend. I am that friend. If you don't want me to tell anyone something, then you can know that I will keep it to myself."

"I have to talk to someone."

"What is it?"

"Well... Uncle Alf... Adolf and I... we... spent a night together."

Amalie was careful not to react. She wanted to know if there was something else about the man that could be used against him. What could he possibly be doing that would cause Geli to change as she had? Geli was still very good in public. She kept up the appearance of the outgoing, carefree, beautiful girl, but those who knew her sensed that something was going wrong, that this... whatever it was that she had with her uncle and his over-protectiveness were taking a toll on her.

"We..." Geli started, but she stopped, once again staring at her feet.

Amalie suddenly felt an unexpected shudder move through her. Was it guilt? She suddenly felt so sad for Geli as Geli sat beside her, obviously in pain, and Amalie was waiting to use her. Amalie had to remind herself what a friend might say, how a friend might comfort another friend at a time like this. Amalie guessed that since Geli and her uncle had had sex, Geli was having trouble dealing with the incestuous aspects of the relationship.

"Geli," Amalie said as she gently took Geli's hand, "it's not such a terrible thing if you might have... you shouldn't feel bad..." Amalie didn't know what else to say until it finally came to her it might not have just been a sexual encounter, that Adolf might have forced her. It was certainly in keeping with Amalie's opinion of Adolf that he might have raped his niece. Amalie suddenly shifted in her chair to face Geli and took her other hand, too. "Geli, did he force you? Did he rape you?"

A single tear ran from Geli's eye, running along her nose and falling to her lap as she continued staring down as though she couldn't raise her head.

Amalie bent down a little, trying to make some eye contact as she softly asked the question again. "Did he rape you Geli?"

Suddenly, more tears came and Geli began to sob. Amalie instinctively put her arms around Geli and began to pat her back softly, whispering into her ear, "It's all right Geli... It will be all right."

Even as Amalie said it, she knew it was a lie. It was the sort of thing you say to calm a frightened child, whether it was true or not. Amalie knew Geli was trapped, and it wasn't just a man, a jealous lover, it was the party too, it was all of these fanatical men. What would they do to a woman who cried rape, pointing a finger at their Fuhrer?

"It's worse," Geli finally began to say through her sobs, "It was disgusting, degrading... It was like a nightmare..."

Amalie was still holding Geli tightly as Geli sobbed at Amalie's breast. Amalie could hardly understand what Geli was saying through her sobbing, but she didn't interrupt her. When Geli stopped sobbing and didn't try to say any more, Amalie pulled away a bit and raised Geli's face by gently taking her chin, while reaching in her purse for a tissue and wiping away a couple of tears before giving the tissue to Geli.

"If he raped you, he can still be arrested, even if he is Adolf Hitler."

"That's not it," Geli finally said, looking around as she talked, still unable to keep eye contact with Amalie, "I wanted to... be with him, but I never thought he would..."

Amalie wanted to push her, she wanted to shout "What? What did he do?", but she kept her calm, waiting for Geli to say what she had to say in her own time.

"He... he..." Geli tried again, but stopped. She wiped away another tear as quickly as it had appeared and then shifted in her seat, straightening up as she prepared to say it at last, to make it real by admitting it to Amalie. "We started by kissing. He said he loved me... and needed me. Only me." Geli suddenly drew a deep breath, interrupting her story with a strangling noise as though she were having trouble breathing. "He picked up that whip. That whip that he carries all the time..." For the first time, Geli looked deep into Amalie's eyes, staring at Amalie, and Amalie suddenly saw the sad haunted look deep in Geli's eyes as she continued, "He wanted me to hit him, to beat him with that whip, to pull off his shirt and beat him." This time it was Amalie who looked away, but only for an instant. She didn't want Geli to think that she was turning away form her. "...and that's not the worst." Geli continued, "He wanted me to..." she began and then stopped again, "Oh God." she said as she hit her own leg, "He wanted me to urinate on him."

Amalie said nothing. She didn't know what to say.

"He's sick." Geli said, "Maybe he just needs someone who loves him, who really loves him. Maybe he can forget about this. Don't you think?"

Amalie was startled by the question at the end of Geli's string of rationalizations.

"Don't you think?" Geli asked again.

"I don't know." Amalie said after a moments hesitation, "I think you should..."

Amalie was interrupted in mid-sentence by Gunther as he walked towards the two women. "Amalie! We're ready to go."

Amalie was happy to be interrupted and turned immediately to answer Gunther rather than trying to finish what she was saying to Geli. "All right. We're coming." She then turned back to Geli trying to think of what to say, but there wasn't anything to be said. "We have to talk about this later."

"It feels better just talking about it" Geli said as she got up and wiped her eyes again, asking Amalie for another tissue so she could blow her nose.

The ensuing car ride was dominated by Gunther and Jakob rehashing the details of the competition. Amalie got out and walked Geli to the front door of the apartment building on Prinzregentstrasse, reassuring her once again and giving her a quick hug before leaving.

"What was that all about?" Gunther asked as Amalie returned to the car.

"Nothing. Geli and Adolf just had a little argument and we were talking about it after the games."

Gunther accepted the explanation and he and Jakob soon returned to their discussion of the games. When they finally made it home to Furstenried, Amalie tried not to be obvious as she soon went to the little writing desk in her bedroom and began to write down a description of the day along with a transcription of her conversation with Geli which she quickly sealed into an envelope and labeled "confidential conversation w/Geli Raubal - 29/10/'30 ", slipping it into the small drawer in the desk just as Gunther came into the room. She pulled out a clean sheet of writing paper in the same motion with which she was putting the completed letter into the drawer, hoping that Gunther hadn't seen the envelope.

"What are you up to?" he asked as he passed by.

"Writing a letter to father about Jakob winning the archery shoot."

"Good news travels fast." Gunther said with a big smile, glowing with pride in his son as though he had taught Jakob everything he knew.

The letter Amalie wrote to her father, the letter she made sure was mailed that evening, did include the news of Jakob's victory, just in case Gunther might some day ask Ethan about the event, but it also included instructions to store the enclosed sealed envelope with the family Bible that she had stolen from Geli's apartment in Vienna.

It was just a week later that Gunther's boss called Gunther into his office. Gunther felt himself tighten up a little, particularly the muscles at the base of his neck. He felt he had a fairly good relationship with his employer, although certainly not like Amalie's relationship with David Frieder. Amalie had invited David and his girlfriend of the moment for dinner on a number of occasions while Gunther had never met socially with Herr Lange. Perhaps it was because Herr Lange was much older than Gunther, in his late sixties as compared to Gunther's thirty-five years, but nonetheless Gunther felt they had a kind of friendship that develops of mutual respect. They were both good at what they did. Herr Lange was a good administrator and Gunther was a good architect. Despite his confidence, however, Gunther was concerned about being called into the office like this.

Every other time he had been in Herr Lange's office, there had been some kind of warning. Herr Lange might have stopped by Gunther's drawing board and said something like "We need to talk about the Borchard building. Come to my office tomorrow after lunch." But this time it was Herr Lange's pretty secretary who had walked over to Gunther's drawing table and stopped, waiting for Gunther to finish the line he was drawing before she looked up after feigning interest in the drawing and brushed the few strands of red hair that had swept down over her right eye.

"Herr Lange would like to see you in his office."

"Now?" Gunther asked, surprised at the breach of the traditional twenty-four hour notice for such an appearance.

"Yes. He says it's important."

Only after Gunther left that day would he figure out that even she knew what the meeting would be about. Herr Lange stood up and motioned to one of the heavy dark wooden chairs as Gunther entered the office. Herr Lange looked out the window once they both sat down and began to speak in a monotone. Gunther watched the expensive fountain pen in Herr Lange's hand which he used alternately as a pointer for imaginary charts and a baton leading an invisible orchestra and finally, just rolling it between his fingers as he finally turned his swivel chair to face Gunther, resting his elbows on the large, dark wooden desk

"...and so, because of these canceled contracts and because of the stock market problems which are effecting so many companies these days..." he said, stopping to take a deep breath before continuing, "We have to re-organize our little company. This is going to be hard for all of us. I have to go back to actually drawing plans..."

"...and me?" Gunther finally asked, the first words he had spoken since entering the office.

"I'm afraid... I am terribly sorry, terribly sorry, Gunther. You're a fine draftsman, a very competent... an artist one might say, but we have to let you go."

Gunther had known as soon as Herr Lange had started talking about the economy and canceled contracts that this was where the conversation was leading, but still, when the words were actually spoken, he felt a sickly panic rise within him. There was a pause until he could finally ask "When will I leave?"

"Well... I would understand if you were upset and wanted to

254

leave immediately, but if you could finish the project you're on now, I do have a couple of small home projects I could send your way if you want to do them on your own."

"Yes," Gunther said, trying to be practical rather than insulted, "I would appreciate that. I should be able to complete the corrections on the Reiger building by next Wednesday."

Herr Lange got up and walked around his desk, extending his hand as Gunther rose. "I can pay you through the end of the month and I'll have Trudi get you the information on those house projects."

Gunther reflexively gave his boss' hand a quick shake and almost found himself saying thank you for the two week severance pay and the other job references, but it caught in his throat and he said nothing as he turned for the door. Herr Lange put a hand on Gunther's shoulder, stopping him as he turned away.

"If there was any way Gunther, any way that we could keep you on, I hope you know that I would..."

Gunther softened at this last gesture. "Yes Herr Lange. I... I would like to thank you for all that you have done. You helped me get started and I am thankful for that."

"I had hoped we could part as friends" Herr Lange said with a weak smile as he gave Gunther a pat on the back. Gunther even managed to return the smile.

Gunther had a hard time telling Amalie about losing his job. He waited for three days before he finally told her just as they got into bed when she turned out the lamp on the bedside table. It wasn't that he was afraid to tell her. He knew she wouldn't turn away from him. It was the way that he felt about himself that bothered him, as though he had somehow failed. He remembered the time after the war when he went without work for so many months and how he felt when Amalie had started working for Frieder and Son. Could he make it on his own as an architect? Would there be enough work if the economy kept going the same as it was? How bad would it get? He suddenly thought of the inflation years and shuddered at the question.

Within a couple of weeks of Gunther losing his job, opponents of the nazis were shocked as the nazis made a huge gain in the national elections. Even the nazi party leaders were surprised as the nazis suddenly became the second largest political party in Germany with one hundred and seven seats in the Reichstag.

While Gunther was happy with the advances made by the party, his main concern was making a living. He kept busy for the next few weeks by finishing up at the firm and bidding everyone good-bye, never to see any of them ever again, and then starting work on designing the houses for the two clients that Herr Lange had referred to him as a token gesture.

He bought a used drawing board and set it up in the corner of the living room. The drawing board seemed huge in the small living room and he thought about taking over the garage as an office, but these plans were always overshadowed by his fear of not being able to make it as a freelance architect when the economy was so bad.

It seemed so strange, watching Amalie go off to work and Jakob leaving for school each day, trying to work in the house as Gertrude went about her chores.

When Gunther and Gertrude had lunch together, it was usually in silence. Gertrude was so used to eating lunch alone that she had nothing to say and Gunther was simply in no mood to talk.

One day Gunther found himself standing at the window after lunch, staring out at nothing in particular as the postman suddenly passed in front of the window, breaking his trance. Even the mail seemed strange. Gunther had never brought in the mail before. It was always sorted out in the small rack on the wall in the kitchen by the time he got home, the bills in one slot, personal letters in another and business correspondence in the third. He stood in the doorway, forgetting to close the door as he leafed through the few pieces of mail.

It felt as if he stared at the letter for ten minutes before opening it. It was a letter from his mother. Gunther had not been to Elsbethen in fifteen years. He had not heard a single word from his father's house ever since their last argument on the subject of his marriage to Amalie when he was on leave during the war. What could possibly move his mother to write after all this time? His father must be dead.

When he finally got the letter open, he found that his father was ill. Oskar Metzdorf had been diagnosed at the beginning of October with lung cancer.

Gunther couldn't believe what he was reading. His first thought was of himself. First he loses his job and now he finds out that his father has cancer. Bad luck comes in threes. Isn't that what they say? What would happen next?

"Are you going?" Amalie asked as they sat down to dinner that night.

"Going?" Gunther asked, caught off guard, lost in thought about how fifteen years had passed since he spoke with his father.

"Yes. Are you going to see your father?" Amalie persisted.

"How come we never visit them?" Jakob asked on top of his mother's question.

"Why?" Gunther asked as though he was in some kind of daze, yet with the kind of incredulity that inferred that Jakob should have known why Gunther never talked with his parents.

"They had a fight" Amalie interjected, answering Jakob.

"Yes" Gunther concurred, "A fight. A fight because I married your mother."

Jakob didn't know how to respond to his father's statement, so he quietly went back to eating his dinner.

"Do you really think I should go see him?"

"Yes..." Amalie said, cautiously venturing an opinion. "We've certainly changed. Maybe they've changed... After all, they did write."

"I suppose that's something." Gunther admitted grudgingly. There was a pause as he thought about it. "I certainly have the time now." he finally said.

It only took a couple of days for Gunther to finish up his work on the house-plans and he soon found himself on a train to Salzburg where he would take a bus to the small town of Elsbethen, some ten kilometers to the south. The last time he had been to Salzburg was when they had taken Jakob to the hospital there after the dog attack and he had thought of going to see his parent's house back then, just to drive by, but he didn't. He didn't even mention it to Amalie.

The house was an uphill walk from the bus stop of about thirty meters. Gunther stopped a moment before opening the wrought iron fence at the foot of the red brick steps which led up to the house. The house had aged noticeably. The yard was still immaculate. The flowers had lost their bloom. The brown stems struggled to stand against a late October wind while a few still stubbornly refused to let go of remaining petals which hung down sadly from what was once the face of a rose here or a chrysanthemum there.

The thick varnish on the heavy oak door had been baked by the sun, cracking the once shiny, even finish into little brown bumps that should have been scraped away years before, but this was how the house had grown sad. A loose tile here and there, cracking paint on window trim... Everything was still in place, but not quite right. How do you knock on a door you haven't seen in fifteen years? Do you approach it like an old friend who has been away or should you be formal, not taking the chance of being embarrassed because you're too friendly when the door can't quite remember who you are?

He didn't have to knock. His mother opened the door as he stood there thinking about it. She must have been waiting for him. Maybe she saw him from the window as he came up the red brick steps. Had she been waiting all morning for him? Had she been waiting all these years for him to walk up those steps?

Marie just looked at him, searching his face for definition of who he was now. Then she looked him up and down. He was a bigger man now, not fat, but filled out, changed from the boy of nineteen to the man of thirty-five. Gunther didn't move. He didn't smile. He didn't reach out although a part of him wanted to reach his hand out, to touch her face. Marie stepped out onto the front stoop and put her arms around her son, around his arms that didn't move from his side. She had her head against his chest, resting in the warmth of his woolen overcoat, as Gunther finally managed to put his arms around her.

"I've come home... to see you... and father... to see if there's anything I can do."

Marie finally let him out of her embrace and took his hand, leading him into the house. The smell of the house brought a kinescope of memories flashing through Gunther's mind, sudden pictures of holiday gatherings, birthdays, school friends and relatives he hadn't seen for so long. He was also caught off guard by the physical change in the house. It had become such a small house! The stairway was shorter and more narrow than it had been when he and his realschule* friends would come charging down from his bedroom and out into the awaiting sport arena that was the back yard. The dining room couldn't possibly have held all the aunts and uncles and cousins who would stop by during the week between Christmas and the beginning of a new year.

"I told you he would come" Marie said softly, with an emotional edge that said that her husband hadn't believed, but she knew that Gunther would not ignore his father in such a time of crisis.

---

* Realschule is the german equivalent of elementary schools.

258

Still holding Gunther's hand, she pulled him into the small den where Oskar Metzdorf sat wrapped in a colorful Afghan which Marie had made years before. His hands rested on his oversized stomach. God! Even his father had shrunk!

The pipe Oskar held produced a steady thin line of sweet smelling tobacco smoke which spread out and dissipated as it rose above Oskar's head while he stared silently at his son.

"Should you be smoking?" Gunther asked after a pause of many years.

Oskar was shocked to hear his son speak. Here he was standing in front of him and now he even talked to him. There was an involuntary twitch as Oskar tried to decide what to do. Should he reply? Was it that easy after all this time, just to start talking? Was small talk enough? He thought all of this in an instant and looked down at the pipe.

"Oh no... I don't smoke it. I stopped cigarettes. I just light this to..." Oskar fumbled around as he gestured at the pipe during his explanation, trying to rationalize how seeing the smoke from the pipe was part of how he stopped smoking cigarettes.

He then calmed down and caught Gunther off guard as he smiled and brushed the afghan aside, standing up and walking over to his son. "How have you been?"

Oskar looked at his son in much the same way that Marie had moments before, looking to see who Gunther was, and Gunther smiled and laughed a little at the casual question. In an uncharacteristic gesture, Gunther actually put his arm around his father and gave a couple of quick pats on the back. "Good father, I've been good."

The conversation between father and son was strained as Marie brought in coffee and then left them to talk. The conversation quickly turned to the common ground of architecture and Gunther was surprised to find that his father not only knew where he worked but that Gunther had been working there for years.

"We went to a dinner party a few years ago... '23 or '24" Oskar explained, "and there was Ethan Stein. Well... your mother had to find out... She asked him how you were doing."

Ethan, Marie and Oskar had all met before when Gunther and Amalie first started seeing each other as teenagers. It seemed it was tolerable to Oskar that his son might go out with a Jewish girl, just as long as he wasn't serious about her. "Wild oats" and all that sort of thing. It wasn't until Gunther announced his intention to marry Amalie that Oskar showed his true colors, denouncing Amalie as a Jewish slut trying to better herself by stealing away Oskar's son. Gunther had known that his father had no Jewish friends and Oskar would occasionally make an anti-semitic remark or tell a vulgar joke, but it wasn't until the engagement that Oskar's blind anger and resentments boiled over, driving his son away. This made Gunther even more determined to marry Amalie, to spite his father.

Then there was the chance meeting at the dinner party. It had been five years since Marie had heard anything about her son, and with everything that was going on in Munich, she couldn't stand it anymore. She had to know if Gunther was all right and so she walked over to Ethan, who had expected that Amalie's in-laws would ignore him, and caught him completely off guard when he turned from one of the guests with whom he was talking to find Marie Metzdorf standing beside him.

They began by exchanging pleasantries and then, with the expression of concern so characteristic of mothers everywhere, Marie asked about her son and his family. They talked for quite a while as Oskar kept an eye on them, seeing how Ethan reacted to Marie, while pretending to be interested in some of the other cliques of guests around the room. Eventually, when he had made a complete circle of the room, Oskar found that he too was standing with Ethan. There was tension between the two men that wasn't there between Marie and Ethan. While Gunther hadn't given a complete report of Oskar's reaction and comments to Amalie and her father, he did make it clear that his father had no interest in associating with Jews. It was an awkward alliance that night as Oskar asked about Gunther and Jakob and, as an afterthought, a politeness, he also asked about Amalie.

It was from this clumsy re-introduction, that Ethan and Oskar began to keep in touch, with the understanding that Amalie and Gunther shouldn't know at that time because, as with so many family conflicts and misunderstandings, the conflict had taken on a life of its own. One irrational act leads to another until no one can actually give a sound reason for their actions. Gunther assumed that his father wanted nothing to do with him and Oskar assumed that his son wanted nothing to do with him, so neither would risk his pride by taking the first step toward re-union.

The relationship between Oskar and Ethan was the strangest result of the problems between Oskar and his son. It's much easier to sustain mindless bigotry when you don't know anyone from the community which you hate, and conversely, of course, it is not as easy to believe the lies of hatred when you have... a friend. Thus came the paradox of Oskar's anti-semitism driving his son away while it was his son's absence that eventually drove his anti-semitism away.

The conversation on that afternoon in late October of 1930 between Gunther and his father certainly didn't cover all of that history though, Oskar only touched on his friendship with Ethan and then shocked his son by saying he had been wrong.

"I even have a Jewish doctor!" Oskar said with a laugh, as though that were the ultimate sign of reform.

The statement suddenly reminded Gunther of the reason for his visit and his manner changed as he asked his father how things were going with the doctor.

"The cancer?" Oskar said as a preface, letting Gunther know that it was all right to say the word "cancer".

"He says it is as best as can be hoped for. It seems the cancer is in just one area."

"He's absolutely sure?"

"As sure as he can be."

"What next?"

"He says they have to operate, to remove part of my right lung."

Gunther looked as if he had just been slapped in the face. For some reason he didn't expect that, but then he couldn't say what he expected. Maybe he had hoped that it wasn't really cancer, that the diagnosis had been wrong. "When?" he asked after a pause.

"I'm going in to the hospital tomorrow."

"Tomorrow? So soon?"

"Well, the diagnosis was made a couple of weeks ago. Doctor Rosenau wanted me to go in the same week that he told me it was cancer."

"Why didn't you?"

"I ..."

"Did you try another doctor?"

"No. I can't really explain it, it doesn't make sense, but even though I believed the doctor, I still couldn't really..."

"You were afraid" Gunther stated with both sympathy and

confrontation.

Oskar sighed and looked down at the floor. He was ashamed even though he had no reason to be ashamed. "It's not easy facing your fears when you've spent most of your life insisting that you're not afraid of anything."

This was a big thing for Oskar to admit. Gunther knew at this moment that his father had changed. He had become more human. Oskar then began talking in a way that Gunther had never heard before, he began talking to his son as a man, two men discussing life.

"I can hold a picture from some time of my life in my mind's eye." Oskar said as he looked at the pipe in his hand which continued to send out its steady stream of smoke rising to the ceiling, "I can even picture myself as though I were an observer of my own life, a bystander watching as the dreams were dreamt and the sins committed and the joys consumed and the pains endured." Oskar stopped for a moment and then looked at his son. "I'm not the one to tell someone how to live their life. I never took risks. I haven't chosen well..."

Gunther didn't know how to respond. His father certainly had reason to be depressed. "It isn't like that." Gunther said, doing his best to sound convincing without actually coming up with any specific contradictions. "We all make mistakes."

Just then Marie came in, telling them it was time for dinner and they all went into the dining room and, after quickly saying grace, began to eat.

"It all started..." Otto said, suddenly interrupting himself with a noisy slurp as the spoonful of venison stew which he was trying to eat as he talked turned out to be hotter than he had expected. "It was just a bad cold" he said once he had swallowed. "Then it got worse, and the doctor, the one Ethan recommended, was afraid it might be pneumonia. He made a photograph..."

"They used the X-ray machine on him" Marie proclaimed in the awkward phrasing of someone who wants to sound well informed, but doesn't really know what they're talking about.

"Yes," Otto acknowledged as he smiled at his wife, "the X-ray machine. Well... Doctor Rosenau said it was bronchitis, but he said he had found something else and he needed another picture. Then a week later he told me I had lung cancer but that it was early."

"If the doctor hadn't made those pictures..." Marie interrupted, at the same time reaching over to touch Otto's hand which rested on the table as he clenched the spoon which he rested on the edge of his bowl as he spoke.

"I wouldn't have known until I got really sick" Otto continued, finishing Marie's statement, "...and by then it would have been too late. Rosenau says I'm lucky that they only have to take part of a lung. Any later and there wouldn't have been anything they could do."

Gunther forced himself to smile as though he believed it would be just a matter of a simple operation, but he knew it was much more dangerous. This would be a major operation and even if the operation went well, there would be a big chance of infection. During the war, Gunther had known a lot of men who had survived battles with relatively minor wounds but then ended up dying from an infection which they got in an army field hospital.

Oskar went into the hospital as scheduled the next morning with the operation scheduled for the morning of the day after that. Gunther and his mother sat in a waiting room of the same hospital where Gunther had brought Jakob after the dog attack years before.

There was a fly that kept making its rounds of the small room, always coming back to rest on Gunther's hand. It became a game where Gunther would hold his hand still, waiting to see it the fly would actually find it's way back and then when the fly landed, Gunther would shake it off, sending it back on its journey around the room. It had been two hours since the operation began and when it was almost noon Gunther's stomach growled and Marie looked up with a start. Gunther just smiled and shrugged his shoulders.

"Maybe we could get something to eat..." he said.

Marie, with an anxious look, just shook her head "no".

"They said even if it went well, we could expect it to take at least another hour" Gunther continued, trying to change Marie's mind.

"I don't know..." Marie said, her shaky voice showing just how nervous she was, "I think we should wait."

"Come. We need to go for a few minutes. It will take your mind off things for a little while."

Marie looked up with eyes that clearly looked for reassurance.

"Come." Gunther said again as he got up and helped his mother on with her coat. They stopped at the nurse's station on the way out and Gunther told the nurse where they were going and that they would be back in just a few minutes.

It was a gloomy, rainy day as they walked out the front door and Gunther couldn't help himself as he thought what a fitting day it seemed for a funeral. He quickly chased the thought away as he tried to convince himself that there was nothing to worry about. His father would be just fine. But he just couldn't stop his mind from wandering. What would happen to his mother if his father died? Did they have any money? Gunther didn't have the slightest idea what his parents fortunes had been since he last saw them. What would it mean to Gunther if his father died?

Marie hardly touched her lunch, so Gunther rushed through his food so that they could get back to the waiting room. Their absence from the hospital hadn't taken Marie's mind off the operation at all as she spent most of the time in the cafe staring out the window up at the third floor of the hospital across the street. Their timing couldn't have been better as it turned out. Just as they came out of the elevator, they ran into Doctor Rosenau who walked over to Marie and took her hands in his. "We're done" he said, "Everything went well and now we just have to watch closely to make sure there are no complications."

"It's over?" Marie said as she finally let a tear run down her cheek, "He'll be all right now?"

"We have to watch him closely for the next couple of days. After an operation like this... We just have to be extra careful."

"I want to see him."

"No, that wouldn't be a good idea right now. He's still under the anesthetic and he needs rest."

"Please..." Marie persisted.

Doctor Rosenau looked at Gunther and then back at Marie and then he sighed. "I could let you go in for just a moment, but I want to warn you that he doesn't look good right now... and he's asleep. He won't even know you're there."

"He'll know" Marie said as though she knew something that the doctor didn't.

Gunther just stood by as his mother went to Oskar's bedside and picked up his hand, gently placing it on top of her own and then covering his hand with her other hand. She looked at him tenderly as a few more tears rolled down her face, but she didn't make a sound as she slowly leaned over and kissed him on the forehead. Gunther put his arm around her as she turned away from the bed and moved towards the door to leave.

It was a long night for Marie as she slept alone in the bed she had shared with her husband for over thirty years. She woke in the middle of the night to the deafening solitude. She missed Oskar's snoring. She laid there staring at the ceiling telling herself over and over again that it would only be a few days before her husband was back home again. Eventually she got up and went down to the kitchen for a glass of water. On her way back to her bedroom, she stopped at the open door of Gunther's bedroom. It had been Gunther's bedroom as a boy and now it was the guest bedroom, but she and Oskar had always called it "Gunther's room" even during all those years of Gunther's exile. She watched her son sleep, listened to his breathing, tried to remember how everything had gone by so quickly and finally went back to bed, only managing to fall asleep after an hour of staring out the window at the cold and distant stars.

Marie was up early the next morning making breakfast, just as she always did, and she and Gunther struggled to make small talk while they ate. They then bundled up against the cold and made their way to the Elsbethen train station, eventually arriving at the hospital in Salzburg just before eight o'clock.

They were allowed in to see Oskar, but still only for a short time. He was still asleep and once again Marie held her husband's hand, but this time his eyelids fluttered and he was suddenly awake and smiling weakly as he looked into his wife's eyes.

"There you are..." Marie said softly, as one might speak to a child.

"I made it through" Oskar replied weakly.

"How do you feel?" Gunther asked.

"It hurts." Oskar said with a grimace, "The doctor says that's to be expected. Rosenau says I'll feel much better in a few days."

"We came in yesterday to see you, but you were asleep" Gunther went on, trying to keep the conversation going and the mood light, "The doctor said you wouldn't even know we were here, but mother insisted that somehow you would!"

"But I did know" Oskar said as he squeezed Marie's hand,

"Your mother held my hand and kissed me on the forehead. Your mother isn't as foolish as you think" Oskar continued, "You should believe in her more."

The three of them talked for a few more minutes until Marie said it was time to go before the nurse came and told them they had to leave. Marie was content now and willing to leave so her husband could rest. She had to be there early that morning to make sure that he was all right. She was afraid he might be too "down" or too "up".

She knew through experiences with other friends and relatives in hospitals that sometimes you can tell a lot about how they would do in the hospital by how they acted. If they were sad or overly worried, they might not make it, and strangely, she had known people who were really happy and bright after an operation who had died suddenly in the night. Oskar seemed to be the same as always, not too happy or too sad. Now she knew that Oskar would do the best he could and the rest would be up to the doctors.

Just as they were about to leave, Oskar called Gunther back, asking Marie to leave them alone for just a minute. Marie left them without asking why, because she knew what Oskar wanted to say. He wanted to make things right with his son. Oskar had told his wife that he wanted to talk with Gunther before the operation because he honestly didn't know if he would live through it, but in all the confusion the right moment just didn't present itself then.

"I just wanted to thank you for coming" Oskar began, "I just thank God that I have the chance..."

"It's all right father," Gunther interrupted, "we've both changed..."

"Yes, but I just wanted to say..." Oskar paused as he tried to reach for one of the eloquent phrases he had rehearsed in his mind, but never said out loud, and now none of them seemed right. "I'm sorry."

Gunther smiled at the way his father had searched so hard for two such simple words, but of course, these were not simple words between the two of them. Terrible things were said many years before when father and son had parted company and these two simple words at this time in Gunther's life meant more than perhaps anything else his father had ever said.

"Me too." Gunther replied.

"No, no" Oskar insisted with a grimace, "It was all my fault, not giving you a chance, not giving Amalie a chance."

"We all make mistakes." Gunther said, "I shouldn't have run away like that. We might have worked it out if..."

There was an awkward pause as they both thought for a moment. "It's all that asinine business about the Jews." Oskar finally said, "After I got to know Ethan Stein... and this doctor. Rosenau saved my life! I just feel like I was such a fool."

"What was the old man saying?" Gunther thought to himself. From one extreme to the other? First he hates all the Jews and now he loves them all? But of course this was not the issue at hand, Gunther thought to himself. This was about a father and son healing old wounds, and Gunther wanted that as much as his father did.

"Well, now it's time for you to rest. Mother and I will be back tomorrow afternoon."

Oskar smiled and Gunther reached for his father's hand, not knowing how to touch him. A handshake wasn't right, so he just held his fathers hand as he said good-bye.

Marie was waiting in the hallway by the door as Gunther came out.

"Is everything ...?" Marie ventured curiously.

"Everything is fine" Gunther said as he took his mothers arm.

Gunther called Amalie from a public telephone the next day to tell her that everything was going well and he would be staying for another two weeks until Oskar was out of the hospital. He also told her about the clandestine communications between her father and his father. Once she was off the phone, Amalie thought to herself that this was a good sign, If her father could keep this secret from her for all these years, she felt better about the confidences which she had entrusted to him about Adolf.

Chapter 11

It was in 1930 that Josef Goebbels invented the myth of Horst Wessel. Horst Wessel was a young pimp who was a nazi on the side. A girl Horst wanted was also involved with another young man who happened to be a Communist and when the two men eventually fought over the girl and Horst was killed, Goebbels said that Horst had been killed fighting for the nazi party against the Communists. From this incident came "the Horst Wessel Lied", the song that became the classic marching song of the Sturm Abteilung as they fought other political factions, especially the Communists, in the streets of Germany, saying that they would not be happy "until Jewish blood came spurting from the knife".

Meanwhile, as the SA was making its presence known in the streets, the nazi party surprised even its own leaders by winning 107 seats in the German Reichstag, compared to only 12 seats won in the elections of 1928. This made the nazi party the second largest political party in Germany, confounding Hitler's opponents and changing the face of the Reichstag as the new representatives chose to attend in full SA uniform, answering the roll call with a loud "Present. Heil Hitler!"

Gunther had managed to get a pass from the front to go home at Christmas for three days just after Jakob turned one-year-old in October of 1917. That was the last Christmas Gunther had spent with his mother and father. That was the Christmas when his father went into a rage about his son marrying a Jew and told Gunther that he was never to come to the house in Elsbethen again.

The Christmas of 1930 saw Gunther, his Jewish wife, their son, and even Ethan Stein, coming to spend Christmas day with Oskar and Marie.

Not only was this the first Christmas that the immediate family had spent together in fourteen years, it was also the first Christmas since the end of the war that Amalie, Gunther and Jakob didn't spend with their adopted family; Gertrude, Klaus and Friedrich.

It was a strange get together with Oskar and Marie lavishing all of their attention on Jakob, whom they hadn't seen since he was a baby, while everyone else expressed concern about Oskar and asked how he had been since the operation. Everyone wanted things to go well and so the day was pleasant enough, but the happiness seemed forced. It had been such a long time since Ethan had seen Gunther and since Oskar and Marie had seen Amalie that none of them knew each other any more and it would take time before they could be more natural with each other. After all of Gunther's expectations, Christmas seemed anti-climactic.

New Years eve was spent back in Munich with Klaus and Katrina, Gertrude, Friedrich and Friedrich's latest girlfriend. Klaus went on at length about the Reichstag elections and how it was only a matter of time before Adolf Hitler would be head of the government. Amalie shuddered at the thought, but joined in with the rest as they toasted the possibility of Adolf's ascension with champagne.

Amalie started to worry about Gunther as the new year began and he couldn't find work. Even though she made enough money for them to get by, Gunther felt that he had to be the one who brought in the most money, that he had to support the family. The tension grew at home and Amalie found that she was glad each day when she would leave for the office, so that she could get away for a while.

Amalie found herself spending more time with Geli as they both tried to spend time away from their uncomfortable situations at home.

A couple of months later Geli had managed to convince Uncle Alfie that they shouldn't take any chances of improprieties between them now that the nazi party had become so much more prominent and he was in the national spotlight. She had been very careful in her approach as she was afraid that he might fly into a rage at the mere mention of their sexual encounter, but instead he was quiet. He couldn't even look at her. She had shamed him. She felt sure that he was relieved when she suggested that they not ever repeat the episodes or even mention them again.

Soon after that, Geli became secretly engaged to Adolf's chauffeur. When Adolf found out, he blamed everything on Emil, the chauffeur, and fired him on the spot, but that didn't stop Geli from trying to break away.

Later in that summer of 1931, Geli confided to Amalie that she had met someone during her last visit to Vienna. She was in love with a painter in Vienna and managed to meet with him a number of times even though Uncle Alfie still kept a close watch over her.

Amalie was worried and tried to convince Geli that she was playing with fire, that she couldn't get away with playing Adolf for a fool, but Geli laughed. Geli had recognized that moment when Uncle Alfie couldn't look her in the eyes. That moment was power. Geli felt that things were turning now and it was just a matter of time before she could get everything that she wanted and she was willing to bide her time.

Amalie was also biding her time. She began to wonder if now was the time to attack Adolf. She thought that since the party had gained power, this might be the right time just as Adolf came into the spotlight, but instead she decided to wait as she watched some strange developments coming out of London.

The American newspaper syndicate owned by William Randolph Hearst had come upon a young man in London named William Hitler. William Hitler was Adolf's nephew, the son of Adolf's half-brother, Alois Jr., who was Alois Hitler's first son, his illegitimate son by the woman who had eventually become Alois Hitler's first wife. Geli had met William one day when Uncle Alfie had called a meeting. Adolf had paid for William's and Alois Junior's passage from England and then summoned Geli and her mother Angela so that the whole family could be addressed. Geli swore Amalie to secrecy as she prepared to tell her what the meeting was about.

"I've never seen Uncle Alfie so mad!" Geli began.

"I told you that you have to be careful" Amalie said, trying to warn Geli again about her secret affair.

"Ja, ja... but cousin William, you won't believe what he said!"

"What?" Amalie said with a smile as she became more interested in the gossip.

"He said that the reporters were very interested when he mentioned that he thought there were Jews in the family!" Geli said with a laugh at the possibility of scandal in the family tree.

Amalie's eyes got big, but Geli only took it as surprise at what she had just been told. Amalie was considering what this might mean to her. The Bible! Did Adolf know about Angela's family Bible?

"Remember," Geli cautioned through her laughter, "you promised not to say anything."

"No, of course not. Was it true?"

"I don't know, but Uncle Alfie was shouting that none of us should ever say anything about our family. He was furious. He said that there were a lot of people just looking for things to use against him and even a rumor about things like that could hurt him."

"Well," Amalie said, trying to appear the loyal follower as Geli's laughter subsided, "I'm sure it's not true."

"Oh, I'm sure it's not true, but it shouldn't really matter." Geli replied.

"But haven't you heard what he says about the Jews?"

"Yes, but that's just politics" Geli said, brushing the comment aside, "politicians say all sorts of things that they don't really mean."

"Geli, just because you have a Jewish boyfriend, don't think it doesn't matter to others. If Uncle Alfie knew that you had a Jewish friend in Vienna He'd go crazy."

"Do you think so?" Geli asked coyly.

"You are playing with fire" Amalie said slowly, scolding Geli and trying to impress on her again how dangerous her game was.

"You worry too much" Geli retorted using the same scolding tone.

Neither Amalie nor Geli could have known that Adolf was so concerned with William Hitler's insinuations, and the rumors that Adolf had heard himself when he was younger about Jews in his family, that he sent Hans Frank, his lawyer, to the Waldviertel region to investigate the rumors.

When Hans returned to Munich after completing his investigation, he was concerned about how his client would react to the findings. Not only did Hans come to the conclusion that there was Jewish blood in the Hitler family, throughout his investigation he kept running into people who said that a reporter, a female reporter from Munich named Liesl Kraus, had been there a few years before asking the same sort of questions. While Han's information was slightly incorrect in that he said it was a son of the Frankenburger family in Graz who had gotten Marie Schicklgruber pregnant when in fact it was a grandson of the Frankenburgers from Graz, he had come to much the same conclusions as Amalie had. The only thing that differed in the investigations was that Amalie had Angela Raubal's family Bible and the confession from Johann Nepomuk Hiedler.

Adolf was, just as Hans expected, enraged by the report, denying it, saying that it was not possible. He then went on to say that he wanted Hans to track down the reporter he had mentioned. Neither Adolf or Hans said it out loud, but they both knew that Liesl Kraus would not live long after she was found. She would just disappear some night, never to be heard from again. Hans would hit a dead end a few days later when he found out that Liesl Kraus had been murdered almost ten years before, but he couldn't shake the feeling that somehow there was more to the story.

It was September when Geli decided to make her move. She knew that she held all the right cards, she knew she could control Uncle Alfie and get away to Vienna. She had lunch with Amalie on the sixteenth and told her that she was leaving for Berchtesgaden the next day to say good-bye to her mother and then she would leave for Vienna from there. Amalie knew that it would be a long time before she would see Geli again, so she embraced her as they were about to part company.

"Remember," Amalie said pointedly, "write to me. Let me know how things are going."

"I will" Geli assured her, "You've been a real friend. It hasn't been easy in Munich." Geli then surprised Amalie with a kiss on the cheek before she pulled away and smiled, giving a little wave as she hurried down the street.

That afternoon, Amalie managed to get out of the office in time to get down to the Hauptbahnhof and see Geli off as she boarded the train to Berchtesgaden. Amalie was relieved once the train was underway. She was happy that Geli made it, that she managed to escape from Uncle Alfie. Amalie had been so worried about Adolf somehow finding out about the family Bible from Vienna and managing to trace it back to her, but she wasn't only worried about herself. She was sincerely concerned about Geli and so she smiled to herself as she walked through the Hauptbahnhof away from the train platforms and down to the U-bahn, boarding the subway for Furstenried station.

"Your uncle called" Angela said once she and Geli got into the villa at Berchtesgaden, "He says you are to go home immediately."

"I am going home" Geli replied curtly to her mother.

"He wants you back in Munich."

"I told him I was going to Vienna."

"Then you had better talk with him."

"We did talk. I don't belong to him. He can't stop me."

"He can" Angela said as a matter of fact, "He said that if you don't come back on your own, he will send someone to bring you back."

Geli's eyes flashed at hearing this threat. "He said what?"

Angela said nothing as Geli fumed for a moment, but then tried to regain her composure.

"I'll go talk to him" Geli finally said with anger in her voice, "I'll talk to him and then we'll see who will stop me from going to Vienna!"

On Friday morning Geli took the train from Berchtesgaden back to Munich. She left her suitcases by the front door of the apartment and when the housekeeper asked if she should have someone take them up to Geli's room, Geli replied coldly that they should be left right where they were, that she would not be staying for long. She started for her room, but then stopped on the stairs and told the housekeeper that when Uncle Alfie got home, he should be told that she was waiting to talk to him. She put a particularly ominous emphasis on the word "talk" which let the housekeeper know that there would probably be another of the shouting matches which had become more and more common over the past few months in the apartment.

Adolf was scheduled to attend a meeting of nazi officials in Hamburg on Saturday morning, so he only intended to stop at the apartment long enough to get ready for the trip. He arrived in the late

273

afternoon with Friedrich Haas and Heinrich Hoffman. Friedrich had done some driving for Adolf after Emil the chauffeur had been fired.

Adolf smiled a little as the housekeeper told him that Geli had returned and was waiting in her room to "talk" with him. Adolf enjoyed having power over her. She had treated him badly many times, humiliated him, but when it came down to it, he owned her. She would do as she was told.

"She can wait" Adolf said, making sure that she heard that he was home, letting her know that she could just wait until he was ready to talk, to lay down the law.

Adolf leisurely went about checking his bags and making sure everything was in order as he supervised the new chauffeur loading the car. After about an hour, Adolf finally walked to Geli's room.

Geli was sitting at her writing desk, working on a letter to a girlfriend in Vienna, writing that she would soon be coming to see her. Geli looked up and stopped writing in mid-word, turning to face her uncle.

"You wished to speak with me?" Adolf said as though he had no idea what topic was on Geli's mind.

"I wanted to tell you something" Geli countered immediately, every word ready and waiting for her uncle. This was to be her declaration of separation and independence.

"..and what is that?" Adolf asked patiently, sure that he was in control, no matter what his niece said.

"I am going to Vienna."

"You are not going to Vienna" Adolf corrected, but Geli persisted.

"I am going to Vienna and you are not going to stop me."

"Why would you think that?" Adolf countered, thinking that he would give Geli enough rope to hang herself.

"Because I don't think you want me here."

"Don't be ridiculous. Why wouldn't I...?

"Because I might be an embarrassment" Geli said pensively.

Adolf felt his control of the situation quickly slipping away. "An embarrassment?" he said with just the slightest, an almost imperceptible, creak in his voice. A creak that Geli instantly recognized as the sound of the knife that she was wielding at his back.

Geli was not stupid, although at times she was a bit too

headstrong, but she recognized this in herself and she instantly tried to back off a bit and appease her uncle. "I love you Uncle Alfie, but I really want to go back to Vienna to live."

"How would you..." Adolf began, but he stammered a bit as he took a step toward Geli while he formulated the question, raising his voice as he went on, "What do you think would embarrass me?"

Geli stood up from her chair at the writing desk and stepped away from the desk, trying to keep distance between her and Adolf. "I just want to leave" Geli shouted back.

"But you just said you love me!" Adolf said angrily.

"Not like that!" Geli shot back.

"Then who, you slut? Is it the new chauffeur? Some delivery boy? Some rag-picking Jew?" Adolf reached a crescendo on the word "Jew".

Geli was crying as Adolf got hysterical and she lashed out at him. "Yes! A Jew! In Vienna... I love him. I love him! Something you wouldn't understand you sick, sick pervert!"

"A Jew?" Adolf now screamed, flailing his arms in wild gestures as he screamed so loudly that he became hoarse, "A Damned Jew!!"

Friedrich was sitting in the kitchen with Heinrich and the housekeeper. He could no longer ignore the shouting as it became animal-like in its ferocity. "I'll see if I can't calm them down" he said as he headed towards the sound of the fight. He arrived at the door of Geli's bedroom just as Adolf lunged at her and threw his fist at her, striking Geli in the bridge of the nose, producing a sickening sound of cartilage being crushed as the blow connected. Geli was almost unconscious as she flew backwards, landing on the floor just beside the writing desk, bumping the desk and knocking over glass flower vase which fell to the floor close to her hand. Geli managed to recover herself just enough to pick up the vase and threw it blindly at her uncle. The thought of Geli fighting back at him when he was so justified in beating her pushed Adolf over the edge into an uncontrollable rage. Just as the vase crashed against the wall, he pulled out his pistol and fired at Geli, the sound of the gunshot coinciding with the breaking glass. She crumbled to the floor from her sitting position. She was killed instantly as the bullet entered her heart.

Friedrich stood at the door, unable to believe what he had just seen. Adolf stood motionless as the pistol slipped from his hand fell into the thick carpet at his feet. Friedrich broke from his trance and ran to where Geli lay on the floor to see if she was still alive.

Friedrich didn't know what to do. He cradled Geli's head for a moment. He thought of how he had loved her and how she hadn't loved him. He then looked up at Adolf. He couldn't tell him that she was dead. Adolf knew it. He didn't need to be told. Friedrich felt like panicking, but he kept his head. He finally stood up slowly and walked over to the door and checked to see that the key was in the lock and then he went over to Adolf and took him by the shoulder.

"She's gone" Friedrich said softly, "There's nothing to be done. we've got to think of you now." Friedrich then lead Adolf back to his own bedroom and sat him down on the edge of his bed.

"I..." Adolf began, sounding distant and hazy, "I didn't..."

"I know it was an accident" Friedrich said, "but now just wait here a minute."

Friedrich then went back to Geli's room. He quickly picked up Adolf's Walther pistol and pressed it into Geli's hand. He tried to make it look as though she had been in the chair of the writing desk and had fallen out when she shot herself. He didn't know what else to do and he didn't have the presence of mind to think out anything more elaborate, although he did try to straighten up the room a bit so that it wouldn't look like there had been a fight. He finished up by locking the door to Geli's room.

"We've got to leave now" Friedrich said as he returned to Adolf who was still sitting on the bed, staring blankly at the wall, "We have to stay on schedule."

"Leave?" Adolf asked as Friedrich's words finally got through to him, "What about the police? There will be questions. An investigation."

"We'll take care of that later. Now we have to leave for Hamburg. We'll make it to Nuremberg tonight."

Friedrich helped Adolf up and managed to get his coat on him. "You've got to get a hold of yourself" Friedrich said, staring directly into Adolf's blank eyes and suddenly Adolf was there.

"Yes," Adolf said, "yes... we'll go to Hamburg..." Friedrich helped Adolf to the stairs but let him walk down to the car by himself as Friedrich stopped by the kitchen and managed to put on a show for the housekeeper, smiling as he told her that Geli was upset and that she had thrown them out of her room and locked the door. "You'd better just leave her alone." he said smiling, "you know how she gets..."

The housekeeper agreed with a wry laugh and got up to bid Friedrich, Heinrich and Adolf a good trip.

Friedrich felt better once they were on their way and putting some distance between them and the apartment. He rode in the back with Adolf, telling Heinrich to stop at the first place where they could make a telephone call once they were out of the city.

"I'll call Max." Friedrich confided to Adolf, "We know a couple of sympathetic policemen."

Once they got to a small inn with a telephone booth, Friedrich called Max and told him to go to a public phone and call him back. He didn't want to take any chances of someone listening in on their conversation.

"There's been an accident" Friedrich said once Max called him back.

"Where?" Max asked cautiously, wondering what Friedrich was up to.

"At the apartment."

"The apartment?"

"Adolf's."

There was a pause as Max began to realize that this must be important. "What do you need?" he finally asked.

"You've got to stay by the phone. I'm... We're on our way to Hamburg."

"The telephone at Adolf's?"

"No, no! Your telephone! Don't go to the apartment. I'll call you in about four hours. Wait by the telephone at your place."

Friedrich then hung up the phone and returned to the car, getting in on the passenger side in front with Heinrich, leaving Adolf alone in the back with his thoughts as the car sped away from the small inn towards Nuremberg.

They were on the road for quite a while before Friedrich finally spoke to Heinrich, but it wasn't that he didn't trust Heinrich. Heinrich had been with Adolf from the start and everyone knew he would give his life if necessary to protect the party, and to him, Adolf was the party.

"We have a problem."

Heinrich looked concerned as he glanced up from the road, only taking in Friedrich's sullen profile since Friedrich couldn't look Heinrich in the eye as he began to plan out a course of action.

"Back at the apartment..." Friedrich continued quietly, as though Adolf would not hear him, "there was an accident."

Heinrich again looked over at Friedrich and this time Friedrich looked him in the eye. "Geli was..." Friedrich tried to think of how best to say it, but he couldn't come up with anything other than the horrible truth. "She's dead" he finally blurted out, quickly averting his eyes and sinking back into silence.

Heinrich was astounded, but kept his composure. "When? How did it happen?"

"She shot herself."

"When?"

"In about an hour from now."

"What?"

"We have to be in Hamburg before word gets out. Adolf has to be seen in Hamburg at the hotel."

"Who knows about this?"

"Only us. We have to be careful. I need your help in working it out."

Heinrich thought for a moment, realizing that Friedrich was asking him how they could best cover it up, obviously to protect Adolf, and he reflexively glanced in the rear view mirror to see how Adolf was reacting to all of this. Adolf was slouched over against the door, staring down at the back of the front seat with an empty, lost and confused look on his face.

"What do you have in mind?" Heinrich asked as he turned back to Friedrich for an instant before turning his attention back to the road.

"It looks like a suicide, but we need do everything we can to make sure that all the pieces fit."

"How?"

"I called Max Amann when we stopped back there. He's waiting for my call when we reach Nuremberg."

"What are you going to tell him?"

"I'm not sure."

"Well, the longer we wait, the better our alibi." Heinrich said as he shrugged a shoulder back towards Adolf in the back seat, indicating that when he said "our alibi", he meant Adolf's alibi.

"We can't wait too long."

"How long do you think?"

"She has to be discovered in the normal course of the day."

"Frau Winter?"

"Yes, the housekeeper. She would call her down for breakfast."

"What if Geli is found now?"

"That shouldn't be a problem. Her door is locked and she asked not to be disturbed."

There was an uncomfortable pause as Friedrich's statement made it clear that this was not just speculation. Geli was really dead and the cover up was already begun.

"Will she cooperate? I mean Frau Winter. Will she do what we say?" Heinrich asked.

"I'm sure of it. Her loyalty, along with money, but we have to keep this as quiet as possible. Max... Frau Winter..."

"Frau Reichert?"

"The landlady? I suppose, and she's been with Adolf for years. He's taken good care of her."

"What about the newspapers? The police?"

"That's what I have to discuss with Max." Friedrich said as he rubbed his eyes wearily, feeling the stress of the situation, anxious to get to Nuremberg and work out the details with Max. "Max knows a couple of policemen and we have to work out a story with Frau Winter and Frau Reichert. There must be matching testimony that everything was fine long after we left."

The road to Nuremberg seemed to stretch out forever.

Friedrich called Max as soon as they got checked into the hotel and once again Max went out to a public phone and Friedrich laid out the whole story along with his plans to protect Adolf. Friedrich was pleased when Max told him that he thought he could take care of the coroner and have the body sent quickly to Vienna for burial. The rest of the story fell into place once Friedrich checked with Adolf to make sure that there was money available to glue everything together.

The story would be that there was no argument between Geli and Adolf and that she was extremely pleasant as she bid Adolf and his escorts a good trip. It would be said that there was a strange sound in the middle of the night and that the housekeeper knocked on Geli's door in the morning and when she didn't answer, the housekeeper called Max, who went to the house and broke the door open. They said that Geli committed suicide because she had wanted to be a singer and she was nervous about an upcoming concert. The coroner would do a cursory examination, but the body was on it's way to Vienna for burial within hours of being discovered.

The newspapers ran stories suggesting that the circumstances of Geli's death were highly questionable, but they had nothing to go on. There was no autopsy. The body was out of the country and the party had worked hard to put out their version of what happened to any paper that would print it.

It wasn't until days later that Friedrich allowed himself to feel something. A night out drinking in a quiet beer hall and then a walk in the English garden with a gentle breeze that seemed to carry distant whispers, voices far away or voices long before. He found a park bench where he sat watching the river. It was past two in the morning and there was a bright, full September moon spilling its silver wash over the trees and grass and into the river. He sat on the bench and stretched out, locking his hands behind his neck and looking up at the stars, at a few sparse clouds illuminated by the moonlight. Then he suddenly sat up straight and looked out at the river as the silver water rushed by. And he cried.

Amalie cried too when she heard. She knew what really happened, or at least she imagined she knew. She had tried to tell Geli how dangerous the game was and she had hoped that somehow she could save Geli. She thought Geli was safe when she had left for Vienna and Amalie didn't even know Geli had come back to Munich until she heard the news of her death. Amalie knew that Adolf was somehow responsible, but she didn't know how. No one in the inner circle was talking. Then she started seeing the newspaper stories that Adolf's people were feeding to the press about suicide. Everyone in the nazi inner circle was waiting to see what might happen to Adolf. Would the authorities believe it was suicide? Geli had slipped through Amalie's fingers.

Amalie even considered in a moment of anger that this might be the time to publish her information on Adolf, but after thinking about it, she decided that she didn't have enough to be sure that he would be brought down.

The scandal of Geli dying in Adolf's apartment and all the rumors that went with it swirled about Munich for months. Adolf was genuinely grieved by Geli's death. He secretly went to Austria to visit her grave even though he was under threat of arrest since the Austrian government of that time had outlawed his nazi party and declared him *persona non grata* in Austria.

Even though Friedrich assured Amalie of the devastation that Geli's death had brought to Adolf and insisted that such sincere grief was proof that Adolf had nothing to do with the tragedy, Amalie was not convinced. Amalie knew the beast and his nature, but she had made her decision to wait and so she appeared sympathetic to poor Adolf.

This, however, was not to be the most difficult event with which Amalie had to contend that September in 1931. Gunther's period of unemployment had been hard on him and the family. He felt he had failed his family and as a result he became sullen and withdrawn. It didn't take much to start an argument with any member of the household, especially Jakob who was now at an age when children are naturally rebellious.

Then one evening after dinner as the two of them sat alone in the living room reading, Gunther told Amalie that he had decided to join the sturmabteilung division of the party. He told her that with his wartime experience and with Klaus' and Friedrich's recommend-ations, he should have no trouble starting out as a group leader and quickly moving up. Gunther made it clear as he spoke that this was not open for discussion, that he had been thinking about it for quite some time and had come to a final conclusion.

Amalie wouldn't really have been able to discuss it anyway. She had denied herself the right to protest when she had tried so hard to be Geli's friend and to be accepted by the nazis as the wife of a devoted party member.

The conflict of who she was and who she had pretended to be robbed her of sleep that night. "What now? What now? What now?" she kept thinking to herself as she lay awake staring at the ceiling as Gunther snored contentedly beside her. She looked over at her husband and wondered who this man was beside her. They had been together for seventeen years. How could he be so stupid? Part of his "declaration" that night had been that the whole Jewish thing was now past. He said all she had to do was listen to Adolf Hitler's speeches and read the newspaper stories to see that he had changed.

Amalie knew what was happening. It was obvious to her. She knew that Adolf was only doing and saying what was needed to win elections. Adolf's only change had been from that of a fanatic with political aims to a politician with fanatical aims.

Her problem, it seemed to her as she lay awake analyzing her life, was that she tried to be too smart. "Maybe it is time for me to leave." she thought to herself. "Divorce? Start over again? Where? What about Jakob?" The more she thought about it, the more she began to feel trapped. She couldn't leave Jakob and she didn't know if he would go with her. The only thing she could come up with as far as a place to stay was going back to Salzburg to stay with her father and the thought of that didn't appeal to her too much. Trapped!

Gunther looked at his watch and saw that he had almost an hour before he had to meet Klaus, so he decided that he would walk to the Brown House rather than taking the U-bahn. He walked casually down Residenzstrasse on his way to Briennerstrasse and he soon found himself standing before Max-Joseph platz. It struck him as stood there that he was on his way to join the S.A. and suddenly he found himself standing within a few meters of the spot where he and Klaus had laid down when the police started shooting at them back in '23. That was the spot. That was where Gunther lay when he saw Adolf jump up from his place on the ground in front of his troops and run to the car that waited to drive him away to safety. Gunther started walking again. He rationalized that all of that had been a long time ago. Things had changed. Adolf had changed his tactics. Adolf wasn't saving himself when he ran, he wasn't afraid, he ran to save the party. He knew the party would someday save Germany and...

Gunther wasn't paying any attention to the people he passed as he looked down at the sidewalk while marching along. He was too busy convincing himself that he was doing the right thing. He looked up for a moment and found that he had passed Briennerstrasse and ended up going back two blocks before turning off Residenzstrasse. He was still twenty minutes early and rather than going inside, he waited on the bench out front for Klaus.

It was less than a minute when Klaus suddenly rushed by, not even noticing Gunther as he flew up the steps of the headquarters.

"Klaus!" Gunther shouted.

Klaus looked around to see who was calling. He smiled as he walked over and sat next to Gunther who had remained seated.

"I thought I was late. You caught me off guard."

"No," Gunther said, "there's still a little time. I hate to seem too eager."

"Right." Klaus agreed, "There's no time to get nervous when you arrive just on time."

"I'm not nervous." Gunther said confidently.

"No, of course not." Klaus said, hesitating for a moment before going on, not knowing how Gunther would take what he was about to say. "Whatever you do," he continued, "don't mention that Amalie is Jewish."

"Of course not!" Gunther replied, "But how far will they go to check?"

"Since she's Austrian, they may not be able to follow up as well as they would in Germany. Make up a maiden name. say that both her parents are dead."

"Brunner." Gunther said as he decided on a new maiden name for his orphaned wife.

"Where did you get that name?"

"One of the men at the front. Joseph Brunner. He always talked about how important his family was, rich and famous."

"Maybe that's not such a good idea then if the family was well known."

"No," Gunther said with a smirk, "it turned out it was all lies. He was killed and I wrote to his family. His mother wrote back to me and it was clear that they were just working people."

They laughed as they got up, but they were silent once they entered. It was a sacred place, like a church, the embodiment of the party, proof of how far the party had come from those nights when they would sit in the back of the Sterneckerbräu arguing while drinking watered down beer.

Klaus, always in control, went up to the desk where a young man in uniform sat typing. He began to tell the young man about Gunther's appointment when he was interrupted by an officer who came into the lobby and began asking the young man about the letter he was working on and another letter that he had yet to begin. The officer was tall and blond with a long thin nose but he looked a bit strange because, although he was thin, he had broad hips, almost like a woman. Klaus was a bit put out when the officer interrupted him, but as the officer began to speak in a funny high pitched voice, Klaus recognized him. Once the officer had finished ordering the young man about, he turned back towards his office, making brief, cold, eye

283

contact with Klaus without a word of acknowledgment, as though he dared Klaus to say anything. He then strode quickly back to his office and shut the door.

"Was that him?" Klaus asked the young man once the officer had closed the door, "The new head of security?"

"Yes, SS Obersturmbannfuhrer Rheinhard Heydrich" the young man recited as he made notes on a letter that Heydrich had just corrected.

"...From the navy? Naval intelligence, right?" Klaus pursued.

"Yes, naval intelligence. Wilhemshaven. Are you a reporter?"

"No, no." Klaus said as though he was being insulted, "I was just curious. I've heard about him, but never met him before."

"You still haven't met him" the young man said with a patronizing tone.

Klaus grimaced with the sort of smile that said he would just as soon have hit the young man as smiled at him and then went on to find out where he and Klaus had to go to see Ernst Rohm, the head of the S.A.

Their acquaintance with Adolf along with Klaus' aggressiveness when it came to his social and political standing got Gunther right to the top as far as joining the sturmabteilung. It wasn't as though he were about to enlist in a military organization, it was more like Gunther was being interviewed for a special job within a successful company.

Rohm was a nasty little man. It was common knowledge that he was a homosexual and he would often comment in casual conversation that terroristic violence was a necessary means to further the parties interests. He had been a soldier who enjoyed war and had the scars to prove it, including an obvious scar in the bridge of his nose that showed in profile where a bullet had cut out a distinct notch.

The interview went on for almost two and-a-half hours, with Klaus sitting in as a character witness for the first hour before being asked to leave Gunther and Ernst alone to continue their talk in private. Klaus alternately sat in the hallway and paced along the wide corridors. He could have left, Gunther had even suggested it, but Klaus wanted to know what went on as soon as Gunther was finished.

Gunther only allowed his exhaustion to show after he had left the office and Ernst had closed the door behind him.

"Well?" Klaus said in an excited whisper, since he only dared to whisper because everything echoed in the large hallway, "How did it go?"

"Well enough, I think." Gunther said with a tired smile, "He seemed to like me."

"Watch out for that!" Klaus said with a laugh, referring to Ernst's reputation as a homosexual.

"No. not like that" Gunther shot back, "I mean he seemed impressed with my record."

"Yes, they like men who worked their way through the ranks rather than those who got their commissions through family connections."

"Yes, that's exactly what he said."

"What else?"

"He took a lot of notes. I think they're going to do a thorough background check."

"Did you tell him 'Brunner'?"

"Yes." Gunther said, but just as he was about to say something else, they came into view of the reception desk and stopped talking until they had passed the young clerk and left the building. "I must call father and tell him about this Brunner thing, make sure he and mother don't say the wrong thing."

It was only a matter of three weeks before Gunther heard that he had been accepted as a group leader. There were no other questions about any of the information he had given, including the references to Amalie Brunner.

Jakob was very proud of his father. Jakob's circle of friends in the youth program saw it as very admirable that his father started off as a group leader. Everything was growing. The youth group, the party, the S.A, and it looked like Adolf Hitler would soon be one of the big leaders of Germany. More and more, Jakob's world became focused on the nazi party.

He was fifteen years old now and beginning to feel more confident in his social world. It all seemed clear and well defined. He knew who to like and who to hate and he knew that he was part of a group that would always be on his side. It was like having two families. He was no longer an only child since now he had his brothers and sisters in the Hitler youth programs.

He would often go to the dances set up through the youth group, but he had still been very shy among the girls even though he was becoming more and more interested in them. He tried very hard not to think about sexual things since the youth groups were often addressed by speakers who would explain how destructive sex could be. He tried hard not to masturbate since they told him what terrible things it would do to his mind and his body, but every now and then he would give in to the temptation and then feel terrible guilt at being so weak. There was one girl in particular that Jakob was interested in. Ingrid Schmidt was the daughter of one of the men who worked at the party headquarters in Munich. She was a year younger than Jakob and had long blond hair which was always braided. She smiled easily at anything that Jakob would say when they ended up talking at one of the youth group parties and she always seemed to want to touch him. She would reach for his hand or touch his arm when she made a point in a conversation and he found that he liked it, yet at the same time it made him feel uncomfortable because he wasn't sure what it meant.

The other boys in the youth group would often sit around after some group sanctioned activity and talk about girls, but Jakob had no way of knowing that most of it was lies. They would tell stories about things they had seen or how far they had gone with a girl or how much girls wanted sex although they couldn't come out and say it and this was the first time Jakob had even heard of such things. By this time he knew the mechanics of sex, but he had never actually seen a girl or a woman with her clothes off. After the first few discussions with the other boys, however, Jakob started to tell the same lies and did his best, as did all the other boys, to try to establish a reputation that would preclude him from being embarrassed by the often heard chants of "virgin" which were accompanied by laughs and finger pointing when the boys began to pick on somebody in the group.

One of the boys he had met on the first day he joined the group had become a good friend. Thomas was the only one to whom Jakob would confide that he was still, in fact, a virgin despite his protestations to the rest of the group. Thomas was in the same position, but he felt that the two of them were a team and somehow if one succeeded in losing his virginity, the other would become anointed by virtue of their friendship. One would live vicariously through the others' great achievement and so he would often try to push Jakob into situations where circumstances looked like there might be good prospects for success and Jakob would do likewise for him.

"She wants you." Thomas whispered into Jakob's ear. They were at one of the group parties in August of 1931 and at last it seemed to Jakob that Thomas might know what he was talking about as he discretely pointed at Ingrid who was smiling at Jakob from the doorway across the room where she had just arrived.

"No," Jakob replied just to be contrary, "We're just friends. We just like each other."

"That's how it is sometimes," Thomas kept whispering in a monotone, "They try to be friends just to get close, but really she wants you to rip off her blouse and lick her tits."

Jakob began to blush violently, unable to retreat since Ingrid was making a bee line across the dance floor towards him just as the tinny music of an old phonograph started playing softly. She was kind enough not to mention the obvious redness in his cheeks as she stood in front of him, ignoring Thomas as she boldly asked Jakob if he wasn't going to ask her for the first dance.

"I don't dance very well." Jakob said apologetically.

"That's all right" Ingrid replied with her characteristic smile, "I've had lessons. I can help you." and with that she took Jakob's hand and lead him to the edge of the dance floor.

Jakob felt awkward and clumsy as he waited for instructions from his teacher.

"Put your right hand here" Ingrid began as she took his hand and reached it around her and placed it on her lower back, giving the hand a pat as though she had just glued it in place, "and hold my left hand out like this."

Jakob could feel that he was still blushing since his face was just as hot as it had been the moment before, especially when Ingrid put her right arm around his waist and gave him a gentle pat on the bottom as she did so.

"Now hold me closer" she continued as she pressed tightly against him. Jakob felt himself becoming aroused and knew that she must feel it as his penis started to press out against her, but Ingrid said nothing about it. She just kept smiling and instructing him how to waltz. "...and move your feet in rhythm to the music. One, two, three, four. One, two, three, four. You're doing fine!"

Jakob finally realized that Ingrid must be aware of his erection, but she obviously didn't care. She didn't say anything and she just kept smiling all the while, eventually even resting her head on his chest as they circled around the floor. He hadn't ever noticed the smell of her hair before, and the way her hair caught the light as they moved. He began to feel more at ease and once the music stopped, he even managed to ask her for the next dance.

After the third dance, Ingrid suggested they might rest for a while and she suggested they go for a little walk. Thomas made a face and smiled as Jakob glanced over and Jakob responded by smiling back as he took Ingrid's hand, escorting her out of the hall.

The dance was in a building within a block of the west bank of the Isar, a ways north of the Deutches museum. The night was warm and bright and it was natural that they would walk towards the river to stand on the Maximiliansbrucke* in the moonlight. They watched the river flowing beneath them for a while and then headed to the walking paths that lead down to the landscaped banks of the river and eventually to one of the ornate black iron benches which was obscured from view by the dense shrubs and undergrowth.

"A nice dance tonight" Jakob said as they sat down.

"Yes," Ingrid agreed without much conviction, as though her mind were on something else, "they usually are nice."

"Usually they're so bright" Jakob continued, trying to keep up the small talk.

"What?"

"The dances. Usually the chaperones have the lights so bright."

"Oh... Yes, you're right"

"But tonight they were just right, like a glow in the room."

"Jakob," Ingrid interrupted, "do you want... would you kiss me?"

Jakob was caught off guard. He had been trying to figure out how he might steal a kiss. He reached over and kissed her, surprising himself as he put his hand on her breast, pressing against the stiffly starched cotton of her blouse and the firm seams of her brassiere. He deftly undid a button on her blouse while still kissing her, fully expecting she would pull away, but she didn't. He felt encouraged and slid his hand under the white blouse, gently pressing on her breast, but he didn't know how to get the brassiere off. He hadn't done this before

* Maximillian bridge

288

and so he contented himself with sliding his hand down to the warm soft skin of her abdomen and then up and down her side slowly as they kept kissing.

He didn't even notice as Ingrid undid another button on her blouse and reached back to undo the hooks of her brassiere. He suddenly found the brassiere sliding down on his hand and was dizzy from breathing so heavily, as though he couldn't catch his breath. He reached up to hold her small breast in his hand and stopped kissing Ingrid as he looked down to see what he held.

Her skin was flushed pink and Jakob put his face to her chest, pressing his cheek to her breast and then turning to kiss it lightly, feeling the heat radiating against his cheek. Ingrid didn't move. She didn't make a sound. She didn't tell him to stop.

"Thomas had been right!" he thought to himself excitedly, "She did want him."

Finally she put a hand on Jakob's head and stroked his hair and then turned on the bench as Jakob moved with her until he was sitting against the back of the bench. Ingrid slowly pulled away from him, looking into his eyes and making no effort to cover her breast.

She caught him off guard again as she suddenly slid her hand down the front of his pants. Jakob had been erect since they were dancing and certainly nothing had changed that since they left the party. Ingrid's fingernail accidentally jabbed at him as she ran her hand down his hard stomach towards his thigh and he jerked back instinctively, afraid of being hurt. Ingrid stopped for a moment and whispered "sorry", but his only response was to stretch out his legs and spread them apart so that she would have room to explore.

Ingrid smiled and continued slowly, feeling her way down, lightly running her hand over his body. "It feels so strange" she said as she gently moved his testicles from side to side until they started to draw up tightly. Jakob couldn't talk. He had never touched himself before in quite that way, that lightly, gently, and he had never had a sexual encounter before and had no idea how it could feel and now that this beautiful girl was touching him like this it sent shock waves through his legs and started his head swimming.

Ingrid then moved her hand up, barely touching it, feeling how big it was. She lightly moved her hand over the skin, up and down, until Jakob couldn't stand it anymore. He quickly undid his pants and reached down, putting his hand over hers and forcing her to grip him firmly. Ingrid giggled because he seemed so frustrated and she liked the thought that she excited him so and made him lose control.

Jakob finally managed to whisper. "Harder", but as he gripped her hand and forced her to pump up and down Ingrid became scared, as though things were going too far and this wasn't just playing anymore.

She tried to let go of him, but that only made Jakob hold her hand even tighter.

"Stop it!" she said, "You're hurting me!" and she pulled away, but Jakob still held her hand.

"Oh God!" he gasped, "Please don't stop. Please don't stop now!" Ingrid kept trying to pull away, standing up and almost breaking free, but Jakob jumped up and wrapped his arms around her, his pants falling down to his ankles as he started pressing himself against her, desperately, uncontrollably rubbing himself against the coarse fabric of her skirt.

Ingrid started crying and saying "no, no...", but Jakob felt out of control, as though he couldn't stop himself. He reached down for her skirt with one hand while still holding her tightly and pulled it up, finally finding skin to rub against. He didn't even try to enter her as he thrust over and over again against the soft skin of her thigh, quickly coming to orgasm.

Once it was over, it was like coming out of a nightmare, he couldn't believe what had happened, he couldn't believe what he had done, that he had been so out of control. Ingrid was crying and frantically trying to brush his semen off her leg as though it were acid burning her skin.

Jakob struggled to pull up his pants. He didn't know what to do. What could he say? He could run. But where? She knew his name. He had hurt her. He had terrified her and now he had to face the consequences.

"I'm... I'm sorry... I couldn't" he looked down at the ground. He was ashamed. How could he have done that? How? How could it have happened?

"I couldn't stop." he offered lamely.

Ingrid stopped crying for a moment and stared at him and even in the darkness he could see the contempt and disgust, the hatred.

"I'm sorry! I'm sorry" he continued, sounding almost as though he was going to cry.

290

"You Bastard!" Ingrid finally spat out at him, "You sick bastard. You disgusting animal." and she took a long swing, slapping him as hard as she could, so hard that her fingers left red marks on the cheek that had only moments before rested against her breast and then she ran off towards the party.

"Wait!" Jakob shouted as he took off after her, "Please."

Ingrid stopped as he came after her. "Don't you dare touch me. If you touch me, my father will kill you."

"No, Ingrid please..."

"What?"

"Please don't tell anyone. I'll do anything. Please, God please don't say anything. I'll do anything. I'll give you anything."

Ingrid's eyes narrowed with hate, but she didn't say anything. She knew she was in control again slowly reached behind herself to re-hook her brassiere and button up her blouse, continuing to stare at Jakob with an expression that dared him to say anything or to move towards her. She finally turned and slowly walked back to the party. Jakob turned and walked in the opposite direction toward the U-bahn station wondering what would happen next. Would Ingrid tell? Would her father come to kill him? Maybe the police would come for him. It was a mind-numbing ride home as his imagination ran wild.

He got home before his mother and father, who had also gone out for the evening, and fell into bed with his clothes on, pulling the covers up over his head and crying quietly, ashamed of what he'd done and wishing that night had never been and afraid of what the morning would bring. When his mother and father asked about the dance the next morning, he just said everything was fine and left it at that. He was grateful for the reprieve that the weekend offered, that he didn't have to worry about whether Ingrid had told everyone at school, but the weekend flew past and he soon found himself walking down the halls of the school, wondering each time someone made eye contact with him if they somehow knew about what happened.

Ingrid knew she didn't need to confront Jakob or tell his friends. She knew that part of her revenge would be making him sweat, making him wait to see what she would do to get back at him. She also knew within hours after the incident how she would take her revenge.

Helmut Puppenspiel was the leader of Jakob's youth group section. In keeping with the policy espoused by the nazi party that the

291

Hitler youth groups should be lead by young people, Helmut was nineteen years old.

Ingrid found Helmut at the Alten Rosenbad restaurant in the Schwabbing district which was frequented by party members and had, in fact, been a favorite meeting place of Hitler himself in the early days of the party. Helmut was laughing with two friends as Ingrid walked up to his table.

"Herr Puppenspiel?" she asked with authority, although it only barely covered the apprehension the fifteen-year-old girl felt as she addressed the youth group leader four years her senior.

"Yes?" he answered with an air of superiority as he looked up at the little girl.

"I need to talk to you about one of the boys in your group."

"Someone caught your eye?" Helmut threw back with an arrogant smirk.

"There is a serious matter which we need to discuss" Ingrid rejoined resolutely.

Helmut realized it was some sort of trouble and he had strict orders to make sure there were no problems or scandals within the youth group. These suggestions came from the party leaders who were beginning to realize the potential of indoctrinating and training soldiers long before they actually become soldiers. Helmut asked his friends to leave for a few moments so that he and Ingrid could talk privately.

"Now then," Helmut began as he motioned Ingrid to sit beside him, "what is it?"

"Jakob Metzdorf."

"Jakob? What's wrong with Jakob? He's one of our best..."

"He tried to rape me."

Helmut stopped in mid sentence.

"Jakob?" he asked after he found his voice again, "but Jakob is a quiet, shy..."

"He did it" Ingrid interrupted.

"When?"

"Last Friday. At the dance."

"At the dance?"

"We left to go for a walk."

Helmut thought for a moment as he took in the information. "Did you tell the police?" he finally asked.

"No."

"Why not? Why are you telling me? Why did you wait to say anything?"

"My father works at the Braunhaus. I don't think the Hitlerjungend should be embarrassed. I just want Jakob Metzdorf out of the HJ so that I won't have to see him ever again."

"You want him thrown out?"

"Yes."

"...and you want me to tell him why?"

"No."

"I suppose you want to tell him."

"Yes. I want to tell him because I know how much he loves it and I want to tell him why this is happening."

Helmut tried not to show any change in his facial expression as Ingrid's plan sank in. "Hell hath no fury..." he thought to himself.

"This assumes that I take you at your word that everything happened as you say" Helmut said slowly as he analyzed the developing situation, "It would be a cruel joke if it wasn't as you said, if you had some other reason to dislike Jakob and just wanted to..."

"Herr Puppenspiel, I could have just told my father and he would take care of it, but you should know that it would be a big mess. This way only you, I and Jakob would have to know."

"And you get to drive the knife into his heart yourself." Helmut imagined saying to the pretty little blond girl, but he only managed a little smile at what a neat package she had made of everything.

"Very well," Helmut conceded, "I'll see Jakob tomorrow afternoon. I'll tell him then."

The next day Helmut sat waiting for Jakob outside the Neue Realgymnasium in Sendlingertores district just as classes let out for the day. "Jakob!" Helmut called out from across the street.

"Helmut?" Jakob said with surprise, not expecting to see his friend here since they were going to see each other in just about an hour at the HJ meeting, "What gives? Aren't we meeting this afternoon?"

"Yes, but there's something we need to talk about."

It made Jakob a little nervous that Helmut was so serious.

"Like what?" Jakob managed to squeak out.

"Let's sit" Helmut said as he walked over to a bench. "Someone came to talk with me yesterday."

Jakob's face was eager with anticipation at what Helmut might say next. Helmut always joked about Jakob going to the Olympics because of talent in archery, or could it be word of a promotion? Jakob knew he was well liked in the group and he did well at all the sporting events. He participated in planning the social events. Maybe he would be asked to lead a squad.

"They... this person... told me there was... an incident." Helmut continued, stumbling through his little speech as Jakob began to tense up. This no longer sounded to Jakob as though it would be a good talk. "An incident at the party last Friday night." Helmut finally finished up in a rush of words, punctuating the accusation by looking Jakob in the eye for the first time since they sat down.

"I... what kind of..." Jakob stuttered as he instantly switched from wanting to offer an explanation to wanting to pretend that he didn't know what Helmut could possibly be talking about, but Helmut pushed ahead, leaving no room for Jakob to confirm or deny what was about to be said.

"A girl says you attacked her." Helmut stated as he looked straight out across the street rather than looking Jakob in the eye.

He spoke in a monotone as he pronounced sentence. "I'm afraid there is no place for that sort of behavior in the HJ. You have to leave... Resign. Because I like you, I'll let you do it yourself rather than letting the other men know."

Jakob was cornered and crushed. He stared down at the gray sidewalk. The HJ was everything to him. All his friends, the sports... the respect he had earned, it all centered around the youth group. He felt like crying as it started to sink in. It hurt. What would he do? He had made a mistake and now he had to pay for it.

"Did she tell the police?" Jakob finally managed to ask in a half whisper.

Helmut was caught off guard by this. He had expected Jakob to stand up for himself, to call the girl a liar, to say that nothing of the kind had happened.

"No." Helmut replied, realizing that Jakob was beaten.

"Will she?"

"I don't think so, she seemed to just want you out of the group."

Jakob was relieved a bit, but then he realized that this was enough. She must have known that. She had taken away everything he had.

294

Helmut felt sorry for Jakob and managed to put his arm around him for a moment with a quick pat on the back. "You'll be all right Orion. It could have been much worse. I understand her father is some official at the party headquarters. Consider yourself lucky that she handled it herself."

Helmut then got up and walked away, quickly disappearing around the corner of the block.

Jakob sat alone on the wall for a while, not knowing what to do next. What would he say to his friends in the HJ? How would he explain it? What would he say to his mother and father?

It was not a coincidence that Ingrid came by at that moment. She had seen Helmut waiting by the school and she was sure that he was waiting for Jakob. She hid and watched as Helmut and Jakob talked and when she saw Jakob's head fall she knew that was the moment Helmut had told him. She felt an incredible rush of excitement at that instant, like a marksman watching as his bullet brought down the quarry. Her bullet had hit home.

When Helmut left, she began to walk towards Jakob. He didn't even notice her until she stood in front of him and spoke. "A pig like you doesn't belong in the HJ."

"I'm sorry" was all Jakob could manage to say to the hate filled face in front of him.

"Now you're sorry!" Ingrid shot back before storming off down the street.

Gertrude was surprised when Jakob came into the house. "You're early!" she said with a smile as she looked up at the clock, "...and late."

"I had something to do at school" Jakob replied, but the truth was that he'd spent the previous hour and more coming up with reasons that he could use to explain to his friends and family when they found out he had resigned.

"Well, you're late for after school, but didn't your boys group meet tonight?"

"Yes, I decided not to go."

Gertrude let the issue drop at that. "Dinner won't be ready for another hour."

"I know. I've got some reading to do."

"Are you all right?"

"Yes, everything is fine" Jakob lied as he went to his room. It seemed like only a few moments later when his mother and father came home and Gertrude was calling him to dinner.

Amalie had had a good day and dominated the conversation for the first few minutes of dinner with the story of a book she had bought for Frieder and Son by outbidding another publisher.

Gunther, on the other hand, had had a rather bad day full of petty bickering and unreasonable requests. When the conversation lulled, he asked Jakob how his day had gone.

"Good."

"Anything new?"

"Not really..." Jakob replied, but then he decided to casually bring up leaving the HJ. so that he would be the one to tell his parents before they had a chance to find out through anyone else. "I decided to leave the Hitler youth program." he said to his dinner plate.

Amalie, Gunther and Gertrude were all shocked since Jakob had been so deeply involved in the group.

"When did you decide this?" Gunther asked.

"I've been thinking about it for some time now" Jakob replied as he began moving his food around on the plate with his fork.

"Why?" Amalie asked, trying not to appear too eager since the news pleased her so.

"A lot of things." Jakob said evasively, which began to frustrate Gunther as he tried to understand what could possibly make his son want to leave the HJ.

"Things like what?" Gunther pressed.

"It's getting too..." Jakob began, "It's like being in the army."

"But that's good!" Gunther insisted, "It teaches you discipline."

"But it's so much. It's not as fun as it used to be." Jakob whined.

"Everything doesn't have to be fun!" Gunther said, raising his voice, "Sometimes the things we don't like are good for us in the long run. We learn through adversity."

"What else?" Amalie asked, interrupting Gunther and urging Jakob to keep talking before Gunther got carried away.

"They're talking about the Jews" Jakob finally offered as though his mother had pulled it out of him, but in reality he knew this was something that would get her support against his father.

Gunther listened intently as Amalie probed this new reason.

"What kind of talk?" she asked.

"They say the Jews should be killed. They're talking about

Grandfather Ethan!"

"You didn't tell them about your Grandfather, did you?" Gunther asked, trying to cover his panic. After all, they would certainly connect Jakob's Jewish Grandfather with Jakob's father as a member of the Sturmabteilung. Amalie looked angry at Gunther's reflexive response to this threat to his job and Jakob knew he had won his mother over. Jakob continued his attack.

"They sing that song; 'When the blood of the Jews is running down our knives, then we all will be happy.'"

"It's just a song!" Gunther said loudly. "I keep telling you it's just talk!"

"I think that's enough" Amalie countered, surprising her husband with the finality in her voice. "Jakob seems to have made up his mind."

"But what will they say if my own son leaves the..."

"This isn't about you" Amalie said calmly.

"He's my son!"

"And what does that mean? That you own him? That he has to do exactly as you do and believe only what you believe?"

Gunther didn't like this argument. He hadn't seen this side of Amalie for quite some time. She had been so agreeable, but now she seemed to be changing. Ever since... If he had to put his finger on it, it seems that just about the time that Geli Raubal killed herself. He said nothing more. He just went back to eating his meal in silence.

Jakob also went back to his dinner in silence, but he didn't feel angry or frustrated. His plan had worked. He turned his mother against his father and kept them from finding out the real reason.

Now if he could just make something like that work with his friends in the HJ, but that would be harder. His friends couldn't be played one against the other like his parents could. Jakob did have an idea, though, that he could use the argument he had tried to pass off on his parents about the HJ becoming too much like the army. He would say he didn't like being told what to do all the time. He could be the rebel. An individualist who was born to lead rather than follow. It was far from the truth and he wasn't sure how he could pull it off, but Jakob didn't think there was any other way.

Chapter 12

Even though the nazi party had won enough Reichstag seats to make it the second largest party in the country in 1930, Adolf Hitler lost the Presidential election of 1932 to Paul von Hindenburg and then in November of 1932 the nazis lost 34 of their Reichstag seats. It once again looked like Adolf Hitler and his party would fade away, but the nazi representatives still remaining in the Reichstag continued to make their presence felt, disrupting the proceedings whenever things went against them.

There were also continuous intrigues regarding the office of Reichschancellor as Hitler tried to get Hindenburg to appoint him to the second highest office in the Weimar government. Hindenburg would have none of it as he personally disliked Hitler. Eventually, however, as three different Reichschancellors came and went, due in large part to the intransigence and disruptive practices of the nazis in the Reichstag, Hindenburg was eventually convinced by a number of advisors that Adolf Hitler was the only man who could hold the government together. The eighty-four-year-old Hindenburg grudgingly appointed Adolf Hitler Chancellor of Germany on January 30 of 1933 although Hindenburg never asked Hitler in person if he would accept the position as he had done with the other Reichschancellor appointees.

Paul von Hindenburg could not have imagined the consequences of his action at that time and he probably thought it was only a temporary political expedient. He clearly underestimated the former corporal and couldn't have seen the road down which Adolf Hitler would lead Hindenburg's beloved fatherland. One can only wonder if it was just coincidence that the old man died within moments of Adolf Hitler passing a law which combined the office of Reichschancellor and President. That was when Hitler became Germany's Fuhrer instead of a Reichschancellor under the President's thumb. The nazis celebrated that day with torch light parades throughout the country and a new oath was issued to Germany's military forces, an oath in which they no longer swore allegiance to the Weimar constitution, but now it was Adolf Hitler alone who demanded their allegiance, for Adolf Hitler had become the state.

The RSHA section of the SS, the National Central Security

Office or "Reichssicherheitshauptampt" of the Schutzstaffel, was where Reinhard Heydrich worked in Munich as head of the party's security police. The Sicher Dienst or "SD", was one of seven departments within RSHA. The organization of the Schutzstaffel was still being developed, including the creation of an office known as the Geheime Staats Polizei. The secret state police which would soon become known all over the world by its shortened name "Gestapo".

Ernst Rohm, the leader of the nazi brownshirts, had only returned from Bolivia in January of 1931 after a self-imposed exile brought on by conflicts between Hitler and himself as to how the party should be run and what the role of the Sturmabteilung should be within the party. This conflict between Rohm and Hitler was not limited to just those two men.

The rank and file of the Sturmabteilung, especially in Berlin, also had problems with the direction that national socialism was taking in Germany. The talk in the S.A. was that the nazis were just becoming another political party, another group of weak men forced to compromise with other interests rather than strong willed leaders who would take the nation by force and bring about the resurrection of the fatherland through national socialism.

"Good morning Rebecca, come in" Gertrude said in a voice that showed pleasant surprise as she opened the door.

"Good morning Gertie."

"...and what has you up and about so early on a Saturday morning?"

"I, uhh" Rebecca stammered as she inched past the doorway at Gertrude's invitation.

"What? Did you need something?"

"Well, Frau Haas..."

"Frau Haas? Suddenly you're so formal. It must be important."

"Maybe I was silly to come over" Rebecca rattled off as she turned for the door.

"Nonsense!" Gertrude countered as she put a hand on Rebecca's shoulder, "Now tell me what you need."

"Well..." Rebecca started, her eyes darting about the floor nervously, "Mother's out... and I don't know where Max is..."

"No wonder." Gertrude said sympathetically, "Your brother is just like my boys used to be. On Saturday morning they were always out of the house before I even had a chance to ask them about their chores."

"Yes," Rebecca continued, a little more at ease, "like I said, mother's gone and Max is gone and I'm supposed to... put some things in the attic and I hoped that maybe..."

"...you wanted Jakob to help you?" Gertrude said, finishing Rebecca's thought while refraining from comment on the obvious ploy to be with Jakob.

"Well, yes" Rebecca answered, still nervous and trying to avoid eye contact.

Gertrude and Rebecca had become friends since they first met months before, and Gertrude suspected for some time that Rebecca was interested in Jakob, but they never discussed it.

Rebecca and her younger brother Max were latchkey children. Their father had died in the Great War and their mother had to work and so Rebecca would stop by to see Gertrude almost every day. Rebecca was a bright girl who often amused Gertrude by talking about her interest in Freudian psychology. It seemed like such an odd interest for a young girl, especially when she tried to explain the strange things psychology taught. The thought of the day that Rebecca, the fifteen-year-old girl, tried to explain to Gertrude, the sixty-six-year-old German housewife, about a concept called "penis envy" would continue to inspire fits of laughter for Gertrude almost until the day she died.

"I'm not sure." Gertrude said sympathetically. "Jakob has been... he hasn't been feeling well lately, but I'll go ask him."

Jakob was having a hard time since he left the Hitler youth He was almost sixteen when he dropped out, an age when it seems more important than ever to fit in and the worst of it was that he had been so popular one moment and then suddenly ostracized the next. Contrary to what Shakespeare said about love, Jakob thought that it would have been better he hadn't been popular in the first place.

Gunther's reaction to his son's isolation was hostile. He had taken a lot of pride in his son's achievements and it seemed to him that Jakob quit without any good reason. He tried to talk with Jakob, to understand him, but after a few weeks of Jakob's withdrawal, Gunther accepted it and ended up becoming more involved in his work and he and Jakob began to drift apart. Perhaps he was more concerned about how these events affected him than how Jakob was doing.

Amalie tried to help, but Jakob pushed her away too, afraid that somehow she might find out the horrible truth. He would shrug his shoulders whenever she tried to talk about it and say that the HJ just didn't suit him anymore. Amalie certainly didn't want to press him to go back since she had never approved of his membership in the HJ anyway, but she knew it was hurting him. In the long run all she could do was write it off to the difficulties of adolescence. Perhaps it was just a phase of rebellion against Gunther. She noticed that it had affected their relationship, but she couldn't decide if that was something Jakob wanted or just an unexpected side effect. Whatever the cause behind it, Amalie worried about Jakob's isolation and the hours spent by himself reading or just laying on his bed with the door to his room closed, saying that he wanted to be left alone.

The knock on the door startled Jakob who was only half awake. "Jakob!" Gertie sang, "May I come in?"

"I'm still sleeping" Jakob called out, at which point Gertrude opened the door just enough to put her head in.

"Gertie! What if I hadn't been covered?" Jakob said sleepily from under the bedding that almost covered his mouth.

"I used to give you baths. You haven't changed that much."

"I hope I have." Jakob said indignantly with an adolescent smirk.

"Come Jakob, it's time to get up."

"Why?"

"I've volunteered you."

"What?"

"Yes, I'm tired of you laying about the house all day. Rebecca needs some help and I said you would."

"Without asking me?" Jakob said, maintaining his indignation.

Gertrude surprised Jakob by sitting on his bed, something he couldn't ever remember her doing before, and then she reached out and brushed the long unruly hair out of his eyes.

"I'm worried about you... You seem so..."

"I'm all right" Jakob interrupted, "I just..."

"Please," Gertrude said, now interrupting Jakob in return, "I would consider it a personal favor if you would help Rebecca put some things up in their attic."

Jakob almost said no, but then as he looked at Gertrude's face, a face filled with concern, not authority, he nodded yes. "It will take a few minutes to wash up and get dressed."

"Thank you liebchen, that's very nice of you."

By the time Jakob appeared in the kitchen dressed and ready to go, Rebecca was just finishing a hard roll and piece of ham that Gertrude had given her for breakfast.

"Where's mine?" he said as though he had been left out on purpose.

"Goodness. You have atrocious manners young man" Gertrude scolded as she took a plate of sliced ham out of the refrigerator and offered it to him.

Jakob smiled as he took the ham with his fingers and chewed a couple of times with his mouth open.

"Jakob!" Gertrude scolded again and Jakob closed his mouth and put a roll in his coat pocket and then took another roll and made a sandwich while simultaneously motioning to Rebecca to follow. "Come 'becca."

Rebecca dutifully scampered after Jakob, turning to smile at Gertrude as she left.

After they walked a few feet, Jakob looked at Rebecca.

"Aren't you going to get in trouble?"

302

"For what?" Rebecca asked, looking puzzled.

"The sandwich."

"What?"

"The sandwich... You ate a ham sandwich."

"So what?"

"I thought you were Jewish."

"Oh" Rebecca said with a blend of indignation and just a hint of embarrassment. "I'm Jewish... Jakob, you're Jewish too."

Jakob kept looking straight ahead as he walked. "Only half" he said curtly.

"According to Jewish law," Rebecca instructed, "you are a Jew because your mother is Jewish. The Jews don't believe like the nazis that you are part this and part that. You are either a Jew or not."

"I am a German."

"So am I" Rebecca said defensively, "My family has lived in Germany for almost six hundred years. My father was killed in the war, fighting for Germany."

Jakob thought about going back on his word to Gertrude and leaving Rebecca there as they arrived at the front gate of her yard, but instead he coolly opened the gate, allowing Rebecca to go first and then followed her into the house.

"These boxes over here" Rebecca pointed out as she breezed through the house. She got up on a chair she had put under the access panel and pulled down the door.

"One of us needs to climb into the attic while the other one hands up the boxes."

"I'll go up" Jakob volunteered.

"Good," Rebecca said with a smile, "I think there are bats up there. I hate going up."

"Thanks" Jakob replied sarcastically.

"Are you afraid of bats?"

"Let's just say I don't care for them much."

"I thought all boys liked bats and mice and snakes and..."

"I thought all girls were quiet and shy." Jakob said as he jumped up and caught the edge of the door frame, showing off as he swung his feet up to the opening and vaulted into the attic.

Rebecca didn't miss a beat in the conversation, but she was impressed. "What do you mean? I'm shy" she insisted.

"Like a pit bull."

"That's not true. At least when I first meet someone I'm shy."

"Like when you first met me?" Jakob challenged as he climbed into the attic, disappearing into the small hole until he turned around and stuck his head out and then his arms, ready for the first box.

"You wouldn't even remember the first time we met." Rebecca counter-challenged.

"Of course I do" he said as she handed him the first box and he disappeared again into the attic and packed the box away in a corner, quickly returning to the opening in the ceiling. "It was on my way to school one morning and there was a downpour and you offered me half of that tiny pink umbrella."

Rebecca smiled at the picture of Jakob crouching slightly under that umbrella with her as they made a dash for the U-bahn station.

"No." she replied simply.

"Of course it was" he protested, "That was the first time I ever saw you."

"No, the first time was when I was over at your house talking with Gertie and you raced in from school and changed into your HJ uniform and than ran out."

"You make it sound like I didn't even see you."

"You didn't."

"Well then, we didn't really meet."

"I met you... Gertie introduced you as you slipped out the door."

Jakob didn't know how to reply to this, so he just let it go by as he reached for another box.

"Are you an anti-semite?" Rebecca asked from out of nowhere. "That's a silly question. You just told me I'm a Jew and now you want to know if I hate 'em?"

"It's not like some people aren't both."

"Well, I'm not..."

"Not which?"

Jakob smiled as he pulled a box out of Rebecca's hands.

"Neither" he said.

"How did you get into the HJ?" Rebecca asked with a look of earnest curiosity. She wasn't challenging Jakob this time, she was just curious how someone with a Jewish mother could get into the Hitler youth program. Jakob said nothing, but that didn't stop her from asking more questions when he returned for another box. "Why did you drop out?"

Again there was silence as he quickly took a box and disappeared.

"...they say you got a girl pregnant..." she said loudly enough so that he could hear her no matter how far he retreated into the attic. It took a moment before he reappeared at the access door and looked down at her.

"Any more?" he asked with anger in his voice as his temper grew short.

"Questions or boxes?" Rebecca asked, working hard to hold back a smile as she realized that she was getting to him, getting through to the stranger who lived only five houses away, the one she had wanted to know for so long.

"Boxes."

"No."

Jakob then made an equal physical display of exiting the attic as he had made of his entry, landing squarely on his feet just in front of Rebecca.

"Would you like some toast and tea?" Rebecca offered.

"Tea?" Jakob tossed back as though insulted, since only women and ridiculous young girls drank tea.

"Coffee, then?" she amended.

"Thank you" he said smugly, thinking that she should have known in the first place that since he was an adult, he would drink coffee. He even managed a smile as Rebecca drifted into the kitchen. For some reason she found herself thrilled at the prospect of making Jakob toast and coffee. She imagined herself as a woman entertaining a gentleman caller instead of just the neighbor offering something to the boy who helped put up boxes in the attic.

"'Becca!"

"Oh no" Rebecca thought to herself as her friends Kurt and Jurgen flew into the living room and through to the kitchen, surprising Rebecca and Jakob in the middle of their domestic episode. She was afraid that they might try to pick a fight with Jakob.

"Metzdorf." Jurgen said with surprise as he fell into one of the chairs at the kitchen table and started eating a piece of the rye toast without even asking, as though it were his own home.

"Hassler..." Jakob acknowledged casually between a bite of toast and sip of coffee. Jurgen was also from the neighborhood and he even went to the same school as Jakob, but he wasn't in the same circle of friends that Jakob had known. Jurgen had, for whatever reasons, made a point of staying clear of anyone involved in the Hitler youth programs.

"Look Kurt," Jurgen said, using the piece of toast to point, "it's Jakob Metzdorf."

"Who?" Kurt asked innocently.

"Orion. The golden boy of the HJ." Jurgen said defiantly as he stared at Jakob, daring him to say anything.

"You're HJ?" Kurt asked with an edge to his voice, confronting Jakob and then looking at Rebecca, wondering why she would have someone from the Hitler youth in her kitchen.

"I was. I'm not anymore. They're getting out of hand." Jakob said as though he had been a pagan who had finally seen the way of God.

Kurt seemed satisfied with the statement, but Jurgen pressed on. "Getting thrown out for getting a girl pregnant isn't the same as leaving because you object to their politics."

Jakob's eyes flashed anger, but he controlled himself. "That," he began slowly, "is a lie they spread to discredit me."

"Prove it" Jurgen challenged.

"How do you prove something didn't happen? Where is this pregnant girl? Where is the baby?" Jakob was calm as he spoke, still finishing his toast and the last of the coffee as he summed up his case. "They didn't want anyone else to leave, so they had to make up some lie about why I left."

After a pause, while Kurt and Jurgen thought about Jakob's version of the story, Rebecca smiled and said she knew it had all just been rumors.

Kurt and Jurgen weren't as quick to accept Jakob's explanation, but it was obvious to them that Rebecca had a crush on him and so they were willing to give Jakob the benefit of the doubt.

Kurt, Jurgen and Rebecca were a group of friends on the outside. They didn't seem to quite fit in at school when they were younger and all three had gone on to higher schooling rather than trade education when they were fourteen. Their career plans all seemed to give insight as to how they dealt with people. Kurt planned on a career in scientific research and he kept trying to qualify and quantify the emotions and motives of others as though he might someday work out an equation of human nature. Jurgen on the other hand was a superior mathematics student who seemed to have chosen to try to understand numbers rather than people. Jurgen was thus quite a social contrast to Rebecca and her pursuit of Freudian psychology.

"Well..." Jurgen said, changing the subject, "are we still going to the museum?"

"That's right!" Rebecca said as she turned to Jakob. "There's a new exhibit at the Deutches museum. Do you want to come?"

Jakob looked at Kurt to see if he would "un-invite" him, but Kurt surprised him by deferring to Rebecca and saying that he should come and that it would be interesting, so the four of them stopped by Jakob's house on the way to the U-bahn to let Gertie know where they were going.

"The museum?" Gunther said as he overheard his son on the way out the door, "Good! It's about time you started getting out of the house."

Gunther had given up trying to do things with Jakob on the weekends and had settled on getting more involved with his work in the SA, but it hadn't been easy since he joined and he rarely talked about his work when he was home. On the one hand he had been with the party from the early days and so there were a lot of familiar faces in the ranks in Munich, but on the other hand he had left after the putsch in '23 which caused some resentment among those same old comrades. Then Gunther had to contend with the momentous defection of Jakob from the Hitler Youth which seemed to bring these conflicts right into Gunther's own home.

Gunther was upset with Jakob's assertion that the youth group was turning against the Jews. Gunther tried to tell Amalie that the song Jakob mentioned was just a song and all the talk about Jews was just rhetoric. He had even talked to some of the SA troops from Berlin where Hitler himself had told the S.A. that they shouldn't bear arms against the Jews and Communists in the streets.

Amalie countered that Hitler's orders were only because of the elections going on at the time and he didn't want any fighting in the streets because it might hurt his chances of being elected. She said that Adolf obviously wanted to appear to be more liberal, a middle-of-the-road candidate who could appeal to Social Democrats and members of the Catholic Central party so that it would be a simple

307

choice between Hitler or the Communists. She was clearly more astute at the nature of politics than her husband as Gunther felt believed in some kind of mystical alliance where national socialism embodied a paradox of a dictatorship that actually represented the will and spirit of the individuals within the nation. A group of people willing to give up their individuality to be free individuals, willing to hand over all power to the state, to its government, so that they might themselves be powerful. It was a form of nazi mysticism that each of these things would naturally follow the other. You had to leave critical thought behind in order to truly be swept up in the dogma of national socialism. Give up everything to the nazis and everything will come to you.

Amalie saw the pretense. She knew it wasn't an oversight that Adolf forgot to mention the elimination of the Jews from his new Germany. There was even a group called the Jewish National Union which supported a proposal by Hitler to deny Jews from Eastern Europe entry to Germany. The German Jews believed that Hitler's shouts of Germany for Germans meant them too.

The most disturbing thing to Amalie though, occurred just a few weeks before Jakob had upset his father with his announcement. On the day of the Reichstag election on July 31, 1932, a Vienna newspaper ran a headline which read "Heil Schicklgruber" with a story about Adolf's father being illegitimate. The story didn't mention Jewish blood in the family, but Amalie was shocked to see it in print and waited to see what kind of reaction there would be to a story that revealed a number of things which had turned up in her own research.

Hitler had lost the election that year for the office of President, but he came very close, winning by far the next majority of votes just below Hindenburg. Apparently the newspaper story, along with other stories directed against the nazis, such as one that revealed correspondence between Ernst Rohm and a psychiatrist in which Rohm acknowledged that he was a homosexual, didn't have much affect on the popular vote and so Amalie came to question whether anything she uncovered would ever make any difference as Adolf became more and more popular.

Political intrigues developed one after another in the new cabinet through the end of 1932 and into 1933 with Hindenburg going through three Chancellors: Bruning, Von Papen and finally General Kurt Schleicher until at the end of January of 1933 it was

308

Adolf Hitler's turn, as leader of what had become the largest political party in Germany, to become Chancellor under President Paul von Hindenburg.

That was a bleak day at Frieder and Son Publishing when the news came in. David and Amalie had pursued many political discussions over the previous months during the Presidential election and then the subsequent run-off election between Hindenburg and Hitler and finally the Reichstag elections which followed soon after the Presidential election. Through all these elections Amalie and David assured each other that with each failure Hitler faced, it meant another nail in his coffin, that the German people would see through the charade and soon all of these ridiculous brown shirts marching in the streets with their flags and slogans would be a thing of the past. They had had their moment and it was just about to pass, but then Hitler somehow managed to sneak in the back door.

David had been Amalie's foil through all that time. She had discussions with him that she could never have with Gunther and now David would share her sense of foreboding while Gunther would be out celebrating the party's victory.

The day that Adolf's ascension to the office of Chancellor was announced, David suggested that he and Amalie should go out for whatever it was that one might call the antithesis of a victory celebration... perhaps a lunch time wake for Democracy in Germany. It was a quiet meal in a small cafe and David uncharacteristically ordered a bottle of wine with the intention of making it two or even three bottles as the opportunity presented itself. It seemed that David had managed to pick just the right place with a similarly minded clientele, because none of the other patrons seemed overjoyed that day even though if they had chosen to strain their ears, they might have been able to detect the distant strains of a blaring brass band playing at the Brown House a couple of miles away.

"The dumplings are a little tough today" David said in passing as he took a bite of the liver dumpling from his soup and glanced over towards the door.

Amalie must have caught it out of the corner of her eye because something told her to look up and she saw the most amazing expression on David's face, as though he had seen a ghost, a welcome ghost.

"What?" she asked as she turned to see what he was looking at over by the door.

"Joseph." David called out, causing a few of the other diners to look at him.

Joseph Hubert smiled as he caught sight of David and Amalie and quickly made his way over to their table.

"What on earth are you doing here?" David continued as he stood up and took his friend's hand, but then decided instead on a great hug.

"I've just now gotten in to town" Joseph said when David finally let go and Joseph reached over to give Amalie a quick peck on the cheek.

"How long are you staying?" Amalie asked as Joseph pulled up a chair from the table next to them and sat down.

"For good!"

"What?" David exclaimed.

"That's right" Joseph said with a smile, "Uncle Max died about a month ago and the sweet old man left me something in his will."

"So why didn't you ever write?" David asked.

"Well, before that all I had was bad news and I couldn't see writing you just to complain. I did all that to mother..."

"What bad news?" Amalie interjected.

"No money, no job... things in America are awful now."

"What about that factory? The one Otto Maus owned. Didn't you get a job there?"

"Sure. Old Otto was as good as his letter of reference and I worked for almost a month until the factory went out of business."

"Oh no." David said sympathetically.

"Yes." Joseph said emphatically as though David was questioning the truthfulness of his statement, "and then a while later I got a job selling radios, but then even that slowed down and they kept the long time employees and let a lot of us new ones go."

"That's terrible!" Amalie commiserated, "but Joseph, things are just as bad here."

"No, that's the great part! Not only did uncle Max leave me enough money to come home, he also left me a majority interest in a textile mill in Dresden which his lawyer assured me is still paying dividends."

"But money's not the only thing," David said, lowering his voice, "haven't you heard? Hitler's just become Chancellor."

"Why are you talking like that?"

"Like what?"

"Like you don't want anyone to hear you. Don't they know Hitler is in?"

"Yes they know, but don't you understand what it means?"

"In America they said things are starting to settle down here."

"Joseph, I've heard that they're already rounding up the communists in Berlin and sending them all off to prison. There are even rumors of executions."

"What does that matter? You're not a communist, are you?" Joseph smiled as he repeated the question, "Are you?"

"My God!" David went on, still speaking in hushed tones after glaring at his friend for a moment, "Are you really that thick? Hitler has always said that the Communists were directed by the Jews. If he's rounding up the Communists today, you can be sure he'll come for the Jews tomorrow."

"There's the problem." Joseph said with a note of triumph as though he finally figured out the flaw in David's logic, "You're afraid for yourself, but don't you see? We're Germans. When Hitler rages against the Jews, he's talking about the kikes... The Russian and Polish Jews."

David was stunned and turned to Amalie as though she might somehow assist in convincing Joseph that there was trouble ahead, but Amalie said nothing. She had already banged her head against a wall too many times trying to make that same argument in her own home.

"Just mark my words," David finally said, "within six months there will be some sort of pogrom in Germany."

"...against the Russian Jews." Joseph added.

"Against all the Jews." David corrected.

There was an uncomfortable pause as David and Amalie went back to eating and Joseph thought about what had been said until he finally turned back to David in a conciliatory gesture.

"There may be trouble for all of us... but surely once all the Communists are taken care of, things will settle down and Hitler will leave us alone. We're an important part of the community."

David just kept on eating.

"Oh, come now... I'm sorry we ever got started on this political shit" Joseph whined, "God knows politics never have been an aid to

311

good digestion."

David managed a weak smile.

"We were already upset about this whole thing when we came in..." Amalie said, trying to help David explain.

"Oh, and then I add fuel to the fire." Joseph said, finishing the thought, showing that he was willing to let it all pass.

"Let's talk about something else." Amalie piped in, "Tell us about America."

Joseph went on for almost an hour about the buildings and the enormity of New York city and stories of the museums and Harlem and Manhattan. Joseph also managed to make a trip to Washington DC one weekend with a girlfriend because they wanted to see the Smithsonian institute, but other than that he had spent all of the last couple of years in New York.

He had managed to get by well enough on his broken English, especially since there was a strong German community in the city and he had found a few different girlfriends during his time there, but they were all German expatriates like himself so, he said with a certain air of superiority, he didn't feel he could really say what American women were like.

Amalie found it amusing that if Joseph had had an American girlfriend that he would then have felt qualified to pass judgment on all American women, but that was the kind of man Joseph was.

By the time they got back to the office, it was almost time to call it a day, especially since neither of them was in the mood to work anyway. David went off with Joseph and Amalie headed for the U-bahn to catch the next train to Furstenried.

When Amalie got home she was told by Gertrude that Gunther had called to say he would be working late. In reality he was out with Klaus and Friedrich. It just so happened that that was the same day Klaus Grunewald retired from the army on the anniversary of twenty years of service to the cavalry at the rank of major and he immediately signed up as a member of the RSHA section of the SS.

The RSHA was a recent division in the nazi party hierarchy at that time. RSHA was a department of the SS which included the security division of the SS, know as the Sicherdienst or rather by the initials "SD". The SD was the department which Rheinhard Heydrich headed.

Klaus, ever the social climber, saw Heydrich as an important man in the party just by the way that Heydrich seemed to have come out of nowhere to lead his department and also because of the rumors which said Hitler was impressed by Heydrich. Klaus, therefore, wanted to get to know Heydrich and wanted to get on his good side, but not so much that he would consider serving in the SD under Heydrich's command.

Klaus saw himself strictly as a fighter, so he chose the Waffen SS as the section to join. He was quickly accepted by virtue of a record that included his continued membership in the party since its beginning, his status as an officer in the regular army and personal contact with Adolf Hitler in the early days of the party and later through Amalie's and Friedrich's friendship with Geli Raubal. He was one of the loyal party members from the putsch of '23 who had stuck with Adolf through thick and thin and was therefore expedited into his new position.

The news of a Hitler Chancellorship which was defeat for Amalie and David Frieder among others, was part of a great celebration for Gunther, Klaus and Friedrich. Actually, it was just another evening spent in a beer hall, like so many before and so many yet to come as the three friends raised their large beer mugs in a toast.

"Our time is here at last! To the future!" Klaus said as he swung his mug close to the others without making contact.

"The future." Friedrich agreed.

They were all in uniform, Gunther dressed in the "brownshirt" uniform of the SA while Klaus and Friedrich were both in the black uniforms of the SS. Friedrich was now a clerk in the SD, helping out with the massive task of putting together files on all of the new party members who had swelled the ranks as a result of the impending rise of Hitler to the Chancellorship with his promises of prosperity for Germany and an end to communist aggression.

"It's been fifteen years now... " Gunther said after they had finished a long drink from their beers. "It seems like a hundred. Wearing a uniform again... It doesn't take much when I close my eyes to hear a master sergeant calling out a marching cadence."

"A twenty year retirement!" Klaus added, trying to out-do his friend, "How's that for old?"

"I remember a lot of times during the war when I never thought I'd live to be thirty years old." Gunther continued, "Now thirty is just another lost memory."

"Well, at least the things we fought for are about to happen" Klaus continued.

"How are things going at the Brown House?" Gunther asked, turning to Friedrich, "They say Heydrich sets up his files in cigar boxes!"

"It sounds good in the newspapers" Klaus said, answering for Friedrich and gesturing as though holding up a newspaper and reading an imaginary headline out loud, "The struggling party exists on the pfennigs donated by its members and other sympathetic working people..."

"I've heard some of the money even comes from America." Friedrich said, responding to Klaus' propaganda.

"I've heard that too," Klaus answered, "but never at headquarters. Lips are tight."

"I wouldn't be surprised..." Friedrich added, "There are a lot of people outside of Germany who would like to get rid of the Communists and would gladly pay us to do it."

"You make us sound like mercenaries" Klaus countered with a challenging edge to his voice.

"No, no" Friedrich said emphatically, "I just meant that they would help supply us so that we can do the job that must be done."

"Well, it's best not to talk about such things..." Klaus said, and even though he said it with a careless lilt, Friedrich felt it was a warning. Operations at the Braunhaus were very secretive and any casual remark might be scrutinized if the wrong person overheard it.

"Speaking of rumors," Klaus continued, turning to Gunther, "I understand you've been doing some talking."

"Talking?" Gunther responded non-chalantly, feeling that his friend was already getting carried away with his new position.

"Yes.... Gunther, you're playing a dangerous game." Friedrich watched in silence as Klaus and Gunther got caught up in their conversational duel as though he weren't even there.

"What the Hell are you talking about?" Gunther asked with rising anger.

"Rumors."

"There are always rumors.... What rumors?"

"You've been telling new men that the Jews are not the enemy."

"But Adolf himself said..."

"He didn't say that!"

314

"Yes, he did."

"No, he said that there should be no incidents during the elections."

This remark hit Gunther because it was exactly what Amalie had said when they argued before.

"This is not a good time to start trouble" Klaus continued, "Remember Walter Stennes in Berlin. The SA almost revolted there. Things are too tense."

"But I haven't said anything..." Gunther started, attempting to minimize his personal campaign of tolerance for Jews based on his "good Jews" and "bad Jew's" rationalization, a campaign that had been effected mostly by Amalie's influence, but also by the Jewish doctor who had saved his father's life.

"We understand" Klaus interrupted with a gesture between himself and Friedrich, cutting Gunther off in mid-sentence, "We know it's Amalie, but you can't let that confuse the issues! There is an uneasy feeling in the Braunhaus, rumors of a possible revolt of the Sturmabteilung here in Munich."

"No. There's nothing like that here" Gunther protested.

"Don't you see?!" Klaus shot back with frustration, "It doesn't matter whether it's true or not. The problem is that some people think it may be true. You've got to make sure that you don't stand out for any reason."

Friedrich was like a student who finally understood the reasoning behind a difficult math question. "You mean that...." he began as he interrupted Klaus, trying to clarify what Klaus was saying, "if they think something might be wrong, they'll look for anyone who..."

"Yes," Klaus continued, finishing Friedrich's thought, "just like in the trenches. The snipers only got the men whose heads showed over the wall."

The reference to snipers in the war brought a nervous laugh of recognition from both Gunther and Friedrich, a bit of graveyard humor which made its point.

Gunther agreed that it would be best not to say anything that could be taken wrong and Klaus, who had only spoken out of genuine concern for his friend, was relieved. They then got down to the business of celebration for Klaus' retirement and subsequent enlistment in the SS and continued their party until long into the night and the early morning of the next day.

February 27th of 1933 was an uneventful day for the Metzdorf family. Gunther made it home in time for dinner which was the exception rather than the rule since the beginning of the year. Just as Amalie and Gunther were about ready to go to bed, there was a report on the radio that the Reichstag building in Berlin was in flames. It was already being declared as an act of arson by Communist agents.

The tone of the report was hysterical as the announcer said that it was believed that one of the men responsible was already in custody. Neither Amalie or Gunther really knew what to make of it, whether it was a single act of violence or if it was just the start of another period like they had lived through at the end of the war. Whatever the case, they went to bed hoping that every thing would be under control in the morning.

The next few days signaled a new morning in Germany. A frightening new morning. Marinus van der Lubbe, a communist from Holland had been arrested in connection with the Reichstag fire, but that would certainly not be the end of it. There would be far reaching consequences stemming from the act of arson on the night of the 27th.

Chancellor Hitler used the incident to exercise emergency powers, issuing a decree the next day which effectively canceled free speech and press along with many other civil rights which one would expect to find in a democratic state. The decree went on to remove the seal of privacy from mail service and telephone communications, freeing government agents to intercept both forms of communication without just cause and the police were also allowed to enter private homes without cause.

Many people, rather than being alarmed by these actions, applauded Hitler's efforts. They knew these actions weren't directed against them and felt it was worth giving up these rights in order to stop the Communists who were now being arrested in large numbers along with suspected Communist sympathizers and just as David Frieder had said a month before, the rumors of executions didn't arouse popular public opposition.

"He just needed an excuse" David Frieder said in a low rumbling voice that frightened Amalie as she sat in his office while he read from the newspaper.

"What do you think it means? Are we next?" Amalie asked.

"We? We as Jews?"

"That too, but I meant as a publishing house."

"Well, I think we're in for something either way. If he suspends newspapers, it's just a matter of time before he sends someone out to check on all the publishers."

"But isn't it just temporary? An emergency decree..."

"There's always a chance of that, but I think he was just waiting for something to happen. Any incident would have worked for him. Maybe I'm just an alarmist, but I think this is just a first step."

David spoke with the air of a fortune teller, believing in the future he predicted and speaking as though it were a vision appearing before him that was so real to him that he might actually reach out and touch it. Amalie knew that it was just an opinion, that David could just as easily be wrong about what might happen, but David's mood of impending disaster made her extremely uncomfortable.

"What do you think we should do?" Amalie asked, "I mean for the firm."

"We might want to review our current projects..."

"You mean we should censor ourselves?" Amalie asked with surprise as she felt that David was going to compromise everything he believed in at the first sign of trouble.

"To an extent."

"What extent?" Amalie asked with an uncontrolled rise in her voice.

"Amalie, it is important in life to choose one's fights. You cannot possibly win every battle. We have to go through the books we're working on and see which ones we really believe in and balance that against the distinct possibility of the government closing us down."

Amalie wanted to argue the point, but it seemed self evident. They could try to go on just as they had been doing, but what good would it do if Frieder and Son was closed down like some of the newspapers?

"I suppose I'd better get a list together." Amalie said with defeat in her voice as she rose from her chair, "Should I call a meeting for tomorrow to go through everything?"

"I don't think so." David answered, "I think I'm going to have to do this myself. These will be hard decisions and I don't think a committee could do it fast enough."

The month of March saw Frieder and Son drop almost a third of it's book production schedule. David lied to a number of authors and printers, using any excuse he could come up with to try to "cleanse" the publishing firm of some of the more left wing projects to which it had committed itself. David's actions were a substantial financial drain on both the company's and his personal assets and there were legal considerations which required him to buy off a couple of authors. He also managed to transfer some works to other publishers whose interest in the profitability outweighed any concern about politics. David was not proud of what he did, but felt certain that a Jewish publisher would soon be targeted by a government which seemed each day to be turning more and more toward the goals of the nazi party which everyone had kept insisting would never be in complete control.

April first of 1933 convinced Amalie of David's prescience when it was announced that because of "atrocity propaganda" by foreign newspapers that there would be a boycott of all Jewish business throughout Germany.

It was the Sturmabteilung which was sent out to stand at the entrances to all Jewish businesses around the country and remind anyone who approached that the business was owned by Jews and that true Germans should take their business elsewhere. The boycott was not violent except for a few isolated incidents. Even many of the new young brownshirts didn't take the boycott very seriously. They felt that the communists were the enemy, not Feldstein the butcher down the block where their mothers had bought meat for years. It was up to Adolf Hitler to educate them.

Amalie and Gunther and for that matter Gertrude and Jakob, didn't mention the boycott once in the three days it lasted. What could be said? Gunther went out each day to organize troops, directing them to different sections of the city with the names of stores to be boycotted while Amalie went to work each day wondering if her own husband would appear at the door of Frieder and Son, shouting at clients that this was a Jewish business and they should consider taking their business to a good German publisher.

It seemed like there was some new decree or law every week restricting rights, especially the rights of the Jewish community. Jews were forced out of the civil service and their numbers were restricted in universities. After a huge May day celebration when a new national labor organization under government control was announced, all the other labor unions were outlawed in Germany.

Meanwhile, the trouble that Klaus had been talking to Gunther about in the ranks of the Sturmabteilung was continuing to develop. The SS was mobilized in Munich on March 9th when a regional commander, or Gauleiter in the terms of the nazi party, by the name of Adolf Wagner along with Ernst Rohm appeared at the office of the Bavarian Minister President demanding that he appoint General Ritter von Epp as a general state commissar.

This was a clear challenge to Adolf Hitler's authority, not only over the entire operation of the SA, but also a challenge to the national governments authority over the region of Bavaria. The demands were not taken seriously and Rohm and Wagner ended up withdrawing without having accomplished anything except antagonizing Hitler and the other party leaders.

Hitler had made promises to leaders of the regular army, the Wehrmacht, that they would be the sole military arm of the nation, not a force in conjunction with the SA as Ernst Rohm had hoped.

Gunther started to spend more time with Klaus. Between the discomfort of the situation at home and the long days of work, he found it easier to talk with his old friend rather than facing his problems.

Klaus had never been much of one for spending time at home anyway. Katrina took care of the boys and that kept her occupied, so Klaus fairly did as he pleased. Not that he was ever unfaithful to his wife, it was more like she was a possession that he had on the shelf at home; pretty to look at and fun to take out every once and again when he felt like it, but not to worry, she would always be there.

Strangely enough, it was a fairly accurate assessment of their marriage from Katrina's point of view too. They had gotten married because they felt that they should be married because that was just the way things were. Katrina wanted children and Klaus wanted boys as heirs to the throne and family name. It was all very convenient and the situation was hardly ever shaken by conflict because they rarely ever interacted on any meaningful level and so there wasn't anything to get upset about. They went to great pains to fit into each other's life and stay out of each other's way.

That was why Klaus looked at Gunther's life as though it were a comic opera. What else could be expected when one married out of one's race? How could Gunther have ever considered marrying a Jew? Now he would have to reap what he had sown, but Klaus, uncharacteristically, didn't rub salt in Gunther's wounds. They kept to safe topics as they wasted their hours downing beer and commenting on the passing parade in the beer halls, fighting their way through to the next day.

Amalie kept herself busy too. She never questioned Gunther about where he had been or why he had been out so late. She spent time working at home and writing letters. One letter was to her cousin Edith in response to the letter Edith had written to Amalie telling her that she had been forced to leave her post as a lecturer on pedagogy because of new legislation against Jews in teaching positions. She had decided to become a cloistered nun and work on her writings which combined Catholic theology with the study of phenomenology which she had pursued at Göttingen University.

Amalie also wrote to her father, being careful what she wrote as she made subtle comments on the way things were going in Munich, afraid that her letter might be opened and read by some government clerk. She went on to say that she would like to visit soon. She knew it was time. She and Gunther were about to celebrate, or at least acknowledge, twenty years of marriage and she knew in her heart that she could not keep trying to make it work. She could honestly say she loved him, even as she knew she had to leave him because things would not get better and they would certainly get worse.

The rest of the year and the beginning of the next was a dream-like paradox as the noose of Hitler's quest for power tightened, yet life had an eirie sense of normalcy for the Metzdorfs. The tension in their household was gradually becoming more pronounced as each member of the family had to work harder and harder to pretend that nothing was wrong. Gunther began taking constant trips out of town on the weekends and working later during the week until it seemed that he only came home to have a late dinner and sleep before going back to his SA duties.

It was a time for daydreams for Jakob as he became more involved with Rebecca and the thought of her swept over him and drew him onto the waves of passion newly found, moving him to places he had never been before. Amalie saw it as a good thing on the one hand that Jakob was getting more involved with Rebecca and her friends as it drew him out after he left the HJ, but on the other hand Jakob was never home any more than his father was. Amalie was concerned about how far Jakob was pulling away from the family, but as far as Gunther was concerned, she was relieved that Gunther wasn't home to drag Jakob back into the nazi fold.

The Christmas of '33 was forced and bleak. Gertrude was with Friedrich and Klaus and Katrina went to visit Katrina's family for the holidays, leaving Amalie, Gunther and Jakob to exchange meaningless gifts and eat a large Christmas dinner garnished with long awkward silences and obligatory compliments to Amalie for being such a good cook.

It was about a month later, one of those dark January afternoons when the sun disappears just after four o'clock, when the night seems even darker because the light abandons us at such an early hour, when Amalie ran into Jakob just as he was about to leave.

"Leaving already?" she asked as she unloaded her briefcase and a couple of manuscripts into a chair so that she could take off her coat.

"A play tonight!" Jakob said with a smile, clearly anxious to be on his way, but considerate enough not to walk out in the middle of the conversation.

"Where?"

"It's a school play... some of Rebecca's friends."

"Oh, Rebecca" Amalie said with a smile, "you two are seeing a lot of each other."

"Silly little kike won't leave me alone." Jakob said with a smile, talking about Rebecca as though he were irresistible to her.

Amalie's eyes flared and she reached over and slapped Jakob hard in the face. "Jakob Metzdorf, You may think you're all grown up and practically on your own, but don't you ever say anything like that again in my presence."

Jakob's face smarted and he felt a tear form in his right eye, but he quickly brushed it away. He thought he had made a good joke. He never used the word "kike" before and had only used it to shock his mother and now he felt terrible because she had taken him seriously.

Amalie stormed out of the room and into the kitchen where she drew a glass of water. There was a twitch in her shoulder, residue of her anger, as Jakob appeared in the doorway. She saw the redness of his eye and took an offensive posture as she stood in front of the sink, expecting him to start spewing some vile nazi rhetoric like his father.

"I'm sorry mother... It was just a joke... a very bad... joke."

He couldn't look her in the eye as he apologized and she melted as he said the words, walking over to him and taking his hand.

"Jakob, I'm sorry I hit you, but that was such a terrible thing to say."

"I know..." Jakob said, still looking at the floor, "...and the strangest thing is that I really like Rebecca."

"Maybe you're just afraid" Amalie said, bending slightly as she tried to look into his eyes.

"Afraid?"

"Maybe you're afraid that you like her more than she likes you and so you pretend not to care."

Jakob thought about it for a moment as they stood there silently. He felt uncomfortable talking about a girl with his mother.

"You can talk to me" Amalie said as she gently touched his chin and raised his face to look at her, "I was a girl once. I might understand more than you think."

Again there was a strange silence as they stood looking at each other.

"and Jakob..." Amalie continued, "I love you Jakob. Don't ever forget how much I love you."

Jakob suddenly realized how long it had been since his mother had said that to him, since he had given her the chance to say it. The strain between mother and father, father and son... all of that, had driven him away from her. It bothered him that he couldn't say it back. For some horrible reason he didn't feel that he could tell his mother that he loved her too, as though he had drifted so far away that the chance to say it was lost. He managed to give Amalie an awkward hug and then turned for the door.

Amalie watched him as he went. She was afraid for him. She worried about how he shut himself off. Had it really been a joke? Was that why he couldn't say that he loved her? He seemed so lost and she didn't know how to reach him.

It had begun to seem as though the gray, snowy winter would last forever when the winter finally gave way to spring. It had been hard for Frieder and Son Publishing that winter as David's fears proved well founded. A number of publishing houses had been closed down and some confiscated by the government under the

Chancellor's emergency power decree and most of those targeted were owned by Jewish families. Most of those efforts so far had been directed at large concerns in Berlin and other parts of northern Germany, not that Munich would be ignored, everything would happen in its time. There was no need to rush. Now was the time for the nazi majority to consolidate its power through the measured pace of legitimate government process rather than fanatical revolutionary destruction.

"Jakob," Amalie said one Monday evening just after dinner in May, "I need to talk to you."

Jakob was uncomfortable with the ominous tone his mother was using and he immediately sat up, laying the book down on the bed beside him.

"The way things are going..." she continued, making a false start. "Jakob, you're just about to get your school certificate" she said, referring to the certificate of maturity that all students get after passing a final examination from secondary schools before going on to a university, "and you might not be able to go to the university here."

Jakob knew what she was talking about, but he had put it out of his mind for some time now, ignoring the fact that he might be subject to the new limitations on Jewish students at the university. Somewhere in the back of his mind he was sure that he could just lie about his mother being Jewish like he had done to get into the Hitler youth.

Amalie continued since Jakob said nothing in response. "...and I thought... now that you've decided on the law instead of medicine... Well, I thought you should consider going to stay with grandfather Ethan in Salzburg. There are two universities close by where you would be sure to be accepted."

Jakob didn't know what to say first. "Leave Munich?" he finally said as though it were inconceivable.

"That might be best." Amalie said reassuringly.

"But I..." he started in a panicky way, "I guess I just never thought of it. Leaving you and father." He added that last little bit as a jab to inspire her to help him find a way to attend the university of Munich so that he wouldn't have to leave Rebecca.

Amalie looked down at the floor as she prepared to deliver another shock. "I was thinking that I would go to Salzburg, too."

323

Jakob couldn't make sense of what she said because the thought seemed to come from out of nowhere. He knew there had been tension between his mother and father and they didn't talk much, but he just thought that was the way all married people acted when they got as old as his parents. He thought most of the trouble was because of the way he had acted, the way he hurt his father by leaving the HJ and the way he hurt his mother by lying about her being Jewish.

Amalie still couldn't look up as she made her confession to her son. "You know your father and I... You know we don't talk. We hardly even see each other... and that seems all right with him... and so I thought..."

"You're going to leave father?!" Jakob asked incredulously. He had only heard of people getting divorced. He didn't even know anyone personally whose parents had gotten a divorce. It was only the subject of dirty jokes among his classmates about sexually desperate divorced women or men freed from the bondage of a frigid wife.

Amalie looked up. "Jakob, please don't say anything. Don't say anything to anyone until I've had a chance to talk to your father."

"You haven't told him yet?" Jakob asked with the same excited tone.

"This is not easy for me." Amalie said with a deep sigh, "It's a hard decision to make. I don't know how to do it "right".

"Maybe if you just talk to father..."

"I don't think that would do any good."

"Have you tried?"

Amalie felt exhausted as she looked into Jakob's eyes and saw the hint of fear, fear of the unknown, of what this might mean to him.

"Promise me you won't say anything. Promise me that you'll think about a university by Salzburg and I'll promise you that I'll talk with your father."

"When?"

"Soon, but don't worry. If it did come down to us leaving, it wouldn't be for some time now. When is your last examination?"

"...end of July."

"Well, don't worry about it. I didn't want to upset you, but I thought you should know."

"Before father?"

Amalie was surprised as this sounded like an attack and she

thought about ignoring it, but then she thought better of it. "Jakob, I know this is hard to understand, but if you think about it, can't you see how far apart your father and I have become. Haven't you noticed how different things are? And do you think he doesn't know these things are happening?"

"And I guess I didn't help much..."

"What do you mean?"

"I know how disappointed father was when I..."

"Oh Jakob! I'm sorry to tell you this, but this isn't about you. This is between your father and me. I'm sorry if you feel like you're in the middle, but you really aren't." Amalie couldn't hold herself back as she moved closer and pulled her son to her, hugging him and giving him a kiss on the forehead. "I know this is a hard thing to understand...and I'm sorry..." she said as she let go and got up, not knowing what else to say, leaving Jakob alone to think about what had been said and to imagine what might happen.

"They think there might be trouble tonight... We need to go out and patrol." Klaus said as he stood in the doorway of Gunther's house.

Months passed since Amalie and Jakob had had their talk and Amalie still hadn't brought it up to Gunther. She wanted to wait until the last minute so that if it turned out that she would be leaving, Jakob would be done with school and ready to leave. She was frozen for a moment as she watched Gunther in his SA uniform join Klaus, who was also in uniform. She didn't recognize them, these two storm troopers in her house.

"We'll probably be late, so don't wait up" Klaus said with a smile to Amalie as they left.

She merely nodded and went back to her newspaper.

It had been raining on and off throughout the day and continued into the evening on that night in late July. The Sterneckerbräu had already become a shrine since Adolf had become Chancellor, a shrine to the humble beginnings of the NSDAP where Adolf first met the members of the struggling group, the place where Gunther and Klaus had first met Adolf. It was Klaus' and Gunther's first stop that evening.

Gunther kept looking around, keeping an eye on the door to see who came and who left and trying to sense the mood of any of his comrades who might pass by. He didn't know what to expect. The rumors of an SA uprising were back and he thought that must be why Klaus wanted him along. The SA would be more willing to listen to an SA Gruppenfuhrer than someone in an SS uniform. It would show solidarity in the face of any trouble.

Klaus, however, was thinking much differently. His bravado and good nature were forced that night because of his unpleasant assignment. An assignment that he had actually requested. Klaus' attentions to Heydrich's activities had gotten him caught up in a terrible twist of party politics. Ernst Rohm had gotten out of hand and had gotten on the wrong side of Adolf's plans for the party. Adolf was going to keep his word to the army that the Sturmabteilung would be brought into line and the night had come to correct the situation. Klaus had heard about the events that were about to unfold and he also knew by the tone of the planning that it would be a severe exercise in discipline. Certain people were referred to as "irredeemable" to the party's true direction.

Klaus knew what that meant, he knew those people wouldn't survive, and then one day he saw a list of names.

Gunther Metzdorf.

He checked it carefully. He even managed to discreetly check to make sure the name wasn't a mistake.

He had tried to warn Gunther. He tried to tell him, but Gunther wouldn't stop and now some clerk had neatly typed his name on a piece of paper with a dozen other names and the list had been initialed by Rheinhard Heydrich of the SD.

The night went slowly as the two friends strolled about the empty streets, stopping every now and again at a different beer hall and then continuing on their way.

Marienplatz was deserted at 2:00 in the morning. The moon managed to peek though rain clouds for just a moment as Gunther, a bit unsteady from all the beer, looked up at the darkened figures in the clock tower of the Neues Rathaus. Klaus had been stalling all night, not knowing if he could do what he had committed himself to. He had said that he would take care of Gunther. He thought it would be better. Why should his friend be arrested and tortured? Why should he go through all that just to die in the end anyway? The moment seemed perfect. It seemed to last forever as Klaus drew his pistol and pointed at the back of Gunther's head.

The gun went off.

Klaus twitched as the pistol jumped in his hand and the flash and echoing report filled the square. Gunther jerked too, but his was the response to the impact of the nine millimeter bullet and he staggered back a step putting out his hand to Klaus so that Klaus might steady him. He didn't even know that it was Klaus who shot him. Klaus took Gunther's hand and let him gently down to the ground, kneeling beside him.

"I'm sorry..." Klaus choked out as he looked at Gunther's bloody face. The bullet had torn away pieces of Gunther's skull above his left eye, allowing his life's blood to rush freely down his cheek and onto his brown shirt, down to the red, white and black armband before falling into a pool on the cobblestones.

It was the sort of thing that Klaus had thought he could do when it was discussed and he got permission to take care of Gunther on his own. He thought it would be an act of mercy, humane and painless. Gunther would die instantly and it would be over. It was for the best that way. But as he knelt there with the pistol in his hand and Gunther gasping for breath, he wanted to take it all back. It was wrong, he couldn't do it. Gunther didn't deserve to die.

"They let me do it so it would be over quickly." Klaus tried to explain to his dying friend.

Gunther's wound stole his voice so that he could only stare at Klaus with a look of surprise.

"It's better this way." Klaus whispered as tears rolled down his face. He petted Gunther's hair. "No torture."

Suddenly Gunther's breathing became uneven as he choked and gasped for air and then tensed up and arched his back for an instant before falling back against the cool cobblestones of the square.

"God, I've made a mess of it." Klaus said to himself quietly, still holding Gunther and seeing the pool of blood on the cobblestones for the first time as the clouds opened again for an instant and the moon looked down, casting silver reflections. The light of the moon illuminated the white of Gunther's eye, the one that wasn't bathed in his own blood, the one that stared relentlessly at his killer.

Klaus heard someone coming down one of the side streets, talking softly, and he just sat there not caring who it might be, not caring if they found him there with the pistol beside him.

He could soon make out the voices of a man and a woman coming closer, but just as he expected to see them with faces contorted in fear and surprise, to hear the woman scream as they came upon him, the voices began to fade. The unknown couple had turned and walked away from the square at an adjacent street, never coming close enough to see Gunther and his murderer lost in the darkness as the moon once again became shrouded in clouds and a hard July rain began to fall and Klaus began to sob openly.

It was late afternoon the next day when the police called, they had been busy. Members of the SA had been arrested all across Germany the night before and throughout the day.

Amalie watched her hand replace the telephone receiver in its cradle as though it were someone else's. She was numb. She hadn't been concerned by Gunther's absence since he had been spending so much time away from home and she hadn't expected any bad news.

Maybe she needed to cry. She couldn't. She had to go identify the body. It seemed so strange that she finally knew she had to leave him and now he had... left her. How could she tell Jakob? When Jakob got home from school that day and found Friedrich, Klaus and Klaus' family there, he knew something was wrong. He stared blankly at his mother when she told him what had happened, that his father had been attacked by a group of men and shot in the ensuing fight, and he just turned and walked out the door. Amalie thought he had just gone out to get some air and was surprised when she realized he wasn't anywhere to be found.

She was still looking out the door when Klaus came up behind her.

"Amalie," Klaus said hesitantly, "I would be honored if you would let me give a eulogy for Gunther."

Amalie tensed up. The last thing she wanted was for this to turn into some kind of honorable nazi military funeral. Even though she had been told it was a group of Communists who attacked Gunther and Klaus and killed Gunther, she knew it was the party that had killed him. They had been killing him for years.

"No" Amalie said with more finality than she had intended and she quickly tried to make her declaration less curt. "I mean I would rather not have a eulogy. Just a service..."

Klaus looked at her for a moment, thinking up an argument to persuade her, but then decided to let it pass.

The mood was stifling as they all tried to make conversation and all Amalie could think of was how much she just wanted everyone to leave. She almost stopped Klaus as he raised his glass of wine and began rambling on, but instead she just hid in the kitchen.

"It all seemed so easy as a child." he began grandiosly, "You just accepted things."

"Why?" he asked the ceiling in pseudo-Shakespearean soliloquy. "I want God to walk down his golden stairway and explain in simple terms why. The time has come for God to account. I don't mean to sound like I'm calling God on the carpet. It would just be nice if we could talk a bit, man to creator, and he could let me in on some of his inside jokes. There is no greater comedian than God."

Everyone else was getting uncomfortable as Klaus continued, not sure what their role was to be. Should they applaud?

There was, instead, a blossoming silence that filled the room until finally Friedrich mercifully suggested that Amalie might like to be alone. Klaus began to insist that this was no time for "the widow" to be left alone, but Gertrude, remembering how it had been when she went through the same thing, agreed that Friedrich was right and Amalie might prefer to be alone for a while. Amalie reappeared from the kitchen and managed a smile for Gertie to acknowledge that she was right and Gertie gave Amalie a warm hug and a kiss as everyone filed out of the house.

"I'll stay with Friedrich tonight" Gertie said, "I'll see you in the morning."

Klaus sidled up to Gertie as she came out. "Now what will she do all alone?"

"She'll cry." Getrude answered sadly with a tear of her own running down her face as she quickly moved away and took Freidrich's hand.

Between fits of crying and trying to listen to the radio and then trying to read, Amalie kept worrying about where Jakob had gone. It had been hours since he had left the house and then she finally realized where he would be. She called Rebecca's mother and asked for Rebecca, but Mrs. Geschwind didn't know where her daughter was. Amalie explained what had happened and said that there was probably nothing to worry about, that Jakob and Rebecca were probably just out talking.

The rain of the previous night had given way to a beautiful starry sky as Jakob and Rebecca sat in the darkness on an iron bench in a nearby park.

"It feels so strange... like I didn't even know him."

"You didn't know your father?"

"I mean... as a man."

"What?"

"I can't picture him when he was a boy or when he was in the army or when he was my age."

"What do you think he was like?"

"I don't know... different, different than me."

"Why?"

"He seemed so certain of things. Everything was clear cut. I don't feel like I know anything."

"Just because he thought he knew something doesn't mean he was right."

"I know, but that's not what I mean. It's not whether he was right or wrong, it's just that he was so sure of himself."

"Are you sure that's so good?"

"Even if he was wrong... Everyone's wrong at sometime or another. I'm not talking about being right or wrong, I just wish I could be as confident..."

Rebecca nodded.

"I don't think he loved me."

The statement was supposed to shock Rebecca and she was supposed to protest, insisting that Gunther loved his son. Her silence spoke volumes.

"He never said it." Jakob continued, "He was happy when I'd win something, like sports, but it was almost like I was something he owned and when I did well it was the same as if he had done it himself."

"Are you mad at him?"

Jakob looked at her with surprise. He hadn't expected that question. "No." he finally answered, "Just sad, I guess."

"It seems to me that if I had all that to say to someone and then they went and died before I could say it... I'd be mad."

Silence.

"I suppose... I'm a little mad."

Rebecca listened patiently and tried to help him keep talking because she knew it was important to him. She knew what it was like to have all of these unanswered questions since her father had died before she was four-years-old. Jakob began to realize something important about "Becca" that night. There are always those people who are more than willing to tell you who they think you are, and there are those who commiserate with you in your confusion, and then there are those special few who stay with you as you fumble in the darkness trying to find your way. Someone who helps you through. She was one of those, willing to listen when you're afraid and talk when you're tired of talking and just be there when you need silence.

They finally found themselves back at Jakob's house. It was so late and Jakob wasn't thinking. He went in and left the door open and Rebecca followed, closing the door behind her. Jakob went to his room and laid down to sleep, but found himself just staring at the ceiling. He was surprised when Rebecca appeared there in the doorway, the moonlight illuminating the soft skin of her face and arms with a gentle glow as she seemed to float towards him. She reached out and took his hand. Her hand was warm and his cold. She squeezed his hand and he pulled her hand to his chest pressing it to the center of him as burning tears blurred his sight and mind. She laid down on the bed beside him.

He wasn't even sure what he was crying for. Was he crying for Gunther, the man, for his father, for the things they hadn't said to each other, for the things they had? It wasn't even these questions that hurt, it was the very real, almost physical, pain that came from knowing that his father was gone forever. Knowing as a man that it was true and yet hoping like a child that if he just wanted hard enough, if he railed and ranted, threw a tantrum, that maybe it would change, maybe God would relent.

Rebecca never said a word. She only drew closer, resting her head on his chest and draping her arms around him as they lay on the bed in the warmth and silence of the night.

Amalie was shocked when she opened Jakob's door the next morning and saw Jakob and Rebecca laying there intertwined. Her first thought was that she should shout and rage, waking them up in a frenzy and chasing them out. That would have been what her mother would have done, but she said nothing. She didn't wake them at all. Suddenly she just found herself looking at them. They were fully dressed, as though they had collapsed into sleep. It seemed natural and innocent. For a moment it struck her like a portrait, unashamed. Then she came to with the unnerving thought that she was staring at her son and his girlfriend. She felt embarrassed and quietly closed the door and leaned against the wall just outside the bedroom. She realized that it wouldn't be long until Jakob left home. He would start at some university next year, if she could still afford it with Gunther gone... Gunther gone. The world had changed again. Her son a man. "My God!" she thought, "only two years younger than Gunther when we married. Only one year younger than me... but he's so young."

Gertrude came in the front door as Amalie stood in the hallway. She headed straight for the kitchen to start breakfast and asked Amalie if she was doing better. Amalie just nodded, not knowing what to do about Jakob and Rebecca, but apparently they had been awakened by Gertrude's activity in the kitchen and realized that they were in an awkward situation.

Rebecca was embarrassed as she came fumbling out of Jakob's room, trying to straighten her wrinkled clothing and unable to make eye contact with Amalie or Gertrude. Gertrude was shocked when she realized what was going on and she glanced over with a scolding look as Rebecca sulked by and then went back to making breakfast without saying a word. Gertrude couldn't approve of such a horrible thing no matter how much she loved both Jakob and Rebecca.

Amalie was sitting in the living room pretending to read a book when Rebecca stopped in front of her.

"Ama... Mrs. Metzdorf" Rebecca stumbled as she tried to explain, "I'm sorry... nothing happened."

Amalie remained expressionless as Rebecca realized what she had said.

"I mean I'm sorry that we...." Rebecca suddenly stopped talking and knelt beside Amalie's chair. "Nothing happened Frau Metzdorf... We just talked. He needed me" she said in a half whisper.

Amalie was caught off guard by this statement. She thought she was in control of this situation, a mother with a right to her righteous indignation at catching her son with a girl in his room. It was one of those strange times when an adult realizes that they are the adult and must react in a certain way whether they truly believe it or not and then she remembered that she knew who Rebecca and Jakob were.

Amalie took the day off work, along with the next week as she had to decide what she and Jakob and Gertrude would do. Gunther's mother and father arrived that afternoon. Ethan would be coming early the next day, in time for the funeral the following afternoon.

Marie couldn't understand why her son had been killed. No one could tell her who this group of men were and why they had shot her son. "A child should not die before the parents" she kept saying at different times throughout the day.

It was hard for Jakob to sleep that night. He woke from a fitful sleep and was frightened as he looked at the window and saw the outline of a man.

"Father?" he whispered loudly, but the figure didn't move. Jakob lay still for an eternity waiting to see what the menacing black outline against the hazy grayness of the night beyond would do.

Finally he reached over for the lamp beside his bed and turned it on. It was only his suit hanging on the curtain rod. His mother must have had his only suit cleaned for him to wear to the funeral the next day and hung it there. Jakob hadn't even noticed it before. Maybe she came in after he had fallen asleep. He turned off the light and tried to get comfortable laying on his side, but finally turned onto his back, staring at the ceiling. He could feel his heart still racing from the moment of panic. He looked down at his chest to see if he could actually see his heart beating. "So..." he thought to himself, "I am the man in the window that I was afraid of."

The strangest images danced in and out of his mind. "I didn't even know him. Would his mother go crazy?" She seemed so calm. She hardly even cried. Didn't she care? She had said she wanted to divorce him...but of course he hadn't cried much himself, especially when there was anyone around. His face actually hurt sometimes from trying to keep a calm controlled expression around friends and relatives. The desire to cry burned at the corners of his eyes, but he wouldn't give in. He wasn't a little boy. He was a man and he would not cry in front of people. It seemed so strange when people came to give their condolences, staring into his eyes intently as if they were studying his face, expecting to see him literally break apart. He was no longer a boy. He had been his father's son, protected and diminished in his shadow, their struggle over whether Jakob was now a man or not was moot between them. Jakob had won through default, the victory was thrust upon him.

The sun was shining when the car came to pick up Amalie, Jakob and Gertrude. They didn't talk as the car worked its way through the streets of Munich to the church. Amalie thought to herself that it would have seemed more appropriate if the weather had been dark and cold and full of rain, as if the world were mourning.

Oskar had arranged the funeral, which was fine with Amalie. She could have done it if she hadn't had a choice, but she felt relieved when Oskar suggested that his son should be buried with a Lutheran service. She couldn't very well have gone to a synagogue to ask if a rabbi would say kaddish* over her husband who happened to be a group leader in the brownshirts.

She had never been to a synagogue in Munich. The last time she had attended any service was when she visited her father in Salzburg. Ethan never asked his daughter whether she went to services because he was sure that he already knew.

The service was pious and impersonal, assuring the family and friends that Jesus was coming to soothe their pain and relieve them of their sorrow, that Gunther was now floating up to the clouds where he would be happy, looking down on them all and waiting until they finally joined him when they achieved their final reward.

Things went quickly the next week. Ethan agreed that they should come to Salzburg and Jakob would certainly be able to find a good university there. Gertrude began to wonder what would happen to her, but then Friedrich surprised her with the news that he had actually managed through the graces of a friendly party member to lease the apartment that the Haas family had lived in before the war. It was a strange twist as Gertrude planned to return to the apartment on Franz Joseph strasse where she had been living when she first met Gunther and Amalie. Things had come full circle. She knew she should be happy now that she had a place of her own and Friedrich was in a position to help her live comfortably, but now she would loose Amalie... and Jakob... and Furstenried. She was 66 years old now. It seemed so hard to start over again.

A few days later, Friedrich was sitting at his desk in his crowded little office, his nose buried in a manila folder when one of the clerks called out with a note of excitement, "Haas! Obersturmbannfuhrer Heydrich wants you in his office. Now."

Friedrich's heart moved into his throat as he rushed down the big hallway to Heydrich's office, stopping at the desk in front of the

---

* The Jewish prayer for the dead.

forbidding, massive red oak door.

"Yes?" the young man at the desk said sternly as Friedrich stood at attention, trying to compose himself.

"Obersturmbannfuhrer Heydrich sent for me... Haas, Friedrich Haas."

The secretary quickly glanced over some notes in front of him and agreed that yes, Friedrich had in fact been sent for, and the young man told him to follow as he knocked on the door and introduced Friedrich.

"Come in Haas." Heydrich said in that unnerving high voice of his, unnerving because it seemed almost funny while the man himself was anything but humorous.

"Yes sir" Friedrich said as he stood at attention.

"No need for that..." Reinhard said as he leafed through papers in a manila folder and motioned Friedrich to a chair, "Sit down." Friedrich tried to get comfortable as his cold superior officer continued reading as though Friedrich wasn't there. "Haas," Rheinhard said, finally putting the folder down on his desk, "our Fuhrer has told me of a great service that you performed some years ago."

Friedrich knew he was referring to the cover up of Geli's murder, but he said nothing, waiting to see what Rheinhard would say next.

"...and you have done well to say nothing. You've been very loyal..."

Rheinhard was trying to read the man sitting in front of him and took Friedrichs silence as a good thing. Even when Friedrich was being complimented, he didn't lose his head and acknowledge his part in the cover up. Then Rheinhard let the silence lay heavy in the room, watching as Friedrich tried very hard to cover up his nervousness and succeeded fairly well.

"I will only ask one question about the past." Rheinhard finally said, staring at Friedrich as though he might bore into his skull with his intent gaze, "Are you the man?"

The question was cryptic and Friedrich suddenly felt his head swimming. "The man?" he thought to himself. The man who killed Geli or the man who covered it up? What was he being asked? "I'm sorry..." Friedrich finally said slowly, "What man?"

Rheinhard wasn't put off by the fact that Friedrich didn't

understand the question. Obviously Friedrich wasn't as intelligent as he hoped, but intelligence wasn't the greatest virtue in such matters. In reality, of course, Friedrich would have had to have been a mind reader to know Reinhard's meaning.

"Loyalty." Rheinhard shot back loudly. "Are you that same man who served so loyally before and can you be counted on to do so again."

The word 'loyalty', even in the early days of the SS was a mystical concept which was nothing less than a direct bond between man and God and the use of that word was always the impetus for dramatic and heartfelt affirmation between an officer and a soldier.

"Of course." Friedrich said emphatically.

Once again Rheinhard paused and considered the man in front of him. "We will need you to go to Berlin." he finally said as he handed Friedrich written orders. "Check with Hans for everything else." he continued, referring to his secretary.

Friedrich remained in the chair to see if there was anything else, but Rheinhard seemed annoyed that he had to bother telling Friedrich that that was all and he could go.

Once outside the door, Friedrich realized that he had tensed every muscle in his body as he sat in that chair in Heydrich's office and he finally relaxed and felt much better as he walked over to Heydrich's secretary to confirm his travel arrangements.

A week later Friedrich found himself in the office of a nameless SS official receiving final instructions for his assignment.

"...and so you will be the Fuhrer's replacement driver."

"Yes sir."

"I cannot stress how important this mission is. If you have any doubts..."

"No sir." Friedrich said loudly and emphatically, an assertion that saved his life since the officer had orders to shoot Friedrich on the spot if he had shown any reticence or questioned the mission, since he had already been briefed on the details of the mission.

Friedrich Haas had been chosen to replace Hitler's chauffeur because of his war experience as a medic, not just because of his prior service to the Fuhrer.

Later that morning he found himself driving Adolf to the estate of Paul von Hindenburg where the old man was sick in bed. Friedrich dutifully followed closely behind Adolf, carrying his large black briefcase as Adolf entered Hindenburg's grand residence.

Hindenburg was 84 years old that year and Adolf wanted an audience to insist that the old man retire and turn the Presidency over to him, but the old man was intractable.

They talked for a while in polite tones that masked the contempt which each man felt for the other. Hindenburg seemed upset with the actions at the end of June when members of the SA were assassinated. The fate of the Sturmabteilung didn't concern Hindenburg, but one of the sideshows of the purge was when Franz von Papen was placed under house arrest. Hindenburg had a personal fondness for his "Franzchen" who had been one of the string of Chancellors since the presidential elections and Hindenburg demanded a promise from Adolf that von Papen would be protected. Adolf asceded, but Friedrich could tell that Adolf was growing tired of the conversation. The only person in the room besides Hindenburg, Adolf and Friedrich was a nurse who sat by the old mans bed in case he should want anything and at this moment, Adolf decided that he was thirsty and asked if the nurse might go out and get a fresh pitcher of water and clean glasses... and ice too, if it wasn't too much trouble. Adolf did his best to be charming as he asked and followed the nurse to the door, closing it and making sure it latched as she left.

Friedrich instantly realized that this was the time to act and knew that he only had a moment or two at the most. He had been instructed earlier that it might become necessary for him to administer a syringe full of an hallucinogenic drug which would eventually bring on paralysis and death.

He opened the briefcase where the syringe was hidden in a pocket as Hindenburg rested with his eyes closed while Adolf made a point of charming the nurse. The old man was taken completely by surprise as Friedrich suddenly jumped on him in the bed and began pulling up the sleeve of the his nightshirt to give him an injection before he knew what was happening. Hindenburg struggled and they wrestled about, but Friedrich quickly bested the old man, putting his knee on the old man's arm to hold it down while he covered Hindenburg's mouth with the bed linens so he could not call out.

During the struggle, Adolf continued to talk for the benefit of anyone who might listen at the door, so that they would think he was still in conference with the Reichs President.

337

Hindenburg was already weak from sickness at this point and even though he was a much bigger man than Friedrich, Friedrich managed to subdue him until the drug took effect.

In the struggle, however, the needle broke off in Hindenburg's arm and Friedrich looked up at Adolf, not saying a word as Adolf continued talking, but pointing at the needle. Adolf couldn't really see what had happened, but it was obvious that something had gone wrong.

There were only a few millimeters of the needle sticking out and Friedrich had to work hard, pinching the skin around the entry wound of the needle to fester the needle out enough so that he could get a hold of it. He finally managed to work it out and set it on the bed table, falling quickly to his knees, looking under the bed for the rest of the syringe. He found it immediately and set it on the bed table next to the piece of needle. He then saw that there were spots of blood all over Hindenburg's nightshirt and realized that he would have to change it. he pulled out a handkerchief and quickly, efficiently, wiped up the spots of blood from the puncture wound and then wrapped the broken needle and the rest of the syringe in the handkerchief and set it on the bedside table.

Adolf, who had been pacing and watching the door nervously as he talked finally turned to Friedrich and asked in a quieter voice, "Are you ready? Are we ready to leave?"

"Not quite. Almost." Friedrich said as he waved Hitler off, indicating that he should go back to his pacing.

Friedrich had noticed that Hindenburg was still bleeding ever so slightly from the needle puncture which had been aggravated by removing the broken needle. He tried to think what to do and noticed a large Meerschaum pipe in its stand on a small table near the bed. He opened the small drawer in the table and was pleased to find matches and pipe cleaners. He took one of the pipe cleaners and lit a match, burning off the bristles of the pipe cleaner, exposing the twisted wires at its core and then returned to Hindenburg as the old man lay helpless, muttering on as the drug began to effect his mind after it had all but paralyzed him, allowing only the most rudimentary movement as the old man might flop an arm across his chest or move his head from side to side. The pipe cleaner was so hot that when he touched it to the small puncture, is sizzled as it came into contact with the skin, thus cauterizing the wound and assuring it wouldn't bleed

338

anymore.

Friedrich knew this was all taking much too long and Adolf was getting more and more nervous. Friedrich then put the burnt pipe cleaner in the handkerchief package so that he would be sure to remove all evidence of the crime. A nightshirt! He had to find another nightshirt and change the old man or the little spots of blood might give everything away. Adolf couldn't imagine what Friedrich was up to as he quickly rifled through a bureau drawer. Friedrich soon fished out another nightshirt that fortunately was the same as the one Hindenburg was wearing and he rushed over and expertly stripped the old man in an instant, a talent he had developed during the war when patients had to be cleaned up fast, and wrestled the new clean nightshirt on him.

Adolf was amazed as Friedrich flew about the room one last time, stuffing the nightshirt and the rest of the evidence into the empty briefcase which he had brought. "We're ready" he said to Adolf as he quickly brushed his hair back with his hand.

Without hesitation, Adolf threw open the doors just as the nurse was returning with the water and glasses, causing her to drop the tray, sending the glassware crashing to the floor as he shouted angrily storming through the waiting room with Friedrich close behind, "The old man is gone! He's completely senile! He doesn't even recognize me!"

Hindenburg's secretary immediately called the doctor and rushed into the bedroom as Adolf and Friedrich left the manor.

Once they were in the car and had actually left the grounds of Hindenburg's estate, Adolf finally asked Friedrich how long it would take.

"From what I've been told, he will be dead by tomorrow afternoon."

Friedrich watched Adolf's face in the mirror as he told him and he was glad to see that the Fuhrer took no pleasure in the news. There was no smile or glint in the eye, as a matter of fact, Adolf looked noticeably saddened, as though he wished it didn't have to be the way it was, but then that was just what Friedrich thought he saw in Adolf's face.

Friedrich was relieved when the train passed through Dachau. He was almost home after his mission. He had been told he had done a great service for Germany and that he would be remembered and

339

rewarded, but somehow he couldn't escape the feeling that he should find a way to protect himself. Today they were grateful and appreciative, but what about tomorrow? What would it take for him to become expendable?

"Amalie, I need to meet you somewhere."

"Friedrich? Is that you?" Amalie asked, thinking she recognized the voice on the phone, but wondering why it sounded so...

"Yes. Could you meet me at the apartment on Franz Joseph?"

"With your mother?"

"No. Alone."

"When?"

"Tomorrow. Wednesday at... 2:00."

"What's going on?"

"It's nothing, really. I just need to talk to you before you leave."

"All right."

"Who was that?" Gertie asked reflexively as she came into the living room.

Amalie was startled and wondered how much Gertie had heard "Oh that? Uh, that was just... David. He wanted me to meet him tomorrow to tie up some loose ends.

"You'll still be able to help me move, won't you?" Gertrude asked with annoyance, afraid that Amalie would go back on her promise.

"Oh, of course. This is just for Wednesday. I'll be free all day Thursday... Don't worry Gertie, I won't let you down."

Amalie found herself getting nervous as she got closer to the apartment, wondering what Friedrich could possibly want to talk to her about. She knocked on the door and found it was unlocked when she tried the knob, so she walked in. Friedrich was sitting in the middle of the front room in the only chair in the apartment, a small wooden folding chair, staring out the window.

"Friedrich?"

Friedrich hadn't heard her come in and jerked his head suddenly toward her.

"I'm sorry," she said, "I didn't mean startle you."

"I was just thinking. This place... all these years."

"I think I'll feel the same way about going back to Salzburg."

"Yes, probably. We get so far away from home sometimes and then when we return, we don't even recognize it. Home doesn't

340

change... we do."

"Friedrich," Amalie said as though she needed to draw him back to the present, "What did you want to talk to me about."

"Things get complicated Amalie." he said wearily, his speech slightly slurred, "I've seen things... done things... that I never would have dreamed..."

"Are you in trouble Friedrich? Do you need money?"

"No, it's not that" he said, shaking his head emphatically. It was clear that he had been drinking and he stopped talking as he tried to pull words together out of a mental fog. He hadn't thought about what he would say when they met and so he was at a loss. "I need someone to trust" he finally said.

"Trust?" Amalie asked, still not knowing what this could possibly be about.

"Yes... Can I trust you Amalie?"

"Of course Friedrich. We've been friends a long time."

"I know. I hoped you would say that. I've got a package... and a couple of letters that I may need some day, but right now it would be best if I had a friend take care of them. Someone who would be out of the country."

"You want me to smuggle something out of the country?"

"It's not like that. It's not something illegal. It's only important to me and a few other people. You wouldn't be stopped by the police or anything. Even if they found it they wouldn't stop you."

"You don't want to tell me what it is?"

"I'd prefer not to."

"Curiosity killed the..." Amalie started to say, but the look on Friedrich's face stopped her. He was very serious.

"Can you do it?"

Amalie thought for a moment. Her instinct was to say yes, but part of her was afraid. "Yes." she finally said and with that Friedrich picked up a small brown box from the floor beside him and offered it to Amalie. She smiled nervously as she took it.

"When are you leaving?" Friedrich asked.

"Sunday. We'll help your mother move tomorrow and finish up everything at the house on Friday and Saturday."

It was hard for Amalie to ignore the box when she got home and she had already decided that she would open it once she got some time to herself when they were in Salzburg, but she had to keep it away from Gertrude and Jakob for the next couple of days.

The house moving for Gertrude was just like all moving days with a bit of confusion, a lot of cleaning and scrubbing and everyone being tired at the end of the day. Amalie had given Gertrude much of the furniture from the house because she didn't want to ship it to Salzburg and store it until she and Jakob found a home of their own while they stayed with her father.

It was hard saying good-bye to Munich, saying good-by to Gertie, to David and his father. Rebecca couldn't even try to pretend that it would be all right when Jakob left. They spent every moment together until it was time to board the train and then she couldn't stop crying even when they stood on the platform waving good-bye and Gertie put her arm around her.

It was a long ride back to Salzburg for Amalie, right back to where she came from such a long time ago, feeling like her life was over.

The Price of Ashes

Part IIII
1938—1944

Chapter 13

The purge of the Sturmabteilung in 1934 began a new phase in Adolf Hitler's plans for his beloved Germany. The purge had been Hitler's answer to the Wehrmacht, the regular army, which was afraid that Hitler would try to replace the Wehrmacht with the SA. Once Hitler had the sworn allegiance of the military, he turned to rearmament. He also began testing the mettle of international adversaries.

Adolf Hitler announced compulsory military service in 1935 and a year later issued orders for German troops to occupy the Rhineland which had been declared a de-militarized zone by terms of the Treaty of Versailles. He won his gamble that neither the French nor the British would intervene and this became his first great feat in the field of international politics. The vast majority of Germans were ecstatic. They believed it was a major step on the road to Germany's redemption from the humiliation of the Great War, a step that didn't cost a single German life. The German nation may have held its breath for a moment as their Fuhrer challenged the Allies, but that breath was soon released in shouts of "Sieg heil!"

Salzburg was as beautiful a city in 1937 as it had ever been for as long as Amalie could remember. The annual Salzburg music festival in August had been world famous for years and once again drew crowds to fill the city. It would not be unusual to see the Duke of Windsor or Marlene Dietrich among the audiences attending performances.

Salzburg was also a dark city in those days. The laughing sparkle of public fountains in the sunlight seemed a lie as strange shadows cast about the centuries-old churches and shops, intermingled with the festive crowds and the music floating through the air. From the house where Amadeus Mozart was born and up to the grayish-white walls and towers of the Festung Hohensalzburg which watched over the "altstadt" district of Salzburg, there was a shadow of fear. The city hidden in the mountains, nestled in the valley of the Salzach River, was suddenly exposed and vulnerable as Adolf Hitler raged in Germany and the Austrian nazis continued to lobby, as they had for more than a decade at that time, for a union with Germany, an "Anschluss."

Relations between Austria and Germany had been strained ever since Hitler came to power in Germany and the Austrian nazis tried to take over the Austrian government in what proved to be an awkward incident for Adolf Hitler. At the same time that Hitler was trying to curry favor with Benito Mussolini in Italy, the Austrian nazis were trying to bring down the Austrian government with whom Mussolini had signed treaties. During the attempted coup in which the Austrian Chancellor, Engelbert Dollfuss, was mortally wounded, Dollfuss' wife and children were on holiday in Italy where they were the guests of Mussolini himself. That early attempt failed, but in 1937 the nazis in both Austria and Germany were calling for Austrian submission to the ideal of a greater Reich ruled by Germany.

Amalie had not returned to Austria specifically to escape the nazis, but it was clear to her that it was a good time to get out of Germany in 1934. She and Jakob had moved in with her father temporarily, but everything seemed so up in the air that she didn't know when they would find an apartment of their own.

The years after Gunther's death were difficult for her-not just because she was widowed or even because Gunther died a sudden, violent death-but mostly because she felt as though she were a refugee running from his murderers. She constantly wondered when

344

they would come for her.

Amalie, like all good Germans, had always been frugal and was also lucky enough to sell her house in Fustenried before the worst legal restrictions against Jews were announced in 1935, the legal code known as "the laws for protection of German blood and honor" or "the Nuremburg laws." Once the Nuremburg laws went into effect, she wouldn't have been able to take the money from the sale of her own home out of Germany.

The only work she could find in Salzburg was as a secretary in a bank, but this had its good points as she began to learn about banking and how to protect what assets she and her father had managed to save over the years.

Ethan's publishing business fell off drastically in those years and it had turned out to be a wise decision when Amalie told her father that she would rather find a job on her own. If she had taken a job with him, they would both have been in the same boat as Ethan was forced to reduce his staff and consider closing down the business that he had worked and fought to build for over thirty years.

It should have been a time in his life when he might have sold and retired, but the rug was being pulled out from under him. His business was devalued because he was Jewish. He lost business and prospective buyers said the business was unreliable. What would they be buying? His name? The name of a Jew in a country that was about to be taken over by the nazis. How much could that be worth? It was a bitter prospect. This was the system that drove men to suicide in those years. A man could work hard all his life to build a reputation, respect for his name, and then along came those people who said that if the name ended in the wrong string of letters, the man behind the name was nothing.

Ethan was not above self-pity, although it would not rule him. Some days were better than others and he probably wouldn't have gotten through it if Amalie and Jakob hadn't been there, but slowly and surely he made a decision to go on.

It was the change in his gentile friends and neighbors that disturbed him the most.

He could somehow forgive, or at least understand, why people with whom he had done business for years drifted away. That was business, and because of the strengthening social stigma of doing business with Jews it was bound to happen. Money, he felt, was reason in itself, separate from the rest of one's life. He couldn't, however, understand the way non-Jewish neighbors looked at him, as though he had somehow changed as they were being swept up in the waves of hatred which the nazis and their propaganda generated. Perhaps that hatred had always been there, like a guttering fire in the morning, and the nazis had only added fuel and fanned it.

Throughout all of this, Jakob buried himself in his studies. His thoughts were mostly about the things he had left behind. He would occasionally go out with a girl, but nothing ever seemed to work out. It just didn't feel right and he could never really say why.

Jakob, Ethan and Amalie were all at home one night when there was a knock on the door. It was a loud, hard knock with a sound of authority. Amalie looked at her father with apprehension as he got up to answer it.

They had all heard the stories. There was something in Germany now called the Geheime Staats Polizei, the secret state police known as "Gestapo" for short. They would come and take people for questioning if they thought they were against Hitler. They had heard of people being shot for trying to escape from the detention camps that had sprung up within weeks of Hitler becoming Chancellor. The bodies would then be cremated and if the family wanted the remains, they would have to pay a price of twenty marks for the ashes. This couldn't have come to Austria now, could it?

Amalie couldn't hear the responses to Ethan's questions. She just sat watching the fire in the living room's small brick fireplace as the crackling wood punctuated Ethan's words.

"Yes?" Ethan said. "Yes, he lives here... where are you from?"

"Jakob?" Amalie thought to herself, "Who would be looking for...", but then Ethan's voice became friendly, inviting the visitor into the house as Ethan went to call Jakob. Amalie smiled and nodded at the young man who knew her name and gave her a friendly greeting, but she couldn't quite place him.

Jakob came down the stairs at a fast clip, well ahead of his grandfather. "Jurgen!" he called out as he landed by the front door. "What are you doing in Salzburg?"

"I'm on my way to Vienna. I was accepted there at a university..."

"You're just now starting the university?"

"Yes, I thought it would be best to get my labor service out of the way."

"Oh, that's right. I forgot all about the two-year labor service... How was it?"

"As good as could be hoped for. They fed us well enough after trying to break our backs..."

"What about Kurt? Did he..."

"Yes, we went in together."

"...and how's 'Becca?"

"Jakob, why don't you invite your friend in?" Amalie called from the living room.

"Oh, I'm sorry Jurgen" Jakob said, putting a hand on Jurgen's shoulder and guiding him into the living room where Amalie was sitting. "What was I thinking? Come in. Sit by the fire and get warm. Mother, you remember Jurgen Hassler from Furstenried?"

"Yes, of course. Would you like some coffee? It's so awfully cold out tonight."

Jurgen smiled impishly. "You wouldn't have hot chocolate, would you?"

"Certainly. It only takes a minute" Amalie replied, already on her way to the kitchen.

"So... how is Rebecca?" Jakob asked, "I mean how are things really going?"

He wrote her regularly, but both he and Rebecca knew they could only say so much in letters. There were questions he could not ask and things that she could not write because the mail could be opened by German officials and Jakob certainly didn't want to bring her any trouble just to satisfy his curiosity. He had not been back to Munich since the end of 1934. A little more than three years. Maybe that was what was wrong. Maybe he loved her more than just as a friend as he had told himself so many times. Was that what kept coming between him and other girls?

"Things are..." Jurgen began, but he just couldn't cover up. "Well..." he started again, "Rebecca and her mother get by."

"Jurgen, you can tell me. Whatever you say is just between us."

"You won't even tell Rebecca?"

"No one."

"Even as a mischling things are very hard" Jurgen said as he opened his coat and pulled a thread which easily slid away and let the lining of his coat fall open. He reached inside and pulled out an envelope. "She sent this with me. A letter for you."

"Mischling?" Jakob asked as he took the letter without opening it, not commenting on the subterfuge.

"Mischling is what they call children of mixed Jewish marriages. When Rebecca heard I was going through Salzburg, she said she wanted to send a letter that wouldn't go through censors."

Just then Amalie came back to the living room with hot chocolate for all three of them. "What is the talk like in Munich?" she asked eagerly.

"Talk?" Jurgen asked.

"We don't know what to believe from what we hear" Amalie said, "Is there any protest? Is there as much talk about Anschluss in Munich as there is here?"

"Everybody talks about the Anschluss" Jurgen answered.

"And everybody is for it?" Jakob asked.

"I haven't heard anyone say anything against it. At least not publicly... ever since Hitler took the Rhineland back. It's like he's God."

"That's what they said at the passion play" Jakob interjected.

"What?" Amalie asked with surprise.

"A friend of mine from school went to the passion play last year in Oberammergau and there was a German tourist sitting next to him. The actor playing Jesus comes on and the German nudged my friend and said 'That is our Hitler' and then when Judas came out he says 'Rohm' under his breath."

"It's like that a lot with the old people" Jurgen agreed. "What they saw destroyed in the war... " Jurgen went on, letting his thought trail away because he didn't know how to put his feelings into words.

"They said things were better for the Jews after the Olympics..." Amalie interjected, changing the subject.

"Just in Berlin. Only until the Olympics were over."

"Well..." Amalie began, but then she drifted into a long silence as she realized how cynical she had grown over the years and she feared that she knew exactly what was going on. Just like she knew that the explanation surrounding Gunther's death was a lie, but she didn't know what the truth was. She saw through the propaganda of German news stories as she tried to find hints of reality, only knowing for certain that there was power being taken piece by piece and that those unfortunate enough not to be in power at the top would certainly be crushed under the weight of that power as time went on.

"Actually, I have some work to do" she continued, excusing herself. "I assume you two have a lot to talk about, so I'll leave you alone."

Jakob found himself still fumbling with the letter as his mother left them sitting in silence.

"How is Kurt?" Jakob finally asked as he found some common ground for discussion.

"He's well... He's off to the University in Gottingen."

"Still in scientific research?"

"Maybe. He started talking about being a surgeon a year or so ago."

"Surgeon? I'm impressed."

"I think that's why he brought it up... to impress people. But don't tell him I said that."

"...and Rebecca is all right?" Jakob finally asked after trying to get back to his original question without seeming too eager.

"Yes" Jurgen said, annoying Jakob with his short answer and obvious ignorance of what Jakob was really asking.

"Is she... Is there somebody she's..."

"What?"

"Is she seeing anyone? Anything serious?"

"Oh!" Jurgen said as the light finally came on, "No, she doesn't go out much. There's nobody special."

Jakob couldn't help but smile at this, but he quickly covered it so that Jurgen wouldn't think he was pleased that she was alone.

"I don't know, but I think that's what she wrote to you about" Jurgen continued, "She talks about you all the time."

"I think about her too" Jakob admitted, looking into the fire as the wood suddenly popped and sizzled, not sure whether he should have said it out loud or not.

"She did say..." Jurgen started slowly, "that she hoped you might... She said she hoped that you two would see each other again soon."

Jakob wanted to tear open the letter and read it right then, but instead he asked Jurgen where he was staying and went on to suggest that Jurgen should spend the night. Jurgen thanked him for the invitation, but explained that he was catching a train later that night for Vienna where a friend would be meeting him at the station.

349

It was that night, after Jurgen left but before Jakob even read the letter from Rebecca, that he decided he would find some way, some reason, to return to Munich as soon as possible. He didn't tell his mother or grandfather about the letter or his decision. He waited until he went to bed to read the letter.

Dear Jakob,

I wanted to write you since I had the chance to get a letter through without worrying about being arrested for saying the wrong thing. We're all afraid now. That may sound like an exaggeration, but it's true. Things have changed so much for us here in Munich. They wrote up something called "the laws for protection of German blood" a couple of years ago and since then they keep adding new restrictions all the time.

My brother Max and I have been issued identity papers which call us "Mischling" which means children of a marriage between a Jew and a gentile. Max is having trouble in school because of all this. When they salute the flag at school in the morning with their "Heil Hitler" and he doesn't raise his hand, he is hit from behind by someone who says that everyone must salute and then the next day when he does salute, he is hit and they say that because he's a Jew, he's defiling the flag by saluting.

Mother has been given certain exemptions because she was part of a "privileged mixed marriage" because father was a war hero, but not Jewish. They put signs on everything now. Jews are not allowed in movie theaters or concerts or parts of the public parks. Every day something reminds you how you are not wanted and yet it's impossible to leave. I was sitting in a movie theater and the lights came up and a man came on stage shouting, asking if there were any Jews in the audience. That was when they first said that Jews couldn't go to theaters and I hadn't heard about it. Everyone started looking around, wondering if there were any Jewish people there and then suddenly someone from the back shouted out "Here! There's a Jew up here." He turned in the man sitting next to him and a policeman showed up from out of nowhere and took the man away. I was terrified that someone would know me and turn me in, but later I found out that because I was a mischling the new law didn't apply to me. The nazis say they want the Jews to leave, but they make people pay so much money for permits to leave that they have to stay.

I know this is a selfish thing to say, but I miss you. I

350

wish I could see you again. I remember the night after your father died and even though it was a terrible thing that happened, I wished that we could stay together like we did that night. I never felt so close to anyone before or since. I think about you all the time. I don't know if you feel the same way, but I hope you do. My worst fear of everything that might happen these days is that I might never see you again.

I love you.

Rebecca

The letter was discomforting. Jakob felt good and bad at the same time, not for the first part of the letter because those were the sorts of things he had expected about how difficult life was in Munich and so on, but the last paragraph seemed unlike Rebecca, like she was asking him to come and save her. That wasn't the way he thought of their friendship. She had always seemed independent, as though it didn't really matter whether he was there or not, but she would prefer him to be there if it was her choice. And then there was that last sentence. "I love you." Maybe she was just scared.

"Love?" Could she really mean that? It had been so long since they had seen each other, but she was right about that night. He had found something there that he hadn't expected. It wasn't sex and they weren't just infatuated with each other. There was something between them that he couldn't describe in words.

He knew that he had to go to Munich.

Within a few days he came up with an idea. He would make the end of the Wittlesbach dynasty in Munich and Kurt Eisner's Raterrepublick the topic of his senior thesis. Jakob convinced his professors of the importance and relevance of such a work and also his need to take a few days to go to Munich to research the subject.

Amalie was not pleased with his plans, to put it mildly. She had been spending her time trying to plan an escape from Salzburg before the nazis took over there, too and while she was fighting to keep one step ahead of the devil, her son wanted to go visit him in his lair.

"Why?" she asked.

"I've been away for so long and I just wanted..." Jakob fumbled through an unprepared and untruthful explanation.

"Do you really think this is a good time?"

He was silenced by this question, asked and answered by its

351

tone, but it certainly didn't cause him a moment's hesitation in his heart. It didn't change his mind, it just showed that his mother was not willing to listen to whatever he said. They both knew this scenario as it was the same one that Amalie and Gunther used to act out. Whenever Amalie would confront her husband, he would stop talking and eventually go on to do whatever he wanted regardless of Amalie's feelings. Amalie was aware of this legacy passed from father to son and so she kept on, even though Jakob hadn't disagreed with her. "You'd be taking an awful chance! Who knows what might happen?" she asked quickly, her voice rising in pitch. "What if something happened and you couldn't make it back here? You've got to think this through. It's possible that if you go, you might not be able to get back."

"Now you're just being ridiculous, mother."

"Ridiculous? Don't you listen to the radio, read the newspapers? Hitler keeps talking about annexing Austria. Who knows what might happen... and what if it happens while you are away?"

"It would only be for a week."

Amalie threw up her arms in frustration. "You can't imagine..." she began, "What if you came back and your grandfather and I had been forced to leave. How would we be able to find you?"

"You're being ridiculous" he repeated.

"Jakob, please..."

"No, I'm going. Next week."

"You still haven't told me why."

Jakob sighed. "I got a letter from Rebecca..."

"Oh, that's it."

"It sounds like things are bad there."

"But what do you think you can do about it?"

"I don't know. I just want to see her."

"It's too dangerous" Amalie said, raising her voice, but Jakob just turned and walked away. Amalie didn't pursue him, but she did talk to Ethan, asking him to try to talk Jakob out of going.

Ethan didn't get any farther than Amalie did and so a week later Jakob fought his way through a deep snowfall on his way to the Salzburg train station.

He started getting nervous for a moment when the train pulled out, wondering if maybe his mother was right. What if something did happen while he was away? There was no turning back now.

It was only about an hour's train ride to Munich. The city was dark and haunting, even in the morning as Jakob broke from the Hauptbahnhof with the eager pace of youth on his way to the U-bahn. The appearance of the city caused him to stop in his tracks. It was unusual for him to pause when he walked. He normally knew where he was going, planning his route before starting out and then walking at a breakneck pace so that he would quickly be done with the inconvenience of walking. This was a much different situation for him though. It was a journey he had decided on against the wishes of his family, something which he planned and committed to and then... he simply did it. He had embarked on a pilgrimage of sorts, that he might personally judge the profligacy of the German people.

But the city stopped him in his tracks. It looked exactly as he hoped it might. Great, wet, heavy snowflakes swirled about the gray buildings and their orange tiled roofs. This was not Munich. This was a memory. He wouldn't know Munich until he spoke with people and found out the mood of the city.

He had planned on taking the U-bahn to the Universitat station by Ludwig-Maximillian Universitat where he would find a travelers pension to stay, but it was still early in the day, so he decided to walk so that he could tour the area. The buildings all looked the same, the Antikensammlung and the Glyptothek and the Braunhaus, the only difference being that now the Braunhaus wasn't the only one festooned with huge nazi party flags.

The Brownhouse was busy with waves of uniformed men coming and going. Brown shirts, the black uniforms of the SS and now a number of the gray uniforms of the Wehrmacht sweeping up the stairs on their way to plan the future of Germany.

He found himself watching the soldiers and thinking that he might even see his "Uncle Klaus" going in or coming out, but then he suddenly felt uncomfortable. Paranoia crept up on him and it entered his mind that they might be watching him watching them, that someone might ask him why he was staring at the nazi headquarters, and so he quickly walked away.

It was a slow time of year for hotels and Jakob had no trouble finding a room in one of the pensions by the university. Once he was settled in he thought he might get something for lunch, but then he realized how close he was to Franz Joseph strasse and decided that it would be a good time to visit Gertrude.

Gertie shrieked with joy when she answered the door and found Jakob standing there. "Jakob! How did you get here?"

"It's for school. I'm staying at the university to do a paper."

"Oh my..." Gertie said, duly impressed with Jakob in his role as scholar and as she calmed down she realized that she hadn't invited him in. "Come in, come in" she bubbled, "Have you eaten?"

"No."

"Well, let me make you a sandwich. Friedrich was over just last night, but he had to go to Berlin. I made a nice ham and I couldn't possibly eat it all. It's a good thing that you're here. Now it won't go to waste. How is your mother?"

Jakob was amused at Gertie's rapid delivery, as though everything she had said was one long sentence, but it was so good to see her again. He didn't even realize how much he had missed her until she opened her door and he saw grandma Gertie's sparkling eyes.

"Mother is good."

"And your grandfather?"

"Yes, everyone is well."

"I was just thinking about your father the other day..." Gertie said as though daydreaming, stopping in the middle of the kitchen on her way to make their lunch, "I can't remember why..." she continued, "Oh, now I have it. Friedrich and I were talking about the first time we met him. He was such a kind man. He invited us to dinner..."

"Yes..." Jakob said reflexively as he sat down, having heard the story many times before.

"Mind you this is just after the war ended. We had no food at all here, Friedrich and I. It really meant something back then for someone to share food."

"During the time of Eisner?" Jakob asked.

"Yes, Eisner... but we mustn't talk of that."

"What?"

"You shouldn't even mention his name."

"Why not?"

"They will think you are a Communist."

"But that's the subject of my paper"

"Oh Jakob, no. It is too dangerous. You have to watch what you say. If someone... misinterprets."

"Dangerous?"

"Jakob, you have been away."

All the while that she was talking, Gertie rushed about the kitchen getting Jakob a sandwich and carefully cutting an apple into wedges for him as she used to do when he was little and then finally pouring coffee for both of them. She then came to rest in the chair next to him as she sighed deeply. "They arrest people for anything."

"Have you heard anything from Rebecca?"

Gertie smiled. "Yes, she comes to see me every week or so."

"How is she? How is her family getting by?"

"They get by."

"They still live in Furstenried?" Jakob asked even though he had received the letter from Rebecca only a little over a week before.

"Yes. Are you going to see her?" Gertie asked with a grandmotherly smile.

"If I have time..."

They passed the afternoon reminiscing and talking about how things had changed since Jakob had left. Gertie insisted that Jakob go to the pension and get his things and bring them back so that he could stay with her for the week. Jakob allowed himself to be convinced, but actually he was happy at the thought of saving the money he would have spent on the hotel and restaurants.

It was a strange feeling that night as he waited to fall asleep in Gertie's extra bedroom. It felt something like a homecoming, but everything was so different. He woke up early the next morning because he wanted to get to Furstenried before Rebecca would leave for work. She had written to him months before that she couldn't get into a university because of the restrictions on the admission of Jews, even Mischlings, and so she ended up getting a menial job in a factory. It was almost seven o'clock when Jakob found himself standing at the gate to Rebecca's yard. He suddenly felt foolish for coming all this way to surprise her and wondered what she would say. The snow was slippery as he worked his way up to the door and knocked. There was a long delay and he knocked again a little louder and turned away from the door, looking over the neighborhood as he waited. He turned around suddenly when he felt someone was watching him and did so just in time to catch an eye peeking out from a curtain and then suddenly disappearing. He then heard someone coming to the door and tried to quickly remind himself of the speech he had prepared to make a joke of his arrival so that Rebecca wouldn't think he came to Munich just to see her.

The door suddenly swung open and Rebecca leapt upon him, wrapping her arms around him and kissing him on the cheek.

"You came!" she said blissfully.

"Well, I..." Jakob stammered, but Rebecca kissed him again before he could go on.

"I knew you would come." she said when she stopped kissing him and just stood there in the snow with her arms around him.

Jakob wondered what he had gotten himself into. He was overwhelmed and for a moment felt like running away, but then he put his arms around Rebecca and held her tightly.

"Oh, it's you. You scared us to death banging on the door like that" Rebecca's brother, Max, said to Jakob as he appeared in the doorway. "I've got to go to school now. Maybe I'll see you later."

Rebecca slipped past Max as they met in the doorway, he going out and she going in with Jakob in tow.

"I haven't spoken to Jurgen, but I assume he gave you my letter." Rebecca said as she pulled him into the kitchen and gestured for him to sit.

"Yes, I..." Jakob started, only to be interrupted again as Rebecca offered him coffee and breakfast.

It was not lost on Rebecca that Jakob had yet to complete a sentence and she decided not to say anything more until he said something about why he had come.

There was quite a silence as she served coffee and then sat across the table waiting for him to speak. Jakob didn't know what to say. He was thinking of different things he might say and then imagining where the conversation might lead and he kept coming back to how he would always end up offering to somehow save Rebecca and he realized how powerless he was.

"Good coffee..." he finally said, raising the cup as though he had to demonstrate exactly which coffee he was talking about. That seemed to be a safe enough topic of conversation.

"Thank you" Rebecca said, trying to hold back a smile. There was another pause as they just sat looking at each other until Jakob finally spoke again. "How are you doing? I mean, really..."

Rebecca stopped smiling and looked down at the kitchen table, studying the grain of the wood as she tried to put her feelings into words. "I don't know... It's been hard, I used to get so mad." She suddenly slapped her hand against the table as she protested angrily, "It's so unfair!"

Jakob was startled and the reflexive twitch which brought him to attention in his chair drew Rebecca's eyes up from the table.

"But the strangest thing is how we grew used to it all" she said calmly, "It seems..." she paused, looking for the right word, but all she could come up with was; "Sad. Sad that we should come to accept it. Kurts father, he's a Catholic, was even sent to the internment camp at Dachau for speaking out against the laws for purity of German blood. They let him out after eight months, but by that time Kurt was in the labor corp. They didn't see each other for almost two years."

"Jurgen didn't say anything..."

"That's what I mean" Rebecca said with excitement rising in her voice again, "We learn what you can talk about and what things are better not to talk about and even though Jurgen knew you and could have trusted you, it was like... like a reflex that he would say nothing. Just in case."

"In case?"

"In case someone was listening."

"It's really that bad?" Jakob asked rhetorically as he shifted uncomfortably in his chair.

"They come for people in the middle of the night. They take them to these internment camps for almost any reason and then you hear every week or so about someone who was shot when he tried to escape."

"We hear the stories in Salzburg, but the papers keep saying that it's just propaganda."

"They call the truth propaganda and then they call their propaganda the truth." Rebecca said with a flourish, but then she spoke softly, as a victim would speak of a tormentor, wanting to say the truth out loud but afraid of how terrible the truth would be once it was spoken. "I think they want us to know... so that everyone will be too scared to talk against them."

Jakob made a sound signifying agreement, but he had nothing else to say.

"What are you thinking?" Rebecca finally asked after another long, awkward pause.

"I don't know, really. It's all so much..." was all he could

357

manage to say.

Rebecca was expecting something. When she saw Jakob standing at the door, she thought he had come for her. To take her with him, to marry. She thought he had come to save her by taking her out of Germany.

"Why did you come?" Rebecca asked, tired of skirting the issue.

Jakob was taken by surprise. It was the moment of truth. He had not even known himself why he had come. "I wanted to see you again."

"Again?" Rebecca said slowly, sadly, " You say that as though you mean you want to see me one last time."

"No!" Jakob said indignantly.

"Then tell me why you came!" she shouted back.

"What do you think?" Jakob shot back, "You think life is like a fairy tale? I can't help you. I can't do..." he thrashed about trying to imagine what Rebecca wanted of him, "...anything. I can't do anything."

Another silence, a house filled with silence... and fear. "I didn't know what to do, but I thought something might come to me if I was here, if we were together" Jakob said as he moved his hand towards hers on the table, just short of touching her.

"Do you love me?" Rebecca asked when she managed to look up at him, into his eyes.

What a frightening question. "Love?" Jakob thought to himself. He had never said that to her before, or maybe he had, but not in that way. He didn't believe he had ever meant it, really meant it, when he had said it to other girls, but this was different. He knew this wasn't the time to lie and he had to ask himself if it was true. Did he love her? Was that why he had come all this way or was he just sorry for her? Maybe he had only come to say good-bye as she accused! Or maybe he too had thought that he might somehow rescue her and take her away.

"Yes" he lied, at least partly a lie, after an almost imperceptible pause which Rebecca ignored.

"Do you want to... to marry me?" she ventured forth cautiously, fearing both possible answers, not knowing if she could accept his pity and marry him so that he would help her leave the country and not wanting to hear him say out loud that he didn't want her.

"Marriage!?" Jakob thought to himself. What a leap for

someone he hadn't seen for three years. How could she even ask such a question?

"I can't get married now. It's a bad time. I have no job, no money." Jakob answered quickly, evading the actual question by rejecting its premise.

"Yes, of course... I was only joking anyway" she said with a smile, letting Jakob off the hook at which point he also smiled, but a pained smile because it had seemed to him to be a bad joke.

"Well then, I suppose you should be going" Rebecca continued.

"Going?" he asked with surprise in his voice, caught off guard again.

"Yes, I have to get to work and since you only stopped by to say hello..."

Her voice was funny, squeaking as she said "say hello" and Jakob knew she was upset, but she was going to pretend that she wasn't hurt as she sent him away.

"I had hoped we could talk..." he said, reaching for her hand as she picked up a coffee cup to take to the kitchen sink, but she pulled away.

"No. there really isn't anything to say." she replied as she leaned against the sink with her back towards him.

Jakob decided that even if she was wrong, at least this would be the time for a tactical retreat. He quietly got up and took his coat from the back of the chair, not saying a word as he put it on and turned for the door. He knew she was crying even though he couldn't hear her or see her face and it hurt him, but there was nothing to be done.

He spent the week doing research at the university, but he took Gertie's advice and skewed the topic of his work so that it was now about the triumph of the Freikorps rather than the rise and fall of the Eisner government. It was a compromise that he didn't take lightly, but he was finally afraid, aware of the dangers after hearing over and over about how one must be careful what one says and does. It's one thing to make light of an over-protective mother, but quite another when everyone gives you the same warning.

It was a pleasant visit with Gertrude and the research went well enough for a credible beginning to a thesis, but the week seemed to be over in just the blink of an eye. Jakob laid awake on that last night before returning to Salzburg, staring at the ceiling and thinking only of Rebecca. She had never been far from his thoughts all week.

He wondered if he should go and see her again in the morning. His train didn't leave until late afternoon, so he would have plenty of time, but why should he go? What could he say that he hadn't already said? He couldn't seem to get comfortable in bed. Even though it was snowing again outside, he felt hot. He constantly twisted and turned, occasionally pulling his pillow out from under himself and beating it into submission before trying once again to get comfortable. Finally he got up to use the bathroom and then went into the kitchen for a glass of milk and a piece of one of Gertie's ever-present cakes.

He then wandered into the front room and sank into an overstuffed chair. His eyes soon grew accustomed to the darkness as he stared out the window at the night and fog which wrapped itself around the city . He watched the white dots of falling snowflakes as they were caught in the glow of a street lamp in front of the apartment building. Nacht und nebel. How can one escape the night and fog?

"What is it Liebchen? What's the matter?" Gertrude startled Jakob when she spoke. She was so used to living alone that she knew instantly when Jakob had left his room and gone into the kitchen and then the living room. She automatically turned on the light, blinding Jakob, intruding on his peace and thoughts. They both squinted and Jakob put up a hand to shade his eyes against the harsh glare of the incandescent bulb. Gertie looked old and tired as she stood before him.

"Nothing. I just couldn't sleep" he said.

"Oh... I suppose you're anxious about going home tomorrow."

"Yes, that's it."

"I'll miss you." Gertie said, obviously sad as she avoided looking at Jakob, pretending to be interested in the snow falling outside. "It was so nice of you to stay here."

"Oh Gertie..." Jakob said in the patronizing tone of youth that doesn't know what it is to be alone, to have been married and had children then finally being all alone, "You really helped me out."

Gertie brushed his thanks away with a wave of her hand, turning her face as though embarrassed. "I didn't do anything. " There was a pause until Gertie spoke again, "You've been so busy, we haven't had much time to talk. Did you get a chance to see Rebecca?"

"Rebecca? Yes... I did see her for a little while."

"She didn't come to see me this week. Is everything all right?"

"Ah, yes. I guess... Like I say, we only talked a little."

"Only a little?"

"Yes, she had to go to work"

"Work? She found work?"

"Yes, she said she's been working at some factory."

"She was, but she told me they let her go."

"She was fired?"

"It's all this craziness about the Jews. They said someone else needed the job..."

"She didn't say a word to me."

"Oh, she must not have wanted you to worry." Gertie said, realizing her *faux pas*.

"What will they do?"

"I don't know. It seems to get worse all the time. Who knows what will happen next? If it were me, I'd leave the country."

"She says they can't afford to..."

Gertie just shook her head.

"Gertie, what about Friedrich? He works in the Brownhouse, doesn't he? Isn't there some way that he could put in a word to help Rebecca's family leave?"

A strange expression washed across Gerties face, perhaps both fear and pain. "Friedrich is... There are some things I can't even say to him anymore. I don't even tell him that Rebecca visits."

Jakob was shocked as he realized that Gertrude was now afraid of her own son.

Gertie took Jakob's silence as accusation, but she wasn't a person who would confront such a thought and so she once again excused Rebeccas situation with a shake of her head and turned back towards her room, stopping at the lamp to extinguish the light before leaving Jakob once again in his lonely darkness.

The early morning found him stepping onto the Furstenried U-bahn platform.

Rebecca looked out the kitchen window at the dark silhouette standing in front of the house and knew it was him. She knew this was his last day and she prayed that he would not leave without seeing her again. She rushed out the front door without even putting on a coat, towards the figure waiting on the sidewalk.

"Oh Jakob, I'm so glad you..." she said as she drew near, but

361

suddenly she realized it wasn't Jakob. She had surprised a complete stranger with her charge through the gate and her exuberant greeting. "I'm sorry... I thought you were..." she said to the stranger as she turned back to the house, but as she did, she almost knocked over Jakob who had just arrived on the scene.

He followed Rebecca up to the door, curious about why she didn't even say hello, but waiting until they were out of earshot to ask Rebecca who that man was that she had been talking to.

"It was just... just a friend." she said, not wanting to embarrass herself. "I'm glad you came back" she continued once they were in the house.

"I couldn't leave like that" Jakob said as he took off his coat, "I need you to tell me if there's something I can do"

"I thought about it since you left. I tried to think about what I wanted. I was so angry at you."

"I know" Jakob interjected.

"I was angry, but I don't even know why. I don't know what I expected..."

Jakob moved towards her and put his arms around her.

"I couldn't leave anyways," she admitted as she reciprocated Jakobs embrace, "I couldn't leave mother and Max here. I just felt trapped. I wanted you to help me escape."

Jakob suddenly found himself kissing Rebecca as she rambled on. "But with the Anschluss coming..." she continued, looking somewhere past Jakob as she tried to concentrate on what she was saying while he kissed her again, "I guess Austria wouldn't be much safer. I don't know where..." She tried to go on, but was no longer able to ignore what was happening, what Jakob was doing, what she was feeling. She stopped talking and pulled away from his embrace enough so that she could look into his eyes for the first time since he arrived. She saw something warm and tender.

"I love you Jakob."

"I love you, Rebecca" he said softly, sadly.

"...and you're leaving today."

"and I'm leaving today... but that doesn't mean I don't love you."

"How can it all be so hard? Why can't we be together?" she asked as she fell against him, burying her head in his chest. A couple of tears ran down her face, but she wasn't crying, not really. "I keep thinking of that night your father died, when we fell asleep together.

I've never felt that close to anyone. Those days just before you left..."

"I think about it too" Jakob said, holding her even closer than before.

Rebecca then kissed Jakob and reached for his hand and led him to her bedroom. She reached for the buttons on his shirt as they stood beside her freshly made bed.

It may have been crazy, It may have been unreasonable, but it seemed to be the only thing that they had to give each other. It was real in an unreal world. It was warmth, and love, and compassion.

The snow had stopped and Jakob thought about the morning spent with Rebecca as he waited for the train to Salzburg and caught a glimpse of the setting sun from the train platform. He had not had many sexual encounters in his life, but the other times he had carefully planned out in advance the who, where and when of the event and how he would go about getting the girl in question to succumb. It was all about sex just for the sake of sex. He hadn't expected this to happen with Rebecca, although if he were to be honest, he would have to admit that the thought of it had crossed his mind as a fleeting fantasy, but this wasn't what he thought it would be. Everything was different with Rebecca. Everything was always different with Rebecca.

When he had told Rebecca he loved her on that first day, it was expedient and insincere, but when he said he loved her a week later, there was suddenly no question, no hesitation. He had been afraid to even think about it before and then suddenly it seemed so obvious. Of course he loved her. The years, the distance meant nothing.

"Then how can I leave her now?" he asked himself. He suddenly thought that he shouldn't get on the train to Salzburg. He could stay at Gertie's and make plans. He would marry Rebecca and they could escape.

He had made excuses before, real and imagined, at Rebecca's suggestion of marriage, but now he just as unrealistically dismissed all possible problems and his mind raced at the thought of how they might elope and escape to Switzerland. The thoughts of escape to Switzerland or possibly even to some exotic faraway land whose name he didn't even yet know started him daydreaming as he sat waiting for his train. How had they gotten to this place, this desperate place? It had happened so gradually, so... Jakob thought of himself as though standing at the seashore as the tide comes in. You see it, you know that the water is moving towards you and you must move out of the way, but then suddenly it is upon you, waves lapping at your heels and only then do you turn and run from the shore.

He then thought about Hitler and how he had admired the Fuhrer when he was a boy in the Hitler youth, Orion the archer. He realized that he didn't really admire Hitler back then, he just knew the man was important, and then of course there had been Friedrich's Geli who actually brought "Uncle Alfie" down to the English garden on that afternoon so long ago. Jakob suddenly thought how he should have killed uncle Adolf. Orion would have been like the American Indians in Otto Maus' western books, Orion would have swept down into the garden on the back of a charging Indian pony and let two arrows slip firmly and deeply into the chest of the tyrannical uncle Alfie. In his daydream Jakob could see the expression of pain and disbelief on uncle Alfie's face as uncle Alfie raised a convulsing hand and lightly touched the shafts of the two arrows protruding from his heartless chest just before falling dead on the bed of finely manicured grass in the English garden.

Jakob smiled a little self-satisfied smile, but then he quickly looked up to see if anyone was watching him, afraid that they might know what he was thinking. He then became upset with himself. How could he sit there and indulge in such ridiculous schoolboy fantasies when he had such terrible problems to think about?

He was so lost in his thoughts about Rebecca that the train to Salzburg seemed to take only a few minutes for the trip that was more than an hour just a week before. He was caught completely off guard when the conductor walked down the passageway calling out "Salzburg. Salzburg station, next stop."

He scrambled for his suitcase and bag full of books and papers just as the train came to a jerking stop and managed to wrestle everything off the train, taking time to get situated once he was on the cold, windy station platform. He decided to take a taxi rather than call Amalie or Ethan to come for him since he had plenty of money thanks to Gertrude letting him stay with her during his visit. Lights glowed in every window of his grandfathers house as the taxi came to a stop and Jakob couldn't help but glance at the house over his shoulder when he was paying the driver, wondering what could possibly move his grandfather to such extravagance.

"Oh Jakob, you're home... Why didn't you call? We would have met you." Amalie said, greeting her son as she skittered into the foyer, stopping on her way from the kitchen to the upstairs with an empty box in her arms.

"Mother..." Jakob said, dropping his bags as he looked around the house, seeing everything in a shambles with crumpled newspapers and boxes everywhere, "What in the world?"

"We're moving, dear."

"Moving!? When? Where?"

"In three days."

"Where? What about the house? What about grandfather?"

"Calm down Jakob. Your grandfather is coming with us. We're all moving to Prague."

"Czechoslovakia? But why?"

"Father got an offer from an old friend for the house and his business..."

"His business! What business?" Jakob said. Both Jakob and Amalie knew that Ethan only went down to his office in pretense that everything was still going well, but neither of them had brought it up before.

"Jakob." Amalie said in a cautionary tone, an admonishment against saying anything that would belittle Ethan, "I said it was a friend of fathers and this friend was... generous. He made an offer that no one else would make."

"but why Prague?" Jakob asked in the tone of a whining child.

"The Anschluss is coming." Amalie declared.

"You've heard something?"

"No, but the way things are going... we've got to get out of Austria. They'll close the borders here just like they did in Germany."

"Now you're just guessing."

Amalie glared at her son, resenting his insulting tone. Amalie was not a rash person and both she and Ethan had talked this over at length before Ethan accepted the offer to sell his house. They knew from what they heard of Germany that if they waited and the nazis took over, Ethan would be at the mercy of any potential buyers for the house and no one would dare give him anything for his business. His friend had offered Ethan less than a fair price, but the friend had done it with the understanding that he would sell it again as soon as he could, sending Ethan more money in Prague. This was quite a gamble for Ethan, but it was the best he could do and he could only hope that his friend would deal with him honestly once Ethan was out of the country as there could be no legal remedy if the friend reneged on the deal and kept all the money.

"I can't come with you" Jakob continued.

"What?" Amalie exclaimed.

"I have to finish school. I have almost six months to go."

"You could go to school in Prague."

"I'd have to start all over again. I don't speak Czech well enough to..."

"There is a large German population in Prague" Amalie countered, "There are separate German universities. You could find German teachers and finish up almost on time."

"But why should I go before we're sure anything is even going to happen? The Chancellor is against the nazis."

"If you wait until it happens, it will be too late. They won't let you out of the country. You'll have to buy your way out like in Germany."

This struck Jakob as he remembered Rebecca. This was the argument that might convince him, but he didn't really want to leave everything behind. He wanted to graduate in Salzburg. He'd never been to Prague.

"I have a friend in Prague who can put us up until we find an apartment..." Amalie went on.

"An apartment?"

"We don't want to spend money on a house."

"Why not?"

"We might need it in a hurry."

"Even in Prague? Don't you think you're going a bit far? the Czechs certainly won't want an Anschluss with Germany."

"We don't know what might happen."

"Oh mother! You really are paranoid."

"Better that I should be over concerned rather than caught by surprise."

"I don't think I want to go to Prague. I'll stay by myself."

"Don't be ridiculous Jakob. The house is sold. We have to move."

"Then I'll find an apartment of my own here."

Amalie was annoyed at her sons defiance, but she wasn't in the mood to keep arguing. She still had a lot of packing to do and she thought she might convince him later if she just let him think about the situation. "If that's what you want, but now we have to pack. There's some dinner in the kitchen. We've already eaten. Please help out when you're done eating. Father's up in the attic and I'm working in the bedrooms."

"What a homecoming" Jakob thought to himself as he slid his suitcase and rucksack into a corner by the front door and went into the kitchen to get something to eat. "Moving? She's crazy!" he said to himself under his breath as he dished up his dinner, "She's hysterical. Everything will calm down soon. All of this will blow over soon."

"So, how was Munich?" Ethan asked as he shuffled into the kitchen, obviously tired after a long day of sorting through memories and packing them up for the move to Prague.

"Good" Jakob said between bites of a sandwich. The conversation stopped as he took a moment to swallow and take a drink of water. "It was just like I remembered..." he finally said.

"Were the nazis out in force?"

"They were like a swarm of wasps building their nest. They were everywhere."

"How was your hotel?"

"I stayed with Gertie."

"Gertie? That wasn't the girl who lived next door, was it?"

"No grandfather. The girl next door was Rebecca. Gertie was... well almost like a housekeeper, but more like part of the family."

"Oh, you mean Frau Haas. Now I remember her. We met at the funeral. How did you end up staying with her?"

"I just stopped in to say hello and she insisted I stay."

"That was nice of her."

"Yes." Jakob said, paying more attention to his sandwich than to the conversation.

"Your mother said you want to stay in Salzburg."

This caught Jakobs attention. "Yes. I'd like to finish up at the university."

"Do you understand what that could mean?"

"Mean?"

"Yes. Have you thought about it, about what might happen."

"You worry too much grandfather."

"Worry too much? Don't you know what it's like in Germany?

Didn't you see anything that's going on?"

"I saw."

"...and don't you know what's going to happen here? The same thing. You have Jewish blood. They could come any time now."

"That's just talk."

"But if it isn't just talk, you could be stopped from leaving Austria after you graduate."

"Mother and I have already talked about this."

Ethan sighed and shook his head, assuming like Amalie that they might be able to change Jakob's mind before they were actually ready to move.

The next couple of days were inconvenient around the house as more and more necessary items succumbed to the growing number of carefully packed boxes filling the house. One could hardly make a meal or get dressed in the morning without quietly cursing about something else that had always been taken for granted, but was now packed away.

It was the night of the second day since Jakobs return from Munich when Amalie began going through the few things in the basement. Most of it was broken old furniture that Ethan had intended to have repaired some day, but he had never gotten around to it. Now it was just so much more for the second hand dealers who were coming in the morning to make an offer on everything that Ethan and Amalie had decided to leave behind. A couple of the pieces of furniture brought back almost forgotten memories to Amalie. There was the rocking horse that she had ridden as a child that she had been forced to hand down to Eleonore.

Eleonore always rode it frantically, to the point where the rails would actually leave the floor and she would bounce across the room. Ethan found it amusing. He told Eleonore that she shouldn't rock so roughly, yet he couldn't seem to help smiling, which encouraged Eleonore to continue misbehaving. Amalie knew that if she had done it, she would have been told that she couldn't play anymore.

Then one day Eleonore fell over and broke the tail and part of the head off. Amalie felt like crying back then when she was five years old, but she didn't. She just got angry, angry at her father. Eleonore couldn't help being such a horrible little girl, that's just the way she was, but Amalie felt betrayed by her father.

Amalie smiled. It was so long ago and it certainly didn't mean anything all these years later, but the memory was so strong. She continued looking around trying hard to see into the corners of the basement. She found herself constantly blocking the light as she would step in front of the single light bulb hanging down from the ceiling by two bare wires, casting her shadow on the very things she wanted to inspect.

There was the small bedside table that her mother had used. Delicate. Carved out of dark walnut with gentle filigree and finely detailed spindles. She remembered it from the day her mother died. Her mother, Ruth, insisted with what little strength she had left at the end that she wanted to finish her life at home surrounded by her family.

Then one day the nurse came into Amalie's room and quietly said "It's time" and held out her hand. They went into her mother's room, standing at the foot of the bed as Eleonore knelt by the bed with her head gently on her mothers outstretched hand.

"Don't be afraid Amalie, Eleonore..." Ruth whispered, her eyes closed, making no effort to raise her head. Just then Ethan came into the bedroom. He had rushed upstairs and was out of breath, his breathing the only sound in the room as he took Ruth's other hand and brought it to his lips, kneeling down at the same time.

"Auf Weidersehen liebchen" he said, his voice cracking as he reached out and stroked her dark hair and then her cheek.

She was gone.

It was as though she had just fallen asleep.

When Ethan began to cry, his daughters knew it was over. Eleonore began sobbing into the bed linens. Amalie stood quietly watching her sister and father. Ethan tried to stand up, bracing himself heavily against the bedside table and there was a sudden, unexpected loud crack as one of the delicate spindle legs broke. It brought Ethan back from his grief for an instant. He picked up the table at that moment and carried it out of the room. Amalie and Eleonore looked at each other, wondering why he would take the time to do that at such a moment.

Amalie now knew why. He would have the rest of his life to grieve, to miss his wife, just as Amalie would have the rest of her life to miss Gunther. An interruption, a moments release from the pain...

Amalie examined the table and it's broken leg. This is where it had stood for thirty years. This was the monument to her mother, not the cold stone block standing in the Jewish cemetery a few miles away.

She then remembered the bible that she had stored down in the basement, the Heidler family Bible so carefully hidden away behind a stack of bricks. Friedrich! She just at that moment remembered that she had put Friedrichs package with that Bible, the mysterious package he had sent with her "just in case it was needed" at some later time. He had never called or written to her about it. Of course he was drunk at the time when he had given it to her just before she left Munich. Maybe it was just some sort of drunken joke. Maybe he didn't even remember it. In fact she hadn't heard a word from Friedrich since she left Munich.

She had thought about opening it as soon as she got to Salzburg, but then she thought better of it and put it away with the Heidler Bible. Now that they were leaving, however, she could no longer resist.

"Father, you've got to come see this!"

"But I'm busy here" Ethan said, annoyed at the way Amalie felt compelled to drag him away whenever she came upon some faux treasure that she hadn't seen in years.

"No, this time it's important" she protested.

"Yes, yes..." he grumbled as he slowly got up and followed her into the basement.

"Where's Jakob?"

"I don't know. He went out with a friend a while ago."

"Good. Close the door behind you."

"Amalie, what kind of nonsense..." Ethan growled, although he closed the door as she insisted.

"I've found something."

Once down in the basement, assured the door was closed and they wouldn't be interrupted, Amalie explained to her father how she had come by the box. She then took the box from its hiding place and carefully laid out the specimens contained therein. Ethan inspected the nightshirt and the broken needle as Amalie read the letter out loud.

"My God! The rumors were true!" Ethan said, still holding the night shirt stained with brown dried blood, "Hindenburg was murdered."

"There's more..." Amalie said, continuing to read the letter out loud.

When she had finished reading the letter which ended by explaining the events surrounding Geli Rabaul's death, Ethan carefully replaced the artifacts and he and Amalie just looked at each other for a moment, at a loss for words.

"He had no proof about the Rabaul girl?" Ethan finally asked.

"No proof, but apparently he was an eye witness."

"But he would never testify..."

"No" Amalie agreed, "I can't imagine he would ever stand in a court and testify. This was all just for... security. He wanted to protect himself from God knows who."

"God knows who? Perhaps Hitler himself..."

"Maybe Friedrich has forgotten about it. I did."

"Something this important?"

"He had been drinking when he gave it to me. I haven't heard from him once in all this time."

"Are you going to try to contact him before we leave?"

Amalie looked at her father. The answer seemed so obvious to her that she couldn't believe he could ask such a thing. "No." she said.

It was such a strange situation that Ethan didn't know whether to be disappointed at her duplicity or proud of her ability to play this game. He only knew for sure that he was clearly out of his element. "Are you going to expose this mess?" he asked.

"No, not now."

"Then what?"

"We'll just take it with us and decide what to do when we're settled."

The next days passed in a flurry of last minute activity as final items were packed, extraneous items sold and everything else was sent off to the rubbish heap.

Jakob remarked as his mother carefully set aside the small broken table from the basement to be sent along to Prague and she told him the story of her mothers death. Even after hearing the story, Jakob couldn't understand why his grandfather hadn't had it repaired. What good was a broken table?

Jakob had made up his mind not to go with Ethan and Amalie to Prague. He moved in with a friend from school and was determined to finish out the school year in Salzburg. He didn't want to run. He didn't want to believe that he could be chased from his home by the same people who had once been his friends and comrades.

The feeling, the strange heaviness in Amalie's stomach as she watched Jakob slowly disappear from sight as the train pulled out of the station, was indescribable. She wanted to pull him onto the train with her. "Come child!" she fantasized herself saying as she would force him to do what was best for him. She couldn't help but think this might be the last time she would ever see her son. She felt angry with her father as she looked at him sitting across from her, staring out the window. He was a man. Why didn't he tell Jakob to forget this nonsense of staying in Salzburg and get ready to leave immediately? That was the way Gunther would have handled it, but now her father looked so... so small. and sad.

It was just then that she realized she was the one in charge now. Her father was counting on her to take care of things and keep them safe. Maybe it was just because of the recent turn of events, the loss of his business and selling the house, but he looked older than he should have, old and tired.

Amalie felt so much better when they got off the train in Prague and saw Hannah Bauer waiting for them. She recognized her in an instant in the crowd even though they had only seen each other a few times in the previous twenty years. Hannah's face had always been a gentle blend of features and colors, a small nose, auburn hair and light blue eyes, and her soft voice. Even though she had changed, she really hadn't changed.

Amalie and Hannah had attended the same university near Salzburg during the war, both of them in the same circumstances of being young brides with young children and their husbands off fighting the war. They kept in touch over the years after Amalie went to Munich and Hannah ended up in Prague where her husband's parents lived. Writing letters regularly, at least one a month, each knew what the other had been through. Amalie had attended the funeral of Hannah's husband, Rolf and Hannah had attended Gunther's funeral.

Hannah and Rolf had bought a big house when they married as they had planned on having many children, but the war changed their plans. Rolf was wounded just a few weeks before the armistice was signed and went into a coma, surviving for almost five years. Hannah was slowly worn out, drained of all hope and prayers until one day he just stopped breathing. She and her daughters survived well enough financially since Rolf's parents were well off and supported them, but the emotional cost was high and Hannah could never find it in herself to take a chance on love again. She knew she would never remarry.

"So, you made it!" Hannah said with a smile, embracing Amalie as she got off the train.

"Oh, Hannah, I can't tell you how much this means to us."

"It's nothing. Now that Erika is married, we have much more space than we need."

Ethan slowly came up beside Hannah and Amalie as they spoke. "Hannah, you remember my father..."

"Of course, Herr Stein...and this is my Karin" Hannah said as she put her arm around the pretty teen-age girl standing next to her.

"Where is Jakob?" Hannah asked after everyone had exchanged greetings.

"He decided to stay in Salzburg...to finish the school year." Amalie said.

Hannah could tell that Amalie wasn't happy about it, but she didn't pursue it.

Over the next few weeks Amalie and Ethan settled in comfortably with Hannah and Karin. They couldn't have made a better choice for house companions if they had interviewed people for the position. The house had five bedrooms, which Amalie made quick note of, planning that Jakob might come to his senses soon and join them.

Jakob, on the other hand, was not doing as well with his choice for a room mate. He had told his mother that his room mate was a stable, reliable old friend and there would certainly be no problems, but the truth was that the young man was a friend of a friend that Jakob hardly knew who was in his first year at the university, his first time away from home, and he was terribly inexperienced in handling his money which meant that he often spent time out drinking with friends and equally as often came up short in paying expenses like rent, heat and electricity. Jakob, however, refused to admit defeat and go to Prague to be taken care of by his mother and grandfather, so he intended to stick it out to the end.

It was in February that Hitler really started to speak strongly and specifically about the destiny of the German peoples that was the

Austrian Anschluss and Jakob began to think that his mother was right, that the Anschluss could happen almost any time in the near future. He thought about taking a weekend excursion to Prague to see how things were going, but then he thought better of it. He was too old to be so skittish. It was time for him to put some distance between his family and himself and this was the perfect opportunity. Once he had his degree... but then of course law school would take so many more years. He could get a job and work his way through law school, just go about his life as though nothing was wrong until all of this national socialist business blew over or at least calmed down a bit.

March started to give some hints that Spring might come. A few warmer days, a little more sunshine and the snow thinning out in the valleys. Both Ethan and Amalie soon felt at home with the Bauers. Hannah didn't seem in any hurry to have the Steins find a place of their own, as a matter of fact, their presence made it a bit easier for her to accept the fact that her daughter Erika had just married and moved out of the house. It's sometimes a sad thing as you get older and discover that friends from your youth, schoolmates for example, just don't seem to fit into your life anymore as you develop other interests and grow apart, but this wasn't the case with Amalie and Hannah. They actually had more in common in Prague than they had had in Salzburg during their days at the university.

Ethan also liked Hannah, often talking about the years that he raised his two daughters after his wife died just as Hannah had had to do after her husband died. Hannah found Ethan to be fascinating. She had never had much contact with Jewish people, even her friendship with Amalie didn't really count as Amalie had spent so much time running away from the Jewish faith, but Hannah and Ethan on the other hand had many friendly discussions about the similarities and differences between Catholicism and Judaism, each of them making a point of trying to learn from the other rather than arguing the correctness of their own point of view.

It was on the morning of March tenth that Erika and her husband stopped by the house. Amalie had gone out looking for work as she had been doing regularly since they got settled in. Hannah had told her daughter that she could have the bureau from her old bedroom since the young newlyweds had to beg and borrow each piece of furniture for their new apartment. Erika was expecting to help her husband carry the dresser out to the truck which he had borrowed from a friend, but Ethan insisted that it was no job for such a pretty young girl.

Ethan smiled at the young man whose name he hadn't quite caught when they were introduced, was it Franz or Hans, just as they were about to lift the bureau. It was heavier than he had expected and he struggled under the weight of it as they awkwardly made their way out of the bedroom to the top of the stairs.

"Stop a moment" Ethan said as they got to the stairs.

"Are you all right?" the young man asked.

"Yes, yes. I just need to get a better grip" Ethan lied as he caught his breath. He then picked up the bureau again and they started the labored journey down the steps. Step down, lower the bureau. Take another step and lower the bureau. One step after another, only a few inches at a time. The young man was getting impatient, but he didn't want to make the old man feel bad so he just kept following his lead.

When they finally made it to the stair landing, Ethan had to stop again.

"Ethan, are you sure you can do this?" Hannah asked as she started up the stairs.

"Oh God!" Ethan said as pain shot through his left arm and he grabbed for it.

"What is it?" Erika asked.

"I... I don't know... I must have pulled..." Ethan said in bewilderment.

"I've seen this before." Erika's husband said as he moved towards Ethan and helped him sit down on the stairs, "It could be a heart attack. There isn't any time to waste. I'll carry you out to the truck and get you to the hospital."

"Don't be ridiculous" Ethan said, trying to brush the young man away, "I can walk."

"No. You shouldn't take the chance." and with that the young man put Ethan's arm around his neck and carried him out of the house.

Erika was waiting alone for Amalie when she got home and told her what had happened. The two of them went to the hospital where the doctor told Amalie that Ethan had most likely suffered a mild heart attack and that he would be all right if he took it easy. Amalie called Jakob as soon as she got home. She didn't want to scare him, but she wanted him to come.

Jakob was on the train for Prague the next morning. He was afraid that his mother had tried to make it sound better than it really was. His imagination ran wild as he pictured himself arriving in Prague just in time for his grandfather's funeral. First his father and now his grandfather. But when he finally arrived at the hospital he found Ethan's room full of people all laughing and talking as though it were a party and there in the center of it all was Ethan, laughing hardest of all.

The next day, the day Ethan came home from the hospital, was the day that the German army entered Austria. Thousands of Austrians were arrested across the country, particularly in Vienna where Eleonore's husband, Louis, was among those rounded up. Even though Louis Hoffman was just a botany professor, the combination of being a Jew and a college professor was enough to put him on a nazi list of dangerous and undesirable elements.

The German invasion of Vienna was the realization of one of Adolf Hitler's earliest dreams. This was the city where he had fallen to the lowest point of his life during his youth, existing off charitable institutions and rare bouts of menial labor. This was also the city where his antisemitic hatreds began to flourish in the pre war period when Vienna was a fading capital of the once great Austro-Hungarian empire which abounded with antisemitic groups distributing pamphlets and books accusing the Jews of all manner of crimes against decent Christian society; from inciting wars from which they might profit to killing Christian children that they might use their blood in Passover matzo. The Jewish community did little to combat these outrageous lies, preferring to keep to themselves and just assuming that the vicious slanders of their enemies would be ignored by the majority of Viennese citizenry, but young Adolf was in this particular instance an avid student.

Vienna was to be cleansed for the Fuhrer, the Jewish population to be dispossessed and degraded and then removed from the capital which Hitler believed the Jews had destroyed. The nazis, both Austrian and German, took great pleasure in the degradation of Viennese Jewry. The Anschluss was their first great success and they reveled in it.

The brownshirts roamed the streets trying to outdo each other in degrading Jews. Old Orthodox Jews who had never in their lives even been without their hats in public, a sign of their devotion to their God, were forced to strip completely as they were beaten and then made to climb trees as the SA mocked them as apes. Other Jews were forced to scrub sidewalks with small brushes as their Viennese neighbors shouted "kike" and "stinking Jew". People who the Jewish population would never have suspected of such hatred were swept up in the anonymity of the mob, cursing and beating whoever the brownshirts pointed out.

It would be weeks before Amalie found out what had happened to her sister and brother-in-law. Just as suddenly as the borders had been opened between Germany and Austria, they were closed between Austria and her other neighbors.

It was funny, albeit dark humor, to watch Jakob go on, ranting and raving about having lost everything that he had left at the apartment in Salzburg and wondering if the university would send transcripts to Prague. Amalie managed to get through Jakob's period of adjustment without ever once mentioning that she had tried to warn him about this very thing.

Once he managed to calm down after a few days he found the transition from Salzburg to Prague relatively easy. Although it was unusual for him to be living in a community where the Germans were a minority, the German community was strong enough and segregated enough that he could live his life pretty much as he had before without putting himself out and going to the trouble of learning a foreign language. He felt Latin and French were enough, along with his smattering of English. It would be ridiculous, it seemed to him, to go to all the trouble of learning Czech or, God forbid, Polish.

Golden Prague certainly had it's charm and history as much as Salzburg or Munich. It was a beautiful city filled with architectural remnants of five centuries past.

Ethan particularly enjoyed telling his grandson the story of one Rabbi Loew who was the chief Rabbi of Prague in the middle of the sixteenth century. It seems Rabbi Loew constructed, or sculpted, a life-size man made of clay. The story is that Rabbi Loew would place a shem, a magic packet, in the mouth of the statue and the statue would come to life and perform menial duties for the Rabbi. The statue had a name. It was called the Golem, although it actually had a first name of Joseph.

The story went on that the Rabbi had to make sure that the Golem was not alive during the Sabbath. When Rabbi Loew forgot to remove the shem during one Sabbath, the Golem went wild, destroying property and terrorizing the citizens of the ghetto. When the Rabbi finally caught up with Joseph Golem and snatched the shem from its mouth, the lifeless Golem dropped to the ground, breaking to pieces.

"... and they say that pieces of the Golem are still kept in the attic of the old-new synagogue to this day" Ethan said with a triumphant flourish as he finished his story.

Jakob looked at his grandfather with skeptical eyes, deciding whether or not to challenge the old man. "You can't really believe that."

"Why not? It's happened again today."

"What?"

"Look at Austria. Lifeless clay-footed Hapsburgs laying about until Hitler puts his hate-filled shem in their mouths and suddenly they're all jumping about shouting Sieg this or Sieg that."

Just then Amalie came rushing into the house breathlessly. "Father, they've arrested Louis."

"Louis? Eleonore's Louis?"

"Yes, yes, I just talked to a woman I worked with in Salzburg and she told me Eleonore had been calling for days trying to get hold of me."

"Days? When did it happen?"

"From what I understand it must have been only a couple of days after the Anschluss."

"But why Louis?"

"I don't know. Maybe it was a mistake, but we have to get a call through to Eleonore."

"Yes... Hannah is out, but I'm sure she won't mind if we call. I'll get on the telephone and see if I can get through to Vienna."

It wasn't until the next day that Ethan finally got a line through to Vienna and found that it was true, that Louis had been arrested by the nazis and was being held somewhere. Eleonore broke into tears again and again as they spoke, trying to regain her composure, but losing it just as quickly each time she thought of her situation. She didn't know where her husband was and she and her two daughters were existing on their meager savings which would dissapear quickly.

"You've got to come to Prague" Ethan said impulsively, "We can help each other if we're all here."

"But I don't have much money, father. If I move It will cost a lot and I won't be near Louis. I have to wait here for him."

Ethan thought for a moment as his daughter waited for a magical response that would save her. "We might have some money to send... I don't know. Amalie has been watching the money. The house in Salzburg hasn't sold yet."

Eleonore's hope evaporated. She was sure Amalie still harbored a grudge because of the way Eleonore had felt about Gunther. Eleonore hadn't even attended Gunther's funeral. She tried to appear sympathetic at the time, but she lied when she told Amalie that she couldn't make the trip to Munich because of the cost, and Amalie knew it was a lie.

"If we skimp... I think we can send two hundred marks" Amalie said that night when she and Ethan talked over her sisters situation.

Ethan thought this was a modest bequest, but he let it go at that. "I don't suppose there's any hope for Louis" he said, moving on to the next matter at hand.

"I can't imagine that he's done anything" Amalie countered, "He's certainly never been politically involved."

"No, just his precious flora"

"I still can't imagine why they arrested him in the first place. You don't suppose they're just arresting all Jews now?"

"Don't be ridiculous" Ethan scolded, "There're too many of us."

"Well it may be that he was only picked up to be questioned. Maybe some of the others at the university were opposed to the nazis and they just picked up everybody, thinking they would question them all and sort out the guilty from the innocent later."

"Do you think they'll just let him go?"

Amalie looked at her fathers eyes. They were hopeful and eager to believe that it was just a silly misunderstanding and that the reasonable men who had arrested Louis would discover their mistake and be nice enough to drive him home and reunite him with his wife. "They'll question him" Amalie said with an ominous tone.

"...but they'll let him go when they find that he hasn't done anything" Ethan said resolutely, trying to convince himself that everything would turn out all right.

"They'll torture him" Amalie said cautiously, not wanting to upset her father, but at the same time wanting him to acknowledge the truth.

Ethan shot a glance as if to say he didn't want to know that and then he repeated himself as if saying something would make it so, "They'll let him go."

Amalie's modest estimate of how much they could afford to send to Eleonore was only slightly tainted with animosity towards her sister. In reality there wasn't much money readily available to them in Prague. Amalie had learned well from her time at the bank in Salzburg and had sent most of her assets to a bank in Zurich knowing that while she wanted her assets liquid, she also wanted them protected. The money she had gotten from selling the house, car and other belongings in Munich along with the payment she had gotten from a life insurance policy when Gunther died had all gone to the bank in Zurich while she, Jakob and Ethan lived austerely off her income from her job at the bank. Later, after the move to Prague, she and Ethan lived off the nominal amount that Ethan had gotten for his house and business.

She knew that the nazis had a nasty habit of confiscating the assets of people they didn't like and she was not fooling herself, she knew that even in Prague they might soon be moving again. Who knew how far Hitler would go? It was only shortly after the Austrian Anschluss when Adolf began making noise about the oppression of Sudeten Germans in Czechoslovakia.

The Czechs, however, were the antithesis of the enraptured Austrians who had welcomed German troops in March. The Czechs were probably the best prepared country in Europe, next to the French with their Maginot line and standing army, to withstand a German assault. That was why Ethan had thought it a good idea for Eleonore and her family to come to Prague. The point seemed moot to Eleonore, however, when her husband Louis came home a few days later, battered and bruised... Even though he had been arrested and beaten, they felt that his release meant he had been vindicated, cleared of any complicity with those who might oppose the Germans. Lightning had struck and they knew lightning didn't strike twice in the same place. They thought they were safe.

For a while they were right, as long as they scrupulously obeyed the newly imported German laws for the protection of blood and honor, as long as they kept up on all of the decrees restricting the movement of Jews within the Reich, as long as they did whatever they were told, they would be all right... for the time being.

The next few months were spent in search of normalcy by Ethan, Jakob and Amalie. Amalie once again found work, this time at a German language newspaper in Prague as a proof reader. She didn't use a hyphenated name there. It was no longer Stein-Metzdorf, but instead just the good German name of Metzdorf. It was important to work and fit in.

Even Ethan found work in Prague. One of his former publishing contacts offered him a job. It was more of a politeness than an actual job, but it gave Ethan something to do and once he got back into a regular work routine he became his old self again.

Jakob found a sympathetic professor at one of the German universities in Prague who was willing to help him get caught up in his studies so that he could get a certificate of completion and prepare to move on to a law school.

The summer passed quickly amid intermittent explosions of German propaganda denouncing Czechoslovakia for atrocities against the Sudeten Germans. It was September when everything came to a head. Hitler's threats and demands that the Sudeten region of Czechoslovakia be annexed to Germany in much the same way that the Austrians had been incorporated into the German Reich moved the Czech government to mobilize its army on the 27th of September in anticipation of a German attempt to forcefully "liberate" the Sudeten Germans.

They were coming. Again. Amalie wasn't sure what they should do. Should they just wait and see or should they try fleeing to Poland? Poland seemed like a bad option. They didn't know anyone in Poland. England seemed like a better chance because Ethan had business acquaintances there whom he had known for years, but they couldn't afford to all go and visas were hard to come by.

They talked it over for a long time and began making lists; what could they do, what couldn't they do, where they could and couldn't go. It all seemed to come down to Amalie insisting that if the Germans came in, Ethan would be in the greatest danger. Judging from what she had heard about conditions in Germany, she and Jakob would be better off because of her marriage to Gunther because of his status as a war hero, but Ethan had no such claim or protection and that, along with his recent heart attack seemed to make it clear that he should get out of the country. It also seemed clear that there wasn't much time left before war broke out.

It was on September thirtieth that Neville Chamberlain landed in England after returning from a diplomatic conference in Munich the day before with Hitler, French ambassador Daladier, Italy's Mussolini and German foreign minister Joachim von Ribbentrop. The newsreel cameras immortalized Chamberlain's sense of triumph as he waved a piece of paper in the air as he deplaned, declaring to the members of the press who had been waiting patiently for him to arrive that the document signaled a new era of friendship between the english and german speaking peoples. "It represents an assurance of... peace in our time" he said.

That piece of paper, in reality, was nothing more than a vague agreement stating that the people of England and Germany should endeavor to maintain favorable diplomatic relations. It was the last thing that the English Prime Minister brought up as everyone was getting ready to leave the conference in Munich. Chamberlain and the French representative had just abandoned Czechoslovakia to Hitler, setting the stage for partition and the eventual dissolution of that country, and Chamberlain asked Hitler to sign the "friendship agreement". "Herr Hitler" glanced at the innocuous sheet of paper and then at the English Prime Minister. He could have laughed at the pathetic nature of the document which would become synonymous with the term appeasement, as synonymous with the term as Chamberlain himself, but Adolph merely called for a pen from one of his subordinates and scribbled a signature just before leaving the room.

Ethan was on a airplane on his way to England the next day. Hannah couldn't quite understand why her friend had been in such a panic to get her father out of the country. The Czech army was ready, even if the French and English had abandoned them. Amalie couldn't afford that kind of naïveté. She had managed to scrape together enough money to get Ethan on a airplane, but that was nothing compared to the effort required to get an exit visa out of Prague during the Munich conference. It took every coin she had to bribe officials, every bit of nerve she had to threaten and cajole others and every bit of dramatic ability she had to gain sympathy from the rest. "He's an old man with a weak heart", "His family is in England and he should be with them", "He's a political refugee who fought for Czech freedom and would be arrested immediately". No lie was too shameless or outlandish and when Ethan was finally on the airplane, his luggage included the package belonging to Friedrich Haas. If Amalie needed to use the information for blackmail to get Jakob and herself out of the country at some later time, the evidence would be safe with Ethan.

The end of the Munich conference seemed anti-climactic in Prague as that city remained part of a diminished Czech republic. Other parts of Czechoslovakia were divided among her neighbors with Hungary and Poland quickly stepping in to devour their piece of the kill like Hyenas moving in after Lions had left the killing ground.

Ethan arrived safely in England. Two months later as everyone tried to settle in again and find something that they could call "normal living", the nazis were let loose on the Jewish population in Germany on the 9th of November. They raged through the streets of big cities and small towns, destroying Jewish business and homes and first desecrating and then setting fire to synagogues.

The official nazi party explanation of the pogrom, delivered to the press by Josef Goebbels, was that the riots were a spontaneous uprising against the dangerous Jewish element in Germany, triggered by the shooting of a German diplomat in Paris by a young Parisian Jew named Herschel Grynspan.

Grynspan said that he shot the German diplomat in response to the mistreatment of Jews in Germany. It was convenient for the nazis that Grynspan acted when he did.

They were ready and waiting for any excuse, particularly those in the higher ranks who wanted to please Hitler by putting his hate-filled rhetoric into action, and how convenient that Grynspan's action had practically coincided with the anniversary of the failed beer hall putsch of 1923. What a perfect anniversary gift for the Fuhrer... Krystalnacht. It was a political expedient to please the one true leader of the nation, a boost to Himmler's and Goebbel's careers. If Adolf had hated grass, then the grass would have disappeared from the German landscape, for the Fuhrer's will was the road to power, regardless of personal belief or morality, in spite of it, in place of it. Crude, vulgar, obscene gluttonous hunger for power. Hitler was become Christ and God that none should be worshipped or obeyed above him.

David Frieder was among those who were arrested on Krystalnacht, the night of broken glass. The pogrom came to be known by that name because of all the shop windows of Jewish owned stores that were broken by Brownshirts and SS troops, most of whom were told to wear civilian clothes so that it would be obvious that it was a spontaneous outburst and not a government sanctioned attack on the Jews. The nazis were going from one Jewish home to the next arresting mostly young men, the ones they thought might oppose the nazis, and sending them off to concentration camps.

David had been home alone writing. He had lost his business in 1937, having managed to hold on longer than most through his own personal appeasement policy towards the nazis. He had done everything he could think of to hold on, including turning over controlling interest to a one time friend who had joined the nazis but considered David, as a Jew, "one of the few good ones in a bad lot". David forced himself to take the insult as a compliment, as his friend had intended. Overnight "Frieder and Son Publishing", after forty-seven years of business, became "Thomas Loescher Publishing". Anything to keep the business going, but it wasn't long before David's one time friend started getting flak for allowing a Jew to hang around, no matter if the Jew's father had started the business, no matter if the son had worked hard and long to build up that business, that he had always dealt fairly and ethically with whomever he had done business. A Jew is a Jew and they could no longer work in any part of the communications industry in Germany. There would be no more Jewish propaganda, no more Jewish communists duping unsuspecting Germans by slipping their nefarious lies into seemingly innocent books or radio broadcasts.

David was writing about Napoleon. It seemed an appropriate topic to David considering the events surrounding the loss of his business. It was the code Napoleon in what became known as the age of enlightenment that established the rights of Jews as citizens within their chosen homelands. The code had been forced on nations conquered by Napoleon as he swept across regions of Europe such as the plethora of tiny kingdoms and states that would become Germany some fifty years later. If one were to pick a year, say 1818, and say that that year was the date which rights were granted (in actuality this occurred over a period of time with the installation of governing bodies in different regions), it would be interesting to consider that many Jewish communities relocated in German regions from England in 1296 when the Jews were expelled from that country and subsequently those Jewish communities spent over five hundred years subject to German laws without any of the benefits of citizenship in those lands.

David thought how ironic it was that France, the country that had produced Napoleon and his code, was the same country that less than seventy-five years later played host to the infamous Dreyfus trial which led Theodore Herzl to create the Zionist movement, demanding that there should be a Jewish homeland in the middle east.

Such were the wanderings of his mind as he sat in front of his typewriter waiting for inspiration. The angry knock on the door made him jump, shocking him out of his daydreams. The figure outlined in the curtained window of the front door was not familiar and just as David was about to move the curtain to see who it was, the jack-hammer fist pounded on the door again, starting Davids heart pounding too hardly got the door open when a voice screeched out "You are the Jew Frieder" in a combination statement-question, but before David could give any response, another man who was behind the man who had shouted rushed in and grabbed David by the arm, almost lifting him off the floor and pulling him outside.

David couldn't exactly say how he got into the truck. He couldn't exactly say that he had been afraid, it was more that he just didn't understand what was happening. How could such a thing happen? Did they really know who he was? Did they mean to arrest him? What next? Where were they going, he and the other frightened animal-men in the truck with him? The smell of that oily canvas draped over the metal frame of the army transport truck would be with him forever. If someone asked him years later what Krystalnacht was like, he would always laugh a haunted laugh and say "It smelled like musty canvas."

They were pulled out of the truck in much the same fashion as they had been put in. Pulled, thrown, kicked and punched, herded in the direction of the door to a police precinct station.

They were all criminals now, all in a large cell, called out one by one and asked questions by a policeman... no, he was one of the SS. He sat at a desk with a typewriter, but there were both police and SS men in the station.

Anyone who protested the questions was beaten. Anyone who

hesitated with an answer was beaten. Anyone who looked the SS man in the eye...

It was good exercise for the nazis that night. They were like sculptors attempting to recreate these shapes standing before them, take these men and turn them into soft clay, shapeless and insignificant. This was terror. When one man sees what happens to another and is willing to do anything to avoid the same fate. Call your mother a whore, your father her pimp, what do words mean in the face of vicious physical brutality? Let them make you say it. You believe that you can keep the truth within yourself. You can't see at that moment that it is the first step towards losing yourself. The first step.

David Frieder answered the questions and soon found himself loaded onto another truck.

The mind rejects certain things at times, things that seem impossible or unlikely. David, smelling musty canvas again as he and a new group of men were tossed about in the back of a different truck rumbling through the cold November darkness, tried to convince himself that everything would somehow turn out all right. Why would they possibly want him? For what? He suddenly felt like crying.

How odd.

It seemed to him that he hadn't cried for years and he began to analyze the situation as though he were just an outside observer somehow floating behind the hapless truck, looking in on its miserable inhabitants and wondering how crying could possibly help. He was amazed at himself for thinking it. Crying!

His mind was swimming. He seemed to be losing himself. Everything was beginning to seem unreal. He suddenly realized that none of the others in the truck had faces, not even the single guard riding at the back, sitting straight and rigid with his rifle ready by his side. The guards face should have been visible in the moonlight, but it wasn't. There were only strange shadows there above the huddled shoulders of the others.

David had no sense of the time when the truck slowed to a stop. He heard a voice challenge the driver of the truck and then the truck lurched forward again for a few hundred feet before coming to a stop. Everyone was ordered out. It was still dark. They were cattle now. They acted like cattle, moved like cattle, they had bought the lie.

The only concern was to avoid any more beatings. They all

386

wanted to live. There was no reasoning here, no appeal to humanity because the guards and officers did not consider their charges human. Move them here, get them into prison clothes, get them to the barracks.

The barracks were raw wood. Bunks were wooden platforms with straw. Three or four men to a "bed". You wore wooden clogs for shoes. The threadworn prison clothes hung on your body. The room had a smell. It was a smell of sickness, the smell of human beings wasting away, but the room was clean. There was a mania for cleanliness. If a man didn't keep things clean enough he would be killed. Not outright, with a bullet, but slowly. They would give him the hardest work, reduce his food ration, withhold water while he worked.

There was no more tomorrow, there was only an endless today. Tomorrow might mean hope, an end to the endless, cruel games the guards would play with inmates, daring them to give the guard a reason to punish or shoot, and there was no end in sight except for death. The memory of yesterdays seemed even more painful than the torture of today because of everything that had been lost and left behind. Today. There was only today.

Chapter 14

1939.

Where could you run if you were a German Jew? Some had money and left Germany in '32 when Hitler first became Chancellor. Others left the country when the Nuremburg laws were announced, but many only had enough to move to Austria or Czechoslovakia or Poland. It became a dark comedy as people tried to run away from nazi terror only to have it follow them as country after country was turned over to Germany with hardly a shot fired. Some Jewish people in Germany had convinced themselves that it was all just a passing terror, but as months became years, a day came when Adolf Hitler's bluff was called and war was about to engulf Europe twenty-two years after the end of the Great War. Jewish hope became an empty dream.

This was the culmination of a time during which the world built the gallows upon which European Jewry would soon be marched. The Evian conference showed the indifference of humanity as England, America, France and many other countries introduced even more stringent immigration restrictions which sealed virtually all escape routes for Jews trying to save themselves from Germany's Third Reich. The English in particular delivered a vicious blow to the chance of Jewish survival in the looming shadow of a world war as the British government issued a declaration which came to be called "the British White Paper" on May 17 of 1939. In 1917 there had been another document issued by that government known as "the Balfour document" which had stated that the British government, which was on the verge of capturing Palestine from Turkey in 1917, supported a Jewish national homeland in Palestine. The White paper of 1939 contradicted the Balfour document, stating that Jewish immigration to Palestine, which had become a British protectorate, would be limited to no more than 75,000 Jews over the following five year period. It was certainly not the only example of a brutal lack of compassion among the nations who considered themselves enemies of fascism. The ocean liner St. Louis steamed into New York harbor in 1937 with a full compliment of Jewish refugees hoping to emigrate to America. They cruised below the Statue of Liberty with its inscription "Give us your tired, your poor, your huddled masses yearning to breathe free...", an inscription written by an American Jew, but they would not be allowed to enter America. The light from Liberty's torch was apparently not meant to shine for them and they were forced to return to Europe.

"...and so, we think it would be for the best if you were to go."

Edith didn't know how to respond. She had assumed that because she was cloistered, she wouldn't have any problems with the authorities.

She had been a teacher in Speyer and was invited to be a lecturer at the Education Institute at Muenster in Westphalia in 1932 just as Hitler was elected to the Chancellorship. It was only about a year later when she was forced to resign because of nazi antisemitic legislation forcing Jews out of all teaching and instructional positions in state run educational institutions.

It was then that she decided to pursue something she had thought about for years, she entered the Carmelite convent in Köln as a cloistered nun.

Her work, beyond her regular duties as one of the sisters, was centered on her writings in which she attempted to wed the philosophical tenets of phenomenology with traditional Catholic theology. During the five years she spent in Köln she finished one of her most important works, "Finite and Infinite Being", and was working on another called "The Science of the Cross". Her books were apolitical, in fact her life was apolitical and the only contact she had with the nazis was when she was required to report regularly to the local police in accordance with the Nuremburg laws of 1935 which classified her as a foreign national, a Jew, even though she had converted to Catholicism in 1922 and had been a cloistered nun for over five years.

"Surely they wouldn't come for me here" she said as she looked up at the bishop. Her eyes didn't show fear, just disbelief. Why would the nazis enter a convent? What possible threat could a cloistered nun be to them that they would go to that extreme?

"I'm sorry to say that they don't have much regard for the mother church" the Bishop answered sadly, turning away from Sister Theresa, as Edith was known in the church, having taken the name of Sister Teresa of Avila upon taking her vows.

"But the concordant..." Edith said, referring to the concordant that Pope Pius XI had signed with the Fuhrer in 1934 in hopes of preserving the sanctity of the church in Germany. The concordant was actually signed by Eugenio Pacelli, the monsignor who was representing the Vatican in Germany at that time and coincidentally the man who would become Pope Pius XII. Little did Monsignor

Pacelli know that Adolf Hitlers drive for power would lead the Fuhrer to try to place himself above God almighty in the everyday consciousness of the German people.

There was an interesting aside, however, a personal experience of Eugenio Pacelli's which explained part of the Popes willingness to negotiate with the nazis. It seems that Eugenio Pacelli was a Monsignor in Munich in 1918 when there was revolution in the streets and he was confronted by a group of Communists who demanded that he abandon his church, the church of the Holy Trinity by the Promenadeplatz, only a few hundred feet from the spot where Anton Arco-Valley would murder Kurt Eisner some months later. The confrontation experienced by Pacelli along with his knowledge that Communism was an atheistic political philosophy turned him to the nazis as the lesser of two evils.

The Bishop waved away Edith's mention of the concordant. He knew it was inconsequential, particularly in the face of the state sponsored Krystalnacht. The nazis had not only visited mass destruction, imprisonment and death against the Jews, to add insult to injury the Jews were forced to clean the sidewalks of the broken glass and further forced on a nation wide scale to pay an indemnity to the government of one billion Deutschmarks for the associated costs of the pogrom.

The injustice was so perverse as to take on a life of its own. A horrific insanity inflicted by the government against its own citizens. No vulgar cruelty was too much. Send men to destroy their homes and businesses and beat and kill them and then make them pay the wages of the men sent to do the work. It was so perverse as to seem comical, and indeed the nazis laughed as they worked, Goering laughing in the Reichstag as he insisted that the Jews pay reparations to the government for their part in the pogrom, the part of the victims.

The bishop knew it was too dangerous for any Jew to remain in Germany even though so many would remain, ignored by the other nations of the world who for nations had espoused the virtues of human dignity and worth, but apparently only for themselves. Edith Stein, Sister Teresa of Avila, was quietly transferred from the Carmel of Köln to the Carmel of Echt in Holland on the last day of the year 1938.

Jakob had done well with his university studies in Prague,

graduating on time and moving on to law studies in the autumn of 1938. He was becoming not only accustomed to Prague, but in many ways enchanted by it.

It had been Karin Bauer who had taken the time to show Jakob around Prague when he first arrived. She liked Jakob, being under the impression that his departure was a daring flight through enemy lines rather than just luck that he had been on his way to visit his mother and grandfather, and Jakob was not quick to correct her. The two of them became friends mostly because it was convenient living in the same house and even though Karin had her own circle of friends, mostly younger than Jakob who was now twenty-two compared to Karin's nineteen years, she was nice enough to spend time with him.

She enjoyed touring Prague with Jakob because of the way he saw the city through the eyes of a stranger, viewing everything as new and exciting, like the first time he saw the sun go down from the Charles bridge as they stood at the foot of the statue of Saint John Nepomuk.

The city had a mystical air to it. strange, dark, narrow back streets waiting to be explored. Bizarre little coffee shops with their haunted and haunting patrons. The paths leading up to Hradcany castle and the few remnants of the centuries-old Jewish ghetto which had, for the most part, been razed before the First World War. Karin was interested in the ghetto mostly because it seemed so foreign. She had a great grandfather, or was it a great great grandfather, who she was told had been Jewish. it didn't seem to matter to her one way or the other except that somehow she felt this relationship made the strangeness of the old-new synagogue and the Jewish town hall a part of her. It somehow called to her, singing a song of things which she had never known.

Jakob loved the look on her face as she took it in. She would be holding his hand, having playfully pulled him along down some strange, dark little cobblestone street as though she had been his little sister bringing him along for protection, and then she would stand there staring at the scene before her, still holding his hand, trying to find some kind of deep personal meaning in the mysterious decaying skyline. Her face was a vision of innocence and curiosity, questing for something unknown.

Over time she introduced him to a strange writer who came from Prague. Not personally, of course, since the man had died some fifteen years before, but she told him he must read the story about the young man who turned into a cockroach and the other story, "The Trial". Even though the writer never said it, she knew the stories were set in Prague. She had been to other cities and she knew that no other was like Prague.

She showed him the house where Dr. Faustus was supposed to have lived. The man made famous in Goethe's book who had made a pact with the devil and had to pay a horrible price in the end.

They talked a lot. Karin was quite bright and enjoyed political discussions and there was certainly a lot to talk about at that time with Hitlers interests quickly shifting from his success in Austria to the plight of the Sudeten Germans in Czechoslovakia and the subsequent diplomatic fiasco on behalf of the English and French. It wasn't until months later when Jakob finally became sure of where he stood. It was in October, after the Munich conference and the beak up of Czechoslovakia, when he joined a group of classmates in a spirited discussion in one of the coffeehouses near the German university in Zelezna, near the old town square. The night had passed quickly and soon it was well past dark as Jakob was making a point in an exchange with one of the women in the group. He was surprised to look up and see Karin there. She wasn't looking at him though. She was staring at the girl he was talking to, as though she were sizing up the other woman.

"Karin!" he said, and then proceeded to introduce her to the others in the group. "What are you up to?"

"Oh, I...we were just... you didn't come home and your m..." she cut herself off before saying that his mother wondered why he hadn't come home, not wanting to embarrass him in front of his friends.

"Oh, the time" Jakob said, also covering up that his mother had sent someone to check up on him. He then explained to his friends that he was staying with Karin and her family and that he hadn't realized how late it was and that he had missed dinner and must be going. He quickly rushed out with Karin, trying to avoid his friends usual insistence that he should stay "just a few minutes more".

Once outside in the night chill, he shuddered involuntarily and wrapped his coat tightly around himself, thinking at the same time that he would say something to Karin about how she embarrassed him, even though she hadn't really, but why take a chance on something like that happening again.

393

"You're cold" she said, interrupting before he had a chance to say anything and she surprised him by putting her arm around him. "My coat's warmer than yours. This'll warm you up faster."

Jakob didn't know what to say to this, so he didn't say anything as they walked. He reflexively reciprocated, putting his arm around her. They hadn't gotten more than a few steps when Karin, trying to be nonchalant, asked "who is she?"

Jakob couldn't help but smile.

"Who?" he asked coyly.

"The girl you were talking to."

"Oh, her. Just a friend of one of the guys."

"A friend of a friend" Karin repeated, giving Jakob a chance to amend his story if necessary.

"Yes. A friend of a friend." After a few steps and a short pause in the conversation, Jakob asked "Why?"

"Why?" Karin repeated.

"Why did you want to know who she was?"

"I was just curious."

Jakob stopped and put his other arm around Karin so that they stood face to face, he with his arms loosely around her waist. "My mother didn't send you out to look for me." he said accusingly.

She smiled and looked down. "Yes she did" Karin lied, unable to look him in the eye.

"You just wanted to know where I was. You're jealous."

"Jealous!?" she said with a laugh, pretending to want to break free of his embrace, but he just pulled her closer.

She looked up into his eyes. It was so cold that they could see their breath in the night air. Jakob kissed her lightly on the cheek and then harder on the lips. He pulled her even closer, pressing his cheek against hers and they just stood there for a moment in the flickering light of a street lamp in the mystical city of Prague.

It was snowing lightly the next morning. It was the Ides of March, 1939, one year and three days after German troops had marched into Austria in the name of Anschluss and now, early in the morning, they came to Prague.

Amalie had a sick feeling in the pit of her stomach. She was finally face to face with that which she had been fighting and running from for so long. It was as though she had tried to kill a rabid wolf in the forest and then found it in her home, ready to pounce. This was that moment. their eyes locked, hers and that which she feared. Feldgrau uniforms marching into Prague.

Hitler had trumped up some excuse involving the government of Slovakia and its disagreement with the Czech president as justification to invade the remaining territory of Czechoslovakia. He knew by their actions, or rather lack of action, in previous months that neither France, Britain nor Russia were interested in going to war over what was about to become the German protectorate of Bohemia and Moravia. Within hours of the arrival of German troops, members of the Czech nazi party were soon roaming the streets of Prague, painting the word "JUDE" or "JID" on Jewish businesses .

"What is it?" Hannah asked as she heard the noise in the street and saw Amalie looking out the window.

"It's the nazis. They've come." The streets were quickly filling with people, the Germans of the Sudetenland cheering the arrival of the German army. They were being liberated.

Jakob opened the window of his bedroom which faced the street and watched the smiling soldiers as they slogged up the street, the line occasionally interrupted by a truck or a tank.

He too looked at the faces of the marching soldiers as his mother had, but he wasn't looking for some mark of the devil, he was looking for familiar faces. Would he see some of his friends from his days in the Hitler Jungend? Would he recognize them after all these years, these boys become men? Would they recognize him? Would they call him friend?

That night at dinner Amalie was quiet and withdrawn.

It was Hannah's turn to make dinner. They all traded off, except for Jakob who conveniently had no idea how to cook and wasn't about to learn. Besides, cooking was woman's work, and even though it was a relatively unconventional household due to the circumstances, Jakob didn't feel he had to become unconventional too.

"Excellent..." Jakob said as he first tasted the braised short ribs.

Hannah smiled at Jakob for the compliment and reflexively looked at Amalie. Hannah's smile quickly faded when she saw Amalie sullenly looking down at her plate as she slowly took a bite. Jakob noticed and also turned. His first reaction was to ask what was wrong, but then he knew. He knew a lot of people who were upset by the arrival of the Germans, but she seemed to be taking it hardest.

"Things seem quiet in the city" Karin ventured, catching Amalie's attention.

"They've only just arrived," Amalie said quietly, "wait until they're settled in."

Jakob found himself wanting to defend them. Maybe because they were the victors, because they could just march in wherever they wanted to without even firing a shot. Maybe he wanted to identify with them because he was a German and not a Czech and all of his friends were German at the university.

"At least it's better than having the Russians invade" he said glibly as he continued eating.

Amalie was annoyed at his cavalier attitude and snapped at him. "It wasn't the Russians who murdered your father."

"Well... the Communists..." he began as he interrupted the constant motion of food from plate to mouth, suspending a loaded fork in mid-air. He had been told it was a gang of Communists who had killed his father and he had never questioned it.

"It was the SS Jakob." Amalie said firmly, "The Sturmabteilung and the SS, the men your father served with. They murdered him and said it was a gang on the street. They murdered him. They murdered hundreds of SA men that night. Anyone who disagreed with them."

There was a sudden chill in the room.

Silence.

Jakob didn't move, still holding his fork between plate and mouth, staring at his mother, meeting her stare. His time in Prague had allowed him to return to another world, a German world of his youth. His mother had tried to fit in so that she could work and so she hadn't mentioned being a Jew for a long time and she exclusively used the name Metzdorf. She had tried to be a German too. How could it be wrong for him to be a German? But she had been lying. She had known who they were all along and she didn't want to be one of them and Jakob finally knew it had been a lie.

He put his fork down after a moment. It was as though he had been pulled to the ground after floating above it for a time. He had stayed in Salzburg because he didn't think that he had to run. He wasn't a Jew. He only left by a fluke and now in Prague he shouldn't have anything to fear.

They killed his father.

His mother was terrified.

It was a moment of truth for this young man. His invincible shield of ignorance was cracked and he had to reconsider the simple answers of his life. He got up and left the table without anyone saying a word and put on his coat, going out into the twilight of the cold March evening. Amalie thought she should stop him since it could be dangerous on the streets at night with the German soldiers newly arrived and nervous, not knowing what to expect from the local residents, but she knew he wouldn't listen.

"Will he be safe?" Karin asked nervously, "Should I go bring him back?"

"No." Hannah retorted quickly, "You can't go out tonight."

"He'll be all right." Amalie said, taking Karin's hand and patting her arm gently, "He just needs to be alone." Amalie even managed a half-smile. She might have even believed it herself.

Why would a man wander the streets at night to consider his problems and find an answer? What could a Prague street lamp know and how could its light help him see? The streets seemed even more haunted than usual that night as Jakob walked along. He only saw a couple of other people as he walked along and they all seemed to be constantly looking over their shoulders. The city suddenly seemed dirty and tired. and afraid.

Jakob turned a corner in the Mala Strava district, almost at the entrance of the Charles bridge, when he saw a soldier standing watch. The soldier was on the same side of the street as Jakob and for a moment Jakob didn't know whether he should keep walking along, cross to the other side of the street or maybe he should just turn around and go back home. "No," he thought to himself, "show no fear." He kept walking.

The soldier walked back and forth slowly in front of his post so that he was alternately walking towards Jakob and away from him. Jakob didn't know that the young soldier was just as wary of him and was attempting to show that he wasn't afraid by turning his back on Jakob as he measured his deliberate pace; four steps east, four steps west.

Jakob felt a bit more at ease as he got closer and saw the soldiers face, a young face, perhaps even younger than Jakob. It seemed like a familiar face, someone who might have been related to any of his friends in Munich, a face with notably gentle eyes. He decided to take a chance and talk to the soldier. "Grüss Gott" he said with a nervous, forced smile.

The soldier was very relieved to hear a German greeting rather than some threatening, indiscernible Czech phrase.

"Grüss Gott" the soldier said with a slight nod.

"Wie geht's?" Jakob continued.

"Quiet" the soldier said as he stopped his pacing.

"Was there any trouble today?" Jakob asked, not sure if he dare be so forward.

"Only a little. Nothing worth mentioning. I don't think anyone was killed." When the soldier said this, he meant that none of the German soldiers had been killed. He didn't even consider any Czech deaths.

"That's good" Jakob affirmed.

"Yes. We weren't really sure what to expect. We..."

The soldier stopped in mid-sentence and came to attention with a Hitler salute as a young lieutenant came through the door beside him. The lieutenant stopped and sized up the situation.

"Soldier, you do know that there is to be no fraternization with the Czechs?"

"Ja wohl, Herr Leutnant!"

"Were you talking to this man?"

"Ja, Herr Leutnant."

"How do explain that?"

"He is German, sir."

"How do you know that? Do you know this man personally?"

"No sir."

"Then how do you know?"

"He speaks German, sir."

Jakob was becoming increasingly uncomfortable during this exchange and started to turn and walk away, but the Lieutenant, who was probably just Jakob's age, raised his hand without looking at Jakob, without averting his intense stare from the frightened soldier, signaling Jakob to stay put and so he did.

"Do you think that there are no Czechs who speak German?"

The soldier did not reply to the lieutenant's rhetorical question and the officer then slowly turned to Jakob.

"Do you have identity papers?"

"Papers? What kind of papers?" Jakob asked nervously, pleading ignorance to the lieutenants question.

"You'll have them soon enough. I'm sure it will be one of the first things the new government does. They'll get things in order." The lieutenant paused slightly as he turned back to the soldier.

"Order." he repeated, "Strength through order and discipline." he said as though repeating a sacred prayer before quickly walking away.

Both Jakob and the soldier sighed in relief as the officer disappeared into the darkness.

"I'm sorry if I got you in trouble" Jakob said.

"It's nothing. I should have seen him coming. He's strict. Everything by the book."

"I know what you mean. I've known some like that. Well, good night. I've got to be getting home."

"Good night" the young soldier said as Jakob also quickly disappeared into the darkness of the Prague night.

Jakob eventually found himself standing on the sidewalk across from Hannah Bauer's house staring at the windows with their soft amber glow caught in drawn lace curtains.

He could feel the cold closing in on him as he stood still and silent in the ocean of darkness, drowning in the night. The cold was trying to force him out of its domain as it swirled and eddied about him unforgivingly, but he would not give in to it. He would not be forced to seek shelter. He would not leave until he was ready. He would not give in to the numbing insistence of his fingers nor the strange feel of the flesh of his cheeks which no longer seemed to be a part of him. It felt as though even the moistness of his eyes were turning to ice. He finally buried his hands in his pockets and leaned against the cast iron bars of an old fence protecting the yard across the street from Hannah Bauer's house.

He saw his mother sitting in a chair reading. What if he never went back? How long would she sit there tonight? Would she still wait tomorrow? He could disappear. Back to Salzburg? Munich? How childish! How stupid! He couldn't go back. He had that Damn Jewish blood in him. She had poisoned him. Damn her. What was he now? Whatever it was, it was her fault.

He stamped his feet against the sidewalk. Now they betrayed him too. "It's not that cold..." he thought to himself. He had been out in colder weather than this. He could stay out all night there on the streets if he wanted to. If he wanted to, but why? Why should he punish himself? It was his feet and hands that were freezing, not hers.

Amalie didn't say anything as Jakob came in noisily with a loud rattling of the door and stamping of his boots. It was comical the way he then paid an inordinate amount of attention to carefully shaking out his coat and putting it on a hanger in the closet. He wanted to make sure Amalie knew she was being ignored. It wasn't until he almost stood behind her that he said "Good night".

"Did you want to talk?" she asked in a motherly tone.

"About what?"

"What?" she exclaimed and then quickly regained her composure. "About your father, of course. What else were we talking about before you ran away."

"I didn't run away" Jakob said angrily, uncharacteristically making no attempt to hide that anger. "I just needed to think."

Amalie looked up and saw the fire in his eyes and pretended to go back to reading her book.

"How long have you known about father?" Jakob continued accusingly.

"Know?" Amalie said, still looking at her book, "No one ever really knows. It's something I know without proof. I don't even need proof."

"Then you don't really have any reason to believe..."

"It all fits together too perfectly" Amalie interrupted as she got up from her chair and faced him, "I know how they work. I know things Jakob. I know how they do things. I know things that could destroy them!"

"What? What do you know?" Jakob said in a crescendo that matched his mother's agitated state, challenging her.

Amalie suddenly realized that she was getting carried away. Could she actually tell her son? Could he keep the secrets? Could she trust him?

"I can't tell you..." she finally said after they stood there face to face, "It wouldn't be safe for you to know."

"When did you first find out?" Jakob asked, pursuing the issue.

"Soon after I first heard about him."

"Who?"

"Adolf Hitler."

"Hitler? What? You must be joking."

"Just after the war..."

"Just after the war? That's twenty years ago!"

"Yes..." she said blankly as he attacked.

"You know something so important and you haven't done anything with it? I don't believe it."

"Done what?" she said loudly with a sweeping gesture and shrug, "It isn't as easy as you seem to think. It wouldn't work to just..."

"This is ridiculous!" Jakob said loudly, cutting her off in mid-sentence, "You're obviously lying, but why? What do you want from me? Do you want me to hate them just because you're a Jew?"

Amalie suddenly slapped him. She even surprised herself.

Jakob didn't move. He didn't reach for his burning cheek. He didn't raise a hand against his mother. He said nothing.

"Jakob, I'm sorry. I..." Amalie began, a tear running down her face as though she were the one who had been hit, but her son turned away and went to his room.

Karin, whose room was just off the head of the stairs, had been awakened when Jakob first came in and had heard most of the louder parts of their conversation. Once Jakob slammed the door to his bedroom, she put on her robe and went downstairs to see if Amalie was all right.

"Amalie?" she said cautiously as she saw Amalie sitting in one of the living room chairs with her head bowed, resting on her hand. Maybe Jakob had hit her, Karin thought, but it hadn't sounded like that when she had been eavesdropping. "Amalie?" she asked again, but this time Amalie was startled and looked up at her.

"Oh, Karin... What are you doing up?"

"I heard... something... and I came down to make sure you were all right."

Amalie brushed away the tears from her face. "All right?" she said with a caustic laugh, "No. I don't think I'm all right."

"Did Jakob... did he hit you?"

"No... no. I hit him"

"Why?" Karin asked incredulously. She had never known Amalie and Jakob to argue, not really argue, in all the months that they had been living in her mother's house. Karin was still young and had yet to learn about the nature of self-deception and terrible secrets. She didn't understand that such things breed anger that waits in the corners of one's life, waiting to rush out unexpectedly and destroy.

"I don't know" Amalie finally responded listlessly.

Karin sat down on the floor at Amalie's feet. Neither of them spoke for a while as Amalie stared off into space. Karin wanted to ask Amalie about the fight, but she didn't know how to bring it up and she was afraid that it might upset Amalie to know that she had been listening in on them.

"I heard you fighting." Karin began cautiously, waiting to see how Amalie would react, but she only continued staring off into space.

"I'm afraid I lied to him..." Amalie said, as if in a daze, "What do they call it? Oh, yes... a lie of omission. I forgot to tell him all these years that he was Jewish. I didn't want it for myself and now he has to fight with it."

"You forgot to tell him?" Karin repeated slowly, her confusion obvious as she looked up at Amalie who made eye contact for the first time.

"It's not easy being Jewish and it's not any easier trying not to be Jewish. It's something you can't run away from."

"Why would you want to run away? Why not just be who you are?" Karin said with the voice of simplicity and youthful idealism.

Amalie thought a moment before responding. "You're lucky Karin. You fit. You're like a bird who flies above it all. We're the foxes running from the hounds, but you'll never have to run. You have the luxury of being unafraid."

"But none of this is your fault. Why is Jakob mad at you?" Karin asked, trying to understand what the fight had been about.

"It's hard to explain" Amalie said wearily, "and I'm really too tired to try. Why don't we just go to bed and talk about this later?"

Karin didn't want to let it go, but she didn't say anything as Amalie got up and left for bed.

Jakob slipped out the next morning without talking to anyone and everyone was quiet at dinner that night. Hannah was the only one who didn't know what was going on. She had gone to bed early the night before and hadn't heard Amalie and Jakob's argument.

"I talked to Walter Hanisch today" Jakob announced from out of nowhere.

Amalie looked at him. "Walter?"

"Walter Hanisch. We attend classes together."

"Oh?"

"Yes. He has an apartment over by the law school."

"and...?" Amalie said, knowing what he was leading up to and wanting him to stop his toying.

"He said he was looking for someone to move in with him."

Karin's heart leapt when Jakob said it. She involuntarily shifted in her chair.

"I've been thinking about it for some time now" Jakob continued, "I think I should move out... be on my own."

"But, Jakob. You're welcome to stay here if you want. We..." Hanna started, but Amalie interrupted. "No. If he wants to leave then he should go."

Karin looked up at Amalie, her eyes pleading for Amalie not to push him out.

"Yes," Jakob said, agreeing with his mother, "I think it's time."

The conversation ended abruptly on that note. Everyone finished eating in silence and Jakob began gathering things that night for his move.

"Do you need help?" Karin asked as she stood in the doorway to his room.

"No."

"Do you have to go tonight?"

"I'm not. I'm just getting things together. I'll move out tomorrow."

"I heard you arguing last night" Karen said as she sat down on the edge of Jakob's bed, "I talked to your mother."

Jakob kept on packing as though Karin weren't there.

"She said she lied to you"

"About what?" Jakob asked non-chalantly.

"It was kind of hard to follow her. Something about foxes and hounds."

"Hounds?"

"That's what she said."

"That's really strange. I had a dream last night about a dog."

"What kind of dog?"

"When I was a boy I had a cocker spaniel named 'Honig'."

"...and you dreamed about Honig last night?"

"No. When I was about twelve, Honig was killed by another dog. I dreamed that other dog was trapped inside a room. The dog

403

was going crazy trying to get out and my father was there trying to keep big double doors closed so that the dog would be trapped, but suddenly the dog started biting him and dragged him into the room."

"How horrible!"

"I couldn't see, but I knew my father had been killed. He had had a pistol, but he dropped it by the door and I knew I had to do something, so I rushed up to the doors and grabbed the pistol and tried to shut the doors just as the mad dog appeared. I closed the door on his neck and tried to hold him as he kept pushing his way out. The dog was incredibly strong and started to push his shoulder through. I finally managed to get the gun up to the dog's head while holding the doors and I pulled the trigger."

"Did you kill it?" Karin asked anxiously.

"The gun misfired." Jakob replied with a wry smile, "I couldn't pull away enough to re-load it and the dog kept snarling and pushing. I turned the gun in my hand, holding it by the barrel, and started hitting the dog with the pistol butt. Blood started to spurt everywhere. It seemed the room was filled with blood and I just kept hitting the dog again and again as blood filled the beast's eyes."

"Did you kill the dog?" Karin asked again insistently.

"I don't know. That's when I woke up."

"It sounds terrible"

"It was. I woke up in a sweat."

"What do you think it means?"

"Means? It was just a dream. A crazy dream."

"You don't think it has some kind of meaning?"

"Like what? Watch out for mad dogs?"

"No!" Karin said, annoyed at his patronizing attitude

"I think it was just because of the argument with my mother. Moving out and everything. It all reminded me of my father and so on."

"Why do you have to go?"

"I'm twenty-two years old. Too old to still be living with my mother."

"But why not stay until you finish school?"

"I don't know... It's too easy, too convenient. It's just time for me to go."

"But what about us?"

This stopped Jakob. He looked up at Karin and then got up

from where he was packing things on the floor and sat on the bed beside her. A couple of tears began to run down her cheeks.

"This won't affect us." he said, trying to reassure her, "I love you Karin."

"I love you." she replied, accenting the word "you" to show how important he really was to her, "But now we won't see each other."

"Of course we will! I'm just moving over by the school. I'm not leaving Prague. We might not see each other all the time, but when we do it won't always be with mothers watching. It will be better this way."

Karin smiled a little at that and Jakob reached over and kissed her.

Just as Karin and Jakob were sharing a kiss, Amalie and Hannah were sharing a pot of coffee in the kitchen.

"Do you think he's really going?" Hannah asked.

"I'm sure he will." Amalie said as a matter of fact, "Once he gets something in his head..."

"Why is he leaving?"

"This whole thing about his father. He's confused and upset. He thinks he can run away from it."

"Amalie, why don't you just talk to him and..."

"I'm not so sure this isn't for the best. He should take some time. He needs to... I don't know quite how to put it. Jakob needs to put the pieces together. He needs to see who his father was and who he is and..."

"...and?"

"I don't know. I just think he's right about being on his own. At least he won't be that far away and maybe..."

"Maybe what?"

"Maybe if they come for me, they won't get him." Amalies facade finally broke. She couldn't look at her friend anymore. She hid her face in her hands. She felt like crying, but didn't.

"If who comes for you?"

"For God's sake Hannah!" Amalie said as she looked up, the tears now starting to come, "don't you know what's happening? As soon as they went into Austria they started arresting Jews."

"Amalie, calm down... Why would they arrest you?"

"Why did they arrest everyone in Vienna?"

405

"I don't know, but surely it wasn't just because they were Jewish. Those people must have done something else. They didn't arrest everyone who was Jewish."

"Hannah, they didn't have to arrest everyone. They have time now. They trapped everyone in Austria. Don't you realize that if Jakob hadn't come to visit father, he would still be trapped in Austria."

This gave Hannah a moments pause, but it all seemed too incredible. Arresting all of the Jews... then what? Why?

"Well I don't think you should worry about that." Hannah finally countered, "I don't think that will happen here. We should just take it as it comes."

They continued talking for a long time, even after Karin and Jakob had gone to bed. It turned out to be a long night, getting ready for Jakob to leave, but a much longer night was about to begin.

Klaus Grunewald leaned back in the old wooden office chair. He had bought the chair second hand. He had been told it was one of the chairs which Adolf had gotten from a party member in the early days of the party when Adolf was setting up a dingy little office in a room rented in the back of the Sterneckerbräu on Herrn strasse. Klaus had been there in the early days and he convinced himself that this was certainly one of the chairs from the first office of the Deutscher Arbeiter Partei.

Things had been going well and he was right in the thick of it. He had known Adolf Hitler since the early days and now he was well acquainted with Rheinhard Heydrich, someone whose fortunes and career were obviously on the rise and he had been told that there was a special mission coming up in the end of August for which he was considered well suited.

Klaus was pleased with the recent turn of events. He believed as the Fuhrer did that it was Germany's destiny to gather all Germanic peoples into one great Reich and Germany's Anschluss with Austria and the acquisition of the Sudetenland in Czechoslovakia was all a part of that vision. Klaus thought grandiosly to himself that he couldn't have done it any better himself.

One day Klaus was called to the Brownhouse for a meeting with Heydrich which, after Klaus had waited for over an hour outside of Heydrich's office, consisted of a rushed conversation as the two walked together when Heydrich had to leave for another appointment.

"This is a very important operation" Heydrich said without looking at Klaus.

"I understand" Klaus replied, although he certainly didn't understand what it was all about. The simple fact that Heydrich said it was important was enough.

Heydrich ignored Klaus' comment. In fact, he didn't even hear it. It was Klaus job to listen, not to comment. "There are a number of squads involved and you will be in one of these squads. Talk to Naujocks*. He'll give you the specifics. You will be with a group responsible for transporting some... 'canned goods'."

Klaus missed a step as Heydrich said this. Heydrich looked at Klaus for the first time and even smiled a crooked little smile.

"I'm afraid I don't..." Klaus began, but Heydrich cut him off in mid-
sentence, still smiling which made his eyes squint even more than usual.

"Talk to Naujocks. Good luck. I've got to go."

Klaus stopped in the middle of the hallway and watched Heydrich hurry away.

It was the end of August when everything came together and Klaus, along with the other members of the "canned goods" group, were given instructions. Adolf Hitler wanted to invade Poland, but wanted it to appear as though Germany had been provoked. The German propaganda machine had been insisting for months that the Poles were terrorizing and murdering the German population within their borders and finally the job was handed to Heydrich to give the world proof of the Pole's bloodthirsty aggression.

Heydrich personally inspected different sites for a Polish invasion along with members of his staff. It was finally decided that the area around Hohenlinden and Gleiwitz would be the scene of "operation Tannenberg". Gleiwitz was the site of a German radio station located close to the German Polish border and this would be the target of the invading Polish army. Heydrich had already cast the roles in his little production and August thirty-first was his opening night. The curtain was scheduled for eight o'clock. Heydrich's subordinates had recruited a number of Polish speaking Germans from the borderlands who were sympathetic to Hitler's policies and

---

* SS Sturmbannfuhrer Alfred Naujocks, a long time operative of Heydrich's

those were the men who would "invade" Germany.

No invasion would be complete, of course, without casualties to show to the international press as proof of Poland's aggression against the Fatherland. This was the mission of the "canned goods" group to which Klaus Grunewald was assigned. They were to transport a dozen prisoners from the nearby concentration camp of Sachsenhausen to the site of the Polish invasion and shoot them there, strategically placing the bodies for maximum propaganda effect. The members of the canned goods squad, except for the leader, weren't told the details of the mission until they had arrived at the radio station with their prisoners, but many of the guards, and many of the prisoners, suspected that it might come to murder.

Klaus was certain from the start that the prisoners would be shot. Why else would they be brought to this obscure place? Heydrich certainly wouldn't allow witnesses. Prisoners couldn't be left alive to tell that the whole thing had been a ruse.

It had been hot that day, unusually hot for that time of year. The countryside was thirsty and covered with tall golden-brown grasses. The radio station was a small wooden shack, weathered and neglected, just big enough for the transmitter, a small studio and a small office.

The sun disappeared just a little before eight o'clock and the operation began with the group of Polish-speaking Germans, who had been dressed in Polish army uniforms and given a brief training session in Polish army regulations, attacking the border post near Gliewitz and vandalizing the station before setting it on fire. They then noisily made their way through the area shouting to each other in Polish and singing Polish songs.

Meanwhile, another group dressed in civilian clothes, supposedly Polish saboteurs, rushed into the radio station and ordered the engineer and the broadcaster to move away from the controls The two employees were then told to stand against a wall in the office as one of the saboteurs held them at gun point and the others began to broadcast in Polish that the hour of freedom was at hand and Polish forces were moving into Germany. The message was then repeated in German, using a heavy Polish accent just as Heydrich's "German forces" back near the border were routing the "Polish invaders" and arresting them.

It was finally time for dispersal of the canned goods. Some of the Sachsenhausen prisoners had been dressed in civilian clothes while others were in Polish uniform. Klaus and an SS lieutenant were let off the truck near the radio station with three of the prisoners in civilian clothes and the truck then continued on towards the site of the border skirmish.

The Lieutenant had drawn his Walther pistol as he was getting out of the truck and now pointed it at the prisoners as he shouted "Line up!" in a shrill voice.

Eggenburger, Henkel and Breitenstein. The three men had names even if Klaus and the lieutenant didn't know it.

"Lieutenant... there is no need to shout" Klaus said in a calm voice.

Rudolf Eggenburger was a young man. Twenty-three years old. It wasn't so long before that everyone who met Rudi was impressed by his clear bright eyes. They were no longer bright. He had a scar just above his left eye, a reminder of what it meant to be a young Communist fighting against the Fascists in the streets of Berlin. He couldn't fight anymore. He had been beaten and starved and forced to work heavy labor to the point of collapse. He was alone. Everyone in the camps was alone. He hadn't seen his family for more than two years. He was ready to die.

"Gentlemen," Klaus continued in the same calm voice, "We have important work for you today. We must wait here for a little while for a truck..." Klaus paced casually as he talked, circling around the prisoners. The lieutenant moved behind the men.

Franz Henkel had been a writer. Not a writer of any great talent or reputation, just a writer who had chosen the wrong things to write about. He had been a prisoner of Hitlers Reich for six years. He had felt that someone had to speak out against the Fascists and that it had finally come to be his turn after so many others had been arrested or deported or had chosen to emigrate.

His turn lasted only a few months when he was turned in by a neighbor for distributing "anti-German propaganda". "Anti-German propaganda" was the term referring to any form of expression or communication that portrayed the new order in anything less than glowing terms. Franz had dared to suggest that the new laws in 1933 restricting the practice of certain professions to Aryans alone might damage German society in the long run and might be just the beginning of a process that would eventually lead all of Germany to ruin.

Four policemen, two in uniform and the other two in suits and overcoats, came to his apartment one evening. They feigned politeness, asking if they might come in and talk with him, but Franz knew they would come in no matter what he said. Franz' heart was in his throat as he sat in his living room with the two officers in civilian clothes while the uniformed officers began going through his apartment, looking through books and papers.

The two officers sitting with Franz seemed completely unaware of the other men rifling through Franz' apartment as they exchanged pleasantries. "How are you this evening, Herr Henkel?", "We understand you are a writer...", "Does someone employ you to write this kind of thing?", "Do you consider yourself a good German?", "Have you lived in Germany all of your life?", "Do you love your country?"

Franz was tongue-tied throughout the ordeal, giving monosyllabic responses and laughing nervously at inappropriate times as his eyes kept drifting to the uniformed policemen going through his things. After a few moments, moments that seemed like hours, one of the uniformed policemen came over to the men talking with Franz and gave a nod to one of the officers.

"Well, Herr Henkel, I'm afraid we must ask you to come with us."

Standing in the darkness, in the trampled grass near the radio station at Gliewitz, Franz couldn't remember any more how he had gotten off that couch in Berlin. He didn't remember the trip to the police station or even the trial. He had only thought back to the apartment because that was the last time he remembered feeling the same way as he felt standing in that field. His heart was in his throat again.

The Lieutenant didn't quite understand Klaus' actions, but Klaus was a superior officer and the young lieutenant wasn't about to question his orders. Klaus was hesitant. How strange this was for Klaus, Klaus who was full of bravado and bluster, Klaus who knew that unpleasant things must sometimes be done for the ultimate good that would come of it. Klaus lit up a cigarette and offered one to the lieutenant. He then shocked the lieutenant, and even himself, by offering cigarettes to the prisoners.

Eggenburger responded dully, putting the cigarette in his mouth and letting it hang there as Klaus offered a light. Henkel didn't smoke and nervously waved off Klaus' offer. Dov Breitenstein actually smiled as he took the cigarette and let Klaus light a new match. Dov watched Klaus' face as the match cast its orange glow on the Aryan.

"So this was the one" Dov thought. This was the animal who would finally kill him. Dov was amused at the courtesy of a final cigarette. A pretense of civility. Dov had been arrested in Berlin on Krystalnacht almost a year before. No reason, no warning, just a group of men going from place to place beating and killing Jews and throwing others in jail, eventually sending them to concentration camps, just because they were Jews. Now he stood in front of an SS officer who offered him a cigarette as though Dov had been found guilty of some crime and was about to be executed according to German law.

Klaus re-joined the young lieutenant standing behind the prisoners. He looked the lieutenant in the eyes as he drew his pistol, a signal that the lieutenant should do the same. The two of them pointed their guns at Breitenstein and Henkel and fired almost simultaneously. The two prisoners fell forward into the sweet smelling grass. Dov was killed instantly, Klaus' bullet had struck him in the heart, but Franz lay writhing on the ground, thrashing through the grass. In his last convulsion Franz turned over and looked at the lieutenant, he and the lieutenant making eye contact before Franz finally became still. Franz' convulsions had been hypnotic. Both the lieutenant and Klaus forgot for the instant that they watched that Eggenburger was still standing there.

Rudolf Eggenburger didn't move. He was already dead. He was just waiting for the bullet that would make it official. The young lieutenant obliged with a single shot to the neck, killing Rudolf instantly.

It took Klaus a moment to recover as he looked over the scene. This was not war, it was the creation of war at the expense of innocents, well if not innocents, at least non-combatants. When did blind obedience to orders to murder innocents become part of the Reich? What a stupid question! Hadn't it been exactly the same with Gunther?

None of Klaus' thoughts were passionate or emotional. He was merely sorting things out. It seemed contradictory, but if this was the way things must be now in order to create a better world, a better world for his sons and their sons, then so be it.

A few minutes later a car came from the direction of the radio station and the bodies were loaded into the car and taken to the station. Klaus watched as the corpses were arranged.

Rudolf was to play the role of the saboteur who had made the announcements, shot by the unbeatable border police and now slumped over the table in front of the microphone.

"Put his hand on the microphone" someone said and the soldier who was situating the body obliged.

Franz was to be the pistol wielding saboteur who held the radio station employees at bay and Dov was cast as the broadcast engineer.

Klaus looked everything over as he was about to leave. He didn't think it was going to work. The three men all had shaved heads. All of the prisoners heads had been shaved, it was standard in concentration camps. The other problem was blood. The men had been shot in the field and had discourteously left all there blood there rather than saving a bit for the station.

The next day, on September 1, Germany invaded Poland in response to Poland's unprovoked attack on the Gliewitz radio station.

No one was fooled. The international press, given a tour of the scene the next day, reported that it was most likely a staged event.

For months Britain and France had been telling Hitler through diplomatic channels that they would not allow him to occupy Poland, but Adolf was gambling that he could once more gain territory with a minimum of expense as he had done in Austria and Czechoslovakia. Chamberlain of Britain and Daladier of France had finally had enough. Two days later their governments declared war on Germany.

Chapter 15

Sitzkrieg. This was the German word coined to describe the period of inaction on the western front from the end of 1939 when the English and French declared war to the Spring of 1940. The English translation was "the phony war".

England spent months mobilizing home defense and an expeditionary force while the French reinforced their first line of defense, a line of heavily armored fortifications called the Maginot line which stretched across their border with Germany and ended at the borders of their allies, the low countries to the north. Certainly the Germans would not cross the borders of these non-combatants in violation of the conventions of modern warfare.

"Herr Stein! Ethan!" Edwin called out as he hurried across the square to intercept his colleague.

"Eddy, how are you?" Ethan responded, using the familiarity that Edwin always insisted upon.

"Well enough... and you? How are things on the West end?"

"Ein bischen schmutzig..." Ethan replied as he took a step back from Edwin and his piercing silver-blue eyes because of Edwin's annoying habit of standing too close to people when he talked to them. "I mean," Ethan continued, translating , "A bit... 'dingy', but comfortable enough." He smiled, proud of his choice of a colloquial word.

"...and no storm troopers."

Ethan's expression changed almost imperceptibly. It was rather unctuous of his friend, this Englishman, to talk about storm troopers after England had abandoned the Austrians and Czechs and then managed to hold itself back from sending any troops into Poland. What would Edwin know about storm troopers?

"Yes, there is that..." Ethan finally responded grudgingly.

"That was rather flippant" Edwin apologized, aware of Ethan's coolness.

"Aahhh." Ethan said with a wave of his hand as though brushing the thought away, "I'm just a bit... what do they say? Blue?"

"Yes, that's it." Edwin said as he sorted through Ethan's Austrian accent, "Feeling blue. It must be the weather. It's a bit different than Austria, isn't it?"

"In Austria we see the Sun once in a while." Ethan replied with a certain conceit of his own.

Edwin laughed. "I guess I'm just so used to this, but I must say I often find myself dreaming of a trip I took to southern Italy a few years back."

"Any trouble with the fascists?"

"The fascists? Goodness, no! It sounds funny when you say it, but of course one thinks of the nazis. It's hard to believe the nazis and the Italians are together. I don't think I ever even saw a soldier when I was there in '35."

Ethan looked at his friend with a sidelong glance as they walked along. Surely the fascists had been there, Edwin probably just didn't notice them. Selective vision. Ethan caught himself as he came up with this second unspoken rebuke and realized that he was upset with

414

Edwin. Actually he was upset with the English in general. They all seemed so remote from what was going on in Europe. Even after war had been declared once the Germans had invaded Poland it seemed that nothing changed. Ethan remembered the day war was declared because it seemed so apocryphal. England had sent out it's diplomatic corps in one last effort of posturing to try to dissuade Hitler from invading Poland, an effort which included the threat of a declaration of war if Germany continued on it's course of conquest. Three days later, on September 3 of 1939, the challenge was unanswered and the British deadline on their ultimatum to the Germans passed, giving Prime Minister Chamberlain no alternative but to declare war at 11:15 in the morning.

At 11:35, just twenty minutes after the declaration of war, the air raid sirens in London began to wail. Everyone rushed for cover and nervous anti-aircraft gun crews waited for their first taste of the salty smoke of German bombs. It turned out to be a false alarm, a false alarm that dragged on for months as the Germans took their time planning their next move while the French and English waited, neither principal of the Anglo-French alliance in any hurry to repeat the experiences of their last encounter with the Germans almost a quarter of a century before.

Ethan's opinion of the English was that while they had certainly been self-deluding, they were not entirely blind. They had taken measures such as establishing food and petrol rationing along with military conscription. They were like the child in the school yard who sees the school bully coming his way. They knew there would probably be a fight, but they stayed back against the wall, putting it off for as long as possible because they knew they would end up with a bloodied nose no matter who actually won the fight.

And then there were the internment tribunals. Certain "Enemy Foreign Nationals", as all emigrates from Germany, Austria and Italy were called as the war loomed close, had been arrested even before the war actually began in September. A decision was made within days of the declaration of war that all enemy foreign nationals would be called up before tribunals to determine whether they should be interned or subjected to restrictions such as not being allowed to travel more than five miles from their home and not being able to own a camera or an automobile. All of these people were classified as either "A"; people who were to be interned for the duration, "B";

people who were to be restricted, or "C"; people who were free to go about as they always had before the war began.

It was Edwin Coopersmith who had met Ethan upon his arrival in London's Victoria station in September of 1938. Edwin had been Ethan's legal representative in England for years for Ethan's publishing business. The two men hardly ever saw each other more than twice a year, but they corresponded regularly and Edwin was happy to put his political beliefs into action by sponsoring Ethan's emigration to Britain.

"Come walk with me" Ethan said, "I'm on my way to work."

"Jane suggested that you come for dinner." Edwin said as they continued across the square.

"What? How did she know we would run into each other?" Ethan asked.

"Oh, I've been looking for you. I told her that I had to find you today to go over some papers."

"Papers?"

"Yes," Edwin said, "a few more things on citizenship."

"I feel like I've already written a book on the subject."

"Well, you have to know the subject to become a subject" Edwin countered with a smile.

"If that's the caliber of your humor Eddy, then it's for the best that you became a lawyer."

"with a caliber like that, I could shoot myself in the foot..."

"Helfen mir Eddy. How does Jane put up with you?"

"She's a good wife. She laughs at me whether I'm funny or not."

"I laugh at you too, Eddy, but it's not because your jokes are funny."

"Speaking of not being funny..." Edwin said as he stopped walking.

"What now? What's wrong?"

"It's probably nothing, but there's talk."

"Talk?"

"About foreign nationals. There's a lot of concern."

"What do you mean 'concern'?"

"With the war and all. People are worried about... espionage."

"Spies? For God's sake Eddy! Most of us only managed to escape with our lives from Hitler."

"I know that. But there are people who think that any refugee

416

might be a spy."

"It's just war paranoia."

"Of course it is, but that won't stop them from setting up..." Edwin's words drifted off as he tried to avoid actually telling Ethan what might happen next.

"Setting up what Eddy?"

"Camps. There's talk of setting up camps for the foreign nationals, but you've got some good connections Ethan and if we can prove your father was a British citizen... with any luck you'll be a citizen before anything happens."

"I was just thinking how strange it is now."

"In what way?"

"Well, Eddy, neither of my daughters knew that my father was British."

"Your own daughters? Why?"

"That's what I mean by strange. I never really meant to hide it from them. It was my mother. She didn't like people to know she had been divorced and remarried. When Amalie and Eleonore were little girls I just told myself that they wouldn't understand and so I didn't see any reason to tell them. When they were older I just never thought of it. This is the first time it ever became important to me."

"It could be crucial" Edwin said. "If you are picked up, arrested or whatever it is the officials have in mind, we'll be in a position to argue that since the Anschluss, Austria no longer exists and as such you are a stateless person. Then we'll argue that by the Act of Anne and the foreign nationals legislation of 1914 that you should be considered a British citizen because your father was a British citizen."

Ethan stopped and turned to Edwin, catching Edwin off guard as he continued on a step and then came back to his friend. "...and you're sure this will work?" Ethan asked.

"Not absolutely. They've enacted special legislation for the duration. These tribunals probably won't be quite like a court of law. War hysteria might have some influence on the proceedings. This isn't something to be taken lightly."

Ethan sighed heavily. "I certainly don't take it lightly, Eddy."

"Of course not... I'm just saying that I can't make any guarantees one way or the other. All you can do now is keep yourself busy. Try not to worry about it too much."

"You've always given me good legal advice Eddy" Ethan said as he extended his hand as they were about to part company, "If you say this is the thing to do, then I'll do it." They shook hands warmly and Ethan started to walk away but then stopped again after a couple of steps. "Tell Jane I'd be glad to come for dinner."

"Tuesday?"

"Yes, that's fine."

Ethan continued on his way, leaving Edwin behind, and was soon standing in front of the book shop where he worked as a clerk. Even though he was already a few moments late, he stood looking in the window. He was looking at himself in the reflection. What happened? He had left Prague to avoid being put in jail or harassed by the nazis and now he was just in a different kind of jail. He had lost his family and friends, his home, and even his homeland. He was sixty-seven years old and yet he felt like a schoolboy being sent away to a distant boarding school, but of course he couldn't talk about such things. There wasn't anyone to talk to. Edwin was much younger, only about forty years old, and Ethan didn't feel that they were close enough to be comfortable sharing such things.

Ethan's English was only passable and his accent gave him away as "one of them" to anyone with whom he came into contact. A Jewish agency in London warned Jewish immigrants that they shouldn't write or speak German in public. He didn't know what to do with the package that Amalie had sent with him.

She had thought the priority was to keep it safe, but it's very safety was the thing that rendered it useless to her. In the course of time from the Austrian Anschluss to the beginning of the war, as Ethan found that it was virtually impossible to communicate with Amalie, he realized that she had outwitted herself. She was playing a game of cloak and dagger, but such a game requires communication. Ethan had months to contemplate the fact that as his daughter's position became more dangerous, the more she needed to resort to blackmail, the less she could actually do to make good on her threats.

Far from London, across the English channel and hundreds of miles across Europe, Jakob looked up from his book as a pretty dark-haired woman entered the library. She smiled at him as she passed by. He returned the smile and nodded, recognizing her from around the campus. He closed the book with a satisfying thud and turned to look at the clock behind him. The huge ancient clock of the law library, nestled within it's ornately carved walnut frame above him, it's face yellowed with age, seemed to erupt within the context of the overpowering silence of the library as the minute hand locked into it's new position, transporting the library at the law school in Prague to a new time.

Karin would be arriving soon to go out to lunch.

He got up and returned his book to the front desk and then gathered up his papers from the study table where he had been working and stuffed them into a battered old valise. Once that was done he allowed himself the luxury of staring out the window into the courtyard. The windows that lined the southwestern wall of the library were a study of symmetry, each dark oak dressed window frame easily big enough to hold a half dozen people, filled with three dozen panes of glass, each pane painted with the snow and frost of the dull gray February landscape.

Karin seemed like a part of that daydream as she danced into the library with her cheeks flushed with the cold and her face lit with a smile.

"Why are you so bright today?" Jakob asked, smirking in response to her contagious smile.

"It's a beautiful day."

"Beautiful? It's about to snow."

"No, not like that. It's mother."

"She's doing well?" he asked passively since she was obviously anxious to tell him something.

"She says that she's in love!"

"In love? With who?"

"We were talking last night and suddenly she asked me how I would feel if she got married again."

"What did you say?"

"I was shocked. I didn't know what to say. I never thought that she would even think of getting married again. It's been such a long time since..."

"Well?" Jakob said impatiently, "Who is he? Where did she meet him?"

"He's Czech!" Karin said gleefully, hardly able to keep her voice down in the library, as though it were something terribly scandalous that would shock Jakob.

"Czech?"

"Yes, she met him a couple of months ago at a dinner party. He

419

works for the city as a manager down at the streetcar office."

"Well, I guess it's steady employment..." Jakob said condescendingly.

"He's a nice man." Karin said, rushing to the defense of her mother's friend, "Wouldn't you be happy for your mother if she was getting married again?"

Jakob thought for a moment before answering, a hesitation which surprised Karin. "I don't know" he finally said, "I suppose It's different now than if I were a child."

"So you don't care anymore?"

"Of course I care... just not in the same way."

"You haven't even asked about her!"

"About mother? You would have told me if there was anything wrong."

"What if it was really bad and I was just avoiding it?"

There was a pause as Jakob studied Karin's face. He thought that surely she was just playing with him. She just wanted to make a point.

"What is it?" he asked.

"What?" she asked innocently as if she had forgotten what they were just talking about.

"Karin is something wrong or not? What kind of game is this?"

"You haven't talked to Amalie in nine months. Don't you think it's about time that you stopped the game that you're playing?"

"It's not a game. It's just the way things go. Children are supposed to grow up and leave their parents."

"Then you aren't angry with her?"

"No... not particularly."

"Then why don't you ever stop by to see her?"

"I've been busy between work and school."

"Every day for nine months?"

"Yes... Between work and friends and..."

"Then why do you always arrange it so that we meet away from the house?"

"Well, I..."

"She thinks you hate her."

"That's not true. I just..."

"If it's not true then do something about it!"

"All right, all right Karin. What do you want me to do?"

420

"Come for dinner."

Back in London a few days later, Ethan found himself before a magistrate in one of the hearings that Eddy had told him would probably not happen.

"I have a report here," began the judge as he peered down his nose through a pair of small spectacles precariously perched on the end of his rather large nose, "and this report states that you have been recently in correspondence with your daughter who lives in..."

"Prague." Ethan said, completing the sentence as the magistrate shuffled through the loose papers of the report.

"Ah yes... Prague. Here it is. But as I understand it she is also an Austrian national..." The magistrate looked down accusingly at Ethan from the bench as he slowly spilled out the word "national".

"Yes, well, she is also a refugee just as I am, but we couldn't afford to all three come to England..."

"Three?"

"Her son, my grandson, Jakob was also staying with us."

"And so you left them in Prague and came alone?"

"Amalie, my daughter thought that it would be best if I came alone."

"Why is that?"

Ethan hesitated for an instant but decided it was best to just tell the whole story. "Her late husband was not a Jew and he was a war hero in the last war and the nazis place stock in that sort of thing and so she thought that I would be in more danger than she or her son."

"Her husband a war hero?" the magistrate asked, arching an eyebrow as though he had finally gotten on to something.

This shook Ethan a bit as he realized his gaffe considering this particular audience and he rushed in to try to clarify what he meant. "The Austrian army" he said quickly with a defining and somewhat apologetic addendum of "against the Russians, not the English."

"Is he in the army now?"

"No... as I said, he was my daughters 'late' husband. He was killed in an automobile accident in 1932" Ethan said, deciding that too much truth would get him thrown in jail, "My daughter is a widow."

"Well, Herr Stein," the magistrate began as he tapped the papers on end to align and square the edges, returning them neatly to their proper folder, "you have some very generous testimonials here from friends and your employer and former business associates, but I'm afraid I'm a little concerned about your family connections. The records here aren't clear... May I ask your age Mr. Stein?"

"I am 67 years old, your honor."

"67? It says 64 here."

"No, your honor. I assure you I am 67. I have my passport right here."

"Would you please hand it to the bailiff, Mr. Stein?"

Ethan waited as the bailiff delivered the passport to the judge and the judge muttered to himself over the document for a moment before looking up. "There seems to be an error in the file here, but I will accept your passport as proof of age. Since you are over the age limit of 60 years old there is no need for incarceration, but for your own safety and in the best interest of his majesty's government I will have to assign you certain restrictions. See the clerk for a set of instructions and they will update your registration card to reflect your foreign national status. Good day."

Ethan was a stunned as he was quickly ushered out of the courtroom so that they could move on to the next case. Restriction was certainly better than incarceration, but it would make life more difficult than it already was. He could be grateful that his work at the book shop was within the five mile limit which the restrictions set on "enemy foreign nationals of questionable allegiance".

The night finally came back in Prague when Jakob was to return to Hannah Bauer's house for dinner. He found himself growing anxious as he showered and dressed, wondering what he would say. Perhaps he was feeling guilty at having been away for so long.

Nothing seemed different, but then it had only been a few months since he had left. The smell of the house in itself was delicious when he arrived. He had been eating very modestly since he moved out, buying soup from the cafe down the street, making cold sandwiches in the small apartment which he shared with Walter Hanisch and so the smell of roast beef and freshly baked bread was a narcotic which drew him in.

"Right on time" Karin said as she stood smiling at him in the doorway.

"I said I would be here" he responded with feigned gruffness,

"Come meet Petr."

"Is that your mother's new..."

"Yes. Petr Hrmeni." she said, interrupting him and taking his arm as she drew him into the living room. "Petr," she continued once they stood before the middle-aged, dark haired man who had taken residence in Hannah's favorite chair and was reading a newspaper, "This is Jakob. He's Amalie's son."

Petr only grunted as he rustled the paper and lowered it enough to make eye contact with Jakob, making some semblance of a nod of acknowledgment before abruptly raising the paper again.

"Jakob's in school to be a lawyer" Karin said with some pride as she pressed on.

"Too many lawyers" Petr countered from behind his newspaper.

"Your German is excellent sir" Jakob commented. He had expected that Petr would speak poor German if any at all and was surprised to hear the clear pronunciation that Sudeten Germans prided themselves on, a German that they considered superior to the softer Bavarian dialects or the sharp and harsh Berlin dialect.

Petr was finally prompted to put his paper down. "Oh... you expected me to speak Böhmakeln?" he said, turning to Karin to explain facetiously, "The Prager Deutsch so typical of ignorant Czechs like myself."

"No sir" Jakob said emphatically, "I was just impressed by... I certainly didn't mean to insult you."

"Of course not. That's the problem with German boys. Even when they don't mean to insult you, they do."

Hannah walked into the room, catching the tail end of the exchange. "Oh Petr, are you picking on our little Jakob?"

"Mother!" Karin objected.

"No Hannah" Jakob interjected, "Mr. Hrmeni is right. I'm sorry sir, I don't know what I expected, but that was rude of me."

"Yes, it was" Petr agreed and then turned to Hannah without missing a beat, "Is dinner ready?"

"A little longer. Jakob, how have you been?"

"Good... Good."

"Your mother isn't home yet. She's been working late. She'll be glad to see you."

Jakob only nodded and Hannah glanced at Karin. Karin had told her that Jakob had wanted to come, but obviously it wasn't so.

"Your studies have been keeping you busy?" Hannah continued.

"Yes, I've been keeping up."

"That explains why we haven't seen you for so long."

"Well, you know how things go... You get caught up and..."

Just then everyone turned as Amalie came in from work. "What a day" she said as she buried her coat in the closet, "I hope you didn't hold dinner for me. I..." She stopped in mid-sentence when she saw Jakob. Karin had planned it as a surprise.

"Everything's just about ready" Hannah said to Karin and Petr, trying to get them out of the room so that Amalie and Jakob could talk, "come to the table."

"I missed you" Amalie said once the others had left the room, "Are you still angry with me?"

"Angry? I wasn't angry."

"Come now Jakob."

"I just... It was just time to go."

"Jakob, I want to talk to you about it. I think we should get all of this out in the open."

"I thought we already did."

"All right, if you don't want to talk, let's just go and eat. At least you're here. Have you met Petr?" She asked as they started for the dining room.

"Yes."

"Something different, huh?"

"What kind of lawyer?" Petr asked as Jakob came into the dining room as though their earlier conversation had never been interrupted.

"A good one, I hope."

"A rich one?"

"I wouldn't mind being well off."

"but at whose expense?"

"Somebody has got to do it."

"Yes, but it would be nice if that somebody cared more about the people they are working for than the money they will get."

"I never said I cared more for the money. I only said that I wouldn't mind if I got some along the way."

"These terrible times. This is one of those times in history when a man should stand up for his ideals before anything else."

"I'd like to think that I always do that."

"That's because you're young. You've never really had to face such things. Soon you'll be in the crucible with fire and heat everywhere. Then you'll find what kind of man you are. You'll get married and have a family. You'll have to consider them when you stand for you principles. Will your children be able to eat if you stand up to something that you think is wrong and lose your job for it? That's when you'll find out who you are."

"I know who I am."

"You know who you think you are. You haven't lived enough to really know. You might find yourself having to do some things that you never dreamed of in order to survive."

"We're going to need a big garden this year." Hannah declared as she brought a small roast to the table. "I don't know when we'll see meat again. I had a terrible time finding this." She then turned to Karin "I'll need your help, dear. You know how terrible I am with vegetables."

"You don't like them?" Petr asked with surprise.

"No, dear. I can't grow them. I'm wonderful with flowers, but for some reason I can never seem to come up with a good batch of tomatoes or beans."

"I'm not much better" Amalie commiserated "but we'll have to do our best with the rationing."

"You know you'll have to hide it" Petr stated.

"Hide it?"

"Yes, of course. Otherwise you'll have to put it in a neighborhood cooperative."

"What?" Karin asked.

"Yes. That's the way they did it during the last war. If you raised a pig or grew some food you had to bring it in and then it was divided by need. If you got caught hiding something you could be arrested and they would say you were part of the black market."

"Then what's the point?" Jakob asked.

"Well, you get to keep a third of it... or you can try to hide it all. It's all a matter of preparation. If you watch the plants and pick them fast, as soon as the vegetables come ripe, and can them as soon as you get them and have a good hiding place ."

"What happens if someone turns you in?" Jakob asked.

"You would turn in your own mother?" Petr countered accusingly.

"No, of course not. I was just wondering what would happen. If someone else were to find out."

425

"You just have to be careful. After all, a lot of other people are doing the same thing."

"Honor among thieves."

"Survival."

"It all depends on the weather this year" Karin interjected, "Last year we could hardly grow anything because of all the rain in the Spring and then such a dry Summer."

"First too much and then not enough" Petr agreed between bites.

"Do you remember that farm we worked on during the first summer of the Great War?" Hannah asked Amalie.

"Oh, of course! How could I ever forget? We were so determined to be independent and not ask anything from our families."

"There was certainly enough food."

"Rutabagas. Rutabagas for breakfast, lunch and dinner. The farmer didn't want to waste his precious crops or meat on us, so as hired hands we always got the same. At least the bread was good. The old woman was a wonderful baker and we always had fresh bread."

"But the work! I never thought I'd live through it all."

Amalie laughed loudly. "You were so happy that winter when you found out you were pregnant because it meant you didn't have to go back."

"...and what about you? It was the same with you." Hannah countered.

The conversation went on like that throughout dinner. Jakob joined in here and there, talking mostly with Karin and Hannah as he and Petr didn't seem to have much in common and he was still reserved when it came to his mother. It was all very well to put on a show, but nothing had been resolved between them and soon he was once again retreating to his apartment.

"Can you do something for me?" Petr asked Hannah a few days later with a curious inflection which she hadn't heard from him before, a way of asking which immediately put Hannah on guard.

"Something like what?" she asked cautiously as she looked up from her lunch.

"It's nothing serious. It's just that I have something to do tonight and I told some friends that I would be out with you this evening."

"...but you won't?"

"Right. I need to go out with some friends."

"...and if anyone asks me, I should say that you were with me." Hannah said, completing the sentence with a lilt as though finishing the telling of a fairy tale to a child.

"You won't do it?"

"What are you up to? Is it another woman?" she asked coyly.

"Would I tell you if it were?"

"Is it important?"

"Yes."

"Is it dangerous?"

Petr hesitated a moment before answering. "Possibly."

"You'll be careful..."

"Of course. It's really nothing. Just a little business."

"I'll go see a movie tonight and tell Amalie that I'm meeting you there."

Petr never told Hannah what he was involved in, but because of the way he would sometimes rage at the Germans when the two of them were alone, she had a good idea.

Petr met Matej as he left work that night. They had known each other since boyhood and each trusted the other implicitly with their lives. They rode their bicycles away from the drab gray stone building which housed the offices of the Prague transit system and were soon coasting down a bumpy cobblestone road on the hill leading towards the Mala Strana district. Martial law had been declared in the middle of November in '39 and it was obvious that it would continue until the Germans were finally driven from Prague.

A cafe' a little darker than the others awaited them, one even more secluded than the rest, already lost in the early winter darkness by the time Petr and Matej walked in. Pavel's wave was discreet as Matej quickly spotted him.

"Pavel" Petr said almost under his breath as he nodded acknowledgment to his comrade while reaching for a chair.

Pavel only grunted in return. Once they were all seated at their table in the back corner of the cafe' Pavel spoke as he looked over the room to make sure no one was listening. "Jiri is ready."

"For God's sake Pavel!" Matej said in a whisper, "Stop looking so suspicious."

Pavel was startled by Matej's rebuke. "I'm sorry. I'm just a little nervous."

"We're all nervous," Petr interjected, " but you can't show it. Who knows who's watching?"

"You're just making me more nervous."

"Don't worry, it will all be over soon." Matej said as he got up, "Pay for your coffee and let's get going."

Petr and Matej went out to their bicycles and waited for Pavel. A few moments later the three of them were pedaling their way along the road on the banks of the Voltava. It was almost half-an-hour later when they rode up to the dilapidated garage on the outskirts of Prague where Jiri was waiting for them.

Jiri walked up as they tried to camouflage their bicycles in the twigs and thorns of a thick patch of undergrowth left bare by the winter. "No one saw you?" he asked.

"Of course not" Matej said. "We wouldn't have come if we thought we were being followed."

"The truck is ready, but we have to be quick about it so I can get it back before anyone notices it's gone."

"Incredible" Pavel said as they entered the garage, "I know you told me, but I don't think I really believed you until now."

"A fresh new military lorry" Petr said with an uncharacteristic smile as he slapped the fender of the truck.

"Let's go" Matej said as he climbed into the back of the truck.

Jiri was the driver. He was a mechanic who worked for a Sudeten German named Heinz Graef who had been put in charge of a group of Czech military trucks which had been confiscated by the Germans. Most of the trucks had been sent to Poland, but a few that had been in need of repairs were left behind and now they were at the disposal of the local officials. They were temporarily "lost". The paper work on them hadn't reached the proper clerk and so on and so forth, resulting in the trucks standing idle in a garage for a period of months. It was Pavel who came up with the idea to borrow one. Resistance to the German occupation in Prague was scattered and unorganized in February of 1940 and so this "mission" was just an idea that these four friends had decided upon. An anonymous act of subversion. A message to the Germans just to let them know that all was not well, that they should not expect the Czechs to just stand by as they were transformed into citizens of a new world empire known as Germania.

428

The four men had only traveled a couple of miles when Jiri pulled the truck up beside an old red brick building with the inscription "nadrazi" (police station) carved into the white stone which made the structural span above the doorway. They had planned the attack for some time. It was an early Tuesday evening when everything was quiet, when only two men would be on duty. Matej was the one who had first heard the rumor and took the time to confirm it. It was this innocent little police station on the outskirts of Prague where a number of confiscated small arms and machine guns had been stored under the watch of a group of collaborationist Czech police officers. Matej quickly jumped out of the back of the truck as it came to a stop and quietly worked his way to the back of the building where there was a tiny basement window painted over with black paint. there was the tiniest chip in this paint where one could barely see into the small store room. There was no light in the room. Matej pressed a flashlight up against the window pane. There was little effect, but as Matej squinted through the hole left by the fallen paint chip there was enough of a faint glow to make out some vague shapes in the storeroom that he was sure were stacked rifles. He got up and rushed back to the others.

"Are we ready?" Pavel asked as Matej reached into the back of the truck for his hat and scarf and shotgun. Pavel had a revolver with only five bullets while Petr had a thick new sledge hammer handle, Matej had a single shot shotgun and Jiri reached behind the seat as he got out of the cab and drew out a big heavy spanner. Their only real weapon was surprise. No one replied out loud to Pavel's question. There were only concerned looks and nods as they each covered their faces with winter scarves and put on hats. They then all started for the door of the police station.

Pavel stopped at the door with the others behind him as he took a quick peak in the station to see who was where. Two police officers were talking. According to what Pavel and his friends knew, these should have been the only people in the station.

They were sitting at their desks, one of them leaning back in his chair with a cup of coffee in his hand, gesturing as he talked, while the other rested his chin on his hand with his elbow on the desk. Pavel opened the door slowly, quietly, just as the officer who was talking made a wide excited gesture relating to the story he was telling, almost spilling his coffee in the process. Both policemen began to laugh as the one tried valiantly to catch himself before he dropped the cup. They both stopped abruptly when they noticed Pavel standing in front of them with his pistol drawn. No one said anything. Pavel was half expecting a dozen policemen to storm in from the back room. He just stood there alone, facing the surprised policeman for what seemed like half-an-hour, but it was only an instant before Petr came in behind him followed by Matej and Jiri.

Petr knew instinctively what to do. He knew he had to terrorize their captives. He brought the sledge hammer handle down with all his strength against the desk closest to him. It sounded like the explosion of a cannon as the hammer handle ruptured the veneer top of the cheap desk. "Down!" he screamed at the policemen. They both fell immediately to the floor and just as fast as that, Petr was on top of them with the rope he had stuffed into his pocket, frantically untangling the rope and almost simultaneously tying both men up, hands together, hog-tying them hands to feet and then tying the two of them together. Petr was in such a frenzy that he didn't even hear the cries of the men as he drew the ropes so tight that he cut off circulation in their hands as he worked. Jiri was suddenly getting in Petr's way as the mechanic joined the melee', rifling through the policemen's pockets looking for the keys that would unlock the storeroom. Matej and Pavel stood watch nervously, Matej facing the back of the station while Pavel watched the front door. Jiri soon had the keys and rushed over to Matej, tapping him on the arm, breaking Matej's trance-like stare at the back door, signaling that it was time to go down to the storeroom. They ran through the back past the four empty jail cells, empty since a dozen prisoners accused of opposing the Third Reich had all just been transferred that morning to Petschek Palais, the Gestapo headquarters in Prague, empty just as Matej had been told they would be by his secret contact. The stairway to the storeroom was dark and narrow, but just as they started down, Jiri tapped his head against a light bulb hanging down in the entryway and groped around for the pull string, igniting the dull glow of an ancient light bulb. The light continued to swing back and forth once Jiri let go, casting strange shadows as he and Matej cautiously wound their way down the musty hallway. There were six doorways in the basement, three on each side of the hallway in perfect symmetry, plank doors made gray by years of dirt.

"It's at the end here" Matej said in a whisper to Jiri as Jiri began

430

to fumble with the ring of keys he had taken from the policeman. Matej reflexively tried the door to see if it was unlocked and the door opened with a creak. He smiled at Jiri as if to say "this is almost too easy", but then his expression instantly changed as the dim light from the hallway spilled into the room revealing another policeman laying on a cot who was starting to wake up from a nap, shading his eyes from the light to see who was in the doorway. Jiri suddenly dropped the keys with a a great jangling noise and lurched for the policeman. The heavy wrench Jiri had brought appeared from nowhere as he brought it down against the top of the policeman's head. Matej was still standing at the door, stunned. The policeman was unconscious and Jiri wasted no time getting back to the keys. "I guess it's the other door" was all he said as he moved across the hall, beginning to go through keys. Matej stared at the motionless policeman on the cot, blood now flowing freely from the gash in his head. It was the moment for Matej when adventure and excitement was transformed into brutal reality. He had known Jiri for years and he never would have thought him capable of such violence. The man might be dying. Why hadn't Jiri just hit him with his fist? They could have just tied this one up like the others...

"Come on. I've got it" Jiri called from the storeroom. Matej pulled himself away. He stood silently in the storeroom with his arms extended as Jiri stacked rifles in his arms and then started back up the stairs.

"What's taking so long?" Petr asked as he met Matej in the hallway. Matej just kept going without answering. Petr's eyes were drawn to the other room as he went down the hall to the storeroom. He was shocked by the sight, but it didn't show in his voice. "Is he dead?"

"I don't think so. He surprised us. I hit him with the wrench. Here, take these." Jiri never broke pace as he handed Petr a load of rifles.

Matej returned with Pavel just as Petr was leaving the room.

"Who's watching the door?" Jiri asked

"This isn't good" Pavel said as he waved his pistol in the direction of the bludgeoned man in the other room, "Let's just take what we can get and get out as fast as possible. One trip for rifles, one for ammunition and then we leave."

The men hurried out with their cargo and then back again for

431

the last trip. Just before leaving, Petr stopped by the two policemen tied up on the floor in the office. "You are Czech and so we won't kill you... this time. You smell like traitors and we will soon kill traitors just as we kill Germans. Remember that."

The four men were soon back at the garage where they prepared the guns by covering each one with grease and then wrapping them in bundles of ten in canvas and then putting the six bundles into a hole that Jiri had dug in the corner of the dirt-floor garage earlier. The boxes of ammunition were also wrapped and buried. It was almost nine o'clock when they finished and Jiri gave everyone a quick handshake before taking off in the truck to return it before anyone would notice it was missing. Petr, Matej and Pavel went out to the brush beside the garage and dug out their bicycles. Pavel knew Matej was upset about the policeman in the basement and stood beside him, giving him a pat on the soldier. "These things happen" he said, "It couldn't be helped."

"I know" Matej replied, "It's just that..."

"What?"

"I didn't want to say it in front of Jiri, but that police officer..."

"You knew him?"

"He was my informant. He was the one who told me about the guns in the first place and now for all we know he might be dead."

"Jesus Christ!" Petr said as he walked over, having overheard what Matej said.

"It couldn't be helped" Pavel repeated.

"Maybe he'll be all right" Petr added.

"I don't know." Matej said, "You didn't see how hard Jiri hit him."

"Come on. Let's get out of here." Pavel insisted, "There is nothing we can do about it. Just go home and for God's sake don't say anything to anyone. Anyone! Not even your family. Even if the Policeman lives, the Germans would hang us for this."

"He's right Matej" Petr agreed, "You have to put it out of your mind. We all knew there would be risks."

"...and remember. None of us is to contact any of the others for at least one month." Pavel cautioned. He then gave Matej another pat on the shoulder and shook Petr's hand firmly before the three men parted company.

Matej and Petr rode along together for a short ways, but Matej

432

suddenly turned down a dark road leading off to the right and Petr found himself riding alone.

England's war with Germany entered a new phase on May tenth of 1940. This was the date the Germans launched their attack in the west. The English and French had both been content to wait for that attack during the time of the Sitzkrieg as both started their slowly turning wheels in motion to mobilize their respective military forces. This, however, was also the time when a new prime minister was appointed in England. It was only three days after the German attack when Winston Churchill's voice came crackling over English radios promising that he would do all he could for the nation even though all he had to give was "blood, toil, tears and sweat". The next day saw the surrender of the Netherlands and two weeks later the British expeditionary force in France found itself caught in a pincer movement by German forces in the area of a small seaport town called Dunquerque. The English and French forces there managed to hold out for a week before being overrun, buying enough time for ships of the English navy and an armada of civilian craft to make a daring evacuation of thousands and thousands of soldiers. It was only two days after Dunkirk when Ethan Stein answered an unexpected knock on his apartment door in London.

"Herr Stein?" the man asked with a decidedly east-side of London accent as he referred to a piece of paper he held in his hand. Ethan sized the man up before answering. Short and heavy-set, the man had a rather unkempt mustache and his small eyes seemed to float atop broad pudgy pouches which mimicked his jowly cheeks. His overcoat was threadbare at the cuffs and the finish of his out-of-date bowler was dull and gray with age. He was obviously a policeman.

"Yes, I am Stein. Ethan Stein."

"I have a warrant here for you... on authority of the crown."

Ethan had known that someone would be around sooner or later. It was the sixth of June, Amalie's birthday. How old would she be now? Forty-five? How could his little girl be 45? But back to the matter at hand, the British parliament had amended its policy on "Enemy Foreign Nationals" on the last day of May in the face of the German assault as the reality of the war struck closer to home. The government had extended the criteria for internment of enemy foreign nationals to include people over sixty years of age. Before May 31, the policy was that foreign nationals from sixteen to sixty years of age would be interned while those over sixty were either A's or B's, but then someone pointed out that even Winston Churchill was sixty-five years old and certainly he would pose a threat to the Germans, so why wouldn't men of his age in the U.K. be a potential danger to his majesty's government?

"Must I go right now?" Ethan asked.

"No, I'm just here to serve you notice. Gather up some things for a few days stay and we'll be around to pick you up tomorrow morning."

The policeman seemed pleasant enough. He had been polite and unobtrusive, as though he had only stopped by to tell Ethan that the neighbors had complained about his dog barking or some other inconsequential transgression against the peace and quiet of the community. A few days? What should he pack for a few days. Would it really only be a few days? He had heard of many people who had been sent away and had not been heard from for months. These couldn't possibly be like the camps in Germany, could they? No, of course not! He should call Edwin and let him know. He should pack food and some money, a couple of books to read... What else? Just clothes. Now he would have no chance of making contact with Amalie or Eleonore, or rather they would have no chance of making contact with him. He had decided a long time before that it would be dangerous to attempt to correspond with them, but he somehow hoped, however unreasonable it may have been, that one of his daughters might somehow manage to get word to him.

"What did he say?" Edwin asked when Ethan called from the pub across the street from his apartment.

"The policeman?"

"Of course! What did he say? is there to be another hearing?"

"He didn't say anything about a hearing, just that I was to go down for questioning and I should bring a bag for a couple of days stay."

"Bring a bag? That doesn't sound good... I hear they're even interning people in 'C' class."

"For how long?" Ethan asked, a squeak in his voice betraying his anxiety.

"I don't know for sure."

"What have you heard?"

434

"I..."

"Come now Edwin. Just say it. What can I expect?"

There was a long pause before Edwin finally answered. "Weeks."

"Weeks?"

"I've heard it's been months for some" Edwin continued reluctantly, forcing himself to tell Ethan the truth.

"Well then..." Ethan said quietly, "I'd better reconsider what I've packed. I'll need the big case. I..."

"Ethan" Edwin interrupted as his friend rambled on, "I'll do everything I can. I'll see if there isn't some way to get you out. Keep your chin up."

"Yes, yes. Chin up" Ethan said sadly, speaking as though in a fog. He hated that expression. It was the sort of thing he thought one would only say to a child. "Give my love to Janie" he said as he hung up the telephone before Edwin had a chance to say anything else.

The next day crept forward in a dense gray fog and incessant rain. Ethan made sure to catch Mrs. Newcombe, his landlady, before she went out to do her morning marketing and tell her that he would be away for a few days. She clicked her tongue and said what a shame it was that "them at the home office don't know what a fine gentleman he was" and how it was all nonsense. Ethan thanked her for her concern and returned to his apartment to wait.

It was hours before a black Mariah pulled up in front of the apartment building and a bobby went up to escort Ethan out. The young police officer shook his head as Ethan dragged a huge suitcase out of the apartment. He offered to take it as Ethan got to the stairs.

"What have you got in here?" he asked as he hoisted the large case to knee level and started walking it down the stairs.

"I thought I might be away for a while." Ethan offered meekly.

"Oh, it shouldn't be more than a few days, a week..."

It turned out that "the questioning" was to fill our forms for internment. There was a young German at the station, also a Jew, sitting beside Ethan who laughed at the huge suitcase Ethan had brought, but when they were both put in a cell together and it was obvious that they were going to one of the camps the young man began to complain that if he had known, he would have packed better.

The transport to the camp was a bleak affair with the unloading

435

of the lorry attended to by a sneering little sergeant with plenty of hatred left over from the previous war who pushed them all along.

Spaghetti was the staple diet, spaghetti with a watery tomato sauce. The barracks were clean but worn, as were the inmates. One of the most annoying problems among the camp population was that the British authorities threw everyone in together. In one camp you would have a group of pro-Germans, a group of ultra-pro-German nazis and a larger group of anti-fascists, especially German Jews, whose reason for emigrating to England in the first place was to escape from Germany and the nazis.

While the anti-fascists kept themselves busy with an eclectic offering of lectures and recitals by anyone who had the desire to speak on their particular field of interest, the nazis would be off in some corner singing their little nazi songs or regurgitating Hitler's party line as though it were a scholarly pursuit and eventually a fight would break out. It happened all the time since the nazis considered it a pleasant diversion from the boredom. They would try to force some of the Jews to raise their hands in a Hitler salute as they sang the Horst Wessel lied and it would start all over again.

By the middle of June the Germans had trampled the low countries without a second thought to their neutrality in order to outflank the French and English forces. After the demoralizing defeat of the B.E.F. at Dunkirk the Germans swung south against the French forces which had been permeated with defeatism since the time of the Sitzkrieg and on June 14 the soldiers of the Wehrmacht stamped their hob-nailed boots against the cobblestones of the Champs Elysees. France quit the war on June 22.

Ethan was sitting on his bunk in the barracks of the internment camp when Aaron, the young German Jew Ethan had met in the police station, sat beside him.

"I can't take this much longer." he said. It had been three weeks since they had been sent to the camp and there was no release in sight. They were allowed to send and receive mail once a week and none of Edwin Coopersmith's correspondence gave Ethan much hope.

"I've got to get out of here." Aaron continued, "I'm a farmer. I've always been outside. This is driving me crazy."

"Don't think about it." Ethan said as he patted Aaron on the shoulder, "You just have to take it as it comes. The sergeant will probably shoot you if you try to escape."

"I've heard there's a way out."

"Out?" Ethan asked with surprise, "How?"

"They say they're sending foreign nationals to Canada and if you volunteer to go you won't be in a camp there."

"Canada?"

"Yes. Why not?"

"Canada?" Ethan repeated with disbelief.

"I'm a farmer. There's land."

"But it's so cold. It's Up by the North Pole, isn't it?"

"It's not that far. Besides, it's better than sitting here until the war ends. What if the Germans invade England ? I'd rather be across the Atlantic."

"Invade? England hasn't been successfully invaded since 1066."

"If anyone could do it, the Germans can."

"You had better not say that too loudly in front of the guards."

"It's not like I want it to happen! There just doesn't seem to be any way to stop them."

Aaron Mendlebaum was not alone in his concern. All across England, even at the highest levels of government, especially at the highest levels of government, there were discussions of a possible German invasion by sea. There were the same kinds of discussions in Germany too, as plans and proposals were drawn up.

Hundreds of detainees, volunteers like Aaron Mendlebaum, were gathered up a couple of weeks later from various camps across England, over two thousand in all, in preparation for boarding the Arandora Star, A British ship bound for Canada. People shouted and cursed the detainees as they were marched through the streets of small towns and villages, thinking that the men were German prisoners of war and the military escorts did nothing to relieve the situation and if any of the detainees tried to explain, speaking from the ranks as they marched, a guard would threaten to beat them if they didn't keep quiet. The conditions aboard the ship were austere, but at least the ship's crew seemed much more lenient than the guards who had brought them to the pier. The boarding took place without incident under misty gray skies and then there was nothing to do but settle in and wait for the ship to disembark.

It was crowded and Aaron considered himself lucky to be sharing a cabin with four other men rather than sleeping on the floor down in the ships hold, even though the cabin was only meant to accommodate two people. The five of them drew straws to see who would sleep on the floor while the others would sleep two to a bunk. Aaron drew the short straw, but he didn't mind. At least he was on his way to freedom.

The crew readied to cast off as twilight neared and the ship was ordered to take position for the small convoy which would zig-zag its way across the Atlantic. The departure times and routes of ship convoys were kept secret as the English tried to keep German U-boats off guard. The Arandora Star's convoy was to sail north along the English coast and then cut across the Irish sea, up past the Hebrides islands and then on towards Iceland and southwest from Iceland to New Foundland.

The Irish sea was relatively calm that night, as calm as the Irish sea ever gets, and the moon shone brightly though long silver wisps of clouds as the sky began to clear.

Aaron went up on deck for awhile and stared up at the sky as he leaned against the railing, taking in the stars and dark blackish-blue sky as two sailors walked past. One of the sailors looked up to see if Aaron was looking at anything in particular and off-handedly commented to the other sailor; "Bad news for us...".

Aaron knew instinctively what he meant. The clearing sky made beautiful silver silhouettes of the other ships which must have made them easy to spot for miles away across the calm sea, a perfect target for German submarines. He imagined what might happen if they were hit. No one had bothered to tell them about lifeboats, or even life jackets, and the ship was so crowded... Even if they had time to evacuate everyone there probably wasn't enough room in lifeboats. His thought about the sinking of the Titanic twenty-eight years before. They hadn't had enough lifeboats, but they were sure that the Titanic was unsinkable as she ventured forth on her maiden voyage. What reason did they have for the Arandora Star? He supposed that he and his shipmates just weren't important enough to warrant proper measures.

And then he saw it.

"God Damn it!" he thought, "It can't be. It can't really be... a periscope."

"U-boat!" he shrieked, "U-boat. Over there."

Suddenly he was joined by a couple of sailors who didn't trust his call, but wanted to see just in case it might be true.

"Here now" one of the sailors said as he rushed up to the deck, "Just calm down mate, Not bloody likely a U-boat this close to port... What did you see? Where?"

"Over there" Aaron insisted as he thrust out his shaking hand, pointing emphatically to a spot right in the middle of the convoy.

"Right there?" the sailor asked with a skeptical laugh, "Don't be daft. They wouldn't be in the middle of the convoy, the cruisers would 'ave spotted 'em"

"I don't see anything" said one of the other sailors.

"But I saw it" Aaron insisted as he let his arm fall to the rail and strained to catch a glimpse of the tiny periscope mast that he was sure he saw trailing across the shallow waves.

"No, no..." the first sailor said as he kept searching the water, "You're just nervous. Imagining things. Don't worry lad, it happens to the best of us. Just don't get everyone up in arms until you're absolutely..." He stopped in mid-sentence as a German torpedo hit home and one of the other convoy ships exploded amid a great shower of water, smoke and fire . "Jee-zuss Chroist!" he said after gulping a short breath. "Alarm! Alarm! U-boat!" The periscope resurfaced just where Aaron had pointed and suddenly the ship erupted with a whelping siren and other ships soon followed suit and turned sharply off course to try to evade the submarine as a cruiser behind them tried to close in, but it was already too late as one of the sailors spotted the bubbling trail of a torpedo cutting through the silver waves. "Torpedo amidships!" came the shout as the sailors scrambled for their battle stations and panic began to set in below deck among prisoners.

Aaron was transfixed as he watched the torpedo heading towards the ship knowing that there was nothing to be done. He wondered if he should jump into the water, but then told himself how stupid that was. "A lifeboat" he thought, "get to the lifeboat", but then he suddenly realized that the torpedo was going to miss the ship and an electric shock ran through his body and he started jumping up and down while holding tightly to the rail, "It missed" he shouted, "the bloody bastards missed us!", but then in almost the same instant out of the corner of his eye he caught sight of another bubbling line sliding through the moonlit waters heading straight for him. This time he didn't wait to see if it would hit or not, but instead ran forward to a lifeboat grabbing onto one of the lowering ropes just as the torpedo impacted on the ship's hull about a third forward of the fantail ripping through the ship and quickly flooding the engine room and lower decks.

Aaron had no way of knowing that the submarine had long since submerged and made a run out of the convoy so that it might slip in again later and take out another ship at its leisure and these tactics were none of his concern. His only thought was getting on that lifeboat. Everything was a blur as he heard the Captain's nasal and inappropriately calm voice giving the order to abandon ship. He had always thought that it took some time for a ship of such size to go down, but the ship started tilting almost immediately as men came pouring out from below decks and racing to the lifeboats. The sailors kept discipline and manned the ropes, getting the boats away quickly, but hundreds of the prisoners were trapped below as water rushed in and panic took hold. The convoy kept moving, leaving the sinking ship behind lest they all become sitting targets for the German U-boat's wolf pack. One of the cruisers stayed back and radioed for help, dropping depth charges and keeping an eye so that the U-boat didn't come back to harass the survivors. That, of course, was the very reason that some U-boat captains did attack survivors; so that a convoy might be weakened while escorts watched over survivors of attacks.

Aaron couldn't look anyone in the eye as he sat huddled in the life boat waiting to be rescued because once the panic was over he felt he had acted like a coward. He didn't know what he should have done, but he knew that his only thought was getting into that lifeboat regardless of what happened to anyone else. He felt that everyone, especially the sailors, were looking at him contemptuously. It wasn't true, though. The sailors hadn't expected anything of him, in fact they thought he had done well to point out the U-boat in the first place and then manage to get into the lifeboat.

Word of the sinking of the Arandora Star and the deaths of hundreds of German and Italian detainees raced across England and brought the whole question of foreign nationals into the spotlight, causing people to ask who the detainees were and why they were being imprisoned. It soon became obvious that many of the victims on the Arandora Star and people in the camps had never been a threat to Britain's national security and groups of citizens began to demand a re-evaluation of the foreign national's classification process.

Back in the detention camp, Ethan heard of the disaster the day after it happened through rumors started by the guards, but he had no way of knowing whether Aaron had survived. Ethan felt very suddenly alone, a feeling that appeared like a gentle rain and then, as he dwelled on it, became a torrent and then a flood overcoming everything in its path. His loneliness was a flood which could cover the world. Why did Aaron have to go? He was his last... running from Austria, running from Prague, being sent to the camp...his last contact with the living world. His pain had come and gone before. It had its limits of time and degree, but this seemed to be the last straw. Ethan had tried to make the best of things in the camp, but Aaron was his only friend and his leaving was bad enough, now he had to die.

Just then two of the nazis walked by Ethan talking loudly and laughing as they always seemed to do, as though they owned the world, and he suddenly felt an overwhelming rage.

"You!" he said, "You did this."

"What are you talking about, old man?" one of the men asked with a smirk.

"He wouldn't have left Germany if it weren't for your kind. You cheap thugs. Vile filthy trash... Animals!"

"Watch your mouth old Jew-pig."

"Old Jew-pig?" Ethan shouted back, finally pushed to the edge, a sixty-seven-year-old man against two strong nazis still in their twenties, but he had the advantage of surprise as he struck, throwing himself at the young man and slamming them both against the wall. One of the nazis, rather than throwing a punch, reached an open hand to push Ethan away, but Ethan was in the perfect position to grab the hand with both of his and he twisted as the three of them fell to the floor landing on the other nazi. The nazi whose hand Ethan was twisting screamed out in pain and strangely, this somehow gave Ethan strength... knowing that they could be hurt increased his rage. He wanted them, these two men as the faces of all Damned Germany, to feel the pain he had felt and put all his strength into twisting the hand until he heard a distinctive "pop" in the young man's wrist. Ethan released the hand and when he did the nazi pulled back with his wounded arm and the other nazi, the one who had been on the bottom as they all wrestled about, tried to scramble out from under them to get at Ethan, but once again Ethan was in an excellent

441

position as he was on top of the other nazi so that his arms were pinned under Ethan and the first nazi so that all Ethan had to do was bring his knee up hard against the second man's face and once again there was an unusual noise as the cartilage in the other nazi's nose cracked. By this time scores of other internees came to see what was happening and joined in the fight on both sides.

The shrieks of the guard's shrill whistles then filled the hall as guards rushed in with batons drawn high and ready to strike down anyone who didn't immediately disperse.

"All right..." The sergeant shouted once things quieted down, "All right you lot. Who is it this time?"

The hall was silent except for the sound of the sergeant's boots against the worn wood floor as he strolled along the path which had been cleared by the guards in the middle of the crowd . He stopped in front of the young nazi who had blood pouring freely from his broken nose.

"...and what happened to you?"

"Nichts" the young man responded curtly, intent on covering up the fact that he had been bested not just by a Jew, but an old Jew at that.

"Nothing?" the sergeant repeated loudly as he reached out and wiped his finger on the nazi's upper lip, holding the bloodied finger up to the man's eye, "Then what the Hell is this?"

"I fell against one of the beds."

The sergeant glared at the man, realizing that he would get nothing out of him and then turned to the rest of the crowd. "Right then, I've had enough of this brawling. It will end today. There will be no mail privileges for the next month and the lights will be put out an hour earlier for that same period. You may all rest assured that any further problems will result in even harsher restrictions." The sergeant paused for a minute to let his words sink in. He thought the prisoners might protest and was prepared to have it all out right there if they did, but no one said a word and after a moment he finally said "Good day gentlemen" and marched out of the hall.

A rumble of muttered curses and comments followed the exit of the majority of the guards, but then the sergeant suddenly reappeared and there was another silence as everyone waited to see what he was up to.

"Bring them in" was all he said as a couple of British sailors with

442

bayonet-fixed rifles marched in and came to a stomping halt by the door and then more men started filing in through the ranks of the escort.

"Who were they arresting now?" Ethan thought as he watched, and obviously the other internees thought the same thing as a new round of murmuring filled the hall.

It was a moment before Ethan recognized a couple of the men coming in. They had been on the Arandora. They must be the survivors... and then Aaron Mendlebaum walked in. Ethan embarrassed himself as he instinctively called out Aaron's name, virtually shouting it and drawing considerable attention, but soon other men were calling out names as the rest of the survivors entered the hall.

Ethan opened his arms as Aaron plodded across the room, exhausted by the ordeal and the walk back to the camp.

"Thank God you're alive" Ethan said as he embraced his friend and patted him on the back.

The sinking of the Arandora Star and the deaths of hundreds of the foreign nationals focused attention on their plight and soon the newspapers were full of stories of innocent, trustworthy people being put in the camps. Public opinion turned against the blanket policy of internment and government officials re-examined internment criteria.

Less than a week after Aaron returned to the camp, the Battle of Britain began as large formations of German bombers crossed the channel at night. By the first week of August both Ethan and Aaron were released from the camp, Ethan because of his age and Aaron because he intended to try emigrating to Canada once again. By the time Ethan returned to his West end apartment the Germans had changed their bombing strategy to include bombing civilian centers as well as British air bases and other military targets. The West end of London, near the shipping district of the Thames docks was battered night after night, leaving Ethan to wonder in passing, but never seriously, if he wouldn't have been better off in the camp. After a few weeks he accepted the invitation of Edwin Coopersmith and his wife to share their country house an hour's train ride to the east of London near the town of Ipswich.

Back in Prague on the day that Ethan moved to his new accommodations, Jiri Molsovice was pushing on a wrench with all his strength when it slipped, causing him to drive his hand hard against the truck's engine block. "Damn!" he shouted as he looked at the blood beginning to flow from the gash at the base of his index finger.

"Vaclav! Get me a rag." he called out to his co-worker, a short, underfed eighteen year old boy who sometimes helped out around the garage, but there was no response. "Vaclav! I've cut myself. Bring me a rag."

Jiri rolled out from under the truck, about to yell out to Vaclav again when he ran into something and quickly looked up to see what it was. It was a boot. A boot on the foot of an SS trooper standing beside an SS officer.

"Jiri Molsovice?" the officer asked.

Jiri said nothing.

"Are you Jiri Molsovice?"

Jiri still said nothing, but as the officer waited for an answer, another SS soldier appeared behind him, almost holding Vaclav off the floor as he pulled him firmly along by the shoulder. The officer slowly and deliberately looked over at Vaclav. "Molsovice?" the officer shouted accusingly as he pointed at Jiri. Vaclav reluctantly shook his head "yes". The trooper dropped Vaclav, pushing him aside as he moved towards Jiri.

Jiri knew what awaited him. He knew what went on at the Petschek Palais in the cells the Gestapo had made in the basement. They had worked so hard to make the cells soundproof, but the screams of the tortured often made their way through.

"Not like that" Jiri thought to himself as he reached for his pocket, "I'm not going out like that."

"Hands high!" the officer shouted as he saw the slight movement, but Jiri had already reached his screwdriver and started his lunge for the soldier closest to him. He caught the soldier by surprise, driving the screwdriver into the man's chest and piercing his heart, killing him instantly. The officer had drawn his pistol and shot Jiri in the arm as there were specific orders to bring him in alive so they could track down the others, but Jiri knew that he was already as good as dead and so he was determined to kill as many Germans as he could before they killed him. He caught the body of the falling trooper he had stabbed and pushed him at the officer, but the officer managed to step out of the way and fired again at Jiri, hitting him in the upper thigh of his right leg, but Jiri was in a rage at this point and just kept on charging towards the officer, pushing on and driving the screwdriver into the officer's side as the officer brought his pistol's muzzle up to Jiri's head and emptied the remaining bullets. Everything happened in the blink of an eye and it wasn't until then that the soldier who had been holding Vaclav managed to fire at Jiri, but he was already dead as he fell to a heap, his face blackened with powder burns and wearing a mask of blood. The officer reached down to feel the wound and as he did he fainted, falling on top of Jiri.

It was a couple of days later when a little blond-haired boy ducked into Petr Hrmeni's garage on a Saturday afternoon while Petr was working on his bicycle. The boy slipped in so quietly that Petr didn't even notice him until he reached over for an oil can and there he was standing by the bench. He was startled at first, but then he smiled. "Well now... who are you?" he asked.

"I'm supposed to tell you that Jiri Molsovice has been killed."

Petr's smile disappeared. "Who sent you?" he asked the little boy, but the boy just backed out towards the door.

"He killed a soldier and an officer before they killed him..." the little boy added, and then he ran out.

Petr walked back to his stool in front of the bicycle and sat down, bowing his head.

While Petr was out in the garage thinking about how Jiri had given his life rather than being captured, Amalie was going down to the cellar to get some potatoes for dinner. She made her way down into the darkness, feeling her way along the cool, damp dirt wall. She was about to reach for the string to turn the light on when a gust of wind caught the door and blew it shut with a resounding crash. She stood motionless, waiting for her eyes to adjust to the dim sliver of light which filtered between the door and its jamb. She had been startled by the door, but now she stood still and listened to the silence. How peaceful it seemed. How safe and quiet. She made out the shape of an old wooden chair in the corner and thought better of turning on the light. She moved towards the chair and sat down. It was wonderfully cool compared to the August heat outside. she found herself reaching out to the wall and touching it, feeling dirt in a strange new way. It felt so foreign, as though she had never felt dirt before. She then scraped some of the dirt onto her fingers. It was remarkably dry, belying its appearance of moisture. She scraped some more of the dirt away and began to daydream. "I could live in here" she thought to herself, "safe... When they come for me like they

445

came for the others I'll run down here. I could live down here." She started scraping more dirt from the wall until she had formed a recess about the size of a large apple. She then stopped and surveyed her work. "I'll need a shovel. I can dig a hole and make a secret room. A secret room where I can live."

"What took so long?" Hannah asked as Amalie returned to the kitchen.

"I was thinking."

"About what?"

"I thought I might move to the cellar."

Hannah laughed, thinking that Amalie was joking, but Amalie continued without missing a beat. "I'll dig a hole in the wall and make a room. I suppose I'll need some wood to hold it up. Maybe Petr can help me."

Amalie walked out of the room as she kept talking to herself about how she would build her room and Hannah suddenly realized Amalie wasn't joking.

Chapter 16

The Autumn of 1941 was the pinnacle of the Third Reich's military achievements. They held the European continent in one greedy hand as they reached for Russia with the other, like a greedy spoiled child who believed he should have it all. Erwin Rommel was in hot pursuit of the British forces in North Africa and the German Luftwaffe was sure to bomb England into submission.

The ancient Tartar beast roared as he stood lord over his domain, demanding allegiance and submission, a crude and primal bloodlust that made these small men believe in their hearts that they could best Beowulf in his lair, and that they had not just the right, but a mission from their pagan god to choose life or death for their pitiful human charges.

It was in September of 1941 that Rheinhard Heydrich came to Prague. He felt there should be no illusions among the Czech people as to their status. They were to submit completely to German rule or be prepared for the harshest consequences. Anyone suspected of anti-German activities could be, and often was, executed on the most casual evidence. Heydrich began a reign of terror as Reichsprotektor of Bohemia and Moravia which was only eclipsed by his role as host of a meeting in a suburb of Berlin called "Wannsee". It was at the Wannsee conference where the destruction of European Jewry was drawn up in gruesome detail and given a name: "The Final Solution".

It was in Wannsee that the old methods of diverting exhaust pipes in to truck boxes and mass shootings were abandoned and the much more efficient method of death camps was devised. How many steps from the train? How many should be spared to work until they dropped and then sent to the gas? How many will they handle each day? Where should the camps be located? What kind of gas should we kill them with? How do we cremate them all? All of the details to be worked out, a thousand details... "Harvesting" the victims: the gold from their teeth, their hair for mattresses, their shoes, their eyeglasses... so many details.

"...and make sure von Burgsdorff reads the text as written" Rheinhard said in passing as he watched himself in the mirror while buttoning up his tunic.

"Durchaus, Herr Reichsprotektor!" his adjutant snapped obediently.

Rheinhard smiled. His new title still pleased him and although he was not a man given to sincere smiles when it came to his work, he allowed himself the luxury in the privacy of his dressing room with only his subordinate present. It was a sly and nasty smile, the sort that a thief would smile after having made off with a great prize. "That's all for now" he said, dismissing his adjutant.

Konstantin von Neurath was the Reichsprotektor of Bohemia and Moravia, formerly known as Czechoslovakia, until Heinrich Himmler and Rheinhard Heydrich decided that it would be in the best interest of the Reich to have an SS leader in charge of the region that Adolf Hitler himself envisioned as "a second Ruhr", a region designated by it's German conquerors to become a major war armament production center. Himmler and Heydrich conspired to replace Neurath with Heydrich by misrepresenting the degree of Czech resistance. It didn't take long to convince Hitler that Neurath was not a well man and that he "should be allowed to convalesce" while Heydrich temporarily assumed the position of Reichsprotektor.

"Any indiscretion, any communication of what has been discussed here tonight," Burgsdorff continued as he read the introduction prepared for him as he addressed the officials assembled for Heydrich's first official appearance in Prague, "would be considered an act of treason and will result in either imprisonment or death."

The statement achieved its intended result as the officers sat in rapt attention while Rheinhard made his grand entrance, striding to the podium and stopping beside it as the audience began to applaud politely. He put his right hand on his hip as he waited for the applause to die down in a gesture that seemed strangely effeminate, strangely so considering the fear that he commanded among these men with his overt threat of death if they dared speak out of turn.

Once the applause began to die down, he dramatically threw his right hand into the air, snapping into a stiff armed nazi salute as he shrieked out "Heil Hitler", drawing an effusive response from the audience as they all returned the salute and bellowed out their reflexive vow of allegiance. Rheinhard relaxed his salute and moved into position behind the podium while the audience continued to roar while he scanned the notes for his speech.

It was a dramatic show. Rheinhard spoke of the destiny of Germany and what was to become of the people who now inhabited the regions of Bohemia and Moravia. Some might be salvageable, others would be candidates for "resettlement in the east", and another portion would be advocates of a position so untenable as to require that they be disposed of, this last group consisting of what Rheinhard called the enemies of the Reich and of course Rheinhard would be the final judge of who was a friend and who was an enemy of Germany.

In the days after his speech, Rheinhard worked quickly to prove his reputation to the residents of Prague as thousands were imprisoned and hundreds were executed. He saw the Universities as breeding grounds for discontent, places where intellectuals were allowed to gather and potentially foment unrest, so as resistance to German occupation increased he simply closed down all the Universities.

Jakob had been sharing an apartment with Walter Hanisch since he had left Hannah Bauer's house. Walter was a friend from school that Jakob had met during one of the casual gatherings when he and his friends would sit at a cafe and discuss the problems of the world and how to solve them. Jakob found Walter to be "volkish", a term the nazis used to mean someone concerned with the people of Germany, more than a German patriot, someone who was concerned with social issues and the well-being of those people.

It was a period in Jakob's life when he wanted to fit in with, if not the nazis, then at least the people who grudgingly supported the nazis. Jakob, on a sub-conscious level, felt that a friendship with people like Walter would make him more German... and less Jewish. He had only to parrot his friend in order to fit in.

That was why it came as such a shock to Jakob when he came home to find two men rifling through the apartment. He didn't say anything. He just stood there watching as though hypnotized while the men continued throwing papers around and emptying drawers until one of them finally noticed him standing there and rushed over, ready to catch him if he should try to run.

"Are you Walter Hannisch?"

"No."

"Then what are you doing here?"

"I share this apartment with him..."

"Oh, then you are..." the man stopped in mid-sentence as he looked over a report which he pulled from his coat pocket, "Metzdorf... Jakob Metzdorf?"

"Yes." Jakob said hesitantly.

"We need to talk with you."

"Why?" Jakob asked as he finally began to find his voice, "What are you doing here? What do you want?"

That was when Jakob disappeared. The two Gestapo officers gathered up their evidence and took Jakob into custody. Walter was arrested as he put his key in the door. A Gestapo agent had been waiting for him.

It was Walter's mother who called Amalie. Monika Hanisch was almost hysterical and began screaming over the telephone as she demanded to know what it was that Amalie's son had done to get both Walter and himself arrested by the Gestapo.

Amalie then shouted back, demanding to know what Monika was talking about.

"When? When were they taken in?"

"Last night" Monika replied as she began to calm down, "the neighbor across the hall said she saw them take Walter away on Thursday night."

"They didn't tell you why they arrested him?"

"Tell me why?" Monika repeated as she began to cry, "They wouldn't even tell me if they had taken him. They said they didn't have any record of Walter or Jakob."

"You're sure it was the Gestapo?"

"Yes, yes. The neighbor said she heard the man say he was with the Gestapo when they took Walter."

Jakob had been taken to Petschek Palais. Named for the wealthy Prague businessman who built the mansion, Petschek Palace was the headquarters of the Gestapo in Prague. The conversion of the building was one of the German's first projects when they entered Prague in 1939. Steps were taken to make the building soundproof so as not to disturb the quiet of the area with the screams of their tortured victims and the basement was redesigned to accommodate more than a hundred people in stall-like cells measuring only one-and-one-half meters by three meters, barely enough room for a small cot and space to walk beside it. There were only windows on the cells on the perimeter of the building while those in the center only had small transoms through which dim light might filter at some time of day.

Jakob was given a smelly, damp blanket on Thursday night and pushed into one of the cells on the west wall of the basement. He stared at the dank little cell as the door clanked shut beside him. He felt like a child. He had just turned twenty-five the month before, but he felt as though someone should have been protecting him. He was innocent of any wrong doing and yet, somehow, these men had seen fit to take him from his home and bring him to this place. Where were his parents to save him? It was only a fleeting thought and, in fact, it disturbed him that he regressed to such a childish thought, but he was in a panic. Everything was suddenly beyond his control. He had considered himself an adult capable of handling whatever might come his way in day to day life. He was independent and mature, and yet all that was now gone as he sat on the thin, urine and sweat stained mattress on the cot.

They had not even told him why he had been arrested.

They came at three o'clock in the morning, but of course Jakob had no idea what time it was as they had taken his watch along with everything else when he had been photographed and finger-printed. They even took his belt and shoe laces to prevent him from doing anything rash. The Gestapo insisted that no one be allowed an easy way out. Their torturing was their business and no one would deprive them of their exercise.

"Where is Walter Hanisch?" was the first question shouted at him. Jakob had been seated in a chair and one of the two guards standing on either side behind him had tied his hands behind his back and tied his feet to the legs of the chair. A single light with its tin shade dangled just above and in front of Jakob's face, blinding him so that he could not see the officer asking the question.

"I don't know," Jakob said with a nervous jangled quiver in his voice, "Maybe the apartment... I don't know."

The question was only a test as Walter had been arrested not long after Jakob and was in a cell just a few meters away in the basement of the Gestapo building. The officer began to pace as he talked.

"You are German..." he said to Jakob in a calm, casual tone

451

which Jakob thought rhetorical until the officer suddenly shrieked out the statement again, striking Jakob in the face.

"You are German!" he said as the sting of a riding crop lashed across Jakob's face.

"Yes!" Jakob shouted back, trying to appease the officer, but then he realized it was the wrong answer, "No, Austrian!"

"Which is it boy? German or Austrian?"

"I was born in Austria" Jakob explained breathlessly, trying to get the words out fast enough to avoid another attack, "but we moved to Munich when I was two years old. We returned to Austria when my father died..."

"When?"

"`34"

"Then why are you in Prague?"

Jakob had to think. He had come for his grandfather when Ethan had suffered a heart attack, but Ethan and his mother had fled the German advance to Austria. That wouldn't sound very good in these circumstances.

"Why are you in Prague?" the officer insisted firmly, but at least he wasn't shouting yet.

"School" Jakob tossed back off the top of his head.

"School?" the officer asked with a note of amusement, believing he had caught Jakob in a lie. "There aren't any schools in Austria?"

"Yes" Jakob replied, wanting to say something to keep the officer talking.

"Why would you come to Prague instead of Vienna or even Munich? There are excellent schools in Munich." The officer was only toying with Jakob, playing a game of cat and mouse until he could get Jakob to admit that he had left Munich and then Austria trying to get away from German occupation.

"I wasn't smart enough" Jakob said with a humility that made the statement sound so degrading as to make it plausible, "I couldn't get into the good schools, so I had to come to Prague."

This admission caught the officer off guard. It was a good story, very believable. A poor student might have to find a "forgiving" institution to overlook a bad school record. "Where did you live in Austria?"

"Salzburg."

Again, it was a good answer. This time because of the

geography. If one was looking for an easier school, Prague was certainly a reasonable trip from Salzburg. There were, however, much greater issues at hand. "How long have you known Walter Hanisch?"

Jakob thought for an instant before answering. He knew that he had done nothing wrong, so it had to be Walter's fault that he had been arrested. The first question was about Walter, so it was obvious that Walter must have been up to something and they thought that he was somehow involved. They couldn't have any kind of proof of anything. He hadn't done anything! At least not knowingly... Jakob tried to think. Had there been any strange favors he had done? Anything delivered, anything... No. Nothing. "I met him through school. It was convenient to share an apartment."

"What do you know about him?"

Jakob didn't know what to say. What did he know about Walter? "He's just a friend."

"A friend? What kind of friend?"

"We just share an apartment. He pays the rent on time... He seems like a good..."

"a good German?" the officer interrupted.

"Yes, I suppose. I've never heard him say anything against the Reich or the Fuhrer. He was happy when the Ger... when we came into Prague." Jakob hoped the officer didn't notice the slip. He wanted to make it clear that he considered himself a German too.

"What does Walter Hanisch do?"

"Do?"

"For money."

"Oh, a job... He's a student, but he also works as... I think he makes deliveries." Jakob stuttered as the officer pressed, not giving him a chance to think what he was saying.

"You think?" the officer asked menacingly, as though he might lash out again.

"I know. I know" Jakob replied quickly and earnestly. "He makes deliveries for a furniture shop."

"What do you know about his family?"

"Nothing... I've only met his parents a couple of times. Just to say hello and..."

"His brother?"

"Brother? I didn't even know he had a..."

453

"You mean to tell me you share the same apartment and you don't know that he has a brother in prison?

"In prison? No! I didn't know he... He never told me. I know he didn't" Jakob was getting excited.

"Come now. You've been friends for over two years and he never once mentioned his brother?"

Jakob realized when the officer said "over two years" that the man knew the answers to many of the questions that he had been asking. It suddenly occurred that this was all a test, that the officer was making sure of what he already knew and hoping that Jakob would slip and admit to something else. Jakob suddenly felt calmer. He had finally made a little sense of it. The officer knew Jakob had done nothing, but he just wanted to make sure of it. All Jakob had to do was keep up with him. "No" Jakob answered simply.

"No..." the officer repeated, realizing that something had changed in Jakob and he had come up to some kind of wall. This was a good time to stop. This was only the beginning of questioning, the start of a process of torture and reprieve, the deprivation of food and water and sleep. The officer was already fairly certain that Jakob knew nothing, but that would not stop the process. From here on it was an exercise, a way for this officer to hone his skills at reducing human beings to their barest elements, to the point where this young man in his charge would soon say or do anything to just stop the pain.

The officer suddenly left the room without saying a word and the two guards untied Jakob and roughly pulled him out of his chair and dragged him out of the room. Just as they left the room, a scream split the silence and Jakob instinctively pulled back against the guard's hold as he turned to see where the scream came from. The guards were immune to the sound of human pain. Neither of them had reacted at all to the sound and they just pulled Jakob along down the hallway back to his cell. The walls were silenced. The scream never passed beyond that place. Jakob was the only one to hear that scream.

Amalie sat on the edge of her bed, staring at the wallpaper pattern. It had become a bit faded there by the window where the sunlight had washed away the bright pink and green, imperceptibly in the sense of time. Had one day been brighter than the next? Was this day more pale than yesterday? It could only be seen as its whole. Yesterday was bright and clean and fresh and today had become

454

older... sadder.

"What day is it today?" Amalie found herself thinking, actually saying it out loud, interrupting her study of the printed flowers with their green stems against the white background that all made up the wallpaper in her bedroom in Hannah's house.

"Friday" she answered herself.

She felt a bit shaken as she realized that she had an appointment for that morning that terrified her. She was to go to the Gestapo building to inquire about Jakob that morning.

She forced herself up in the same manner as if someone had stood in front of her and taken her hands and pulled her up to her feet. She stopped at the window and looked out at the cobblestone street. The sky was streaked with wisps of clouds and held up by the piercing dark claws of the trees fallen victim to autumn which then suffered their sentence of winter.

It was December. The fifth. It had been several weeks since Rheinhard Heydrich had come to Prague to replace Konstantin von Neurath to enforce the iron discipline that the Fuhrer demanded for the protectorate of Bohemia and Moravia. Amalie remembered Heydrich from Munich when her husband and Klaus Grunewald had been so excited that he was the new leader of the SD back in '33. This must have been the man ultimately responsible for Gunther's death, Amalie thought to herself, and now he had taken her son.

"Do you want me to come with?" Hannah asked as Amalie came down the stairs.

Amalie thought for an instant. "Would you?" she finally asked with a wince.

"Of course. I've got my coat right here... I thought you were going to ask me, but..."

"I didn't know if you wanted to get involved."

"Oh Amalie! You should know that I'll always be with you. I just wasn't sure whether you wanted me to tag along or if you thought it would be best to go alone."

"Hannah, the truth is that I'm so afraid that I don't know if my legs will get me there. They're already shaking and I haven't even left the house."

Hannah smiled and embraced her friend. Amalie began to cry.

"What am I going to do?" Amalie sobbed, "I don't even know why they arrested him."

Hannah patted Amalie's back as she held her. "It will be all right. It's probably just a mistake. You'll have everything cleared up in a few minutes and they'll let you bring him home with us."

Amalie pulled back a bit so she could look into Hannah's eyes to see if it were true, if Hannah really believed such a miracle was possible, and Hannah's expression did nothing to betray her doubts. Amalie even allowed herself some hope.

It was a long trip from Hannah's house through the city to Petschek Palais. The gray, oblong building was bleak and forbidding. No warmth showed through the windows, only reflections of the darkened sky awaiting another snowfall. The climb up the steps seemed interminable, getting closer and closer to the center of terror. This was a nazi trademark. You must climb up to reach them. Humanity itself was beneath them. They were a lofty goal attainable only by the pure, the Aryan ideal.

The entryway was wrapped in two great marble stairways with a reception desk set strategically in front between them. Guards with machine guns were stationed at the foot and top of each stairway as well as a guard on either end of the clerks desk.

The clerk was just finishing up filling out a form as Amalie entered. His pleasant attitude was a marked contrast to the surroundings. "Yes...?" he asked as he looked up at Amalie and Hannah.

"My son... I..." Amalie started, trying to get the words out, but they wouldn't come. The clerk sat patiently waiting for her to gather herself up when Hannah interrupted. "Her son has been... brought in for questioning. She was hoping to see him."

The clerk turned to a file drawer beside him. "I'm not certain if it is possible. What is your son's name."

"Metzdorf, Jakob Metzdorf" Amalie answered.

"Metzdorf..." the clerk repeated as he leafed through the files, "Yes, here we are. Metzdorf, Jakob. Twenty-five. Mala Strana district..."

"Yes. That's him" Amalie said with great effort to stay calm.

"He is one of Obersturmbannfuhrer Kleist's cases. The best I can do is to see if the Obersturmbannfuhrer is available to speak with you."

This may have seemed to be a kindness on the part of the clerk, but actually it was just another part of the process. If a prisoner was being particularly difficult, it was often valuable to remind the prisoner that his or her family was also vulnerable. If the prisoner was not cooperative, his family might also be arrested and questioned.

Obersturmbannfuhrer Kleist was available at the time. He was having coffee with one of the other officers when the messenger sent by the clerk found him. "What is it Lemke?" he asked.

"Someone's mother is at the desk."

The officer with Kleist could not repress a sardonic smile.

"You're much too cynical, Friedrich" Kleist said to the other officer, "Who is she here for?" he continued, turning to the messenger.

The messenger looked at the note from the clerk. "Metz... Metzder..."

"Metzdorf." Kleist confirmed, "I'll be right there."

"Metzdorf?" Friedrich asked with surprise.

"Yes, a boy. Jakob Metzdorf. Do you know him?"

"If it's the same boy. I haven't seen him in six or seven years. Is he from Munich?"

"Salzburg" Kleist answered, but then corrected himself "No, I believe he did say he lived in Munich for a time."

"What's it all about?"

"That anti-government propaganda ring. It seems his room-mate was a delivery boy. I don't think the Metzdorf boy was involved."

"What was the room-mate's name?" Friedrich asked with a smile.

"What are you up to, Friedrich?"

"I want to be her white knight. Come riding in at the last minute and save the day. Now come on Gerhard, what's the name of the room-mate?"

"Hannisch, Walter Hannisch."

"Are you going to see her now?"

"I suppose I could."

"Use room 27. I'll watch through the mirror."

Kleist, Obersturmbannfuhrer Gerhard Kleist, strode down the hall with his boots clicking off a military cadence as he thought about his approach to this new situation. He decided that he would follow the usual line, obsequious politeness until they were out of sight and carefully hidden away in room 27 and then he would press the game

457

the same way he had with the son. He would accuse the mother of protecting her son even though she knew he was distributing anti-German propaganda and then he would sit back and see how she would respond.

Amalie and Hannah stood waiting at the foot of the stairs for the answers to Amalie's questions. There were no chairs for people to use while waiting. They were not supposed to be comfortable.

"Frau Metzdorf?" Gerhard asked, not sure which of the two women was Jakob's mother.

"I am Amalie Metzdorf" Amalie said clearly, steeling herself for the confrontation.

"This way please" Gerhard said as he motioned for her to follow.

"Is my son here?"

Gerhard stopped in mid step. "Did she really expect him to discuss such things here?" he thought to himself. Obviously she didn't understand the rules... He was in charge and he was not to be questioned.

"If you will just come with me, we can discuss all that in private."

It sounded ominous to Hannah. It sounded like the way all those terrible stories began, the stories about the Gestapo that always ended with "...and he was never heard from again."

"Is it all right if I come along?" Hannah found herself asking, surprising even herself when she said it.

Gerhard turned to Hannah, about to explain how that was not possible when Amalie reached for Hannah's arm. "That's not necessary", Amalie said with a forced little smile, "I'll be fine. Why don't you go on and do your shopping and I'll see you later at home."

"Are you sure?" Hannah asked, "I could wait for you..."

"No. Go ahead. I don't know how long I'll be."

There was nothing left to say as Amalie started up the stairs with Gerhard, but Hannah couldn't seem to turn away. She just stood there watching them until they disappeared down the hallway and then she listened as their footsteps faded away.

Gerhard opened the door to a sparsely furnished office and stepped aside so that Amalie could enter first. There were no windows, just a glaring fluorescent ceiling fixture which seemed to wash the life out of everything in the room. A green metal desk. two metal office chairs. The required print of a painting of Adolf Hitler hanging on the wall alongside a small mirror which seemed out of place with a companion small wash basin on a table below it.

Gerhard took his place behind the desk after offering Amalie a seat and then began silently going through three file folders. The silence went on for a few moments until Gerhard finally popped up from the file folder he was holding, just enough to expose his eyes as he looked down at Amalie. "Jakob Metzdorf?" he finally asked.

The question caught Amalie off-guard since she thought she had already made that point clear. "Yes," she said, "Jakob Metzdorf. He is my son and I was wondering... I had heard rumors that he had been arrested. Of course I'm sure it's some kind of mistake. He would never do anything wrong. I know he..."

"Frau Metzdorf," Gerhard interrupted, "Do you know a 'Walter Hanisch'?"

"Walter? Yes, Walter is the boy Jakob lives with. They share an apartm..."

"And do you mean to tell me that your son didn't know what this Hanisch was up to?"

"...Up to? I don't know what you..."

"We have proof that Walter Hanisch is part of a group of traitors printing and distributing treasonous slander against the Third Reich."

Friedrich was unmoved by the exchange as he watched through the one-way mirror and listened over the speaker. It always intrigued him to watch these sessions and the effect was not changed by the fact that he was personally acquainted with the subject. At one point Amalie looked up at the mirror, only because she wanted to look away from Gerhard and she certainly didn't want to look at the print of Hitler. Friedrich sank back from the mirror. It was as though she had looked him directly in the eye, looked at him accusingly as if to ask how he could allow this to happen to her. Perhaps it was different when he knew the person. Some long hidden trace of guilt at the thought of this game, a game that was often a matter of life and death. It was time to go in. He would put an end to this.

"...and your maiden name?" Gerhard asked Amalie just as Friedrich left the observation room, making his way to room 27.

"Stein."

"Stein?"

459

"Yes."

"Frau Metzdorf... Are you Jewish?" "My parents are Jewish. Well, my father. My mother died when I was young."

"Then your son is Jewish?"

"Jakob's father was not Jewish..."

"Then he is a mischling."

"Mischling? Yes, I suppose so."

"Frau Metzdorf, it seems then that your son has lied on his registration forms."

"What?"

"He has said that he has no Jewish blood."

Gerhard and Amalie were both startled as the door opened. "Gerhard, I was... Oh I'm sorry, I didn't know you were..." Friedrich said, lying as he pretended to see Amalie for the first time in seven years. "Amalie?! Amalie Metzdorf, is that you? I don't believe it."

Amalie was so relieved to see a familiar face at that point, even though it was a familiar face atop an SS uniform, that she stood up and embraced Friedrich.

"Oh Friedrich!" she said as she held him, turning her back on Gerhard. Friedrich hadn't expected such a warm reception and he just smiled at Gerhard as Amalie held him for a long moment.

"Friedrich," Gerhard said sternly, bringing the conversation back to the climactic moment when Friedrich had interrupted, "Frau Metzdorf and I were just talking and it seems that her son is in a bit of trouble."

"That Hannisch mess? I'm sure Jakob wasn't..." Friedrich countered

"No. It's something else. It seems he lied on his registration papers."

"What?" Friedrich asked as he finally realized that something else was going on, "In what way?"

"He lied about his mother being Jewish."

Friedrich looked at Amalie for an instant. "Of course she was Jewish" he thought to himself. He knew it somewhere and yet they had all overlooked it back then. It had seemed so ordinary back then. It was just something they never talked about, but now here it was and Jakob could go to prison for lying about it.

Friedrich didn't know what to say.

"Friedrich," Amalie said, "Could we talk about this alone?"

460

Amalie knew what to say. She had brought papers with her. She had brought a Photostat of Friedrich's confession in the Geli Raubal murder. She had brought a Photostat of the Heidler death bed confession. She knew what to say and was just about to say it to Gerhard when Friedrich had entered, but it would be easier to say to Friedrich, and Friedrich would know it was true.

"I..." Friedrich stammered until Gerhard stepped in.

"If you want to handle this Friedrich, that would be fine with me."

"Yes, yes" Friedrich said as he stumbled while turning to the door, trying to gather his thoughts, "Amalie, let's go to my office."

Amalie watched Friedrich as he walked slightly ahead of her. He had lost most of his hair since they had last seen each other. It reminded her of how he had been the youngest of them, Klaus, Gunther and herself, but then he was only three years younger than she. Three years seemed like so much back then, but so little now.

Friedrich went into his office with Amalie in tow and sat down behind his desk. There was none of the obsequious pretension as with Gerhard. Friedrich had thought he would come in and save the day with a bit of play acting and now there was a real problem. Rheinhard Heydrich, still the head of the Gestapo, epitomized the term "rabid anti-semite" in both his personal and public life. His demagoguery in playing up to Hitler's and Himmler's, hatred for the Jews was the key to his inordinate power in relation to his position. Heydrich had shown that he would be their Iron warrior, unswayed by pity for any Jew. He was ready to step into the role as Germany's avenger for the crimes which the Jews had committed against Germany. He would go to any length to find a solution for Europe's Jewish problem. All this meant that it would be hard for Friedrich to find some way to make an exception for Jakob. At least he was a mischling and not a full Jew.

"This is very serious." Friedrich began as he finally addressed Amalie who had been waiting patiently for him to speak.

"But Friedrich, you know how Jakob is for Germany. My God! He was in the HJ before it was mandatory..."

"No, not the Hannisch nonsense. We've talked with him and we feel confident that he had nothing to do with that. It's this other matter. Lying about his... background."

"Couldn't we just say he made a mistake? We've never been practicing Jews. We could just say he didn't understand."

461

"I don't know if that would be enough. He might have to spend some time in jail. I think we might be able to make it short... maybe just a year... but I don't know for sure."

Amalie sat up straight in her chair, as though she had been hit in the chest and pushed back. She hadn't dreamed when she first saw Friedrich that he would say such a thing, and at that it seemed that he felt he was doing her a favor by talking about only a year in prison, a year in prison because she was Jakob's mother. She suddenly felt as though she were a mother who had passed a disease on to her child and now she would have to stand by and watch him suffer.

"No." she said resolutely, "my son will not go to jail."

"Come now Amalie, I'll do everything I can, but we have to be realistic. You have to see that it might come down to that no matter what we do. Jakob has committed a crime by lying on his registration form and... well, it's just bad timing. With the new Reichsprotektor..."

"Heydrich" she said heavily, as though the name in itself was a prison term.

"Yes, Reichsprotektor Heydrich. He was sent to take care of the problems here with partisans and resistance to the Reich. We have very strict orders to enforce all the rules and laws. Things will be less... severe... later on, but now he has to get complete control and that means being harsh in many cases. I don't know what..."

"Friedrich" Amalie said, interrupting him as he rambled on about order and discipline, "Jakob will not go to jail."

"Oh, come now Amalie, haven't you heard a word..."

"Friedrich, have you forgotten who you're talking to?"

The question seemed astonishingly threatening, but Friedrich couldn't think for the life of him what it was that she was talking about.

"What do you mean? You mean my mother? Amalie, I will always be grateful for the way you and Gunther took in my mother when I had to go away, but I'm afraid that doesn't have any bearing on..."

"Your mother? Friedrich, is it possible that you don't remember? Were you really so drunk that last night that you forgot?

"What last night?"

"That last night you came to my house in Munich before Jakob and I left for Salzburg."

"No, I don't really..." he said hesitantly, trying to remember what might have happened, "it was a long time ago." He suddenly perked up with shock. "We didn't... I mean I didn't do anything... I..."

"No" Amalie said with a sharp edge to her voice, "of course we didn't do anything like that."

"I'm afraid I don't remember."

"Then let me refresh your memory" Amalie said with the confidence of one who holds all the cards and knows it, "This is a copy of the letter you gave me that night. You said you might need some help some day and that I should take it out of the country and keep it for you."

Friedrich took the letter and started to read his own confession as Amalie went on. "The original is safe with friends both here and in England."

Friedrich's face began to pale as he read his own handwritten confession which he had forgotten from so long ago, the delivery in a state of drunken paranoia which he had forgotten.

"The robe and needle" he whispered to himself as he read, the memory rushing back to him and filling the room.

"If anything happens to me," Amalie continued without emotion, "this letter and the rest of the package you gave me, along with other valuable bits of information which I understand Reichsprotektor Heydrich himself has been looking for, will be released to the international press for inspection. You, more than anyone, knows the validity of this information."

Friedrich crumpled the letter in his hands, banging his clenched fists on the desk with a resounding report as he stared at Amalie as though he had just been shot.

"How could you do this to me?" he growled.

"To you?" Amalie repeated with amazement. "Do this to you?" Her voice began to rise. "You tell me that my son should go to prison for a year because I am a Jew and you ask how I can do this to you?!"

There was a pause for a moment. Neither knew what to do next. Amalie spoke first. "It's for Jakob. Don't you understand Friedrich? I can't let you hurt him because of me. I just want my son back."

"Do you realize what a dangerous game you're playing?" Friedrich countered, thinking that it might not be too late to talk her out of it. "Amalie. We could forget this ever happened. I wouldn't tell anyone. You just give me what you have and I'll destroy it. I will do my best for Jakob, but I'll tell you now that you had better consider

463

what might happen if you keep this going."

Friedrich began to get animated as he spoke, gesturing as he got up from his chair, "They'll always be after you, just waiting for the moment that you slip and then you'll lose everything. We're not talking about a few months in jail. I'm telling you Amalie, they'll hurt you every way they can. They'll kill everyone you love and then when you think they can't hurt you anymore, they'll begin the torture."

Suddenly he was crouching beside her, on one knee as though he were pleading while she stared straight ahead at the desk, and he spoke in a hoarse whisper, a terrifying rasp that said he knew what he was talking about, "Unspeakable things, the kinds of things you couldn't imagine in your worst nightmares. It will be Hell on Earth for you Amalie. They'll tear your body apart piece by piece and make sure that you stay alive while they do it so that you can watch them. They're sick sadistic animals Amalie. They love it. They volunteer to do it! They challenge each other to make more pain, to make it last longer, to do it... better."

It took all of Amalie's self control to keep herself from shaking. She had known Friedrich for a long time, had seen him in many different surroundings and situations, and she knew that he was not an actor. He was not the sort who could make up something like this. She knew that it was something he must have seen, that he must have spoken with, known the "men" he was talking about.

"Friedrich..." Amalie said slowly and deliberately as she composed herself, "I have known you for many years. In good times and bad. I love your mother. I do not want to hurt you..."

"Then what? What do you want?"

"I want to walk out of here with Jakob. Now. Today."

Friedrich sat behind the desk and studied her. "Wait here." he said as he got up and left the office, closing the door behind him.

Amalie wasn't altogether sure if it was a good sign or not, but she felt it must be. Unless he thought it was some kind of bluff. Certainly she couldn't get word out to Ethan to carry out her threat in England and she hadn't made any plans for someone to publish the letters in Prague, but Friedrich couldn't possibly know that it was all bluff.

She waited in the little office for over half-an-hour and then it suddenly occurred to her that if it were a trap, Friedrich wouldn't have just left her there, free to wander off. He would have locked her in. Did he? She had been so unnerved that she couldn't think if she had heard him lock the door. She decided to get up and try the door. She walked over and touched the brass knob, just holding it for a moment until she worked up the courage to turn it ever so slowly until it either stopped or until she heard a click which would tell her it was unlocked.

Click.

Was that it? She could just walk out? ...but that wasn't what this was about. It was about Jakob, but if Friedrich left her unattended then that must mean he was going for Jakob. Unattended? Maybe there was a guard standing on the other side of the door. She had seen two guards by one of the other doors as she and Friedrich had come to his office. Maybe they were outside this door now. She was still holding the doorknob tightly, turned open, held as tightly as she was now holding her breath. She would open the door a crack and see if there was a guard. Just as she managed enough of a crack to see outside, the hall was filled with the loud "click-clack" sound of two soldiers marching smartly down the hallway. She held the door as she closed it, holding it back so that it wouldn't make a sound. They were coming for her, to take her away. The sound of her heart pounding filled her ears so much so that she hardly noticed as the sound of the soldiers boots against the hard tile floor faded away as quickly as it had come. They went right past the office. She opened the door once more to make sure. There was no one in the hallway. Friedrich must have gone for Jakob.

She spent another half-hour vacillating between an impending dread that they might yet come to take her away and an elation that Jakob might soon be free. She was startled as the door knob turned and she stood up abruptly, ready to face whatever happened next.

She didn't say anything when Jakob came in, she only put her arms around him and held him. His eyes were dark and she could feel him shaking. He hadn't had much sleep in the past few days.

"I talked to Kleist," Friedrich said as he followed Jakob in, "he said that as a favor to me, he never talked to you Amalie. Jakob must go in of his own accord and tell them that he made a mistake. He'll get off with just a warning."

"What do we do now?" she asked, still holding on to Jakob who made no attempt to pull away.

"Leave" he said in a low voice.

465

Amalie began to usher Jakob out the door when Friedrich unexpectedly put a hand on her shoulder. "Remember this Amalie. You were lucky, lucky that I was here. Be careful who you talk to."

She didn't care what he said. It had worked. She had gotten Jakob out. Jakob was in no state of mind to ask what Friedrich meant, in fact Jakob wouldn't even remember being released.

Hannah peaked around the corner as she heard someone unlocking the door and pushing their way in from the cold. She expected to see Petr come in and stomp the snow off his boots, but suddenly there was Amalie and Jakob and she rushed down the hallway to meet them.

"Is he all right?" she asked anxiously as she took his other arm.

"Yes," Amalie answered, "I think he'll be fine. He just needs sleep. Help me get him up to bed."

Amalie and Hannah were just returning downstairs as Petr got home from work. "Amalie!" he exclaimed as he saw her, "I thought you would still be with Jakob."

"Yes, I've just brought him home."

"Home? Here?"

"Yes. He's upstairs asleep."

"How on Earth did you manage that?"

"It was all a mistake. I just talked to them and..."

"What does it matter how?" Hannah interrupted, scolding her husband, "He's out and safe."

"Yes, yes, of course" Petr said apologetically as he put an arm around Amalie's shoulder, "I was just surprised. You must be terribly happy."

"I'm just tired..." Amalie said as she moved to a chair in the living room and fell into it, "I was so worried all the time I was there."

The three of them went on talking and Amalie made up a story about an apologetic officer immediately releasing Jakob to her, but Petr had some idea that it wasn't the truth.

Resistance in Prague had been growing slowly but steadily in numbers since the incident at the police station with Jiri and Matej and there was much better communication among those involved. Petr had heard through a friend about Walter Hannisch even before Jakob was arrested and he knew that Walter had been caught dead to rights with anti-nazi propaganda and would certainly be going to prison, possibly even sentenced to death. It didn't seem possible that

466

Jakob would be released like this. Petr had never heard of, could not even imagine, an officer of the SS being apologetic and moving so quickly to release a prisoner. He was sure there was more to the story.

A few kilometers away, in a small town outside of Prague, at the same time that Amalie was settling in and beginning to feel better, the SS had organized a forced labor contingent made up of civilian prisoners. They were to convert an old Hapsburg fortress garrison founded in 1780 by Emperor Joseph II and named in honor of his mother, the Empress Maria Theresa, into a prison camp. Having been built in the name of Empress Theresia, the town which grew around the fortress was given the name "Teresin" and the converted fortress was being made into a German Konzentrationslager known as "Theresienstadt".

And a few hundred kilometers away from that, a group of Polish carpenters and laborers were also getting off a train. They had been conscripted as workers from Krakow for the German army and transported to a building site a few miles out of a small town called Oscwiecm to build another labor camp which would be called Birkenau, although the name of Birkenau labor camp would soon be overshadowed by the name of the camp which would soon thereafter be built within sight of Birkenau, but not as a Labor camp. Auschwitz would be built for an altogether different purpose.

Klaus Grunewald had enlisted with the SS just as the nazis had come to power and by the end of 1941 the German SS was busily working on a solution to Europe's "Jewish problem". Wherever German armies advanced in the east, they were soon followed by SS men belonging to the "einsatzgruppen", the squads which would move into towns and villages with their specially designed trucks and begin by segregating the Jews into some large building in town, a school, a warehouse, a synagogue... the nature of the building wasn't important as long as all of the Jews from the town could be held within. They would then be loaded into the trucks and taken from the building for transport to some unnamed destination, but it was soon after the doors of the trucks were closed that the victims found out the terrible secret of these trucks, that the world famous truck manufacturing company which had built these trucks had modified them at their factory, venting the exhaust pipes directly into the airtight body of the truck. The human beings who had been forced into the trucks were dead by the time the truck arrived at it's unnamed destination: a place somewhere in a nearby forest where workers had already dug a pit to be used as an unmarked mass grave.

Klaus found that it wasn't hard to find the Jews either. They were listed as Jews on tax records or sometimes he would first find the Rabbi of a village and tell him that if he didn't write up a list of all of the Jews in the town, then he and his family would be executed on the spot and all the other Jews found would be killed. A Rabbi in such a position could not imagine that all his friends and acquaintances would be murdered regardless of what he did, so he believed that he would be saving lives by cooperating with Klaus.

This was simply another aspect of the terrorism which the Germans used so effectively. How could the Rabbi know that his actions were futile? Whether he cooperated or not, the results would be the same. The only difference being that his cooperation would make the job go quicker and that was Klaus' goal: expediency. "Let me kill you quickly because I must hurry off to kill many others before I am done."

When you ask how it was done, know that this was the fulcrum, that the Rabbi was uncertain and Klaus was not, that the victim still believed in the tenets of a society and the murderer had somehow become the legitimate force of the society. Ask yourself this question: if you were stopped by a policeman on the street for some ambiguous reason, would you suspect that his ultimate goal, that the purpose he knew of from the moment he saw you, was to kill you? If you have any respect for authority, any trust or faith in basic human dignity, then your answer is probably "no". Even beyond that, even if you had heard rumors of such murders in far off places, you probably wouldn't want to believe that such things happen, that they could happen to you. You would still want to believe that your life could not be taken so easily, so arbitrarily. Such a death would not only be a violation of what you believe of human society, but an even greater crime against the most basic human morality. Cold blooded killing is the realm of the insane, not a policy of governments. To begin to understand, you must first stop asking how the victims could have allowed themselves to be killed and begin to ask how the murderers could have allowed themselves to do it.

David had been released from Dachau in 1940, about a year-and-a-half after he was arrested on Krystalnacht. He didn't know why he had been released anymore than he had known why he had been arrested, beyond, of course, the crime of having been born a Jew. He had gone to live with his father when he was released, as he had no other place to go. The "authorities" had confiscated everything in his apartment when he had been arrested. They took everything, whether it had value or not. All of his manuscripts were gone, every personal item. All the little things that one collects over a lifetime as momentos; pictures, postcards and letters, the little stuffed bear he had as a baby that his mother insisted he keep for when he had a son or daughter of his own someday and even the little tin locket that his mother had given him just before she died with her picture as a young girl. He was 47 years old, but felt like a hundred. He had given his life to his work and never gotten married, so now he was alone.

David's father Sam was 72 and had given his hobby of watching politics a strange twist, he tried to combat his disenfranchisement with knowledge as though knowing what might happen could protect him from that fate. Sam knew about the einsatzgruppen. Such a straight-forward statement doesn't do justice to the situation. In a time when the Jewish population had been deprived of all rights due citizens of the country in which he lived, when rumors outnumbered the stars in the heavens and many of those rumors seemed inconceivable and ridiculous, Sam had sifted through all the information that he could find and had come up with the truth. It's like saying that a blind man could describe the face of a man he had never heard of nor met.

"They are killing them" he would say to David whenever the subject of the East would come up. David never replied. He couldn't deny it and yet the thought was too mind-numbing, that men, women and children were being murdered just because they were Jews. Even in light of that realization the peculiar nature of humans came into play. Sam believed that the German Jews would be spared, that the nazis were only killing the Polish Jews, the Jews who would not assimilate into German society, the Jews who were ancient and backwards, who were an embarrassment not only to the nazis, but even to the sophisticated German Jews.

"How bad would it get?" was the question Sam and David dared not ask themselves. Pogroms ended. They knew it would end someday, but when?

Not far away from Sam and David in Munich, Rebecca

Geschwind wasn't wondering about such things... She was just trying to keep everything together from day to day. That night she was putting her son, Thomas, to bed. She whispered the end of a bedtime story to him as he nodded off to sleep and then gently kissed him on the forehead. She had named him Thomas after her grandfather. He was just a little over three years old now and he never knew his father... nor did his father know him.

In Vienna, Louis Hoffman and his wife Eleonore and their daughters didn't wonder about such things either. They were sure that the worst was already upon them, that the worst had already happened and things would soon start to get better once the Russians were defeated and the Germans felt content with their conquests.

Ethan Stein, separated from his family, living alone in England, asked himself every night how long it would be until he could return to his family.

In Prague, Ivan was a bit annoyed at the rapid pounding of his heart. He had thought that he might control his fear and anxiety through sheer determination. He had thought about this meeting the night before and told himself specifically that it was nothing to worry about and that he need only keep repeating that to himself and then he would finally believe it and thus be able to stay calm. It was the nervous ones that always got caught. At least in his estimation. People who were nervous tended to forget details and, worst of all, people who are nervous always look guilty. He smiled to himself as he put out the tiny bit of cigarette that he had held so carefully as it started to burn his finger and thumb. Even a child knows that it is a bad thing to look guilty... you tend to get into trouble for things which other people have done, the wrong place at the wrong time as they say, but when you look guilty and you are guilty...

Janu seemed to dance up to the table in the cafe' as she moved towards the very pale, thin young man whom she was supposed to meet that night. She was formed of natural grace and beauty, the sort of woman who could never grow old in the eyes of a man, the sort of woman who seems older than she is when she is a child and much younger than her age when she is a woman. She let the newspaper fall carelessly on the table by Ivan's hand as she moved close to kiss him.

"What a day!" she said as she pulled a chair close to Ivan and sat down.

"Was there trouble?" Ivan asked under his breath, in a

clandestine tone that annoyed Janu. She was trying to be nonchalant and open in the way that two lovers might talk when they met over a bottle of wine after a long days work and here was Ivan sounding like a spy.

"No, not really," she said with a laugh and a playful nudge against his shoulder, "it was just so busy. There is so much going on at the station these days."

"Oh..." Ivan acknowledged with a laugh, a nervous little laugh.

Janu put her arm around him and gave him another little kiss, this time on the cheek, and pulled him towards her, rocking a little from side to side. "...and how was your day?"

A deep blush began to roll across Ivan's face as he looked at her, finally realizing as he tried to translate her actions into a coded message that she just wanted him to loosen up and be more at ease. He smiled and sighed a deep sigh. "Fine. My day was fine."

Neither of them looked more than twenty years old. Even though Ivan could not leave behind his stiff and stilted demeanor, it would have been hard to believe that these two young people sitting at a table in a little cafe' were anything more than children trying to navigate the awkward stages of a new courtship. They talked for a little while longer until Janu pulled her coat on and said that they should get going if they were to meet their friends. Ivan stood up and helped her with her chair and coat before picking up the newspaper and slipping it into a pocket which a friend had sewn on the inside of his coat. They then walked casually out of the cafe', bidding the waiter goodnight and then quickly turning down the first side street they came to. They embraced as they came to a little courtyard as though they were about to kiss goodnight, but this time when they pressed their faces close Janu whispered to Ivan. "This is the first of three lists. We must meet again on Wednesday and Saturday." She then let go of him and disappeared down one of the narrow little side streets.

Ivan walked quickly to the nearest tram stop. It was almost six o'clock and the curfew was at eight. He would have to hurry to meet his next contact and make it home before then.

Petr was sitting in the little cafe' where he, Matej and Jiri had met almost three years before. A radio played a German song in the back room, but it could be heard clearly in the bar since there were so few people there and none of them was talking above a whisper. He was thinking about that particular meeting, the meeting that ultimately resulted in Jiri's death. He thought about Jiri often, many times replaying the picture in his mind of Jiri riddled with bullets, laying on the floor of the garage, He wondered why he tortured himself so with that picture and finally decided that perhaps it was a way of reminding himself how dangerous this business was, or maybe he wanted to remind himself of why he kept at it. It was certainly more dangerous now with "the blond beast of Prague", as Heydrich had come to be known, sitting up in Hradcany castle indiscriminately issuing death edicts to any who might cross his path.

The title was a joke to Petr. Heydrich had achieved a title... he was a member of the nobility in the ignoble and obscene realm of arbitrary death. The story was going around Prague that Heydrich had visited St. Vitus, the place where the royal jewels of Bohemia were kept. When he heard that the crown was cursed, that if any but the royal heir to the throne of Bohemia should place the crown upon his head, that man would be cursed to die soon after, Heydrich laughed and insisted on placing the crown on his own head. The priest in attendance awaited divine intervention, but to no avail. Heydrich contemptuously tossed the crown back onto the pillow where he had found it and swaggered out of the room unscathed. One cannot be sure, but perhaps every Czech who heard that story wondered why the blond beast wasn't struck down then and there.

Petr saw Ivan before he actually saw him, his head jerking toward the door as he needed to confirm what he already knew. Ivan made no gesture of recognition as he worked his way over to Petr's table and quickly sat down. The man behind the bar quickly appeared at the table. Ivan was just about to pull the newspaper from his coat and was startled when he looked up and saw the bartender standing there looking at him. There was fear in Ivan's eyes, but the bartender, who had known Petr for some years and had some idea of what was going on but was not the sort of man who would get involved in such things one way or the other, pretended not to notice. "What would you like to drink?" he asked Ivan, who managed to stutter the word "beer".

"For God's sake, get hold of yourself!" Petr whispered to Ivan.

"Yes, yes... I'm fine." Ivan said in a normal voice, "It has been a long time. and how is your wife?"

Petr just rolled his eyes at Ivan's pathetic attempt to cover up his anxiety and just then an announcement came over the radio that the Fuhrer was going to deliver a speech. Petr looked over to the bartender and caught his eye, pointing to the room with a twisting gesture of his hand that suggested turning off the radio, but the bartender merely shrugged as Hitler began to mumble and then rage over the airwaves. "If they come in," the bartender explained, referring to the German soldiers, "and I don't have it on, I'll get in trouble."

Petr just shook his head and the bartender turned away. "Let's get out of here." but just as he stood up and pulled out some money to pay for their drinks, an SS trooper and a man in a trench coat entered the bar. It was obvious that the man in the trench coat was Gestapo just by the look of him, the smell of him. The man in the trench coat stood by the door and looked everyone over and almost everyone stopped for a moment at one point or another and nervously glanced over at him as he surveyed the room. Ivan discretely pulled out his newspaper as he talked to Petr, pretending not to notice the Gestapo man, and set the paper on one of the chairs beside him. The Gestapo man was busy walking over to the bartender.

"You. Do you serve Jews in here? Are there any Jews in here?" the Gestapo man asked in a loud voice.

The bartender looked up with a start. "What's that? What did you say? I'm sorry, but we were trying to listen to the Fuhrer's speech."

The Gestapo man hadn't even realized the speech was on and, just as the bartender had intended, he was taken aback. A couple at one of the tables began to smirk, but they stopped the instant the Gestapo man looked over at them.

"A filthy Czech telling me about a speech by the Fuhrer?" the Gestapo man started in a low growl as he addressed the bartender, about to launch into a tirade, but he was met by the bartenders own tirade. "Czech?!" the bartender started, "My family is from Passau. We are as German as you are. We are the Sudetendeutscheren that the Fuhrer freed in '38. ...and about the Jews. I have never served Jews in here and I never will. I am insulted that you dare say it!"

The Gestapo man stared at the bartender for a moment and then looked around the bar at the patrons once again. Nobody dared return his look. "Ja," he finally said, "Good. That is the way it should

473

be. Heil Hitler!" He then motioned to the trooper and they marched out.

Ivan let out a sigh of relief once he was sure the unwelcome visitors were far enough away. At just about the same time, a man and woman who had been sitting at a dark little booth in a corner of the bar rushed up to the bar and the man pumped the bartenders hand in an emphatic handshake and said something quietly to him as they quickly left. It seemed quirky to Ivan.

"What was that all about?"

"Silly ass," Petr chastised, "They're Jews, of course."

Ivan just shook his head. Even he, with his youth and naiveté, knew that if the bartenders bluff had failed and the Gestapo man had found the Jews, then everyone in the bar would have been scrutinized and the newspaper would have been found and the list and...

"Let's go, and this time I mean it."

Ivan was almost to the door when he remembered the newspaper on the chair and ran back to get it, handing it to Petr as they left.

"Here, you forgot your paper." Ivan said in a stilted, unnatural cadence as though trying to recite a prepared speech, "Janu said we should get together again soon... Wednesday and Saturday look good." He turned and walked away as soon as they got outside.

Petr sighed and turned in the opposite direction, heading home. He wondered how anyone could have thought that Ivan was ready for this kind of work.

Once he got home, Petr went directly to the kitchen where he found Hannah finishing up the preparations for that evenings dinner, just as he had expected, and he asked how much time it would be before they would be ready to eat.

"About half-an-hour."

"Good. I've got a few things to do out in the garage."

He looked about the yard as he slogged through the slushy snow on his way out to the garage, allowing himself to feel nervous for the first time that evening. It seemed to him that this was the time to be nervous, when everything seemed to be going perfectly and he might begin to think that he was safe. He suddenly had a fantasy of SS storm troopers rushing out from the bushes around the yard with their schmeisser sub-machine guns blazing, cutting him to pieces in his own back yard. He succumbed to an involuntary shudder as he forced the pictures out of his mind and pulled up the collar of his coat.

The garage door let out a loud moaning creak as Petr swung it out towards himself, leaving it open so that the moonlight would illuminate the room enough so that he could find the string for the light fixture which dangled from the ceiling. Once the bare bulb flooded the garage, Petr closed the door and pulled down the latch which locked it from the inside and began to stuff newspaper and kindling into the small cast iron stove in the corner. The small windows in the garage had been painted over with black paint years before because of the blackout restrictions and so Petr felt a certain degree of security as he finally pulled out the newspaper which Ivan had given him and began to rifle through it looking for the list which Janu had risked her life to get and pass on to the Czech resistance.

Janu was a clerical secretary in the central railroad offices through which the Germans sent their train routings and also information on cargo for verification at various checkpoints on route. She was one of many clerical workers who made sure that cargo lists of specific railroad cars matched the master lists of any given train, that is to say, any changes in groupings of cars as goods were distributed throughout Bohemia and Moravia. One of the newer types of cargo manifests was the listing of Jews and political prisoners by individual's names as a single type of cargo making up complete trains as they were being transported from the west into the recently completed concentration camp at Teresin which the Germans called "Theresienstadt". Janu was new to the partisans and as they didn't want to take any chances in being betrayed or on her being caught, she was not told who they were looking for. She was only asked to provide the entire list of names for a specific day.

It was these lists which Janu was spiriting out to her contacts. The partisans were trying to find one of their leaders, a woman named Zena Marusin who had managed to avoid summary execution by the Gestapo and was, according to their informants, about to be transported to the "kleine Festung", or "little fortress" as it would be called in english, at Theresienstadt.

The little fortress was a whitish-gray stone tower just past the red brick walls of the main camp at Theresienstadt where anyone who caused trouble in the camp was sent for special treatment and also a place where SS Totskopf guards would tend to other enemies of the

Reich.

Petr slowly ran his finger down the hand-written list, working to interpret the writing. The handwriting, presumably Janu's, was neat and handsome, but the ink had been smudged in several places, probably as a result of the writer working quickly and being interrupted constantly as she worked, having to repeatedly hide the paper and then pull it out later to continue.

Zena's name was not on the list. Petr checked the list, made up of two very full pages, three times, paying special attention to the smudged names to make sure he hadn't misread them. Name after name slipped past his finger, anonymous, meaningless names... Eleonore Hoffman. "Eleonore Hoffman..." he thought to himself as his finger paused. Why was that name familiar? Maybe his mind was just playing tricks. It wasn't such an unusual name. Perhaps he merely wanted to recognize one of the names, to somehow make these people mean something to him as he so casually passed over them all.

"No. Wait. Wasn't that the name of Amalie's sister?" Petr thought to himself as he lifted his finger from the list and pressed it thoughtfully to his lower lip, trying to remember, " She had talked about her sister often before and the husband. What was his name? Louis. Yes, that's it. The college professor. Louis Hoffman."

Petr then quickly ran his finger back down the list to Eleonore Hoffman's name and there below it was Louis Hoffman. There was an instant then that Petr almost smiled, as though he had a feeling of victory that one gets when sure that he has trapped an enemy, but then he was just as quickly ashamed at having felt it. Amalie was not the enemy, but Petr knew there was something strange about her from the way she had managed to get Jakob out of Gestapo headquarters some three months before. She could conceivably have been an agent, but that seemed a rather remote possibility. Whatever it was, Petr was sure that this would be the means to find out. She certainly wouldn't let her sister and brother-in-law and their children be sent to Theresienstadt if she had the means to prevent it.

He rested his arms on the work table, slouching over the list as he thought about how he would manufacture the intrigue which would make Amalie finally lay out her cards in this game of poker, when someone rattled the door knob. He bolted upright and, in an uncharacteristic burst of energy, reflexively went for the cast iron stove, disregarding the pain as he burned his fingers opening the door

476

of the stove and tossing both pages of the list inside.

"Petr" Karin called from outside, "mother said to come and get you... dinner is ready."

He quickly opened the door of the stove again when he realized that it was only his step-daughter looking for him, but the lists had already been reduced to shiny, black wrinkled cinder-sheets. No matter. He had already seen everything that he needed, but he would have liked to have passed them on to his superior. Now his superior would have to settle for Petr's report.

Hannah, Karin and Amalie were just sitting down at the table as Petr came into the kitchen. He stopped for a moment as he realized that something was missing. "Where's Jakob?"

After a week of recuperation around Christmas time, during which time he was attended to with loving concern by Karin, Jakob decided that even after his ordeal he wanted to go back to the apartment he had shared with Walter. Even though Walter had been sentenced to two years in prison for his part in distributing anti-nazi leaflets, Jakob didn't feel at all uncomfortable in finding a new roommate and going on as though nothing had happened. That was a talent of Jakob's, his ability to neatly package everything and put it quickly behind him as though nothing could affect him.

He did, however, end his boycott of his mother, suggesting that he would come and visit every Wednesday and Sunday evening, coincidentally at dinner time.

This was why it took a moment for Petr to realize what was missing on that cold March evening. He had to remind himself it was Wednesday and then it followed that Jakob should be there, sitting close to Karin and sharing their food rations...

"I don't know" Amalie said, responding to Petr's question.

"I haven't talked to him since Monday" Karin added.

"He's probably just late... He'll be here" Hannah concluded.

"Yes. I'm sure you're right" Petr said off-handedly as he began to eat, "after all, he seems to lead a charmed life." Petr was careful when he said it, not showing the coy smile which he felt tugging at the corner of his mouth as he took a noisy bite of a hot potato and gravy.

They all heard the rattle of the front door as Jakob came in and shook off the cold. He made his apologies for being late and asked everyone how they were as he took his place beside Karin and helped himself to the stew Hannah had made. It was a pleasant enough dinner with everyone sharing in the conversation, even Petr who usually didn't say much when he was eating. He surprised Amalie by asking her about her family, if she had heard anything recently.

Jakob asked Karin if she would like to go to a movie that evening and so they left as soon as they finished dinner. Hannah was busy clearing the dishes and insisted that Amalie needn't help since Amalie had done it all by herself the night before when Hannah wasn't feeling well.

Suddenly Amalie found herself alone with Petr in the living room. It occurred to her that Petr was acting strange that evening and that he must be up to something, but then she dismissed the thought, deciding that he was just in a good mood and she was being overly suspicious. Petr was sitting by the radio, reading a newspaper, and Amalie was trying to get into a book she had been reading for days when she suddenly noticed out of the corner of her eye that Petr wasn't really reading the newspaper. She glanced over quickly to see what he was doing. He was holding the newspaper up, but just enough so that it would cover his face and he could still see over it. He was watching Hannah as she cleared the table. "Now, that is strange" Amalie thought to herself. She found herself peeking over at Hannah in the kitchen, too. What was Petr looking at her for? When Hannah had cleared everything off the table and was over at the kitchen sink where she was out of sight of the living room, Petr looked over at Amalie only to find that she was already looking at him with a quizzical expression. He managed a weak smile, but it quickly disappeared as he moved his chair a little closer to her's and then slid to the edge of the seat so that he was closer yet.

"How..." Petr began, trying to bring up Eleonore and Louis, but then he decided to start with something different, "How was work today?"

"Work?" Amalie repeated with surprise since she had already discussed her day with Hannah at the dinner table while Petr sat beside them. "Work was fine."

"Good, good" he responded tritely as he was obviously distracted trying to think of what to say next.

"What is it Petr?"

"Amalie... I have some friends..."

"Yes?"

"Sometimes they know things, tell me things..."

"Things?"

"Yes. They tell me things that they find out, but I can't tell you how or where they hear these things."

"What is it Petr? What are you trying to tell me?"

"Amalie, you know all about the KL in Teresin, don't you?"

"I've heard of it."

"and you know they're sending Jews there."

"I thought it was political prisoners."

"That too, but now they're starting to send more Jews."

"From where, Prague?"

"Even from Vienna, well, important Jews from..."

"Important?"

"People who are well known. Especially those known outside of the country. It's for propaganda."

"Why are you telling me? Is it someone..."

"Your brother-in-law. It seems he must be well known in his field."

"Louis?" Amalie said with a start, but then she spoke out loud as she thought to herself: "Yes, of course. I guess I never thought about it, but he always seemed to be heading off somewhere to lecture on his precious plants." She then looked Petr in the eye. "Does that mean Eleonore and the girls too?"

"Yes. The whole family."

"When?"

"As near as I can tell, they should be arriving any day now. Tomorrow or the next day."

Amalie thought for a moment as she considered the news. "Will they be all right?"

"I don't know. From what I've heard of the political prisoners in Teresin, the Communists and Social Democrats... It's harsh."

"But are they in danger? Are they in danger right now?"

"If they do as they are told and don't try to escape..."

"Louis? Eleonore? Escape?!" Amalie replied, almost laughing at the thought of Louis attempting something so daring, "I couldn't imagine them taking any chances, especially if the girls are with them."

"Well then, they should be fine for the time being, but..."

"What?"

"There are rumors."

"What kind of rumors?"

"There's no proof. Just stories. From Poland."

"But this isn't Poland!" Amalie exclaimed, as though there was a magic boundary separating those places where terrible things happened from the place where people were kept safe. She had already heard the stories from Poland. You could get in trouble for telling such stories. You could get in trouble for just listening to such stories.

"No, of course it isn't." Petr said as he took Amalie's hand and patted it gently like a concerned uncle comforting a little girl who has just found out that her pet dog is missing.

"What can I do?"

"I don't know. I don't think there's anything that can be done. That's why I wasn't even sure if I should tell you."

"No, Petr. I'm glad you told me. At least I know what's going on. I hate not knowing more than anything else. At least I can..."

"Can what?" Petr asked with a certain controlled intensity as he felt she was about to confide in him.

"So, what are you two whispering about?" Hannah asked as she dried her hands on her apron while entering the living room.

"Whispering?" Amalie repeated, trying to cover up, "No, we were just talking about Jakob and Karin."

"Yes," Petr agreed, "things seem to have cooled off between them."

"Oh, I don't know..." Hannah said as she thought about it, "I think it just shook Jakob up when they..." She stopped in mid-sentence as though mentioning Jakob's arrest would bring misfortune. "I think he and Karin might be thinking about getting more serious."

"More serious?" Amalie said with a laugh.

"Perhaps." Hannah continued, preparing to explain her statement, "Maybe he knows what life is like now, that they aren't children anymore and it might be time to..."

"...to settle down?" Petr said with a smile, finishing Hannah's thought.

"Why not? It could happen like that." Hannah said defensively.

Karin, meanwhile, pressed against Jakob's arm, resting her head against his shoulder as they sat watching the movie. He didn't pull away, but he didn't put his arm around her like he used to do before. Karin looked up at him with big puppy-dog eyes hoping that he might smile or laugh at her and gather her up in his arms, but he didn't even notice. He just stared at the movie screen.

Jakob leapt to his feet once the movie was over, helping Karin on with her coat and quickly ushering her up the aisle and out of the theater.

"Can we stop for coffee or hot chocolate?" Karin asked as they hurried along.

"Hot chocolate? That's a bit optimistic, isn't it?" Jakob joked, referring to the food rationing.

"Well, coffee then."

Jakob only spoke to order when they stopped in at the small coffee shop. Beyond that he just stared out the window at the dark, gloomy buildings lining the street.

"Where are you these days?" Karin finally asked.

"What?" he said reflexively as he came out of his trance, "Oh, you know. Work or the apartment. That's all."

"That's not what I mean." Karin shot back, "You seem so far away."

He looked into her eyes for an instant and then turned away, as though he really couldn't explain to her because she couldn't possibly understand. "I'm lost. I can't even finish school now", he tossed his arms on the table and leaned closer to Karin, gesturing widely with his hands as he began speaking in a whisper. "Since the arrest, when I had to register as a mischling... They don't let Jews practice law and even if a half-Jew can work in a law office, nobody hires them. I wouldn't even be able to get a job if I could graduate."

"Things can't go on like this forever. Maybe we can go someplace else."

"There's no place to run to. Everything's different now. I'm a Jew. It's something you can't run away from."

"Jakob, what are you talking about?" Karin said with an uncharacteristic intensity, "I always knew. Nothing has changed for me. You were the one who was always running away from it, not me."

"I just...", he stopped in mid-sentence and stood up, tossing a couple of coins on the table "Let's get out of here." .

Once they were out on the street he started talking again. "I

481

can't figure out what my father was doing..." he said as they walked home, taking Karin by surprise. "He was a part of it."

"Of what?" Karin asked, not knowing what Jakob was talking about.

"He was a party member."

"I know. I heard your mother talking to my mother once."

There was a pause in the conversation as they walked. Karin tried not to let Jakob see as she looked at him out of the corner of her eye. His face was sad and serious.

"I can't believe it's been eight years since he died."

They kept walking.

"I've been thinking about Walter a lot."

Karin didn't know if he was expecting some kind of reply. He had always avoided the subject of his roommate's arrest.

"Walter and I were friends. We talked about things. We talked all the time, but now I don't know who he was."

"Does he remind you of your father?"

"What?" Jakob asked with surprise, stopping in mid step.

"Your father" Karin answered, defending her question, "You were talking about your father and then you started talking about Walter."

"Oh, I see what you mean. No, I was talking about... Well, I told you I was in the HJ when I was a boy."

"The Hitler Jungend? I don't get it."

"It's us."

"Us? You and me?" Karin asked, utterly confused and thinking that somehow her original fear was about to be realized and he was finally getting around to telling her that he didn't want her anymore.

"No. It's as if they define the truth. My father, Walter, my friends. They always said the same things, but none of it meant anything. The words and what really happened. They're everywhere. The newspapers, radio, the movies, they're in the streets and in the schools. I began to believe them, I began to believe, and then to know, that there was something wrong with my mother and her family for being Jews."

"I know."

"You know? I never said anything."

"Yes you did. All the time. Not right out, but it was always there. We all knew it."

482

Jakob was silenced. He was like a little boy caught in a lie, embarrassed and angry, wanting to deny the lie, but unable to.

"I've never dared to tell you because you've been so..." Karin was so overwhelmed that she could hardly get out the words that she had wanted to say for so long, "It's not the Jews like they say. The nazis are animals. They kill anyone who gets in the way."

"Shhh." Jakob said as he put his arm around her and started them walking again, "If someone heard you..."

"I've watched you for so long now and I've been afraid." she continued, " I don't know why you go along with your eyes closed. Is it your father? Is that why you..."

"I don't know. I suppose I thought I was safe if I was with them and against who they were against. This thing with Walter has changed things. He didn't have to do it. He wasn't one of 'them', the people who had to be afraid. I don't know why he did it and I never got a chance to talk to him about it."

"I think you do know why he did it."

Jakob looked at her. His reflex was to deny this too, but he didn't say anything. He did know why. Walter just had the courage that Jakob couldn't seem to find.

"I'm thinking of joining the resistance." he said as he straightened up from the hunched over position he had assumed when he had told Karin to keep her voice down. It was clearly bravado. He didn't believe it anymore than Karin did. It was only true in the sense that the thought crossed his mind, not that he would ever actually do it.

"Because of the arrest?"

"That's only a part of it. I kept trying to hold on to something that wasn't really there. I wanted to be a part of it, I guess because they seemed invincible. It seemed so sure that they would win and I guess in the back of my mind I thought there would only be two kinds of people: the conquerors and the conquered. I didn't want to be one of the conquered."

They arrived at Karin's house just as Jakob finished his self-absorbed soliloquy and he stopped at the gate to the yard.

"Aren't you coming in?" Karin asked. He just forced a half smile. "You aren't even going to come in and say goodnight to your mother?" she continued, trying to coerce him.

"No. You tell her goodnight for me." Jakob said as he leaned forward and gave Karin a gentle kiss on the cheek before walking away.

She stood there watching him as he walked away, waiting until he was out of sight before going inside.

Hannah was just coming downstairs towards the front door as Karin came in. "How was the movie?"

"Fine."

"Isn't Jakob with you?" she asked with surprise since Jakob usually came in with Karin after a date and helped himself to something to eat.

"No, he had to get home. I'm going to bed. Good night."

"Is everything all right?" Hannah asked, concerned with the curt, dull tone of her daughter's voice.

"No, I'm just tired."

Hannah made way for her daughter to pass on the stair landing as Karin went up to her room and then went into the living room where Amalie was reading.

"I guess Jakob and Karin had a fight."

"Oh, are they home?"

"Karin is. Jakob didn't even come in."

Amalie clicked her tongue. "That is a bad sign..." she said in a playful way, as though she knew that it couldn't be a serious problem between her son and Hannah's daughter.

"You're right" Hannah agreed, taking Amalie's meaning "It's probably nothing. Well, I'm off to bed."

"Good night." Amalie said, pretending to drift back into her book.

"Petr!" Hannah called out to her husband who she knew was around somewhere, but she didn't quite know where, "I'm going up to bed!"

"I'll be up in a while" came a response from the cellar.

"I can never imagine what he does down there all the time" Hannah muttered to herself as she started up the stairs.

Just as she topped the steps, Petr came out of the cellar, waiting in the doorway for an instant to be sure that Hannah continued down the hallway to the bedroom. Amalie glanced at him over the top of her book as he quietly worked his way into the living room and sat down beside her.

"Heydrich" he said, "Heydrich is the key."

484

She didn't know what he meant by it. She had hoped he would come to talk with her about it, about Eleonore and Louis and the girls, since they hadn't had a chance to talk all evening with Hannah coming in and out all the time, but this caught her off guard.

"The Reichsprotektor?" she whispered.

Petr just looked at her.

"You mean to get Eleonore and Louis out?"

"Of course. What else would I be talking about?"

"Why wouldn't I just go to Teresin and talk to someone at the camp?"

"Don't be stupid! Seidl would probably throw you in right behind your sister"

Petr's statement was like a splash of cold water in Amalie's face. She and Petr had always been... awkward. Neither really knew quite how to talk or act with the other. Their only common bond had been Hannah and each had assumed that the other, through their bond with Hannah, had to be a fairly decent person, but they had never really gotten on together. This was the first time Petr had called Amalie stupid, indeed the first time he had ever been short with her. Any time before when he was upset or annoyed with her, he simply removed himself from the situation by leaving the house.

"Who?"

"Siegfried Seidl. Seidl is the commandant of Theresienstadt."

"Then what do you suggest?" Amalie asked pointedly after regaining her composure.

"From what I understand, the camp is administered from Berlin. That's why I think you have to go to Heydrich, because he's the representative of Berlin here in Prague."

"But what could I say? How would I get through to talk to him?"

Petr let the question hang there. This would be the moment of truth.

"Petr? What is it?" Amalie persisted after waiting for a response.

"I've got to ask you a question Amalie. It's a hard question. It's hard because it means that we have to trust each other. I have to trust you in order to take the chance of asking you, and you have to trust me in order to answer."

Amalie didn't know what to make of it. He had said more to her that night than he had said in all the months they had known each other and none of it made sense to her.

"When Jakob was arrested," Petr finally began, "What did you do, what did you say to get him released? Do you know someone or are you somehow connected to..."

"Are you asking me if I work for the Gestapo?" she asked stoically.

"No, I just..."

"Well, I don't."

"That's not it. Amalie, I'm just trying to help and I just..."

"Petr, how could you even ask? How could you think it? After all this time in the same house..."

"It just seemed so strange."

"What? What seemed strange? What have I ever done that could make you believe such a thing?"

"You walked into Gestapo headquarters where your son was being interrogated and walked out with him under your arm an hour later."

"But he was innocent. He hadn't done anything."

"Since when has that mattered to the Gestapo?"

"The officer I talked to was... He was a nice man. He thought I was pretty. Is that so hard to believe? That he took pity on me?"

Petr didn't respond for a moment. He took his time pulling a cigarette out of his shirt pocket and lighting it, taking a long slow drag as he looked Amalie in the eye. She knew from that look that he didn't believe her. He wanted her to know that.

"Amalie, I just wanted to help you and your sister. If you can't trust me, then let us forget the whole thing here and now. It's getting late and Hannah will be down in a minute wondering what's kept me so I'm going to bed. You think about what I've said. I won't bring it up again. If you decide to trust me, then you'll have to tell me."

It wasn't until Petr disappeared up the stairs that Amalie realized she had been gripping the book that she had been trying to read all night so tightly that she had bent the hard cover. She felt alone. She wasn't sure if she could trust Petr at all. What if he was a Gestapo informant? What a joke that would be, the informant accusing her of being an informant. There was no one she could talk to about it.

She went to bed.

The next day she could hardly think of anything else. She wandered through an uneventful workday at the printing company

486

and finally made it home, finding Hannah bustling about the house as she finished her daily chores. They made small talk for a while as Hannah swept the hallway until Hannah caught Amalie off guard with an unexpected question.

"So, what were you and Petr talking about for such a long time last night after I went up to bed?"

Hannah smirked as she caught a glimpse of Amalie's startled expression out of the corner of her eye.

"We were just talking about work and... oh yes, we were talking about Karin and Jakob. and other things. Just talking."

"So you're not trying to steal my husband away from me?"

Amalie laughed. The relationship between Petr and Amalie had always been so obviously strained, so "proper" and distant in all the time they had known each other.

"I'm glad you two are getting along" Hannah said in counterpoint to her previous suggestion, but when Amalie stopped laughing abruptly, Hannah looked up to see what was wrong. "Hannah, I've found out some terrible news... It's Eleonore and Louis. I've heard they're being sent to the camp in Teresin."

"Oh no."

"...and I don't know what to do. I've got to ask you something. I couldn't come out and ask Petr..."

"Ask him what?"

"If he knew anyone who might... Does he know anyone in the German command."

"No! Why would you even think that?

"I was hoping. I thought that since he works with..."

"No, it's just the opposite. He works with them because he has to, but he hates..."

Hannah caught herself before she went too far. She knew it was dangerous to get carried away when talking, even in her own home.

"Amalie, we've known each other for a long time and you've been living here since..."

"...and I've always been grateful, for what you've done for all of my family."

"Yes, and I was always glad to help, but this is..." Hannah faltered, her voice breaking, and she leaned the broom against the wall and joined Amalie sitting on the stairs. Just as she sat down, the broom fell over, making a ear-shattering bang as it slapped against the polished wood floor. Hannah let out a little shriek as they both jumped.

"...as if I weren't already nervous enough." Amalie said as she took a deep breath.

"You don't know who to trust these days..." Hannah said sadly. Amalie listened quietly, wondering if they were still talking about the same thing.

"Amalie, I'm going to take this chance. I'm going to take a chance with our very lives and tell you something... I think Petr works with the resistance. I don't know for sure. He's never said it to me, but I think he's involved with them."

While Amalie and Hannah were discussing the fate of Amalie's sister and brother-in-law, Klaus Grunewald was resting in a hospital a couple of hundred kilometers away in a remote area of Czechoslovakia, a mental hospital out in the country far away from the war.

The doctor who was assigned Klaus' case was looking over the file before talking to his patient. Klaus had had a nervous breakdown. Another officer found him sitting on the floor in the corner of his office quietly repeating the words "so much to do" to himself over and over.

"So, Major Grunewald, what can you tell me about why you're here..." the doctor said as he pulled up a chair beside Klaus' bed.

"I don't really know. I would guess it was just fatigue. I was having a lot of trouble sleeping."

"Sleeping? What kind of trouble?"

"I just couldn't seem to get comfortable. I would lay there and..."

"...were you tired?"

"My God, yes! I would be so tired that I couldn't stand up, but then when I went to sleep..."

"You did sleep then?"

"No. That was the strange thing. I would fall asleep and think I had been sleeping for some time, but then I would awake with a start and find that I had only been sleeping for a few minutes and then I couldn't get back to sleep at all."

"What woke you?"

"I don't know."

"Was it a noise or... perhaps an 'itch' of some sort?"

"No. Nothing like that."

"Dreams? Did you have nightmares?"

"Not that I recall. I don't dream."

"You don't dream?"

"No."

"Come now Major. Everyone dreams."

"Not me. I haven't for the longest time."

"That's very hard to believe. It's more likely that you just don't remember your dreams. What is the last dream you can remember?"

"The last dream?" Klaus repeated thoughtfully as an image flashed in his mind of the recurring nightmare he had experienced after he shot Gunther Metzdorf, the dream of a bloody river sweeping them both along as they fought to simultaneously drown and save one another. "I don't remember my last dream." he finally said.

"Well then... I'd like you to keep paper and pencil here by your bed . Now that we've talked about dreams you'll probably start to dream and I want you to write down whatever you remember as soon as you wake up."

That night Klaus lay awake in bed. He was restless and edgy as he thought about sleep and the possible dreams he might find there. He fought against the sleeping pills the nurse had given him until finally, lost in the tossing confusion of fatigue, he slipped away. He awoke with a start, thrashing wildly as he sat up. He knew something was terribly wrong as he came out of sound sleep. There was something jabbing him in the side. He turned to look and found that he was lying on top of someone. It was a bony elbow that was jabbing him and he suddenly realized that it wasn't just one person, he was lying in a pit of bodies. He looked around and suddenly saw Katrina, his wife, naked and dead, her body just one of the many. He saw his son Hans, but not as the husky seventeen-year-old of 1942, he was looking into the dead, opaque eyes of a little boy of three or four, naked and dead, laying on the mountain of bodies.

"Shhh!" came a little boy's voice from beside him. It was Ernst, another of his three sons, also a little boy, four or five-years-old, laying naked amongst the other naked bodies smeared with blood. "Don't say anything" Ernst continued, "He's coming to finish the wounded. Pretend you're dead and he might just pass by."

Klaus looked up. It was the ravine. That ravine by Kiev where they had been ordered to kill the Jews in the fall of 1941, thousands of them, tens of thousands. He had been one of the officers in charge. They forced the Jews to undress and then go stand by the edge of the ravine, facing the open pit filled with the bodies of men, woman and children who had already been killed. A soldier of the einsatzgruppen would then rake their bodies with machine gun fire and they would fall into the pit, bodies on top of bodies, a moaning writhing mountain of humanity. If they were lucky, they died instantly. The rest would be smothered by others falling on top of them and die slowly of their wounds. The officers would circle the pit looking for survivors and shooting them with their pistols. The operation even drew tourists; off-duty soldiers and a group of German engineers working nearby. Klaus saw himself walking along the wall of Babi Yar with his pistol out, shooting anyone who moved. He came closer and as Klaus looked up at himself on the edge, he saw himself smile and then he shot Ernst who shook with a violent twitch and then lay still in the midst of the other dead. Klaus started crying.

"You bastard!" he shouted at himself up on the rim. The Klaus standing above him only laughed as he aimed the pistol at himself in the pit and fired.

Sweat was pouring down his face as he woke up again. This time he was back in the hospital. He picked up the pad of paper and the pencil, held it for a moment and then laid it back on the table. He wouldn't get back to sleep that night.

That afternoon the doctor returned to see how he was doing.

"Any dreams?"

"No," Klaus said, "nothing."

Chapter 17

Politics is a strange game, even in wartime, perhaps especially in time of war. Eduard Benes was the head of Czechoslovakia's government in exile in Britain, but there was a functioning government in Germany's protectorate of Bohemia and Moravia which felt they were doing just fine without the interference of the government that had fled in the face of German aggression. Benes felt he had to take action to show that he was actually in charge of the Czech soul and not the collaborators in Prague. There weren't many ways to actually prove this, however, and so the Benes government spent months searching for a means to assert themselves. They finally decided that the way to gain respect of the Allies, in particular their British hosts, and thereby assure that when the war was over that they would be returned to power in Czechoslovakia, was to instigate Czech resistance against the Germans. Little could Eduard Benes know, as is so often the case with politicians tinkering away behind the scenes to assure their own position, the terrible chain of events he would set in motion by his self-serving actions.

"Thank you for coming Herr Stein."

"You may call me 'Mr.' Stein. I speak very good English. I've been here for some time now."

"Yes, I see here that you emigrated in '38."

"Correct. Soon after the Anschluss."

"We understand you spent some time in Prague?"

"Yes. My daughter and I... and my grandson. We stayed in Prague after the Anschluss. My daughter and grandson are there still, to the best of my knowing."

"...and why is that?"

Ethan felt an involuntary twitch. So this was to be an interrogation after all, even if they did call it a "voluntary de-briefing" for anyone who wanted to help the war effort.

"They couldn't afford the trip. I was to go first and then, when they got the money, they were to come later, but the Germans entered Prague before they could get away."

"I see you spent time in a camp... released in '40?"

"Ja. An English camp. They let me out because of my age. I am now 69 years."

"Clean bill of health..."

Ethan didn't know quite what to make of that statement. Perhaps the officer meant his politics, or maybe he had some medical record in the dingy beige file that he kept leafing through as he asked his questions, the file that was clearly stamped "Enemy Foreign National" in red ink across its face.

"Do you know anything of military matters Herr Stei... I mean, Mr. Stein?"

"In what way, military?"

"Did you have a chance to observe any military facilities in Austria before you left? In Salzburg?"

"No. If you mean the Germans, once again I left just before they got there. We left Salzburg two months before the Anschluss, although my grandson only left the day before they came."

"The day before? Why did he wait so long?"

"He didn't want to leave. He only came to Prague by accident. He came to see me in the hospital and that just happened to be the day the Germans entered Austria."

"Why didn't he want to leave?"

"He was... he was young. Just a boy. He thought he knew better than his mother and me. He wanted to be a man. By himself."

"Oh, I see. Just at that age, eh? Time to get away from mother and strike out on his own."

Ethan allowed himself a faint smile as the British office became more relaxed and familiar. "Ja, that's it."

"What about your son-in-law? It says here that he was a... party member?"

Ethan was embarrassed. He was also a little angry. It was so obvious. The officer makes him comfortable with a bit of talk about how understandable it was about Jakob and then he asks about Gunther.

"Ah... yes... Gunther was killed in '34"

"By whom?"

"What does that matter?"

"Do you know who was responsible?"

"We don't know. Myself, I think it was the purge. The SS."

"Where does your daughter live?"

"The last I heard, she was still living with her friend on the street called Busovice."

"A man friend?"

"No, no. Nothing like that. A woman. Another widow named Bauer, Hannah Bauer."

"Is your daughter a party member?"

"A party member!? She's Jewish!"

"She was married to a party member."

"Yes, but that was long after they were married. That was in the early days. She didn't know what a nazi was. We hadn't even heard of them back then."

"Why did she stay with him?"

"That would seem to be a question you would have to ask her."

"She never talked with you about it?"

"My relationship with my daughter was... There was a period of time when we didn't talk."

"... and why was that?"

Ethan glared at the officer. "I don't know that it's any of your business. I thought we were to talk about things relating to the war."

"I'm sorry. I didn't mean to offend you, but we are hoping to make contacts in certain cities and one way is if we make contact through family members. I was just interested in how your daughter

493

might feel about the Germans in Prague."

Images flashed in Ethan's mind of his departure from Prague. The conversation with Amalie about the package he brought with him to England, the evidence from the murder of Hindenburg and the other papers. He had decided to come in and talk with the intelligence service because he hoped that it would somehow help Amalie and Eleonore, but he didn't know if he should say anything about the package. On the one hand he knew that they would probably demand the evidence be turned over at once, but on the other hand he felt helpless doing nothing with the package.

The time had come in Prague. After a few days of sparring about, Amalie and Petr had come to an understanding. Amalie told Petr she had "valuable information" and he told her, in vague terms, about his connections with a Czech resistance group. He insisted that the only way to help Eleonore and her family was by making contact with Heydrich, a face to face meeting where she would threaten international publication and exposure. Plain and simple blackmail.

Petr had nothing to lose by this tactic. His goal was to disrupt the Germans in any way that he could, and this seemed as good a way as any. If Heydrich ignored the threat and Amalie published whatever she had, it would make good propaganda for the underground. If Heydrich believed Amalie on the other hand, then Amalie could certainly be useful to the resistance movement.

"We have set up a meeting."

Amalie was startled. "A meeting? With the Reichsprotektor? When?"

"The first Tuesday in May. The fifth."

"Two weeks? Why so long?"

"He's a busy man."

"What do I say Petr? What did you tell him?"

"Me? I didn't talk to him. It was set up through other people. He doesn't even know your name."

"What was he told?" Amalie asked as she raised her hands to her head, "My God, what am I supposed to say to him?!"

"You just have to tell him what you told me. That you have some information..."

"...and then what? They arrest me on the spot?"

"No. We have something else arranged."

"What?"

494

"I don't know exactly. I was told that it was best if we didn't know. That way we couldn't betray them."

"Betray them? What about me, alone in Gestapo headquarters?"

"You will have to trust them."

"Trust them? They don't even trust me enough to tell me what will happen and I'm supposed to give them blind trust?"

"Amalie, have you forgotten that you were the one who came to me, who asked me to help you? Don't forget that I am here with you. You could betray me, and I'm willing to take that chance."

"I would never betray you."

"You don't know that until the time comes. No one can be sure what they would do if the Gestapo" Petr stopped. He didn't want to scare her, but he wanted to make his point. "No one."

There was a moment of silence as they both became lost in their thoughts, Amalie worried about the whole thing and Petr trying to organize it all in his head.

"I'm already compromised because we live in the same house. I can't do any more work for the resistance unless something changes. They'll check my background, and Hannah and Karin, and watch us all carefully."

"Then we should tell Hannah and Karin." Amalie said thoughtfully as she followed Petr's exposition.

"I'm not sure."

"We have to tell them something" she insisted.

Petr glared at her. This was one of the things that always got in the way between them. She never let him just say something. She always challenged him. Not like Hannah and Karin. He knew Hannah and Karin would be satisfied with whatever he chose to tell them, but Amalie would cause trouble and insist that they knew everything. He felt it would be too much of a risk if they knew.

"For God's sake, can't you just take my word for it!" he shouted unexpectedly, "It is safer for them not to know! Don't you care about their safety?"

Amalie was beaten down by the barrage. She was already nervous and on edge and this seemed unfair. She was sure that she cared about Hannah and Karin even more than Petr, but she didn't say anything. She knew he was hard and cold and she often wondered why Hannah ever married him, but she said nothing.

It was hard getting through the next days. The thought of her

495

impending meeting with Heydrich was never far away. It came to her a number of times that she should just ask Petr to cancel the whole thing, but then she thought of Eleonore and the girls and it steeled her resolve.

"Your 2:00 appointment is here Herr Reichsprotektor" barked the young SS captain who served as Heydrich's secretary.

"Who is it?" Reinhard asked without looking up from the paper on his desk, annoyed that he had to ask.

"I'm afraid I don't know Herr Reichsprotektor. If you recall, this is the meeting that was scheduled..."

"Oh, yes. That's right. Today is our mysterious guest." Heydrich said, looking up and addressing his secretary. "The man who..."

"It is a woman Herr Reichsprotektor" the captain interrupted.

"A woman..." Heydrich said with a smile, "The woman who has information of 'a most important nature to the well being of the German Reich'."

Heydrich stood up and walked to the front of the desk. "Well, send her in. Send her in. Such an important person must not be kept waiting. And Artur, make sure we are not disturbed."

Amalie was determined not to show fear. Petr had told her "these men are like dogs, wild dogs... they smell fear".

"Good afternoon, Fraulein." Reinhard said, playing a game of congeniality as he extended his hand to take Amalie's, raising her hand to his lips, but not actually kissing it.

"Good afternoon, Herr Reichsprotektor." Amalie replied as Reinhard directed her to sit in a chair beside the highly polished and ornate desk while he returned to his chair.

Just then the telephone rang and Heydrich snatched it up before the first ring ended. "I said we were not to be disturbed!" he said in a very firm voice.

"This is not your secretary." the voice on the other end said calmly.

Heydrich glanced at Amalie and then turned slightly away from her as he continued the conversation. "Who is this?"

"This is a friend of the lady seated beside you."

"What? What are you talking about?"

"I have called to make sure that you understand that she is not alone. We have managed to get into your headquarters and make a direct line to the telephone in your private office and even now we can see you and the woman."

"That is impossible."

"Hold up your hand Herr Heydrich."

"What?"

"Raise your hand and extend your fingers. I will tell you which hand and how many fingers."

"What kind of game is this?" he as..ed and then turned to Amalie accusingly, "Who is this on the telephone? Where are they?"

Amalie was taken completely by surprise and wasn't even completely sure that Reinhard was talking to her.

"Well, who is it?" he persisted as he cupped the receiver in his hand and glared at her.

"I...I... how could I know, Herr Reichs...?" Amalie stammered.

Reinhard turned back to the telephone and began shouting into the receiver "...Tell me who this is right now or I'll have this bitch arrested and shot!"

Amalie was terrified as she listened without any idea of what was happening.

"Now, now, Herr Heydrich... by the by, you extended two fingers of your left hand as he held the telephone receiver up."

"Do not toy with me," Reinhard said slowly in an ominous tone which was incongruous with his high pitched voice, yet it was all too clear how dangerous he was, "if you want her to get out of here alive."

"Herr Heydrich, we have only telephoned you as a courtesy so that you would know that the woman is serious and that she is not alone. You should know that we could have killed you just now, but this is more important than that. Listen to her Herr Heydrich. She has important information and I'm sure you will agree to let her leave once you have talked with her."

A loud click let Reinhard know that the conversation was over. His first impulse was to call in his officers and have them search the building, but he realized it would surely turn up nothing. There would be time for a search later. Now it was time to talk with this woman. His anger was overcome by curiosity. He loved a good competition and this seemed to have the potential to be an excellent game.

"You have the advantage of me" Reinhard said once he had regained his composure and turned all his attention back to Amalie.

Amalie was still reeling from his telephone references to having her arrested and shot and she couldn't imagine what possible advantage she might have attained.

"Your name." he went on, as though there had been no threats a moment before and he was just continuing the polite protocol he had begun when she first entered the room, "You know my name, but I don't know yours."

"Amalie" she said as though suddenly waking out of a dream.

"Amalie... A lovely name. I suppose you don't have a last name. No. No one ever does in these matters. It isn't done."

"Herr Reichsprotektor, I have come to ask for your help." Amalie said, thinking that she could start just by asking for help and hopefully she wouldn't have to resort to blackmail.

"My help?" Reinhard repeated with a note of incredulity, realizing how lost she was.

"I have a friend who has somehow... I'm sure it is a mistake. Somehow my friend has been sent... I can't imagine how it happened, but I've been told my friend has been sent to the Theresienstadt camp."

"Would you like a glass of water? Perhaps some coffee or tea?"

Amalie was stunned by the non-sequitur "Yes, a cup of coffee would be..."

Reinhard picked up the telephone. "Artur, please bring in a cup of coffee for my guest."

"Now, who is this friend, Amalie?" Reinhard asked politely, assuming that she would name some partisan leader in the kleine Festung, thereby confirming Gestapo information on who was who and letting him know by her request just who the most important inmate was in the prison.

They were then interrupted by an SS trooper in white gloves who brought in a coffee tray.

Reinhard waited patiently for the name as the coffee was served and Amalie took a first sip and smiled at him.

"There now... where were we? Ah, yes. Who was this friend of yours?"

"Professor Louis Hoffman... and his wife... and two daughters. They are from Vienna and I can't imagine why they were..."

"A Professor? In what field?"

"Botany."

"Botany?"

498

"Yes. Plants."

"Of course. and what is your relationship to this man?"

"The Hoffmans are friends of the family and we were worried..."

"Hoffman... A Jew?"

"I think he might..."

"If they are in a camp, they must be an enemy of the Reich." Reinhard pronounced.

"Oh, I'm sure not. Louis would never do anything..."

"If he was a Jew trying to teach children in Vienna..."

"I don't believe he has taught for months now, Herr Reichsprotektor."

"What exactly is it you want me to do?"

"I was hoping you could look into it and..."

"Why?" Reinhard asked, his voice beginning to rise, "Why would I look into this like some clerk dealing in the filthy details of the life of some dirty little Jew?" Reinhard then rose from his chair, leaning over his desk, "Why? I don't understand what you are doing here."

Amalie was backed into a corner. She had been afraid from the moment she walked in the door, but suddenly she was calm. She had feared it would be like this and now that it was, her fear was gone, as were her illusions that she might not have to resort to blackmail.

"I am here so that we might come to an understanding." she said, pointedly leaving out the title 'Herr Reichsprotektor' as she said it.

"An understanding? What kind of understanding?" Reinhard asked as he sat back down.

"I have some information, Herr Reichsprotektor, which would be... embarrassing. It would most likely cause a crisis in the government."

"Fascinating" Reinhard said with a smile. "Of all the people who have come into this office... A woman comes in and actually tries to blackmail me. What is it? A child somewhere? Some little bastard to be presented to a Gauleiter? You'll have to give me some particulars if you expect to get out of here Amalie, some very impressive particulars."

Amalie was unfazed. "I actually have a number of pieces of material, but today I have only brought a photographic print of a document. A document, I might add, that is safely out of the country and held by someone awaiting instructions. By that I mean that if I am not able to contact them, then it will be published."

Amalie handed Reinhard the photographed pages of the confession of Johann Nepomuk Heidler, confessing the Jewish birthright of Alois Hitler, Adolf Hitler's father. She waited patiently as Reinhard quickly skimmed over the pages. She then took great satisfaction as Reinhard went over the first page one more time, this time carefully running his finger over the key text. She knew that he knew it was legitimate. What she couldn't have known was that this had been the exact thing Heydrich had been looking for throughout Austria for four years. The Austrian prime ministers Dollfuss and Schuschnigg had intimated that they had such information, but after the Anschluss Reinhard had failed to turn up any documents as he searched from Salzburg to Austria. Now here it was in his hands.

"An obvious forgery!" Reinhard declared as he tossed the pages at Amalie.

Amalie smiled.

Reinhard didn't give an inch. "Do you understand what the penalties for forgery are in the Reich, Amalie? ...and I think you should understand that this sort of thing... in wartime, this could easily be considered treason. Do you know the penalty for treason?"

"We..." Amalie said hesitantly as she realized all at once that there really was a 'we', "are prepared to publish this information."

"All for this... what was his name? Hoffberg? Hoffstein?"

"Hoffman."

"Yes. Hoffman. You're willing to risk everything for this Hoffman?"

Amalie didn't reply since the answer was already obvious. There was no turning back now.

"We will need time to check into all of this, to find your Hoffman friend."

"Of course. I will be back next week." Amalie said as she stood up.

Reinhard rose and met her at the door, blocking her way. "May I see the document again?"

"Certainly. I have a number of duplicates if you would like another."

"No. This one should do" Reinhard said with a smile as he took her arm and led her to the outer office.

Amalie fought to maintain her calm as he held her arm. It was clearly the gentle hold of an escort rather than the grip of a jailer, but she knew it was meant to unnerve her.

"What day will you return? I'll have Artur make an appointment."

"I think it best if I surprise you, Herr Reichsprotektor."

"You already have surprised me, Amalie."

Amalie managed a weak smile in reply and then walked confidently out of the office, firmly closing the door behind her. Reinhard stood at the door, raising his hand to silence Artur who was about to reprise him of the details of his next meeting. Reinhard was listening to Amalies footsteps. Once she had closed the door behind her, her measured pace turned into a quick trot, just short of a dead run. Reinhard smiled.

"Artur, I want a complete investigation on her. The only name she gave was Amalie."

"Is that all?"

"Yes. Have somebody ready all next week to follow her as soon as she comes in and I want a search of all the buildings that can be seen from my window. Send in Dietrich and Messner. I'll give them the details."

"This afternoon?"

"Now. Immediately."

Amalie was already well out of Hradcany and down the steep decline heading towards the Charles bridge. She wanted to head away from home, away from anything that might connect her to family or friends. She might be followed. She stopped suddenly as she passed by a non-descript storefront with the name "Petterink" above the door, a small shop dealing in the design and building of specialty furniture, and looked back to see if she could spot anyone following her.

Believing she had made good on her escape, she turned down a narrow street and continued on her way.

Inside that store, Petterink's, a boy of twelve sat in a corner by the window whittling away at a stick of pine, hoping to bring forth a handsome pony from the warm wood with its interwoven streaks of orange, white and yellow. This boy's name was Josef. Josef whittled there because his brother had been arrested by the nazis and sent to a labor camp in Germany.

Josef had always admired his brother and wished that he could be like him with his excellent standing at the university and his ability to make friends with anyone, to win the respect of almost everyone he knew, except of course the nazis. It was when the brother joined the protests against the Germans that he was arrested and sent away and that was when Josef truly learned to hate the Germans. His hatred was the reason that he jumped at the chance to be a lookout for Petterink. Not the old man Petterink who owned the store, but his son, Stephan, who had known Josef's brother and asked Josef if he wanted to "help out" against the Germans. Josef watched out the window as he carved, and if a German, whether he be civilian or soldier, came into the shop, Josef was to stomp twice on the floor.

Stephan Petterink was down there below, in the basement with two other men named Josef. Josef Valcik and Josef Gabcik were in hiding. These two men had been trained as commandos by the British and had parachuted into Czechoslovakia in late December of 1941 with another commando on a mission supported by Eduard Benes, the former president of the Czechoslovakian republic and the leader of the Czech government in exile in England.

"When are we moving?" Valcik asked nervously of his host.

"We were told to wait for Kubis. He's on his way" Stephan answered through the pale fog of cigarette smoke.

"When?" Gabcik asked insistently.

"Soon." Stephan reiterated, "They might wait until dark before coming in, but he will be here by tonight at the very latest."

"It's the waiting that's maddening." Gabcik said as he ground out a cigarette butt on one of the ancient planks of a rickety old table, "I'll do the job. I'm not afraid, but let's just get it over with."

"The time has to be right" Valcik countered, "If we rush into it we might miss him and just get ourselves killed in the process."

"Killed? Not me. I met a beautiful girl in London before we left. I promised I'd be back."

Valcik laughed. "I thought you had a girl in Brno."

"She's for after the war. Linda is just 'for the duration'."

"Well, let's have a go at another hand of cards."

"I'm going up." Stephan said as Valcik began dealing, "Remember, if you hear two knocks on the floor, kill the light and be ready to head out toward the river if someone comes to the first door."

502

There was a huge old door with a notoriously squeaky hinge which opened onto the hallway that led to the door to the cellar and that first door could be clearly heard as it vibrated through the old floor boards. It was a perfect and natural warning alarm. The cellar where Gabcik and Valcik were waiting was actually an old coal room, separate from the rest of the cellar and with a small door which, while out of sight, exited close to an alley. There was even a rusted ladder for access to the roof in the small vestibule where the door let out to the alley so that if they saw their escape blocked in the alley, they could go up to the roof and work their way across to other buildings.

Stephan went up through the small workshop and out to the front where Josef was contentedly working on his carving.

"How is it coming?"

"Good. Look at the mane. The wood gives it such a pretty color."

Stephan took the sculpture and studied the pony's flowing orange mane. "You're getting better all the time. You'll be an expert carver before this war is over."

Josef smiled, but said nothing. He knew that jokes were a luxury. If you let yourself talk too freely, even with friends, you might make a mistake when it really counted and so even this little boy told himself to be careful with every word.

"You go home. I'll take over here."

They only kept watch from the window during business hours. Once the night came they posted a man on the roof. Stephan had run a wire up from the cellar to the roof, mixed in with the telephone wire so that it looked inconspicuous. The wire connected a switch on the roof with a bell down in the cellar as a warning system if the Germans should appear. It was an elaborate system considering that the commandos would only be staying in that particular cellar for a couple days, but the importance of their mission dictated that they take whatever precautions possible. The Germans had known of their presence within days of their arrival in Czechoslovakia, so by May they had been on the move for months, just barely managing to stay ahead of the Germans. Although hot on their trail, the Germans didn't know the objective of the commando's mission.

Stephan looked up from a book he was reading just as someone appeared outside the storefront window and headed for the door. It was one of his contacts. Stephan got up and went behind the counter.

"Good afternoon."

"Yes" the man nodded in acknowledgment, "Is the cabinet finished?"

"Not quite. Everything should be together by this evening. When do you want it delivered?"

"That's not definite. Can you store it?"

"Until the weekend, but no later."

"We need to see if the trolley man can take delivery." The man said, referring to Petr Hrmeni.

"I've heard he's not feeling well. He said his uncle will soon be moving in with him to keep an eye on him." Stephan said, meaning that Petr had gotten word to him that the Gestapo might be watching Petr constantly, although he didn't go as far as to tell Stephan about Amalie and Heydrich.

Amalie and Petr tried to be subtle once she finally made it home after her round about journey home, but Hannah knew there was something going on when Amalie went out to the garage after dinner just "to see what Petr was up to". Once they were alone, Amalie told Petr about the meeting and the strange telephone interruption and Petr explained that it must have been from the contact who had set up the meeting in the first place. They, the people who were higher up in the resistance organization than Petr, had contacted Petr that afternoon and had decided that the next meeting would be on the following Wednesday. Amalie would arrive at Hradcany un-announced just as Rheinhard Heydrich arrived at his office, hopefully giving them the element of surprise, and then there would be a diversion set up for Amalie's exit although Petr hadn't been told what form the diversion would take. Petr had been told that from that day on contact between Petr and the others would be kept to a minimum and he was to immediately destroy any sort of records that he might have.

There was quite a buzz among the small group in Heydrich's office who had been informed in vague terms of Amalie's visit. The search of buildings outside Reinhard's window had turned up nothing, which indicated to Rheinhard that this was a serious threat. All of the offices in the nearby buildings where someone might have been able to watch Rheinhard and Amalie were occupied by German military personnel and the investigation showed no opportunity for someone to get in and out of any of those offices undetected. The three storerooms that might have been used as observation posts had no telephone lines and there were sentries routinely posted on rooftops in the Hradcany area. Whoever had made that telephone call was very adept. Even the telephone line connection which made the direct link to Heydrich's office telephone was so ingenious as to be untraceable. Whoever had done this was very good at it.

"The information which she has given me appears to be authentic" Rheinhard said as he ran his fingers through his hair while trying to put the pieces of this puzzle together. "She had a decidedly German..." he continued, but then quickly corrected himself, "Bavarian accent. It could have been Austrian."

"Possibly Sudetendeutscherin?" Captain Dietrich offered.

"More likely Austrian if the blackmail involves..." Obersturmbannfuhrer Messner began, about to finish his sentence with the name "Hitler" as he made the connection between Hitler and his birthplace at Braunau am Inn in Austria, but he decided against it. If Rheinhard Heydrich had decided to omit the name of the Fuhrer from this investigation, Messner didn't want to be the one to bring it up.

Rheinhard looked up at Messner as he spoke. The look in Reinhard's cold blue eyes was that of an attack dog which had just posed itself, holding perfectly still, leading an observer to wonder whether the look foreshadowed a vicious attack or a wagging tail. "We should not overlook the possibility that she may be Austrian" he finally agreed, inwardly amused as he saw Messner's almost imperceptible reaction of relief as the slip passed. Rheinhard enjoyed the power, the power of fear which he commanded in even his own close associates.

"Shall we try to make a sketch?" Dietrich asked.

"Yes. Have an artist come and talk to Artur. I'll look at it after he's done. She said she'll be back next week. I want a camera installed by Artur's desk by tomorrow morning. She shouldn't know she's being photographed."

"It is of primary importance that we appear to accede to her demands until we can determine the true nature of the threat."

"Of course, Herr Reichsprotektor."

"She must not know she is being followed when she leaves here. We have to find out how many are involved and take them all at once."

They continued to iron out the details of their counter-attack against Amalie and her group of traitors until they were sure that they would be completely prepared for her next visit. A Gestapo man was assigned each day to wait in an adjoining office, an agent who was to be costumed in a slightly worn suit so that he would blend in with any average crowd of Czechs in the city, ready at an instants notice to follow her. There were also agents posted inconspicuously outside Hradcany in the park. They were to take up the chase once the first agent had followed Amalie outside and identified her as the target. The first man would then conveniently allow her to outrun him so that she would believe she had made it out safely while the other agents continued the chase.

"This is the dress you will wear on Tuesday. The twenty-seventh, that's when we're going." Petr said as he surprised Amalie by walking in to her bedroom unannounced, checking the hallway as he entered to make sure that neither Hannah nor Karin saw him. "...and this hat and veil."

"...but....where did it come from? Why a veil? Why do I have to..."

"They contacted me yesterday. Don't worry. I checked your closet to make sure it fits."

"You went through my closet?

Petr smiled. "We have no secrets now."

"When?" Amalie asked, wanting to know what time she was to be at Heydrich's office.

"10:00. It is important that after the meeting you make it to work on time as though nothing happened. When do you start work?"

"9:00."

"That's not good." Petr said as he thoughtfully stroked his chin. After a moment as Amalie watched, waiting for him to come up with a solution, Petr pointed a finger upwards to signal that he had an idea. "I have a friend who's a dentist. Tomorrow is Friday and I'll call him to schedule an appointment for you and you can tell the people at work that you won't be in until noon on Tuesday. There shouldn't be any problem with the time. Everything has been arranged and with any luck you will only be in Heydrich's office for fifteen minutes. He's usually very punctual."

At Petschek Palais, just as Amalie and Petr were discussing their plans for the meeting, Messner and Dietrich were verifying the undercover detail for the next morning.

"How many men in all?" Dietrich asked as he opened his fountain pen and brought out a small notebook while waiting for a response.

"Four. Five if you can convince the Obersturmbannfuhrer to let me come along." Friedrich Haas replied.

"Another one who wants to play at espionage?" Dietrich asked with annoyance.

"No, no... It's just that this one sounds intriguing. A mysterious woman walks into Heydrich's office, trying to blackmail to get some partisan released from a camp. You must admit it takes some courage."

"...or stupidity."

"Maybe both. I'd like to come along."

"We're not sure when she'll be back. It could be any day this week, any time of day."

"I can be there tomorrow and Wednesday. Maybe I'll get lucky."

"All right then. Just do as you're told and stay out of the way."

The morning dawned clear and bright blue on that Prague Tuesday in May. Heydrich's open, green Mercedes rolled up to Hradcany at 9:45. The scene in front of the castle gates past the gardens was not unusual for a weekday. A bit of traffic, not much since the castle district was on the opposite side of the Voltava river from the parts of Prague where most business interests were located, and a few pedestrians including a group of school-children on an outing in the nearby park.

Amalie arrived by tram a couple of blocks from the castle gates. She noticed the car in an alley with it's hood up and the man in the blue shirt pretending to work on the engine. This was her escape route. She was told it was more dangerous to try to pick her up closer to the castle, so a distraction had been planned for when she was leaving so that she could get back to the car undetected and then hopefully avoid being followed.

She finally arrived at the gate of the castle where the sentries asked for her papers, but this time she knew they were expecting her and so she didn't have papers with her. This alone was a crime, but she had to take the chance, she had to be bold.

"I am here to see the Reichsprotektor. Tell him that Amalie is here."

The sentry looked at her dubiously, as though she were probably crazy, but he called Heydrich's office anyway and, much to his surprise, was told to let her pass.

Friedrich, who was sitting on a bench a few yards from the gate doing such a good job pretending to feed the pigeons that he never even saw Amalie coming, looked up when he heard the name "Amalie". His first reaction was surprise. "Amalie?", he thought to himself as he got up from the bench and walked to the gate to see if it were "his" Amalie, "What would Amalie be doing here?". Dietrich, who had been watching the gate from across the street, couldn't believe that Friedrich was walking to the gate. He would ruin everything. Friedrich, however, was in shock as it all became clear. He realized that Amalie was the mysterious woman, the blackmailer. She was going to tell Rheinhard Heydrich about Friedrich's involvement in...

Friedrich's mind began to spin. He jerked involuntarily as Dietrich slapped a hand on his shoulder and asked incredulously "What are you doing?".

"I just... I saw..." Friedrich tried to explain, but he stopped as he realized that he didn't dare say it.

"I don't give a Damn what you saw. Get out of here. I won't stand for you making a mess of this."

"No, no." Friedrich said quickly, knowing that he had to stay there if he was going to do anything about Amalie, "I'm sorry, I just wasn't thinking. Don't worry, I'll..."

"I'm sorry Hauptsturmfuhrer Haas. We can't take any chances. I'm afraid I'll have to ask you to return to your office. We'll take care of this."

Friedrich looked at him pleadingly, but then there was a sudden flash of anger in his eyes. "But I've got to..." he said, stopping in mid-sentence as something else came to mind. "All right." he said, suddenly calm, "I'm sorry if I've caused any problems."

"Good. Now please just go back to your office. I'll call you later and tell you how things work out."

There wasn't anything left to say, so Friedrich finally acquiesced, thanking Dietrich for his offer to keep him informed. Friedrich decided, however, not to leave. He would return once he

508

was out of sight of Dietrich and the others.

In the castle, Amalie once again found her way to Reinhard's office. She felt ridiculous in the veil, but she kept it on none the less, following Petr's instructions to the letter. She didn't know as she stood in front of Artur's desk that she was being photographed.

"Well, Frau Amalie." Rheinhard said once they were alone in his office, "What is the game today?"

"Game, Herr Reichsprotektor?"

"Yes, what do you want today?"

"Nothing has changed. The release of Hoffman and his family."

"I would be happy to do that, but I'm afraid I can't quite yet."

Amalie waited for him to continue as he moved around his desk and sat on the corner in front of her.

"You see, my people tell me that they cannot determine that the Photostat that you gave me isn't a forgery. I'm afraid I need more to go on before I can help you."

Amalie had thought he might demand more, so she had carefully edited one of the copies of Friedrich's writings which she then handed to Rheinhard.

"What is this?"

"An interesting article, Herr Reichsprotektor. Perhaps you remember the tragic suicide of Geli Raubal in Munich some years ago? This is a somewhat different account of what happened that night."

Rheinhard had not been involved in the events surrounding Geli Raubal's death, but because of the extensive files which he kept, files on friends as well as enemies of the party, he had known for quite some time about what had really happened in Adolf Hitler's apartment on that night in 1934 and now he held in his hands an accurate, possibly an eyewitness, account of that evening.

It was the very blankness of his expression which told Amalie that she had hit her target. He must have known that the first document, the Heidler deathbed confession was true and accurate even though he discounted it, but now it was obvious that he knew this second bit of evidence was an authentic document and that Amalie and her associates were a real threat.

"How do you want this handled?" he finally said after spending a few moments going over the papers.

Amalie was caught off guard by this apparent surrender, but she kept calm. She had considered over the previous few days what exactly she should ask for. "Papers. I will need papers for the Hoffman family and five others to leave Prague. The papers must be for Switzerland."

"In what names?"

"What?"

"The five additional... travelers. What are their names?"

"Blank. They must be blank, of course. Something that entitles the bearer to travel to Switzerland."

Rheinhard hadn't really expected her to reveal the names, but he couldn't resist trying. What a great joke it would have been! "You understand it will take time for the Hoffman's to be released. Some things are difficult even for me."

Amalie knew it was a lie intended to keep her off balance and buy time for the SS to track her down, but since she felt secure that they wouldn't identify her and since she needed time to get Hannah, Petr, Karin and Jakob together for a trip to Switzerland, she let it pass.

"Very well. And I assume I will then be given the original documents..."

"...when we are in Switzerland."

"In Switzerland? How do you propose that?"

"I assumed I would send it by courier, but if you have a better suggestion, I will consider it."

"I would think we should exchange the documents for this Hoffman family right here in Prague." Rheinhard said defensively, as though Amalie were questioning the honor of the Third Reich.

"In Prague!?" Amalie said with a start, unsettled by the ludicrous nature of the suggestion.

"I give you my word as Reichsprotektor that you will be allowed to travel unmolested to Switzerland once I have received all of the originals and copies of the material."

"I'm afraid I cannot accept those terms, Herr Reichsprotektor. We must be on neutral ground before I would be willing to turn over the documents."

"...and I am not willing to turn over the Hoffmans unless I am sure that..."

"And so we have a stalemate." Amalie interrupted.

Rheinhard was not the sort of man who allowed interruptions.

"Apparently we both need a bit more time to consider the details. We should meet again in the next few days while the Hoffmans are being processed out of the camp."

Amalie was not pleased with the suggestion, but since she had really not considered other options for the exchange, she agreed that it might be best. With that she bid Rheinhard good day and left the office. This time she didn't run as she left. She had instructions from Petr that she was to stop at the first lavatory she came to as she went to her right out of the office where someone would give her instructions. She didn't know what to expect as she entered the room. She smiled as she looked in the mirror and there behind her she saw a face peek out above one of the toilet stall doors and then the door opened to reveal another woman dressed exactly as she was, veil and all. A double! They had sent someone to mislead the Gestapo by acting as Amalie's double.

"Quick, put this on." the woman said in a hoarse whisper as she handed Amalie a plain gray skirt and jacket with a military style cap. Apparently Amalie was to walk out as some sort of SS office worker.

"What do I do with this?" Amalie asked, referring to the dress, hat and veil.

"In the toilet water tank."

It was only when the woman spoke again that Amalie realized....

"My God! You're a man!"

"Quiet!" Ivan whispered as he put his hand to her mouth. "This isn't a joke. I may have to outrun them, so they sent me instead of a woman, besides, I have regular clothes on underneath this. They'll be looking for a woman and I'll suddenly turn into a man." He looked at the door as they heard footsteps approach as though he expected someone to walk in on them. He continued once the footsteps had passed. "I'll go out now. You wait for a couple of minutes before you leave."

Amalie went into one of the toilet stalls and sat down. She thought of laughing. The thought of the strange man in a dress, like something out of a crazy cabaret show, but she was so rattled and nervous that she just sat there shaking, looking at her watch every few seconds as she waited for a couple of minutes to pass before leaving.

The Gestapo man Heydrich had assigned to follow Amalie was in hot pursuit of Ivan as soon as he left the washroom. Once Ivan appeared outside of the building on his way to the gate, a subtle hand gesture from a man across the street signaled a man on a horse drawn hay wagon to start his way up the street. Just as the wagon came close to the gate, a car came up beside the wagon and side-swiped it, knocking off the wagon wheel and sending the wagon driver tumbling into the street along with the better part of his load of hay. The driver of the car and the farmer then started yelling at each other at the top of their lungs, the driver of the car accusing the farmer of cutting in front of him and the farmer yelling that the other man was crazy.

The incident had the desired effect on the sentries at the castle gate as one, with his machine gun at the ready, went over to see what was going on while the other tried to watch the post and the accident at the same time. Ivan slipped past the sentry, but his real goal was to convince anybody following him that he was Amalie. It worked too well.

Friedrich had been in a panic ever since he saw Amalie go into the SS offices and, after considering his options, decided that he had no choice other than to kill her. Either he killed her and stopped her from saying anything more to Heydrich or he would be arrested and shot as a traitor. He remembered as he waited in the nearby park how they had been friends, how Amalie and Gunther had taken in his mother during the bad times after the war, but he still kept coming to the same conclusion. Whatever Amalie was up to would surely result in his own death.

He watched the gate steadily even as the noisy accident in the street drew most everyone's attention and then he saw her. She walked calmly past the one remaining sentry without even being challenged and made her way down the street, adjusting her hat and veil as she came closer to the place where Friedrich waited in a stand of brush in the park. He had gotten a good look at the dress and hat even though he couldn't make out her face. He kept telling himself that he had to do it as she walked towards him, as the pumping of his heart roared in his ears, and then she was there in front of him.

"Amalie!" he shouted as he leapt up from the bushes and fired a shot, narrowly missing Ivan's right ear as he reflexively looked to see who was shouting. Ivan started to run as Friedrich tried to aim with his hands shaking furiously. "God forgive me!" he shouted.

Suddenly the air was filled with the sound of gunfire. It wasn't just Friedrich's gun. Dietrich had run out when he heard Friedrich shouting and when he realized that Friedrich was shooting at the woman, Dietrich shot at Friedrich.

Friedrich spun around to face Dietrich as a bullet burned into Friedrich's shoulder, then another bullet cut into his stomach as he tried to fire at Dietrich. He just wanted to stop Dietrich from shooting at him. "No, no, no, no, no...." Friedrich said pathetically as a final bullet hit him in the face and he fell forward into the grass.

Dietrich walked up to Friedrich's body. "Crazy bastard..." he said as he looked down at the corpse, "What was he doing? Why...?" He then walked over to the other body. Friedrich had killed the woman. She had tumbled up in a pile against the iron stake fence surrounding the castle grounds. It wasn't until he was within a few feet that he realized something was strange. He moved the hat away with his foot and saw that it was a man. He shook his head and walked over to a bench where he sat down as the other agents came over to see what had happened.

Amalie heard someone call her name from a distance as she walked past the sentries, but she couldn't tell who it was. She froze for an instant, but then as everything started to happen all at once down the street, it was obvious that it wasn't about her and she kept walking.

She soon arrived at the alley where a car and driver were waiting for her. Neither of them said a word as she made good her escape, showing up at work on schedule after her morning dental appointment.

Petr had spent his day at the transportation office trying to keep his mind off Hradcany castle and what might or might not happen there in the morning. By the time he got home from work he could hardly stand the thought of just having to sit and wait to see if Amalie came home at all.

"Did everything go all right today?" Petr asked as soon as Amalie walked in.

"Don't you know?" Amalie said with a resentful edge to her voice as though Petr were somehow orchestrating everything and then just sitting back to enjoy the action.

"How would I know? I told you they wouldn't chance making contact with me anymore once this was all underway."

"Well..." Amalie said as she took off her light sweater, the sweater which she had put on when she changed clothes yet one more time after she met the car in the alley and before she finally arrived at work, "There was something going on as I left his office, but they weren't after me so I just kept going."

"Something going on? What?"

"I don't know. I could have sworn somebody called my name."

"What about the decoy? Did he make it out?"

"That man in the lavatory? My God, I couldn't believe it! A man dressed like me. I didn't know what was going on."

"That's the way it's supposed to be. The less a person knows, the better for all concerned. But did you see what happened to him?"

"No. I didn't see him. Oh no, you don't think he... I didn't even think about it. I was so relieved just to get out of there that I didn't think..."

"This part about someone calling out your name... this is bad. Even if the Gestapo knew you as Amalie, I don't think they would call you by name, I don't think they would even stop you until they thought they had everyone." Petr bit his lower lip as he thought about it, trying to come up with an explanation. "If someone you knew betrayed you..."

"Who?" Amalie asked in disbelief, "You're the only one I've told about any of this."

"...and if they knew you, how could they mistake the decoy.... They would have had to have known the dress and veil. They would have to have known that Amalie had an appointment with Heydrich..."

"It doesn't make any sense."

"We could be in trouble."

"Do you think they know who we are?"

"I think... it's going to be a long night" he said with a grimace. "Tomorrow I can try to find out what happened, but tonight we just have to wait."

"Should we leave?" Amalie asked after considering Petr's statement.

"What about Hannah and Karin?"

"I mean all of us... Jakob, too."

"...and go where?"

"I don't know. I thought you knew people who did this sort of thing."

"We don't even know if there's anything wrong yet. Now that I think about it... if something had gone wrong, why wouldn't they have picked you up at work? ... and me too, if they knew about me. It's been over five hours."

"So you think we'll be alright?"

"Yes, I think so. Let's just not say anything to Hannah or Karin."

"I think we should talk to them."

"Why?"

"When I was with Heydrich today... I told him I wanted safe passage for my sister and her family to Switzerland."

"So?"

"I also told him I wanted five extra sets of travel papers, papers without names so that whoever had them could use them."

"What?!" Petr said loudly, causing Amalie to shrink back, "We can't leave. This was only a... a test, a test so that we could see if we couldn't get others out, too."

"A test? You never told me that. How do we get others out if I hand over the papers after Eleonore and Louis are across the border?"

"We don't hand over the papers."

Amalie just stared at Petr. He must have known what he was saying. He was playing with Eleonore and Louis' lives, not to mention the fact that he was using the word "we" freely.

"I think that's enough" she said with a note of finality, "You seem to have forgotten that I'm the one with the papers."

"And do you think you could have gotten this far without me?"

Amalie thought about it for a moment. The answer was obviously "no", but she still didn't know if any of their efforts would actually get Eleonore and her family out of Theresienstadt. The question she was asking herself in response to Petr's question was "How far have we gotten?".

That doubt, wondering if she would ever get the travel papers, plagued her as she and Petr continued to argue until he finally relented and agreed to let her tell Hannah and Karin. It seems that Amalie was, after all, holding the better hand. Her control of the documents, especially the ones in Ethan's possession in England which she only hinted at to Petr, was the final word.

She called Jakob and told him that he needed to come over so that they could talk about something important. Once everyone was there, she gathered them in the living room and told them that it was time to leave and that she had the means for them all to go to Switzerland. Jakob objected most strenuously, but Hannah and Karin weren't very keen on the idea either. Then Amalie laid out in rather vague terms the events of the previous day and insisted that they really had no choice but to leave.

At the same time Amalie was delivering her speech on politics and survival to her friends and family, Josef Gabcik and Josef Kubis, two of the parachutists who had arrived in Czechoslovakia the previous November from Britain were preparing for their mission. They checked their grenades and cleaned their British Sten machine guns and went over the plan one final time: who was to be where, when would they be there, how would they escape...

The next morning Petr and Amalie went to work as usual, he to the transit office, hoping to get some information on what had happened the day before, and she to the printing factory, where she hoped to make it through the day without having the Gestapo burst in to take her away. On that same morning Gabcik, Kubis and Valcik were on their way across the river to a hilly district named Kobylisy where the road wound dangerously down to the bridge that lead towards the heart of Prague.

Gabcik waited nervously at the edge of the sidewalk with his hands in the pockets of his raincoat as people passed by to catch the bus on their way to work. He smoked a cigarette. and then another. and then another. Kubis was waiting a little further up the sidewalk with his briefcase, maybe twenty or thirty feet, back away from the sidewalk near some bushes, just in case something went wrong and Gabcik needed help. Valcik was further up the road, within sight of Gabcik so that he could signal him with a flash of light from a small mirror when the car came by.

The car was late. First half an hour, then an hour and longer... They had been waiting almost six months for this moment and this final delay was almost unbearable, but they had to remain calm. They had to stand among the crowd without looking conspicuous. It was almost 10:30 when Gabcik saw a flash of light and finally caught sight of the small, open Mercedes.

The secret training they had undergone in Scotland told Josef Gabcik that he must try to get in front of the car, hopefully when it had stopped for whatever reason, and fire from there. He would have a better chance of hitting the target as it came toward him than he would have if he tried firing at the car from the side as it flew by. There would also be less chance of hitting innocent bystanders that way.

The car stopped. A group of people were boarding a tram as the car drew near and a man suddenly darted across the street. The chauffeur stopped and waited for the man to cross and that was Gabcik's cue. He entered the street and turned towards the car, opening his raincoat and leveling his Sterling machine gun at the passenger.

Jammed! The machine gun wouldn't fire as Josef stood there in front of the Reichsprotektor's car ready to kill Reinhard Heydrich. The chauffeur accelerated as Gabcik stood in the street, unable to believe what was happening. He had stood within two yards of "the butcher of Prague", and his gun had jammed! There was nothing to be done. He threw down the gun and ran.

Josef Kubis had been watching all of this with equal disbelief, but once the events registered in his mind, he acted. This was why he was there. He picked up the briefcase and started moving towards the car, fishing one of the two bombs, a Mills bomb, out of the briefcase and then letting the briefcase fall to the ground as he moved into the street and pulled the pin.

He threw the grenade at the car as it moved quickly around a hairpin curve. Heydrich had stood up in the back seat and was shouting something to the chauffeur as he pointed at Gabcik running up the street. The grenade exploded as it was about to land near the right rear wheel of the car.

Rheinhard jumped out of the car and started shooting at Gabcik and yelling as the would-be assassin ran up the hill and out of sight followed by Kubis and Valcik. Once the assailants were out of sight Rheinhard staggered and dropped his pistol, putting his hand to his abdomen and looking down to see that he was bleeding. Bits of metal and fabric from the seat of the car had been shot into his body from the force of the explosion.

"They tried to kill Heydrich" was a whisper that ran through the streets of Prague like a drunken madman. There was both fear and jubilation in the voices that passed on gossip ranging from "They made a mess of it. He'll live." to "He's already dead, but they're not releasing the news.".

In Berlin, Wilhelm Canaris heard the former. Canaris and Heydrich were compatriots of a sort. Canaris was the head of Abwehr's intelligence services while Heydrich was in charge of the Gestapo and the Sicherdienst, the internal security police of the nazi party. They had been friends in the beginning with Canaris, the older of the two by seventeen years, acting as teacher to Rheinhard in the nature of espionage and military intelligence. They often found themselves in opposition, though, as the years went on and they each struggled to gain the greater share of power for their own offices. The two men seemed to epitomize the tenets of their respective offices. Heydrich's thirst for power within the nazi party was like that of a vampire's thirst for blood; vulgar and self-centered, while Canaris, although equally self-centered, had some vestige of conscience. Canaris, as a member of the Wehrmacht*, recognized an historical context, past and future, of the actions of the Third Reich. Canaris may not have always acted the part of the conscience of a civilized man, but at the very least, he was aware of that conscience.

"So Hans, they believe he'll live?" he asked his subordinate as they talked freely in Wilhelm's office.

"Almost certain." Hans said curtly, as though disappointed.

"Careful Hans," Wilhelm said with a scratchy little laugh, "we mustn't enjoy this. People will get the idea that we don't care much for dear Rheinhard."

"Hans..." Wilhelm continued after a bit of thought , "I'd like you to clear your schedule for a few days. I want you to go to Prague to see how he's doing."

"Go to Prague?" Hans protested as he got up from his chair, "But I'm sure they'll keep us abreast of..."

"Hans. You've got to think ahead." Wilhelm said as waved for Hans to sit, "There must be a lot of confusion at Hradcany right now."

"Confusion?"

"Yes, what with dear Rheinhard in the hospital and all of those secret files of his just laying about unwatched..."

Hans smiled. "When shall I leave?"

"Tomorrow."

---

* The Abwehr, the department of military intelligence, existed within the Wehrmacht in the same way that all governments have military intelligence gathering departments. The RSHA, on the other hand, existed within the nazi party as an enforcement branch of party policies.

Chapter 18

The war had been going well for Germany up until 1942, but suddenly there were portents of the future, like clouds of smoke on the horizon telling one that a fire was raging in the distant forest and was on its way. Adolph Hitler's hysterical proclamations of June, 1941 that Moscow would be overrun and Russia conquered in a matter of weeks rang hollow. The Russian winter of 1941 halted the German invasion and the siege took as great a toll on German troops as it did on Russian civilians.

Josef Stalin, the Russian leader who had taken control of the Soviet government on the death of Vladimir Lenin in 1924, did as much to damage the Russian military as any German commander. In a continuing fit of paranoid delusion, Stalin had purged the military leadership of his country throughout the 1930's. His fear of counter-revolution within the Union of Soviet Socialists Republic led him to question the allegiance of military officers from the highest to the lowest ranks which resulted in highly publisized trials which often resulted in death sentences for the accused.

Stalin's paranoia further moved him to ignore military intelligence from his British and American Allies who had warned him of the impending German invasion weeks before Germany's operation Barbarossa swept the Russians out of Poland and far within the Russian borders.

It was only the Russian winter which saved that country in 1941. Eventually Stalin acknowledged intelligence reports which stated that the Japanese were not preparing to invade Siberia and this allowed him to move large numbers of winter trained troops from Siberia to the German front which became the turning point in the Russian campaign.

In late 1942 American troops entered the European war as they invaded North Africa, first taking on the Vichy French forces and then moving against the Germans. In a matter of months the German's would be driven out of Africa by the combined British and American forces.

"He's dead?" Viktor Letschek asked his friend Antonin who was relating the fate of Rheinhard Heydrich.

The two men had stopped and climbed down from their wagons to talk for a moment as they passed each other on the dirt country road near their small flat patches of farmland. Viktor was brushing away the flies drawn to the pungent, sickeningly sweet smell of the cow manure which filled his wagon. He was used to the smell. It was the flies that he couldn't stand.

"Of course he is!" Antonin exclaimed, "How could you not have heard? It was days ago. He died in the hospital from his wounds."

"Did they catch the men who killed him?"

"No, but they've arrested many people. More every day."

"It's terrible, these Germans... but one knew it would happen like this. I knew when I heard he had been attacked that there would be retributions."

"So you don't think they should have done it?"

"It's none of my business. I just take care of myself and my family" Viktor replied, "These young men, hardly more than boys... They don't think. They kill the German governor and what good does it do? Now the Germans will kill Czechs and a new governor will be sent." Viktor threw up his arms to accent this final statement, punctuating the gesture of futility with a shrug of his shoulders.

"...but I'm sure if I don't bother them," he continued, " they won't bother me."

"No one is safe." Antonin said ominously, "They could arrest anyone at any time."

"Why would they bother with us?" Viktor said as he climbed up on his wagon and took up the reins, "We haven't done anything."

Viktor didn't give the conversation a second thought as he worked in the fields that day or later as he and his wife and daughter ate their dinner. He sang a lullaby to his 5 year old daughter Katje when he tucked her in to bed and then went back to the kitchen. He and his wife, Anna, sat talking at the table about how the day had gone and the next days work that lay ahead when they heard a truck coming, and then another. There wasn't usually any traffic in the small village at that time of night, a little after nine o'clock. Normally there was hardly a soul to be seen until midnight when the workers came home from the steel mill in Kladno, but they all walked or rode bicycles.

Then they heard the voices. There was shouting and the barking of dogs and suddenly a gun shot. Viktor's heart began to pound. "Soldiers" he thought, wondering they were up to as Anna got up and went to the window.

"Be careful" he cautioned her as she looked out and he got up and moved to the other side of the window. They could see another truck pull up about a hundred yards away and soldiers jumping out of the back, quickly assembling into a line as an officer barked out orders which Anna and Viktor couldn't quite make out.

"What do they want?" Anna whispered as she hid behind the worn blue window curtain.

"They're after somebody..." Viktor responded as yet another truck passed by the window, "but why are there so many?"

"Pull the curtains" Anna said as though it might somehow protect them.

Viktor drew the curtains obediently, leaving a small sliver of space between them so he could continue to watch. "They're all over" he said, his voice trailing off. "It was just a dog that got shot. I saw them throw it against Dmitri's house."

"What should we do?" Anna asked anxiously.

"There's nothing we can do. I'm sure they've surrounded the town. Maybe it's trouble with the steel workers again. Maybe there's been more sabotage and they've come to round up the workers. You go to bed. I've got some reading to do. I'll come in a little while."

Viktor was not a man to read, so Anna knew he was just making an excuse to stay and watch the street. She left him to his vigil.

Hours passed and nothing happened beyond the shouting and rushing about the streets and Viktor began to believe that he and his family wouldn't be involved in whatever was happening. He had been dividing his time between watching at the window and sitting in an old upholstered chair in the living room gradually spending more and more time in the chair than at the window until finally he drifted off to sleep in the chair.

A thunderous pounding on their front door launched Viktor from his chair with his heart pounding in response and brought Anna rushing into the living room in her nightgown.

They had come for Viktor!

"What do we do?" Anna asked in a panicked whisper.

Viktor's eyes instinctively searched the room for escape, but then he remembered Katje asleep in her bed. In that instant he knew he had to give himself up so that Anna and Katje might be safe.

"You go to Katje and stay with her" he said in a voice that was suddenly calm, "I'll answer the door."

Anna looked at her husband with wide, frightened eyes and was just about to protest when the front door suddenly exploded and a half dozen German soldiers rushed into the room, two of them pointing their rifles at Anna and Viktor as the others began to ransack the house.

"What do you want?" Viktor shouted and just as the soldier with a gun trained on Viktor told him to keep his mouth shut, Katje's scream pierced the air and Anna tried to run to her daughters room.

"Katje! Katje!" she shouted as the soldier guarding her brought his rifle up across his chest and forced her back.

The other soldiers then came into the kitchen, one of them holding Katje with his arm around her middle as she cried and screamed for her mother. He dropped her to the floor and told her to shut up as he pushed her towards Anna with his boot.

The soldier in charge of the squad then brushed the others aside as he addressed Viktor. "Your wife is to gather all your valuables. You must come with us and she and your daughter will join you in the commons when she is done." The soldier then turned to leave after delivering his curt summons, ignoring Viktor as he tried to ask what it was all about.

When Viktor repeated his question, a soldier behind him thrust a rifle butt into the small of his back and told him to shut up and start walking.

There wasn't anything valuable to gather up in the Letschek household except Anna and Viktor's gold wedding bands and a locket which Anna had been given by her grandmother. She dutifully fished the locket out of it's hiding place in the dresser drawer in their bedroom and reported to the soldier who had stayed behind to escort them outside.

Anna looked out at her neighbors who were already lined up in the center of the village as her escort pushed her out into the night. They were all so quiet. The only noise was the shouting of a soldier here and there as they ordered the villagers to stand in two rows, the men standing in a row in front of the women and children, and the occasional sound of barking and then a sudden gunshot as a dog was killed while trying to protect his master.

The fear that floated over the gathered villagers was as thick and dark as the smoke spewing from the Kladno steelworks. They tried not to show it. Children soon began to cry and their mothers held them tightly. The men stood stiffly and stoically as the German soldiers strutted up and down the lines of victims, planting their boots solidly and contemptuously on the soil of Lidice, on the soil of Czechoslovakia, with the self-righteousness of conquerors turned sadists.

None of the people of Lidice could have known the bizarre circumstances, the tenuous thread which linked them to their fate and brought about the occupation of their village. It all began with a strange, anonymous letter which had been addressed to a woman using only her first name and sent to the factory near Lidice where she was employed. The owner of the factory opened and read the letter in which a nameless man wrote to say that he was leaving and could not see the woman anymore. The plant owner, without any basis for his assumption, jumped to the conclusion that the anonymous man who suddenly had to leave must have been one of the men who had assassinated Rheinhard Heydrich. Acting on that assumption, the factory owner sent the letter to the Gestapo, saying that they should arrest the man so that the reprisals against innocent people might end. The Gestapo investigations in the area turned up nothing definite, but they did discover that a family named Horak in the village of Lidice had a son who had moved abroad before the war. In the Gestapo's zeal to find the assassins, they leapt to the conclusion that the son must have been one of the parachutists and that the villagers must have hidden him and helped him in his mission. None of it was true.

The villagers had no idea why they were being gathered in the night, they only knew that anything could happen when the Germans rounded people up, anything... But nothing good. It might be forced labor. It might be reprisal. Everyone had heard the stories of people being rounded up in Prague and executed over the past three years.

Viktor looked over as Anna and Katje were brought to the line behind him. Katje was crying and wiping her tears with her sleeve as Anna held her other hand and led her. Katje sniffled and looked up at the line of men and saw Viktor looking at her. He forced a smile.

"Papa!" Anna shouted and ran towards him, breaking free

Anna's hold. The soldier ran after her, catching her by the collar of her dress a few yards before she reached Viktor and pulled her back, lifting her up roughly by the dress as though it were a harness. Katje screamed and Viktor turned to go to her, but his neighbors in line held him as an SS sergeant shouted "Stay where you are!"

Anna did, however, run to Katje. Just as she was about to take her daughter from the soldier, he threw the little girl at her mother. "Keep your little brat close or you won't be so lucky next time."

Anna's first reaction was to thank the soldier for not shooting Katje, but she said nothing, she just moved quickly to join the line of women and children.

Once all the houses were cleared and everyone lined up, the officer in charge began to shout out accusations against the people of Lidice and the Czech people in general in what he called "the cowardly and heinous attack against, and murder of, the beloved and noble Reichsprotektor of Bohemia and Moravia". Many of the villagers began to look around nervously at each other and wonder if anyone had been involved. Had someone in Lidice brought this down on their neighbors?

"The women and children will get on the lorries and the men will stay" shrieked the officer at the top of his voice.

The men looked for their wives and children, mothers and sisters, and they looked at each other, wondering what this meant. The officer then shouted that they should look straight ahead and that they would see their women and children soon enough.

The trucks were soon revving up their engines and lurching away into the night, heading for the school in the next town where the women and children would await their fate. The soldiers remaining with the men of the village were then ordered to close in around them and start them walking.

No one dared speak as they marched along. Viktor allowed himself to wonder if this was the end. Was this the way he would die? No, of course not! But then why were they being marched out of the village instead of taken away in trucks? Could they just be out of trucks? No, that's ridiculous. They must have known how many people there were in Lidice. They must have had a count of how many women, how many children and how many men. They knew everything, didn't they?

Viktor could hardly see where he was going in the darkness,

darkness suddenly black as pitch as a patch of clouds covered the moon, as though the moon itself couldn't bear to witness what was about to happen and drew a curtain of clouds so that it wouldn't have to watch. Viktor just kept his eyes on the ghostly figures of his neighbors moving ahead of him and followed. When he stumbled over a stone in the road a soldier's head twitched back to see if someone were trying to escape. Viktor looked straight ahead. Never look them in the eyes. Just like with a wild dog. If you look a wild dog in the eye, he might think you are challenging him and suddenly lunge for your throat.

The night was peaceful around them, the world was peaceful around them. Viktor's mind started to wander as the group shuffled along, raising a cloud of dust on it's way to... How could he be in this place, this dream? Suddenly the thought was there again: "is this how he would die?". How strange it was. When the thought first occurred to him, it was as a remote and easily rejected concept from somewhere far in the back of his mind and yet it returned and seemed more plausible and then it returned again and it seemed possible and then it returned again. Then it seemed real.

He saw the barn at Horak's farm. Or possibly he just knew it should be there and he only thought he could see it in the darkness. Then there was a light.

The officer in charge of the mission had driven ahead to Horak's farm accompanied by a truck with a few soldiers to catch anyone who might be luckless enough to be there. He then waited for the rest of the soldiers and the men from the village at which time he had the headlights of his car and the truck turned on the barn.

The soldiers at the barn then started some last minute preparations as dawn began to break. They went into the house and soon returned with mattresses, leaning them against the barn. Viktor got a sick feeling as he realized what they were doing. The mattresses were there to stop bullets from ricocheting off the stone wall. This was going to be the end after all. Unless... Maybe it was just posturing, a frightening gesture to coerce a confession from some guilty party or to convince someone to turn in his neighbor. The only problem with that tactic was that Viktor had nothing to confess and no one to turn in. He didn't know that all of his neighbors were in the same position. There wasn't anything to tell the officer.

Then it began. There were no questions. No interrogations.

Three soldiers lined up side by side in front of the wall and one of the other soldiers took one of the villagers, a boy of fifteen, by the shoulder of his coat and pulled him over to the stone wall in front of the mattresses. The soldier didn't say a word. He didn't tell the boy to stay, he didn't tell him what was going to happen, he didn't tell the boy why it was going to happen. He just let go of the boy's coat and the boy watched the soldier walk back to the other villagers and just as the soldier took another man by the shoulder, the report of three rifles ended the world.

The boy hadn't even looked at his murderers. He thought there would be more to it than that. It couldn't be that simple. It couldn't be that fast. He thought he had a moment left of his life to see the world, he thought they would tell him what he had done and he thought there would be enough time to look into the eyes of the soldiers. They wouldn't kill him then. How could they? He hadn't done anything. They would know that. They wouldn't go through with it.

The next man was brought to stand almost on top of the boy. The boy's hand rose slightly from the dew drenched grass in a last pathetic gesture and then fell just as the three rifles exploded again.

And again.

And again.

No one wept. No one begged. They only waited. They knew they were already dead and nothing would change that. They thought about their past and their families. Some wondered how these men could do this while others accepted that this was war, brutal and unreasoning. Still others didn't bother with such thoughts in their last moments, they thought of it as though it were an accidental death, they had just been in the wrong place at the wrong time.

Viktor thought how it was too late now to do anything. If only they had all fought the Germans when they had first come into the village. They should have... "No" he suddenly thought, "We couldn't have done anything. We didn't know they were coming. We didn't know it would come to this. We have no weapons. We..."

A hand firmly grabbed his coat and pulled him along. His heart was pounding so hard that he could feel it in his temples. He was sure anyone looking at him could see his face twitching. He wanted to calm down. He didn't want the soldier to see that he was afraid. Damn them! Damn them! Damn them! Damn them! He couldn't gather his thoughts. It was as though his mind were grasping for thoughts the way a winded man gasped for breath.

"Anna."

"Katje."

"Mother."

He couldn't see the killers. He only saw the trees past them, the fields beyond them, his home, the home where he grew up, his grandmother, his father, the dog he had loved when he was a boy. He saw the sunrise. The Sun behind the murderers. He felt its warmth.

God.

A sound like the crackling of a dry log in the fireplace. A burning... The Sun exploded into a white, a whiteness that filled the world. He couldn't close his eyes against the brightness of it. It was everywhere. It was everything.

A few days later, in Berlin, Hans Beyfeurt rushed down the hallway with his overloaded briefcase. He didn't have a moment to spare if he was to make his appointment with Admiral Canaris.

"Ah, Hans... How was your trip?" Wilhelm asked as his subordinate entered Wilhelm's office.

"Very good. Excellent, in fact." Hans said with a smile.

"Excellent? That sounds very promising."

"It is. You won't believe what I've come up with. It was a perfect moment of opportunity. There was confusion in their offices, especially considering the pressure that the Fuhrer put on Frank* to find the assassins. I walked in and said I had been sent from Berlin to inspect their records as part of the investigation and some little corporal all but fell over himself handing over documents."

"Anything we don't already know about?"

Hans quickly opened his briefcase and found a paper that he had been sure to leave on top. He handed it to Wilhelm without a word, an action which immediately alerted Admiral Canaris to the importance of this piece of paper since Hans rarely did anything without comment.

"The confession of Johann Nepomuk Heidler as given to Father..." Wilhelm began to read. Hans remained silent as he watched Wilhelm read. He was waiting for the moment that Wilhelm would realize what he held in his hands.

"My God! This is fantastic." Wilhelm said with a twinkle in his

---

* Karl Hermann Frank. Rheinhard Heydrich's successor as Reichsprotektor of Bohemia and Moravia.

eye as he lowered the paper and addressed his aid, "Where did it come from?"

"Heydrich's office."

"Yes, of course." Wilhelm said impatiently, "I mean where did he get

it from?"

"I couldn't get the whole story. The corporal only said that a woman came in with it within the past week or so."

"Do they think this woman was involved in the assassination?"

"No. If this document is legitimate, then I would guess it was some sort of extortion plot."

"They tried to blackmail Rheinhard?" Wilhelm asked with a note of surprise. "She's lucky he's dead!"

"There is one other thing..."

"What is it?"

"It seems they took a photograph of the woman with a concealed camera" Hans said as he once again fished through the depths of the corpulent briefcase before producing the photograph for the admiral's inspection.

"A veil..." Wilhelm said as he looked at the picture of Amalie, "Is there a name?"

"She used the name Amalie, but no last name. Of course it probably wasn't her real name."

"Did they have anything to go on?"

"Apparently she had just given Heydrich an ultimatum, but he died before..."

"Do you know if she's contacted anyone else? Perhaps Frank's office."

"I don't know. The people in Frank's office weren't as willing to talk with me as the man in Heydrich's office was. They wouldn't confirm or deny anything and I tried not to let them know what I had."

"The trick then my dear Hans is to see to it that this 'Amalie' woman contacts us."

"But how?"

Wilhelm took out a cigar and unwrapped it as he thought for a moment, eventually holding the cigar between thumb and index finger, tapping it against his lower lip before lighting it. He took a long draw, turning the tip to a brilliant orange and then exhaling a great gray cloud of smoke as he finally answered with a question. "Do we have good people in Prague?"

"People in Prague?" Hans asked with surprise since the Abwehr's intelligence was directed against the allies and generally didn't include having agents in occupied areas as that was the realm of the SS and the Gestapo, "No, we don't have any. There's no reason we..."

"Come now Hans." Wilhelm cajoled, "I don't mean our agents as such. I mean don't we have some sympathetic friends. For God's sake, there's been an enormous German community in Prague for quite some time. Our people must know people and so on. We need some connections and we don't have much time. We could talk to someone who knows people in the resistance. Use your imagination Hans! We could put word out that we are the people to contact now that Rheinhard is dead. We could put a notice in the paper."

"What? A notice?"

"Amalie," Wilhelm began as though he were reading the notice from an imaginary newspaper held in his hands, "Uncle Willy needs to talk to you since the death of our friend."

Hans looked at his superior as though the old man had gone mad. "Uncle Willy?" he asked incredulously.

"Hans, I think we might have a great opportunity here and we mustn't let it slip through our fingers. If this woman has proof and we can acquire that proof..."

Hans flashed a smile at the thought of it before returning to the consideration of how that goal might be achieved. "I'll find out who has connections with the Sudeten Deutches."

"Quickly. Today. We have to move fast or this will probably fall into the lap of that idiot Karl Hermann and he'll make some horrible mess of it," Wilhelm admonished, "or worse yet that little monster Heinrich might get his sticky little fingers in it. We don't want that."

"No, Herr Admiral."

"Absolutely no, Hans! ...absolutely." Wilhem trailed off as he once again began to tap his lower lip with his smoldering cigar while slipping into deep thought, contemplating how they were going to handle this intriguing situation.

Prague, beautiful Prague, stank of stale blood and hatred in those days and weeks following the assassination of Rheinhard Tristan Heydrich. The adults in the village of Lezaky, east of Prague, were all murdered after German investigators had found a transmitter there which had been used by the parachutists. Kubis and Gabcik, along with other members of the resistance were betrayed by one of their own, Karel Curda, who led the Gestapo to the Karl Borromaeus church where more than a hundred were hiding. They were all killed in the German assault. The assassination brought such terrible reprisals from the Germans that the goal of Eduard Benes' government in exile, to bring more Czechs into the service of resistance organizations, was unrealized. Even to the extent that the Benes government denied any role in the assassination.

The renewed wave of oppression by the German occupation forces against the Czech people in general in response to the death of the Reichsprotektor was nothing new for the Jewish population. The concentration camps specifically designed to murder vast numbers of people, that is to say Auschwitz-Birkenau, Chelmno, Sobibor, Treblinka and Belsen-Bergen, were already in full operation by that time. The first victims had been those in the East, especially Poland, but through the summer and autumn of 1942 the deportation of Jews was in full swing across occupied Europe, including the Netherlands.

It was in the Netherlands that a group of Catholic Bishops issued a pastoral condemning Germany's treatment of the Jewish population of Europe. The intrinsic flaw in the reasoning of the Dutch Bishops was that they believed they were reasonable men protesting an injustice in an appeal to other reasonable men, they believed that God's law required them to stand up for the oppressed Jews. Little did they know that Adolf Hitler believed he was God... and the SS agreed with him.

A day dawned bright and hot, hot even in mid morning in the Dutch city of Echt when the SS squad approached the convent of Carmelite nuns. This was to be the day of warning for the Bishops, a disciplining of these unruly Catholics who felt they could reproach the greatest leader the German nation had ever known or would ever know. It was to be the day when SS troops would show them that God would not shield and protect them.

A Lieutenant named Helmut Weispfennig waved one of the four troopers who accompanied him to the heavy oak door, indicating that the soldier should knock, as though the act of knocking on a door was beneath the dignity of an SS officer. They waited impatiently for a short moment as they eagerly considered the task at hand and then when no one answered, Helmut motioned again for the soldier to knock. When another moment passed without answer Helmut began to order the door broken in, but just then they heard the scraping and clanking of the lockworks as someone laboredly pulled the heavy door inward. A bespectacled and supremely wrinkled old nun, hunched over with age, peaked out from the door with an engaging smile, the same smile she had for every stranger regardless of position or occupation. "Gud Dag" she said to Helmut, who ignored the old woman's politeness.

"Please summon whoever is in charge" he said curtly as the soldiers then pushed through the door, almost knocking the old woman down. Helmut then followed in, strutting with the pretension of a true Aryan and SS officer. He sniffed at the air. He didn't like the smell of the place. It smelled of piety and old women. Off in another room he could hear Organ music and assumed that it must be the chapel.

The nun did as she was bid, going to the office of the mother superior and telling her that there was a most insistent young man to see her, one of those impatient Germans.

Helmut didn't wait for the mother superior to introduce herself, nor did he even wait for her to reach the bottom of the stairs as she came to talk with him.

"I am Obersturmfuhrer Weispfennig. I have been sent to collect the Jewish whore, Edith Stein and the priest, Berghorst. We know you have been hiding them here."

"They have not been hiding young man, Sister Teresia has..."

"Obersturmfuhrer Weispfennig." Helmut corrected, referring to her colloquial use of the term "young man".

The mother superior had dealt with his sort before, and so she acquiesced. "Yes, of course... Sister Theresa has not been hiding Herr Obersturmfuhrer Weispfennig. She has been regularly reporting to the local police as she has been ordered. She hasn't made any effort to..."

"Will you send for her or must we find her ourselves?" Helmut interrupted.

"She is in prayers. It will only be a moment."

Helmut didn't wait. Once again he motioned for the troopers to act, which they did with zeal as Helmut pointed toward the chapel as he issued orders. "You two with me. You two find the priest."

The two with Helmut burst in on the nuns who were in the middle of their daily devotionals in the chapel.

Once again Helmut casually followed the troopers as a hunter might follow his dogs when they flush birds out of the tall grasses. Helmut rather enjoyed the fear he inspired in people as he performed his duties. He liked the way he looked in his black uniform. It made him feel taller. It was the uniform that had drawn him to the SS. He knew that even when he was afraid, he didn't look it as long as he was wearing the black cloak. There was power in the weave of it, the power of life and death, the sense of inescapable, omniscient power. Even though he was only twenty-three years old, there was the mystical link of age which the fraternity of the SS taught. He was immortal, ancient and new, molded in the cast of the pure Aryan avenger.

He pulled a photograph out of his pocket and began moving through the chapel, holding the picture beside the face of each woman he passed. "Damned ugly penguins!" he said to one of the troopers, "They all look alike." He laughed at his own joke and continued down the row of pews, checking each nun to see if she was sister Teresia. He finally came to a woman in her fifties, a woman with quick dark eyes, eyes that seemed to speak volumes of dignity and gentleness.

Helmut was unmoved, save for a sly smile which crept across his thin, pointy little face as he realized he had found his quarry.

"You are the Jewish whore, Edith Stein?" He shouted accusingly as he reached out and threw back the cowl of her habit revealing her closely cut hair.

Edith stood her ground. "I am sister Teresia Benedicta of the cross, named in blessed memory of Teresia of Avila."

"None of your lies, Jewish slut! Are you Edith Stein?"

"I was Edith Stein."

Just then the mother superior came up behind Helmut. "Herr Obersturmfuhrer, I'm sure there's been some mistake. Sister Teresia has been with us for years. She's been a Catholic for over twenty years."

"She still smells like a Jew."

"But surely a cloistered Catholic nun is no threat to..."

"I only know what I have been told and I have orders to bring this Jewish cow in." Helmut said tiredly as he took Edith by the arm and guided her towards the troopers who closed ranks around her.

"But Herr Obersturmfuhrer," the mother superior continued as she tried to maintain her calm, "I am certain this is all a mistake. Where are you taking her? Who can I talk to?" .

"She is going to the police station. I don't care where she goes after that... I assume some camp." Helmut answered, and with that he motioned for the little parade to begin as the four storm troopers escorted Edith out of the chapel and out to the waiting truck. They were soon joined by the other troopers and the middle aged priest who was also being arrested to teach the Bishops a lesson.

Edith and Father Berghorst sat expressionless as the soldiers made crude jokes about the Jewish nun while the truck moved through the city to the police station. Two of the soldiers quickly jumped out when the truck reached its destination and the other two pushed Edith and Father Berghorst to the gate of the truck into the waiting arms of the first soldiers who roughly pulled their prisoners off the truck, letting Father Berghorst fall to the ground as they pulled him out. Edith moved to help the priest, but one of the soldiers pulled her back. Father Berghorst pulled himself up from the cobblestones and began to dust himself off just as the soldier beside him pushed the priest with his rifle butt towards the door of the police station.

Obersturmfuhrer Helmut Weispfennig laughed and joked as he presented his prisoners to the desk sergeant, telling how he had found the priest and nun and brought them in, as though he had performed a great act of courage, bringing in these terrible enemies of the German state.

Obersturmfuhrer Weispfennig was blind to the injustice of Edith and father Berghorst's position. He couldn't see them as human beings because of the stone which lay deep within him, the cold hard stone upon which was carved his God. His God hated the Jews. This God was protected by all that Helmut was, all of his life and thoughts and fears. His God was his father and mother, his children, his country and all that he believed in. This God could not be touched by the outside world, nothing would turn him away because this God saved him from the frightened cowering child that he was, this God brought him from darkness and told him who he was. That was why he would not be swayed by the pitiful corpses of his enemies. He had no ear for the shrieks of the children of his enemies. He would not confuse his enemies lives with the fate of humanity.

The interrogation at the police station was like countless others when people were arrested solely because of their name. One of the men questioning Edith slapped her because she didn't answer fast enough. Father Berghorst fell when he was pushed into a cell, having hurt his foot when he fell from the truck, and was kicked by the policeman who had pushed him "for good measure". They were "processed" and given new identification cards for their transfer to the Westerbork concentration camp.

It was the afternoon of the next day when Edith finally arrived at Westerbork, one of the German concentration camps in Holland where they gathered their victims, a collection point before they were sent East.

There were thousands of people crowded into Westerbork, all kinds of people, certainly Jews, but also anyone else who didn't fit into the scheme of ideal German society. Homosexuals, Communists, intellectuals who might oppose Hitler, Catholic Priests such as Father Berghorst who might have preached against the Third Reich, Jehovah's witnesses, and so many others filled camps across Europe.

The smell of the place hit you first. The camp's sanitary facilities, toilets, showers and kitchens, had been built to accommodate no more than two thousand people, but the camp constantly swelled to four, five and even six thousand people. The July heat aggravated that oversight, creating a veritable cloud of a foul mix of feces, urine and body odor. There was no wind, not a breath of air.

Edith couldn't help covering her nose and mouth as she moved through the crowd, but she removed her hand from her face as soon as she saw the looks on peoples faces. She thought they might feel she was somehow shunning them and she didn't want anyone to think that. In reality, the people were staring because of her battered face and shorn hair... and the remnants of her nuns habit. She had received a final beating before leaving the police station. A young German soldier, a Catholic, felt that she, as a Jewess, had defiled the sisterhood and he laid a punishing, closed fist blow across her left cheek which soon turned her eye black and blue.

Father Berghorst stopped and knelt before a man who was laying in the dirt and filth. The man was wearing all the clothes he owned, shirt upon shirt, coat upon coat, and had fainted from the heat and the sickening stale air.

Edith kept moving until she heard the sound of a woman screaming. She moved through the dull gray and brown crowd until she came to the place where a woman sat by the fence, surrounded by the crowd which had left her a small semi-circle of space in the dirt as they stared at her numbly. She held a baby in her arms and rocked it from side to side as she kept screaming a sharp, cutting animal-like scream. The woman wasn't crying, which was why it seemed even stranger than it was.

Edith assumed that the baby must be dead as she stood with the rest of the crowd watching for a moment, assessing the situation. She was sure the woman had lost control because of her child's death.

Edith pushed through the crowd and walked over to the woman. The woman didn't seem to see her. She just kept screaming and rocking, although she was becoming hoarse.

Edith sat down beside the woman and put her arm around the woman, pulling her close. The woman continued to scream hoarsely into the folds of Edith's dress. Edith held her. After a moment, the hoarse screams stopped and the tears came, not great flowing tears because the woman was dehydrated and no longer had tears within her, but a misty stream across her tired face.

Edith took that moment to look down at the young body the woman held in her arms. She was startled as she folded back the blanket when baby reached for her finger. The baby was alive. He looked well and healthy. Edith didn't know what to think then. She didn't know what had happened to this poor woman in her arms, what she had lost or what she feared losing so much that it broke her.

For Edith, the next few days at Westerbork were like drifting off to a fitful sleep just before the nightmare was to begin. Then the day came when Edith's name appeared on the list of names posted for those who were to gather for the next train. They were told it was the train to a place of resettlement, to a place which the benevolent German government had set aside for their enemies to live in peace apart from the noble Aryans.

The train was made up of boxcars in various states of repair, some new, some old, just as one might expect of any freight train. The few small windows which had been cut into some of the boxcars were covered with barbed wire while the majority of boxcars were nothing more than wooden ovens in the heat of the sweltering summer.

"Raus!" "Schnell!" The rabid, barking words fell out into the festering afternoon like the sweat pouring from the brow of both victims and the criminal animals who beat and prodded the victims onto the train. It didn't take long for the train to fill and soon their was a sound moving from the head of the train to the end, a sound that could have been the dropping of a guillotine blade. "Shoop. Thunk." It was the closing and locking of the doors on each car.

Edith had lost track of Father Berghorst and didn't know if he was even on the train. She looked over the darkened car as her eyes became accustomed to the dim light. She tried counting the people as a mental exercise to get her mind off the heat and stench. Fifty-one, fifty-two...seventy, seventy-one... She would lose count and start over again, but it didn't bother her since there was nothing else to do. It was so crowded that one couldn't even sit down and she wasn't ready to try to make conversation yet. Her highest count was eighty-seven, although she wasn't sure if that was right. Eighty-seven people in a boxcar roughly four meters wide and ten meters long. Her calculations were interrupted as a man standing next to the man standing next to her suddenly dropped to the floor as though someone had pulled his legs out from under him.

"Water..." he whispered, but there wasn't any water to be had. They had been underway for hours and it wasn't a surprise that someone collapsed, in fact there were others at the opposite end of the boxcar who had fallen without Edith even being aware of it, the surprise was that anyone was still standing at all.

"Help him over here" Edith said to the man next to her, motioning that the fallen man should be set up against the wall of the car. The man she spoke to just stared at her. Maybe he didn't understand her. Perhaps he didn't speak German. Whatever the reason, Edith moved through the crowd to the man who had fallen and managed to get hold of him by his coat and dragged him to the wall by herself. There wasn't anything else she could do for him since there wasn't any water or food. The only concession the Germans had made to the idea that human beings would be traveling in the boxcar was a bucket which had been left in the corner for use as a toilet.

Edith tried talking to the man as the train rumbled on and on, attempting to comfort him. It was the next morning when the train stopped and the door was opened. The bright morning Sun was raw and cutting as it sliced into the crowd. The people shaded their eyes and a loud moan emanated from deep within them, a confused sound from those who were assaulted by, and yet welcomed, the light of day. A confused sound from those who feared their tormentors and yet welcomed the angry looking soldier who threw stale crusts of bread at them as though throwing a hand grenade into the crowd and laughing as he watched the subsequent struggle for life as the victims fought a bloody battle for each crumb divided among them.

A supply of water brought another frenzied battle. A single bucket with a single tin cup at the bottom, a bucket just like the one used as a toilet, was passed in as the toilet was passed out to be emptied. Once the toilet was dumped by one of the prisoners and returned, the water bucket was withdrawn and the door was locked down again. It was then an hour of waiting until the train began to move again. Somehow the waiting seemed to be worse than moving. Probably because movement meant that the tortuous journey would be that much closer to the end.

Edith's journey was much different than many other deportees from the Netherlands. These other deportees were victims of what one might call the German sense of humor, or more appropriately, their constant attempts at duplicity regarding the fate of the Jewish population in Europe. These other deportees, the wealthy and influential among the Jewish community, were allowed to take luggage and whatever possessions they could carry with them as they boarded regular passenger trains on their way to resettlement in the East. Few suspected the true nature of their fate until they stood before a crowd of vicious camp guards and snarling dogs and kapos, until they stood at the foot of chimneys belching out sickeningly sweet black smoke which obscured Sun and Moon.

People began to die in the boxcar which continued to rumble Eastward with Edith and her doomed companions. The stench of death was now added to the horrible smell of the place, but by then every nose was numb to the foulness of it. Edith tried to help however she could, comforting those about to die and trying to comfort those who had loved the dead.

Days passed. Two. Three. Four. Time had no meaning. They handed corpses out to the guards whenever there was a stop for water or, more rarely, when some kind of old or spoiled food was thrown into the car. There was more room to move about as the dead made way for the living and barely living. Wild eyed men, women and children sitting in the squalid darkness, forgetting who the enemy was, beginning to think that it was the others who were alive with them in the car, these others who challenged them for their pathetic pieces of stale bread and a few drops of water. What animal survives in a wilderness of humanity? Trying desperately to hold on to a thread of consciousness of who they were and repeating over and over a silent prayer that this couldn't be real.

The train stopped and started, hesitated, shuddering and trembling as it moved to its final destination, ready to unload its freight in a twilight world. Three headed dogs and animals that stood upright with prodding sticks forced everyone out of the cars and into the new open darkness, out from the staleness of their boxes and into a moaning, screaming night of searchlights and hoarsely shouted orders.

"Here!"

"There!"

"Fast!"

"Get over there! now!"

Each order bitterly punctuated with a kick or punch or a thick wooden cane brought down against someone's back.

The prodding animals had the deceptive faces of human beings, but anyone who dared to look into their angry eyes, searching for some hint of pity or compassion, found that the faces were only masks. These "men" had taken the power of life and death to their breast, they drank the blood as though it gave them greater life. They were drunk with the taste of it. The evil of their acts took on a life of its own as though it were the skeleton that held them, the food that fed them. They were dead, too, just like their victims, but they were undead. It was the baseness of their cruelty alone which animated them as they left all belief in humanity behind for the sake of those who considered themselves above the most basic laws of even their own God, for even their own God had carved in stone that man shall not kill, but once killing is begun, it is that much easier the next time and the time after that.

Sister Teresia and Edith Stein stood in a line awaiting the flip of Mengele's hand. Left, right. Left, right. Life, death. Another step. Another.

"Look at that, Siggy" said an SS guard who was standing with his friend, lighting a cigarette as they took a break and watched the crowd.

"What?" Siggy asked as he looked over the nameless group of people before him.

"There, by the front..." Tomas said as he pointed at an obscure figure in black.

"A nun?"

"Probably a damn Jew hiding out."

"What about it?"

"Let's take her for a walk."

The two guards casually walked over and Tomas took Edith by the collar of her habit without saying a word and pulled her away. No one said anything. Edith didn't question where they were going, none of the other guards asked why she was being taken... The abduction was a non-act, a life so trivial and meaningless that it didn't even warrant comment. Siggy and Tomas marched her across the field towards a brick building. The way Edith was being pulled along didn't even allow her to look up to see the whole building, just the orange and brown bricks rising from the grass.

"Are you a Jew?" Tomas growled as they moved towards a door.

"I am Sister Teresia of the Carmel of..."

"I asked if you are a Jew, you piece of shit."

"I have been a nun for eight..."

Tomas threw her up against the brick wall, pinning her with his arm across her chest as he shouted "You have one chance to live, bitch. Tell me the truth. Are you a Jew, you fat whore?"

Sister Teresia, already tortured and shattered by the journey, was about to wretch as she convulsed involuntarily in the face of the attack.

"Are you?" Tomas continued, "Are you a..."

Just then Sister Teresia's head lurched forward as she tried to vomit, but she had neither food nor water enough in her system to produce anything. Even so, Tomas leapt back and let her fall to the ground.

Sigmund laughed at his friend as he cursed at the tortured nun.

"Shut up!" Tomas shouted at Siggy, "You think that's funny? You think its so damned funny?"

Enraged, Tomas grabbed the back of Sister Teresia's habit while she crouched in front of him, still wretching. He kicked open the door of the building and threw her inside.

The men inside were startled by the invasion and stopped their work for an instant as they waited to see what happened next.

"You" Tomas said to one of the inmates who stood in front of the iron cradle which he was about to load before pushing it in through the cast iron door, "Come here."

The man was little more than a skeleton, given enough to keep working as one of the laborers who was spared the gas chamber or bullet as long as he proved useful. His eyes were rimmed with dark circles set deep within his gaunt face.

"A present for you" Tomas said with a vicious smile which contorted his face, a smile lit by the dancing flames licking out from the cast iron portals of the crematorium. "This crazy Jew cow gave herself to Christ, as though Christ would accept her vile disgusting..." Tomas' thought trailed off as he looked down at Sister Teresia.

"Christ doesn't want her, so you can have her."

The man stared at Tomas in dull incomprehension.

"Fuck her Jew. Fuck her. I'll bet she's never been fucked. She's too ugly, but you don't mind, do you?"

The man continued to stare. He knew he was as good as dead no matter what happened next.

"Don't you hear me, you stupid little kike? Take off your pants. Don't you know how it's done?

When the man still didn't move, Tomas pulled out his pistol. "Do it" he shouted and the man dropped his pants.

Tomas laughed hysterically as the fires seemed to glow even brighter as he went out of control. "Look at him Siggy! Look at that pathetic little..." he stopped in mid-sentence and knelt down by Sister Teresia's face, "But you want it, don't you, you old slut?"

He once again dragged Sister Teresia by her clothes, throwing her at the man.

"Take it, bitch. Take it in your hand. Put it in you mouth!"

Sister Teresia had not shed a single tear since she had been arrested. She had not shown her fear. She had been strong and caring for those around her, trying to care for the sick and beaten, but now it was over. She put her face against the cement floor and sobbed.

"You pathetic little man" Tomas said to the exposed man standing over Sister Teresia, "You can't even get hard, can you?"

The man stood there, unanswering.

"Then what good is it?" Tomas said and aimed his pistol at the man's genitals and fired. Even Siggy was shocked at how far this was going, but Tomas wasn't done yet as the man laid on the floor writhing in pain. "And you get to go for a ride." Tomas said as he grabbed Sister Teresia's habit one last time and tossed her onto the iron cradle with the same effort one might use tossing a sack of flour into a wagon. He then pushed the cradle forward with all his strength, with the strength of all the blind, mindless rage within him, and propelled Sister Teresia into the fires.

"She didn't scream..." Siggy said with astonishment as he stepped over to Tomas. Tomas said nothing. He only stared into the fire, but he couldn't see the body of Sister Teresia within the furnace, he couldn't make out any shape or form. There was only the "woosh" sound of the flames being drawn upward. It was as though she had disappeared.

Siggy stepped closer and his foot brushed against the castrated crematorium worker still writhing in pain on the floor. He looked down at the man and simultaneously drew his pistol, putting a bullet in the man's head. Tomas was startled by the shot, thinking for just an instant that the shot had been fired at him, but then he realized where he was. He was God there. There were no other predators.

Chapter 19

The German defeat at Stalingrad and the subsequent surrender of thousands and thousands of German troops signaled the most decisive turning point of the war against the axis powers. They had been able to retreat from North Africa, but Stalingrad represented the worst loss of troops and material ever suffered by German forces. 1943 found them retrenching as they awaited the Allies next move, but the execution of the final solution continued unabated, in fact, the rate of deportation was even stepped up as the nazi killing machine was made more and more efficient.

Within Germany, the German people, most notably college students and other young people, were turning against the war. On February 18, 1943, Hans and Sophie Scholl were arrested as they tried to pass out anti-nazi literature by throwing it from a second floor landing into the foyer below of a Munich University building. They were seen by a building superintendent and immediately detained by the man until Gestapo agents could arrive. Sophie Scholl, 21 , and her brother Hans, 24, were members of a German resistance group known as "the white rose" . Within six days after their arrest, they were both tried, convicted of treason against the state and beheaded by guillotine in a German prison.

"Oh my God" Amalie said as she read the letter.

"You are to report to..." the letter continued.

"What is it?" Hannah asked as Amalie gripped the paper tightly in her hand, crumpling it.

"They've changed the laws again. Jewish wives and husbands of special marriages have to report now."

Amalie couldn't have known that this turn of events was only made possible by her own actions months before. It wasn't until she went to Gestapo headquarters to get Jakob released that German officials even became aware of her existence. The Czech government didn't have those sorts of records on a Frau Metzdorf, that her maiden name was Stein and her family was Jewish, and she had no occasion to give out that information to anyone else when she and Ethan first came to Prague. Of course, she wouldn't have done anything differently if she had known that saving Jakob would have exposed her in this way, but as it was, not knowing what led to her "arrest", it made the Germans seem omniscient to her.

"Oh no..." Hannah said as she rushed over to see the letter.

"What do I do?"

"Wait 'til Petr comes home. When are you to report?"

"The day after tomorrow."

It had been six months since the death of Rheinhard Heydrich and Amalie was paralyzed by fear. This was how she always reacted to adversity, making an attempt to change something in her life and then just dropping everything and hiding from the world if something went wrong. This time, however, she was not alone. When she had gathered everyone together and told them what was going on and how they would all be leaving for Switzerland, Hannah, Karin, Petr and even Jakob grudgingly agreed.

She was right to be afraid since Wilhelm Canaris had made it a priority for his adjutant to find the woman who had tried to blackmail Heydrich. Petr had heard about the efforts of the Abwehr intelligence agents in Prague through his connections in the resistance movement and had warned Amalie that they must .

"There's only one thing to do." Petr said decisively, "We must contact one of these men looking for you and see if they are willing to renew negotiations for the documents."

The resistance had dwindled significantly in numbers since Heydrich's death and the subsequent blood purge of Bohemia and

Moravia. Just as the German command had planned with it's terroristic response, when the Germans proved their readiness to murder the innocent, the Czech people realized that no one was safe as long as the nation was occupied by Germans and that by joining the resistance they would endanger their entire families.

Petr thought about going through the chain of command within the resistance, but rejected that idea as he realized he would have to give all of the details to new people whom he didn't really know. Many of the men he had worked with before Heydrich's assassination were now dead, some in connection with the assassination, others only because they were in the wrong place at the wrong time when the Germans were rounding up people for retribution killings.

"Jakob" came the thought flashing in his mind. "Of course!" he thought. Jakob had gone underground to avoid the forced labor brigades which claimed so many young men throughout the city. Soldiers would descend upon a busy street, blocking both ends of the street and then go through the people they had trapped like fishermen would go through their nets, picking out appropriate fish to send to work for the Reich.

Jakob had already done some minor work for the resistance, delivering packages and such, and so he had developed a sense of the streets and how to avoid soldiers and how to identify Gestapo men and avoid them also.

Petr knew, however, that even as he developed this plan of attack, it wouldn't keep Amalie from reporting for resettlement.

"I have to go?" Amalie asked with surprise, since she had been waiting to hear Petr's great rescue plan when he had told her that he had a solution that he needed to discuss with her.

"I think it's best. Most likely it would be Theresienstadt because of your status, your late husband. If you try to hide, we would all be under suspicion, maybe even arrested, and then we couldn't do anything to help us all get out of the country. Besides, with agents looking for you, they'd never look in one of their own Konzentrationslager."

"But how long?"

"A few weeks at most. I think once we make contact things should go fast, one way or the other."

"One way or the other?"

"Amalie, we've known all along that this is a gamble."

"At least I would be able to see Eleonore."

"If she's still there."

"Still there?"

"They transport people to the East. To still be there, she and her family either have to be important enough to keep in the camp or they must be very lucky."

"What do we do if they've gone East?"

Petr didn't want to tell her what he knew about being sent to Poland. He had heard the stories through the resistance and he knew that being sent East most likely meant death. The time had come for Petr when he was thinking about his wife and daughter and himself. He wanted to save them and himself and Amalie could do that if things worked out.

"We'll have to deal with that when the time comes. We have to believe that they're still in Teresin."

Jakob couldn't come to the house to say good-bye on the morning Amalie was to report. It was too dangerous. Someone might be watching the house, waiting for just such an opportunity to arrest him.

Amalie had never felt so alone as that morning. She had tried to be brave and insisted that neither Hannah nor Karin go with her to the freight yards where these last Jews of Prague, except for those who had gone into hiding, were to wait for a train.

Amalie was surprised at the number of people at the collection point. There were about two hundred or so men and women. She wouldn't have guessed there were that many mixed marriages in the area. It all seemed very quiet. All of them were middle-aged or older since children were not affected by this new amendment to the Law for the Protection of German Blood and Honor.

The next surprise was two standard train coaches that pulled up at the collection area. She had seen pictures and heard stories about the cattle cars used for Jews and had expected to make the short journey amid straw and manure, but instead it was a quiet and orderly boarding of the train, all quite civilized without any shouting or abuses by the guards accompanying them, in fact the guards even politely helped some of their charges to board. Except for the guards and the extremely somber nature of the passengers, it could have been any weekend outing to the country. The passengers didn't talk amongst themselves, even though the guards hadn't told them that they couldn't. Fear was the greatest guard of all.

Amalie didn't know what to expect when she arrived at the camp, but she wasn't prepared as the train came to a stop and another train was being unloaded ahead of them. The guards receiving them were much different than the ones that had come with them from Prague. The Theresienstadt guards were Czech policemen who had enlisted their services to assist the Germans and they were eager to impress their superiors with their ability to instill and maintain the strictest discipline and order among the newly arriving camp prisoners. A few German soldiers with submachine guns watched as the Czech guards went about their duties, shouting and snarling, hitting people with canes and pushing them to the registration tables where prisoner's passports were inspected and then confiscated along with whatever valuables the officials found in bundles or suitcases. Amalie had only packed clothes and some food, having left everything else with Hannah for safe keeping.

People were everywhere. The inmates who watched the newly arriving prisoners were, gaunt and emaciated men, women and children who stood just past the barricades at the entrance of the camp where the new arrivals were being processed. The area just ahead of Amalie was an area for families closed in with electrified and barbed wire fence just in front of the brown brick wall of the one-time military garrison.

Amalie searched all the faces she could see while she was being questioned, hoping to catch a glimpse of Eleonore or Louis or the girls, but none of these people looked anything like them. Unless... Could they have changed so much? Could Louis' pleasant, pudgy face now be like these others? How old was Eleonore now? Forty-five? It had been years since they had seen each other. Could Eleonore now look like these other tired, worn-out old women?

She wandered through the cobblestone streets of the ghetto once she had been told where to go. She was lost and alone. She floated among the others as the antithesis of a ghost among the living, for she was the living among these many ghosts. She looked over the faces as one might look through photographs, wondering how an old picture might translate into that present day. Could that be Eleonore? Could that man be Louis?

There were tens of thousands of people in the camp, every corner filled in the garrison originally built to house five thousand troops. The styles of buildings varied according to when the were built, brownstone here, white plaster there, with the heart of the ghetto, the garrison itself, surrounded by the massive brick walls standing some twenty feet above street level. The commandant of the camp had his office in a central building of the garrison, a building with a fenced-off yard which was the administrative center of the camp.

Amalie noticed for the first time as she stared at the administration building that the sky had clouded over since she had started out to catch her train. Something caught her eye as she looked up at the looming storm clouds, an officer coming down the steps of the administration building. She stood there with her suitcase in hand, watching the man as he limped down the stairs. There was something so familiar about the balding gray haired man, something about the way he moved, the way he motioned to brush back hair as he put on his hat, hair that was no longer there, something... She was startled, so startled that an involuntary twitch, a reflex action, turned her away from him. How could it be? What kind of cruel joke had sent Klaus Grunewald to this same horrific place?

She quickly walked away. She wasn't ready to deal with him yet. The picture of him, that one quick glance, was etched in her mind. He looked even more stiff and intolerant than she remembered from Munich. It had been eight years since she had seen him last and his face had become severe, lines that had only been suggested in those days in Munich now clearly and sharply cut down his face like scars, lines that defined a harsh and joyless soul.

"Oh my God! Amalie!" came a shout from across the street as Amalie turned a corner.

Amalie tried to find the face in the crowd, but she didn't recognize anyone until a woman broke from the crowd and ran towards her.

"Eleonore?" Amalie whispered. Eleonore's jet black hair, pulled back and tied, was now painted with broad strokes of gray. She had lost a lot of weight, especially around her face which left empty skin hanging about her jowls. She looked like the other timeworn, weary women of the ghetto.

"Eleonore..." Amalie repeated, but this time out loud for her sister to hear, "I can't believe I found you."

"How long have you been here?" Eleonore countered.

547

"Just today. A few hours."

"Have you reported to the Jewish council?"

"No. They told me to... just a minute. I wrote it down. Report to..."

"Don't bother with that. The council does better at that one thing. I'll take you there."

"Eleonore," Amalie interrupted hesitantly, afraid to ask the question that leapt to her mind, "what about... How is Louis."

"Oh, yes. He's here. The girls, too. We're doing as well as can be expected. It's horrible. You won't believe it. No food. Beatings... and worst of all, they send people out of here, to the East."

"East?"

Eleonore looked around to make sure that no one was listening before whispering to her sister. "They never come back. There's never a word from them, just the stories from others. They say they're being killed. To be sent to the East means death."

Back in Prague, Petr made contact with Jakob through the resistance and they set a time to meet.

"...and so, you are the one who should make contact with this man. I found out that he isn't with the Gestapo. He's with the Abwehr."

"The Abwehr?" Jakob asked, "Why is the regular army..."

"Have you ever heard of Wilhelm Canaris?" Petr challenged.

"Canaris? No."

"Admiral Wilhelm Canaris is the head of German military intelligence. It seems that he and Rheinhard Heydrich were friends."

"...and so this Canaris wants to avenge Heydrich? But they already found the assassins. Wasn't everyone killed at Borromaeus church?"

"No, it's worse than that. They were sent to find a woman named 'Amalie'."

"What?"

"They must have found a file or..."

"...and they know about mother?"

"No, not really. For some ungodly reason she used her real first name when she was talking to Heydrich, but it's just as well since he probably assumed it was a lie."

Jakob just shook his head.

"So now that your mother is at Teresin, we need to try to finish what she started. I think we can contact this Canaris and get her and your aunt out of there and get all of us out of Czechoslovakia."

"How?"

"First things first. Make contact with the Abwehr agent and then we'll figure out how to get through to Canaris."

"Where do I find him?" Jakob asked.

"You don't. I'll find him first and set up a meeting for you. I want him to think that we are part of a group."

"When?"

"I think I can find him tomorrow or Wednesday. I'll try to set up your meeting for Saturday night in a crowded place. I'll be there too, out of sight, just in case."

There was a bar in a hotel in Wenceslas square by the national museum which was such an institution that Czechs continued to go during the war even though off-duty German officers would also frequent it. The Czechs would laugh at things that didn't matter and talk quietly among themselves, occasionally throwing furtive looks around the room to make sure no one was listening too closely lest some innocent statement draw attention. This was why Petr chose the place, because neither Czech nor German would seem out of place there.

It was busy, just as Petr had promised, on that Saturday night as Jakob sat at a small table in the corner. He kept looking up whenever anyone came near the table, trying to decide if this person or that person could be Canaris' agent.

Adele Baldrika was drinking Compari as she sat at the bar. She had aquired a taste for it in Venice before the war when she first started working for military intelligence as they constantly monitored the political mood of the Italians and their military status. She nonchalantly watched Jakob in the mirror behind the bar as she waited for 7:00, the appointed time of their meeting. He was underfed, bordering on gaunt, but even from a distance she was struck by his piercing silver, blue eyes. She was amused by his nervous expression and his awkward, uncomfortable movements as he waited. She knew she already had the upper hand.

She walked over to the table just as the chimes of a clock over the bar faded into the cacophony of the many voices and different languages throughout the room. Petr's reflexive thought as he saw her walk over to Jakob was that she was interested in him, but then he realized she must be the agent. Jakob wasn't as quick, looking up at her with that searching gaze but immediately discounting her. He was expecting some innocuous gray little man, not a tall, pretty woman.

"My drink is almost gone. Won't you buy me another?" she asked as she draped her coat across a chair, brushing her hair away from her face as she sat down.

"I'm sorry," he replied as he scanned the room, "but I'm waiting for..."

"I understand you're a friend of Amalie's."

Jakob stopped in mid-sentence. She had his complete attention. "Yes, I needed to talk..."

"We know."

"We have certain information that we..."

"We know all about that, too."

"This might go a little faster if you let me finish a sentence" Jakob said abruptly as his eyes flashed.

"I don't know... I think it's going fast now" Annette noted dryly.

"I need to talk to Canaris."

"We would like to talk to Amalie."

"After."

Adele paused a moment as she considered the exchange. "Who are you?" she finally asked.

"A friend of Amalie's."

"A friend?"

"Yes. I know what she knows and can speak for her."

"Why didn't she come."

"That would have been foolish. We had to find out who you are."

"Why shouldn't we just arrest you and torture you until you tell us everything?"

"Because we both know this isn't just about information. It's about evidence. Proof."

"You don't expect the Admiral to come here."

"No. I thought I would be making a trip to Berlin."

"We leave tomorrow morning at 8:00" Adele confirmed as she decided that Jakob was a legitimate contact, "Meet me at the station on platform 10."

Jakob didn't say anything more. He just got up and left.

Petr saw Adele smile a wicked smile as she watched Jakob leave. Petr wondered if that meant it was a trap or did the woman just feel that Jakob was in over his head? In whatever case, Petr waited to make sure Jakob wasn't followed and then left too.

Petr and Jakob talked over the meeting that night in Jakob's little room, a hiding place in the basement of a friend's house. He had been underground for months by that time, having gotten forged papers with Petr's help in the name of Anton Eberhard. He had to have a German name because he still hadn't learned much of the Czech language even though he had been living in Prague for five years. It was just as well, though, since it was easy for him to blend in with the other Sudeten-Deutsch in Prague. He could count on a little money from various friends now and again and his mother had left a little for him with Hannah when she went to Theresienstadt. He managed to get ration coupon books under his false name and so he was getting by well enough.

"You've got to be careful" Petr cautioned, "in Berlin, you're out of your element. A strange city... You're going into the lion's den"

"I'm nervous enough, Petr. If that's all you have to say, then you should go so I can get some sleep."

Petr glared at him. "They might torture you."

"I know."

"If you say anything, we might all..."

"For God's sake Petr! I know! I know. We've been over this before. I know what's at stake. I won't betray anyone. Remember, I've been questioned before and I know what they do."

"Keep reminding them that we're waiting to hear from you, that if we don't..."

"Only as a last resort." Jakob countered, "They can't think I'm scared."

He knew the train ride to Berlin was going to be a long one as he and Adele sat across from each other and he tried to be calm, feigning interest in the view of the Czech countryside as it rushed by. Pictures flashed in his mind of the Gestapo questioning him about Walter Hannisch at Petschek Palais when Adele flashed a nazi badge to the conductor who asked for their tickets. Jakob had told Petr that there was nothing to worry about if they tortured him as though his last experience with the Gestapo had made him strong.

In reality he was terrified at the thought. He put on a front, but he knew that if he had known anything about what Walter was doing, he would have told the Gestapo officer. He would have told them anything to make it stop. They go inside you to places where you never imagined anyone might go. If it were just physical, it would be rape, but it was even worse. They break into your mind. They take away all the illusions of your identity which once let you think of yourself as inviolable and let you know just how helpless and vulnerable you are. Once they've driven you to your knees, how do you stand again? They force you to redefine yourself as a human being, as something less.

He was afraid not only for himself but for his mother and friends too, because now he did know things and he didn't know if he could go through questioning without breaking. He could only pray that it didn't come to that.

"What are we supposed to call you?" Adele asked as she took out a cigarette and slowly lit it, ending with a flourish as she let her silver cigarette lighter snap shut with a distinct snap.

"Anton."

"Anton... I like it. I had a puppy named Anton before the war. Are you Jewish?"

"Jewish?" Jakob answered with surprise, but only because the question came out of nowhere.

"Yes. I just wondered. Not that you look it, but from what I've heard..."

"What have you heard?"

Adele smiled and waved a finger at him. "Anton! It's never that easy."

Jakob didn't realize that he had slid forward ever so slightly as he asked the question until he drifted back in frustration at Adele's coy reply.

They switched trains in Dresden to an express train to Berlin, arriving a little after 9:00 that night. There was tension in the air throughout Berlin. This was after the German defeat in Stalingrad and a sense of foreboding hung heavy in the city. Everyone, whether they talked of it or not, was waiting for the Russian response. If they could defeat the German armies in the field, how long could it be before they took the offensive?

Adele seemed oblivious to the bleakness of the city as she cut through the crowds with Jakob in tow on her way to Canaris' headquarters. They were expected and she certainly wasn't going to be the one to keep Wilhelm Franz Canaris waiting.

Allied bomber raids on Berlin were about to force the Abwehr to move its offices from the rambling old buildings located on the Landwehr canal to Zossen, some 30 kilometers to the south of Berlin. At the time of Jakob's visit, however, Admiral Canaris was still ensconced within the winding hallways and catacomb of rooms which had once made up a group of fashionable homes on Tirpitzuferstrasse, homes which had served as a headquarters for the Abwehr since the time of Kaiser Wilhelm II.

Adele had called from the train station so that Admiral Canaris was waiting for them in a small conference room when they arrived at the Abwehr offices. Wilhelm's dark blue suit coat hung on a coat tree behind him as he sat at the head of a heavy oak table with his shirt sleeves rolled up, going over some papers.

"Admiral Canaris" Adele said by way of introduction as she directed Jakob to a chair across the table. "And Admiral," she continued, "this is our new friend 'Anton'."

Wilhelm looked up, taking off a pair of reading glasses as he did, sizing Jakob up before speaking. "Anton?" he repeated after a moment.

"Yes," Jakob answered awkwardly, "Anton." He was surprised at Canaris' appearance. The man seated before him had a friendly face, unlike the harsh, scowling expressions he was used to with military officers in the Gestapo.

"and you are here at the request of...?"

"Amalie."

"Yes... Amalie. That's it. We've heard some interesting things about Amalie, but I'm sure you know all about that."

"I know the general nature..."

"Why is it that Amalie hasn't contacted us herself?"

Jakob was becoming unsettled as Wilhelm began probing. "She... We weren't sure if this was a legitimate contact..."

"And you are a sacrificial lamb?"

Jakob's heart began to pound. He knew it was meant to be a joke, a very dark joke, but the thought of torture was suddenly there, haunting him. "No," he said, composing himself, "I am a volunteer."

"Oh, I see." Wilhelm said patronizingly, "Courageous, immortal youth. What have you come for?"

"...but you were looking for us..." Jakob answered with confusion.

"So I did. We are in the business of gathering information and we understand that Amalie is offering a bit for sale."

Jakob nodded in response.

"Is there anything you can tell me about it. Something to convince me that you are the one we should be talking to."

Jakob cleared his throat. He had thought about what he would say all during the train ride from Prague. Say enough, but not too much. "We know about... There is evidence suggesting... Ah, we have certain facts about high placed officials that would be embarrassing..."

"Well, a little embarrassment isn't such a terrible thing. Should we really be worried?"

Jakob paused. He knew Wilhelm was trying to unnerve him and get him to say too much. "Certain important officials would be extremely compromised by..."

"Who?" Wilhelm asked, cutting Jakob off again.

"Who?" Jakob repeated as he tried to decide if he would be going too far to mention Adolf Hitler specifically.

Wilhelm knew the answer to the question, just as any good lawyer knows the answers to the questions he asks a witness on the stand. The important thing is to get them to say the words, to come right out and confirm what everyone knows. "Yes," he continued, "It's time to lay down your cards young man. Who are we talking about?"

"The Fuhrer."

A little smile crept almost imperceptibly across Wilhelm's face. Jakob saw the smile, but didn't know if it was there because he had made a mistake by implicating Adolf Hitler or if it was because the Admiral was somehow pleased that the Fuhrer might be vulnerable.

"...and what now?" Wilhelm asked as he sat back slightly in his chair.

Jakob's sense of relief filled the room. Storm troopers had not rushed in and carried him off to some dank cellar. He had made it through the first step. "There is a problem." he began, feeling his way through the rest of the negotiations, "There are a number of... components. There are different pieces of evidence and one of them requires that I go to England."

"England?" Wilhelm repeated, but this time his voice showed genuine surprise. Germany's intelligence gathering in England was virtually non-existent since the early days of the war. The apprehension of German agents in England had been made a priority by the Crown even before war was declared. That policy was pursued with such ferocity that virtually all German agents were uncovered and arrested within the first year of the war. Anyone that German intelligence did manage to get past the English Navy, English Army and the English public in general could only be effective for short, single objective missions. They would be in and out in a matter of hours.

"A package of evidence was sent there before the war."

"All that time? Are you sure it's still there?"

"It was sent with a very reliable courier."

"What about the bombing? Your man could have been killed, the package destroyed." Wilhelm was still playing the game as he said it, still trying to get an upper hand.

Jakob had always assumed that his grandfather was all right just because he was in England and that was the first time he realized that something might have happened to Ethan. "No." he said, "We've been in contact. Everything is fine."

Wilhelm didn't detect the lie as he watched Jakob's eyes. "Delivering you to England is a difficult undertaking."

"But, of course, you can do it."

Yes, yes... We can do it. I think it would only be fair, however, that if we were to help you get to England, that you should do something for us."

"Something?"

"You say that you are in touch with this... Amalie, and that you need to get to England to help us, but you can't tell us exactly what it is that you need to do. This leaves us rather in the dark. Very well, if you need to keep your activity secret, then so be it, but we must have some reason to believe that you are committed to helping us."

"What are you asking me to do?"

"We need you to terminate an agent."

"Terminate? You want me to kill someone?"

"You don't need to know all the details. I'll just say he is a double-agent who is leaning a bit too far to the other side."

"But why me? Shouldn't you have somebody who's done that

sort of thing before?"

"Strangely enough it doesn't work that way. If you have someone constantly taking care of these sorts of things he has a much higher chance of being caught. It's better to use a novice with a single mission in mind. They never see him coming and he's most likely... expendable."

"Expendable? You mean it doesn't matter if I get away or not."

"Frankly, no. That's how you prove yourself to us. If you can accomplish the mission and get away, we'll have some idea what you're made of. We'll give you some training and get you to England, but after that you're on your own."

Jakob returned to Prague the next day. They only allowed him a day to get ready for his short, intensive course in espionage tactics. He let Petr know what had happened, but told him that if he managed to get word to Amalie that he shouldn't tell her about Canaris' extra assignment.

Jakob's first thought was that he could do it easily, that he could kill this anonymous man without hesitation. He told himself that it was all part of the war. He was now a soldier in his own unique way and he would have to kill another soldier. He hadn't had time yet to consider what it would mean to kill a man up close, to see his face and overcome whatever he saw in that man's face.

The guards of Theresienstadt were mostly former Czech Policemen who volunteered their services to the German Reich. This was certainly not unique to the former region of Czechoslovakia. All through Europe the nazis found allies from among the ranks of conquered nations who sympathized with their ideals of racial superiority and conquest. One of these Czech guards, however, was a member of the Czech underground.

Vasek Zapotocky's role was to be a guard. He was not to draw attention to himself or attempt any foolish heroics. He was told to follow the lead of the other guards, to be as cruel as they were and not to speak of politics. He dare not stand out in any way or he would be useless to his comrades. His assignment was to smuggle messages in and out of the camp and get information to the underground about the status of prisoners. When Zena Marusin was brought to the Kleine Festung, the same Zena Marusin Petr had been looking for when he found out that Amalie's sister and brother-in-law were on their way to the camp, it was Vasek who let the underground know of her arrival.

He saw her as she was marched into the Kleine Festung and heard her screams as he patroled the streets of the camp that night. Vasek was the one who was told to get four of the camp inmates to cut down the bodies of the dead. Zena had been hanged as the sun rose that morning along with two other prisoners from the little fortress. She had been tortured until her face was almost beyond recognition, but she never told her Gestapo tormentors anything about the operations of the resistance.

It was Vasek who got word to Amalie about the progress of her plan although she never knew it was him. Notes were left in places where only she would find them, left at odd times when she couldn't imagine anyone being around to leave them. One day she found a note scrawled on a piece of old newspaper which read "Orion goes to England". It took her breath away. Jakob? To England? How? There was no one to ask about the cryptic message and certainly no one, not even Eleonore, who she would tell. Somehow Jakob was getting to England, but she didn't know if he was getting away or if he was making contact with her father to follow through on the blackmail plot.

Amalie had been in Theresienstadt for almost a month. She and Eleonore had grown very close in their adversity, closer than they had ever been before. Life was very hard there. Food was scarce and the ghetto was horrifically overcrowded. The old people died off like flies. The Jewish council tried to keep the inmates busy with concerts, lectures and other distracting entertainments, but there was a growing resentment of the council as people began to see them as privileged and separate from the majority. Council member's families were not subject to deportation to the East. They got better food and more of the few privileges available to inmates and this often came down to the difference between life and death. Some of the inmates openly expressed their view of the council members as collaborators.

The days passed with a numbing slowness. People who were coming into the camp were beginning to pass on rumors that the war had turned and that the day might soon come when the Germans were defeated, but these people were soon washed through what the Germans called the "sluice". The insidious nature of Theresienstadt was that while it wasn't one of the nazi's death camps, it had become a way station for Jews and other prisoners on their way to the death camps in the East, most notably Auschwitz in Poland. Theresienstadt was the anteroom to Hell. For all the people in the world who claimed not to know about the murder of Jews in Poland, there were those in Theresienstadt who knew with all certainty that the trains going East meant death. It was no question or secret there. They knew.

The trains would come and swell the camp population to even more difficult dimensions, including a yard in front of the former garrison fenced in with barbed wire and referred to as the family camp. It was incongruous to hear the laughter of children playing against such a macabre backdrop, but that is the nature of children that they might adapt and survive.

Amalie had watched a train leaving the camp for the East after she had been there a couple of weeks. She didn't know why she hadn't been picked. It was only luck. She watched as the train pulled away, heard the sounds of people groaning as the train started off, jerking and throwing people around inside the cattle cars as they began the final leg of their journey.

She was also there when a train came in. She wondered where they were from as the guards quickly and brutally forced them out of the box cars and into the processing yard where their few possessions would be confiscated and they would be issued Theresienstadt identification papers.

She heard German, Bavarian German. They were from the South. She looked over the crowd trying to see a familiar face, but then she realized it was useless. The chance of her seeing... Was that David? She tried to get closer as she saw the thin, pale man with worry lines etched on his face.

"David?" she called out.

The man looked up with a start. It had been so long since anyone had known his name. "Yes?" he asked, still dazed and confused from the long, harrowing trip from Munich.

"David. Is that you? Do you remember me?"

It seemed to take his eyes forever to focus on her face and before he responded Amalie looked down at the man laying at David's feet. "Oh my God! Sam? Is he all right?"

"Amalie?"

"Yes David, it's Amalie. Your father, is he...?"

"He needs help. Can we get him some water? There was no

water. It was such a long trip and there was nothing to eat..."

"We don't have much here either. I'll help you. Let's get him to my room."

"They've assigned us an apartment." David said, still dazed, as though he thought everything would be all right now that they had arrived. He seemed to think they would be taken care of in some kind of Jewish retirement community just like the German propaganda portrayed the relocation centers in the East.

"Everything's ready in my room David. Let's go there first."

Sam was hardly able to get up as Amalie supported him with his arm around her shoulder and David wasn't much help as he trudged along with them.

"Help me Louis" Amalie said as she saw her brother-in-law on the street.

"Who is it?" Louis asked as he took Sam's other arm, brushing David aside.

"Sam Frieder from Munich. And that's David. I worked for David in Munich."

They carried Sam into Amalie's small room and laid him on the bed. David knelt down by his father and tried to make him comfortable. Louis whispered to Amalie as he left, "He doesn't look good." Amalie was frozen in the doorway. She had seen so many of the old people die. They died on the trains, some held on for a few days and still others seemed to be doing all right in the camp, that is to say as well as anyone could, and then a morning would come when they just didn't wake up.

She watched the man who she barely recognized as David kneeling next to his dying father, the father who had also been her friend. She couldn't stand there any longer. "I'll go get some water" she said. David looked up, his eyes filled with an overwhelming sadness, but he said nothing.

Amalie was stung by a cold, cutting wind as she crossed the street to the latrine with its long row of stamped tin sinks each hung below a small mirror. She stopped for a moment and looked in the mirror as she let the water run in the tin cup she had brought with her. It had been a long time since she had studied her face in a mirror. The lines were so deep and clear. She remembered how surprised she was when she saw Eleonore's gray hair on that first day in the camp, but now as she looked she saw that her hair had even more gray than her sister's.

"Mrs. Metzdorf?" came a voice from the doorway.

Amalie turned to see a thin, pale young woman holding the hand of a little boy.

"Yes?" Amalie answered hesitantly.

"I can't believe it's you! It's been so long."

Amalie just stared blankly.

"You don't remember me..." the young woman said sadly, "Your son and I were friends. I lived a few houses..."

"Rebecca?" Amalie interrupted.

"...Yes." the young woman said as she managed a weak smile.

"You were on the train this morning?"

"Yes. My mother, my son and..."

"This is your son?"

"Yes."

"He's so handsome." Amalie said as she walked over to them, "Is your husband with you, too?"

"No."

"Is he all right? Is he still in Germany?"

"I don't know where he is."

"Oh, that must be terrible. I'm so sorry. A lot of people get separated. Sometimes they show up..."

"Mrs. Metzdorf, I..."

"There's no need for that. Call me Amalie."

"Amalie... Where is your son?"

" I don't know. He was here in Prague, but I haven't had any word for some time. No one can visit here."

"I wanted to tell him..."

"Tell him what?" Amalie asked, but as she asked, Rebecca looked down at her son in such a way, brushing his hair back just the way Amalie always had to do with Jakob when he was a boy, and suddenly Amalie knew before she really knew.

"I don't want to hurt you Amalie. I don't want anything. This might not be the right time, but with the way things are, I have to tell you now while I have the chance... Jakob is Thomas' father."

"What?"

"Just before the war, before the Anschluss. Jakob came to Munich. Something to do with school... and we..."

"The Anschluss? ...Yes, I remember. We were in Salzburg and

left for Prague just before they came."

"I couldn't get word to him. I know it must be a shock..."

"...and you had to take care of..." Amalie began, but stopped in mid-sentence, having forgotten the little boy's name.

"Thomas."

"You had to take care of him all by yourself?"

"I was still with my mother. My brother Max helped out, too wherever he could."

"Rebecca, I've got to get back to my room. Someone else who came in on the train this morning is very sick and I just went out for some water. Come with me."

Amalie tried to tell Rebecca as much as she could while they walked back to Amalie's cell. "You'll see where I live and you can come back after you get settled. I should warn you that they sometimes separate the children from their parents. It depends on how much room they have. A lot of the children live with the orphans up in the attics. Don't fight them if they separate you. They might cut off your rations. If you are separated, don't worry. You'll still be able to be with him most of the time and after a little while you might be able to bribe them for another room where you can all stay together."

"But we don't have anything to bribe them with."

"Don't worry about that now. We'll come up with something." Amalie said as she stopped and looked down at Thomas. "My Grandson..."

"Yes." Rebecca answered, expecting Amalie to embrace Thomas or kiss him.

"I have to go." Amalie said as she looked Rebecca in the eye. Rebecca could see that Amalie had to tear herself away.

Amalie didn't even notice the other people as she crossed the street. She didn't see the little girl reaching up to her, sitting on the sidewalk begging for food.

David's hand was on his father's forehead as Amalie came back to the room and offered him the water. David took the cup and pressed it to Sam's lips. A small line of water ran down Sam's cheek.

"He's got a fever. It started yesterday."

"Has he eaten?"

"I don't think he can. He goes in and out. Can you get any food? Soup or something like that?"

"We don't get much. We've been getting rotted potatoes lately,

561

but you can usually get some good pieces off of them. I can make a thin soup... But you've got to go now and find out where you're staying. You'll get in trouble if you don't and that won't do Sam any good."

David looked at her. He knew she was right, but he didn't want to leave because he was afraid his father would die while he was away. "You'll stay with him?" he finally asked.

"Of course, David. I'll..."

"Aunt Amalie?" came a voice as Sophie Hoffman, the younger of Amalie's two nieces, appeared at the door. She didn't say anything more when she saw that Amalie wasn't alone.

"Sophie, dear, this is a friend of mine from Munich and his father. I've got to stay with Sam. Could you tell your mother that he needs a little soup?"

"Yes Aunt Amalie." Sophie answered and then disappeared from the doorway as quickly as she had come.

"There." Amalie said to David, "Now everything is taken care of. You can go and find out where you're assigned. Don't worry about Sam. I'll take care of him."

She could see that David was overwhelmed by it all. It was as if he couldn't speak for all the emotion that was welling up within him. Then he suddenly put his arms around her. She could hear the tears in his voice. "I never thought I'd see you again. I never thought I'd see anyone that I used to know. God put you here. God put you here Amalie, just to remind me that he exists."

"Go David. Go now. Everything will be all right."

In a secret training facility not far from Wilhelm Canaris' new Abwehr headquarters at Zossen, outside of Berlin, Jakob's training was just ending as Rebecca, David and Sam arrived in Theresienstadt. The people who trained Jakob knew that there was something unusual going on because Jakob had arrived in the middle of the training session in progress and was kept separate from all of the other trainees. No one talked about it though, because this was their business. They knew what they needed to know and kept everything else to themselves.

Jakob's graduation ceremony came in the form of an escort on a train bound for Wilhelmshaven during which he was briefed on last minute details of his mission before boarding a submarine which would take him to the English coast. The captain riding with him in the staff car told him that the man he was to kill might not be where he was supposed to be. Their information was old and all they had now was a rumor that had filtered through to one of their few contacts left in England that Gerhard Kruger, Jakob's target, had been reassigned. Kruger was an operative who had been planted in England long before the war started. Kruger's mission began soon after Adolf Hitler started splashing about in the waters of international politics by sending troops into the Rhineland in 1935 for what Hitler considered his first step towards reclamation of German honor by forcing French occupation troops off German soil.

The truth was that Gerhard Kruger was the son of a German merchant and an English mother in Egypt. When he went to England in 1935, it was under the name of Cecil Baker, claiming to be from an English family who fought the Boer in South Africa and then moved to Egypt where he was born. He spoke impeccable English thanks to his mother and through various contacts along with forged credentials and other papers he managed to enter the English Foreign Service soon after his arrival in Britain. The Abwehr would periodically give him information over the years to pass on to the British, information carefully chosen to be current yet non-threatening to German plans, so that he could pass it on and receive credit for his initiative and thus be in line for advancement.

It worked very well for the Abwehr until they began to suspect that he had become a double agent, a suspicion that seemed confirmed by the fact that he was one of the very few to survive the English round up of German agents in Britain. He claimed that his position was compromised and that he had to keep a low profile, waiting until something very important came up, but Canaris didn't believe the report. Admiral Canaris was sure Kruger had been turned to the English side and knew that he had to stop him. Kruger couldn't cause much trouble at the moment, but Admiral Canaris was concerned about the future. an unexpected turn of events, such as an invasion of the continent, might suddenly give value to a heretofore innocuous bit of information in Kruger's possession.

This was where Jakob came into the picture. Canaris knew instinctively that Anton Eberhard, the name Jakob was using, was his best chance of sending someone to eliminate Kruger. Anton was a motivated young man, motivated by whatever personal mission he had in England. Admiral Canaris was willing to wait and see how this young man would play out his cards, but it was also an excellent opportunity to take care of the Kruger affair.

Jakob was given identity papers along with ration cards and money. He had gone over every detail of Cecil Baker's life in England many times, although now he had to consider that Baker might have moved. Jakob didn't fight the training. He felt he had been a coward for not getting into the war in some way. There was no army for him to join and he had never been in a situation in the resistance where he might have to kill anyone so he allowed himself to be immersed in this idea of killing Cecil Baker as a part of the war. It was a real and tangible act of war. Even though he was killing this man for German intelligence he convinced himself that it was for his own purposes, that he was somehow in control of the situation and the assassination of Cecil Baker was just a part of the plan to save his family and friends in Prague.

On top of everything else, Jakob had only a vague idea of how he would contact his grandfather. He knew about Edwin Coopersmith, but as far as where Ethan lived, the only address he had was for the apartment on the West end where Ethan had lived in 1939. For all he knew, his grandfather might not even be alive, but this was a prospect that he never allowed himself to consider.

Streaks of orange, pink and red slipped through the heavy cloud cover across the horizon as Jakob entered the submarine station. He had never been to the ocean before. His only experience with England had been through school. He excelled in spoken English and every Englishman he met commented on how well he spoke their language, but he had only met a few and perhaps they were only being kind. The training in the Abwehr camp was only like a bandage on a gaping wound. They expected to keep Jakob alive just long enough to complete his mission and then it was up to him if he made it back.

The submarine was remarkably small. He had expected something enormous to match the propagandist's exhalations of the gallant German wolf packs which brought England's navy to its knees, but it was only a smelly, cramped, steel tube into which he descended.

The English channel was deceptively calm as the submarine left its cement stall in the submarine base, but Jakob soon began to feel the rise and fall of the channel swells. He was a source of amusement for the young sailors as he began to feel sick and stagger down the narrow passage way to the head to vomit over and over again.

The crossing to England seemed endless as they took a route to the north to avoid detection. They traveled on the surface to make time until they were to the north of their drop target. When they were within range of known destroyer patrols along the English coast they submerged and started their approach to the drop zone. Everyone was quiet. These men were all experienced even though they were very young, most of them even younger than Jakob, but they were still nervous about trying to land someone in England. It showed in their eyes.

The weather had taken a turn for the worse during the crossing and when they surfaced as they came to the little bay where Jakob was to be taken ashore, the wind was sending huge waves crashing over the deck. Two sailors scrambled onto the deck with a rubber raft and Jakob in tow. The sailors knew to hold on to the railing around the deck gun as they inflated the raft, but Jakob was almost taken over the side by the first wave rushing over the steel grate deck. One of the sailors managed to grab him by the sleeve and throw him against the rail just in time as the wave washed Jakob's feet out from under him. Jakob was about to thank the sailor, but it was clear from the sailor's expression that Jakob's inability to take care of himself was a great annoyance and the sailor had only saved him in the way he might grab for a box of cargo about to go off the deck.

"Hold onto those straps" one of the sailors shouted at Jakob, referring to the straps on the side of the rubber raft which was being tossed five feet or more above the deck as it road the swells of the stormy waves. Jakob couldn't imagine how he would even get into the tiny raft, but it wasn't something he had to worry about. In the next instant the two sailors physically picked him up and threw him sprawling onto the "floor" of the raft with his small satchel hitting him in the back as it flew in after him. The sailors then timed the rise and fall of the waves so that they could each in turn jump into the raft. Jakob was amazed at how they just went about their business without saying a word, each knowing his job and doing it without consideration of the danger. They were soon making their way slowly to the rocky shore as the sailors paddled furiously against the waves which somehow seemed to be coming at them from all directions. Jakob lost track of the shore as he huddled down against the incessant stinging spray of saltwater. He was sure they were being washed out to sea away from the submarine, but he didn't say anything to the others, he only prepared to drown.

"Out!' came a shout above the sound of the storm and Jakob looked up to see one of the sailors looking at him with wild eyes. Jakob was confused. Was this some kind of order to abandon ship? But why would they leave a raft? Even if it were sinking, where would they go? Then he looked around to see if the raft was sinking just in time to see a patch of gravelly shore slip up under them, a great wave disappearing beneath them as though a magic carpet had made a perfect landing.

"Out!" the sailor shouted again, knowing that they had to make their way back to the submarine as quickly as possible because even in weather like this there was a chance that they might be seen and they knew the English navy would go all out to destroy a submarine so impudent as to try to land someone on British soil. Jakob tumbled out onto the beach with his bag, which had miraculously survived the ride. He had no more than checked out the condition of his bag when he looked up to find that the sailors and their rubber raft had disappeared and the submarine was nowhere in sight amidst the darkness and the turbulent eruptions of the ocean, even there within the sheltered bay.

He made his way up the steep hills to a small shelf-like plateau below the cliffs that watched out over the bay. He could see through the gray darkness out to the bay now, now that he was well above the waves, and was surprised to see that the submarine was still there. He even believed he saw the little raft bobbing up and down close to the conning tower, suggesting that the sailors had just made it back in the same time that it took him to climb the hills. He watched as the conning tower then slowly disappeared beneath the waves. He was completely on his own.

He was about twenty kilometers north of Ipswich and he had to make his way to London. He knew there was no time to waste since many of his papers were dated for the next couple of days. He decided the bad weather wasn't so bad since people might be less suspicious of a man who showed up looking like a pathetic drowned dog rather than a dark and mysterious stranger.

It was past 5:00 on Tuesday morning when he finally got to Ipswich. He couldn't take the chance of trying to board a train in one of the smaller towns or villages as there was too much of a chance that he would be noticed as a stranger. He had to blend in where people couldn't know everyone, where one more man wouldn't be the talk of the town.

There was no way that he could have known as he walked to the train station that he passed within a hundred meters of the house where Ethan Stein had been living for the previous three years. His plan was to meet with Ethan first, before taking care of the Cecil Baker problem so that he could get out as quickly as possible after the killing.

His first stop when he arrived in London was the address Ethan had given Amalie on the West end where he was staying when he first got to England. When he found that the address had been bombed out and that Ethan had "moved to the country", his next stop was a second-hand shop where he picked up a used valise. He needed it as part of his cover story when he made contact with Edwin Coopersmith.

"Solicitor Coopersmith?" he asked as he stood at the door of Edwin's law office.

"Yes?"

"I need to get in touch with a client of yours"

Edwin sized up the young man standing before him. "I'm sorry... Who are you?"

Jakob had been told during his Abwehr training that many Germans had been arrested in England at the start of the war because of paranoia about espionage and that, in fact, the vast majority of German agents were picked up at that time. He then knew how he would find out Ethan's whereabouts if Ethan wasn't still at the address he had given Amalie before the war broke out. From that information he decided on his course of action when at the assumed the most arrogant demeanor possible and did his best impression of a clenched-jawed, south-of-England accent. "I'm with the foreign office. We conduct periodic checks on foreign nationals by contacting various acquaintances... Check with different people at different times, that is... to make sure all the stories match."

"the stories?" Edwin asked, annoyed at the presumption that he would lie.

"Oh, I certainly don't mean anything by that. It's just the job, you understand. Do as we're told and so on. Eh, what? Ours is not to question why, and so on..."

"Quite..." Edwin agreed dubiously.

"So, if you would just..."

"May I see your credentials? Do you have a badge or something?"

Jakob thought things were going smoothly until Edwin asked for identification. He didn't have anything to support his impersonation since this had been his own idea, completely separate of the Abwehr's training or knowledge. "Am I to understand that you don't wish to cooperate? I'm sure you realize that in times of emergency like this, the government must exercise certain..." he rambled on in an ominous tone, trying to bluff his way through.

"They aren't talking about internment again, are they?" Edwin countered with hostility.

Jakob had no way of knowing what his grandfather had been through. He didn't know that virtually every foreign national had been arrested and questioned at some time and that most spent some time in a British detention camp, but he didn't dare show ignorance. He shot back an answer as quickly as Edwin had made the accusation: "No, of course not. "

Edwin grudgingly relented at that point, feeling there was really nothing he could do protect Ethan. "He lives in Ipswich. South of the train station. He's registered with the police there, of course. Why don't you just check your records?"

"Sir, we know what our records say. We're just verifying them through other sources."

"That is the most ridiculous..." Edwin began indignantly.

"It may well be sir, but I don't question my orders." Jakob said, cutting him off.

"Well, that's all I have to say about the matter. If you have any more questions about Mr. Stein, you'll have to ask him yourself because I refuse to say anything behind his back."

Jakob acted as though he had been properly chastised and put in his place even though he had nothing else to ask. "Yes, sir. I'm sorry you feel that way. I'm just doing the job I was given to do and I have to believe that it is somehow valuable to the war effort. We all have to do our part after all, don't we sir?"

"Good day" Edwin said curtly as he closed the door in Jakob's face.

A smile crept across Jakob's face as he walked away, but just for a moment. He was pleased with his job of acting, but now he had to work out his plan. If only he had known his grandfather was in Ipswich. Now he had to decide if he should take care of Cecil Baker first and then go back to Ipswich or should he see Ethan first and then come back to London to take care of... Yes, that was it. He had two days. It would all work out.

He spent the rest of the morning verifying that Cecil Baker hadn't moved as the rumors at Abwehr training camp suggested. He even saw him as he came out of the bank on his way to lunch. It gave Jakob a chill when he recognized Cecil's face through the mist of the bleak April morning. Jakob had gone through the training and seen countless photographs of Cecil Baker, but this was the instant that made it all real. The game of "hide and seek" was over, the game of "spies" was over. Now he saw the man that he had agreed to murder. From the safe distance of Germany he had convinced himself that he could do it, but now he was overwhelmed by the thought. He ran from it. He headed for Victoria station to board the train to Ipswich.

It didn't take long for Jakob to track down the "elderly Austrian gentleman" as he asked people living in the neighborhood of the train station for information while he once again introduced himself as an officer of the foreign office. He was soon knocking on the door of a ramshackle little cottage close to the train station just as Edwin Coopersmith had said. Ethan blinked when he opened the door. His first instinct when he saw the stranger standing in front of him was that it was his grandson, but logic forced him to dismiss the thought as it would certainly be impossible for Jakob to suddenly show up in England. "I'm sorry," he said as he explained his strange reaction, "but you reminded me of someone... Can I help you?"

Jakob was also shocked. He was surprised by his grandfather's appearance. He had become shorter, shrunk in the five years since Jakob last saw him, and his hair had gone completely white instead of the familiar black with streaks of gray. "Grandfather?"

"My God!" Ethan whispered in amazement, "It is you, Jakob! How did you... ?" He stopped in mid-sentence and embraced his grandson as tears filled his eyes, but then he quickly stopped and looked around to see if anyone was watching. "Come in. We can talk here. Do you think anyone saw you come here?"

"Yes, but it's not a problem. I've told them that I'm with the foreign office checking up on you and they fell over themselves trying to help."

"I can't believe it! This is incredible! How did you get here?"

"you won't believe it, grandfather. Are you sure no one will interrupt us or hear us?"

"Yes, quite sure."

Jakob took a breath before giving Ethan the news. "Mother is in one of the concentration camps."

"Oh God, no!"

"Yes... and so is Aunt Eleonore and her family. That's why I'm here. I can't tell you everything because it would be dangerous for you, but I've come for the package that mother sent with you."

"Package?"

"Yes. The package" Jakob said impatiently as he teetered on anger, "Something about Hindenburg and Hitler. Some letters or something." Even as he said it, terrible thoughts flashed through Jakob's mind: "What if Ethan couldn't remember? What if he had lost it?"

"Oh, yes... yes. I have it here. It's a small box as I recall. Up in the attic."

They immediately went up to the tiny attic and searched through the musty boxes amid the other lost odds and ends until Ethan finally pointed out a small wooden box in the corner. Jakob pulled it out and began inventorying the contents. It was just as his mother had told him, the blood spattered nightshirt and the broken needle along with Friedrich Haas' letter detailing both the murder of Paul von Hindenburg and the murder of Geli Rabaul. Petr Hrmeni had told Jakob before he left Prague that the Germans would take whatever he might bring back from England, so he should only let them have enough to show that Amalie's information was valuable. Jakob decided to write his own letter, telling only the story of the Hindenburg murder, and putting that in the box. He took the original letter and sewed it into his coat, hoping that he might get it past the Abwehr.

"This is it" he said to his grandfather as he made sure everything was ready, "I'm going to leave it with you. I have to go to London tonight and then I'll be back at the Ipswich station at 7:00 tomorrow night. You'll have to meet me there with the box. I don't suppose you have an automobile...?"

"No."

"Well, then... You'll have to leave it somewhere where I can just pick it up on my way through."

"Why don't you just come here?"

"I can't. It will be late" he said with hesitation and suddenly he couldn't make eye contact with his grandfather, "...and they might be looking for me."

Ethan was startled as the implication registered. "Looking for you? Why would they... What are you doing tonight?"

A sullen expression overtook Jakob as he imagined his grandfather eyeing him accusingly.

"Don't answer" Ethan continued. "You're right. It would be best if I didn't know."

They sank into a terrible silence for a moment. It had been so long since they had seen each other and their reunion should have been joyous, but now they struggled awkwardly with the situation.

"They have lockers at the train station. Maybe you should take the box with you. That would draw less attention than wandering through the city at odd hours."

"Yes. You're right."

There was another awkward pause. Jakob felt so guilty because of what he had to do the next day that he couldn't stand being with Ethan. He had to put his sense of right and wrong aside if he was to carry out the task of killing Cecil Baker and he suddenly felt that his grandfather was judging him even though Ethan had no idea of the events that were about to unfold.

"I've had a great deal of time to think" Ethan began, "All this time away from everyone I... I don't think I should have left."

"You wouldn't have survived" Jakob said as he once again looked Ethan in the eye.

"I don't feel as though I've survived here. I've lost everything."

"They would have taken you away if you had stayed. At least here you're free."

"Jakob, I promised myself that if I ever saw you again..." a single tear started down Ethan's cheek as he strained to keep his composure, "I promised myself I would tell you how much you mean to... I want you to know how much I love you. How much I have always loved you and..."

"It's all right grandfather," Jakob said as he put an arm on the old man's shoulder, "I know."

It was one of those moments when one generation tries to reach another and neither completely sees the other. Jakob saw an emotional old man, perhaps even thought it a sign of weakness, while Ethan saw his whole life and was in full realization of what was important to him, what was important in life, and wanted to magically pass that on to his grandson before it was too late for him.

"I've got to go now" Jakob said as he embraced Ethan, "I won't see you again for awhile, but if this all works out we'll all be together soon."

The trip back to London was uneventful and Jakob quickly found a cheap hotel room where he could settle in for a good rest before the next days work.

He dressed very carefully the next morning as he got ready for the mission. He had two weapons to choose from. He carried a small caliber semi-automatic pistol in a holster on his ankle and a stiletto-type commando knife on a harness around his shoulder and neck that he could quickly draw out of his collar. He had been shown the best ways to use the knife and was told that the most effective was to come up on his victim from behind, grab the victim with his left arm around the man's body so that he could hold down the victim's arms, and slip the long blade of the knife down into the opening of the collar bone to the side of the neck. The determining factor would be opportunity. How would he get Cecil Baker alone?

His rendezvous with the submarine was set for 2:00 in the morning, but the last train to Ipswich was at 11:00 PM. That gave him only sixteen hours to find the right time and place, kill Cecil and then get to the train station.

He threw away the valise and everything else except the forged papers and money and then waited down the street a few hundred meters from Cecil's house while Cecil came out to the bus station. Cecil looked just like any average English businessman as he sat on the bench in his dark coat with his black bowler and his umbrella leaning against his leg as he read the morning newspaper.

Jakob sprinted up to the bus as Cecil boarded and got on behind a couple of other people. After a few blocks he suddenly realized that they weren't heading in the direction of the bank where Cecil worked. He felt panicky, but he stayed where he was. He was just a few seats behind Cecil and there was no way Cecil could get off the bus without Jakob.

Jakob's imagination started to get the better of him. What if Cecil somehow knew that Jakob was there to kill him? Maybe he was leading Jakob into some kind of trap. He didn't have long to think about such things since Cecil was soon gathering up his things and moving to the door. Jakob waited until some other people got up so that he wouldn't be right behind Cecil when he followed him.

They were at a train station. Jakob suddenly realized that he didn't have any time left. Mr. Baker was obviously about to leave and it would be too obvious if he left with him. Jakob's heart began to pound. Should he shoot him and then just run? No. There it was, just in front of him. The answer: A crowded bridge over the railroad tracks leading to the platforms.

Jakob started to weave his way through the crowd. No one paid much attention to him since he was just one of a number of men rushing through the crowd, although they were just rushing to catch their trains while Jakob was trying to catch up with Cecil. He caught up with Cecil just as Cecil stepped onto the bridge. Jakob grabbed him by the coat. The man turned suddenly. It wasn't Cecil! Jakob must have lost him in the crowd.

"I'm sorry, I thought you were..." he said as he let go of the man and then turned to find Cecil.

Jakob was startled as he turned to find that Cecil was right behind him, in fact, he ran right into him. Everything was instinct then. Jakob grabbed him by the coat and wrestled him a couple of steps over to the railing. Cecil was caught so completely off guard that instead of fighting back, he spent his effort just trying not to fall. Cecil thought it was just an awkward stumble. He couldn't have known that Jakob was trying to kill him as everything happened all at once. When Jakob had pulled Cecil to the railing, which was little more than waist-high, Cecil was already off balance and it required little effort on Jakob's part to flip Cecil over the railing. Cecil grabbed for Jakob, catching Jakob's coat to keep from falling, but Jakob brought his fists down hard against Cecil's hands and broke free of his hold. Cecil fell some fifteen feet on to a train which was speeding under the bridge.

Jakob ran as soon as Cecil let go and so he didn't see the way Cecil's body bounced off the train, landing limply on to the next track like a rag doll with all the stuffing knocked out of it. Jakob did hear the shrill scream of a woman on the bridge though, as people came

573

running from all directions to see what had happened, crowding in towards the footbridge. Jakob suddenly stopped running as he decided to that it would be best to get lost in the crowd. He began to walk parallel to the train tracks, trying to look like all the other people who were looking down at the tracks to see what had happened. He was soon out of the area of the train station.

He made his way back to Victoria station and immediately boarded a train for Ipswich. He wasn't sure what he would do next, but he wanted to get out of London and the time on the train would be time to think.

Everything had gone so quickly with Cecil Baker that it would only be 11:00 in the morning when he arrived in Ipswich, leaving him fifteen hours to stay out of sight. He decided that his best option would be to hide out in the country, so once he arrived at the Ipswich train station he only stayed long enough to get the package from the locker before starting the long hike to the pick up point.

He walked for hours along the roadside, ducking out of sight on the rare occasions when a car or someone on bicycle might pass by, until he came to a little patch of woods close to the ocean where he stopped to rest for a couple of hours. He had traveled about seventeen of the twenty kilometers by that time, just as the Sun was setting. It was a beautiful night, but all he could think about was how hungry and tired he was and how he didn't dare sleep because he might sleep right through until morning and how he couldn't go foraging for food this close to the pick up point because he might be seen and get caught as he waited around for the submarine. He didn't even dare light a fire to keep warm. He huddled against the trunk of an ancient evergreen, making himself comfortable on the thick bed of fallen needles, and waited for the right time to start the last leg of his hike.

Suddenly there was a strange warmth around his ear, moist and hot. Jakob drifted in and out of a fog. He had fallen asleep. He froze, every muscle in his body tensing as he realized what was happening. Someone was there beside him. He would have to kill whoever it was. Jakob didn't even open his eyes until he was ready to move. He leapt up and pulled out his knife as he threw his body toward whoever it was standing over him. All at once he realized it was a fawn that he had pushed over and pinned against the tree. He caught the slightest reflection of the moonlight in the big brown eyes of the startled young deer and began to laugh out loud, partly because it seemed so funny, but mostly as a release of the incredible tension. He was surprised as he sat back against the tree to find that he was shaking all over and then he suddenly thought about the time. He scrambled out from under the tree in a panic so that he could see his watch in the moonlight. He could still make it if he moved quickly.

The ocean was calm as he got to the bay. It was a beautiful scene, but not the sort of thing an agent hopes for when the submarine sent to pick him up stands out starkly against the moonlight reflecting on the calm water. Jakob had made it just in time as he saw a raft half way between the submarine and the shore. The pick up went smoothly and he was soon having a sandwich aboard the submerged submarine on it's way back to Wilhelmshaven.

Petr had been right in his assumption about Canaris and his Abwehr. Jakob was greeted by two men as soon as the submarine came to dock who told him he was to leave for Berlin with them immediately. It was a long ride to Canaris' new headquarters outside of Zossen. They arrived late at night, but even so, Jakob was told that the Admiral would soon be there to talk to him.

"How did everything go?" Wilhelm asked as Jakob was ushered in to the Admiral's office.

Jakob was clearly annoyed as he took a seat across the desk from Wilhelm. "Am I under arrest?" he asked.

"Arrest? No... let's just say you're being 'debriefed'. Just like any good spy. I assume the Kruger problem has been taken care of... "

"Kruger? Oh, yes. Cecil Baker. He's dead."

"Well done. I hope it wasn't too much of a problem."

Jakob changed the subject rather than going into detail about the killing. "They've taken my package..."

"Did you think we wouldn't?"

"No."

"I thought as much." Wilhelm said with a wry little smile, "You wanted us to have a sample."

"Something like that... The Hindenburg affair, that's the least of what we have."

"Impressive."

Jakob was pleased by the admiral's comment, but he was also very cautious. "What will you do with it?"

Wilhelm's forehead filled with wrinkles as he furled his brow. "I

575

don't think I've ever heard before of a case where the blackmailer asks how the ransom money should be spent."

"How long will I be kept here?"

"We have to make sure Kreuger is dead."

"There's no way he could have survived."

"Ah, now Anton" Wilhelm replied, using the pseudonym Jakob had given when he first contacted the Abwehr, "This is where the problems start arising. I don't know you well enough to take your word for things and we don't have a very reliable operation in England. We can't always get into the right places to verify information. We have this newspaper" Wilhelm paused as he tossed a carefully folded London newspaper on to the desk so that Jakob could see the article about the killing. Jakob was surprised to see a rather good sketch of himself below a headline reading "murder suspect eludes police".

"But we can't be sure quite yet" Wilhelm concluded. "British intelligence is quite good at giving out news stories at times, telling us just what we want to hear."

"So we wait." Jakob said with

"It shouldn't be long. Then we'll let you run along back to Prague."

"Run along?" Jakob asked dubiously, "Just like that?"

"Not to worry. We'll stay in touch. You see my dear Anton, by doing this little job for us you have given me a little 'on, off' switch. It wouldn't be very good if your friends in the resistance found out that you had killed an English agent, would it? If you don't work with us, we'll just switch you off."

In Theresienstadt, Amalie had been waiting for weeks to hear from Petr or Jakob. The conditions were getting worse in the camp. Thousands of people were being brought into the camp just as thousands had been sent out days before, but it was soon obvious that more were coming in than had been sent East.

They often had to stand in the courtyard for hours while they were counted every day when the commandant ordered a roll call. That one was the worst. The one before the deportation. They all stood there for hours and hours, six, eight hours, longer. The Jewish council was making up the list. They had just been told that eight thousand were to go and they must send them out. If the council didn't decide then the council and their families would be the first on the cattle cars. "Who would that help?" they rationalized as they agreed to put their marks upon the heads of the damned. Should the sick go because they would die anyway? The old? What chance did they have in Theresienstadt? Should whole families go so that they would be together or should the parents be sent and the orphans cared for in the attics of the Theresienstadt town hall and stores?

These were decisions made by men who convinced themselves that they were fit judges and that they could help by doing the job of choosing who would stay and who would go to the East.

In the middle of all the confusion, Amalie was summoned to the commandant's office.

For some strange reason she was sure that she would be talking to Klaus Grunewald. She had not talked to him in all the weeks since she had seen him there on the steps of the commandant's office and she had tried to convince herself that he had forgotten her.

"Sit there." a corporal commanded as he pointed to a chair in a drab little office. She looked around after the corporal left her alone, closing the door behind him. The desk in front of her was old and abused. It certainly wasn't the commandant's office. She thought to herself that this was just an extra room where they questioned people, not a place for torture, but the place where they started with small talk to size up somebody before getting serious.

A Captain came into the office from a side door, crossing in front of Amalie without acknowledging her presence. He carried a thick stack of files in one hand as he held another file close to his face. He slapped the stack of files loudly on the desk and sat down, all the while still reading the open file. He continued to read while Amalie sat quietly and patiently.

"Now then," he finally said abruptly, "you are this 'Metzdorf' woman?"

Amalie simply nodded her head in agreement.

"Please speak up when you are addressing me." the captain said with a nasty edge to his voice as he cocked his head to the side.

"Yes, sir. I am Amalie Metzdorf."

"...from Munich and then Salzburg and Prague?"

"Yes, Herr captain."

"We have some interesting information here. It seems that we are to provide you with some special considerations."

"Considerations?" Amalie asked, but she was almost certain that

577

it had something to do with Jakob's trip to England.

"Yes. It seems that you and your family are to be exempted from transport. It seems the Abwehr is doing some sort of investigation and somehow they think you might be of value."

"My family? There are a few other people..."

"We thought this might happen. It's all in the hands of the Abwehr, so you are to give us all the names and they will make a decision on who shall be exempted."

"...and food? Will there be more rations?"

"You are a Jew in Theresienstadt. Don't get greedy. You're lucky to get this."

Amalie knew she was supposed to be terrified, but she wasn't. She was sure she was in a position to bargain. "We need double rations" she said as she stared the captain in the eye, "We need double rations just to live."

There was venom in the captain's gaze as he stared back. "We shall see."

Amalie was then dismissed from the office and she immediately went back to her room to write out the names of those she would take with her.

There was no writing paper to be had, but she always made a point of picking up whatever scrap paper she could find; a piece of a poster or an old notice that had been nailed on a wall or anything blowing around the street. She had a small piece of a discarded pencil which she carefully sharpened and then she started writing.

Eleonore and Louis and their daughters. Sam and David Frieder. Rebecca Geschwind and her little boy and Rebecca's mother. Amalie had also been surprised to find that there were others in the camp that she knew. Otto Maus, the writer from Ried with whom she had worked, the one who wrote stories about the American west in the frontier days, had been in the camp for months. It seems he was regarded as a substantial writer. It was even rumored that the Fuhrer himself had read some of Otto's books when he was a boy.

Another surprise came one day when Joseph Hubert, David Frieder's boyhood friend from Munich, was pushed out of one or the dark, fetid box cars into the bright, unfamiliar sunlight of the Theresienstadt yard.

There were two dozen people in all. Amalie was cynical enough to put down the names of some people she had only met in the camp, thinking that the German captain might not grant protection to all of the people she had named and so she would need some extra names that she could cross off.

She was ready to go back the next day and bargain with the captain, but the guards wouldn't let her enter the building. She would have to wait for him to call her.

It was two days later when she was ordered back to the office. It was the same game as she was once again left waiting in the office, but this time it was almost two hours before the captain stormed in and slammed a new stack of files down on the old desk. He took a deep breath and let it out in a loud sigh as he brushed back his hair with his hand. "Refresh my memory." he said tiredly, "What is this about?"

"I'm Amalie Metzdorf" Amalie said hesitantly, "We talked the other day. You said there were special considerations in my case and I should write down the names of my family and..."

"Ah, yes. Metzdorf. Very well. What do you have?"

"These are the others..." Amalie said as she handed the paper to the captain, "I think they..."

"Very well." the captain said, cutting her off, "You may go."

"But I..." Amalie stuttered.

"That is all." the captain said slowly and distinctly.

Amalie didn't know what to make of it and so she got up and left. The cold wind stunned her as she walked past the guards and down the steps. She wondered to herself if it was all some kind of a trick. Had she given them a list of special victims? Instead of saving her family, had she condemned them to torture until she told her captors everything they wanted to know?

There was nothing to do but wait. There was no one she felt she could talk to about what was happening and so she didn't want to talk to anybody because it was all she could think about. She laid on the straw covered wooden bed on top of the small, frayed woolen blanket in her tiny room. She was paralyzed with fear. She knew a storm was coming, a storm that she had called up, and she thought it might destroy everyone she loved.

"Amalie" David called out urgently as he stuck his head in the doorway, "It's father...Can you come?" He was gone before she had a chance to answer, but she jumped up and ran out the door, soon catching up to him and leaving her concerns of the previous moment behind.

"What is it?" she asked as she tried to catch her breath.

"I'm not sure. He just started shivering and saying how cold he was and then he started to break out in a sweat."

They rushed into the white-washed cement building with its catacombs of tiny cells and quickly made their way through the maze of hallways to the small room that David and his father shared, a room hardly big enough for the two small cots and the battered little table pressed between them. David froze in the doorway as he saw his father laying still in the cot with his eyes closed. Amalie pushed past him in the doorway and knelt down beside Sam, taking his hand in hers. Sam suddenly lurched up with a start. "What? What is it?" he asked the empty air in front of him.

Amalie had expected the worst. She was sure Sam had died like so many of the older people, so she was startled when he lurched forward. "Nothing's wrong..." she said as she regained her composure, "Are you all right, Sam?"

"Yes. I'm just so tired." He said as he turned on his side and went back to sleep.

David's reaction during all of this was a half-smile, half cry as his voice broke and he let out a funny little squeak as he sighed in relief.

"He's all right for now." Amalie pronounced

"I don't know what to do anymore." David said as he sat down on the other cot, "I don't know what's wrong."

"He seems to be doing better."

"Do you really think so?" David asked, obviously hoping for Amalie to encourage him, "he's been doing better than when we got here, but he never got over being deported. That cattle car took something out of him, something that had kept him going before."

"Hope?" Amalie asked.

"He's been through a lot." she answered, "Considering everything, yes. I think he'll be fine."

"Everything has been so hard. I was surprised that we weren't on that last transport to the East." he said sadly because he knew there would be another. transport to the East soon enough. Surely they would be on the next one.

"I know..."

"Of course you do. We all do. They think we're all the same, but

we're so different and now here we all are thrown together

It wasn't until last year that I started going to Shabbat services... I hadn't gone since I was a boy. Father was going and he asked me to go with him to a friend's house. We had lost almost everything by then..."

"Did it help?"

"Help? No, that's not it. It was... 'Teshuva'. The return. It was the last place to go, the only thing left, and it brought us back to ourselves."

"What do you mean?"

"We had tried so hard to fit in as Germans, generation after generation, but they kept telling us we weren't Germans. Then we found out who we were and what we had been running from. We are Jews and we finally learned that that was enough. We remembered that it was a holy thing to be a good Jew, that we were chosen to receive the Torah and all the persecution that went along with it. The Germans have decided to make Hitler their God and they chose us to pay the price for their apostasy." David stopped for a moment. He had been looking down at the floor and he looked up at Amalie, smiling weakly as he continued, "Even here they have services."

"I know. I've heard about it."

"...but you don't go."

"No. I haven't..." Amalie began, but she stopped in mid sentence as the door suddenly swung open and one of the guards entered.

David and Amalie just stared blankly at the man, waiting for him to speak.

"Frieder?"

"Yes?" David answered.

The guard's only reply was to drop a sack on the floor in front of David before walking out and closing the door behind himself.

"What is it?" Amalie asked as David moved towards the bag and opened it.

"Food!" David exclaimed, "Why would they give us more food?"

"That should help Sam." Amalie said, ignoring David's question. She knew the food was the answer to the request she had made of the captain. She suddenly knew that it might all work. They could get out.

"Yes, of course, but why did they give it to us?" David repeated as he held up a loaf of bread.

Amalie had been standing all the time that she and David had been talking, but now she sat down on the cot beside him. "David, I know why they did it. It was because of me."

"Because of you?"

"I think I've found a way out."

"What on earth are you talking about?"

"David, I think I can get us out of here. You, me, Sam... my family... I think we can all get out."

"Amalie," David started as he eyed her suspiciously, wondering if she was losing her mind, " are you all right?"

"Yes. Just listen David." she said impatiently, "I've made a bargain with them. I had some papers they wanted and I think I can trade the papers to get us out."

"How? How can you hide anything in here? The guards would find anything you..."

"No, the papers aren't here."

"Then how can you get them. The minute you tell them where..."

"No, listen David. Listen!" Amalie said loudly as her frustration became apparent. "Jakob is outside..."

"Your son, Jakob?"

"Yes, of course. He can help us and this food is the proof. He must have done something so that the nazis believe me. That's why they gave us the extra food. It's a sign of good faith."

"What is it all about?"

"Things I discovered before the war, back when Gunther was in the party. I even know one of the officers here. He was a good friend of Gunther's"

"What kind of things?"

"Information about Hitler himself, information about the rumors of Jewish blood and other things."

"But you're... That's just as bad as they are!"

"David! What do you mean? It's nothing like that."

"Of course it is. They made it a crime to be a Jew and you're playing up to that."

"David, I'm trying to save us. I'm doing everything I can to save my family and friends. I'd do anything I could to keep them safe."

582

"But don't you see that for everyone you save, someone else will be taken in their place?"

"That's not true," Amalie said, the words all seeming to rush out at once, "They're taking everyone. There isn't anyone left behind who will be taken if someone steps out of line. They're killing everyone."

"I just can't agree with this. You're making a deal with the devil. They say it's a crime to be a Jew and you're agreeing with them when you accuse him of being a Jew."

"I don't care! I do not care! I have to save my family and this is the only way. I can't afford your ethics."

"But Amalie, how will you live with yourself? Later, after all of this is over, how will you live with yourself?"

Amalie became quiet, but her words were intense as she responded. "I will live through it David. That's all there is now. We know what's happening out there. Here they die from shortage of food and medicine. Out there someplace they're being murdered. I believe that. I don't want to believe it, but I do and I'll do whatever I can to save myself and the rest of my family."

Chapter 20

April 19, 1943 was the day when the survivors of the Warsaw Ghetto rose against the Germans using whatever guns they could smuggle, steal or take from German soldiers they had killed during the battle. Only 70,000 of the 1940 population of 500,000 Jews in Warsaw were still in the walled-off Jewish ghetto by that time. The majority of those people had been transported to death camps, most notably Treblinka.

German troops were about to begin the final phase of making Warsaw "Jew free". In the years following the heroic uprising there would be those who asked why these people hadn't risen up sooner against their oppressors. Why hadn't these unarmed citizens, a minority in any of the countries where they were persecuted, risen up against the best armed and trained military force the world had ever known up to that time?

These German soldiers called themselves Christians and believed that Christ died for the sins of man, but for whom did six million Jews die? Did they die for the nazis? Did they die for all the countries that closed their doors to Jewish immigrants? Or was it just to show us how easy and mindless death is, to remind an entire world of our responsibility not just for Abel, but Cain as well?

April of 1943 drifted somewhere within the eye of the storm for Prague. Heydrich's body had been buried in Berlin some ten months before drenched in a moribundly glorious nazi funeral with full military regalia. He was eulogized tenderly for possessing "an iron heart", a reference that was meant as a compliment. The death which had been so brutally avenged was now just a memory for the survivors.

Petr Hrmeni struggled through the doorway of Petterink's furniture store with a chair in one hand and a broken leg from the chair in his other. He had never been to Petterink's before, but he had heard that this was the place where Heydrich's assassins had been hidden for a few days before the attack. There weren't many people left in Prague by the Spring of 1943 who were willing to oppose the German occupation after the nazi's bloody revenge. That was why Petr was delivering the chair himself.

The man behind the counter waved Petr into the back. Petr let the chair fall in a pile on the floor next to one of the work benches and looked over at one of the workmen. The other man looked out a window at something. Petr couldn't see that he was checking with a lookout across the street who had watched Petr come in and was waiting to see if anyone was following. The workman then nodded to Petr and Petr quickly made his way to the basement. They had done some masonry work in the basement since the time when Josef Gabcik and the others were there. The room now had a false wall at one end. It had taken months to do since they couldn't just bring in all of the materials at once since it would arouse suspicion. They had to sneak in a bag of mortar with a load of lumber here and a few bricks with another load there until they finally had enough. The door to the newly created room was in the floor. You had to crawl through a tunnel under the wall to get into the room which was only two meters wide. It was a very long room, though, because the wall ran the length of the basement so that it would blend in. The room was almost six meters long. Perfect for pacing back and forth as you waited.

Jakob had gone underground again since returning from his meeting with Admiral Canaris. He had told Petr about the Cecil Baker killing, but Petr told him not to tell anyone else. Petr had never heard of Kruger, Cecil Baker's real name, and so he assumed that he wasn't from the Czech area. He also assumed that since this Kruger was originally a German agent, the other members of the Czech resistance would understand that the killing had been necessary just in case word did leak out that Jakob had killed this man.

Jakob aimed his pistol at the trap door as he heard someone coming through the tunnel. Even when he heard the three knocks, a pause and a final knock that was meant to identify the visitor as friendly, he still kept the pistol cocked and aimed at the trap door.

Petr looked up blankly at the pistol muzzle which greeted him. "You seem edgy."

"I've been waiting here for two weeks now."

"I know. I know."

"No, you don't know" Jakob said as he put up the pistol and Petr climbed out of the hole. "I haven't been outside for a minute. I shit in a can. Pacing back and forth is the only exercise I get. You don't know what that's like."

"Fine." Petr said curtly, after all he had just been trying to sympathize, "I don't know what it's like."

"I've started having dreams about killing Kruger..."

"Try to put it out of your mind" Petr said as he brushed off the dirt from the tunnel.

"Put it out of my mind?" Jakob asked as he sat down in one of the two rickety old chairs on either side of the small table in the middle of the room.

"You've got to put it behind you" Petr continued as he sat down in the other chair.

"Do you know what it's like to kill a man with your bare hands?" Jakob asked earnestly, but an angry, impatient look on Petr's face made it clear that he knew exactly what Jakob was talking about.

Jakob just sighed and shook his head. "How is Karin?" he asked, changing the subject.

"She's good, but we don't have time for that now. I've got news."

"What news?"

"From your mother. Well, about your mother."

"She's all right?"

"Yes. She heard about your trip to England. Apparently she's been bargaining within the camp on the strength of your success."

"Bargaining? I thought the bargain was already made. Our freedom for the rest of the papers."

"She's upped the stakes. Food for herself and family... and she's added others."

"Others?"

"There are some other names here." Petr said as he handed Jakob a piece of paper, "She's gathered quite a group. The logistics of getting everyone out might prove..."

"My God." Jakob said with astonishment as he read the names.

"What is it?"

"Rebecca Geschwind."

"Who?"

"She was... I knew her in Munich. Her name is on the list."

Anyone else might have asked why the name surprised Jakob or what this woman had meant to him, but Petr wasn't interested. He let it drop and went on with his planning. "...getting that many people out," Petr mused, "It's too many for a truck. "

"Train?"

"Could we put them through that?" Petr asked with concern as he looked up at Jakob, "I suppose it makes sense. They send trains out to the East. One more car mixed in shouldn't raise suspicion."

"They could take them out in their own boxcar with a regular train" Jakob added, " and let it off on a siding. Then reroute it to Switzerland."

"I'll get word to Amalie. She'll need to get blank travel papers for Hannah, Karin and me. And you, of course. And then she can negotiate for the train."

"Do you think they'll do it?"

"A train to Switzerland? Yes. I don't think it's too much. The papers are in a Swiss bank. There's some money involved to bribe Swiss officials. Amalie could turn over the information on the deposit boxes..."

"At the train? Wouldn't they want to make sure everything was there before they let anyone go?"

"Of course..." Petr said, pausing as he thought about it, "of course they would."

"They could wait in the train while a messenger was sent to verify..." Jakob offered.

"...But then they might just turn the train back once the messenger returned. It's too great a chance of double cross."

"So Mother and the others would have to be safely in

Switzerland before the exchange?"

"But then the Germans wouldn't have anything to bargain with. They would never agree to that."

They discussed the plan for awhile until they came to an agreement about how things should be handled.

"I want to go in." Jakob said as they wrapped things up.

"In?" Petr asked, "In where."

"Theresienstadt. I should be the one to explain everything to mother."

"Are you crazy? We already have a system for getting messages through. It would be too dangerous to go there."

"But the plan needs to be perfect. Details have to be confirmed. It's worth the risk."

"Why do your really want to go?"

"Who would she trust more than me?"

"But for God's sake, you're in hiding!"

"Then no one would expect me to show up in a concentration camp."

Petr sighed heavily and shook his head. "There is a chance, a small chance, but a chance, that we could get you inside. However... It would be much harder to get you out."

Jakob and Petr went over a map of the camp so that Jakob would know where to find Amalie once he was inside. Then they waited. They were waiting for a rainy day, hoping that the rain would lessen the guard's enthusiasm for checking on everything and everyone who came and went from the camp.

It took a few days to work out the arrangements and then there was the wait for the right weather, but within a week and a half Jakob found himself crouching in the back of a wagon filled with old potatoes in various stages of decay.

Everything hinged on Vasek Zapotocky. Vasek was the guard in Theresienstadt who worked with Petr and the resistance on occasion. Because part of Amalie's negotiations were financial, Vasek was particularly motivated to help. Vasek knew the farmer who was making deliveries and convinced the farmer to bring Vasek's friend Mirek to unload for him. On the day before and the day after Jakob's visit, Vasek would conceal Mirek in the camp so that when Jakob came in to unload the potatoes, it would be Mirek who would go out with the potato cart while Jakob stayed in the camp for a night. The next day Mirek would stay in the camp while Jakob went out and then the morning after that Mirek would appear from within the camp to unload the cart.

Jakob got out of the cart in the drenching rain and began to unload the potatoes into the crib behind the kitchen as Vasek stood watch with his machine gun. Jakob had never seen Vasek before and had only been told that the guard who would be watching him was friendly to their cause. It occurred to Jakob, though, that he had no way of knowing if this was the right guard. He couldn't be sure. things could always go wrong and if this was the wrong man...

Jakob loaded potatoes into two buckets and carried them into the kitchen. He dumped them into a huge kettle in the kitchen and as he did a young man who was the same size and build as Jakob, even wearing the same clothes, took the buckets from him and went out to the yard. That was it. That was everything. He was in. The other man was Mirek and he would go out with the cart when it left.

The previous weeks, the mission in England and the time hiding out in Petterink's cellar, had left Jakob gaunt and drawn. He didn't look out of place in Theresienstadt. The rotting potatoes in the cart had assailed his senses as he traveled the ten kilometers to the camp, but now he found that the whole camp smelled like that and much worse. Death and decay. People with ashen gray faces, children begging in the streets of the camp from people who themselves hadn't had enough to eat.

The other people in the kitchen didn't say anything about Jakob's presence. They had been bribed by Vasek not to say anything about what they might see for the next couple of days. It didn't take much to buy their silence. A couple of extra rotten potatoes was a fortune.

Jakob was careful not to be too fast or direct as he made his way to Amalie's cell. He kept his eyes down as he moved down the street, trying to match his pace with the other people he came across. There was no one in the room when he got there, so he sat on the cot and waited.

Amalie stopped as she came to the door of her cell. She somehow knew that something was out of place and she slowly peeked around the door before she went in. "Jakob!" she exclaimed, looking around outside to make sure no one was watching before she rushed in and sat beside him, putting her arms around her son. "How did you get here? What's happened?"

Jakob assured her that things appeared to be going as they had hoped and he told her the details of Petr's plan for getting everyone out of the country.

"He's sure it will all work?" Amalie asked about Petr.

"There are no guarantees."

"No, but..."

"We both think it's the best chance."

There was a pause as Amalie thought about it all and Jakob got up and went to the tiny window, standing to one side of the window so as not to be seen as he cautiously surveyed the yard.

"Jakob" she said hesitantly, "I have to tell you something... It's quite a surprise, at least to me."

"What ?" he asked as he continued looking out the window.

"You remember Rebecca Geschwind?"

"Of course. I know all about it. I know she's here."

"You know everything?"

"Everything?" he repeated, looking at her.

"Thomas?" she asked.

"Thomas? Thomas who?"

"When Rebecca and her mother came here, she had a little boy with her... Her son, Thomas."

"Her son? Rebecca married?" he asked as he sat back down on the cot, "Was her husband with her?"

"She isn't married."

"Well, the father... was he with her."

"No. The father..." Amalie started, but she couldn't find a good way to say it, so all the words came out at once. "Rebecca says he's your son. She says You're the father."

Jakob was stunned. It was the last thing he had expected. "Me?!"

"Don't you think it could be...?"

"A son?" he said, not responding to Amalie, but just letting the thought sink in.

"Could he be your son?"

"I... I don't know. How old is he?"

"She said it was just before the war, just before Austria..."

Jakob looked at his mother. "Does he look like me?"

"The eyes..." she said.

590

"We did... just before I left Munich. We didn't plan it... it was just so hard to leave her there. Everything was so mixed up. Neither of us thought we would ever see each other again."

Jakob slouched forward with his head in his hands, massaging his neck as the muscles tightened. "Yes, it could... He could be my son."

Amalie put her arm around him.

"What about Karin?" Jakob continued, "What do I tell Karin."

"It was a long time ago. A mistake." Amalie said as she tried to comfort him, "Karin will understand."

"I don't know what to do."

"I think you need to talk to Rebecca."

"That's funny..." he said as he looked her in the eye, "That was why I wanted to be the one to come here. I wanted to see you, but once I found out she was here I had to... I had to see her, but I never dreamed of anything like this."

"You wait here." Amalie said resolutely as she stood up, "I'll get Rebecca and bring her here. It might not be safe for you to be prowling around. We only have an hour before curfew."

Jakob sat in the frigid darkness nervously anticipating Rebecca's arrival. There had been an excitement about sneaking into the camp, an anticipation of seeing his mother and Rebecca, but now he had a moment of silence to take in the atmosphere of Theresienstadt. It was ugly and stale and he could still smell that vague foulness in the air that had hit him when he first arrived. He suddenly felt a panicky desperation as it crossed his mind that something might go wrong with the switch the next morning and he could be trapped in the camp.

It was cold and forbidding and ominous. He had to touch the wall to see if it felt the same as it looked. The dank, cold cement seemed to run through his hand like electricity. It was real. It was all real.

"I can't believe you're here." Rebecca whispered as she swept into the room, taking Jakob by surprise as he quickly pulled his hand away from the wall. "You look well" she lied as she closed the door behind her.

"It's so cold." was all Jakob could say, trying to explain what he had been doing when she came in, but Rebecca hadn't even noticed.

"Amalie said that she told you about Thomas..."

591

Jakob thought to ask if she was sure it was his son, but he didn't say anything.

"I've thought about you," she continued, "but I never thought I'd ever see you again."

"There have been others." Jakob said.

"What?" Rebecca asked, obviously confused.

"Other women." he said, "I've been involved with..."

"That's not what this is about" Rebecca said, "I just wanted you to know." There was a pause as each of them considered what to say next.

"Are you married?" Rebecca asked.

"No." Jakob said as he started to pace in the tiny room.

"But you love her?" Rebecca asked, not knowing about Karin specifically, but just assuming that there was another woman in Jakob's life at that time.

"We've been... We were thrown together."

"Convenience?"

"Damn it!" Jakob said, slapping the cold cement wall, "God Damn it. It shouldn't be like this."

There was another awkward pause as Rebecca sat silently on the cot and Jakob stood there leaning against the wall.

"Come with me" Rebecca finally said after a moment.

"Where?"

"Just come."

Rebecca took Jakob's hand just like she used to do so many years before. She looked cautiously out the door before pulling him along. and they crept through the street to one of the other buildings. No one said anything as they passed the different rooms although many of the other inmates gave surprised looks as they saw Rebecca and the strange young man pass through to her room.

There was a little boy with unruly thick brown hair curled up in a rat's nest of straw and a worn wool blanket riddled with holes.

There was something new born in Jakob in that instant. It was a feeling he had never known before, a feeling of warmth and... and... a feeling that there had been something missing that he hadn't even known about before and now here it was. Sleeping quietly and gently in front of him. So small and helpless, so handsome, so beautiful. His son.

Rebecca had also been looking wistfully at Thomas, but she was amazed when she looked up from the tiny figure curled up in the corner to see Jakob's face in the dim light filtering into the room. "You're crying!" Rebecca whispered.

Jakob quickly brushed the single tear out of the corner of his eye. "Thomas?" he asked, changing the subject, questioning where Rebecca had gotten the name.

"For my great grandfather on my father's side."

Jakob then looked Rebecca in the eye as he realized something. "Why are you here?" he asked her, "You're a mischling like me."

"When they came for mother I wouldn't let her go alone."

"You're joking." he said incredulously.

"No. I made such a fuss that they said I could..."

"A fuss?"

Rebecca smiled. "I kicked and screamed. They were happy to order me out."

"...even though it meant bringing Thomas here?"

"I just couldn't let mother go alone" she said, drifting into silence as she looked back at Thomas. "He's so much better since your mother got us more food." she continued, "I don't now how she did it, but I'm so grateful."

"She didn't tell you what it was all about?"

"No. I was hoping you would tell me what's happening."

Jakob paused a moment as he decided how much to tell her. "It's best that you don't know everything," he started, "but you should be ready to leave here on a moment's notice"

"Leave? But it's impossible to escape."

"Don't ask me how and don't tell anybody what I've told you. Just be ready."

"When?"

"A week... A month... Anytime."

The next day's switch with Mirek went as smoothly as when Jakob had entered the camp. They had been lucky that there hadn't been one of the commandant's midnight role calls or a surprise check by the guards through the inmate's barracks and cells, but that was because the commandant had been busy that evening. He had been up late discussing details of an assignment with Hans Beyfeurt, Admiral Canaris' assistant who had coincidentally come from Berlin on the same day that Jakob had slipped into the camp.

The next day Hans Beyfeurt sat with his feet up on the desk as he waited for Klaus Grunewald. Hans was not the sort to put up his feet, but he was playing a role for this assignment.

"Grunewald?" he asked as Klaus strolled in, unimpressed.

"Major Grunewald" Klaus corrected as he shot out a stiff-armed nazi salute and then took off his winter coat, turning his back on Hans as he hung it on the coat tree in the corner of the office.

"Major? but wasn't it Colonel?" Hans asked with a stinging tone of superiority.

"I understand you wanted to talk to me" Klaus countered coolly as he sat in the chair in front of Hans' desk.

"Do you know why?"

"I haven't the slightest idea."

"We know quite a bit about you Major Grunewald."

"Of course you do..."

"Not just your service record."

Klaus just raised his eyebrows a little as an implied question, as though he were asking to hear more without bothering to dignify Hans' remark by asking the question out loud.

"We know about your time in the hospital" Hans continued.

"What is your point?" Klaus asked coolly.

"...and your life in Munich before the war" Hans continued, ignoring Klaus' question, "We have quite a bit of information about that... "

Klaus was fifty-two years old. He felt comfortable in the role, past the time of childish insecurities, used to the respect given to an officer in the German Waffen SS, but now this Abwehr officer was quickly stripping him of that self-assurance. Klaus tried to hide his anxiety as Hans Beyfuert continued the game of cat and mouse,

"We have an interesting situation developing. One of those devious little Jews in your charge is actually trying to blackmail her way out of your vacation resort."

"My Jews?" Klaus asked, questioning why he should be held accountable when Seidl was the commandant and Klaus was just a subordinate officer.

"You are just as responsible as any of the other officers... besides, we came up with an interesting note on you. You see, we at the Abwehr like nothing better than to dig up useful information. Well, of course, one doesn't always know what might be useful in the future. It was only a few months ago that we gained access to some of the records of Rheinhard Heydrich. One can't help but admire the fastidious nature with which the Reichsprotektor's office gathered and filed information. You actually knew the Reichsprotektor when he first arrived in Munich, didn't you?"

"Around then." Klaus said evasively

"It seems no one was exempt from his... probings." Hans added.

Klaus coughed a forced little cough just so that he could put his hand to his mouth so that he could wipe off the thin line of perspiration forming on his upper lip.

"Oh, that's right." Hans said as though a thought had just popped into his mind, "I didn't mention the name of our little trouble-making Jew... actually a Jewess I should say."

Hans reached into his pocket and took out a gold plated cigarette case as he continued speaking slowly "Amalie." he said as he took a cigarette from the case and tapped the end on the table, "Interesting woman." He then lit the cigarette, drawing a couple of puffs before continuing. "She married an Austrian."

Klaus shifted uneasily in his chair. He had known Amalie was in the camp within a week of her arrival. He had heard some talk about the extra rations given to her and her family, but he paid no attention. He thought it best to ignore her and hoped she would do the same for him. All of his memories of her had changed through the passing years. He had rewritten the story in his mind and heart over that time. His story now read that Amalie had been the cause of Gunther's death, regardless of who had pulled the trigger on that rainy night in 1934.

"You killed her husband." Hans said coolly, snapping Klaus out of his drifting thoughts and back to the stifling little office.

"I was ordered to..." Klaus started to explain.

"How strange..." Hans interrupted, pretending to be confused at the contradiction, "There is a note here saying that you requested..."

"I...I wanted..." Klaus stammered, "I wanted to save him the humiliation"

"I don't suppose it mattered what you wanted when his wife found out."

"I don't believe she knows."

"Oh? How interesting." Hans said thoughtfully, "But, of course it doesn't matter. Our only concern is that you know this woman and we need you to work with us."

"To do what?"

"The wheel is about to turn. We have only to play out a last scene in our game. "

"What do you want from me?"

"Amalie believes that she will win this game. She thinks she can blackmail a high official into letting her go, but how would that look?" Hans asked sardonically.

"And...?"

"And so we want you to convince her that she is right. That everything will work out just as she planned it."

"What was her plan?"

"That she and her group would be sent to Switzerland where she would turn over some documents."

"What docu..." Klaus started, but he cut himself off in favor of a more diplomatic question, "When? When does all this happen?"

"Soon enough. We have a few details to finish. I would say that within the next two weeks."

"What do I do?"

"You will be our go between. You will keep Amalie apprised of the plans."

"That's all" Klaus asked, wondering why they would go to all the trouble of involving him.

"You will also accompany them on their journey. We thought that you might build her confidence. Can you be..." Hans stopped in mid-question as he looked for an appropriate word, "Cordial?"

"Cordial?" Klaus repeated, "Of course. Amalie and I were... friends. I think we understood each other."

"Have you talked with her here in the camp?"

"Don't be ridiculous. This is much different now. I couldn't possibly..."

"But now you can?"

"Well, certainly. This is also different. Now that I have..."

"Can you kill her?"

"What?"

"I mean" Hans said as he looked directly into Klaus' eyes just like a snake charmer would stare at a snake, "there may be a time when you must do what's best for the Fatherland. Can you kill her if you have to?"

"After befriending her?"

596

"Yes."

Klaus paused for a moment, but he knew the answer. "Yes."

"Without hesitation?" Hans continued.

"Yes."

"Good..." Hans said with a note of finality as he passed the first hurdle in Canaris' plan.

It was a few days later when Petr Hrmeni climbed back up through the trap door in the cellar of Petterink's furniture shop to talk with Jakob again.

"They're moving."

"From the camp?" Jakob asked, "When?"

"by the end of next week"

"Will we know the exact day?"

"I think so, but not more than three days notice."

"What about You and Hannah and the girls?"

"I guess we're a good faith gesture."

"What?"

"We're getting our papers... and that includes you, before they leave Theresienstadt."

"What do you think about it?" Jakob asked as he began to pace, "Can we trust them?"

"The travel papers will be blank, just like we told them, but they might try to arrest whoever picks them up..."

"I don't know" Jakob said, shaking his head as he looked up at Petr, "I just don't know. It all seems straight forward. Maybe they want the package so badly that they'll play along, but I just don't trust them."

"That's because you're getting smart in your old age" Petr countered with a smile, "The Germans shouldn't be trusted." Petr leaned back in the chair, resting his head against the wall as he started tapping his fingers on the table while he considered the possibilities. "They might not give us any trouble if they were trying to show your mother that everything was going fine and she had nothing to fear from them. She is, after all, the only one who can give them what they want in this whole mess."

Jakob stopped pacing and sat across the table from Petr. "If I were a nazi..." Jakob began slowly, "I would let you and me and the girls go through unmolested and then wait for that critical moment when mother tells them what they want to know. I'm sure they'll have some way to verify the information before they let her go, but of course they couldn't let her go then."

"You think they'll kill her after they get what they want?"

"If the tables were turned... If we had a German blackmailer in our hands..."

"We would have to kill him. He would still be a threat."

"Exactly." Jakob agreed somberly.

"Everybody..." Petr continued reflectively.

"I think so." Jakob agreed again, "They'll kill everyone who's with her on that transport."

Vasek Zapotocky was drinking coffee in the gate house in Theresienstadt while Jakob and Petr were discussing the possibility of Amalie's plan ending in disaster.

"You!" a German SS officer shouted as he stomped into the gatehouse, pointing at Vasek as though the finger were a lethal weapon, "and you!" he continued as he pointed at one of the other three Czech guards sitting at the table, "Come with me."

Vasek shrugged his shoulders in response to the look from the other chosen guard as they got up and followed the officer.

When Vasek got out outside, the officer was standing in front of a group of two SS troopers with machine guns escorting six prisoners who had obviously just arrived in the camp. They all appeared to have been beaten, although in different ways.

"This one" the officer said as he flipped the expensive leather gloves he held in his left hand to indicate a man who had been severely beaten about the face to the point where his eyes were almost completely swollen shut, "goes to the commandant's office. Take him and wait for me there."

The prisoner flinched as Vasek put a hand to his shoulder to get him moving towards the camp headquarters. Vasek had seen it many times before. Some of the other guards thought it was funny when a prisoner flinched and would get rough with them, punching them or hitting them with the butt of their rifles. Vasek wasn't that kind of man. He didn't want his fellow guards to think he was sympathetic to the prisoners, but he never went as far as to join in on their petty abuses.

The prisoner, Gottfried Berendt, was a young German national who had moved to Czechoslovakia just before the war. He was resigned to his fate and so he didn't resist the guards. Gottfried had been arrested for distributing literature encouraging resistance to the German occupation. He had been brought to the Kleine Festung after being questioned by the Gestapo. This would be his last stop as they tried to get him to name others involved in the conspiracy against the Reich. Gottfried would never tell them anything, though, and so his fate was sealed the moment a Gestapo agent had placed a hand on his shoulder as he carried his briefcase full of flyers up a street in Prague.

Now it was Vasek who placed a hand Gottfried's shoulder, guiding him up the steps of the headquarters and inside.

"Major Zimmerman sent us" Vasek said to a young SS Corporal sitting at a desk by the door, "Where do you want him?"

"Take him in there and wait with him" the corporal answered as he pointed to one of the doors across the hall.

Vasek did as he was told, followed by Gottfried and the other guard. There were only three chairs in the office, two to the right of the door and the other was the swivel chair behind the desk. Vasek motioned for Gottfried to take one of the chairs by the door while Vasek sat in the chair behind the desk. The other guard stopped in the doorway as he saw Vasek sitting behind the desk and smiled. "You'll get in trouble" he said to Vasek as he closed the door.

"That's my affair."

"You think so?" the other guard asked as he sat beside Gottfried, "You don't think they'll roast my ass, too?"

"You worry like an old woman" Vasek replied, "Why don't you get us some coffee?"

"Yeah... yeah." the guard said as he got up and left.

Gottfried stared at Vasek. He wanted Vasek to look at him, to see what they were doing to people. He wanted to burn his face into Vasek's eyes.

Vasek, however, did his best to avoid eye contact with Gottfried and so he looked around the room until his eyes came to rest on some papers on the desk. The corporal in the entry way had assumed that since Hans Beyfeurt and Major Grunewald had left the office, they were done with their business, but Hans had left his paperwork on the desk.

Vasek made it his business to avoid things that didn't concern him. Since he occasionally did things to help his friends in the resistance he wanted to make sure that he didn't get caught up in anything by mistake. He didn't want to do anything that might look suspicious because the appearance of wrongdoing might lead to an investigation that would uncover things he actually had done. But here was this map on the desk.

It was a map of Southern Europe from Czechoslovakia to Switzerland with a train route drawn in blue pencil and red pencil. The two lines coincided as they started from Teresin and headed east, but then, a few Kilometers out of Prague, the red line turned east, cutting across Germany through the Alps and stopping just short of the Swiss border. The point where the red line ended was circled in red with the note "Swiss Border Station 37" also written in red.

"What are you looking at?" Gottfried asked as he squinted through his swollen eyelids at Vasek as Vasek poured over the map. Vasek shot a menacing glance to Gottfried but said nothing.

Gottfried had no reason to say what he was about to say. He knew there was no way out of his current situation, but he couldn't help making an observation about Vasek. "You're not like the others, are you?" he continued.

"Shut up!" Vasek snapped, looking up just in time to see a shadow through the frosted glass window of the office door. He immediately pushed back from the desk and stood up, moving towards Gottfried. He expected the other guard to come in with two cups of coffee, but instead it was the Corporal from the front desk with a menacing looking Colonel.

"I'm sorry, Colonel Beyfeurt" The Corporal said nervously as he rushed in, "I thought your business was completed and..."

"Just get them out!" Hans said through clenched teeth.

Vasek pulled Gottfried up by the arm, trying to get him out before the German officer became even more upset.

That night the moon rose with an eirie, brilliant orange face, so big as it sat on the horizon that you might think it was about to overtake the Earth on its journey through space. It was finally starting to feel like spring as the night breeze gave up its winter bite. It was still cold, but no one would freeze to death in the camp that night.

Amalie had spent the day in the family camp with Eleonore's family. It was called the family camp because the fenced in yard was meant to accomodate families while the barracks within the garrison walls were communal barracks. There were, however, also some rooms in various buildings within the garrison which had been made into small "apartments" for the "prominente", the famous among the Jewish prisoners who might occasionally be put on display for the International Red Cross or other visiting dignitaries to show how well the Theresienstadt Jews were being treated.

The family camp was nothing more than a staging ground. Jews being brought to Theresienstadt were held there as a stepping stone to the extermination camps in the East which was why the German SS often referred to the Theresienstadt ghetto as "die Schleuse", meaning "the gate". While many Jews across Europe would go directly to the extermination camps from their point of origin, hundreds of thousands were sent in small groups from different areas, especially from within Germany itself, to Theresienstadt until it was convenient to transport them to the killing centers. It might seem strange that Germany was not the first place to be made "Judenrein", or "Jew free" by the nazis, but then the nazis felt they knew where every Jew in Germany was, and so they had the time to take care of them at their leisure.

The swelling population of the camp set off a series of rumors among the people who made up the stable base of Theresienstadt's inmates, the people who were too important for whatever reason at the time for the SS to exterminate. "The camp is getting too full" the prominente' would say, "They'll be sending some East soon."

Amalie's sister, Eleonore, had heard the rumors and was getting nervous. She sent Sophie to get Amalie and she and Amalie had spent the afternoon going back and forth about what Amalie was up to as the two of them carefully washed the family's threadworn clothes and secretly prepared the extra rations for that day. Eleonore wanted to know where the extra food came from, a question she hadn't asked before, and then she wanted to know what Amalie knew about another train taking people East. Eleonore was startled when Amalie replied "I'm working on it."

Eleonore had expected Amalie to say that she knew nothing. Amalie's answer sent Eleonore into hysterics. She wanted to know everything that was going on. She also demanded to know how it was that Amalie dared to hide the truth from her. For Eleonore, the very thought of not being in control was disturbing enough, but to find out that her own sister somehow had a say in what was about to happen and had kept it all secret, pushed her over the edge .

Eleonore began to scream and threaten and cry all at the same time. Amalie then surprised her with a sharp, stinging slap. "I'm trying to save your life" Amalie said sternly as she grabbed Eleonore's hands and held them down as Eleonore tried to fight back. "Your life! Your children's lives... There's nothing you can do! You mustn't tell anyone or you could destroy our chances. For once in your life you have to trust me."

Eleonore began to sob and Amalie managed to put her arms around her sister just as Sophie and Rachel came in. "What's wrong?" Sophie asked.

"We heard shouting" Rachel added, "What's happened?"

"It's nothing girls" Amalie said as she let go of Eleonore and stood up. "nothing..."

That was when Amalie went back to her cell. She opened the door and was shocked when she saw someone sitting in a chair in the corner of the darkened cell.

"Come in" the man said, "I've been waiting here for quite some time."

She couldn't see him, but there was something familiar in the voice. "Klaus..." she whispered.

"I was surprised when I found out you were here." he said casually.

Amalie just stood silently by the door.

"I didn't think we should be seen meeting" he continued, "It wouldn't look good for either of us."

Memories of Klaus came flooding back to Amalie as he went on. The self-righteous arrogance that had turned her against him so long ago was still there. She could tell even in just those few words, the way he sat, the way he spoke. "Why are you here?" she finally asked with a bristling annoyance intended to hide her fear.

"You're not happy to see me?" Klaus countered sarcastically.

"It's been a long time." Amalie said, "We don't have to pretend now. Not here."

"I can't really tell you why I'm here because I haven't been told everything that's going on" Klaus began tersely. He didn't like being a pawn ordered around in such a way, especially since it involved Amalie.

"Someone from the Abwehr has contacted me." he continued, "It seems they know that we were..."

Klaus was about to use the word "friends", but as he looked at

602

Amalie, he couldn't bring himself to say it. "That we knew each other" he finished.

"Has something gone wrong?" Amalie asked.

"No. Nothing is wrong. I've just been sent to tell you about the details. You'll be leaving."

"When?" Amalie asked anxiously.

"One week."

"How?"

"You'll be going by train. For some reason the Abwehr wants to keep this all quiet and so you'll be leaving on the next transport."

"Transport?" Amalie asked with alarm, "To the East?"

"Yes." Klaus answered, letting the word sink in because he enjoyed the fear it inspired. "But your boxcar will be let off at a siding" he continued after a pause, "and routed off to the West."

"Switzerland?"

"From what I understand" he said with a grudging nod.

"Next Tuesday?" Amalie asked, wanting him to confirm that she had heard correctly.

"Tuesday." he repeated.

Amalie put out her hand to catch the door frame. she felt light headed. It was almost over.

"I don't suppose you would care to confide in an old friend?" Klaus asked, "What's this all about?"

Amalie actually smiled. "Is there anything else you have to tell me?" she asked.

"No" Klaus said as he stood up. He wasn't going to wait around for Amalie to insult him by dismissing him. "That's all for now. I'll keep in touch."

He reached for the door, but stopped as he held the door knob. "Of course it would be best not to tell anyone..."

"Of course." Amalie agreed curtly. After all, she knew the rules of this game better than he.

It seemed impossible for Amalie to keep track of time as she waited for the fateful day. Just as it seemed the hours were dragging on endlessly, a day would slip away and then another would suddenly dissapear until Amalie finally found herself wide awake on the evening before the transport was to arrive. Amalie had never known Vasek Zapotocky by name or that he had been her contact with Petr and she heard nothing of the buzz among the other guards and officers when Vasek disappeared in the middle of the week.

She couldn't sleep at all that night, but she stayed on her cot, waiting, until she heard a scream split the early morning before dawn. Instinctively she knew what it was. The guards were forcing people out into the yard for a roll call as a long train of box cars rumbled along the rails leading up to the camp.

Amalie wandered out into the street under the slightly intoxicating, confusing influence of lack of sleep. The world was in the prolonged twilight of a winter that had stayed too long and a Spring which was hesitant to appear. The absence of snow left the streets and the parade ground covered in a dust settled over the winter months.

Amalie saw the looks on the faces of the dying and the soon to be dead, but they couldn't see her. She knew she wasn't one of them. She was about to be free and she suddenly thought of the conversation she had had with David Frieder. Was one of these people going to be taking her place? Was she murdering them? It had all been clear before, the need to survive and save the lives of her family. She knew it was the only thing to do. She thought to herself that It must just be the lack of sleep that was confusing her now.

Everything was orderly and quiet in the beginning. People lined up for the selection process and waited, but once the doors were opened on the boxcars, intermittent cries and shouts came up from the crowd as families were separated and the guards began driving people in. The noise escalated and the dust began to rise as people shuffled along and were forced into the boxcars by guards who were now using canes to beat people as it became difficult for people to push into the boxcars.

Everyone that Amalie had named when she talked to the German officials had been separated from the rest of the inmates and loaded on to the last boxcar. Even though Amalie felt sure that Klaus had told her the truth about the boxcar being re-routed, it was still unnerving being part of the thousands packed into the stifling boxcars.

She was relieved when she entered the car, even though it was a pathetic scene with Eleonore crying in one corner with Rachel and Sophie gathered in her arms, Sam Frieder being helped on by David and Louis and the rest of the occupants huddled into piles on the floor. Sam had taken a turn for the worse when he heard that they would be on the train.

Amalie's relief came from the fact that no one else was in the boxcar besides those she had named. The boxcar seemed almost empty compared to the others and just as the doors were being slammed shut down the line of cars, a couple of sacks were subtly thrown into Amalie's boxcar. Little Thomas scurried over to the door to see what was in the bags. "Food!" he said in his little voice and then he pulled a large canteen out of the bag that he could barely hold with his little hands and shook it.

Everyone in the boxcar knew by then that something was going on, but they didn't dare hope that they were somehow saved. Everyone just looked about at each other with unasked questions reflecting in their eyes.

The train moved out at a slow and labored pace. Once the rhythm of the wheels on the rails became steady and regular, Rebecca was the one who crossed over to Amalie. "Will we...?" Rebecca started to ask, but she couldn't get it out in one breath, "Are we going East?"

"No." Amalie answered simply.

"Of course we are" Eleonore screamed, "Can't you see? Something is wrong! We're going to the gas!"

Amalie looked at her sister, but didn't say a word. The others scattered around the car didn't know what to think and there was a long period of silence as everyone thought about what fate awaited them. The silence passed as time wore on. One becomes tired of being afraid and eventually a plateau of normalcy comes to the situation. David and Louis began to talk and then Otto Maus and Joseph Huber joined in. They talked about things completely unrelated to their present situation and as they did, the others conversed and relaxed around them. The undercurrent of fear was fading until the train began to slow down and everyone was silent once more as they wondered what was happening.

The train came to a stop. Everyone expected something to happen, but there was nothing. No shouting or shooting, No guards pulling them out or beating them. Nothing. They waited in ignorance for more than two hours. The Sun rose in that time and little pinpoints of light appeared on the western wall of the boxcar. The only sound was Sam Frieder's loud snoring. It was a comical counterpoint to the underlying tension and no one, including David, did anything to stop it. Then suddenly there was a loud clanking of metal against metal. There was no sound of an engine and Otto Maus asked "What is it? What are they doing?" loud enough for everyone to hear.

"We're being disconnected from the train" David answered.

"What does it mean?" Rebecca asked from the other end of the car.

"We're changing direction" Amalie said quietly, triumphantly.

Just then the doors opened, letting in a welcome breeze to cleanse the hot stagnate air, and as if to confirm Amalie's pronouncement, blankets were thrown in. Incredibly, the door was left open.

"Blankets?" Louis asked, "Why on Earth...?"

"We're going to the mountains." Amalie answered, and this time she smiled. It was true. It was all going to work.

Everyone began to talk excitedly, but then suddenly a German officer appeared, standing in front of the doorway. Everyone quieted down again.

"I trust everyone is well" Klaus said to no one in particular, "If you pass out the empty canteens, we will refill them and be on our way."

They went about their chores, gathering canteens, passing out the bucket they used as a toilet and generally cleaning out the boxcar when they heard an engine struggling to pull the rest of the train, the other Theresienstadt Jews, eastward. No one commented on it. They all knew what it meant, a look even flitted across little Thomas' eyes, that look a little boy has when he knows he is doing something wrong and hopes that he won't be caught. They couldn't think about it though, because now they had hope and they were waiting for their own engine which finally came to pull them along with the Sun.

It was hours before the boxcar started getting cool and Rachel passed out the blankets. The cold was salvation and so no one complained, in fact Rachel was greeted with smiles as she went from family to family. They began steep climbs and long curves around mountains. The train went on at a steady pace, much faster than they had traveled that morning on the heal of the eastward bound train. They went on until afternoon in the mountains and then the train began to slow down.

Amalie had gravitated to Rebecca, Thomas and Rebecca's

mother. Amalie and Mrs. Geschwind spent hours talking about Munich and how things had gone after Amalie left in 1934. There was a lull in their conversation just as Amalie heard the sound of the engine slowing down.

"Are we going up again?" Rebecca asked Amalie.

"I don't think so..." Amalie answered.

"Then why..?"

"We may be there" Amalie said, "or maybe it's just time to do business."

"Business?"

Amalie didn't answer. She just looked at Rebecca with a look that said "don't ask".

Everyone got nervous as the train came to a stop and then the door suddenly slid open with a loud scrape and slam. There stood Klaus again as the door opened, but this time he was flanked by two SS troopers with machine guns cradled in their arms. "We will give you water again, but you must all stay on the train..." Klaus announced loudly, lowering his voice as he continued. "All but you" he said as he made eye contact with Amalie.

Amalie hadn't even realized that Rebecca had taken her hand until she tried to get up. She looked at Rebecca with a forced smile. "I'll be all right." She said as she pulled away and walked to the door where one of the troopers helped her jump down.

She froze as she looked around once she was out of the boxcar. There was a building just ahead of the train and on the small wooden structure were signs declaring "Passport Control" and "Switzerland". There it was. She could walk to it. If she were to run right then she might even make it to freedom before the machine guns could cut her down. But, of course, there were all the others still waiting on the train.

"We have kept our part of the bargain" Klaus said as they walked, "Now it is time for you to fulfill your part."

The building was divided neatly in half with the German officials on one side and Swiss border officials on the other. Klaus stopped at the door to the German office and opened it for Amalie.

"We have people in Bern, Zurich and Geneva waiting just for your call" he continued, "Now it's your turn. Where must they go? Who do we call?"

Amalie hesitated for an instant, but then she decided that she believed Klaus and his business-like manner. She thought it was all going to be just as simple as he made it seem. Make a telephone call, they go to the safety deposit box and then the train crosses the Swiss border. "Zurich" she said simply.

The call went through quickly and easily and German agents were soon on their way to the bank she named with the information necessary to gain access. Once again they spent time waiting. Amalie was accompanied back to the boxcar where everyone asked her what had happened.

"We are at the border" she said solemnly, "There is nothing to do now but wait. It should all be over soon."

There were smiles and tears as her words sunk in and everyone allowed themselves to relax. Amalie had no sooner told them that they would have to wait for a while when the train began to move forward and everyone became excited, some gasping with surprise while others were praising God for their deliverance, but then they realized that the train was only moving off the main track. It was then that Amalie realized how helpless they were as they waited, but she decided that she had to trust Klaus. She knew it was a strained alliance, but it was all she had to hold on to.

Klaus was sitting in the office drinking coffee and trying to relax as the Sun was setting. He almost dropped his cup when the phone rang. A sergeant handed him the telephone and the German Abwehr agent in Zurich told him that everything had gone just as Amalie had said.

Klaus hung up the phone heavily. His orders had made it clear that once the information was verified he was to dispose of Amalie and the others. The border station was a ruse, a building pre-constructed and placed fifteen kilometers from the actual Swiss border on a siding and manned by German soldiers. All that was left for Klaus now was to order his men to get everyone off the train and take them to a wooded area past the tracks and shoot them. His mind flashed back to Babi Yar and the dreams he had had afterwards.

Klaus slowly took off his hat and brushed back his hair. "Take them out and shoot them." he said brusquely to the sergeant at the desk across from him.

The Sergeant got up immediately and headed out the door, calling all the soldiers together in front of the border station. Klaus sat in the building alone as the sergeant gave instructions to the soldiers. Just as Klaus was about to get up and join the others, he saw something flash past a window at the back of the building. He went over to the window, but couldn't see anything in the snow. He thought it must have been his imagination, a flashback from Babi Yar. He put on his coat and went out the door just as the sergeant ordered the troops to march.

At that moment, Vasek was climbing up on the train engine. "Step back!" he shouted at the engineer, but the engineer reached for a large spanner. Vasek fired his pistol in the air as a warning and the engineer stepped back. "I'll kill you." Vasek said as he leveled the pistol at the man's head, "You can either get the train across the border or die here!"

Klaus and the others heard the shot and the Sergeant began shouting at the soldiers to spread out, but it was too late. Four machine guns began firing from around the building and from a stand of pine trees several meters in front of the train. It was a murderous cross fire which cut down the entire company virtually still in formation. None of the soldiers could even see where the enemy machine gun fire was coming from, so the few machine gun bursts the Germans managed to get off were completely futile. Every soldier fell into the snow, painting the slush in front of the counterfeit border station with bright red pools and speckled patterns surrounding the bodies.

Everyone in the boxcar thought they were being shot at and people started screaming and shouting. Some of the men banged on the walls as though they were animals caught in a trap, as though they might break down the sides of the boxcar and get out. The screams and cries continued even after the shooting had stopped and the partisans were coming out from their hiding places.

There were only eight partisans, but they were sure that the German contingent accompanying the boxcar would be small, and they were right. There were only six troopers along with the sergeant and officer. The odds had been one to one. The partisans were lucky in this because not only couldn't they find anyone else willing to go with them all that way, there was also the concern that a larger group would have been much too noticeable and harder to move all the way from Prague. They had spent four days working their way from Prague and across Austria to Switzerland, having left as soon as they had gotten forged copies of the travel papers which the Abwehr had delivered to Petr's contacts as part of the original agreement with Amalie. Amalie had insisted that along with her transport, the Abwehr must deliver four sets of open travel papers for Jakob, Petr, Hannah and Karin. Petr made use of these papers, having as many copies forged as he could within the space of two days. The partisans used these papers on and off during their travel as they tried to vary their mode of transportation through their journey just in case anyone might suspect them. They had taken a gamble on the limited information which Vasek Zapotocky gave them about the route and destination of an unexplainable transport heading towards Switzerland. Vasek decided that this was the time when he would make a final commitment to the resistance.

Inside the car, once the shouting had subsided, David had insisted that as a final desperate act they should wait for the door to open and then jump on the first man at the door so that some of the others might get out and make it across the border. None of them had yet realized that they were not really at the Swiss border and so they thought their flight would only be a matter of a few hundred meters. The other men agreed and so they waited in front of the door, each man's heart pounding as they heard the latch being moved and the door begin to slide.

Jakob threw down the machine gun he had been firing once he was sure all the soldiers were down and ran to the train. He undid the latch on the boxcar and began to pull the door open. "Rebecca!" Jakob called as he slid the door open, "Mother!"

David, Louis and Otto, being the first men at the door, fell out of the door as it opened, tumbling on top of Jakob. Amalie had caught sight of Jakob in the instant before David and the others leapt and tried to stop them.

"No!" she shouted, "It's Jakob!", but the others had already started pouring out of the boxcar. It was pandemonium as everyone who could run poured out of the boxcar. They saw the station and started running toward the "Switzerland" sign, many of them not even noticing the squad of dead German soldiers in the snow.

They ran until Petr and one of the other partisans appeared from the side of the building and called out that they had been saved, that there was nothing to fear and that they were safe.

Rebecca hadn't heard Jakob call out her name, but when she came to the door to get out she immediately saw him. He had quickly

610

recovered from being knocked over and was trying to calm the people running past him. She couldn't believe her eyes and she jumped into the snow, falling to her knees and then, struggling back to her feet she made her way over to him. She reached out her hand to touch his face to make sure he was real and he smiled at her. She started crying and he took her in his arms. Amalie had come to the door with Mrs. Geschwind and Thomas, stopping them before they joined the mad rush. Thomas stood watching his mother for a moment. The only time Jakob had seen Thomas, Thomas was asleep on his cot in the camp.

"Who is that?" he asked as he stood between his two grandmothers.

"That" Amalie said as she, too began to cry, "is your father."

It didn't take long for Petr to get everyone back to the train and explain that the border station was a ruse and that they had to continue on to the real Swiss border.

"But we can't cross through the border all at once" he explained, "We will have to split up into smaller groups and make crossings at different places along the border. We have forged papers for a dozen people, but that was all we could get made up on short notice, so the children, the old and the sick will go through the border station. Everyone else will have to make the harder crossing."

Vasek had convinced the engineer, albeit at gunpoint, to help them and so they were all to ride the train until they were within a couple of kilometers of the border where the people without forged papers would get off and start their cross country journey with the partisans to guide them.

Jakob, Petr and Vasek rode in the Engineer's cab to keep an eye on everything. Jakob leaned close to Petr so he could be heard over the noise of the train engine as it strained on an incline. "Do you think we'll all make it?" he asked.

"We'll be close..." Petr said, "If no one gets lost in the dark, I think there's a good chance."

Considering Petr's cynical nature, Jakob considered this a virtual guarantee that everyone would make it.

Back in the boxcar, David and Louis talked as they looked over the snow-covered mountainside through the partially open boxcar door.

"I think we'll make it" Louis said, "We've come so far... so close... I'm sure we'll make it."

"I don't know... "David said.

"You don't think we'll make it?" Louis challenged with surprise in his voice.

"I don't mean that" David answered as though he had been caught in a daydream, "I just get this feeling that we've cheated. We were so close to... It's not hard to imagine that we might have kept on going with the rest of them."

"East?"

"Yes. Gone East with the rest of them to die. For all we know they may all be dead right now."

"Would you rather die with them?" Louis asked rhetorically.

David just looked at him. The expression was an uneasy one. "I don't want to die. No more than anyone else would, but..."

"I wonder what the world will be like" Louis said as he looked out at the snow covered Alps, "They don't know what they're doing. No one will ever know just what has been lost. The people they killed... there could have been statesmen, physicians, religious leaders who might have healed the world... all gone."

"Smoke up the chimney..." David said, half joking in cynical, black humor, "You're right, though... But even beyond that... One has to wonder what will become of mankind when they see how easy it is to destroy nations. What kind of justice could possibly redeem us? We'll all pay the price, the cost of those ashes thrown into the ocean. Ashes spread through forests and scattered in wild flower beds..."

"The price of ashes..." Louis said to himself as he looked at David for an instant before his gaze returned to the snow covered Alps rolling past the train.

Back in the snow behind them, amid the waste of German soldier's bodies left from the ambush, Klaus Grunewald's body suddenly rolled over. Snow which clung to his sweating face melted almost instantly. The bicep of his left arm was shredded and his blood was creating a crimson slush in the snow. He crawled to the dead soldier closest to him and pulled a scarf from around the boy's neck, using it to tie off his arm. He then took the boy's combat knife and looped the handle in the scarf to twist the scarf tightly, making a tourniquet that slowed the flow of blood. He then passed out. He had no idea how long he had been out when he woke up. It was dark and cold. He pulled coats off a couple of the soldiers and struggled, half-walking and half crawling, to the office. He went inside and rested for a while before trying to rekindle the wood fire in the stove in the corner of the office. The partisans had been efficient enough to cut the telephone line at some time before or after the attack, but he hoped that someone would be sent out to see if something had gone wrong when he failed to report in. If only he could stay alive.

List of characters from "The Price of Ashes"

"The Price of Ashes" is an historical fiction novel which follows the Metzdorf family from the end of the First World War and on through the next three decades to the turning point of the Second World War.

An "F" preceding the name indicates a fictional character while "N" indicates non-fictional characters. The text dramatizes certain historical events while taking a certain amount of license with other events which have never been completely documented with historical fact.

F- Alfred and Otto .... Friends of Richard Werthers.

N- Max Amann .... Part of the nazi inner circle from the early days of the party whom Adolf Hitler had met as a soldier during the First World War.

F- Sister Angelina .... A nun who taught with Edith Stein in Speyer.

N- King Tut Ankahmen .... An Egyptian pharaoh whose tomb was discovered in the 1920's. King Tut's name came to be associated with both the curse on his tomb that said that death would follow any who desecrated his burial place and the Egyptian artifacts, especially the riches of gold, that were found in the tomb.

F- Anna and Lissa .... Two girls from one of Edith Stein's class at the Catholic school where she taught in Speyer.

N- Count Anton Arco-Valley......... Count Arco Valley wanted to join the Thule society, a group very much like the nascent nazi party, but was denied membership because he was half Jewish. In an attempt to impress the members of the Thule society and thus gain acceptance, he assassinated Kurt Eisner, the head of the Bavarian Republic.

N- Prince Max von Baden .... The German Reichschancellor who oversaw the transition of power from the abdicating Kaiser Wilhelm to the new Weimar Republic under President Friedrich Ebert.

F- Cecil Baker .... See Gerhard Kruger.

F- Erika Bauer............................. The older of Hannah Bauer's two daughters.

F- Hannah Bauer .... A friend of Amalie's from college, Amalie renews their friendship in Prague when Amalie and her father leave Austria just before the Austrian Anschluss.

F- Karin Bauer .... The younger of Hannah's two daughters.

F- Rolf Bauer................................ Hannah's late husband.

F- Father Berghorst .... A priest arrested along with Edith Stein in Echt.

F- Hans Beyfuert .... Admiral Wilhelm Canaris' adjutant

N- Otto von Bismarck.................... 19th century German statesman many credit with the founding of a unified German state in 1871.

F- Father Brumgart .... A retired priest from the Dollersheim parish in Austria.

N- Admiral Wilhelm Canaris .... The head of German military intelligence during the Second World War.

N- Neville Chamberlain .... The Prime Minister of England from 1937 to 1940. Chamberlain's name has become synonymous with the policy of appeasement which allowed Germany to annex Czecho-slovakia prior to the outbreak of the Second World War without ever firing a shot.

N- Winston Churchill.................... Prime Minister of England during the Second World War.

F- Edwin Coopersmith .... Ethan Stein's legal business representative in England who helps Ethan when Ethan emigrates to England before the war begins.

F- Jane Coopersmith..................... Edwin Coopersmith's wife.

N- Edouard Daladier .... The Premier of France during the Munich crisis in 1938.

F- Matej Damek .... A Comrade of Petr Hremni in the Czech resistance.

N- Emily Dickinson...................... 19th century American poet.

N- Marlene Dietrich .... A world famous German actress who left Germany when the nazis came to power.

F- Dietrich................................... One of Reinhard Heydrich's SD officers involved in the investigation of Amalie Stein-Metzdorf during the Second World War in Prague .

N- Engelbert Dollfuss.................. The Chancellor of Austria during Adolf Hitler's rise to power in Germany.

N- Friedrich Ebert........................ Ebert was the leader of the German Social Democrat party in 1918 who became the first President of the Weimar Republic which replaced the monarchical rule of Kaiser Wilhelm II of the Hohenzollerns at the end of WWI.

F- Rudolf Eggenburger................. Three prisoners taken from
F- Franz Henkel   Sachsenhausen concentration
F- Dov Breitenstein   camp and killed in 1939 as part of the "Gliewitz incident"

N- Kurt Eisner............................. The Social Democrat leader of the post-WWI government of Bavaria which replaced King Ludwig of the Wittlesbach dynasty in that region.

N- Hans Frank.............................. Adolf Hitler's lawyer who eventually rose to be an important member of the nazi party as governor general of Poland. Frank was the man who implemented the destruction of Polish Jewry.

F- Annaliese Frankenburger.......... see Johanna Hiedler

F- David Frieder........................... A Munich book publisher at the end of WWI, he was the head of Frieder and Son Publishing which his father, Sam, had started years before. Amalie Metzdorf started working for David as an assistant copy editor in February of 1919.

F- Sam Frieder .... The father of David Frieder, Sam was the founder of Frieder and Son Publishing. He retired before the end of the First World War and made a hobby of following the tumultuous political scene in Germany.

N- Josef Gabcik .... Three of the Czech expatriates trained
N- Jan Kubis   by the British as commandos and
N- Josef Valcik   parachuted into Czechoslovakia to carry out various missions of sabotage and assassination for the allies.

F- Max Geschwind .... Rebecca Geschwind's younger brother.

F- Rebecca Geschwind.................. A girlfriend of Jakob Metzdorf, her family

lived in the same neighborhood in
Furstenried district of Munich

F- Thomas Geschwind.................. Rebecca Geschwind's son.

N- Joseph Goebbels .... The nazi party's minister of
propaganda. Goebbels was
headquartered in Berlin long before the nazi
party received the majority votes under the
Weimar elections which brought them to
power.

N- Herman Goering..................... A WWI flying ace who became a confederate
of Adolf Hitler's in the early days of the nazi
party and eventually head of the German
Luftwaffe during WWII.

F- Klaus Grunewald .... Gunther Metzdorf's front line comrade from
the First World War, a conservative, right wing
militarist.

N- Herschel Grynspan .... A Jewish youth who shot a minor German
diplomat in Paris to protest of the
mistreatment of Jews in Germany in 1938.
Grynspan's actions were cited by the nazis as
the act which precipitated the pogrom
against the Jews known as "Krystalnacht".

F- Friedrich Haas .... Another friend of Gunther's, a young
German who Gunther befriends while the
two of them are looking for work in post-
WWI Munich. Friedrich had been in the
medical corps as an ambulance driver and so
qualified in Gunther's mind as a member of
"the brotherhood of front-line soldiers"
which later became a qualifying phrase of
the emerging nazi party.

F- Gertrude Haas........................... The mother of Friedrich Haas, she is
representative of the working middle class of
Germany during the revolutionary and then
the Weimar period in Germany.

F- Manfred Haas .... Gertrude Haas' late husband. Friedrich Haas'
father.

F- Monika Hanisch....................... Walter Hanisch's mother.

F- Walter Hanisch .... Walter was Jakob Metzdorf's roommate in
Prague just before WWII. He was arrested
for distributing anti-nazi propaganda.

F- Hans, Peter and Stefan.......... Friends of Ernst Toller in post WWI Munich.

F- Jurgen Hassler.......................... A school friend of Rebecca Geschwind.

N- Theodore Herzl........................ Known as "the father of modern Zionism", it was Herzl, along with Emile Zola, who came to the defense of Captain Alfred Dreyfus of the French army in a famous case of government sanctioned antisemitism which came to be known as "The Dreyfus Affair".

N- SS Obersturmbannfuehrer
Rheinhard Tristan
Eugen **Heydrich** .... The head of the SicherDienst in Munich before the nazis came to power in Germany, he was eventually appointed as Reichsprotektor of Bohemia and Moravia. Heydrich, as a subordinate of Heinrich Himmler, was the coordinator of the Wannsee conference, the meeting where nazi officials coined the term "final solution" in reference to the nazi policy of genocide against the Jews.

N- Hiedler family .... Hitler was a misspelling of the name Hiedler in church records when Alois Hitler was legitimized in 1876.

N- Johanna Hiedler .... a mixed cast of fictional and real
N- Johann Georg Hiedler   ancestors of Adolf Hitler.
N- Johann Baptist Polzl
N- Johann Nepomuk Hiedler
F- Annaliese Frankenburger
F- Edmund Hiedler

N- Heinrich Himmler .... Head of the nazi SS which included the Gestapo and Totskopf or "deaths head" divisions responsible for the murders of European Jews resulting from the nazi policy of genocide.

N- Paul von Hindenburg................ The head of the German high command during the First World War who became president of the Weimar republic after the death of Friedrich Ebert in 1925.

N- Adolf Hitler............................. Leader of the National Socialist German Worker's Party (Nationalsozialistische

Deutsche Arbeiterpartei)

N- Alois Hitler .... Adolf Hitler's father

N- Alois Hitler Jr........................... Adolf Hitler's half brother.

N- Klara Hitler nee-Polzl............... Adolf Hitler's mother

N- William Hitler......................... A nephew of Adolf Hitler.

F- Louis Arthur Hoffman............... Amalie's brother-in-law, married to her sister Eleonore.

F- Eleonore Hoffman (nee Stein) .... Amalie Metzdorf's sister.

F- Rachel Hoffman .... Louis and Eleonore's eldest daughter.

F- Sophie Hoffman .... Louis and Eleonore's younger daughter.

F- Katrina Holzman .... Klaus Grunewald's wife.

F- Honig..................................... The name of the Springer Spaniel which Gunther buys for Jakob on his eighth birthday. "Honig" translates to "Honey" in English, referring to the color of the dog's coat.

F- Petr Hrmeni .... A Czech national who marries Hannah Bauer in Prague. Petr is also a member of the Czech resistance.

F- Joseph Hubert .... A longtime friend of David Frieder. David Frieder is Amalie's boss.

F- Janu Hudak.............................. A Comrade of Petr Hremni in the Czech resistance.

F- Johann and Thomas .... Friends of Jakob's in the Hitler youth, a political, fraternal and athletic club for boys associated with the nazi party.

N-Gustav von Kahr .... One of the leaders of the Bavarian provincial government at the time of Hitler's beer hall putsch on November 9th, 1923.

F- Obersturmbannfuhrer
Gerhard Kleist .... The SS officer who questions Jakob Metzdorf when he is arrested in Prague.

N-Eugen von Knilling.................. One of the leaders of the Bavarian provincial government at the time of Hitler's beer hall putsch on November 9th, 1923.

F- Liesl Kraus .... A reporter with a Munich newspaper. Amalie assumes Liesl's name during her investigation of the Hitler family.

F- Gerhard Kruger......................... A German Abwehr agent during the Second World War, Gerhard assumed the name "Cecil Baker" as a cover name and eventually became a double agent for the English.

N- Jan Kubis .... see Josef Gabcik

F- Kurt .... A school friend of Rebecca Geschwind.

F- Viktor & Anna Letschek
and their daughter, Katje............... A farm family from the village of Lidice in Czechoslovakia.

N- Eugen Levin............................ A Communist revolutionary sent from Moscow to revitalize the faltering revolution in Munich in 1919.

N- Karl Liebknecht........................ A contemporary of Rosa Luxemburg, Liebknecht protested the First World War and agitated for Communist uprising in Germany after the war. Liebknecht was imprisoned during WWI until the Social Democrats released him and he once again took up the Communist cause.

F- Thomas Loescher...................... The man who takes over Frieder and Son publishing after nazi anti-semitic legislation forces David Frieder out.

N- Rabbi Loew and
F (?)- the Golem........................... While Rabbi Loew was an actual rabbi in Prague in the 16th century, the myth of the Golem said that Rabbi Loew had created a man-like creature out of clay which he could control with magic.

N-Otto von Lossow........................ One of the leaders of the Bavarian provincial government at the time of Hitler's beer hall putsch on November 9th, 1923.

N- Marius van der Lubbe............... The man convicted of setting a fire at the German Reichstag building which became Adolf Hitler's justification for imposing emergency powers.

N- Erich von Ludendorff............... The Quartermaster General of the German High Command during the first world war, Ludendorff was the man who orchestrated the surrender of Germany, the abdication of

Kaiser Wilhelm and the succession of the Social Democrat party as leaders of the new Weimar Republic. The position of Quartermaster General was a relatively minor position in the high command, but due to Ludendorff's aggressive and imposing military successes at the beginning of the war, he was able to exercise more authority than would normally be acceptable for an officer of that rank.

N- Rosa Luxemburg .... "Little Rosa", born of Jewish parents in Poland, was a communist activist in Germany before, during and after the war. She was jailed for her activities during the war, but was released when the Social Democrats took over.

F- Zena Marusin .... A leader in the Czech resistance who was arrested and imprisoned at the Kleine Festung at the Theresienstadt concentration camp near Prague.

N- Franziska Matzelberger .... The first wife of Alois Hitler (Adolf Hitler's father), she was the mother of Angela and Alois Jr. Angela Hitler married Leo Raubal and their daughter was Angela "Geli" Raubal, Adolf Hitler's niece with whom he had an affair.

F- Otto Maus .... A middle-aged author of books on the American old-west, Otto was a client of Frieder publishing who lived in Ried, Austria. Amalie, as an agent of Frieder and son, worked with Otto on the publication of some of his books.

F- Aaron Mendelbaum .... A young German immigrant in London who is imprisoned with Ethan Stein in an English "Enemy Foreign Nationals" internment camp during the early months of the Second World War.

F- Messner .... One of the German SD agents working out of Rheinhard Heydrich's office in the SS headquarters at the Petschek Palais in Prague during the Second World War.

F- Amalie Stein-Metzdorf .... The protagonist of "The Price of Ashes", Amalie was born in Salzburg, Austria in

621

1895 to Ruth and Ethan Stein. The Steins are reform Jews. Amalie is the wife of Gunther and mother of Jakob, her only child.

F- Gunther Metzdorf .... The husband of Amalie, Gunther served in the Austrian infantry in WWI on the Russian front. Gunther moved his family to Munich at the end of the war.

F- Jakob Metzdorf .... Amalie's son, Jakob was born in 1916

F- Maria Metzdorf .... Gunther Metzdorf's mother.

F- Oskar Metzdorf .... Gunther Metzdorf's father.

F- Jiri Molsovice .... A comrade of Petr Hremni in the Czech resistance.

N- Amadeus Mozart .... 17th century composer.

N- Benito Mussolini .... Leader of the Italian fascist party which took over the Italian government in 1922. Adolf Hitler as head of the German nazi party sought to emulate Mussolini's early successes.

N- Alfred Naujocks .... A subordinate of Rheinhard Heydrich's who worked with him in a number of clandestine operations.

N- Konstantin von Neurath .... The first Reichsprotektor of Bohemia and Moravia who was replaced by Rheinhard Heydrich at the end of 1941.

F- Mrs. Newcombe .... Ethan Stein's landlady in London.

N- Czar Nicholas II .... Czar of Russia at the turn of the century and during the First World War, Nicholas Romanoff was a cousin of Wilhelm Hohenzollern, both men being descended from Queen Victoria of England who was their grandmother. Nicholas II was deposed during the Russian revolution in 1917 and subsequently he and his family were murdered by members of the Bolshevik faction. It was rumored that Nicholas' youngest daughter, Anastasia, and his son, Alexeyavich, somehow escaped the slaughter. The rumor is still alive in light of a recent discovery of the burial site of the Romanoff family where the bodies of the two youngest children were not found.

F- Pavel Novak............................. A Comrade of Petr Hremni in the Czech resistance.

N- Eugenio Pacelli .... A Monsignor in Munich during the First World War, he became Pope Pius XII prior to the Second World War.

N- Franz von Papen...................... One of a succession of Reichs-chancellors under Weimar President Paul von Hindenburg before the appointment of Adolf Hitler, von Papen was a favorite of Hindenburg's and was eventually appointed as ambassador to Austria until the Anschluss in 1938.

N- "Blackjack" Pershing................ The general in command of the American Expeditionary Force, the American military contingent sent to France during the First World War.

F- Helmut Puppenspiel .... The leader of Jakob Metzdorf's Hitler youth group.

N- Geli Raubal .... Angela "Geli" Raubal was Adolf Hitler's niece, the daughter of his half-sister Angela and her husband, Leo Raubal.

N- Frau Reichert........................... Adolf Hitler's landlady at the room he rented on Thierschstrasse before moving to Prinzregentenplatz, Hitler asked Frau Reichert to move with him to the Prinzregentenplatz apartment.

N- Joachim von Ribbentrop .... German foreign minister under Adolf Hitler.

N-Hans Ritter von Seisser.............. One of the leaders of the Bavarian provincial government at the time of Hitler's beer hall putsch on November 9th, 1923.

N- Ernst Röhm .... The head of the Sturm Abteilung, the military arm of the nazi party also known as the brown shirts, before the 1934 purge.

F- Doctor Rosenau........................ The doctor who operated on Gunther Metzdorf's father, Oskar Metzdorf.

N- Maria Schicklgruber................. Alois Hitler's mother, Adolf Hitler's paternal grandmother.

F- Ingrid Schmidt......................... A girlfriend of Jakob Metzdorf in Munich .

N- Kurt von Schuschnigg.............. The Austrian Chancellor who succeeded

Englebert Dollfuss.

N-Hans Ritter von Seisser............. see Gustav von Kahr

N- Edith Stein .... A Jewish philosopher from Breslau, Germany who converts to Catholicism and eventually becomes a Carmelite nun and theological writer. There is a fictional relationship in the book whereby she is a cousin of Amalie Stein-Metzdorf.

F- Ethan Stein .... Amalie's father. Ethan was the owner of a publishing house in Salzburg, Austria before the Second World War.

F- Ruth Stein............................... Amalie's mother who died from influenza when Amalie was 12 years old.

F- Father Strachler .... The parish priest in Dollersheim before Father Brumgart.

N- Gregor Strasser....................... One of the leaders of the Sturm Abteilung, the military arm of the nazi party also known as the brown shirts, in Berlin before the nazi purge of 1934.

N- Ernst Toller............................. A Munich playwright who lead a bloodless takeover of the Bavarian government after the assassination of Kurt Eisner and then, after he was deposed by the Communist leadership of Eugen Levin, he led revolutionary forces in battle against right wing "Freikorps" units which tried to take over Munich.

N- Josef Valcik............................ see Josef Gabcik

F- Helmut Weispfennig .... The SS officer who arrested Edith Stein at the Carmel of Echt.

F- Karl Werthers .... A friend and co-worker of Manfred Haas.

F- Richard Werthers..................... Richard's father and Friedrich Haas' father worked together for many years and the two sons had a casual friendship as boys. The two hadn't seen each other for years when they meet again in the story. Richard was drafted towards the end of the war and just finished his training as the war ended and was swept up in the revolutionary fervor of 1918-1919.

N- Horst Wessel .... A Berlin pimp who was also a member of the nazi party. Wessel was killed in a fight over a woman by a man who happened to be a member of the Communist party. Josef Goebbels then created a myth that Wessel had died fighting for the nazi party and a song was soon written celebrating this myth, a song which included such warm sentiments as "when Jewish blood drips from the knife, then we will all be happy".

N- Kaiser Wilhelm .... Wilhelm Hohenzollern was the last German Emperor, ending two hundred years of Hohenzollern rule (apart from their role as rulers of Prussia prior to that period) which began with the unification of Germany by Otto von Bismarck in 1871.

N- Duke of Windsor .... King Edward VIII of England who abdicated the throne of England in 1936 so that he could marry Wallace Simpson, an American divorcee.

N- Frau Winter .... Anny Winter was Hitler's housekeeper at the Prinzregentenplatz apartment in Munich.

F- Vasek Zapotocky .... A member of the Czech resistance, Vasek was a former Prague police officer who becomes a guard at the Theresienstadt concentration camp in Czechoslovakia.

F- Zeigel .... A nickname for one of Friedrich Haas' co-workers. The translation is "brick"

F- Ivan Zeleny .... A Comrade of Petr Hremni in the Czech resistance.

****